# interface

# interface

STEPHEN BURY

BANTAM BOOKS
NEW YORK TORONTO LONDON
SYDNEY AUCKLAND

INTERFACE

A Bantam Book / May 1994

All rights reserved.
Copyright © 1994 by Stephen Bury
Book design by Chris Welch

Library of Congress Cataloging-in-Publication Data

Bury, Stephen.
    Interface / Stephen Bury.
        p.   cm.
    ISBN 0-553-37230-0
    1. Presidents—United States—Election—Fiction.   I. Title.
PS3552.U788I58   1994
813'.54—dc20                                                                    93-2051
                                                                                   CIP

Published simultaneously in the United States and Canada

PRINTED IN THE UNITED STATES OF AMERICA

RRH      0 9 8 7 6 5 4 3 2 1

*To Wilbur*

# interface

# the state of
# the union

## CHAPTER ONE

William Anthony Cozzano's office was a scandal. So it was whispered in the high councils of the Illinois Historical Society. For over a century, under dozens of governors, it had looked the same. Then Cozzano had come along and moved all the antique furniture into storage (Abraham Lincoln was the greatest man in history, Cozzano said, but his desk was a piece of junk, and Stephen Douglas's side chair was no prize either). Cozzano had dared to move *electronics* into the frescoed vault of the governor's office—a thirty-six-inch Trinitron with picture-in-picture so that he could watch C-SPAN and football at the same time! And his chair was no antique, but a high-tech thing with as many adjustable features as the human body had bones. He had suffered enough abuse, he claimed, in Vietnam and on the frozen turf of Soldier Field and didn't deserve to be mangled by some antique chair day in and day out, Illinois Historical Society be damned. That chair was everything Cozzano wasn't: fat with padding and glossy with petal-soft leather where Cozzano was lean and craggy and weathered, a man who had waited his whole life to look the way he did now, as if carved from a block of white oak with a few quick strokes of an adze.

Cozzano was sitting in the chair one night in January, holding a fountain pen as big as an uncooked hot dog in his left hand. Cozzano returned to his home in the small town of Tuscola every weekend to mow the lawn, rake leaves, or shovel snow, so calluses made a dry rasping sound as his writing hand slid across the paper.

The fountain pen looked expensive and had been given to him by someone terribly important a long time ago; Cozzano had forgotten whom. His late wife, Christina, used to keep track of who had given him what and send out little notes, Christmas cards, and so on, but since her death, all of these social niceties had gone

4

straight to hell, and most people forgave him for it. Cozzano found that the pen's bulk fit his hand nicely, his fingers wrapped around the barrel without having to pinch it like a cheap ballpoint, and the ink flowed effortlessly onto the paper, nib scrawling and calluses rasping, as he signed the endless stream of bills, proclamations, resolutions, letters, and commendations that flowed across his desk like blood cells streaming in single file through the capillaries of the lung—the stately procession that sustained the life of the body politic.

His office was on the second floor of the east wing, directly above the capitol's main entrance, overlooking a broad lawn decorated with a statue of Lincoln delivering his farewell address to Springfield. The room had only two windows—tall narrow north-facing ones that were blocked even from the late afternoon sun by the north wing and the soaring capitol dome. Cozzano called it the "arctic circle"—the only part of Illinois that was in darkness for six months out of the year. This was a somewhat obscure and technical joke, especially in these days of endemic geographic ignorance, but people laughed at it anyway because he was the Governor. He kept his desk lamp going all day, but as the sky had darkened and as he worked into the night, he had not bothered to turn on the overhead fixtures, and he now sat in a pool of illumination in the middle of the dark office. Around the edges of the room, innumerable pieces of decoration reflected the light back at him.

Each governor decorated the office in his own way. Only a few things were immutable: the preposterous fresco on the ceiling, the massive doors with brass lions' heads mounted in their centers. His predecessor had gone in for a spare, classical nineteenth-century look, filling the place up with antiques that had belonged to Lincoln and Douglas. This impressed visitors and looked nice for the tour groups who came by every hour to launch flashcube barrages over the velvet rope. Cozzano had banned the tour groups, slamming the doors in their faces so that all they could see was the brass lions, and turned the office into a cluttered Cozzano family museum.

It had started on the day of his first inauguration, with a small photo of his late wife, Christina, placed on the corner of his historically inaccurate desk. Naturally, photos of his children, Mary Catherine and James, came next. But there was no point in stopping with the immediate family, and so Cozzano had brought in several boxes containing pictures of patriarchs and matriarchs going back several generations. He wanted pictures of his friends, too, and of their families, and he also needed various pieces of memorabilia, some of which were chosen for sentimental reasons, some for purely political ones. By the time Cozzano was finished decorating his office, it was almost filled with clutter, smelling salts had to be brought in for the Historical Society, and, as he sat down for the first time in his big leather chair, he could trace the entire genealogy and economic development of the Cozzano clan, and of twentieth-century Illinois, which amounted to the same thing.

There was an old aerial photograph of Tuscola as seen from its own water tower in the 1930s. It was a town of a few thousand people, about half an hour south of the academic metropolis of Champaign-Urbana and a couple of hours south of Chicago. Even in this photo it was possible to see gaudy vaults in the town cemetery, and Duesenbergs cruising the streets. Tuscola was, for a farm town, bizarrely prosperous.

In an oval frame of black walnut was a hand-tinted photograph of his great-grandfather and namesake Guillermo Cozzano, who had come to Illinois from Genoa in 1879. In typically contrary Cozzano fashion he had bypassed the large Italian communities on the East Coast and found work in a coal mine about thirty miles southwest of Tuscola, where soil and coal were the same color. He and his son Giuseppe had gone into the farming business, snapping up one of the last available parcels of high-quality land. In 1912, Giuseppe and his wife had their first child, Giovanni (John) Cozzano, followed three and five years later by Thomas and Peter. All of these events were recorded in photographs, which Cozzano would be more than happy to explain to visitors if they made the mistake of expressing curiosity, or even allowing their eyes to stray in that direction. Most of the photos featured buildings, babies, or weddings.

John Cozzano (photo) lost his mother to influenza at the age of six and, from that point onward, lived his life as if he had been shot from a cannon. During his high-school years in the vigorous 1920s he held down a part-time job at the local grain elevator (photo). By the time economic disaster struck in the 1930s he had worked his way up into the management of that business. With one foot in his father's farm and the other in the grain elevator, John was able to get the family through the Depression in one piece.

In 1933, John fell in love with Francesca Domenici, a young Chicago woman. As evidence of his fitness to be a husband, he decided to buy an enormous stucco Craftsman house on a tree-lined brick street on the edge of Tuscola (photo). Even by the standards of Tuscola, which had an inordinate number of large and magnificent houses, it was a beaut: three stories, six bedrooms, with a full basement and a garage the size of a barn. All of the woodwork was black walnut, thick as railroad ties. He was going to buy the place for five hundred dollars from a railway company man who had gone bankrupt. At this time, John had only three hundred dollars in the bank, and so he was forced to borrow the remaining two hundred.

This quest eventually led him to Chicago, and to the doorstep of Sam Meyer (photo), formerly Shmuel Meierowitz. Sam Meyer operated a number of coexisting businesses out of a single storefront on Maxwell Street, on Chicago's near west side (photo). One thing he did was lend money. Sam's son was named David; he was a lawyer.

Every Italian person John Cozzano had ever spoken to for more than about ten minutes had spontaneously warned him of the danger of borrowing money from Jews. He had accepted these warnings at face value until he overheard Anglo-Saxons in Tuscola warning each other, in exactly the same terms, of the dangers of borrowing money from Italians. John borrowed the money and bought the house. As soon as he had cleaned all the junk out of the basement and taken care of a dire flea infestation, he went back up to Chicago and proposed to Francesca.

He bought a ring from Sam Meyer on credit and they were married in Chicago in June 1934. After a short honeymoon at the Grand Hotel on Mackinac Island (photo), they moved into the big house in Tuscola. Within eleven months, John had repaid all of his debts to Sam Meyer, and he discovered that, contrary to legend, it was possible to carry on a financial transaction with a Jew without forfeiting your shirt, or your immortal soul.

This planted a seed in his mind; he might be able to buy the grain elevator on credit and get rid of the feeble old man and the incompetent drunk whom he had been working for. John spent the rest of the 1930s buying the elevator and then trying to develop it into something bigger: a factory to convert corn into other things. Francesca spent the same time trying to get pregnant. She had four miscarriages but kept trying anyway.

As of the beginning of 1942, when America entered the war, John Cozzano, Mr. Domenici, Sam Meyer, and David Meyer were partners in Corn Belt Agricultural Processors (CBAP), a successful corn syrup production facility in Tuscola, Illinois (photo). John and Francesca were the parents of a brand-new baby boy, William A. Cozzano (photo), who by that time was the fourth grandchild of Giuseppe. He was, however, the first grandson. Everyone who laid eyes on the new baby predicted that he would one day be President of the United States.

Thomas joined the army, was sent in the direction of North Africa, but never got there; his transport ship was sunk by U-boats in the North Atlantic. Peter found gainful employment as a Marine sniper in the Pacific. In 1943 he was taken prisoner by the Japanese and spent the rest of the war starving in a camp. John was both too old and, as a farmer, too strategically important to be sent off to war. He stayed home and tried to keep the family enterprises afloat.

War required lots of parachutes. Parachutes took a hell of a lot of nylon. One of the feedstocks required to manufacture nylon was cellulose. One excellent source of cellulose happened to be corncobs. And John Cozzano's factory had been throwing away corncobs by the hundreds of tons ever since it had gone into production. The heap of corncobs that rose from the prairie outside of Tuscola had now become the highest point in several counties and could be seen from twenty miles away, especially whenever pranksters set fire to it (photo).

Sam Meyer contacted everyone he knew. A lot of these were recent immigrants from Central Europe and were only too happy to invest in a parachute factory, knowing that it could have only one conceivable practical use. John got the nylon production unit up and running just in time to throw out a very low bid on a very large government contract. The next year, Allied shock troops poured into Normandy borne on billowing canopies of Cozzano nylon (photo).

Peter came back from war with bad kidneys and a bad leg. While he was not well equipped for doing physical labor, he performed a useful role as troubleshooter, figurehead, and conversationalist for CBAP until he died of kidney failure in 1955. His father, Giuseppe, died two months later. During the interval between the war and these deaths, things had gone smoothly for the Cozzano family, except for the annihilation of the ancestral farmhouse in 1953 by a tornado (photo).

Two times in two months, the entire Meyer clan, led by Samuel and David, came down from Chicago to attend funeral services. Hotel rooms were scarce in Tuscola and kosher kitchens nonexistent, so John and Francesca put the Meyers up in their big stucco house and did what they could to provide them with acceptable cooking facilities. Francesca learned to keep a blowtorch handy so that Sam Meyer's son-in-law, a rabbi, could perform a ritual cleansing of her oven (photo).

During these visits, William Cozzano, now thirteen, shared his bedroom with a number of younger Meyers, including David's son Mel, who was the same age. They became friends and spent most of the time down the street at Tuscola City Park playing baseball, Jews versus Italians (autographed baseball in glass box).

A year later Samuel Meyer died in Chicago. The Cozzanos all came north. Some of them stayed with the Domenicis, but the Meyers returned the favor by giving other Cozzanos a place to stay. Mel and William shared a mattress on the floor (photo).

After that, Mel and William stayed in constant touch. They liked each other. But they also knew they were the eldest sons of families that had accumulated much and that if they screwed up and lost it, it would be no one's fault but their own.

*The remaining space* in the office was filled with William A. Cozzano's personal memorabilia:

A black-and-white photo of his parents, the Olan Mills logo slanted across the bottom, shot in a makeshift traveling studio in a Best Western motel on the outskirts of Champaign-Urbana in 1948.

An assortment of six-inch-high capital letter *T*'s, made from cloth, mounted under glass, along with a corny photo of the seventeen-year-old Cozzano, pigskin tucked under one arm, other arm held out like a jouster's lance to straight-arm an imaginary line-backer from Arcola or Rantoul.

Diploma from Tuscola High.

A photo of William with Christina, his high-school sweetheart, on the campus of the University of Illinois, where they had both attended college in the early sixties.

A wedding picture, the couple flanked by eight rouged and false-eyelashed sorority belles on one side and seven tuxed and pomaded University of Illinois football players, plus a single Nigerian graduate student, on the other.

Diploma (summa cum laude) with major in business and minor in Romance languages.

A battered and abraded football covered with thick stout signatures, marked ROSE BOWL.

Two photos of Cozzano in the Marines, mounted side by side in the same frame: one, picture-perfect William in full-dress uniform, staring into the distance as though he can see a tunnel of light in the sky at one o'clock high, JFK in glory at the end of the tunnel, asking William what he can do for his country. The second picture, two years later: William Cozzano in a village in the Central Highlands, unshaven, eyes staring out alarmingly white and clean from a smoky face, a slack-jawed, inadvertent grin, a Browning automatic rifle dangling from one hand, a cherubic Vietnamese girl sitting in the crook of the other arm with her left leg wrapped in fresh white gauze, staring up at him with her tiny mouth open in astonishment; Cozzano was smiling through a crazy weariness that threatened to bring him to his knees at the next moment but the girl sensed that she was safe there.

Another glass mount, but instead of cloth letters this one had forged medallions hanging on colorful satin ribbons: a purple heart and a bronze star from Cozzano's first tour and another purple heart and a silver star from his second, surrounded by a flock of lesser decorations.

Baby pictures of Mary Catherine and James.

An illuminated parchment from Pope John XXIII superfluously blessing their marriage.

A picture of his father on a fishing trip in Alaska, shortly before his fatal heart attack.

A photo of Cozzano in his Chicago Bears uniform, sitting on his helmet to keep up and out of a sideline morass, black grease on his cheekbones, blood hardening on his knuckles, grass stains on his shoulder pads.

Pro Bowl rings from a couple of different years in the Nixon and Ford administrations.

The last formal portrait of Christina, shot just before she had been transfigured by radiation and chemotherapy; this one also said "olan mills" and had been shot in a slightly nicer motel room in Champaign-Urbana by the same photographer who had done Cozzano's parents in 1948.

A photo of William giving a victory speech on the front lawn of the family house in Tuscola, flanked by Mary Catherine and James.

Autographed photo of William with George Bush at The Peking Gourmet Restaurant in Arlington, Virginia, a harshly flash-lit amateur snapshot, Cozzano and Bush eating Peking duck in shirtsleeves and yukking it up.

Cozzano jogging around Camp David with Bill and Hillary Clinton.

An invitation to a White House dinner from the current President.

*The dome of* the Illinois State capitol was built on foundations of solid stone seventeen feet thick. Cozzano needed to keep all of this stuff in his line of sight while he worked, because these pictures and souvenirs were his foundations.

Cozzano was reading a letter that he was supposed to sign. He knew that he should simply do it, but his father had told him that he should always read things before he signed them. Since a large part of Cozzano's job involved signing things, this meant that he often worked late. He was holding his big pen in his left fist, nervously popping its cap on and off with the ball of his thumb.

The intercom made a gentle popping noise as Marsha, his secretary, turned on her microphone in the next room. Cozzano startled a little. Marsha had a talent for finding things to do, and when Cozzano stayed late she often hung around for a few hours and did them. Her voice came out of the speaker: "The State of the Union speech is about to begin, Governor."

"Thank you," Cozzano said, and shut off the intercom. "I guess," he added, to himself.

Cozzano reached for the remote control and turned it on to C-SPAN—he could not abide the network anchors—just in time to see the cameras pan over the ritualistic standing ovation given every president, no matter how incompetent. Continuing to thumb buttons on the remote, he caused a little window to open up in the corner of the screen, running the Comedy Channel's live coverage.

The egregious hypocrisy of the scene disgusted him. How could those assholes cheer the person who was leading—wrong, *failing* to lead—the country into disaster?

Eventually the applause died down, and the Speaker of the House reintroduced the president. There was a second obligatory standing ovation. Cozzano scoffed, shook his head, rubbed his temples with the palms of both hands. He couldn't take it. The cameras swept the section where the president's wife and family sat, smiling bravely. The president pathetically waved his arms to quiet the ovation, and then began his speech.

A year from tonight, I hope to stand on the West Front of this great building and begin my second term as your President.

(cheers and applause, mostly from one side of the hall)

He proceeded to do some ritual complaining about the usual topics: the budget deficit and the national debt. Just as predictably, he blamed it on the usual suspects: gridlock in Congress, the growth of entitlements, the insurmountable power of PACs, and, of course, the need to pay interest on the national debt, which had grown to something like ten trillion dollars. The only mildly interesting news coming out of the speech so far was that he intended to adopt a Rose Garden strategy during the coming election year, staying at the White House and doing battle with the two-headed monster of the deficit and the debt. This was the only responsible thing he could have done; but Congress applauded him deliriously.

It was all so completely predictable, so politics-as-usual, that

Cozzano was lulled into a near coma, trapped between boredom and disgust. Which made it all the more shocking when the bombshell hit.

We must either cut entitlements—the payments made to our senior citizens on Social Security, and sick people on Medicare and Medicaid—or we must cut the interest that is paid to the national debt. Now, granted, we borrowed that money. We must pay it back if we can. And we most certainly will make our best effort to pay it back. But not at the expense of the sick and the old.

(applause and cheers)

Our debt is the result of our own sinful irresponsibility in fiscal matters, and we must accept the consequences of those sins. But I am reminded of the words of the great Russian religious figure Rasputin, who once said, in a similar time of economic troubles, "Great sins demand great forgiveness."

(applause)

Let us not forget that we owe this money to ourselves. Surely we can find it in our hearts to repent from our economic foolishness and to forgive ourselves for the mistakes that were made by ourselves and by our predecessors.

(applause)

This nation was founded upon a great social contract. A contract in which people banded together to form governments in the defense of life, liberty, and property. This noble experiment has lasted for more than two centuries. Written into the contract by our founding father Jefferson was the assertion that if government violates the contract, the people have the right to overthrow it. This is the basis of the glorious revolutionary tradition that serves as a shining light of inspiration for the entire world.

(applause; cheers)

Tonight, in the spirit of Jefferson, I call for a new social contract. I am proposing to the Congress, and to the American people, the Declaration of Fiscal Independence.

(applause)

In short, my fellow Americans, I propose as a first step to place a cap on the percentage of our budget that can go toward paying interest on the national debt. The exact level of this cap, and the details of its implementation, are subject to discussion and agreement between my staff and Congress—and I'm sure that we can look forward to many lively discussions on this issue.

(laughter)

But regardless of the details, the message is the same. Great sins demand great forgiveness. Let us now forgive ourselves, so that we may go forth into the brave new world of the third millennium with a clean slate and a clear conscience.

(thunderous applause and cheers)

Let the message go forth to the world that the country of the third millennium will be the United States of America and that its opening breaths of life were sounded in this noble hall on this great evening.

(ten-minute standing ovation)

It was an outrage, pure and simple.

Having failed over his entire term in office to do anything about the budget deficit, the President was now going to patch it up by allowing America to weasel out of its financial obligations.

Which was bad enough in and of itself; but he was also trying to portray this measure as an act of Lincolnian fortitude on his part.

Cozzano felt an atavistic desire to fly to Washington, climb up on that podium, and slap the President across the face. It was the same brute, animalistic impulse that came into his head when he imagined someone hurting his daughter. His heart thumped powerfully a few times. He realized that he was being primitive and stupid, and tried to calm himself down. There was no point in thinking these things.

Still Cozzano did not sign the letter on his desk—a thank-you note to the Prime Minister of Japan for his hospitality during Cozzano's visit last week. His powerful fingers gripped the smooth in-laid barrel of the pen. The rhodium alloy nib, charged with just the correct amount of French ink, was poised a few millimeters above the grainy surface of the buttery cotton-fiber stationery that Coz-zano used for personal correspondence. But when Cozzano moved the pen—that is, when he did the thing in his mind that, ever since he had been inside his mother's womb, had caused his fingers and his hand to move—nothing happened. His eyes tracked across the paper, anticipating the pen's course. Nothing. The President spoke on and on, stopping every few sentences to bask in adulation.

Cozzano's hand sweated. After a while, the pen fell out of his fingers. The nib dove into the paper and slid straight across it like a plow skidding across hard prairie. It left a comet-shaped streak of blue-black on the page, whacked down flat, and rocked side to side for a few moments, making a gentle diminishing noise.

He cursed under his breath and a strange sound came out of his mouth, a garbled word he'd never heard before. It sounded so unfa-miliar that he tried to look up, thinking that someone else might be in the room. But no one was here; he had spoken the word himself.

When he moved his head it threw him off balance and pulled him toward the left. His left arm had gone completely limp. He saw it slide off the desk but he didn't quite believe it, because he didn't feel it move. The cuff link, a cheap hand-me-down from his father, popped against the sharp edge of the tabletop. Then his arm was swinging at his side, eased to a halt by the slight mechanical friction of his elbow and shoulder joints.

He slumped back into the chair's comfortable, Cozzano-shaped recesses. His right arm slid off the desk as he did so and he found that he could move it. He was sitting comfortably in his chair now, sagging leftward. He saw his intercom and knew that he could punch the button and call Marsha. But it was not clear what he should say to her.

His eyes drooped half shut, the sound of the roaring, stomping, howling, and applauding Congress closed in on him like a nail keg lowering over his head, and in his confusion, he lost his will. He was entirely too tired to do anything, and why bother to fight it? He had accomplished enough for several lifetimes. The only thing he'd missed out on so far was having some grandchildren.

That, and becoming President, which he was going to do before the year 2000. But he wasn't sure if he really wanted that awful job anyway.

## CHAPTER TWO

The State of the Union was never a big event in Cacher, Oklahoma. Forty-eight-year-old Otis Simpson yawned and looked at the wall clock, just for the record. It was 02:46:12 Greenwich Mean Time. He turned the sound off. The speech had devolved into endless waves of applause. Commentators were beginning to break into the sound track in hushed, solemn tones, stating the obvious: "the President shaking hands with congressional leaders as he makes his way out of the room." Soon the analysts would come on and tell Otis what he had just watched, and Otis definitely didn't need that. The only opinions that mattered would be coming in via fax and modem during the next few hours. His job was to stay awake in the meantime. So he triggered the other monitor and began to keep one eye on an HBO flick, already in progress.

Otis had inherited his mother's tendency toward bulk, his father Otho's awkward looks, and a light regard for basic hygiene. The many folds in his ample frame contained an inexhaustible supply of sweat-blackened lint balls, and his thinning hair failed to conceal the skin ailments that plagued his scalp. He had never married. His mother had died giving birth to him. He served as a trusted assistant on his father's work, the full extent of which he never fully understood.

Otho Simpson, eighty-six, had, as was his pattern, gone to bed at 00:00:00 Greenwich Mean Time. This time was as good a bedtime as any other and was easy to remember. Otho and Otis lived belowground, in a former lead mine, and did not pay much attention to the diurnal cycle upstairs. Their job was to gather and respond to information from all over the world, from all twenty-four time zones, and so there was not much point in trying to hew to a particular schedule. Otho was spare and gaunt, hampered by persistent urinary tract infections that filled whatever room he was in with a disconcerting odor and caused continual pain. Unlike his son, Otho had a mind that, had he chosen, could have earned him a Nobel Prize in economics or physics or at least made him a very rich man in a more conventional sense. Instead, he had become an accountant of sorts, and spent his life looking after a body of investments with a total cash value in the neighborhood of thirty trillion U.S. dollars.

These assets did not belong to any one specific person or entity, as far as Otho could tell. They belonged to a coordinated international network of investors. Otho didn't know who these people were. He wasn't supposed to know and he probably wasn't supposed to think about it. But he did think about it from time to time, and he had drawn some conclusions based on circumstantial evidence. Most of them were individuals, many were families, some were corporations. Their net worths varied from a few million dollars up to tens of billions. Judging from the hours when they liked to do business, most of them must be living in American and European time zones, with a few in the time zones that were used by Japan, Hong Kong, and Australia. He only knew one member of this organization by name, one Lady Guenevere Wilburdon; she was his contact and his boss.

In the last half century, especially after the death of his wife in 1948, Otho had rarely left Cacher. Several times a week he would hobble onto the lift, ride it several hundred feet straight up to the surface and go for a stroll through the ruins of the town, taking in what passed for fresh air in Cacher and feeling the sun on his skin. But he felt most comfortable down below, in the subterranean capsule that was his home, surrounded by twenty feet of solid reinforced concrete, breathing filtered air and drinking distilled water.

The capsule had been built during the early fifties by a huge international contractor called MacIntyre Engineering. It was built to exactly the same set of specifications used for the control capsules of Minuteman silos—easy enough, since MacIntyre had constructed most of those. Any information that could conceivably influence the performance of the economy—public and proprietary, open and secret, from hard data to vicious gossip—was funneled into the capsule over a variety of communications links. Otho read every word of it and used it to manage the investments of the Network. His life was rather solitary and he had not seen a movie in a theater since *The Sound of Music*, but he did not care; the honor of being the anonymous manager of a significant fraction of the assets of what used to be called the Free World sufficed to give him a value-laden life.

Several hours after the conclusion of the State of the Union address, at 06:00:00 GMT, a digitized chord sounded from one of the workstations, waking Otis up. A window materialized on the screen and filled with columns of numbers. This was normal; it happened every day at this time.

A chorus of faint humming noises was emanating from a stainless steel rack carrying several dozen identical fax machines. Otis was surprised to note that nearly all of the machines suddenly had long strips of paper dangling out of them, and several were still active. Most of his father's clients took a hands-off approach and rarely, if ever, bothered him with specifics.

Otis went to the workstation and scanned the numbers: a statistical summary of how the Network's investments had performed during the last twenty-four hours, and initial responses to the State of the Union Address from the stock exchanges in Delhi, Novosibirsk, Hong Kong, Singapore, and Tokyo. All of the capital markets were sharply down. Commodities, especially gold, were soaring uncontrollably.

The digital clock on the wall clicked to 06:10. Otis went in to wake up Otho. Otho and Otis slept in steel-framed bunk beds in a small room just off the communications center.

"Daddy, the figures for yesterday are in."

Otho sat up in bed without hesitation, as if he'd never been asleep. Another workstation was next to him on a bedside table. He reached out with one withered hand, grabbed a mouse, and chose a few commands from the menus on the screen. A copy of the financial tables materialized. He put on a pair of extremely thick glasses that made his eyes look the size of baseballs.

The numbers for the first part of the day weren't bad. But the State of the Union address had changed all that.

"We got a lot of faxes too," Otis said, handing his father a thick sheaf of slick, curly paper, covered with notes from all over the world, many handwritten.

"Jesus Christ," Otho said, "what did that son of a bitch say?"

"Daddy, I turned the sound off on him and watched an HBO movie."

"Probably not a bad idea. Pull up the CNN monitor tape and rerun the speech for me—no, hold it, I can't stand the thought of watching him. Download a transcript off the news wire."

"Okay, Daddy."

Ten minutes later, Otis brought back the transcript. Otho scanned through it, looking for a few key words, and went almost instantly to the concept of forgiveness. Deep vertical crevices appeared in the middle of his brow and he let out a feeble stream of air through pursed lips.

By this time Otis knew he was in for a long night, so he turned on the bedside TV set and punched up CNBC.

"That bastard has just got every bull and bear in the world going insane." Otho set the faxes down on his bedside table and slipped his feet into a pair of slippers by the bed. "But he's half right. This country has problems. Someone needs to do something or all of its investors will get screwed."

"Investors?"

"Yup. America used to have citizens. Then its government put it up for sale. Now it's got investors. You and I work for the investors."

Otis regarded his father with the mixture of respect, fear, and awe that he had shown since he was a child. "What's going on, Dad?"

"It was just a matter of time before some politician actually became stupid enough to mention forgiving the national debt."

"Like Senator Wright?"

"Yeah. Who died in a plane crash. But obviously the President thought it sounded like a catchy idea."

"How are you going to handle this, Daddy?"

"Crank up the word-processing software. I'm going to do the first round-robin report since the Cuban Missile Crisis. This is too big for me to just fly off the handle—I have to provide the Network some options."

Otho's joints creaked and ground audibly in the nearly perfect silence of the capsule as he made his way out of bed, over to a stainless steel toilet, and from there into the control center. He sat down in front of a large high-resolution monitor and began jotting down a few options, as they came into his head. Later, he could rework them into deathless prose:

a. Pull investment out of the U.S. national debt—absorbing the loss immediately—and explore new areas, such as purchasing the larger part of the former Soviet Union;

b. Do nothing and hope that the American political structure will muddle through;

c. Intervene directly in American politics in order to return it to a certain sort of stability and to insure our long-term investment in the debt;

d. Suggestions?

He then directed his system to send out the message in encrypted burst-mode fax transmissions. Beyond vague geographical indications, he did not know to whom the faxes would go. When he had taken control of the Network's finances fifty years ago, it had been stipulated that all communication would be to code-identified participants.

The returns came in remarkably quickly. In the aftermath of the President's speech, everyone important was awake right now, regardless of time zone.

With the exception of a few Middle Easterners who wanted the Network to invest massively in the Muslim-dominated republics of the former Soviet Union, most of the Network liked the third option. The clincher was a fax from Lady Wilburdon, the acting chairperson, who noted, "You have done well for us, and we place our trust in you. Put your country back in working order."

He spent a few minutes doodling with an old, well-worn slide rule. Back in the early seventies he had purchased a couple of the first pocket calculators and, as a mathematician, been horrified by their illusive precision. The slide rule was a far more trustworthy and illuminating guide to the numerical world.

The United States had borrowed ten trillion dollars since the onset of Reaganomics. A significant fraction of that debt was now owned by the Network. Those loans were supposed to bring in a certain fixed amount of interest every year. The cap proposed by the President would reduce that income by an amount on the order of a few tens of billions of dollars per year—possibly even more, if the country went into a deeper crisis and made further cuts.

In the long run, then, the Network stood to lose hundreds of billions of dollars from the measures that the President had just proposed. Otho was therefore justified in spending real money here —easily in the tens of billions. This was more than enough to throw an election. Perot had nearly done it for just a few hundred million.

Otho knew perfectly well that his Network was not the only organization of its type in the world, and that he was not the only person running through this sort of a calculation tonight. It wasn't enough just to mess around with an election; everyone would be getting into that game during the next few months. The important thing was to do it well, and not just on an ad hoc basis but as part of a coherent long-range strategy.

If the Network planned carefully and wasn't too obvious about it, it could go far beyond managing the outcome of this one election. It could actually erect a system that would enable America's investors to have a permanent say in the management of their assets. It would eat up a lot of the Network's liquidity, but by moving some money around, Otho would be able to free up enough to assemble quite a little war chest. The markets had all gone to hell anyway, providing a perfect cover for the enormous shifts he would have to make in the next couple of days.

The more he thought about it, the more he was convinced that it was a sound decision. He should have done it a long time ago. The fact that he hadn't probably proved that he was obsolete, or something.

The United States of America had served its purpose. It was time to cash her in. Like a big creaky old corporation, her individual parts, intelligently liquidated, were worth more than the whole. She still had the best damn military money could buy, as the Iraqis had discovered during the Gulf War, and she still came up with new ideas better than anyone. Under new, fiscally responsible management, she could still perform well, pay her debts, and provide a tolerable standard of living for her citizens. Otho needed to make sure that that management was provided by the Network and not by one of the other entities with which the Network competed.

He sent out a fax to Mr. Salvador telling him to swing by Cacher for a face-to-face. That was the hard part; he had never been good at the interpersonal stuff. Then he got down to the work he did better than anyone else in the world: sending out sell orders, shuffling assets, arranging his pieces on the board.

In simple numerical terms, liquidating the Constitution of the United States was not the biggest or the most difficult job Otho had ever undertaken. For some reason it made him nervous anyway. Since the Kennedy assassination he'd had nothing but contempt for politicians. But he wasn't attacking a particular president here; he was attacking the institution of the presidency. Meddling with primal forces. He moved slowly, made mistakes in his arithmetic, forgot things, kept going back on his own decisions. It was an unfamiliar sensation to be agonizing about his job. Images kept coming unbidden into his mind, clouding his thoughts: FDR declaring war on Japan, the moon landings, D-Day, football games on Thanksgiving, Lou Gehrig's farewell speech.

More than once his fingers came to a dead stop on the keyboard as these and more personal, more emotional memories surged uncontrollably through his mind. He wondered if senility had finally touched him. Finally he had to get up and hobble over to their little kitchen and take the bottle of vodka out of the freezer. He knew that he was doing the right thing here, that if he didn't, someone else would. But it hurt.

By 10:00:00 GMT, the communications room was once again quiet. Otis woke up from a short nap and went in to check on Otho.

From the dark room, a thin voice almost chanted, "Well you know, this country once worked real well, when we had values that people believed in."

Otis saw the empty vodka bottle on the table, still fogged with condensation, and realized that his father had just gotten drunk for the first time in three decades. "What do you mean by values?"

"They were code words like *honesty, hard work, self-reliance* . . . myths, actually, to motivate the people to accept the natural inequities found in a market system. In the old days, contract was sacred:

divorce, bankruptcy, fraud, were taboos for the average people. The rogues of course, the robber barons were beyond that. We have to return the country to those values so that there won't even be a thought to renege on the debt."

"Daddy . . ."

"Yes, boy?"

"How will you do it?"

"I think I'll hand this one off to Mr. Salvador. He's an ambitious fella. He obviously wants to take my place a couple of years down the road, or whenever Lady Wilburdon decides to replace me. He's an asshole, and there's a good chance he'll get killed or ruined trying to do this. And if he survives, he'll be a better man for it."

"Daddy?"

"Yes, boy."

"Good night, Daddy."

## CHAPTER THREE

"Look, it's *not* like this is some kind of a—" Aaron Green said. Then a cautious instinct took control and he brought himself up short. He was looking over the epaulets of the security guard at a large red sign on the wall: DO NOT MAKE JOKES OR COMMENTS REGARDING WEAPONS OR EXPLOSIVE DEVICES.

"It's not a *what?*" said the guard in front of Aaron, a wiry older white man. Aaron was still trying to decide where to begin when the guard spoke the dreaded words: "Step over here with me, sir."

Aaron followed the guard over to a table, just beyond the picket line of metal detectors, still within the dreaded security zone. Beyond it lay the concourse, a pacifist utopia full of weaponless citizens streaming in an orderly fashion toward their gates. In the overpriced bars and overpriced restaurants, business-suited travelers stood, drinks in hand, below television sets, watching the President deliver his State of the Union address.

"What do we have there, sir?" said the guard behind the table, the chief of this beady-eyed, polyethnic truth squad. He was a very

wide, convex black man with a deep voice and he was trying to
sound open-minded and jolly. He was wearing an ID flasher with
the name BRISTOL, MAX.

"It's a piece of electronic equipment," Aaron said, setting the case
on the table.

"I see. And can you open this up and show it to me?" Bristol said.

The case was largely full of gray foam rubber. A rectangular
cavity the size of a couple of shoe boxes had been excavated from
the center. Filling this cavity was a white steel box with ventilation
slots cut into the top. The box was exactly the right width to fit into
a standard electronics rack.

The plan was that one day, a whole lot of these things would be
stacked together in racks, racks lined up next to each other, hundreds in a single room. The room and the equipment would be
owned by big media companies in L.A. They would buy all of the
stuff from Green Biophysical Systems, of which Aaron Green was
the founder, chief technologist, president, and treasurer.

With the lid of the case open, the upper half of the faceplate was
visible. It had no controls, knobs, or anything, just a single red LED
with the word POWER printed underneath it, and, in big letters, the
Green Biophysical Systems logo, and the acronym IMIPREM.

The power cord was coiled up in a separate niche in the gray
foam rubber. Yet another niche contained an item that Aaron hoped
they wouldn't notice: a cuff. Hard plastic shell lined with black
foam, for comfort. He wondered what the guards would think of
that.

"Looks interesting," the guard said. His insincerity was palpable.
"What is it?"

Aaron took a deep breath. "An instantaneous, multiplexing, inte-
grating, physiological response evaluation and monitoring device."

"What does it do?"

*It doesn't blow up.* "Well. It's a little bit like a polygraph."

"I need to see it work."

"What?"

"I need to see your IMIPREM work," Bristol said.

Aaron pulled the IMIPREM out of its foam rubber nest and set it
on the table. Then he uncoiled the power cord, fit one end into a
three-pronged recessed socket on the back of the unit, and plugged

the other end into a wall outlet near the table. The little LED came on. "There," he said.

Bristol raised his eyebrows and looked extremely dubious. "That's all it does?"

"Well, it does a lot more than that, naturally," Aaron said, "but it has no interface, per se, except through a computer. See, if I could hook this up to a computer, it would produce all kinds of meaningful output."

"But the only thing it'll do right now, here, for me, is turn on this little red light," Bristol said.

Aaron was trying to come up with a diplomatic way to say yes when they were interrupted by another person. He was carrying a laptop computer. He was holding the device out at arm's length.

"Tick, tick, tick, tick!" the man was saying. But he pronounced it "teeuhk, teeuhk." He was one of those southerners who could add syllables to words and make it sound good. "And then somewhere over Newark—BOOM! Haw, haw haw!"

The old guard grinned and guided him to the table.

"Sir," Bristol said.

"Howdy," the man with the computer said. "This is a Compaq— more bang for the buck than IBM! Haw haw!"

As Aaron watched in disbelief, Bristol exchanged a friendly, knowing grin with the big southerner.

"Got a Gamma Prime CPU, a gigabyte drive, and three pounds of Semtex," the southerner said.

He had a smooth, trombonelike voice that could be heard for miles. All of the metal detector guards were looking at him and chuckling. The businessmen filing through the metal detectors, picking their pocket change out of the plastic buckets, were looking at the southerner with appreciative grins, shaking their heads.

He was tall, probably a couple of inches over six feet, had love handles, an unexceptional suit, a high forehead, the beginnings of jowls, a florid complexion, eyebrows raised up in a perpetually surprised or skeptical expression, a tiny little pursed mouth. "Whoa, looks like I got some competition here!" he blurted, eyeing the IMIPREM in mock wonder.

Then his whole face changed; suddenly his eyes were narrowed and darting, he had become secret and conspiratorial, shooting sidelong glances at Bristol, Max. "Abu Jihad!" he hissed at Aaron. "Praise be to Allah! We have perfected a nuclear device capable of fitting under an airline seat!"

The big guard and the southerner joined together in loud, booming laughter. "I got a glass of bourbon with my name on it in that bar by the gate," the southerner finally said, "so let me crank this thing up for you and get on out of here. If you don't mind, sir," he added to Aaron, courteously enough.

"Not at all."

The man snapped the computer open and folded back the top to reveal its screen, a flat, high-resolution, color monitor. Aaron had other things to be worrying about right now, but he couldn't help staring at the man's computer; it was one of the nicest and most powerful laptops you could buy, certainly one of the most expensive. These things had only been on the market for a couple of months. This one was already worn and battered around the edges.

The southerner hit the on button, hollering "BOOM!" so loud that Bristol actually startled a little bit. Then he laughed.

The screen came alive with windows and icons. From a distance, Aaron recognized about half of the icons. He knew what this software did. He could guess that the southerner did a lot of statistical analysis, desktop publishing, and even desktop video production.

"Sir, would this do the trick?" Bristol was saying.

"Yo!" said the southerner, giving Aaron a dig on the arm. "He's talking to you!"

"Huh?" Aaron said.

"Would this computer be capable of talking to your machine there?" Bristol said.

"Well, yes, if it had the right software loaded onto its hard drive. Which it doesn't."

"Oh, I see what's going on," the southerner said. Suddenly he stuck out his hand toward Aaron. "Cy Ogle," he said. "Pronounced, but not spelled, like mogul."

"Aaron Green."

Cy Ogle laughed. "So you have to show this guy here that your box won't blow up when we reach our cruising altitude. And until you hook it up to a computer, it won't do anything except turn on that little red light."

"Exactly."

"Which don't mean jack to him, because that light is about the size of a grain of rice, and for all he knows the rest of the box is full of black powder and roofing nails."

"Well . . . "

"You have the software with you? On floppies? Well, load it in there, and let's take this baby for a spin."

Aaron couldn't believe the guy was serious. But he was. Aaron fished the diskette with the IMIPREM software out of his briefcase and popped it into the drive on Ogle's machine. A single-typed command copied the files onto Ogle's hard drive.

In the meantime, Ogle had already figured out what to do with the cable: he ran it from the back of the IMIPREM into the corresponding port on the laptop.

"Okay. Ready to roll," Aaron said.

Aaron unbuttoned his shirt cuff. He fished the plastic cuff out of the case and snapped it snugly around his exposed wrist.

A ten-foot cable dangled from the cuff. Most of it was coiled up and held together by a plastic wire tie. Aaron plugged it into the back of the IMIPREM.

A new window materialized on the screen of Ogle's computer. It was a moving, animated bar graph. Half a dozen colored bars, of different lengths, fluctuated up and down. At the base of each bar was a label:

BP     RESP     TEMP     PERSP     PULS     GSR
NEUR

"It's monitoring my body right now. See, the bars stand for blood pressure, respiration, body temp, and a few other things. Of course, this is its most basic level of functioning, beyond this it's capable of an incredible number of different—"

Ogle's hand slammed down on Aaron's shoulder and gripped him like a pair of barbecue tongs.

"I'm an undercover agent for the Bureau of Alcohol, Tobacco, and Firearms," Cy Ogle said, "you're under arrest for conspiracy to commit terrorist acts on board an airliner. Don't move or you'll be shot!"

"What!?" Aaron screamed.

"Just kidding," Ogle said. "Haw, haw!"

"He's right, look at the bars," the guard said.

Blood pressure and just about everything else had suddenly shot way up. As they watched, and as Aaron calmed down, the bars subsided.

"Thanks for the demonstration, sir, it was very interesting," the guard said. "Have a nice flight."

Then Bristol turned to look down the concourse. Aaron and Ogle were both looking that way too; some kind of generalized disturbance seemed to have broken out. But it wasn't hooligans or terrorists. It was businessmen in suits, stampeding out of the bars and restaurants where they had been watching the President on TV. They ran down the concourse, knocking travelers and sky caps aside, and began to scuffle over the few available pay telephones.

Ogle chuckled indulgently. "Looks like the President made a corker of a speech," he said. "Maybe we should hook your machine up to *them*."

*As it turned* out, they were on the same flight, sitting across the aisle from each other in the first row of first class. Coach was full of shuffling grannies and beefy sailors; first class was mostly empty. Ogle worked on his computer for the first hour or so, whacking the keys so rapidly that it sounded like a hailstorm on the tray table, occasionally mumbling a good-natured "shit!" and doing it again.

Aaron pulled a blank tablet of graph paper out of his briefcase, uncapped a pen, and stared at it until they were somewhere over Pittsburgh. Then it was dinnertime and he put it away. He was trying to organize his thoughts. But he didn't have any.

After dinner, Ogle moved from the window to the aisle seat, right across from Aaron, and then startled Aaron a little by ordering them both drinks.

"Big presentation," Ogle said.

Aaron heaved a sigh and nodded.

"You got some kind of small high-tech company."

"Yeah."

"You developed this thing, spent all your venture capital, probably maxed out your credit cards to boot, and now you got to make some money off it or your investors will cash you in."

"Yeah, that's about right."

"And the cash flow is killing you because all the parts that go into these things cost money, but you don't actually get paid for them until, what, thirty or sixty days after you ship 'em. If you're lucky."

"Yeah, it's a problem all right," Aaron said. His face was getting red. This had started out interesting, gotten uncanny, and now it was starting to annoy him.

"So, let's see. You're going to L.A. The big industry in L.A. is entertainment. You got a device that measures people's reactions to things. A people meter."

"I wouldn't call it a people meter."

"Course not. But that's what they'll call it. Except it's a whole lot better than the usual kind, I could see that right away. Anyway, you're going to go meet with a bunch of executives for movie and television studios, maybe some ad agencies, and persuade 'em to buy a whole bunch of these things, hook 'em up to man-on-the-street types, show 'em movies and TV programs so they can do all that test audience stuff."

"Yeah, that's about right. You're a very perceptive man, Mr. Ogle."

"What I get paid for," Ogle said.

"You work in the media industry?"

"Yeah, that's a good way to put it," Ogle said.

"You seem to know a lot about what I do."

"Well," Ogle said. All of a sudden he seemed quiet, reflective. He pushed the button on his armrest and leaned his chair back a couple of inches. He leaned his head back and closed his eyes, curled one hand around his drink. "High-tech has its own biorhythms."

"Biorhythms?"

Ogle opened one eye, turned his head a bit, peered at Aaron. "Course you probably don't like that word because you are Mr. High Tech, and it sounds to you like cocktail-party pseudoscience."

"Exactly." Aaron was beginning to think that Ogle knew him better than he knew himself.

"Fair enough. But I have a legitimate point here. See, we live under capitalism. Capitalism is defined by competition for capital. Would-be businessmen, and existing businesses seeking to expand, fight for the tiny supply of available capital like starving jackals around a zebra leg."

"That's a depressing image."

"It's a depressing country. It's not like that in other countries where people save more money. But it's like that here, now, because we don't have values that encourage savings."

"Okay."

"Consequently you are starved for capital."

"Right!"

"You had to get capital from venture capitalists—or vulture capitalists, as we call them—who are like the vultures that feed on the jackals when they become too starved and weak to defend themselves."

"Well, I don't think my investors would agree."

"They probably would," Ogle said, "they just wouldn't do so in your presence."

"Okay."

"Venture capitalism is risky and so the vulture capitalists hedge their bets by pooling funds and investing in a number of start-ups at once—backing several horses, as it were."

"Of course."

"But what they don't tell you is that at a certain point a couple of years into its life cycle, the start-up suddenly needs to double or triple its capitalization in order to survive. To get over those cash flow problems that occur when orders suddenly go from zero to more than zero. And when that happens, the vulture capitalists look at all of their little companies and they cull out the weakest two-thirds and let them starve. The rest, they provide with the capital they need in order to continue."

Aaron said nothing. Suddenly he was feeling tired and depressed.

"That's what's happening to your company right now," Ogle said. "You're, what, three years old?"

"How'd you know that!?" Aaron said, twisting around in his seat, glaring at Ogle, who remained quiescent in his big fat chair. He was almost expecting to see a crew from *Candid Camera* filming him from the galley.

"Just a lucky guess. Your logo," Ogle said, "you designed your logo yourself."

Again Aaron's face reddened. He had, in fact, designed it himself. But he thought it was fairly professional, a lot more so than the typical home-brewed logo. "Yeah, so what?" he said. "It works. And it was free."

"Okay, this is ridiculous," Aaron said. "How did you know that?"

"If you were old enough to have made the cut—if you had passed through the capitalization barrier—you would have immediately gone out and hired professional designers to spiff up your corporate image. The vultures would have insisted on it."

"Yeah, that was going to be our next step," Aaron said.

"That's okay. That speaks well of you, as a scientist, if not as a businessman," Ogle said. "A lot of people start with image and then try to develop substance. But you are a techie and you hate all that superficial crap. You refuse to compromise."

"Well, thank you for that vote of confidence," Aaron said, not entirely sarcastically.

The flight attendant came through. They each ordered another drink.

"You seem to have this all figured out," Aaron said.

"Oh, no, not at all."

"I don't mean that to sound resentful," Aaron said. "I was just wondering—"

"Yes?" Ogle said, raising his eyebrows very high and looking at Aaron over his glasses, which he had slid down his nose.

"What do you think? You think I have a chance?"

"In L.A.?"

"Yeah."

"With the big media moguls?"

"Yeah."

"No. You don't have a chance."

Aaron heaved a big sigh, closed his eyes, took a gulp of his drink. He had just met Ogle but he instinctively knew that everything that Ogle had said, all night long, was absolutely true.

"Which doesn't mean that your company doesn't have a chance."

"It doesn't?"

"Course not. You got a good product there. It's just that you don't know how to market it."

"You think I should have gone out and gotten a flashy logo."

"Oh, no, I'm not saying that at all. I think your logo's fine. It's just that you have a misconception in your marketing strategy."

"How so?"

"You're aiming at the wrong people," Ogle said, very simply and plainly, as if he were getting annoyed at Aaron for not figuring this all out on his own.

"Who else can I aim at with a product of this type?"

Ogle squeezed his armrest again, leaned forward, allowed his seat to come upright. He put his drink on his tray table and sat up straight, as if getting down to work. "You're right in thinking that the media need to do people-metering kinds of stuff," he said. "The problem is that the kinds of people who run media companies are not going to buy your product."

"Why not? It's the best thing like it. It's years ahead."

Ogle cut him off with a dismissive wave of the hand. "Doesn't matter," he said flatly, and shook his head. "Doesn't matter."

"It doesn't matter how good my product is?"

"Not at all. Not with those people. Because you are selling to media people. And media people are either thugs, morons, or weasels. You haven't dealt very much with media people, have you?"

"Very little."

"I can tell. Because you don't have that kind of annoying, superficial quality that people get when they deal for a living with thugs, morons, and weasels. You are very earnest and sincere and committed to certain principles, as a scientist, and thugs and morons and weasels do not understand that. And when you give them an explanation of how brilliant your machine is, you'll just be putting them off."

"I have spent a hell of a lot of time finding ways to explain this device in terms that almost anyone can understand," Aaron said.

"Doesn't matter. Won't help. Because in the end, no matter how you explain it, it comes down to fine, subtle technicalities. Media people don't like that. They like the big, fabulous concept." Ogle pronounced "fabulous" with a mock-Hollywood gush.

Aaron laughed rather hotly. He had seen enough media people to know this was true.

"If you come to a media person and you want to do a miniseries about the Civil War, or Shakespeare, or the life of J. S. Bach, they will laugh in your face. Because nobody wants to watch that stuff. You know, intelligent stuff. They want pro wrestling. Media people who try to do Shakespeare get fired or go broke. The only ones who survived long enough to talk to you are the ones who backed pro wrestling. And when you come up to them talking about the fine points of your brilliant technology, it makes them think of Shakespeare and Leonardo da Vinci, which they hate and fear."

"So I'm dead."

"If you rely on selling to media people, you're dead."

"But who else needs a device like this one except for media people?"

"Well," Ogle said softly, sounding almost surprised, as if he hadn't gotten around to considering this question. "Well, actually, I could use it. Maybe."

"You said you were in media," Aaron said.

Ogle held one finger up. "Not exactly. I said I worked in the media industry. But I am not a media person, per se."

"What are you?"

"A scientist."

"And what is your field of study?"

"You, Aaron, are a biophysicist. You study the laws that determine the functioning of the body. Well, I am a political biophysicist. I study the laws that govern the functioning of the body politic."

"Oh. Could you be a little more specific?"

"People call me a pollster," Ogle said. "Which is like calling you a palm reader."

## CHAPTER FOUR

Eleanor Boxwood Richmond heard the State of the Union address on the radio, but she didn't really listen to it. She was driving a borrowed car down abandoned streets in Eldorado Highlands, an aborted suburb ten miles north of Denver. She had borrowed the car from Doreen, who lived in the trailer next to hers, several miles to the east, in the town of Commerce City.

In case the police tried to phone with any news of her husband, Eleanor had dropped her football phone out her kitchen window, pulled it across the gap between her trailer and Doreen's, and fed it through the window of Doreen's bedroom. Eleanor's husband, Harmon, for whom she was searching, had obtained the football phone free of charge by subscribing to *Sports Illustrated* some years ago. Now the *Sports Illustrated*s were still showing up on time, every week, while Harmon himself, depressed by unemployment and bankruptcy, had become more and more erratic. Some things you could at least count on.

Eleanor felt foolish and humiliated every time she spoke on the football phone. It did not make looking for a job in the banking industry any easier. She would sit there in her trailer, which would be baking hot or freezing cold according to the outside temperature. She kept the windows closed even in summer so that the screaming of Doreen's kids, and the heavy metal from the trailer on the other side, would not be audible to the person she was speaking to. She would telephone people wearing dark suits in air-conditioned buildings and she would hold the little plastic football to the side of her head and try to sound like a banker. So far she had not gotten any jobs.

Back in the old days, when the whole family had lived together, happily, in their big house in this suburban development in Eldorado Highlands, they had had a phone in every room. In addition to the football phone they had had a sneaker phone; a cheap little Radio Shack phone that would always go off the hook unless you set it down firmly on a hard surface; and a couple of solid, traditional AT&T telephones. All of these phones had disappeared during the second burglary of their trailer and so they had been forced to get the football phone out of storage and use that instead.

Eleanor Richmond had not seen her husband, Harmon, in two days. For the first day, this had been more of a relief than anything else, because usually when she did see him, he was half-reclined on their broken-backed sofa in front of the TV set, drinking. From time to time he would go out and get a McJob, work at it for a few days, quit or get fired, and then come back home. Harmon never lasted very long at McJobs because he was an engineer, and flipping burgers or jerking Slurpees grated on his nerves, just as talking on the football phone grated on Eleanor's.

The neighborhood that Eleanor was driving through had been built on a perfectly flat high plains ranch in the early eighties. All of the houses were empty, and three-quarters of them always had been; as you drove down the curvy streets, you could look across yards that were reverting to short-grass prairie, in through the front windows of the houses, all the way through their empty interiors, out the back windows, across a couple of more yards, and through another similar house on another similar street.

Eleanor and Harmon Richmond had purchased their house brand new, before the carpet was even installed. It was early in the Reagan administration. Harmon worked for a medium-sized aerospace firm that sold avionics to the Defense Department. Eleanor had just finished raising their two children to school age and had reentered the workforce. She had started out as a teller for a bank in Aurora and been promoted to customer service representative in fairly short order. Soon she would be branch manager. Eleanor's mother, a widow, had sold the ancestral town house in Washington, D.C., and moved out to a fairly nice retirement community a short distance away.

They were doing pretty well for themselves. So, when the houses around them remained empty, for a month, then six months, then a year, and the value of their house began to fall, they didn't get too worried about it. Everyone makes a bum investment now and then. They were well compensated, the mortgage payments weren't that bad, and they could easily cover their expenses, including the monthly payment to Mother's retirement community.

Times had actually been good for several years. They should have taken advantage of that to squirrel some money away. But the Richmonds were the only people in their respective families who had managed to make the breakthrough to the middle class, which meant that each one of them had a coterie of siblings, nephews, nieces, and cousins living in various ghettos up and down the East

Coast, all of whom felt they had a claim on what they all imagined was the family fortune. They wired a lot of money back East. It didn't come back.

They broke even until the early nineties, when Harmon's company got LBO'd, and the financiers in New York who had bought it began to break it up and sell off the little parts to various people. The particular part of it that Harmon worked for got sold to Gale Aerospace, a defense contractor based in Chicago. They gave him a choice: move to Chicago or move to Chicago. But they couldn't move to Chicago without selling their house, which now was worth half what they had paid for it. Harmon got fired.

The following year, the bank that Eleanor worked for was bought out by a huge California bank that already had millions of branches all over the area—including one that was directly across the street from the one where Eleanor worked. They closed her branch and she lost her job.

The foreclosure on their house had not been long in coming. They had bounced around from one big apartment complex to another for a few years and finally wound up in the trailer park in Commerce City, next to Doreen. They still had two cars, a 1981 Volvo wagon that they had bought used, and a rather old Datsun that did not work anymore and was parked, permanently, in front of the trailer. Harmon had taken the Volvo with him when he disappeared, stranding Eleanor in the trailer.

She had sought him everywhere else. Now, just for the sake of being complete, she was back in the old neighborhood.

It was amazing how quickly you forgot the street patterns. It was almost as if the people who laid these things out wanted you to get lost. She drove for a quarter of an hour down the winding lanes, courts, and terraces, flipping U-turns in circles. The voice of the President of the United States continued to whinny from the radio. The words seemed almost devoid of meaning and the rhythm of the speech was constantly broken up by outbursts of applause and cheering. The pale, desiccated prairie grass, dusted with powdery snow, reflected the moonlight through the windows of the empty houses. Many of the streets had never been finished; the asphalt would simply terminate and become a hard-packed arroyo lined with uncompleted houses, their naked studs and unconnected plumbing lines projecting into the dry air like the rib cages of dead animals.

Finally she saw some landmarks that reminded her of where she was, and her old reflexes took over, guiding her automatically through the twists and turns.

Their house sat up on a little rise at the end of a cul-de-sac, a lollipop-shaped street that broadened into a circle at the end. Their house was right at the top of the lollipop, looking down the length of the street and out over a nice view of the Rockies rising into the night sky with the lights of Denver lapping up against them.

The house shone tonight in the moonlight. The "White House." They had called it that partly because it was white, and partly because moving into it had made them feel like they were white people.

It was meant ironically. Feeling like a white person had never been one of Eleanor Richmond's big goals in life. She had grown up in the heart of Washington, D.C., and had often gone for weeks at a time without seeing a single white face. People would come in from other parts of the country and complain about how the system was stacked against them: the cops and the judges and the juries were all white. But in D.C., the cops and judges and juries were all black. As were the teachers and the preachers and the nuns who had educated Eleanor. She had never gotten the sense that being black singled her out in any way. In some ways that had actually made it easier for her and Harmon to settle down in a predominantly white middle-class area.

Still, moving into a white house in a suburban development in Colorado had made her feel like a pioneer on the edge of the wilderness. She had often longed to jump into the Volvo and drive back to D.C. It felt better if she joked about it, and so she called it the White House. And when her relatives from D.C. came out to visit and bum money off of them, she laughed and joked about the White House all the way from the airport, so that by the time they got there, and saw just how white it was, they were ready for it, and they didn't take her for some kind of traitor.

When she pulled into the old cul-de-sac, the White House was dead ahead, sitting up on its little hill, and it was all lit up from

within. The only house within a mile that was lit up. Someone must
have broken into it and turned all the power back on at the circuit
panel.

Someone named Harmon.

Eleanor braked Doreen's little car to a halt, there in the handle of
the little lollipop street, and sat for a couple of minutes, staring
through the windshield, up the hill, at the White House full of light
and good cheer.

The Volvo was not visible anywhere. But the light inside the
garage was turned on. Once he'd gotten the power restored, he
must have used it to open the garage door, and parked the Volvo
inside, just like in the old days.

Eleanor was trying to make up her mind what she should do
now. Because her husband had clearly gone crazy. Either that, or
gotten so drunk that he might as well be crazy.

She was tired of having crazy relatives. Her mother had
Alzheimer's. They had moved her to a much cheaper nursing home
and might have to move her into the trailer any day now. She was
basically crazy. Her kids were both teenagers, hence crazy by definition. Now her husband was crazy.

Eleanor Richmond was the only person in the whole family who
was not crazy.

Not that she wasn't tempted.

Eventually she reasoned that, crazy or not, it wouldn't do her
husband any good to wind up in jail. He might think, in his own
crazy, drunk mind, that he still owned this house. But he didn't. The
Resolution Trust Corporation owned it; they had taken it over from
the defunct savings and loan that had foreclosed on it. Eventually
the RTC would probably sell it to speculators who would come and
strip out the usable wiring and carpets, or maybe just bulldoze the
whole thing down to its floor slab and turn the neighborhood into a
dirt-bike track or a toxic waste dump. Eleanor knew that this house
was walking dead, a real estate zombie, and that it was going to be
wasted. But that didn't change the fact that they didn't own it anymore and Harmon could go to jail for having broken into it.

Maybe going to jail would do Harmon some good. Shame him a
little, snap him out of his depression.

But she kept saying that to herself every time something bad happened to them and it never worked; he just got more depressed and bitter. He didn't need any more shame.

She'd better go get him. Once again, Eleanor, the solid one, the noncrazy maternal figure, would bail everyone else out. Someday she would have to indulge herself and go crazy a little and let someone else bail her out. But she didn't know anyone who was up for the job.

*The front door* was unlocked. The house smelled funny. Maybe it had been shut up for too long, baking in the sun that poured in through the windows all day, peeling all kinds of fumes and chemicals out of the paint and the carpet and making the air stink. She left the door open.

"Harmon?" she said. Her voice echoed off every wall.

There was no answer. He was probably dead drunk in the living room.

But he was not in the living room. The only things there, the only sign that Harmon had been in the place at all, were a few tools dropped on the floor in one corner of the room, over by a little broom closet where they used to store the slide projector and the Monopoly game and the jigsaw puzzles.

The door to the broom closet was open, the tools spilled out on the floor next to it. A hammer and a crowbar. Eleanor would have known that they were Harmon's even if he had not carefully painted RICHMOND on the handle of each one, in her nail polish.

The thin strip of trim that ran around the door had been removed entirely and thrown on the floor, little nails poking up into the air. Uncovered drywall had been exposed where the piece of trim had covered it up, and Eleanor could see dents in it where Harmon had inserted the crowbar.

The door opening was lined with another piece of trim, a doorjamb with a little brass strike plate about halfway up where the latch of the door would catch. Harmon had tried to pry this jamb off.

Eleanor squatted down in the doorway and put her hand on the doorjamb. An uneven ladder of pencil and ball-point pen marks climbed up the wood. Each mark had a name and a date written next to it: Harmon Jr.—age 7, Clarice—age 4. And so on. They reached all the way up to nearly Eleanor's height; the last one was marked Harmon Jr.—age 12.

Harmon had tried to pry the jamb off and take it with him. But the wood was thin and cheap, and under the twisting force of his crowbar, it had split in half down the middle, half of it remaining nailed down to the door frame, the other half pulled halfway out, white unstained wood exposed where it had shattered.

She wondered how long Harmon had been sitting there on their broken-backed sofa in the trailer in Commerce City, his beer in his hand, meditating over this doorjamb, planning to come and take it away. Had it been eating away at him ever since they had moved out?

Clarice's birthday was next week. Maybe he intended to give this to her as a birthday present. It had great sentimental value, and it was free.

"Harmon?" she said, again, and heard it echo again off the bare walls of the house. She went to check the bedrooms, but he wasn't in any of them.

The sound of music finally drew her to the garage. Faint, tinny music was coming out of the Volvo's stereo. It was barely audible through the mud room door. She went into the garage.

Harmon was sitting in the driver's seat of the Volvo, reclined all the way back. Once she got the door open, she recognized the music: Mahler's Resurrection Symphony. Harmon's favorite. Years ago, on their first trip to Colorado, they had parked on the summit of Pike's Peak and listened to this tape, loud.

She walked quietly up the flank of the Volvo and looked in the driver's window. Harmon had leaned the seat all the way back and folded up his jacket to make a little pillow on the headrest. His eyes were closed and he wasn't moving.

The keys were in the ignition, in the ON position. The tank was empty. The engine was dead. The volume on the stereo was turned all the way up. The tape had been running for hours, possibly even days, auto-reversing itself back and forth, playing the symphony over and over again, running the battery down until hardly anything came out of the speakers.

Harmon was dead. He had been dead for quite some time.

Before she did anything else she reached inside the car and pounded the garage door opener clipped to the sun visor. The big door creaked open, letting in a rush of fresh clean air and opening up a clear glittering view of the suburbanized foothills.

It was a very sensible thing to do. Eleanor Richmond did it because she was not crazy, would not allow herself to be crazy, would not allow herself to succumb to the poison gas that her husband had used to kill himself. Her kids and her mother needed her and she could not indulge herself the way Harmon had.

She did not want to look at Harmon or touch his body and so she went and sat on the front steps of the White House for a while, letting tears run down her face and shatter her clear view of the lights of Denver. She did not have any shoulder to rest her head on and so she scooted over to one end of the step and leaned against the white vinyl siding of the house, which gave a little under the weight of her head.

After a while, she walked back in through the open front door and went back into the living room. She picked up her husband's crowbar from where he had thrown it away. The floor was dented beneath it; he must have hurled it down there in a rage when the door jamb had shattered. From there he had probably gone straight to the Volvo.

Eleanor worked the point of the crowbar underneath the portion of the doorjamb that was still nailed down, and prying gently, a little at a time, moving the crowbar up and down its length, worked the jamb loose from the frame of the house. It held together okay and she knew that a little Elmer's glue would fix it right up. She would ask Doreen's boyfriend to nail it up to the wall of the trailer and then she would have Clarice and Harmon, Jr., stand against it and she would measure their height and mark their progress. They would roll their eyes and say it was stupid, but they would secretly love it.

Every few seconds, all the way through this, she remembered, with a shock, that her husband was dead.

She carried the doorjamb out and fed it in through the open window of Doreen's car. It still stuck out a little bit but it would be okay for the drive home. Living in Commerce City, watching Mexicans, she had learned that you could get away with letting just about anything hang out the windows of your car. She backed out of the driveway and turned around in the big circle and left the White House beyond, driving aimlessly into the heart of her old neighborhood, looking for another house with lights in it, a house where they might have a working telephone.

# the ride

## CHAPTER FIVE

Marsha Wyzniewczki's relationship with her boss had never been ceremonious. When he didn't answer for the third time, she got up from her desk, worked up a good head of steam accelerating across ten feet of office floor, and threw her full hundred and ten pounds against one of the two tall, narrow, Lincolnesque doors that separated her office from the Governor's.

A small old gray man was hunched over in the Governor's chair, in a pool of light in the dark office. Marsha had to look at him for several seconds before she was completely sure that this man was William Anthony Cozzano, the tall sturdy hero who had entered the office a few hours ago, ruddy from his afternoon jog up around Lincoln's Tomb. He had somehow been transformed into *this*. A wraith from the VA Hospital.

A mother's reflex took over; she groped for the wall switch, lighting up the office. "Willy?" she said, addressing him this way for the first time ever. "Willy, are you all right?"

"Call," he said.

"Call whom?"

"Goddamn it," he said, unable to remember a name. This was the first time she had ever heard him utter profanity when he knew that she was listening. "Call her."

"Call whom?"

"The three-alarm lamp scooter," he said.

Cozzano flapped his right arm, causing his whole body to bend perilously to that side, and pointed across the office at his wall of pictures. "Three-alarm lamp scooter."

Marsha couldn't tell which picture he was pointing at. Christina? The little Vietnamese girl? One of the bridesmaids? Or his daughter, Mary Catherine?

Mary Catherine was a doctor, three years out of medical school.

She was a neurology resident at a big hospital in Chicago. The last time the Governor had gone to the city, he had visited her apartment and come back chuckling about one detail of her life: She spent so much time on call and slept so little that she had to have three alarm clocks by her bed.

"Mary Catherine?"

"Yes, goddamn it!"

Marsha went back to her little cockpit, where she sat all day, irradiated on three sides by video screens. Sliding a computer mouse around on the desktop, she located Mary Catherine Cozzano's name and slapped a button. She heard the computer dialing the number, a quick tuneless series of notes, like the song of an exotic bird.

"South Shore Hospital switchboard, may I help you?"

Cozzano's voice broke in before Marsha could say anything; he had picked up his extension. "The budlecker! Make the budlecker go!" Then, infuriated at himself: "No, goddamn it!"

"Excuse me?" the operator said.

"Mary Catherine Cozzano. Pager 806," Marsha said.

"Dr. Cozzano is not on call at this time. Would you like to speak to the doctor who is?"

Marsha did not understand that the following words were true until she spoke them: "This is a family emergency. A medical emergency."

Then she dialed 911 on another line.

Then she went back into the Governor's office to make sure that he was comfortable in his chair. He had slumped over to one side. His right arm kept lashing out like a gaff, trying to hook onto something sturdy enough to pull his full weight, but the surface of his desk offered no purchase.

Marsha grabbed the Governor's upper left arm in both of her hands and tried to move him. But Cozzano reached across his body with his right hand and gently, firmly, pulled her hands loose. She watched his hand for a moment, confused, then noticed that he was staring directly into her eyes.

He glanced significantly at the telephone on his desk. "Fuck me," he said. "Get the maculator!" Then he closed his eyes tight in frustration and shook his head. "No, goddamn it!"

"The maculator?"

"The old Egyptian. Glossy head. He'll fix this muggle. Get the boy of my father's acehole! Ace in the hole."

"Mel Meyer," she said.

"Yeah."

That was an easy one; Mel was the second preset on the Governor's phone, a one-button job. Marsha picked up the phone and pushed that button, with a sense of relief that made her decisive. Mel was the guy to call. She should have called him first, before calling the ambulance.

She ended up having to try a couple of numbers before she reached him on his car phone, somewhere on the streets of Chicago.

"What is it!" Mel snapped, getting things off to a typically brisk start.

"It's Marsha. The Governor has had a stroke or something."

"Oh, no!" William A. Cozzano said. "You're right. I had a stroke. That's terrible."

"When?" Mel said.

"Just now."

"Is he dead?"

"No."

"Is he in distress?"

"No."

"Who is aware of this?"

"You, me, an ambulance crew."

"Is the ambulance there?"

"Not yet."

"Listen carefully." In the background, Marsha heard honking, the squealing of tires, the dim filtered sound of other motorists shouting at Mel, their voices Dopplering weirdly as they veered and accelerated around him. He must have pulled onto the shoulder, sidewalk, or wherever else he saw clear space. Mel kept talking smoothly and without interruption. "You don't want an ambulance there. Even at night the Capitol is crawling with media jackals. Damn that glass wall!"

"But—"

"Shut up. I know you have to get him medical attention. Who's on security detail? Mack Crane?"

"Yes."

"I'll call and tell him to get Willy into the dumbwaiter. You take the stairs down to the basement—don't wait for the damn elevator, don't talk to any press—and find Rufus Bell, who's down in the boiler room, smoking Camels and waiting for the lottery numbers to come up on TV. Tell him that the Governor needs his help. Tell him to clear a path to the civil defense tunnel."

Then Mel hung up. Marsha was saying, "Civil defense?"

The Governor was smiling at Marsha with one side of his face. The other side was expressionless. "He is a smart back," he said. "No! You know what I mean. Do what he said."

The Governor's offices were separated from the rest of the capitol by a huge glass wall that completely sealed off the east wing. Just inside the glass wall was a generously sized reception area, furnished with leather chairs and davenports, where visitors waited to see the Governor or his staff. Right up against the glass was a security desk where Mack Crane or another member of the Governor's security detail was always stationed, twenty-four hours a day, keeping a sharp eye on anyone who approached from the direction of the rotunda. Mack was a plainclothes Illinois cop, bald head fringed with straight, steely hair, wearing an unfashionably wide tie over a short-sleeved shirt. By the time Marsha had made it out of the Governor's office, through her own office, and out into the reception area, Mack's phone was already ringing, and as she punched her way out through the glass doors, heading for the Rotunda, she could hear him saying, "Hi, Mel."

Rufus Bell was downstairs in his little asbestos empire, smoking unfiltered Camels and watching television on a little black-and-white set he had poised on an upended bucket, when Marsha drove her shoulder into the steel door of the boiler room. Something in her manner caused him to rise to his feet.

"This is an emergency," she said. "The Governor needs your help."

Bell flicked his cigarette into a coffee can full of water, scoring a direct hit from ten feet away, simultaneously punching the TV's off switch with a knee. Then he just stared at her and Marsha realized he was waiting for instructions.

"Is there a civil defense tunnel or something?"

By way of saying yes, Bell strode over to a big sheet of stained and lacquered plywood bolted to a wall. The plywood had dozens of cup hooks screwed into it. A key chain dangled from each cup hook. He grabbed one.

"Willy's coming down," Marsha said. She swallowed. "On the dumbwaiter."

Rufus froze solid for a long moment, then turned around and looked searchingly at Marsha.

"You need to clear a path from the dumbwaiter to the civil defense tunnel. Big enough for a stretcher."

Bell shrugged. "Shouldn't be hard," he said, exiting the room. He was a big round man with a rolling gait that looked slow, but Marsha had to hurry to keep up.

As they came into the hallway, Bell turned and held the key chain out to her, suspending it by a single one of its myriad keys, held between his thumb and forefinger. "You want me to clear that hallway, you gotta do the tunnel yourself. End of this hall, take a right, go to the very end."

Marsha had thought that she knew her way around the state house but now was beginning to feel lost and uncertain. But Bell was staring at her remorselessly, holding the key chain right up in her face, and she had to do it. She took the keys, getting a firm grip on the important one, and ran down the hallway.

"Yo!" Bell said, "you'll need this!"

She turned around to see Bell holding up a thick black rubber-coated flashlight. He clicked it on, waved it back and forth a couple of times, and underhanded it to her down thirty feet of hallway. She plucked it out of its spinning trajectory with a one-handed grab, shattering two fingernails, and spun on her heel.

Behind her she could hear a tremendous clattering; looking back she saw Rufus beginning to shove entire file cabinets this way and that. That was all she took in before she turned down the next corridor.

It was built from several different kinds of masonry pieced together and then painted the same color, a thick glossy industrial yellow. The ceiling was obscured by bundles of heavily insulated pipes and ventilated steel conduits carrying thick black electrical cables. The corridor was narrowed by flimsy steel cabinets and racks lining the walls, stuffed with maintenance supplies, gutted Selectrics, and ancient civil defense biscuits.

The door at the end of the hall was small, heavy, and almost too dimly illuminated to see. A heavily yellowed cardboard sign was stuck to it, bearing the FALLOUT SHELTER emblem. Once it was unlocked, it took a mighty tug just to budge it. Then it opened slowly and steadily, with the momentum of a battleship, and slammed into the wall hard enough to knock off chips of the thick old yellow paint. Beyond was a circular tunnel stretching away, ruler-straight, for as far as the beam of the flashlight could penetrate. It was barely high enough for her to enter without stooping. Cold air oozed out and flowed over her shins.

She aimed the beam at the floor, because her main concern at this point was to notify any vermin of her approach so that they would at least have the option of getting out of her path. Then she ducked through the low frame of the door.

Running down the tunnel, she tried to figure out which direction she must be going now. Her trip down the stairway had gotten her all spun around. She decided that she must be going north, under Monroe Street, toward the squat limestone building, the former steam plant, that housed the Illinois Emergency Services and Disaster Agency.

Finally she reached the end of the tunnel. There was another massive blastproof door here, which opened using the same key; clearly Rufus Bell had been through from time to time, oiling the lock and the hinges. She threw the bolt and put her shoulder against the door, the silky filaments of her blouse snagging on the rough layers of rust and flaked paint.

But it seemed to open by itself. Brilliant light poured through. She was looking into a wide hallway in another basement somewhere. Four people were staring at her in amazement: one custodian and three emergency medical technicians, fully equipped with a gurney and several big fiberglass equipment cases.

One of the EMTs, a tiny, athletic-looking young woman with a short bristly haircut, peered down the length of the tunnel. "Does that lead somewhere?" she said. "I guess it does."

•   •   •

*The capitol only* had three passenger elevators and they all opened directly onto the Rotunda, a yawning four-story-high well where privacy was pretty much out of the question. But buried in the wings of the building were large dumbwaiters used by house, senate, and gubernatorial staff to shuffle cartons of papers back and forth. They were easily large enough for a person, even a big person like Cozzano, to sit in.

Marsha led the EMTs through the basement, and into the storage room under the east wing where the Governor stored inactive files. Along the way they picked up Mack Crane, who was loitering in a corridor intersection, keeping a sharp eye in the direction of the stairs that led up to the first floor, looking for what Mel Meyer had referred to, alternately, as "jackals" and "witnesses." Marsha could not help darting one glance up the stairs. She was expecting a phalanx of photographers and video crews, poised to capture her wide-eyed expression so that they could splash it up on the front page of the *Trib* tomorrow. But the top of the stairs was guarded by a sentry line of orange cones warning of a WET FLOOR. Bell must have done that; while no one was really afraid of a wet floor, anyone who knew the ways of the statehouse would try to avoid walking through the middle of one of Bell's mopping projects and earning his undying enmity and noncooperation.

The dumbwaiter was stopped in the storage room, doors flung open. Governor William A. Cozzano was sprawled out on the basement floor with his head and shoulders cradled in the lap of the janitor who was talking to him softly. Bell did not look up as the gurney approached. He said something to Cozzano, something about "medevac." He slipped one arm under Cozzano's shoulders and one under his knees and picked the two-hundred-fifty-pound Governor up as if he were a six-year-old.

"Just leave him there," one of the EMTs said, but Bell stepped forward and gently laid Cozzano out full length on the gurney, ready for transport.

*The EMTs worked* over Cozzano for a few minutes. Then they rolled him out into the corridor and back toward the civil defense tunnel. Marsha glanced up the stairs as they went by and saw the knees and feet of a nocturnal journalist heading for the first-floor men's room.

The gubernatorial stretcher, with its motorcade—the EMTs, the secretary, the cop, and the janitor—moved quickly and silently through the basement, down the tunnel, and into the basement of the building that Marsha had glimpsed earlier. No one said anything except for Cozzano, who said, jovially, "Why is everyone so wallpapered?"

The janitor in the other building was holding the freight elevator for them. They all rode it up to the ground floor, along a short hallway, and out through a roll-up steel door and into a parking lot where an ambulance was waiting. The cold air of the January night came through Marsha's blouse as if she were naked. She pirouetted slowly, looking around, trying to establish her bearings.

The ambulance had backed into a three-sided nook that opened out onto an empty gravel parking lot covered with gray hard-packed snow. They were in back of a one-story building of rough-hewn limestone. This building had a notch taken out of its corner, and the back wall of that notch contained the roll-up door. The building was separated by a gap of just a few feet from a much larger seven- or eight-story building whose solid, windowless back wall formed the third side of the nook.

The big building was the Illinois State Armory, which also housed the Illinois State Police. The small building from which they'd just exited was the Emergency Services and Disaster Agency, its roof studded with funny-looking antennas. Marsha, who'd been working in the capitol for twenty years, was astonished to realize these things: that the Governor of Illinois had a secret escape route, a vestige of the Cold War, a secret bolt-hole to escape from atomic attack and deliver himself into the protection of the Illinois National Guard.

She wondered how many other secrets about the capitol and the office of the Governor, and about this Governor himself, she had never learned or even suspected. She wondered why she'd never been told about these things. And she wondered how Mel Meyer had known. For Marsha the acquisition of knowledge had always been an orderly process pursued in public schools, but Mel was different, Mel came by his knowledge in mysterious ways. He didn't even have a government job, he was just the Governor's lawyer and friend, he hardly ever came to Springfield, and still he carried all the secret blueprints and phone numbers in his head.

As the EMTs were pulling the doors of the ambulance closed on Cozzano, she saw Bell standing there, staring at Cozzano through the rear windows. As the driver shifted the transmission into forward gear, the ambulance's backup lights flashed once like heat lightning and illuminated Bell's face, burning the still image into Marsha's retinas. Bell's forehead was wrinkled in the middle, his eyebrows angled upward in the center, his eyes were glistening and red. As the engine revved, he suddenly straightened up, clicked the heels of his boots together, and snapped out a salute.

Cozzano was staring back at Bell through the tiny windows in the back of the ambulance. The Governor moved his right arm, heavy with blood-pressure cuff and intravenous lines, and returned the salute. The ambulance moved forward on twin jets of steamy exhaust and angled across the parking lot, headed for the trauma center at Springfield Central Hospital, less than a mile away.

## CHAPTER SIX

As soon as Dr. Mary Catherine Cozzano got on the down elevator, headed for the parking garage, she began to go through a ritual she had developed for passage through hostile territory. She hauled the strap of her purse up over her head so that it ran diagonally across her body, snatch-proof. It hung on her right hip so as not to interfere with her pager, which was clipped to her left hip. She unzipped the purse, pulled out her key chain, and clenched it in her right fist so that the keys stuck out from between her fingers like spikes on a medieval weapon. As she carried her keys in her purse, she observed no size limitations; her key chain was as sprawling and ramified as a coronary artery, branching out to include a miniature Swiss Army knife, a penlight, a magnifying glass (all freebies from drug companies), and a stainless steel police whistle. The whistle dangled on a thick length of metal rope. She got it between her thumb and index finger, ready to use. She had already made sure that she was wearing her running shoes—not high heels, not boots —and a pair of scrub pants that offered her legs freedom of movement. That was a given, because these were the only clothes anyone could tolerate on a thirty-hour shift in a sprawling hospital.

Finally, as the elevator was passing downward through the lobby level and into the subterranean parking levels, she reached into her purse and pulled out a black box that fit neatly into her left hand. It was rectangular with a bend near one end. The bent end was concave and sprouted four blunt metal prongs about a quarter of an inch long, making it look like the mouthparts of a tremendously magnified chigger. The prongs were symmetrically arranged: an outer pair that stuck straight out from the end of the device, and an inner pair, closer together, angled toward each other as they sprouted from the concavity. When Mary Catherine found the box inside her purse, it fell naturally into her hand in such a way that her index finger was resting on a black button, just under the crook, near the prongs. Mary Catherine pulled it out of her purse, held it up away from herself, and pulled the trigger.

A miniature lightning bolt, a purplish-white line of electrical discharge, popped between the two inner prongs. It created an alarming, crusty buzzing noise that seemed to penetrate deep into her head. The spark whipped and snapped in the air like a slack clothesline caught in a November wind.

She tested it like this, every day, because she was William A. Cozzano's daughter, and because her father was John Cozzano's son, and everyone in their family learned, when they were very young, not to be sloppy, not to assume, not to take anything for granted.

Then the elevator doors opened, like the opening curtain on a cheap horror film, and she was staring into a low-ceilinged catacomb, filled with greenish, inexpensive institutional light that was hard on the eyes but did not really seem to illuminate anything. These were the tombs where doctors and nurses buried their cars while they worked. Most of the cars were shambling zombies, long since turned undead by the depredations of mobile chop shops that cruised up and down the ramps night and day.

During these trips through the catacombs, Mary Catherine liked to tell herself that her chosen specialty gave her an advantage in self-defense: she could diagnose people from a distance. By the way they walked, by the reactions on their faces, she could tell active psychotics from healthy, run-of-the-mill radio thieves.

Mary Catherine was not the kind of woman who would carry a weapon in her purse. She was not sure what kind of woman would, but certainly not her. She did it anyway. At first it had been a concession to her father. Ever since the death of her mother, her father's concern for her safety had become an obsession with him. When she had moved into her apartment, he drove up from Tuscola with all of his tools and spent a weekend reinforcing the deadbolts, putting bars on the windows, caging her in from the outside world. The people who lived in the apartment across the air shaft—an extended family of Brazilian immigrants—spent most of that weekend gathered in the living room, almost as if for a family portrait, staring in astonishment as the Governor of Illinois dangled halfway out of a sixth-story window sinking bolt hole after bolt hole into the brick window frames with a massive three-quarter-inch electric drill that he had borrowed from one of his farmer cousins.

The next time her birthday rolled around, Dad had given her a small, neatly wrapped box. Mary Catherine had been embarrassed and flushed with gratitude, thinking it was a necklace—and coming from Dad, it was sure to be too formidable to wear. But when she had gotten it out of the box, it turned out to be a stun gun instead. A fitting weapon for a neurologist.

Dad had never observed any limitations on his life. He saw nothing remarkable in assuming that one day he would be President of the United States. He had always assumed that Mary Catherine would feel the same way. He always told her that she could do anything she wanted with her life, and while she never doubted him, she always took it with a grain of salt. And when he first became aware that, as a woman, she was in danger in ways that he was not, and that this danger limited what she could do, he was deeply troubled. He refused to accept it for a long time. But he was starting to understand and was trying to find ways to exempt her from the regulations that society imposed on all women. Because, goddamn it (she could hear him say), it just wasn't fair. Which was all the reason he needed to do anything.

*She was halfway* to her car when her beeper detonated, scaring her half out of her scrubs. She had been awake or virtually awake for thirty-six hours and was running on a lean, rancid blend of caffeine and adrenaline. One reflex told her to grab the beeper and push the button that would make it shut up. The other reflex told her to pull the trigger on her stun gun and get it up into the solar plexus of any bad guys who might be in her vicinity. The reflexes got a little confused and the two little black boxes collided, the stun gun and the beeper, and the stun gun won; the beeper went silent.

(a) This was no time to stand still and figure out the problem and (b) as of thirty minutes ago, she was no longer on call. This had been a mistake on the part of the operator. She had paged the wrong doctor. Sooner or later, they would figure it out, they always did. Right now, Dr. Cozzano needed to get home and sleep.

When she got back to her apartment, her answering machine was taking down a message from a man whose voice she did not recognize. She just caught the tail end of it as she was coming through the door: ". . . condition is stable and he's under the personal care of Dr. Sipes, who of course is a very fine neurologist. Thanks. Bye."

She recognized the name Sipes; he was on the faculty of the Central Illinois University College of Medicine and he showed up at all the conferences. Apparently this call had come from downstate, where some colleague had a question about something. Didn't sound urgent; she would call him back later. She turned down the volume on the answering machine, locked all of the locks that Dad had installed to keep her safe, fed the cat, and went into the bathroom.

There was a mirror in the bathroom. Mary Catherine had not looked in a mirror for something like a day and a half. She took this opportunity to see if she still recognized herself.

Her father was the Governor of Illinois, which meant that this face of hers showed up on television and in the newspapers with some regularity. She had to look respectable without being dowdy. She was also a doctor, so she had to look smart and professional. She was a resident, so she had no money and couldn't spend any time at all worrying about how she looked. And she was the product of a small town in Illinois and had to go back there every couple of weeks and not seem uppity and strange to her old Girl Scout chums.

Once you left the city limits of Chicago you were in Big Hair Territory. Mary Catherine had been the only girl in her high school who had escaped the syndrome. She had extremely thick, black, luxuriant Italian hair with a natural wave that, during the humid summers, turned into a curl. She would have preferred to shave her head for the duration of the residency. Dad was never happy unless she let it grow down to her waist. In compromise, she had settled on a cut that let it hang just above her shoulders.

She showered and climbed into bed with wet hair. A few bits of mail had arrived, notes and cards from friends and family members in other parts of the country, and she leafed through them by her bedside lamp. Her eyes could not trace the handwriting, and the contents penetrated her brain only feebly. It was a waste of time. She reached to turn off the ringer on her telephone, but discovered that it was already turned off. She had probably turned it off the last time she had attempted to get some sleep, whenever that was. The time was 9:15 P.M. She set her three alarm clocks for five o'clock in the morning. She tossed the pager and the stun gun onto her bedside table. The pager no longer responded when she pushed the TEST button. Apparently the stun gun had fried its microchips.

When she woke up, the bedside clocks all read within a few minutes of 9:45 and someone was pounding rhythmically on her front door with a heavy object. For a moment she thought she had overslept and that it was 9:45 in the morning, but then she realized that it was dark outside and her hair was still wet.

It sounded like someone was trying to break in with a sledge-hammer. She pulled on jeans and an ILLINI sweatshirt, went to the door, and peered out through the peephole.

It was a cop. The wide-angle view in the peephole made his body very large and his head very small, amplifying his already coplike appearance. He had a huge L-shaped billy club in one hand and was patiently ramming the butt of it into her door. Standing behind the cop was a man in a trench coat with his hands in his pockets. He was shorter than the cop, so that the peephole magnified his face rather than his body. It was Mel Meyer.

"Okay!" she shouted. "I'm up." She sounded cheerful and ready for anything, even though she was neither. Women of the prairie did not bitch, nag, or whine.

Then she thought: why is Mel here?

Dad had as many lawyers as a mechanic had wrenches. He embodied a large business, a fortune, a few charities, and the state of Illinois, and lawyers came with all of those things. They were always around. Always calling Dad, taking him to dinner, coming over to his house with papers to sign. Sometimes she couldn't tell which were his friends, which were his business associates, and which were actually representing him. To Mary Catherine, lawyers had always seemed as common as air, the taxi drivers, bag boys, and janitors of the world of affairs.

But if all those other lawyers were William A. Cozzano's army, then Mel Meyer was the stiletto strapped to his ankle. Mel was the eschatological counselor of the Cozzano clan, drafter of wills, executor of estates, godfather of children, and if the whole world turned to decadence and strife one day and civilization collapsed, and Dad were trapped on a hilltop surrounded by the heathen, Mel would shoot himself in the head so that Dad could use his corpse as a rampart. He was small, bald, rumply, tired-looking, lizard-eyed, and didn't talk much, because he was always thinking everything out two hundred years into the future.

And now he was standing in her hallway, with a cop, quiet and motionless as a fire hydrant, hands in the pockets of his trench coat, staring at the wallpaper, thinking.

She undid the locks and opened the door. The cop stepped aside, clearing a wide space between Mel and Mary Catherine.

"Your pa needs you," Mel said. "I got a chopper. Let's go."

*Springfield Central had* started out as your basic Big Old Brick Hospital with a central tower flanked symmetrically by two slightly shorter wings. Half a dozen newer wings, pavilions, sky bridges, and parking ramps had been plugged into it since then, so that looking at it from the window of the chopper, Mary Catherine could see it was the kind of hospital where you spent all your time wandering around lost. The roofs were mostly flat tar and pea-gravel, totally dark at this time of night, though in areas that were perpetually shaded, patches of snow glowed faintly blue under the starlight. But the roof of one of the old, original wings was a patch of high noon in the sea of midnight. It bore a red square with a white Swiss cross, a red letter *H* in the center of the cross, and some white block numerals up in one corner. Well off to the side, new doors—electrically powered slabs of glass—had been cut into the side of the old building's central tower.

It made her uneasy. This wasn't Dad's style. As the governor of one of the biggest states in the union, William A. Cozzano could have lived like a sultan. But he didn't. He drove his own car and he did his own oil changes, lying flat on his back in the driveway of their house in Tuscola in the middle of the winter while frostbitten media crews photographed him in the act.

Zooming around in choppers gave him no thrill. It just reminded him of Vietnam. He took this to the point where he probably wouldn't have known how to get a chopper if he had needed one. Which is why he had to have people like Mel, people who knew the extent of his power and how to use it.

"We have limited information," Mel said, on the way down. "He suffered an episode of some kind in his office, shortly after eight o'clock. He is fine and his vital signs are totally stable. They managed to extract him from the statehouse without drawing a whole lot of attention, so if we play this thing right we may be able to get through it without any leaks to the media."

In other circumstances, Mary Catherine might have resented Mel's talk of media leaks at a time like this. But that was his job. And this kind of thing was important to Dad. It was probably the same thing that Dad was worrying about, right now.

If he was awake. If he was still capable of worrying.

"I can't figure out what the problem would be," Mary Catherine said.

"They're thinking stroke," Mel said.

"He's not old enough. He's not fat. Not diabetic. Doesn't smoke. His cholesterol level is through the floor. There's no reason he should have a stroke." Just when she had herself reassured, she remembered the tail end of the message she'd heard on her answering machine, the one that mentioned Sipes. The neurologist. For the first time it occurred to her that the message might have been about her father. She felt a sick panicky impulse, a claustrophobic urge to throw the helicopter door open and jump out.

Mel shrugged. "We could burn up the phone lines getting more info. But it wouldn't help him. And it would just create more potential leaks. So just try to take it easy, because in a few minutes we'll know for sure."

The chopper made an annoyingly gradual soft descent onto the hospital roof. Mary Catherine had a nice view of the capitol dome out her window, but tonight it just looked malevolent, like a sinister antenna rising out of the prairie to pick up emanations from distant sources of power. It was a tall capitol but not a big one. Its smallness always emphasized, to Mary Catherine, its unnatural concentration of influence.

Springfield liked to bill itself as "The City Lincoln Loved." Mel always referred to it as "The City Lincoln Left."

Mel and Mary Catherine had to sit inside for a moment and let the momentum of the rotor spin down a little. When she got the thumbs-up from the pilot, Mary Catherine put her hand on her hair and rolled out onto the white cross in her running shoes. She had thrown a trench coat on over her sweatshirt and jeans, and the buckle whipped back and forth on the end of its belt; the wintry air, traveling at hurricane speed under the rotor blades, had a wind chill factor somewhere down around absolute zero. She didn't stop running until she had passed through the wide automatic glass doors and into the quiet warmth of the corridor that led to the central elevator shafts.

Mel was right behind her. An elevator was already up and waiting for them, doors open. It was a wide-mouth, industrial-strength lift big enough to take a gurney and a whole posse of medical personnel. A man was waiting inside, middle-aged, dressed in a white coat thrown over a BEARS sweatshirt. This implied that he had been called into the hospital on short notice. It was Dr. Sipes, the neurologist.

She was used to being in hospitals. But suddenly the reality hit her. "Oh, god," she said, and slumped against the elevator's pitiless stainless steel wall.

"What's going on?" Mel said, watching Mary Catherine's reaction, looking at Dr. Sipes through slitted eyes.

"Dr. Sipes," Sipes said.

"Mel Meyer. What's going on?"

"I'm a neurologist," Sipes explained.

Mel looked searchingly at Mary Catherine's face for a moment and figured it out. "Oh. Gotcha."

Sipes's key chain was dangling from a key switch on the control panel. Sipes reached for it.

"Hang on a sec," Mel said. Since he had emerged from the chopper his head had been swinging back and forth like that of a Secret Service agent, checking out the surroundings. "Let's just have a chat before we go down to some lower floor where I assume that things will be in a state of hysteria."

Sipes blinked and smiled thinly, more out of surprise than amusement; he wasn't expecting folksy humor at this stage in the proceedings. "Fair enough. The Governor said that I should be expecting you."

"Oh. So he is talking?"

This was a simple enough question, and the fact that Sipes hesitated before answering told Mary Catherine as much as a CAT scan.

"He's not aphasic, is he?" she asked.

"He is aphasic," Sipes said.

"And in English this means?" Mel said.

"He has some problems speaking."

Mary Catherine put one hand over her face, as if she had a terrible headache, which she didn't. This kept getting worse. Dad really had suffered a stroke. A bad one.

Mel just processed the information unemotionally. "Are these problems things that would be obviously noticeable to a layman?"

"I would say so, yes. He has trouble finding the right words, and sometimes makes words up that don't exist."

"A common phenomenon among politicians," Mel said, "but not

for Willy. So he's not going to be doing any interviews anytime soon."

"He's intellectually coherent. He just has trouble putting ideas into words."

"But he told you to expect me."

"He said that a back would be coming."

"A back?"

"Word substitution. Common among aphasics." Sipes looked at Mary Catherine. "I assume that he doesn't have a living grandmother?"

"His grandmothers are dead. Why?"

"He said that his grandmother would be coming too, and that she was a scooter from Daley. Which means Chicago."

"So 'grandmother' means 'daughter' and 'scooter—' "

"He refers to me and all the other physicians as scooters," Sipes said.

"Oy, fuck me," Mel said. "This is gonna be a problem."

Mary Catherine had a certain skill for putting bad things out of her mind so that they would not cloud her judgment. She had been trained that way by her father and had gotten a brutal refresher course during high school, when her mother had fallen ill and died of leukemia. She stood up straight, squared her shoulders, blinked her eyes. "I want to know everything," she said. "This Chinese water torture stuff is going to kill me."

"Very well," Sipes said, and reached for his key chain. The elevator fell.

All that Mary Catherine was doing, really, was coming to the hospital to visit a sick relative. The chairman of the neurology department did not have to guide her personally through the hospital. She was getting this treatment, she knew, because she was the Governor's daughter.

It was one of those weird things that happened to you all the time when you were the daughter of William A. Cozzano. The important thing was not to get used to this kind of treatment, not to expect it. To remember that it could be taken away at any time. If she could make it all the way through her father's political career without ever forgetting this, she'd be okay.

Dad had a private room, on a quiet floor full of private rooms, with an Illinois State Patrolman stationed outside it.

"Frank," Mel said, "how's the knee?"

"Hey, Mel," the trooper said, reached around his body, and shoved the door open.

"Change into civvies, will ya?" Mel said.

When Sipes led Mel and Mary Catherine inside, Dad was asleep. He looked normal, if somewhat deflated. Sipes had already warned them that the left side of his face was paralyzed, but it did not show any visible sagging, yet.

"Oh, Dad," she said quietly, and her face scrunched up and tears started pouring down her face. Mel turned toward her, as if he'd been expecting this, and opened his arms wide. He was two inches shorter than Mary Catherine. She put her face down into the epaulet of his trench coat and cried. Sipes stood uncertainly, awkwardly, checking his wristwatch once or twice.

She let it go on for a couple of minutes. Then she made it stop. "So much for getting that out of the way," she said, trying to make it into a joke. Mel was gentlemanly enough to grin and chuckle half-heartedly. Sipes kept his face turned away from her.

Mary Catherine was one of those people that everyone naturally liked. People who knew her in med school had tended to assume that she would go into a more touchy-feely specialty like family practice or pediatrics. She had surprised them all by picking neurology instead. Mary Catherine liked to surprise people; it was another habit she had picked up congenitally.

Neurology was a funny specialty. Unlike neurosurgery, which was all drills and saws and bloody knives, neurology was pure detective work. Neurologists learned to observe funny little tics in patients' behavior—things that laymen might never notice—and mentally trace the faulty connections back to the brain. They were good at figuring out what was wrong with people. But usually it was little more than a theoretical exercise, because there was no cure for most neurological problems. Consequently, neurologists tended to be cynical, sardonic, remote, with a penchant for dark humor. Sipes was a classic example, except that he appeared to have no sense of humor at all.

Mary Catherine was trying to make a personal crusade of bringing more humanity to the profession. But standing by her stricken father's bedside crying her eyes out was not what she'd had in mind.

"Why is he so out of it?" Mel said.

"Stroke is a major shock to the system. His body isn't used to this. Plus, we put him on a number of medications that, taken together, slow him down, make him drowsy. It's good for him to sleep right now."

"Mary Catherine told me that guys of his age, in good shape, shouldn't have strokes."

"That's correct," Sipes said.

"So why did he have one?"

"Usually stroke happens when you are old and the arteries to your brain are narrowed by deposits. This patient's arteries are in good shape. But a big blood clot got loose in his system."

"Damn," Mary Catherine said, "it was the mitral valve prolapse, wasn't it?"

"Probably," Sipes said.

"Whoa, whoa!" Mel said, "what is this? I never heard about this."

"You never heard about it because it's a trivial problem. Most people don't know they have it and don't care."

"What is it?"

Mary Catherine said, "It's a defect in the valve between the atrium and the ventricle on the left side of your heart. Makes a whooshing noise. But it has no effect on performance, which is why Dad was able to join the Marines and play football."

"Okay," Mel said.

"The reason it makes a whooshing noise is that it creates a pattern of turbulent flow inside the heart," Sipes said. "In some cases, this turbulent flow can develop into a sort of stagnant backwater. It's possible for blood clots to form there. That's probably what happened. A clot formed inside the heart, eventually got large enough to be caught up in the normal flow of blood, and shot up his carotid artery into his brain."

"Jesus," Mel said. He sounded almost disgusted that something so prosaic could fell the Governor. "Why didn't this happen to him twenty years ago?"

"Could have," Sipes said. "It's purely a chance thing. A bolt from the blue."

"Could it happen again?"

"Sure. But we're keeping him on blood thinners at the moment, so it can't happen right now."

Mel stood there nodding at Sipes while he said this. Then Mel kept nodding for a minute or so, just staring off into space.

"I have eight hundred million phone calls to make," Mel said. "Let's get down to business. List for me all of the other human beings in the world who know the information that you just gave me. And I don't want him being wheeled around this hospital for everyone to look at. He stays in this room until we make further arrangements. Okay?"

"Okay, I'll pass that along to the others—"

"Don't bother, I'll do it," Mel said.

*It was like* the old days in Tuscola, when a hot, portentous afternoon would suddenly turn dark and purple and the air would be torn by tornado sirens and the police cars would cruise up and down the streets warning everyone to take cover. Dad was always there, guiding the kids and the dogs down into the tornado cellar, checking to see that the barbecue and lawn chairs and garbage can lids were stowed away, telling them funny stories while the cellar door above their heads pocked from the impacts of baseball-sized hailstones. Now, something even worse was happening. And Dad was sleeping through it.

And Mom wasn't around anymore. And there was her brother James. But he was just her brother. James wasn't any stronger than she was. Probably less so. Mary Catherine was in charge of the Cozzano family.

*Sipes and Mary* Catherine ended up in a dark, quiet room in front of a high-powered Calyx computer system with two huge monitors, one color and one black-and-white. It was a system for viewing medical imagery of all kinds—X-rays, CAT scans, and everything else. This hospital had had them for several years already. The hospital where Mary Catherine worked probably wouldn't get one until sometime in the next decade. Mary Catherine had used them before, so as soon as Dr. Sipes set her up with access privileges, she was able to get started.

After a while, Mel somehow tracked her down and sat next to her without saying anything. Something about the darkness of the room made people hush.

Mary Catherine used a trackball and a set of menus and control windows to open up a large color window on the screen. "They put his head in a magnet and baloney-sliced his brain," she said.

"Come again?" Mel said. It was funny to see him nonplussed.

"Did a series of CAT scans. Had the computer integrate them into a three-dimensional model of Dad's melon, which makes it a lot easier to visualize which parts of his brain got gorked out."

A brain materialized in the window on the computer screen, three-dimensional, rendered in shades of gray.

"Is this the way doctors talk?" Mel said, fascinated.

"Yes," Mary Catherine said, "when lawyers aren't around, that is. Let me change the palette; we can use a false-color scheme to highlight the bad parts," she said, whipping down another menu.

The brain suddenly bloomed with color. Most of it was now in shades of red and pink, fading down toward white, but small portions of it showed up blue. "When lawyers and family members are present," Mary Catherine said, "we say that the blue parts were damaged by the stroke and have a slim chance of ever recovering their normal function."

"And amongst medical colleagues?"

"We say that those parts of the brain are toast. Croaked. Kaput. Not coming back."

"I see," Mel said.

"Been taking a stroll down memory lane," Mary Catherine said. "Check this out." She played with the menus for a moment and another window opened up, a huge one filling most of the black-and-white screen. It was a chest X-ray. "See that?" she said, tracing a crooked rib with her fingertip.

"Bears-Packers, 1972," Mel said. "I remember when they carried him off the field. I lost a thousand bucks on that fucking game."

Mary Catherine laughed. "Serves you right," she said. She closed the window with the chest X ray. Then she used the trackball to rotate the image of the brain back and forth in different ways to reveal selected areas. "This stroked area accounts for the paralysis and this small one here is responsible for his aphasia. In the old days we had to figure this stuff out just by talking to the patient and watching the way he moved."

"I detect from your tone of voice that you think this is all basically superficial crap," Mel said.

Mary Catherine just turned toward him and smiled a little bit.

"I like video games too," Mel said, "but let's talk seriously for a moment here."

"Dad's mixed dominant, which is good," Mary Catherine said.

"Meaning?"

"He does some things with his right hand and others with his left. Neither side of the brain predominates. People like that recover better from strokes."

Mel raised his eyebrows. "That's good news."

"Recovery from this kind of insult is extremely hard to predict. Most people hardly get better at all. Some recover quite well. We may see changes over the course of the next couple of weeks that will tell us which way he's going to go."

"A couple of weeks," Mel said. He was clearly relieved to have a specific number, a time frame to deal with. "You got it."

*"Guess what?"* Mel said to the Cozzanos the morning after the stroke. It was six A.M. None of them had slept except for the Governor, who was under the influence of various drugs. James Cozzano had arrived shortly after midnight, driving his Miata in from South Bend, Indiana, where he was a graduate student in the political science department. He and Mary Catherine had spent the whole night sitting around in the Executive Mansion, which was nice, but not exactly home. Mary Catherine had tried to sleep in bed and been unable to. She had put on her clothes, sat down in a chair to talk to James, and fallen dead asleep for four hours. James just watched TV. Mel had spent the same time elsewhere, on the telephone, waking people up.

Now they were all together in the same room. The Governor's

eyes were open, but he wasn't saying much. When he tried to talk, the wrong words came out, and he got angry.

"What?" Mary Catherine finally said.

Mel looked William A. Cozzano in the eye. "You're running for president."

Cozzano rolled his eyes. "You swebber putter," he said.

Mary Catherine gave Mel a wary, knowing look, and waited for an explanation.

James got flustered. "Are you crazy? This is no time for him to be launching a campaign. Why haven't I heard about this?"

His father was watching him out of the corner of his eye. "Don't squelch," he said, "it's a million fudd. Goddamn it!"

"I spent the whole night putting together a campaign committee," Mel said.

"You lie," Cozzano said.

"Okay," Mel admitted, "I put together a campaign committee a long time ago, just in case you changed your mind and decided to run. All I did last night was wake them up and piss them off."

"What's the scam here?" Mary Catherine said.

Mel sucked his teeth and looked at Mary Catherine indulgently. "You know, 'scam' is just a Yiddishized pronunciation of 'scheme'—a much nobler word meaning 'plan.' So let's not be invidious. Let's call it a plan instead."

"Mel," Mary Catherine said, "what's the scam?"

Cozzano and Mel looked soberly at each other and then cracked up.

"If you turn on that TV in a couple of hours," Mel said, "you will see the Governor's press secretary releasing a statement, which I wrote on my laptop in the lobby of this hospital and faxed to him an hour ago. In a nutshell, what it says is this: in the light of the extremely serious and, in the Governor's view, irresponsible statements made by the President last night, the Governor has decided to take another look at the idea of running for president—because clearly the country has gone adrift and needs new leadership. So he has cleared his appointment calendar for the next two weeks and is going to closet himself in Tuscola, with his advisers, and formulate a plan to throw his hat into the ring."

"So all the media will go to Tuscola," James said.

"I would guess so," Mel said.

"But Dad's not in Tuscola."

Mel shrugged as if this were a minor annoyance. "Sipes says he's transportable. We'll use the chopper. More private and presidential as hell."

Cozzano chuckled. "Good backing," he said. "We'll go to the buckyball."

"What's the point?" James said. He actually shouted it. Suddenly he had become upset. "Dad's had a stroke. Can't you see that? He's sick. How long do you think you can hide it?"

"A couple of weeks," Mel said.

"Why bother?" James said. "Is there any reason for all this subterfuge? Or are you just doing it for the thrill of playing the game?"

"People my age get their thrills by having good bowel movements, not by playing games," Mel said. "I'm doing it because we don't yet know the full extent of the damage. We don't know how much Willy is going to recover in the next couple of weeks."

"But sooner or later . . ."

"Sooner or later, we'll have to come out and say he's had a stroke," Mel said, "and then the presidential bid is stillborn. But it's better to have a nice little planned stroke at home, while trying to lead the country, than a big ugly surprising one while you're picking your nose in the statehouse, don't you think?"

"I don't know," James said, shrugging. "Is it?"

Mel swiveled his head around to look directly at James. His face bore an expression of surprise. He was able to mask his emotions before they developed into disappointment or contempt.

Everyone had always assumed that James would one day develop from a bright boy into a wise man, but it hadn't happened yet. Like many sons of great and powerful men, he was still trapped in a larval stage. If he hadn't been the son of the Governor, he probably would have developed into one of those small-town letter-of-the-law types that Mel found so tiresome.

But he was the son of the Governor. Mel accepted that. He didn't say what was on his mind: *James, don't be a sap.*

"James," Mary Catherine said, speaking so quietly that she could barely be heard across the room, "don't be a sap."

James turned and gave Mary Catherine the helpless, angry look of a little brother who has just had his cowlick pulled by his big sister.

Mel and the Governor locked eyes across the bedspread.

"Hut one!" Cozzano said.

## CHAPTER SEVEN

Gangadhar V.R.J.V.V. Radhakrishnan, M.D., Ph.D., had not cracked a skull in seventy-nine days and he was not happy about it. Even the shaven-headed thugs stamping out license plates ten miles down the road at the New Mexico State Men's Reformatory would get rusty without their daily quota of practice on the license-plate stamping machine. For a neurosurgeon, eleven weeks without pressing the madly vibrating blade of the bone saw against a freshly peeled human skull was intolerable.

In order to crack a skull he had to get to a decent hospital. In order to reach a decent hospital from here, he had to use the Elton State University airplane. But every time he needed it, the football coach had taken it out on a recruiting trip to L.A. or Houston. This was in direct violation of Dr. Radhakrishnan's contract with Elton State, which stated that he would have access to the airplane as needed.

The only person who could help him was Dr. Artaxerxes Jackman, the president of Elton State University, and Jackman had to be approached in the right way. Jackman had a Ph.D. in education and higher administration. It was almost criminal fraud to call him a doctor, but, in the academic sense, a doctor he was. Dr. Radhakrishnan had not spent most of his life in his native India without figuring out that important positions are quite often filled by undeserving swine, who must be deferred to in any case.

His own father was a case in point. Forty years ago, about the time Gangadhar had been born, Jagdish Radhakrishnan had been a rising young idealist in the Nehru administration. That very idealism had led to an appointment on the Railway Corruption Enquiry

Committee of 1953. Jagdish had carried out his responsibilities zealously, refusing to pull his punches even when it became evident that he was getting close to many a high-ranking official. He found himself summarily transferred to a low post in the Sheet Mica Price Controller's Organisation, where he had languished ever since, living only for the achievements of his two sons: Arun, the golden boy, the firstborn son, now a member of Parliament, and to a lesser extent, Gangadhar.

Gangadhar V.R.J.V.V. Radhakrishnan knew that the faculty of Elton State University was, in the academic world, roughly equivalent to the Sheet Mica Price Controller's Organisation, and that if he ever wanted to get out of this place he would have to show more discretion—more savvy—less boneheaded idealism than his father had back in the 1950s. For half a year he had been trying, diplomatically and politely, to get in for a face-to-face with Dr. Jackman, but their meeting kept getting postponed.

Before he even veered into the parking lot of the Coover Biotechnology Pavilion, blood balloons began to detonate on the windshield of his full-sized, one-ton, six-wheel-drive Chevy pickup truck. He kept driving even though he could no longer see through the windshield. If he was lucky, he might run over an animal rights activist and then claim it was an accident. The truck was not in a mood to slow down; it was heavily laden with fifty-pound sacks of Purina Monkey Chow. He had just paid for the monkey chow himself, with his own money, down at the grain elevator—the closest thing there was to a skyscraper in Elton, a white tubular obelisk sticking up above the railroad tracks on the edge of town. He had talked to the grinning windburned Nazis, given them his money, endured their snickering at his accent and their remarks about his heavy winter coat.

"So what do you do with this stuff? Fry it up or just eat it cold?" one of them had said, as they were piling the monkey chow into his truck.

"I feed it to brain-damaged lower primates," Dr. Radhakrishnan had said. "Would you like a sample?"

The one thing they valued him for—that gave him potential status as a human being in their eyes—was his monster truck: 454

cubic inches of V-8 power, double wheels on the rear axle, a thick black roll bar brandishing great mesh-covered Stalag 17 searchlights that could pick out a shrew on a rock in a midnight windstorm across two miles of chaparral. He had traded in a BMW for this coarse and ungainly machine halfway through his first winter here, almost two years ago, when he found out that the ultimate driving machine simply did not go in a six-foot snowdrift.

The double-edged windshield wipers smeared blood across the windshield in gory arcs, giving him a partial view of the loading dock. It wasn't real blood, of course. After the first few attacks, they had decided it was politically incorrect to use the real stuff and they had switched to Karo syrup with red dye in it. In the cold February air, it congealed on contact. Dr. Radhakrishnan preferred the real blood; it was easier to wash off.

A dozen of his grad students and lab techs were waiting for him around back at the loading dock. Dr. Radhakrishnan pulled up to it and left the motor running. They jumped into the back like a commando team and formed a human chain, passing the fifty-pound sacks of monkey chow up across the dock and into the freight elevator. Radhakrishnan had a total of fifteen grad students: four Japanese, two Chinese, three Korean, one Indonesian, three Indian, one Pakistani, and one American. They had learned to work together well at times such as this, even the American.

He pulled his empty truck around into the parking lot. Dr. Radhakrishnan had a reserved parking space near the entrance. Right now half a dozen activists were occupying it with their bodies, staging a die-in. Most of them were just doing it in their Levi's and Timberland's, but the star of the show was a person in a gorilla suit with a big steel colander over his head with a pair of jumper cables clamped onto it. The gorilla spazzed out and died grandly as Dr. Radhakrishnan's blood-soaked four-by-four cruised past in low gear, a shattered balloon fluttering from the radio antenna, and parked in an unreserved spot farther from the door.

They thought they were going to force Dr. Radhakrishnan to change his ways by making him feel bad. They thought that the way to make him feel bad was to make him feel unliked. They were desperately wrong on both counts.

He shoved a magnetically coded ID card into a slot, punched in a secret code, and the door opened for him. This new facility had been built securely, because they knew that the animal rights people would try to find a way in. They didn't have a chance; they were like raccoons trying to break into a missile silo.

The top floor belonged to Radhakrishnan and his crew. He had to punch in more numbers to get out of the elevator lobby. Then he smelled home. It had the sharp disinfectant smell of a doctor's office with a low undertone of barnyard.

A baboon was sitting in a stainless steel chair in the Procedure Room, wrists and ankles loosely taped in place. The baboon was anesthetized and did not need to be restrained; otherwise, the tape wouldn't have held him. All it did was fix him in a convenient position.

The entire top of the baboon's skull had been removed to expose the brain. Park and Toyoda were under the hood, as it were, working on the baboon's electrical system. Toyoda had his hands in there, maneuvering a narrow probe with a miniature video camera on the end of it. The output of the video camera was splashed up on a big-screen Trinitron. Nearly inaudible high-pitched ticking and whistling sounds emerged from the headphones of his Walkman; he was listening to some particularly noxious form of American music.

Park held a retractor with one hand and a mug of coffee in the other. Both of them ignored the baboon and kept their eyes on the TV set. It was providing live coverage of the interior spaces of the baboon's brain: a murky universe of gray mush with the occasional branching network of blood vessels.

"A little bit left," Park suggested. The camera swung in that direction and suddenly there was something different, something with hard, straight edges, embedded in the brain tissue. It did not seem to have been dropped into a hole, though; it seemed as though the brain had grown around it, like a tree growing around a fence post. The object was a neutral, milky white, with a serial number stamped into the top. Any layman coming in off the street would have identified the substance as teflon. It was just translucent enough that one could make out, inside the teflon shell, a sort of squared-off sunburst pattern, like the rising sun flag of the Imperial Japanese Navy, etched in silver against a neutral gray background. At the center of that sunburst was a tiny square region that contained several hundred thousand microscopic transistors.

But neither Park nor Toyoda nor Dr. Radhakrishnan looked at that part of it. They were all looking at the interface—the boundary between the sharp edge of the teflon casing and the brain tissue, with its infinite, organic watershed system of capillaries. It looked good: no swelling, no necrosis, no gap between the baboon and the microchip.

"A keeper," Toyoda said, grinning, pronouncing this newly acquired bit of American slang with great precision.

"Bingo," Park said.

"Which baboon is this?" Dr. Radhakrishnan said.

"Number twenty-three," Toyoda said. "We implanted three weeks ago."

"How long has he been off the antirejection meds?"

"One week."

"Looks like he'll do well," Dr. Radhakrishnan said. "I suppose we should go ahead and give him a name."

"Okay," Park said as he slurped uncertainly at his lukewarm java. "What do you want to call him?"

"Let's call him Mr. President," Dr. Radhakrishnan said.

*Two men were* waiting for Dr. Radhakrishnan in front of his office. It was unusual, this early in the morning; Dr. Radhakrishnan's secretary wouldn't even be here for another half hour. One of the men was Dr. Artaxerxes Jackman, of all people, looking somewhat grumpy and astonished. The other man was a stranger, a man in his forties with sandy blond hair. He was wearing the best suit that Dr. Radhakrishnan had ever seen west of the Mississippi, a charcoal-gray number with widely spaced stripes, sort of a City of London number. Both men stood up as Dr. Radhakrishnan entered the room.

"Dr. Radhakrishnan," Jackman said, "no one was here so we just figured we'd set up and wait for you. I want you to meet Mr. Salvador here."

"Dr. Radhakrishnan, it's a pleasure and an honor," Salvador said, extending his hand. He wore no jewelry except for cuff links; when he extended his arm, just the right amount of cuff—plain, basic white—protruded from the sleeve of his jacket. He did not go in for the crushing American style of handshake. His accent was definitely not American either, but beyond that, it was as untraceable as a ransom note.

"You are up bright and early," Dr. Radhakrishnan said, ushering Mr. Salvador into his office. Jackman had already departed, slowly and reluctantly, casting glances over his shoulder.

"No earlier than you, Dr. Radhakrishnan, and certainly no brighter," Mr. Salvador said. "Jet lag would not allow me to sleep later and so I thought I would get an early start."

Dr. Radhakrishnan handed him some coffee. Salvador held the mug out in front of him for a moment, examining it like a freshly excavated amphora, as though he had never seen coffee served in anything other than a cup with a saucer. "Comanches," Salvador said, reading the mug.

"That is the name of the football team associated with this institution," Dr. Radhakrishnan said.

"Ah, yes, football," Salvador said, his memory jogged. He was showing all the signs of a man who had just flown in from some other hemisphere and who was trying to get cued into the local culture. "That's right, this must be high football territory. The pilot told me that we are on mountain time here. Is that correct?"

"Yes. Two hours behind New York, one ahead of L.A."

"I didn't know that such a time zone existed until this morning."

"Neither did I, until I came here."

Salvador took a sip of coffee and sat forward, all business.

"Well, I would love to indulge my weakness for endless small talk, but it would be wrong to waste your time, and it is rude for me to sit here being mysterious. I understand that you are the world's best brain surgeon."

"That is flattering but not exactly true. I could not even aspire to that title unless I devoted myself to doing procedures."

"But instead you have chosen to devote your career to research."

"Yes."

"It is a common career choice among the very finest medical minds. There's more of a challenge in trying something new, isn't there?"

"In general, yes."

"Now, it is my understanding—and please correct me if I say something stupid—that you are developing a process to help persons who have suffered brain damage."

"Certain types of brain damage only," Dr. Radhakrishnan said, trying to be discouragingly cautious; but Mr. Salvador was not even slightly deterred.

"As I understand it you implant some kind of device in the damaged part of the brain. It connects itself to the brain on one side and to the nerves on the other, taking the place of damaged tissue."

"That is correct."

"Does it work with aphasia?"

"Pardon me?"

"A speech impediment—caused, say, by a stroke?"

Dr. Radhakrishnan was badly thrown off stride. "I know what aphasia is," he said, "but we do our work on baboons. Baboons can't talk."

"Suppose they could?"

"Speculatively, it would depend on the extent and the type of the damage."

"Dr. Radhakrishnan, I would appreciate it very much if you would listen to a tape for me," Salvador said, pulling a microcassette recorder out of his pocket.

"A tape of what?"

"Of a friend of mine who recently became ill. He suffered a stroke in his office. Now, as luck would have it, this took place while he was dictating a letter on a tape machine."

"Mr. Salvador, excuse me, but what are you getting at here?" Dr. Radhakrishnan said.

"Nothing really," Salvador said, good-humored and unruffled as if this were an entirely normal procedure.

"Are you about to ask me for some kind of a medical opinion?"

"Yes."

Radhakrishnan had a canned speech cued up, about how the doctor/patient relationship was extremely solemn and how he could not even dream of diagnosing a patient without hours of examination and the all-important paperwork. But something stopped him from saying it.

It might have been Mr. Salvador's unpretentious and offhand manner. It might have been his personal elegance, his obvious status as a member of the upper class, which made it painful to bring up such banal issues. And it might have been the fact that he had been escorted here personally by Jackman, who would not have bothered to do so unless Mr. Salvador were very important.

Mr. Salvador took Dr. Radhakrishnan's silence as permission. "The first voice you will hear will be that of my friend's secretary, who discovered him after the stroke." And he started the tape rolling. The sound quality was poor but the words were clear enough.

"Willy? Willy, are you all right?" The secretary sounded hushed, almost awed.

"Call." This command did not sound finished; the man wanted to say, "Call someone," but he could not summon forth the name.

"Call whom?"

"Goddamn it, call her!" The man's voice was deep, his enunciation flawless.

"Call whom?"

"The three-alarm lamp scooter."

"Mary Catherine?"

"Yes, goddamn it!"

*"That's all there* is," Mr. Salvador said, switching off the machine.

Dr. Radhakrishnan raised his eyebrows and took a deep breath. "Well, based on this kind of evidence, it's difficult—"

"Yes, yes, yes," Mr. Salvador said, now sounding a bit annoyed, "it's hard for you to speculate and you can't say anything on the record and all that. I understand your position, doctor. But I am attempting to engage you in a purely abstract discussion. Perhaps it would have been better if we had met over dinner, rather than in such a formal setting. We could arrange that, if it would help to get you in the right frame of mind."

Radhakrishnan felt miserably stupid. "That would be difficult to arrange in Elton," he said, "unless you are very fond of chili."

Mr. Salvador laughed. It sounded forced. But it was nice to make the effort.

"Speaking very abstractly, then," Dr. Radhakrishnan said, "if the stroke hit his frontal lobes, he may very well have personality changes, which my therapy could not fix. If that part of his brain was spared, then the cursing probably reflects frustration. Your friend, I would wager, is a successful and powerful man, and you can imagine how such a man would feel if he could not even say simple sentences."

"Yes, that puts it in a new light."

"But I can't say much more than that without more data."

"Understood." Then, offhandedly, as if asking for directions to the men's room, Salvador said: "Can you fix the aphasia, then? Assuming your off-the-cuff diagnosis is correct."

"Mr. Salvador, I hardly know where to begin."

Mr. Salvador took out a cigar, a mahogany baseball bat of a thing, and scalped it with a tiny pocket guillotine. "Begin at the beginning," he suggested. "Care for a cigar?"

"To begin with," Dr. Radhakrishnan said, accepting the cigar, "there are ethical questions that entirely rule out performing an experimental procedure on a human subject. So far we've only done this on baboons."

"Let us do a little thought experiment in which we set aside, for the time being, the ethical dimension," Mr. Salvador said. "Then what?"

"Well, if a doctor were willing to do this, and the patient fully understood what he was getting into, we would first have to build the biochips. In order to do this we would have to take a biopsy a few weeks ahead of time, that is, take an actual sample of the patient's brain tissue, then genetically reengineer the nerve cells—in and of itself, hardly a trivial operation—and grow them in vitro until we had enough."

"You do that here?"

"We have an arrangement with a biotech firm in Seattle."

"Which one, Cytech or Genomics?"

"Genomics."

"What is their role?"

"They implant the desired chromosome and then culture the cells in vitro."

"They grow them in a tank," Mr. Salvador translated.

"Yes."

"How long does that phase last?"

"A couple of weeks usually. Cell culture is dodgy. Once we had gotten the cultured cells back from Seattle, we would fabricate the biochips."

"How long does that take?" Mr. Salvador was obsessed with time.

"A few days. Then we would proceed to the implantation."

"The actual operation."

"Yes."

"Tell me about that."

"We identify the dead portions of the brain and remove them cryosurgically. It's rather like a dentist drilling out a cavity, cutting away damaged matcrial until he hits a sound part of the tooth."

Mr. Salvador winced exquisitely.

"When we do this on baboons, we do it in a specially constructed operating room here that is not sterile. It is not even minimally fit for humans. So in order to do this operation on a human, it would be necessary to build a specially designed operating theater from scratch. The operating room would probably cost more than this entire building in which we are sitting."

This last statement was intended to scare Mr. Salvador off, but it seemed only to bore him. "Have you ever got to the point of drawing up plans and specifications for such a facility?"

"Yes, in a speculative way." Anyone who knew the first thing about grantsmanship always had that kind of thing lying around, to demonstrate the need for far greater amounts of money.

"May I take a copy with me?"

"The plans are on disk. You'll need a fairly powerful Calyx system just to open them up."

"Is that some sort of computer thing? Calyx?"

"Yes. A parallel operating system."

"It it something that one could buy?"

"Yes, of course."

"Who makes it?"

"It's an open system. So there are many such machines on the market—mostly aimed at engineers and scientists."

"Who makes the best sort of Calyx machine?"

"Well, it was invented by Kevin Tice, of course."

Mr. Salvador smiled. "Ah, yes. Mr. Tice. Pacific Netware. Marin County. Superb. I shall see if Mr. Tice can supply us with a nice machine that will run his Calyx operating system."

Dr. Radhakrishnan assumed that Mr. Salvador was employing a bit of synecdoche here. But he was not entirely sure. "If you do get access to a Calyx machine, with the proper CAD/CAM software, these disks will run on it."

"Then I would be delighted to take a disk with me, with your permission," Mr. Salvador said. Without further discussing that issue of permission, he continued, "Now, what happens after the operation?"

"Once the implantation had been performed, if the patient did not die in the process, there would be a period of a few weeks in which we would keep him on antirejection meds and monitor him closely in order to make sure that his body did not reject the implant. Assuming it worked, he would then have to be retrained. The patient tries to move the paralyzed part of his body. If the movement is correct, then we instruct the chip to remember the pathway taken by the signals from the brain into the nerve. If it is incorrect, we instruct the chip to block that path. Gradually, the good paths get reinforced and the bad ones get blocked."

"How do you instruct the chip? How do you give it feedback, as it were, once it is implanted inside the patient's head?"

"It includes a miniaturized radio receiver. We have a transmitter that simply broadcasts the instructions directly into the patient's skull."

"Fascinating. Utterly fascinating," Mr. Salvador said, sincerely enough. "And what is the range of this transmission?"

"I'm sorry?"

"Well, how far away from the transmitter can the patient be?"

Dr. Radhakrishnan smiled the same smile he had used with Jackman. "You misconstrue me," he said. "We do not use radio transmission because we need to talk to the patient's biochip from a distance. We use it because this enables us to communicate with the biochip without using an actual wire through the skull into the brain."

"I see, of course," Mr. Salvador said dismissively. "But radio is radio, isn't it?"

Dr. Radhakrishnan smiled and nodded. He could not find any way to disagree with the statement "radio is radio."

## CHAPTER EIGHT

Aaron Green faked it for a whole week, throwing his IMIPREM into the trunk of his rented Dynasty every day and hawking his wares up and down the length of Wilshire Boulevard. Then he got up one morning, rummaged through his briefcase, emptied out the pocket where he stuffed people's business cards, and pulled one out. Plain black ink on white paper: CY OGLE—President—Ogle Data Research, Inc.

Ogle was the guy. The man who had taken one quick look at his IMIPREM, in the least auspicious circumstances, and recognized its value. A guy as smart as Ogle didn't need any sales pitch. No fancy presentations.

Aaron had known ever since their conversation on the plane that he would eventually make this phone call. But he had forced himself to stick to the original plan for a week anyway.

Enough of that. The card listed offices in Falls Church, Virginia, and Oakland, California. Hardly auspicious. Aaron dialed the number in Oakland, steeling himself for a lengthy round of telephone tag.

"Hello?" a man's voice said.

"Hello?" Aaron said, caught off guard. He had been expecting a secretary.

"Who's this?"

"Excuse me," Aaron said, "I was trying to reach—"

"Mr. Green!" the man said, and Aaron recognized him as Cy Ogle himself. "How are you doing down there in Holl-ee-wood? Are you having a *fabulous* time?"

Aaron laughed. He had assumed, on the plane, that Ogle must

have been drunk. But now he sounded the same. Either Ogle was drunk all the time, or never.

"I don't think I'll be putting my handprints in cement anytime soon."

"Had many interesting conversations with those big media moguls?"

Aaron decided to test Cy Ogle. "They're all teflon golems."

"And all of your scientific arguments just slide right off their high-tech, nonstick surface," Ogle said without skipping a beat.

"What's going on?" Aaron asked. "You answering your own telephone now?"

"Yup."

"It's just that I figured, being president of your own company and all, you'd have a secretary or something."

"I do," Ogle said. "But she's a real good secretary, so I'm not going to waste her time having her answer the phone."

"Well," Aaron said, "I don't want to waste *your* time. You must be busy."

"I'm busy pushing on the gas pedal and keeping this old gas-guzzler between the white lines," Ogle said.

"Oh. You're driving?"

"Yeah. Going to Sacramento to sell the Governor a bill of goods."

"Oh. Well as long as you and I were on the same coast—"

"You thought we should get together about your IMIPREM."

"Exactly," Aaron said. He was pleased that Ogle still remembered the acronym.

"Let me ask you one question," Ogle said. "Could you make it small?"

"The IMIPREM? What do you mean?"

"It's big now. Bigger than a breadbox, as we used to say. Got a big old power supply built into it, I would guess. Is there any intrinsic reason you couldn't miniaturize it? Make it portable? Say, Walkman sized, or even smaller, like wristwatch sized?"

"It would be a major project—"

"Stop trying to be a business executive," Ogle said. "I don't want your opinion of this from a major project point of view. I want you to do what you do best. Now, a V-8 engine can't be small; it won't work. But a calculator can be small. Is the IMIPREM a V-8 engine or a calculator?"

"A calculator."

"Done. Now stop worrying about all this business shit. Go to Disneyland."

"Huh?"

"Or the Universal Studios tour. Or something. I won't be back until tonight."

"Okay."

"This afternoon, before traffic gets screwed up, go to LAX and take a shuttle up to San Francisco and a car will meet you. Bring everything."

"Gotcha."

"We got a new project underway, since I last talked to you, that you are going to just love," Cy Ogle said. "You are just going to love it."

Then Ogle hung up the phone.

*Aaron considered showing* up in the full set of Mickey Mouse ears, just to prove that he had in fact gone to Disneyland. But he decided at the last minute that this would be just a little bit too off-the-wall. So he opted for a simple, oversized, 100 percent cotton Goofy T-shirt. A T-shirt was more conservative than a set of ears, and Aaron had a feeling that Cyrus Rutherford Ogle would relate better, somehow, to Goofy.

When he came off the plane in San Francisco, a man was standing by the gate holding a hand-lettered sign that said A. GREEN. The driver seemed to read everything in his face, and ventured into the torrent of deplaning businessmen to take Aaron's IMIPREM case out of his hand before Aaron had even identified himself.

The driver was named Mike. He wasn't a uniformed chauffeur or anything like that, just a normal-looking black kid of eighteen or twenty, wearing a black T-shirt. Quiet, courteous, and efficient. After a brief wait by the baggage carousel, Mike led him out to a navy-blue Ford Taurus with an oversized engine and lots of antennas (innocuous but powerful; correct but not ostentatious; comfortable but not decadent) and drove him up the freeway to the Bay Bridge and across to Oakland, surging from lane to lane (decisive but not reckless). They exited shortly after getting into Oakland and then cruised down into a semirenovated downtown area and from there into a not-so-renovated area on the fringe of the waterfront warehouse district.

A number of the buildings down here were well on their way to being trashed, but as usual in California, there were a few nice ones that stood out, not so much because they'd been perfectly maintained, but because they had been well-designed to begin with.

One of the best was a big old Art Deco Cadillac dealership, a glass-walled flatiron of a building set in the angle of two diverging avenues. The ground floor was huge and wide open, with ceilings that looked some twenty-five feet high, completely wrapped in tinted glass. That was the showroom; behind it, farther back into the block, was garage space. Above this ground floor were four or five additional floors of office space. On top of the building, the word CADILLAC was written large in orange neon script, looming over the intersection in letters that must have stood twenty feet high. Beneath that, mounted high on the prow of the building, was a big clock, a full story high, its numbers and hands outlined in more neon. The neon worked but the clock didn't.

Most of the big windows were in surprisingly good shape. A few of them had fist-sized holes in them, backed up with sheets of plywood, and the wide, double glass doors that had once beckoned would-be Cadillac buyers into the dealership had been rebuilt in plywood and painted black. The upper floors of the building looked empty. A few yellowed windowshades hung askew. It wasn't until Mike pulled the Taurus up in front of the black plywood doors, and Aaron saw the street number spray-painted across them in orange, that he realized this address matched the one printed on Cy Ogle's business card.

Once Aaron entered the showroom, his eyes adjusted well enough to see that it was mostly empty. No desks, no Cadillacs. He pulled the door shut behind him and latched it using a big, old-fashioned hook and eye.

The formerly high-gloss floor of the showroom was covered, patchily, with swaths of bleak off-brown indoor-outdoor carpeting,

and the occasional half-unrolled length of battered and scarred gray
foam rubber. A gridwork of black iron pipes hung down below the
ceiling, and a few dozen theatrical spotlights were clamped onto the
pipes here and there.

Other light fixtures were affixed to tall, telescoping poles
mounted on tripods. The tops of these devices had big white um-
brellas on them to serve as reflectors; the effect was that of a sparse
field of gigantic sunflowers. Heavy black electrical cables, bundled
together with gray tape, snaked all over the floor.

It was a stage. And the stage had props, scattered around irratio-
nally: a couple of heavy, impressive wooden desks. Plastic plants.
Several bookshelves loaded with books. But as Aaron found when
he looked at one of these, it was fake. There were no books on the
shelves. What looked like a line of books seen on edge was a hollow
plastic shell. The entire bookshelf weighed all of about twenty
pounds.

There were some muffled clunking noises, and some lights came
on at one end of the room. Aaron could only see about half of the
showroom floor from here, the rest of it had been blocked off by
flimsy partitions.

Finally he made out the streamlined pear shape of Cyrus Rutherford Ogle, standing next to a gray steel circuit-breaker box bolted
to the wall, clunking lights on and off.

"Goofy," Ogle said, "my favorite."

"Oh. If I'd known, I would have brought you a souvenir."

"I get a souvenir every time I meet with one of my clients, haw
haw haw," Ogle said. "Come on back, my offices are back here, such
as they are."

"Interesting building," Aaron said.

"We figured we'd leave the big CADILLAC up on the roof," Ogle
said, "to attract Republicans."

Aaron walked toward the back of the showroom, picking his way
over cables and rolls of carpet padding.

"You might wonder why a man who has been described as a cross
between Machiavelli and Zeffirelli would hang out in Oakland.
Why not Sacramento, where the politicians are, or L.A., where all
the media scum hang out?"

"The question had crossed my mind," Aaron said.

"It's a tug of war. Closer I am to Sacramento, the better it is for the politicians. Closer I am to L.A., the better it is for the creative talent."

"You're closer to Sacramento. So I guess the politicians win."

"They do not win, but they predominate. See, media people have no scruples. They will go anywhere. Politicians have no scruples either. But they like to act as though they do. And it is beneath their sense of artificial dignity to go all the way to L.A. because they still think that I am just a huckster and it makes them think that they are groveling to the false gods."

Ogle turned his back on Aaron and led him through a maze of partitions.

"So why not set yourself up in Sacramento, if media people will go anywhere?" Aaron said, strolling after him, looking around.

"Media people will go anywhere, but I won't. I won't go to Sacramento because it is a dried-up shithole. And San Fran is too damn expensive. So here I am, the best place I could ever be."

They were approaching some kind of an elaborate construction, a room within a room. It was a three-dimensional webwork of two-by-fours surrounding and supporting a curved wall. An old-fashioned, lath-and-plaster wall.

One side of the construct had been slid away so that Aaron could see inside. The room as a whole was elliptical in shape, now split open like a cracked egg.

Ogle noticed his curiosity and gestured at it. "Go on in," he said. "Nicest room in this whole place."

Aaron sidestepped the unadorned beams of the wooden framing and passed through the gap into the oval room.

There was a nice desk in here. It was an office. An oval office.

It was *the* Oval Office.

Aaron had seen the real Oval Office in the White House once when his high-school band went to Washington, D.C. And this was the same. If the two halves were slid back together, it would be an exact replica.

"It's perfect," he whispered.

"On TV it's perfect," Ogle said, ambling into the room. "On film, it's just pretty good. Good enough for the yokels, anyway."

"Why would you need something like this?"

Ogle tapped the big leather swivel chair with the palm of his hand, spinning it around toward him, and fell into it. He leaned the seat back and put his feet up on the presidential desk. "Ever hear of the Rose Garden strategy?"

"Yeah, vaguely."

"Well, the White House is a busy place, what with all of those tour groups traipsing in and out, and as I said, most of the media types are here in Cal. Sometimes it's more convenient to pursue the Rose Garden strategy right here in Oakland."

"I didn't know you operated at that level," Aaron said. "I didn't know you worked for presidential candidates."

"Son," Ogle said, "I work for *emperors*."

"*In the* 1700s, politics was all about ideas. But Jefferson came up with all the good ideas. In the 1800s, it was all about character. But no one will ever have as much character as Lincoln and Lee. For much of the 1900s it was about charisma. But we no longer trust charisma because Hitler used it to kill Jews and JFK used it to get laid and send us to Vietnam."

Ogle had broken a six-pack out of a junky old refrigerator behind the "Oval Office" and set up the cans on the presidential desk. Aaron had pulled up another chair and now both of them had their feet up on the desk and beers in their hands.

"So what's it about now?" Aaron said.

"Scrutiny. We are in the Age of Scrutiny. A public figure must withstand the scrutiny of the media," Ogle said. "The President is the ultimate public figure and must stand up under ultimate scrutiny; he is like a man stretched out on a rack in the public square in some medieval shithole of a town, undergoing the rigors of the Inquisition. Like the medieval trial by ordeal, the Age of Scrutiny sneers at rational inquiry and debate, and presumes that mere oaths and protestations are deceptions and lies. The only way to discover the real truth is by the rite of the ordeal, which exposes the subject to such inhuman strain that any defect in his character will cause him to crack wide open, like a flawed diamond. It is a mystical procedure that skirts rationality, which is seen as the work of the Devil, instead drawing down a higher, ineffable power. Like the Roman haruspex who foretold the outcome of a battle, not by analyzing the strengths of the opposing forces but by groping through the steaming guts of a slaughtered ram, we seek to establish a candidate's fitness for office by pinning him under the lights of a television studio and counting the number of times he blinks his eyes in a minute, deconstructing his use of eye contact, monitoring his gesticulations—whether his hands are held open or closed, toward or away from the camera, spread open forthcomingly or clenched like grasping claws.

"I paint a depressing picture here. But we, you and I, are like the literate monks who nurtured the flickering flame of Greek rationality through the Dark Ages, remaining underground, knowing each other by secret signs and code words, meeting in cellars and thickets to exchange our dangerous and subversive ideas. We do not have the strength to change the minds of the illiterate multitude. But we do have the wit to exploit their foolishness, to familiarize ourselves with their stunted thought patterns, and to use that knowledge to manipulate them toward the goals that we all know are, quote, right and true, unquote. Have you ever been on TV, Aaron?"

"Just incidentally."

"How did you think that you looked?"

"Not very good. Actually I was kind of shocked by how strange I looked."

"Your eyes looked as if they were bulging out of your head, did they not?"

"Exactly. How did you know that?"

"The gamma curve of a video camera determines its response to light," Cy Ogle said. "If the curve were straight, then dim things would look dim and bright things bright, just as they do in reality, and as they do, more or less, on any decent film stock. But because the gamma curve is not a straight line, dim things tend to look muddy and black, while bright things tend to glare and overload; the only things that look halfway proper are in the middle. Now, you have dark eyes, and they are deeply set in your skull, so that they tend to be in shadow. By contrast, the whites of your eyes are intensely bright. If you knew what I know, you would keep them fixed straight ahead in their sockets when you were on television, exposing as little of the white as possible. But because you are not versed in this subject, you swivel your eyes around as you look at different things, and when you do, the white part predominates and it jumps out of the screen because of the gamma curve; your eyes look like bulging white globes set in a muddy dark background."

"Is this the kind of thing that you teach to politicians?"

"Just a sample," Ogle said.

"Gee, it's really a shame that—"

"That our political system revolves around such trivial matters. Aaron, please do not waste my time and yours by voicing the obvious."

"Sorry."

"That's how it is, and how it will be until high-definition television becomes the norm."

"Then what will happen?"

"All of the politicians currently in power will be voted out of office and we will have a completely new power structure. Because high-definition television has a flat gamma curve and higher resolution, and people who look good on today's television will look bad on HDTV and voters will respond accordingly. Their oversized pores will be visible, the red veins in their noses from drinking too much, the artificiality of their TV-friendly hairdos will make them all look, on HDTV, like country-and-western singers. A new generation of politicians will take over and they will all look like movie stars, because HDTV will be a great deal like film, and movie stars know how to look good on film."

"Does any of this relate to me, or are we just speaking in the abstract here?" Aaron said.

Cy Ogle rotated his beer back and forth between the palms of his hands, as if attempting to start a fire on the tabletop.

"A human being cannot withstand the scrutiny given to a presidential candidate, any more than a human being could survive the medieval trial by fire, in which he was forced to walk barefoot across hot coals."

"But people did survive those trials, didn't they?"

"Ever taken a fire-walking course?"

"No. But I've heard they exist."

"Anyone can walk barefoot across hot coals. But you have to do it right. There's a trick to it. If you know the trick, you can survive. Now, back in medieval times, some people got lucky and happened to stumble across this trick, and they made it. The rest failed. It was therefore an essentially random process, hence irrational. But if they had had fire-walking seminars in the Dark Ages, anyone could have done it.

"The same thing used to apply to the modern trial by ordeal. Abe Lincoln would never have been elected to anything, because random genetic chance gave him a user-unfriendly face. But as a rational person I can learn all of the little tricks and teach them to my friends, eliminating the random, hence irrational elements from the modern trial by ordeal. I have the knowledge to guide a presidential candidate through his trial in this, the Age of Scrutiny."

"What kinds of tricks?"

Ogle shrugged. "Some are very simple. Don't wear herringbone patterns on TV because they will create a moire pattern. But some of them are—and I do not use this term in a pejorative sense—fiendish. That's where you come in."

"I gather you want to use the IMIPREM to monitor people's reactions to political debates, or something."

"Don't ever say IMIPREM again. I hate that word," Ogle said. "It's a clumsy high-tech name. It's the worst trade name ever invented. Right now, your device is going to get subsumed into a larger group of technologies. It is going to become one very important element in a large and extremely complicated technological system. The name for that system is PIPER. Which stands for poll instantaneous processing, evaluation, and response."

"You asked me if I could make it small enough to be portable," Aaron said.

"That I did."

"You want to have your poll subjects carry these things around with them. You want to monitor their reactions to the campaign in real time. That's *poll instantaneous processing*. And *evaluation* must mean that you're going to feed all the data into your computers so that you can analyze and evaluate the incoming data as fast as it arrives."

"You are very perceptive," Ogle said.

"How about *response?*"

"How about it?"

"I understand the instantaneous processing and evaluation. But how can you *respond* to a poll instantaneously?"

"As I said," Ogle said, "your device will be only a small part of a large system."

"I understand that. But I'm asking—"

"Similarly, you, Aaron, will be only a small part of a large organization. Not the leading man anymore. A small price to pay for financial security, wouldn't you agree?"

"Yes. I'm just wondering—"

"One of your responsibilities, as a part of this large team, will be to use your head a little bit and not try to delve into matters that are remote from your own little sphere. You can't understand everything."

"Oh."

"Only I, Cyrus Rutherford Ogle, can understand everything."

"I was just asking out of pure curiosity."

"What is this the Age of, Aaron?"

"Scrutiny."

"Guess what is going to happen to you and your company when you become part of the PIPER project?"

"We will get scrutinized."

"Guess what is going to happen, then, if you insist on asking infelicitous questions, out of pure curiosity?"

"I will get roasted alive on hot coals."

"Along with me and everyone else involved in PIPER, including my clients."

"Say no more, I will be discreet."

"Good."

"I'm just trying to figure out what my responsibilities will be in PIPER."

"To work with our chip people and miniaturize your device. I have already made an appointment with some clever fellows at Pacific Netware, up in Marin County. We will go up there tomorrow and meet with them, like medieval monks gathering in a remote orchard, and we will build high the flame of, quote, rationality, unquote."

## CHAPTER NINE

Tuscola in late morning was silent except for the whistles of hundred-car freight trains thundering north-south along the Illinois Central or east-west on the B&O, and the occasional distant blatting noise of a truck downshifting on the highway. Cold winter sunlight was slanting in through the beveled-glass windows surrounding the front door, forming a spray of little rainbows on the aging shag carpet that covered the living room floor. Cozzanos had always placed a premium on warmth over exquisite taste and so they had shag carpet. William A. Cozzano had known for a long time that there was good oak flooring under there and had been resolving, for the last twenty years, to peel up the carpet and sand it and refinish it. It was one of those things that would wait until his retirement.

But he wouldn't be able to do it now. There was no way he could handle a big floor sander. He would have to pay someone to do the work for him. He had always done his own work on his own house, even when it meant waiting until he had a free weekend.

The street was made of red brick. So was the sidewalk. The bricks were heaved up from place to place by the roots of the big oak trees in the front yard. In other spots they were gradually sinking into the lawn. Kids from the afternoon kindergarten class were ambling down the sidewalk on their way to the Everett Dirksen Elementary School two blocks away, which had been retrofitted into a former hospital. They took no notice of the house. Older kids, who could read the words THE COZZANOS on the little sign hanging on the lamppost in the front yard, always stared and pointed, but the kindergartners didn't. Cozzano recognized a grandnephew twice removed and tried to wave, but his arm didn't work.

"Goddamn it," he said.

When he moved his tongue, a wave of drool crested over his lower lip and ran out the left side of his mouth. He felt it running in a thin stream down onto his chin.

Patricia came back into the room, of course, just in time to get a good look at this. She was a local girl, former babysitter to James and Mary Catherine, had worked in Peoria as a nurse for some years, and was now back home in Tuscola, working as a babysitter again. This time for William. Before the stroke, she had treated William Cozzano with awe and deference.

"Whoops, did we have a little accident there?" she said. "Let's just wipe that right up." She took a diaper out of her pocket and ran it up Cozzano's chin, a brisk uppercut. "Now, here's your coffee—decaf, of course, and pills. Lots of little pills."

"What are those pickles?" Cozzano said.

"I'm sorry, William, what did you say?"

He pointed to the little plastic cup that Patricia had set down next to him, filled with colorful circles and oblongs.

Patricia heaved a big sigh, letting him know that she'd rather he didn't ask such questions. "Blood pressure, anticlotting, heart stimulation, elimination, breathing, and then of course some vitamins."

Cozzano closed his eyes and shook his head. Until two weeks ago he had never taken anything other than vitamin C and aspirin.

"I put some skim milk in your coffee," Patricia said.

"I take it purple," Cozzano said.

Patricia beamed. "You mean you take it black?"

"Yes, goddamn it."

"It's just a little hot, William, so I wanted to cool it down a bit so you wouldn't burn your mouth when you took your medicine."

"Don't call me that. I'm the coach," Cozzano said. Then he closed his eyes and shook his head in frustration.

"Of course you are, William," she said in a buttery voice, and put the little cup of pills into his right hand. "Now, down the hatch!"

Cozzano did not want to take the pills, merely because he did not want to give Patricia satisfaction in any way. But at some level he knew that was puerile. So he tossed the pills into his mouth. Patricia took the cup from his hand and gave him the coffee, which was tepid and beige. Cozzano had gotten in the habit of drinking black full-roast coffee, and the only kind available around here was the sour greenish grocery-store variety. He lifted the mug to his lips and forced down a couple of big, awful swallows, feeling the pills crowd together in his throat and stick halfway down his esophagus. He would rather leave them stuck there than drink any more of that small-town coffee.

"Very good!" Patricia said, "I can see you have a knack for this."

Cozzano was accustomed to being a superman and now he was being praised by a Big Hair Girl for his ability to take pills.

"Would you like to watch a little TV?" Patricia said.

"Yes," he said. Anything to get her out of the room.

"What channel?"

Why didn't she just give him the remote control? Cozzano heaved a big sigh. He wanted to watch channel 10, CNBC. In his condition, one of the few things Cozzano could do was manage the family's investments. And in the economic chaos that had been unleashed by the President's State of the Union address, they needed a lot of management.

"Five million," he said. "No, goddamn it!"

"Well, sometimes it seems like this cable TV has about five million channels, but I don't think I can do that!" Patricia said in a high, inflated tone, her I'm-making-a-joke voice. "Did you mean to say channel five?"

"No!" he said. "Twice that."

"Two?"

"No! Three squared plus one. Six plus four. The square root of one hundred," he said. Why didn't she just give him the remote control?

"Oh, here's a news program. How's that?" Patricia said. She had hit one of the network stations. It was a little one-minute news break at the top of the hour, between soap operas.

"Yes," he said.

"Here's the remote control in case you change your mind," she said, and left it on the table next to him.

Cozzano sat and watched the little news break. It was totally inconsequential: presidential candidates cavorting around Iowa in a series of staged media events. The caucuses were in a week and a half.

Cozzano could have won the caucuses without lifting a finger. People in Iowa loved him, they knew he was a small-town boy.

Anyone who lived in the eastern part of that state saw him on TV all the time. All he had to do was pick up a phone and get nominated. Looking at the candidates on TV, he was tempted to do just that and put an end to all of this nonsense.

Senators and governors were out in the snow, picking up baby livestock, milking cows, standing in schoolyards wrapped up in heavy overcoats, tossing footballs to red-faced blond kids. Cozzano chortled as he watched Norman Fowler, Jr., billionaire high-tech twit, walking across the hard-frozen stubble of a cornfield in eight-hundred-dollar shoes. The wind chill was thirty below zero and these guys were standing out on the prairie without hats. That said everything about their fitness to be president.

Cozzano's family had always told him he ought to run for president one day. It sounded like a nice idea, bandied across a dinner table after a couple of glasses of wine. In practice it would be ugly and hellish. Knowing this, he had never seriously considered the idea. He had known for some time that Mel had quietly organized a shadow campaign committee and laid the groundwork. That was Mel's job; as a lawyer, he was supposed to anticipate things.

Of course, now that Cozzano had had a stroke and couldn't run, he wanted to be President worse than anything. He could make a phone call and a few hours later a chartered campaign plane would be waiting for him at the airport in Champaign, and suddenly literature and campaign videos would be piled up in heaps all over the United States. Mel could make it happen. And then Patricia would wheel him up onto the plane, drooling for the cameras.

This was the hardest phase of recovering from the stroke. Cozzano had not yet readjusted his expectations of life. When his high expectations collided with reality, it hurt like hell.

The news break metamorphosed into a commercial for cold medicine. Then the anchor person came back on to tell America when the next news break would be. And then a new program started up: *Candid Video Blind Date.*

Cozzano was so disgusted that he could not change the channel fast enough. It was as if this tawdry program would cause him physical damage if he watched it for more than ten seconds.

The remote control was on the table to his right, on the good side of his body. He reached over for it, but she had put it a little too far back on the table; the heel of his hand could touch it but his fingers couldn't. He tried to screw his arm around into a kind of self-induced hammerlock, but in his disgust he was doing it so hastily that he just ended up knocking it farther back on the table. It shot backward, flew off the table, and buried itself in the shag carpet. Now it was stuck between the table and a bin full of old newspapers: a two-week accumulation of the *Trib*, *The New York Times*, and *The Wall Street Journal*, none of which he would ever read.

He couldn't reach the damn thing. He would have to ask Patricia for help.

On the screen, the hysterical applause of the crowd had subsided and the host was warming them up with a few jokes. The humor was crudely sexual, the kind of thing that would embarass even a ninth grade boy, but the crowd was eating it up: in a series of reaction shots, Big Hair Girls and fat middle-aged women and California surfer types jackknifed in their seats, mouths gaping in narcotic glee. The game show host grinned devilishly into the camera.

"Goddamn it!" Cozzano said.

Patricia was washing some dishes in the kitchen and had the water going full blast, she couldn't hear him.

He didn't want Patricia to hear him. He didn't want to beg Patricia to come into the room and change the channel on the TV for him. He couldn't stand it.

He couldn't stand this TV program either. William A. Cozzano was watching *Candid Video Blind Date*. Across town, John and Giuseppe and Guillermo were turning over in their graves.

All of a sudden tears came to his eyes. It happened without warning. He hadn't cried since the stroke. Suddenly he was sobbing, tears running down his face and dripping from his jaw onto his blanket. He hoped to god that Patricia didn't come in.

He had to stop crying. This wouldn't do. This was too pathetic. Cozzano took a few deep breaths and got it under control. For some reason, the most important thing in the world to him was that Patricia not find out that he had been crying.

Sitting there in his wheelchair, trying not to look at the television set, Cozzano let his eye wander around the room, trying to concentrate on something else.

In the far end of the living room, a pair of heavy sliding doors led into a small den. Cozzano had never used it for much. It had a small roll-top desk where he balanced his checkbook. A beautiful antique gun case stood against one wall. Like all of the other furniture in Cozzano's house it had been made out of hardwood by people who knew what they were doing back in the nineteenth century. There was more solid wood in one piece of this furniture than you would find in a whole house nowadays. The top half of the gun case was a cabinet for long weapons, closed off by a pair of beveled-glass doors with a heavy brass lock. A skeleton key projected from the keyhole. Cozzano had half a dozen shotguns and two rifles in there: all of his father's and grandfather's guns, plus a few that he had picked up during his life. There was a pump shotgun that he had used in Vietnam, an ugly, cheap, scarred monstrosity that spoke volumes about the nature of that war. Cozzano kept it in there as a reality check. It made a nice contrast between the fancy guns, the ornate collector's items that various rich and important sycophants had given him.

Above and below the long weapons, a few handguns hung on pegs. The bottom half of the gun cabinet consisted entirely of small drawers with ornately carved fronts where he kept his ammunition, oil, rags, and other ballistic miscellanea.

Sitting in the next room in his wheelchair, Cozzano tried a little experiment. He reached up into the air with his right hand, seeing how high he could get. He was pretty sure that he could reach high enough to turn the skeleton key on the gun cabinet doors. And if not, he could always haul himself up out of his wheelchair for a few moments and carry all his weight on his right leg. The cabinet was massive and stable and he could probably use it to pull himself up.

So he could probably get the doors open. He could pull out one of the guns. It would probably make the most sense to use one of the handguns, because the long weapons were all enormous and heavy and would be awkward to maneuver with only one hand.

The .357 Magnum. That was the one to use. He knew he had ammunition for it, stored in the upper right-hand drawer, easy to reach. He would pull the pin that held the cylinder in place and let it fall open into his hand. Then he would drop it into his lap, letting it rest on the blanket between his thighs. He would grope in the drawer and pull out a handful of rounds. He would insert a few of these into the cylinder—one would suffice—and then snap it back into place. He would rotate the cylinder into position to make sure that one of the loaded chambers was next up.

Then what? Given the power of the weapon, it was likely that the bullet would come flying out the far side of his head and hit something else. There was an elementary school nearby and he could not take any chances.

The answer was right there: across the den, opposite to the gun case, was a heavy oak bookcase.

Cozzano couldn't see it from here. He reached down and hit the joystick attached to the right arm of his wheelchair. A whining noise came out of the little electric motor and he began to move forward. Cozzano had to do a little bit of back-and-forth to get himself free of the living room furniture, then he swung around back of the sofa and into the den. He spun the wheelchair around in the middle of the den and backed himself up to the wall next to the bookcase.

It was perfect. The bullet would emerge from his head, hit the side of the bookcase, and if it penetrated that inch of hardwood, would go right into the back cover of the first volume in a commemorative edition of the complete works of Mark Twain. No bullet in the world could make it all the way through Mark Twain.

So freedom was within reach. Now he just had to think it through.

Suicide would void his life insurance policies. That was a minus. But that didn't matter so much; his wife was already dead and his kids could support themselves. In fact, his kids didn't need to work, they had trust funds.

His body would be discovered by Patricia. That was a plus. He would not want to put a family member through that kind of trauma. It was a good bet that his brains would be splattered all over the room. Patricia was a medical professional who would be psychologically equipped to handle this, and Cozzano felt that the experience would be good for her. It might make her into a little less of a sugary lightweight.

He wondered if he ought to leave some kind of a note. His roll-top desk was right there. He might be able to scrawl something with his right hand. He decided against it. It would look pathetic, written with his wrong hand. Better for him to be remembered for what he had done before his stroke. For anyone who knew him, *Candid Video Blind Date* running on his TV set was suicide note enough.

Besides, Patricia might come in and discover him writing it. Then, he knew, they would take away the guns and anything else that he might use to hurt himself. They would shoot him full of drugs and mess with his brain.

And maybe they would be right. Maybe suicide was a stupid idea.

Of course it wasn't a stupid idea. Suicide was a noble thing when done in the right circumstances. It was the act of a warrior. Cozzano was about to fall on his sword to spare himself further humiliation.

And now was the best time to do it. Before his spirit was broken by the drool on his chin and by the numbing onslaught of daytime television, before his feeble new image was discovered by the media harpies and broadcast to the world.

The doctors had said that as time went on, he might have additional strokes. This meant he might become even more pathetic, incapable of taking his own life.

Cozzano had never been sick. Cozzano had always known that, barring the odd drunk driver or tornado, he was going to live until he was in his eighties.

Decades. Decades of this hell. Of watching *Candid Video Blind Date*. Of looking at that horrendous shag carpet and wishing he was man enough to handle a big floor sander. It was unimaginable. Cozzano hit the joystick and rolled across the room to the gun cabinet.

There was a sharp rapping noise. Someone was knocking on the window.

Cozzano turned the wheelchair halfway around and looked. It was Mel Meyer, standing out on the porch, waving to him.

## CHAPTER TEN

Mel Meyer saw some boys on the shoulder of the interstate checking the tie-downs on a flatbed truck carrying a piece of farm machinery. He pulled into the left lane to give them a safe berth, and as he shot past them he realized that the boys were about sixty and forty years old respectively. They only looked like boys because, on this cold February day, they were wearing denim jackets that barely came down to their waists. Culture shock again. You'd think he would have gotten used to it by now.

Mel understood intellectually that these people had to wear short jackets because it gave them greater freedom of movement while they worked, and he also understood that their mall-dwelling females wore pastel workout clothes and running shoes at all times because they were more comfortable than anything else. But to Mel they all looked like children. This was not because Mel was some kind of a snob. It was because he was from Chicago and these people were from the entirely separate cultural, political, and economic entity called downstate.

To make anything work between two such disjointed places there had to be the equivalent of diplomats—people who, in another context, had once been defined as "men sent abroad to lie for their country—in both senses of the word." The intra-Illinois diplomats were the old family law firms in the major and minor towns of the state. These professionals lacked the partisanship to have a killer impulse for their clients. Instead they saw life in terms of each side winning, if at all possible.

In Chicago there were perhaps a hundred families such as the Meyers, ranging through the Polish, Slovak, Irish, Ukrainian, Hungarian, and even WASP sections of town, who kept the lines between the two Illinoises open and flowing, working in enterprises legal and illegal. It was perhaps the purest and most professional group in Illinois, and the Meyers were masters of the guild.

Shmuel Meierowitz's son David, even though he was a Conservative Jew, had the skill and honesty to gain the trust of even the most bigoted downstate ambulance chaser. Generations of lawyers from Cairo, Quincy, Macomb, Decatur, and Pekin (home of the Fighting Chinks) knew that the Meyer family's word was good. It was not particularly surprising, then, that the Cozzanos had encountered the Meyers, and that they had formed an alliance.

Since then, a lot of Meyers had put a lot of miles on various cars, driving back and forth. Shmuel normally rode the Illinois Central, but David cruised up and down U.S. 45 in the stupendous Cadillacs and Lincolns of the 1950s and 1960s, and Mel scorched the pavement of Interstate 57 in a succession of Jaguars and Mercedes-Benzes.

Mel had defined his very own Checkpoint Charlie, the official dividing line between Chicago and downstate. He drove by it everytime he took I-57 south from the heart of the city. It was out in one of the suburbs, Mel had never bothered to find out which, where traffic finally started to open up a little bit. The landmark in question was a water tower, a modern lollipop-shaped one. It was painted bright yellow, and it had a smiley face on it. When Mel saw the damn smiley face he knew he had passed into hostile territory.

The flatness of downstate was, in its way, just as stark and awe-inspiring as Grand Canyon or Half Dome. He had been down here a thousand times and it always startled him. The settlers had come here and found an unmarked geometric plane; anything that rose above that plane was the work of human beings. When Mel had first come this way it was mostly grain elevators, water towers, and ranks of bleachers rising up alongside high-school football fields. These artifacts were still there, but nowadays the most prominent structures were microwave relay towers: narrow vertical supports made of steel latticework, sprouting from concrete pads in cornfields, held straight by guy wires, drum-shaped antennas mounted to their tops. Each antenna was pointed several miles across the prairie in the direction of the next microwave relay tower. This was how phone calls got bounced around the country. These things were all over the place, crossing the country with a dense invisible web of high-speed communications, but other places you didn't see them. In cities they were hidden on the tops of buildings, and in places with hills, they were built into the high places where you couldn't see them unless you knew where to look. But out here, the buildings and hills had fallen out from under the phone company and their invisible network had been laid bare. It was not merely visible, but the single most obvious thing about the downstate landscape.

It caused Mel to wonder, as he skimmed across the prairie on I-57, its four lanes straight as banjo strings, paralleling the equally straight Illinois Central railway line, whether downstate had some magical feature that might expose another network, a network that had, so far, so perfectly hidden its workings in the complexity of the modern world that Mel wasn't even sure it existed.

*Cozzano beckoned Mel* into the house and rolled forward into the living room.

"Hey, Willy, how are you?" Mel said, coming in the front door. He spun a stack of newspapers into Cozzano's lap: the *Financial Times* was on top, and Cozzano could see the red corner of the *Economist* sticking out underneath. Mel pounded Cozzano on the shoulder, peeled off his heavy cashmere overcoat, and, oblivious to the fact that it cost more than a small car, tossed it full-length onto the sofa where it would pick up dog hairs. "What is this shit on the TV?" he said. He went up to the set and punched buttons on the cable box until he got CNBC. Then he turned the volume down so it wouldn't interfere with the conversation.

"Hey, Patty," Mel said. "You need to do any medical stuff with Governor Cozzano in the near future?"

Patricia had no idea how to deal with people who were not from Tuscola. She just stood in the dining room, glowing fuzzily in her peach-and-lavender sweatsuit, drying her hands, looking at Mel, completely baffled and uncertain. "Medical stuff?"

"I am asking you," Mel said, "if the Governor will be needing any specific medical attention from you in the next few hours—medications, therapy, anything like that. Or are your duties going to be strictly domestic in nature—making food and taking him to the bathroom and stuff like that?"

Patricia's eyes looked down and to the left. Her mouth was slightly ajar. She was still completely nonplussed.

"Thank you," Mel said, reaching his arms far apart to grab the handles of the big sliding doors that separated the living room from the dining room. He drew them shut with a thunderclap, closing off their view of Patricia. Then he went to another door that had been propped open and kicked out the doorstop.

"In or out, Lover. Command decision!" he snapped.

Lover IV, the golden retriever, scurried into the room and got out of the way as the door swung shut.

"You gotta take a leak or anything?"

"No," Cozzano said.

"You look good, for a guy who's exhausted."

"Huh?"

"You've been working so hard thinking about the campaign that you have collapsed from exhaustion," Mel said. "You're taking a week or two off to recover. In the meantime, your able staff is filling in for you."

Mel plopped down on the couch next to Cozzano. He began to rub his chin with his hand. Mel had a thick and fast-growing beard and shaved a couple of times a day. For him, chin rubbing was something he did when he was taking stock of his overall situation in the world.

"You were going to blow your brains out, weren't you?"

"Yeah," Cozzano said.

Mel thought it over. He didn't seem especially shocked. The idea did not have a big emotional impact on him. He seemed to be weighing it, the way he weighed everything. Finally he shrugged, unable to deliver a clear verdict.

"Well, I've never been one to argue with you, just offer advice," Mel said.

"Yes no."

"My advice right now is that it is entirely your decision. But there may be factors of which you are not aware."

"Oh?"

"Yeah. I'm sure you're probably thinking what it would be like to spend twenty, thirty years this way."

"You win the Camaro!" Cozzano said.

"Well, it's possible that you may not have to. I'm getting, uh, shall we say, *feelers*, from people who may have a therapy to cure this kind of thing."

"Cure it?"

"Yeah. According to these people you could get back a lot of what you lost. Maybe get back all of it."

"How? The melon is dead."

"Right," Mel said, not missing a beat, "the brain tissue is toast. Kaput. Croaked. Not coming back. They can rewire some of the connections, though. Replace the missing parts with artificial stuff. Or so they say."

"Where?"

"Some research institute out in California. It's one of Coover's little projects."

"Coover." Cozzano chuckled a little bit and shook his head. DeWayne Coover was a contemporary of Cozzano's father. Like John Cozzano, he had gotten lucky with some investments during the war. He was a billionaire, one of those billionaires that no one ever hears about. He lived on some patch of warm sandy real estate down in California and he didn't get out much except to play golf with ex-presidents and washed-up movie stars. His granddaughter Althea had gone to Stanford with Mary Catherine and they had been on the fringes of each other's social circles.

John Cozzano and DeWayne Coover had had a number of dealings during and after the war and had never really hit it off. Some people liked to believe that there was some kind of rivalry between the two men, but this was a completely off-the-wall idea. Coover's success dwarfed that of the Cozzano family. He was in an entirely different league.

"I got a call from one of Coover's lawyers," Mel said. "It was on an unrelated thing. A leukemia thing."

After Christina died of leukemia, Cozzano had founded a charitable organization to research the disease and assist victims. DeWayne Coover, who had a penchant for big medical research projects, had been a major contributor. So it was not unusual for Cozzano's people to talk to Coover's people.

"So I'm talking to the guy, and it's about some kind of trivial question relating to taxes. It comes into my head to wonder why this guy, who is a senior partner in a big-time L.A. firm, is talking to me about this issue, when it's so tiny that our secretaries could almost handle it. And then he says to me, 'So, how's the Governor doing these days?' Just like that."

Cozzano laughed and shook his head. It was incredible how word got around.

"Well, to make a long story short, he's been dumping bucks into researching problems like yours. And he's definitely putting out feelers."

"Get more phone books," Cozzano said.

"More information about it? I knew you'd say that."

Cozzano raised his right hand to his head, shaped like a pistol, and brought his thumb down like a hammer.

"Right," Mel said, "a bullet to the head is the most experimental therapy of all."

## CHAPTER ELEVEN

The next time Dr. Radhakrishnan heard from Mr. Salvador was ten days later, when two packages arrived in his office, courtesy of GODS, Global Omnipresent Delivery Systems. One of them was a small box. The other was a long tube. Dr. Radhakrishnan paused before opening them to marvel at their pure, geometric perfection. In India, as in most of the United States, mail was a dusty, battered, imperfect thing. Mail came wrapped up in protective layers of inexpensive, fibrous brown paper, tied together with fuzzy twine that looked like spun granola; the contents burst through the wrapping at the corners, skid marks trailed along every side, and the shapes of the packages and envelopes always came just a bit short of the geometric ideal. Addresses were scrawled on it in magic marker and ballpoint pen, antique-looking stamps, fresh from the engraver, stuck to it, annotations made by various postal workers along the way.

That was not how Mr. Salvador mailed things. When Mr. Salvador mailed something, he went through GODS. The biggest name in the express-mail business. Mr. Salvador's mail was not made of any paper-based substance. No fibers in there. Nothing brown. The wrapping was some kind of unbreakable plastic sheeting with a slick teflonesque feel to it, white and seamless as the robe of Christ. Both of the packages were festooned with brilliantly colored, glossy, self-stick, plasticized GODS labels. None of the labels, nor any other parts of the packages, had ever been sullied by human handwriting. Everything was computer-printed. Every one of the labels had some kind of bar code on it. Some of the labels contained address-related information. Some contained lengthy strings of mysterious digits. Some pertained to insurance and other legalistic matters, and others, like medals on an officer's chest, seemed to be purely honorific in nature.

The color scheme consisted of three hues; every check box, every logo, every stern warning and legal disclaimer on every label was in one of these three hues. The hues all went together perfectly and they looked great, whether they were on the packages themselves or on the neatly pressed NASA-style coverall worn by the fetching young woman who had delivered the packages, obtaining Dr. Radhakrishnan's signature on a flat-screened notebook computer that beeped and squealed as it beamed his digitized scrawl back to the remote computer inside the glossy, tri-hued GODS delivery van. The woman was cheery, confident, professional, apparently taking a little time off from her normal job as a trial lawyer, aerobics instructor, or nuclear physicist to do some life-enriching delivery work. Dr. Radhakrishnan, the world's greatest neurosurgeon, had felt small, dirty, and ignorant before her. But before he could ask her for a date, she was out the door, having more important things to do.

Dr. Radhakrishnan opened the box first. There was no tape; the magic white wrapping stuck to itself. As he pulled it apart, stickers and labels tore in half, and he got an intuition that, perhaps, part of the thrill of receiving such mail was that you got to dramatize your own importance by tearing it apart. It was like ravishing an expensive, salon-fresh call girl.

Inside the wrapping was a featureless hard plastic box, white and unmarked, that had to be opened using some trick that Dr. Radhakrishnan could not figure out right away. When the box had been penetrated, the entire contents turned out to have been sealed in plastic wrap, like a glass in a motel room. Dr. Radhakrishnan knew that in the context of American culture, to seal something up in plastic was to honor it.

The contents turned out to be a short stack of unmarked 3.5-inch floppy disks. He remembered that he and Mr. Salvador had had a discussion about the Calyx operating system, so, on a hunch, he popped one of the disks into the Pacific Netware workstation on his desk.

The systems were compatible. There were a few files stored on the disk, all in a standard format used for color images. They all sounded like medical scans of one type or another.

Dr. Radhakrishnan opened some of them up and checked them out; these files were all pictures of the same man's brain. The man had suffered a stroke that had, to judge from the position of the two affected areas, probably interfered with his speech and caused some paralysis on the left side. Interestingly enough, the affected parts of the brain were isodense, which is to say that they had the same density as the healthy parts of the brain surrounding them. This indicated that these pictures had been taken within a few days of the stroke.

It did not take much imagination on Dr. Radhakrishnan's part to realize that he was looking at the brain of Mr. Salvador's friend. Mr. Salvador was implicitly asking him a question: is this the type of damage that you can fix?

And the answer was yes. In theory. But the facility that would be required to do the work did not exist and wouldn't exist for years, even with preposterously optimistic assumptions about grants and funding. Oh, you could build one any time you wanted, if you had the money. But who had that kind of money?

Dr. Radhakrishnan eventually outsmarted the latching system on the tube. Rolled up inside was a thick stack of poster-sized sheets of paper.

In his cluttered lab it took some doing just to find a table large enough to unroll them. Finally he chased Toyoda out of the coffee room, where he had been watching MTV, and cleared off the counter, wiped up a few spills with a napkin, and unrolled the pages across the wood-grained Formica. Unrolled, the stack of sheets was nearly half an inch thick. They were all the same size, and all covered with precise, colorful drawings.

Flipping quickly through the stack he saw floor plans, elevations, detailed renderings of individual rooms. The top sheet was an elevation. It portrayed a modern, high-tech structure perched on a piney bluff overlooking the sea. There was a modest parking lot, a satellite dish on the roof, lots of windows, an outdoor cafeteria, even a bicycle path. Looked like a nice place to work.

The second sheet was an elevation of an entirely different building. This one was in an urban setting. It had an austere sandstone color with a few darkly tinted windows set up above street level. It was also high-tech, but at the same time it was strikingly Indian: he could see the classic motifs of Hindu architecture, updated and streamlined. The materials were unusual: reinforced concrete where it counted, of course, but sandstone and marble on the outside, even some traditional inlay work.

The third sheet showed the same building from a higher angle, revealing a central, glassed-in atrium lined with offices and abloom with lush flowering tropical plants. Behind it, a neighborhood of low, blocky concrete structures stretched toward a somewhat more built-up district a few blocks away, centered on a huge circular roadway lined with shops and offices.

Dr. Radhakrishnan was shocked to recognize the ring road: it was Connaught Circus, the solar plexus of his home city of New Delhi. Once he figured that out, everything snapped into focus, he understood which direction he was looking in, recognized the shapes of the Volga Hotel and the glass front of the big British Airways office on the Circus, the entrances to the underground bazaar.

He knew exactly where this building was. It had been drawn in on the site of the Ashok Cinema, a memorable, if decrepit structure, where Papa had taken him to movies as a child. Right in between Connaught Circus and the India Gate, close to the seat of government, embassies, everything.

If this building—whatever it was—was really under construction, or even being contemplated, it was news to him. He should have heard about it by now, because fancy new high-tech structures did not spring up every day there. Dr. Radhakrishnan did not know what this building was, but he could recognize high-tech architecture when he saw it. It seemed that someone had ambitious plans to create a sort of silicon ashram.

Maybe this was some sort of an investment opportunity. Or maybe they were trying to attract researchers to this new complex. But it had to be a far-off fantasy on someone's part because if ground had been broken in Delhi—if this plan had even been whispered—Dr. Radhakrishnan would have heard about it. He was not the most well connected Delhian by a long shot, but he knew people and he stayed in touch.

He continued paging through the stack, trying to glean some clues. The drawings alternated between the two buildings: the one on the bluff above the sea and the one in Delhi.

Space was set aside for offices, R&D, laboratories, operating rooms, and even a few private bedrooms, complete with all of the equipment you would expect to see in a state-of-the-art intensive-care ward. Evidently these buildings were for biomedical research of the most advanced sort.

The building in Delhi included one operating theater that was especially large and complicated. Dr. Radhakrishnan found a detailed plan of the room and went over it carefully, growing more and more certain as he did so that he had seen this before: it was an exact reproduction of the specialized operating room that he had described to Mr. Salvador. The one that Mr. Salvador had taken with him on those disks.

The plans for Radhakrishnan's ultimate operating theater had simply been dropped whole into the blueprints for a new building. But it wasn't a hack job. The systems had all been integrated into their surroundings. The plumbing lines, the electrical wiring, the gas lines, all went somewhere. Subtle modifications had been made without changing the essential features. In fact, the room had been improved in several ways. Engineers had been at work on this. Very good engineers.

Dr. Radhakrishnan was beginning to experience a prickly, hot feeling centered on the back of his neck, as though he were the victim of a joke or psychological experiment. He shuffled quickly through the stack, trying to get clues, looking for a point of reference. But he couldn't find anything that explained whether this was reality or fantasy, who had these plans drawn up, or why.

Until he got to the last sheet, which showed an elevation of the front entrance of the building in Delhi. The doorway was surrounded by a massive masonry frame. The material had a rich red hue, the color of Indian sandstone. The name of the building was carved into a flat square stone next to the door, a Rosetta stone in English and Hindi:

DR. RADHAKRISHNAN V.R.J.V.V. GANGADHAR
INSTITUTE OF BIOMEDICAL RESEARCH—DELHI BRANCH

He read it over several times, as though this were the first time he had ever seen his own name written down.

He sifted back through the stack, looking for elevations of the building above the ocean. Finally he dug up an elevation showing it from ground level, with a concrete marker set into the ground by the entrance to the parking lot:

ROBERT J. COOVER BUILDING
DR. RADHAKRISHNAN V.R.J.V.V. GANGADHAR
INSTITUTE OF BIOMEDICAL RESEARCH—
CALIFORNIA BRANCH

Finally, a clue here. Robert J. Coover was a very rich man. A billionaire. The building in which Dr. Radhakrishnan was standing was the Coover Biotech Pavilion; Coover had had it thrown together a couple of years ago when he decided that biotechnology was the wave of the future.

It made sense, in a way. This Elton State thing had just been a fishing expedition, a stratagem to attract promising talent. Now that Dr. Radhakrishnan's project with the baboons had succeeded so brilliantly, Coover understood that it was time to pull away and get serious about forging ahead. And Dr. Radhakrishnan was ready to do some forging.

It was 9:30 A.M., one of the few times of day when he and his brother in Delhi might be awake simultaneously. In Delhi, the opposite side of the world from Elton, it was 10:00 P.M. and Arun would probably be watching the news on his television set.

Dialing India was always an adventure. He got through eventually and reached his brother at his home in one of the pleasant colonies on the outskirts of the metropolis, where government officials lived with their air conditioners. As he had anticipated, the English language version of the news was running in the background. The sound quality on the phone was very bad and Arun had to run over and turn the television down in order for them to get through the obligatory several minutes of family-related small talk.

"Me? Oh, I'm fine, everything is going well enough," Dr. Radhakrishnan said. "I heard some—some rumors about a new development in the city and I wanted to ask you if you knew anything about them."

"What sort of rumors?"

"Has anything been happening lately with the Ashok Cinema?"

A silence. Then, "Ha!" Arun sounded satisfied, vindicated. "So news of this heinous crime has even reached Elton, New Mexico!"

"Only the most tenuous reports, I can assure you." Dr. Radhakrishnan did not want to put his brother off by explaining to him that if a hydrogen bomb were dropped in the middle of Connaught Circus, it probably wouldn't show up in the American media unless American journalists were killed.

"I knew it would come out eventually. Little brother, it is corruption and CIA intrigues. Pure and simple. That's the only explanation."

"Are they planning to do something to the theater?"

Arun laughed bitterly. "Let me catch you up on events. The Ashok Theatre does not exist anymore, as of yesterday!"

"No!"

"I kid you not."

"I knew it was decrepit but—"

"It is more decrepit now. They have smashed it to the ground. Within twenty-four hours the site was picked clean by a million harijans. They came from every quarter of the city, like piranhas, descended on the rubble before the dust had settled, and carried away every piece of the building. Why, my secretary says that today they had earth-moving equipment there, digging a basement!"

"But . . . who is 'they' in this case?"

"Guess."

"I can't."

"MacIntyre Engineering. The right hand of the CIA!"

Like many Indian politicians of a certain age, Arun liked to find the CIA everywhere. Gangadhar, having spent some time in the States and gotten an idea of the way that large American institutions actually operated, had his doubts. He had come to realize that MacIntyre Engineering would be a far more fearsome multinational corporation if it had nothing whatsoever to do with the United States Government.

"Since when are you such a cinema buff anyway?" Gangadhar asked.

"What do you mean?"

"Why is this such a heinous crime? The Ashok Theatre was a dump. It was high time for it to be torn down anyway."

Arun sighed at his brother's naivete. "It is not so much what they did as the way they did it," he said.

"How was that?"

"They swaggered. They came into town like pirates. Little brother, it was like the old days, when the Brits or the Yanks would charge in and do as they pleased."

"But Arun, we are a sovereign country. How could they—"

"A sovereign country run by men." Arun sighed. "Corruptible men."

"They bribed their way in?"

"Gangadhar, do you have any idea how long it would normally take to obtain all the permits to raze a theater and begin construction of a new structure?"

"Weeks?"

"Months. Years. MacIntyre did it in days. They only got here a week ago. The telephone lines were smoking, Gangadhar, so many of their people were phoning in from the States, calling all the right officials, sending round limousines to take them out to lunch. I have never seen anything like it."

Someone was rapping on the frame of Dr. Radhakrishnan's door. He looked up to see yet another delivery person from GODS carrying a package. This one was the size of an orange crate.

"Just a moment, I have to sign for something," he said. He beckoned the courier into his office, signed his name on the notebook computer with a nonchalant flourish, and waved him out. He withdrew a penknife from his desk drawer and began to cut the fiberglass tape that held the top of the box in place. It was a thick-walled styrofoam sarcophagus.

"Do you have any idea what sort of structure they intend to build?" Dr. Radhakrishnan continued.

"If they had gone through the normal channels, I would, but the ink is hardly dry on the blueprints, the workers themselves probably don't even know what they are building. The pace of the construction is frantic. They have actually purchased a local cement factory for their own private use! Gangadhar, everyone says that America has gone downhill, but you would never believe it if you could come here and see this. The only parallel I can think of is the Manhattan Project."

"Did I ever tell you about the time I went to the Taj Mahal?" Dr. Radhakrishnan said, suddenly, on a whim.

"I don't know. Why?"

Dr. Radhakrishnan had gotten the lid off the styrofoam box. The walls were three inches thick. The interior was filled with a swirling fog of dry ice. He waved his hand over it to dissipate the cryogenic mist. In the middle of the container, neatly packed between large chunks of dry ice, was a small rack made of clear plastic, about the size of a cigarette case. It was made to hold several narrow glass tubes. At the moment, it held two of them.

"I was standing there looking at some of the inlay work on the north wall of the structure. Magnificent stuff. And this group of Americans was there. Had come all the way around the world to see the Taj Mahal. It was beastly hot, must have been forty-five degrees.

They were all dirty and tired and as usual there were pickpockets all over the place. And one of them said, 'Hell, we should just build one of these things. In Arizona or somewhere.' "

"You're kidding."

"Not at all. He thought that they would just raise some money and replicate the Taj. And all the other Americans just nodded as though that were a perfectly reasonable idea."

"It's unbelievable."

Dr. Radhakrishnan had opened the little case now, taking care not to burn his hands with the intense cold, and removed the two narrow glass tubes. Each one was mostly empty except for a small dark wad of material near one end. He raised them up toward the light.

"They have no values of any kind," he said. "Nothing means anything to them. The Taj is just a construction project, a particular manipulation of assets. And whatever they're doing on the Ashok Theatre site is more of the same."

He saw a glint of red and realized that the dark wads must be tissue samples of some kind, which had presumably leaked a bit of blood against the glass walls of the tubes before they had frozen. He stepped over toward his window to allow the winter sunlight to illuminate them a little better.

Arun's voice sounded far away. "Maybe they're building a Taj in Delhi so they don't have to take the bus all the way to Agra," he joked.

Dr. Radhakrishnan said nothing. He had recognized the contents of the tubes.

Mr. Salvador had mailed him pieces of two people's brains.

## CHAPTER TWELVE

From two thousand feet above the California coast, Dr. Radhakrishnan could see the whole thing taking shape. This was one of those especially nice corporate jets with oversized windows: a Gale Aerospace Gyrfalcon. The windows gave him a panoramic view of the entire parcel: there was the flat, sandy plain where the future position of the private landing strip was already marked out with little fluorescent orange flags. There was the gravel access road, which was rapidly being transmuted into asphalt by a road crew. There was the grove of trees that would be turned into a little park where the workers could recreate. And finally, high above the pounding white crests of the Pacific, there was the rocky bluff where the facility itself would be constructed.

Was being constructed.

"My god," Dr. Radhakrishnan blurted. "It's half finished."

Mr. Salvador smiled. "This sort of rough structural work always goes surprisingly quickly. I suppose that putting on all the doorknobs will take eons. Care for another cigar?"

The coastline passed beneath them. The afternoon sun was now slanting in through the windows on the left side of the Gyrfalcon.

Dr. Radhakrishnan still didn't know how to take all of this. He had been thinking about it for days and still hadn't figured it out. It was way too much. Totally unrealistic. He had scraped for money and recognition his whole career. Now he was getting everything. The Manhattan Project, as Arun had said. This could not be happening. But it was happening.

His instincts told him that there was no rational explanation for this frantic expenditure of money. But that was a closed-minded attitude not befitting a scientist. He was not a businessman. Who was he to say that it didn't make financial sense?

Dr. Radhakrishnan V.R.J.V.V. Gangadhar belonged on this business jet. And he deserved his research institutes also. It was altogether fitting and proper.

*"I couldn't help* noticing you had some newspapers in your briefcase," Dr. Radhakrishnan said. "I didn't get a chance to pick one up this morning."

"Yesterday's *New York Times*," Mr. Salvador said.

"Oh," Dr. Radhakrishnan said disappointedly. "I was hoping to take a look at the stock quotes."

"Say no more," Mr. Salvador said. He put his cigar down and moved to the front of the cabin. He sat down in a leather swivel chair in front of a portable communications setup that was built into the forward bulkhead of the Gyrfalcon, just behind the cockpit. It included a telephone and a fax machine, a keyboard, and a couple of flat-screen monitors. The fax machine had been oozing paper almost since the moment they had taken off in Elton, and by now a long curlicue had piled up beneath it on the deck. "These Gale birds are pricey but they have peerless avionics," Mr. Salvador continued, punching away on the keyboard.

A stock ticker materialized at the bottom of one of the monitor screens, scrolling from right to left. "Can you make this out from where you are?"

"Yes, I can see it very clearly, thank you."

"I should have anticipated your interest and had it running when you came aboard. My apologies."

"Oh, I'm not that much of a player," Dr. Radhakrishnan said, embarrassed by the fuss. "But I have a bit of stock in Genomics, that company in Seattle. When we began working with them, I was so impressed that I decided to buy in."

"And it's been moving rapidly of late, making you a nervous wreck," Mr. Salvador said.

"Exactly. Takeover rumors. I told my broker to sell at eighty-three."

"Then you made out brilliantly."

"I did? What do you mean?"

"Genomics was just bought out by Gale Aerospace this morning. At eighty-five. You called it exactly."

"Gale Aerospace now owns Genomics?" Dr. Radhakrishnan said. He was relieved and delighted. But he also thought it was just a bit eerie. He glanced around at the interior of the jet's cabin as if it might be able to tell him something.

"Yes."

"Why would a rocket and missile company want to own a scruffy little genetic engineering firm in Seattle?"

"Diversification!" Mr. Salvador said. "An intelligent enough strategy in this age of world peace, wouldn't you say?"

"Yes. Now that you mention it, it does seem perfectly logical."

"While we happen to be on the subject of tissue culture, did you get my other package? The tissue samples?" Mr. Salvador said.

Tissue samples was a nice word for it. "I did," Dr. Radhakrishnan said. "They were good clean samples. Whoever took them for you knew his business."

"We try to hire well," Mr. Salvador said.

"This is the first opportunity I have had to work with human brain tissue," Dr. Radhakrishnan said. As he delivered this sentence, he slowed down, sensing that he was on slick footing.

Mr. Salvador smiled understandingly. "I know that the regulations on these things in the States can be quite stifling."

"Exactly. Anyway, I, uh, or we, my students and I, were not sure exactly—we have so little experience." Dr. Radhakrishnan knew that he was groping pathetically, but Mr. Salvador kept smiling and nodding. "We have, anyway, initiated the cell culturing process with those samples . . . sent them on to Genomics. There were a few false starts—"

"Naturally. That's how science works."

"—but the samples you gave us were so, well, generous, so large, that we had a lot of margin for error. I am almost surprised, well . . ."

"Yes?"

"Of course human brains are larger than baboon brains, so my perspective is skewed just a bit, but if I were to take samples of a human brain that were so large, I would"—again, he sensed he was on slick footing—"well, let us say that in America, with its malpractice hysteria, where you always have to cover your tail—"

"Ridiculous." Mr. Salvador agreed.

"—lawyers—"

"Carping and niggling and backfilling," Mr. Salvador said. "In some ways, Doctor, America is the best place in the world to do research. In other ways, with its litigiousness, it is a terrible place. We think that India and America may be able to complement each other in this respect."

*He was so good.* "Exactly. Mr. Salvador, you have a knack."

"I am so pleased that we are able to see eye to eye on this," Mr. Salvador said.

"How are the, uh, patients doing, by the way?" Dr. Radhakrishnan said. "Ha! I almost called them specimens."

"Call them whatever you like," Mr. Salvador said. "They are doing well. You will be able to examine them shortly. Of course we would not have selected them for inclusion in this program if they had not already suffered neurological damage, so this makes answering your question somewhat problematic."

"Yes, I see your point."

"Well. I don't mean to wear you out with all this technical chit-chat. We'll be taking the great circle route to Delhi," Mr. Salvador said. "We'll make refueling stops in exciting places like Anchorage and Seoul. There's a private cabin on the other side of that bulkhead where you can get some rest, and while you're there I'm sure that Marla will be happy to give you a massage or engage you in conversation or whatever it is that would make the time go faster."

"Ah," Dr. Radhakrishnan said. "I thought I smelled perfume."

"As you can see, Mr. Coover is a consummate host. My job does not come with such fringies, but I have more than enough to occupy myself." Mr. Salvador nodded in the direction of the communications rig on the bulkhead.

"You are a busy man," Dr. Radhakrishnan observed.

"Great things are afoot," Mr. Salvador said with uncharacteristic gusto. "For certain people, this is a fascinating time to be alive."

Dr. Radhakrishnan certainly felt that way. "How long have you been working for Mr. Coover?"

Mr. Salvador paused before answering, his face alert, his eyes glittering. He was not thinking about how to answer so much as he was studying Radhakrishnan's face. He seemed, as usual, ever so slightly amused. "I wouldn't make unwarranted assumptions," he said.

Dr. Radhakrishnan wanted to pursue this line of questioning but he had realized that, by asking about Mr. Salvador's background, he had blundered into the realm of bad taste. And that was much worse than bad morals or bad manners for a certain kind of person.

However, he sensed without having met her that Marla would be a much more accessible person on all levels. "I'm going to freshen up," he said, nodding toward the private cabin in the back.

"Take your time and relax," Mr. Salvador said, "it's a long way to India."

. . .

*In his usual* style, Mr. Salvador had gone to great lengths to make Dr. Radhakrishnan feel at home in Delhi, even though Delhi *was* his home. A large suite had been rented out at the spectacular Imperial Hotel, an aptly named pile sitting at the end of a palm-tree-lined drive just off Janpath. It was just south of Connaught Circus and less than a mile from where the institute was being constructed. Mr. Salvador had rented out a couple of floors of the hotel. During the course of the long flight across the Pacific, Marla had developed quite an infatuation with Dr. Radhakrishnan and insisted that she be allowed to stay in Delhi for a while; Mr. Salvador had grudgingly granted her a suite of her own, just down the hall from Dr. Radhakrishnan's. Mr. Salvador was staying at the other end of the hall in lesser but still opulent surroundings.

When Dr. Radhakrishnan arrived at the Imperial, a pleasant surprise awaited: his entire extended family. They all cheered and hugged and kissed him right there in the parlor of his suite and then moved downstairs to a banquet room for a lengthy dinner. Dr. Radhakrishnan felt like a conquering hero back from the wars, being welcomed home by the maharaja with a royal feast.

After that, Marla had to nurse him through a day or two of hangover, fatigue, and jet lag. When he finally felt ready, he called for a car and told the driver to take him southward down Janpath into the New Delhi South Extension, where, he had been assured, the temporary laboratories of the Radhakrishnan Institute were bustling away.

On his way out of the hotel, he met a young American fellow in the elevator. Dr. Radhakrishnan could have met this man in Antarctica and still recognized him immediately as an American high-tech entrepeneur. He was in his early thirties. He had longish hair that had probably been cut in the mirror at home. He had a beard. He wore glasses. He was dressed in blue jeans, sneakers, a decent enough striped white shirt, and a crumpled wool blazer. He was carrying a briefcase in one hand and a rather formidable laptop computer in the other.

And one other key point: unlike everyone else he had met since the beginning of the flight to Delhi, he did not make any effort to brown-nose. "Hi, you must be Radhakrishnan," the man said. "I'm Peter Zeldovich. Most people I work with call me Zeldo. That's my handle on most e-mail systems. Nice to meet you." He put his laptop on the floor of the elevator and stuck out his hand; Dr. Radhakrishnan shook it, limply and reluctantly.

"Gotten over your jet lag yet?" this man said as they took the elevator down to lobby level.

Dr. Radhakrishnan had already forgotten his proper name. He was terrible with names. Now he knew why everyone called this person Zeldo. His real names vanished instantly from memory; Zeldo lingered unremovably on the doorstep of the mind, like a steaming turd left behind by a stray dog. Hopefully they would not be working together very much.

Naturally they would not have to work together. It was Dr. Radhakrishnan's institute, he was in charge, he could send Zeldo back to his festering West Coast bachelor pad whenever he got to be too annoying. Which might not take very long, at this rate. "Heard you were on your way in to the Barracks, so I thought I'd hitch a ride with you," Zeldo said as they exited into the lobby.

"The Barracks?"

"Yeah. That's what we've been calling the temporary institute. Guess you haven't seen it yet."

"Why would you call it by that name?" Of course it was superfluous even to ask questions like this; these breezy American chaps had to have nicknames for everything.

"Because that's what it is. It's down south, on the edge of this military zone—"

"The Defence Colony?"

"Yeah." Zeldo reached for one of the doors, almost colliding with the turbaned doorman who opened it for him.

Dr. Radhakrishnan had only been back in the civilized world for a couple of days, but now it felt as if he had never left, and as if the years in Elton were nothing more than a frigid nightmare.

"Anyway, the temporary lab facilities are set up in these barracks-type buildings. Soviet concrete things, you know. It'll be okay for the time being, I guess."

Zeldo had the presence of mind to allow the driver to open the car door for him, and he slid into the seat ahead of Dr. Radhakrishnan. He folded up his long legs so that his knees were pressed against the back of the driver's seat and piled the briefcase and the computer on his lap. The driver pulled out onto Janpath, ignoring the painted lanes and creating his own, in the traditional local style.

"I'm the chiphead from Pacware," Zeldo said, as if Dr. Radhakrishnan were supposed to know what that meant.

"What is Pacware?"

"Pacific Netware. I design logic devices—chips—for them."

"Am I to gather that you are connected, in some way, with my institute?"

Zeldo gaped at him. "Sure," he said. "I'm doing the hardware design on the silicon portion of the new model biochips."

"I was not aware that a new model was required."

Zeldo shrugged. "New models are always required," he said. "Hardware design is a fast-moving target. You don't update your designs every few months, you're working with Stone Age technology."

Dr. Radhakrishnan was finding it very difficult to keep his temper under control. Perhaps he was still just a bit irritable from his travels. For him to come home in triumph and finally to receive the recognition he deserved, and then to be stuck in an elevator, and a car, with this laid-back Yank who told him he was back in the Stone Age—

But he held his tongue, because he had an inkling that Zeldo might be half right. The chips they put into the baboons were off-the-shelf models with limited capabilities. It was a basic fact, with electronics, that if you designed a customized chip to do a particular job, it could work thousands of times faster than an off-the-shelf model.

If Zeldo could do his job properly and build a new, specialized chip for this purpose, it might vastly improve the capabilities of Dr. Radhakrishnan's implant.

Actually, bringing in a "chiphead" from a hot company like Pacific Netware was a brilliant idea. He wished he had thought of it himself. He wondered who *had* thought of it.

"Did they try to set you up with a babe?" Zeldo said.

"I'm sorry? A babe?"

"Yeah. A chick. You know, a prostitute."

Dr. Radhakrishnan wished that Zeldo had not used this word.

"They did with me," Zeldo said. "Bought me a first class ticket on British Airways to get me over here from San Francisco. Soon as I get on, this incredible woman sits down next to me. She was playing footsy with me before we even pulled away from the gate. God, she was a hot lady."

Dr. Radhakrishnan smiled conspiratorially. "You liked her, eh?" he said.

"Well, she didn't have a lot going for her intellectually," Zeldo said, frowning, "and I'm involved in a monogamous relationship at home."

They did not converse much more until they arrived at the Defence Colony, whose gate was guarded by heavy machine guns in sandbag nests, manned by eagle-eyed Sikhs. The Sikhs let them through without opening fire; a minute or two later they were at the Barracks.

They had obviously been constructed to house troops assigned to guard duty and other low-level work in the Defence Colony. Because this was Delhi, and the Defence Colony was prestigious, they were actually quite nice, for barracks. Each building was thirty or forty meters long, wide enough for a row of beds down either side with a broad aisle down the middle. They were all concrete and concrete block, with tin roofs, and it was clear that they had been hastily painted and retrofitted with better electrical service and air-conditioning. The Radhakrishnan Institute now occupied two of these buildings. Building 1 was filled with offices and laboratories. Building 2 was filled with beds. The beds were filled with brain damage cases.

Strokes were generally not a major health problem in India. The classic stroke patient was a fat old smoker and though many people smoked in India, few people were fat and many did not have the opportunity to get old. Fortunately, from the point of view of a researcher, any time you got nearly a billion people living and working in conditions not notable for safety, you did not have to rely on strokes in order to see a broad and deep spectrum of brain damage.

On his initial inspection of Building 2, Dr. Radhakrishnan saw a fascinating assortment of unfortunates who had been combed from the slums. It seemed that Mr. Salvador had some sort of connection with the Lady Wilburdon Foundation, a British charity group that operated free clinics and hospitals all over India. Mr. Salvador had exploited this connection, recruiting medical students from all over the country as brain damage talent scouts who would scan incoming cases and let him know of any promising prospects. In addition to the two whose brains had already been sampled, Dr. Radhakrishnan saw a man who had had a brick dropped on his head in a construction site. A soldier shot through the brain during ethnic violence in Srinagar. A lunch delivery boy from Delhi who had been thrown off his motorcycle rickshaw in a collision with a lorry. A street kid from Bombay who, in trying to do a second-story job on an old colonial structure, had slipped and fallen twelve feet; a spike on the wrought-iron fence had entered his open mouth, passed up through his palate, and impaled his brain.

Even by Western standards, the care these patients were receiving was fairly generous. The building was no architectural gem, but it was clean and well maintained. It was not lavishly appointed with high-tech equipment, but it was well-staffed with attentive nurses and nursing students who were clearly doing all they could to see to the patients' individual needs. And none of these patients was paying a single rupee. Most of them had no rupees to begin with.

Building 1 had its own generators, a pair of brand-new Honda portable units delivering a hundred and twenty volts of all-American sixty-cycle power. The juice was filtered and conditioned through an uninterruptible power supply and then routed through shiny, freshly installed conduit to a generous number of galvanized steel junction boxes, bolted to the barracks walls every couple of meters, studded with American-style three-prong outlets. All of this had been set up so that Zeldo and his ilk could fly straight in from California, drop their whores off at the Imperial, and plug their computers and other more arcane devices straight into the wall without having to deal with the awful culture shock of incompatible plugs and voltages. More to the point, the Honda generators would not flicker, spike, brown out, and black out as the Delhi grid was apt to. No precious data would be lost to unpredictable Third World influences.

Zeldo and a couple of other slangy pizza-eating beards from

America had laid claim to one end of Building 1 and set up their own little outpost of heavy metal music and novelty foam-rubber sledgehammers for pounding on their workstations when they got frustrated. They had even erected a sign: PACIFIC NETWARE— ASIAN HEADQUARTERS. On his way in, Dr. Radhakrishnan had noted the presence of a freshly installed satellite dish, and he could not help but suppose that they were connected to that.

Mr. Salvador had his own little nook at the other end of the building, as far away from the foam rubber sledgehammers as he could get. He was not in at the moment, but Dr. Radhakrishnan knew Mr. Salvador's style when he saw it: a heavy antique desk, comfortably scuffed, an electric shoe polisher, and every communications device known to science.

The intervening space was all at Dr. Radhakrishnan's disposal. At this point it was all new, empty desks and new, empty filing cabinets. A few people had already moved in. Supposedly, Toyoda was on his way in from Elton and might have already arrived. There were also a few promising Indian graduate students whom Mr. Salvador had managed to recruit away from their positions in America and Europe, and there were signs that some of these people had already arrived, claimed desks, and gotten down to work.

At the moment there was nothing for Dr. Radhakrishnan to do except sit down with a big stack of medical records that had been assembled on the head cases in Building 2, and sort through them, looking for patients with the right sort of brain damage.

*A couple of* hours after Dr. Radhakrishnan arrived, a patient named Mohinder Singh was brought in. He was a lorry driver from Himachal Pradesh, way up north in the foothills of the Himalayas. He had been driving down a mountain road with a bundle of half-inch pipe lashed to the back of his lorry. The pipes were apparently of different lengths; some stuck out farther than others. His brakes had gone out and he had gone off the road and slammed into something. The bundle of pipe had shot forward. The longest one had come in through the back window of the truck, struck him just behind the ear, passed all the way through his head, and emerged through one of the eyeballs. A nearby road crew had used a hacksaw to cut off most of the pipe, leaving only the portion that was stuck through his head, and he had been evacuated to a nearby Lady Wilburdon Charities clinic where he had been noticed by one of the talent scouts.

He did not look very promising at first. It seemed likely that the pipe had smashed things around quite a bit inside there and bruised large portions of the brain. But Dr. Radhakrishnan had not gotten to where he was by being hasty and superficial. He shipped Singh down the road to the All-India Institute of Medical Sciences for a series of head scans.

AIIMS was India's foremost medical research institute and it was only a couple of minutes away from the Barracks along the Delhi Ring Road. They would be able to take some excellent pictures of Mr. Singh's brain with the equipment they had there. And, in a stroke of luck, the chunk of pipe that was still embedded in Mr. Singh's head was made out of copper, a nonmagnetic substance; they would be able to run him through an NMR scanner without turning it into a projectile.

Dr. Radhakrishnan was stunned to learn that the pipe had gone through his head almost three days previously. He must have been in great pain, but he refused to acknowledge it. From the head down he was well-nourished and in perfect health. This was one patient who was not going to go into shock every time they put a needle in his arm.

When Singh came back from AIIMS with a stack of films and scans piled on his chest, Dr. Radhakrishnan was pleasantly surprised. The pipe was thin-walled, cut off fresh and sharp on the end that had gone through Singh's head. As best as Dr. Radhakrishnan could tell from trying to interpret the images, it had sliced its way through the soft, gelatinous brain tissue, rather than shoving it around and bruising it. It had acted almost like a core sampler.

Once the pipe was taken out and some of the mess cleaned up, assuming that Singh did not get infected, which was simply a question of antibiotics, he was going to be an ideal candidate for therapy.

"Not a whiner," Mr. Salvador said, when he came by later to inspect. "Robust. Positive attitude, as far as I can tell. Willing to try just about anything. He reminds me of the chap in the States."

"What chap?"

"Whom you heard on the tape. Whose scans you looked at."

"Ah, yes."

A thrilling sensation suddenly washed over Dr. Radhakrishnan's body. A wave of adrenaline seemed to be rushing through his circulatory system like a chemical tsunami. He opened his eyes a little wider and blinked a few times as though he had just stepped out into bright warm sunlight after a long winter in Elton, New Mexico, and his body rocked from side to side just a little bit, its stance and balance changing as he stood up straighter, breathed a little deeper. The jet lag vanished. He looked around him, suddenly taking in the room with the frighteningly intense glare of a raptor soaring on a mountain thermal. His hands tingled, almost as if the saw and the drill were already there, buzzing away, slicing heedlessly through bone, penetrating into the core of some other human being.

Mr. Salvador could take his Gyrfalcon jet and his cars and his institutes and his hotel suites. He could take them all back to America. It wouldn't matter. This was the feeling that Dr. Radhakrishnan V.R.J.V.V. Gangadhar lived for.

All of the nurses and orderlies in this part of the barracks had risen uncertainly to their feet. "What are you waiting for!?" he snapped. "This poor man has a pipe through his head! Let's get it out."

## CHAPTER THIRTEEN

"I'm going to be real straight with you," Mel said.

"Somehow I'm not surprised," Mary Catherine said.

They were sitting together at a corner table in an old-fashioned family-type Italian restaurant. The restaurant was across the street and down the block from the hospital where Mary Catherine had spent most of the last four years. When families of stricken patients had to eat, they gathered around the big circular tables here and glumly plunged their forks into deep, steaming dishes of lasagna, like surgeons around an operating table.

"Your dad is not a happy camper right now," Mel continued. "And it's going to get worse in a week or two, when we have to come out and tell the public that he has suffered a stroke. I don't know how he's going to react."

She slapped her menu down on the table and stopped even pretending to read it. "Enough, enough," she said. "What the hell are you saying?"

"Your dad would rather die than live the way he is now," Mel said.

Mary Catherine kept looking and listening for a few seconds, until she finally realized that this was all there was to it. If Mel had been talking about anyone else, "he would rather die" would have been a figure of speech. But not with Dad. She could just imagine him, sitting down there in Tuscola, making the executive decision that it was time to die, and then formulating his plan.

"That's enough," she said. "That's all you have to say."

Then she closed her eyes and silently let tears run down her face for half a minute or so.

She opened her eyes, rubbed her face with her napkin, blinked away the last tears. Mel was sitting with his hands folded together, patiently waiting for her to finish. Out of the corner of her eye she could see a hefty waitress loitering with her pad and pen. The help here knew how to deal with grief. The waitress was trying to figure out when it was okay to approach the table.

"Okay, I'm ready to order," Mary Catherine said, louder than she had intended.

The waitress approached. Mel hurriedly snatched up his menu and began to scan it; he wasn't ready. Watching him, Mary Catherine suddenly felt a lot of affection for good old Mel, trying to pick out an entrée, any entrée, because Mary Catherine was ready to order.

"I'll have the fettucine with pesto and a club soda," Mary Catherine said.

"Some kind of baked noodle thing without any meat," Mel said.

"Lasagna? Manicotti?" the waitress said. But Mel could not be bothered with details; he didn't hear her. "And a glass of white," he said. "You want a drink, Mary Catherine?"

"No thanks, I'm working," she said. Finally the knot went out of her throat and she felt better. She took a couple of deep breaths.

"All clear," she said.

"You're handling it well," Mel said. "You're doing a good job of this."

"I suppose he has a little plan all worked out."

"Yeah. The den. Sometime when there's no kids out in front of the house, I would guess."

"He'll probably use the big shotgun from Vietnam, right?"

Mel shrugged. "Beats me. I'm not privy to all his decisions."

"You know, James and I always used to get into trouble when Patricia was babysitting us as a kid. And Mom and Dad would come home and be just shocked." Mary Catherine laughed out loud, blowing off tension. "Because Patricia was such a nice girl and why were we being so mean to her?"

Mel laughed.

"So now I'll have to go home and give Dad a hard time for wanting to shoot himself while Patricia's babysitting him." She heaved a big sigh, trying to throw off the aching feeling in her ribs. "But it's really hard to talk to him when he's in that—that whole situation he's in now."

"See, he's acutely aware of that. And that's why he made this decision."

"So why are you here?" she said. "Is this an official message from Dad?"

Mel snorted. "You kidding? He'd kill me if he knew I was telling you this."

"Oh. I thought I was being given one last chance to go down and talk to him before he did it."

"No way. I think I caught him in the act. Lining up his shot," Mel said. "Now he's too embarrassed to actually do it for a while."

"Well . . . of course I want him to live. But I have to admit killing himself now would be a lot more true to his nature."

"Absolutely," Mel said. "And it would give him a chance to get in a last dig at Patricia, which is incentive enough."

Mary Catherine laughed.

"But he's not gonna do it," Mel said.

"Why not?" It was unusual to think of Dad making up his mind to do something, and then holding back.

"There's one possibility we are investigating. A new therapy that might bring him back to where he was."

"I haven't heard of any such thing," Mary Catherine said.

Mel set his briefcase up on the table and snapped it open. He pulled out a manila envelope and handed it to Mary Catherine.

Inside was a stack of a dozen or so research papers, mostly reprints from technical journals. On top was an eight-by-ten black-and-white photograph of a rakishly modern, high-tech structure on a bluff above the ocean.

"What is this place?"

"The Radhakrishnan Institute. They do heavy-duty neurological research. Those papers describe some of the work they've been doing."

Mary Catherine set the photograph aside and began to flip through the research papers.

"I thought you might be interested in seeing some of that stuff. It's all gibberish to me," Mel said.

Mary Catherine frowned. "I'm familiar with these papers. I've seen them. All in the last three years."

"So?"

"Well, the stuff described here is all fairly basic research. I mean, in this one here, they're talking about a technique to grow baboon brain cells in vitro and then reimplant them in the baboon's brain."

"So?"

"So the date on the paper is three months ago. Which means it was probably written sometime last year."

"So?" Mel would continue asking this question until hell froze over or he understood what she was getting at.

"So, it's like these guys just invented the wheel last year, and now they're claiming that they can make a car."

"You're saying it's a hell of a stretch between putting some new cells into a baboon's head, and fixing your dad."

"Exactly."

"How long would it take to cover that ground?"

"Well, I don't know. It's never been done before. But I would think it would take at least five or ten years, if everything went well."

"Why would they—"

"They're neurosurgeons, Mel. Neurosurgeons are the ultimate macho shitheads of the medical world. Nobody can stand them. Their solution to everything is cold steel. But they can never really do anything."

"What do you mean? Cutting a hole in a guy's brain seems like doing a hell of a lot."

"But there's no cure for most neuro problems. They can chop out a tumor or a hematoma. But they can't really cure the important problems, and, because they are macho shitheads, that drives them crazy. Clearly, that's the motivation behind this research. And the inflated claims."

Mel pondered this one for a while.

Mary Catherine sipped on her club soda and watched Mel ponder it. As usual, it seemed that this affair had a lot of dimensions that he wasn't telling her about. A gray winter light was shining in through the window, bringing all of the wrinkles in Mel's face into high relief, and suddenly the look on his face seemed frighteningly intense to her. "This is a tough one," he finally said, shaking his head. "Too much emotional shit getting in the way. Can't think straight."

"What are you thinking, Mel?"

Mel shook his head. "Five or ten years. See, I haven't really talked to anyone yet. All I get is feelers. These feelers are so subtle I can't even tell if they are really there. Like this here"—he pointed to the photograph and the papers—"came in the guise of a fund-raising mailing. They wanted to know if your dad wanted to contribute to this thing. But it's no coincidence. I know that for damn sure."

"Have they offered to fix Dad's brain, or not?"

"Absolutely not, and you can bet they never will," Mel said. "They will wait for us to ask them. That way, if it goes wrong, it was our idea. But from the way they are acting, you would think that they were ready to put him under the knife tomorrow."

"So here is the sixty-four thousand dollar question," Mary Catherine said. "Does Dad believe that these people can fix him up? Does he believe it enough to keep him from killing himself?"

"For now, definitely. He won't do it today, or tomorrow. But . . ." Mel stopped in midsentence.

"But if I blab my big mouth and say that this is highly speculative and might be five or ten years down the road, that's different," Mary Catherine said.

"I don't like to put this pressure on you," Mel said, "but yeah, I think you have a point there." He reached across the table, grabbed the photograph, and held it up. "This keeps him alive. It's his hope. It's all he has right now."

"Well, that's good," Mary Catherine said.

Mel gave her a penetrating look. "How is it good?"

She was taken aback by the question. "It keeps him alive, like you said. And even if it does take five or ten years before this surgery can be performed, we can keep his hope alive until then. And then, maybe someday, we'll have him back."

Mel stared at her morosely. "Shit. You've got it too."

"Got what?"

"That same look on your face as Willy had when I told him about this." Mel slapped the picture facedown on the table, broke eye contact, looked out the window, started rubbing his chin.

"What are you thinking about?" she prompted him after a few minutes.

"Same thing as ever. Power." Mel said. "Power and how it works." He heaved a big sigh. "The power that some unheard-of thing called the Radhakrishnan Institute is suddenly wielding over the Cozzanos." He heaved another big sigh. "And over me."

"Your emotions getting in the way?"

"Yeah."

"Get a detached opinion, then."

"That's a good idea. I should talk to Sipes down there at the U."

"Don't. Sipes is a big-time researcher in these fields."

"So he's a good guy to talk to, right?"

"Not necessarily. That means he has theories of his own. Theories that may compete with Radhakrishnan's."

"Good point. Very devious thinking by your standards," Mel said with cautious admiration. "Why don't you go check it out yourself?"

Mary Catherine was startled. She blushed slightly. "I thought the idea was to be objective," she said.

"Objective is nice. It's a cute idea," Mel said, "but there's nothing like family, is there?"

"Well—"

"Suppose we did find some supposedly objective doctor to check this Radhakrishnan thing out for us. Would you really take his word for it?"

"No," she admitted, "I'd want to go and see this thing for myself, before Dad went under the knife."

"Done. I'll hire you, on an hourly basis, as a medical consultant for Cozzano Charities," Mel said. "Your job will be to investigate the medical qualifications of research programs that we are considering donating to. And right now we are considering a donation to the Radhakrishnan Institute."

"Mel, I'm a resident. I can't take time off."

"That," Mel said, "is a political problem between Cozzano Charities and the director of your fine hospital. And I have been known to involve myself in politics from time to time."

## CHAPTER FOURTEEN

During the wintry depths of his depression, his seasonal affective disorder in Elton, New Mexico, Dr. Radhakrishnan would have settled for any kind of surgery at all. He would sit in his house, looking out the windows into the dim blue light, which would sift down from the sky like a gradual snowfall, and watch the neighbors' dogs sniff and dig into snowbanks, and wonder how one went about getting one's hands on a dog, and whether it was technically illegal to do brain surgery on one, just for practice. Now that he was back in the saddle, though, he was starting to get picky.

In this phase of the project, they were working on Mr. Easyrider and Mr. Scatflinger, not their real names. The samples of brain tissue that had been overnight-expressed to Dr. Radhakrishnan in Elton had belonged to these two men.

It was not entirely clear what their real names were. Both of the patients were in the category of found objects. Neither one was neurologically equipped to identify himself, and if either of them had been in the habit of carrying identification, it had been removed by other persons before they had come under the purview of the authorities. Before Dr. Radhakrishnan arrived to impose some sense of decorum on the Barracks, the Americans (naturally) had come up with these names. Like everything else that bubbled up over the rim of the icky cultural stewpot of America, the names were pervasive and sticky and could not be scrubbed off once applied. Actually, for a while they had referred to Mr. Scatflinger as Mr. Shitpitcher, but this was completely unacceptable—the nurses could not even bring themselves to say it—and so Dr. Radhakrishnan had changed it.

Mr. Easyrider had been run over by a motorcycle. They could not be positive about this, since there were no witnesses to the event, but the motorcycle track running over the side of his head provided telling circumstantial evidence. The resulting trauma had caused a subarachnoid hemorrhage, which is to say that a blood vessel had burst inside his head and bled internally, killing part of the brain.

Mr. Scatflinger, née Shitpitcher, had been employed in heaving cow manure onto a trailer. The trailer had tipped, an avalanche had taken place, and his legs had been underneath it. There were major broken bones. A fat embolism formed at the site of one of these breaks, passed up into his heart, and then apparently crossed over from one side of his heart to the other through a small congenital hole. From there it was pumped straight up his carotid artery into his brain where it caused a massive stroke. This was known as a paradoxical embolism.

If Dr. Radhakrishnan were to take certain doctrines of his religion absolutely literally, he would not be allowed to have any contact with either Mr. Easyrider or Mr. Scatflinger. Yet today he was going to carve great holes in their skulls and implant fresh biochips. Of course he was wearing gloves, so technically speaking he wasn't coming into contact with them. But this was a technicality.

Anyone who adhered, at least nominally, to any religion that was invented millennia ago by people who ran around in burlap and believed that the Earth was built on the back of a turtle—that is, any of the major religions—ran into little dilemmas like this on a regular basis. The Christians practiced ritual cannibalism. Whenever he flew between the West and India there was always at least one Muslim on the plane who had to get out the in-flight magazine, check out the route map on the back page, triangulate against the position of the sun, and try to figure out in which direction Mecca lay. And when the ambulance had brought a Chiricahua Apache in to the Elton State University hospitals with a severe brain bleed that needed emergency surgery, Dr. Radhakrishnan had not had time to consult all of the religious authorities in order to figure out whether Hinduism allowed him to touch an Apache. He just gloved up and dove in there. At a certain point one had to just shrug, stop looking over one's shoulder theologically, and get on with life. Perhaps in some later life, at some more mystical plane of existence, Dr. Radhakrishnan would find out whether or not he had broken any cosmic rules by touching an Apache in New Mexico, or by touching Messrs. Easyrider and Scatflinger here in Delhi. In the meantime, like everyone else, he had to translate the arcane precepts of his ancient religion into a somewhat looser and vaguer set of rules called ethics, or values.

"*I am waiting* for the biochips," he said into the telephone. "Waiting and waiting and waiting."

There was a brief silence on the other end of the line, or what passed for silence. Indian telephones had a sort of organic quality. Not the sterile silence of American fiber-optic linkups. On one of these phones, one felt that one was plugged in to the electromagnetic fabric of the entire universe; the phone system just one huge antenna picking up emanations from other telephones, television and radio stations, power lines, automobile ignition systems, quasars in deep space, and stirring them together into a thick sonic curry. This is what Dr. Radhakrishnan listened to while he was waiting for Zeldo to come up with another excuse for not being ready.

"There's just one more bug that we really ought to get rid of," Zeldo said. "Twenty of the best guys in the business are going over this code line by line."

"Twenty? You only have four people there!"

"Most of the work is being done in California. Over a satellite link," Zeldo said.

"Well," Dr. Radhakrishnan said, "while your team is sipping espresso in Marin County, my team is standing in a hallway here at AIIMS with two brain-damaged patients on gurneys, waiting."

A long silence, the sonic curry poured forth from the telephone. "I don't know what to tell you," Zeldo said. "It's not quite ready."

"Did you hear about the programmer's wife?" Dr. Radhakrishnan said. "She is still a virgin. Her husband just sits on the edge of the bed every night and tells her how great it's going to be."

Zeldo did not laugh. Dr. Radhakrishnan was beginning to get that tingly feeling in his hands.

He stuck his head out of the office and looked down the hallway. Mr. Scatflinger was lying on the gurney, quiescent, his head freshly shaved, blue lines drawn on his scalp like the rhumb lines of an ancient navigator.

"Can you or can you not reprogram this thing remotely, after implantation?"

"We can modify the software. That's how we're programming it as we speak. It's sitting in the culture tank and we're talking to it over the radio."

"It's finished."

"No."

"Put the culture tank into the truck and get it over here now. That is an order."

The chip consisted of a silicon part—the part that Zeldo was responsible for—surrounded by an inert teflon shell, connected on either end to brain cells that had been grown in a tank in Seattle. The only way to keep those brain cells alive was to supply them with oxygen and nutrients. The biochip sat in a tank full of a carefully pH-balanced, temperature-regulated, oxygenated chemical solution that Zeldo and the other Americans referred to as "chicken soup." The soup gave the brain cells everything they needed to stay alive, except for intellectual stimulation. The chip was only a couple of centimeters long in its entirety and so the tank itself wasn't that large, just a few liters in size. But it was attached to a variety of machines to keep it properly balanced and regulated, so the apparatus as a whole ended up being roughly the size of a vending machine. It rolled around on oversized rubber wheels, and it had enough built-in backup battery power so that it could be unplugged from the wall for up to half an hour. All of this portability was needed, for the time being, because of the far-flung nature of this enterprise. The chips had first been incarnated in Seattle, placed into this tank, and then rolled on board a specially chartered GODS jet, where the support systems had drawn power from the airplane's generators. From the Indira Gandhi International Airport, the whole mess had been transported to the Barracks for debugging. Now it had to be shipped down the road to AIIMS for the actual surgical procedure. Each time it was trundled from one place to another it had to survive on battery power for a few minutes.

Zeldo and his cohorts referred to the apparatus as the Cabinet of Dr. Caligari. They hauled it around in the back of a truck. The truck poked its way slowly down the Delhi Ring Road, pulled off into the parking lots of AIIMS, and backed up to a loading dock. The back door flew open and there were Zeldo and his hackers, surrounding the Cabinet of Dr. Caligari, all blinking lights and bubbling tubes.

There was an interval of half an hour or so, during which the patients were prepared for surgery, the operating room people got scrubbed and gloved, and Zeldo and his crew got the Cabinet of Dr. Caligari transferred across the hospital to the operating theater, leapfrogging from one power outlet to the next, down hallways and up elevators. Then Dr. Radhakrishnan just had to perform a couple of operations.

It was strange, and possibly ludicrous, to be doing both Mr. Easyrider and Mr. Scatflinger at the same time. Each operation was a major event in itself. But there were many strange and ludicrous things about the way the Radhakrishnan Institute was currently functioning. As they went over the plans for this day, they had all shared a creepy, unspoken feeling that they were extending themselves years beyond where they really ought to be, and that many things might go wrong.

The operations were conceptually simple. Incisions were made along the lines that had been drawn on the patients' shaven heads. Flaps of scalp were peeled back and the bleeding was cauterized or clamped off. When the actual skull was exposed, Dr. Radhakrishnan cut through it with a bone saw.

A polygon of skull, a trap door of sorts, was cut into the side of the head and saved for later use. Still, the brain itself was not exposed; they looked through the hole at a tough inner membrane, the brain's final layer of protection. When this was flapped out of the way, they were looking at actual brain matter.

"*It was a* debacle. I am personally ashamed. I will never do anything like that again. The level of incompetence makes me physically ill. I may shoot myself," Dr. Radhakrishnan was saying.

"Have a drink," Mr. Salvador said. This was easy to arrange because they were sitting in the bar of the Imperial.

"When I am tense I bite my lip. Today I think I have swallowed half of my own blood supply."

"Think of it as opening day for a new business venture," Mr. Salvador said. "It's always a debacle."

"Even *debacle* does not do justice to this day," Dr. Radhakrishnan said. "It was an apocalypse."

Mr. Salvador shrugged. "That's why we make mistakes, so we can learn from them."

"One gets very impatient, doing research for years and years. The pace is so gradual. After a while you say, 'I wish I could just get on with it and put one of these things into a human brain and see what happens.' But this business today reminds me of why we take years and years to get ready for these things."

"The patients are both alive. All's well that ends well."

A waiter came by and gave Dr. Radhakrishnan another drink. Mr. Salvador tossed some rupees onto the table. "Why don't you take that with you?" he said. "I have something to show you."

"What?"

"Let's go for a spin."

*The former site* of the Ashok Theatre had been surrounded by a barricade twenty feet high. In places it consisted of chain-link fence with tarps stretched across it. In places it was pieced together with scraps of wood. In and of itself the fence was a considerable invest-ment; the materials that went into it could have housed thousands.

Things did not become much clearer after Mr. Salvador and Dr. Radhakrishnan had gotten past the guard at the gate. Most of the site was filled with a scaffolding. It was just a dense three-dimen-sional web of steel, with some parts of it additionally shored up with wooden beams. So far most of the work was being done in iron; the scaffolding was intertangled with another web of reinforcing rods.

The density of activity was incredible. The site seemed to con-tain several workers per square yard, all doing something as fast as they could. Several cranes were active, moving giant prefabricated constructs of reinforcing rod into place.

"All reinforced concrete. So it looks like hell until we pour," Mr. Salvador said.

Dr. Radhakrishnan would have gotten lost in a second, but Mr. Salvador knew his way through the tangle. He led him fearlessly into a passage that cut through the heart of it, straight in toward the center, brushing past workers the entire way. He noticed along the way that he was now walking on planks. Looking down between gaps, he could see straight down one or two stories. The place was extraordinarily well lit with thousands of electric lights strung on long yellow cords. Hundreds more workers were down below them, bending more steel rods into place. Large amounts of concrete had already been poured down there.

As they approached the middle, Dr. Radhakrishnan could see glimpses of more concrete through gaps in the scaffolding. It was a sort of squat concrete obelisk, rectangular in cross-section, rising straight up out of the foundation below them, up to a height of three stories above their heads. It was large enough, perhaps, to put a volleyball court on each level. The walls had a few rectangular openings on each level where, presumably, this part of the building would later be connected to adjacent rooms or hallways. Thousands of reinforcing bars sprouted from the walls at the levels of the floors-to-be and along the locations of future walls, giving the whole tower a bristly, hairy appearance. The bare concrete walls, still so new and clean they were almost white, had already been partly obscured by conduits, plumbing, and ductwork that grew up and snaked around the structure like tropical vines climbing a tree. Craning his neck to look up toward the top, Dr. Radhakrishnan could see the louvered enclosures of large pieces of machinery mounted on the roof, probably air conditioners and electrical generators.

The obelisk was connected to the surrounding scaffold work by a couple of catwalks, giving it the appearance of a keep in the center of a medieval castle. When they walked across the bridges into the building, they passed through some kind of a cultural divide. Everyone working inside here was Korean, Japanese, or American, and they were speaking English to each other with varying degrees of proficiency. Some of them were wearing smart, clean coveralls, and some of them were wearing ties. Two or three big Calyx computer systems were already up and running, nice ones with huge color screens, and engineers were using them to zoom in on various subsystems.

"This, of course, is the essential core of the operation," Mr. Salvador said. "The only part that you will really need in order to continue your research. It will be ready to use in a week. As long as you don't mind walking through an active construction site in order to reach it, that is."

"Not at all," Dr. Radhakrishnan said.

## CHAPTER FIFTEEN

Merely scooping out a hole in a man's brain and dropping in a biochip was not enough. It was like assaulting a supercomputer with a Skilsaw and then throwing in a handful of loose silicon chips.

The biochip had to be connected into the brain tissue in billions or trillions of different ways. All of the connections were microscopic and could not be made by the hand of any surgeon. They had to grow.

Brain cells didn't grow. But the connections between them did. The network of linkages was constantly shifting and reconnecting itself in a process that was usually described as "learning." Dr. Radhakrishnan did not really care for this terminology because it contained a value judgment. It implied that every time new synapses were formed inside a person's mind it was because they were memorizing Shakespeare or being taught how to integrate transcendental functions. Of course, in reality most of the internal rewiring that went on in people's brains took place in response to watching game shows on television, being beaten up by family members, figuring out the cheapest place to buy cigarettes, and being conditioned not to mix plaids with stripes.

As soon as it had seemed like a safe bet that Mr. Easyrider and Mr. Scatflinger were going to live for a while, they were transferred back to the Barracks in a specially equipped ambulance. They were laid side by side in a separate room that had been built into one end of Building 2. They were connected up to numerous machines, wired into a support system. Each of them had a red polygon on his head, a U-shaped welt, hairy with black sutures, marking the boundary of the flap that had been peeled back during surgery.

In the center of the area outlined by the surgical scar, a bundle of lines was plugged into the patient's head. It passed through the middle of the flake of skull that had been neatly sawed out by Dr. Radhakrishnan's bone saw. While Dr. Radhakrishnan had occupied himself with implanting the biochip, a lesser surgeon—more of a technician, really—had drilled a few holes through the disembodied chunk of skull and implanted a plastic connector. The connector was about the size of a dime and was really a cluster of smaller connections: half a dozen tiny tubes for passing fluids in and out, and a miniature, fifty-pin electrical plug, a nearly microscopic version of the port on the back of a computer. Since most communication between the biochip and the outside world was supposed to happen over the radio, only a few of these fifty pins were hooked up to the biochip itself. Most of them were hooked up to sensors that monitored the patient's condition and to the electrostimulus system that was supposed to encourage the growth of new connections between brain and biochip.

When the operation was finished, this connector peeked through the skin, somewhat in the fashion of a wall socket. The researchers could then interface with the patient by sticking a matching plug into the socket; when it was stuck in properly, all of the fluid and electrical connections were made in an instant. So many tubes and wires were crammed together in this bottleneck that they seemed to explode from the side of the patient's head. Some of the connections ran directly to various pieces of bedside machinery that monitored pressure inside the skull, delivered drugs, or helped to oxygenate the brain tissue in the biochip. Others were taped to the head of the bed, from which they ran over to the nearest wall, passed through a hole, and ran through a conduit that connected the two buildings.

The people in Building 1 saw Mr. Easyrider and Mr. Scatflinger as media entities, nothing more. No odors, no fluids, just images on TV monitors, tracings on oscilloscopes, graphics on their Calyx workstations, and the occasional disembodied sound effect coming out of a speaker. This, Dr. Radhakrishnan reflected, made it a lot easier to deal with them objectively.

*There was not* much to do for the first few days. The brain cells in the biochip had not yet had time to connect themselves up to the patients' brain, so the chip was neurologically inert, just a dead piece of shrapnel embedded in the head. Then, one morning at about three o'clock, computer screens all over Building 1 suddenly came alive as a neuron in Mr. Scatflinger's brain hooked up with a neuron on the fringe of the biochip.

As soon as Dr. Radhakrishnan got there, they popped the corks on a few bottles of champagne and then stood under the monitor for a while, watching the data stream by. Zeldo did some typing on his workstation and brought up a new window on the screen, this one showing a running graph of the brain activity.

"Someone go shine a light in his eyes," Dr. Radhakrishnan said.

"Yes, Doctor!" said one of his Indian grad students. He ran out of the building, pulling a penlight from his pocket. A few moments later the grad student was visible on the closed-circuit monitor that had been showing live coverage of Mr. Scatflinger from Building 2. All eyes flicked back and forth between the closed-circuit set and the computer monitor as the grad student leaned over the sleeping Mr. Scatflinger, peeled back one of his eyelids with his thumb, and shone the penlight into it.

The graph jumped. The crowd went wild.

"Well done, Doctor," someone was saying. It was Mr. Salvador, shaking his hand, offering a cigar. "Remarkable success, especially under the circumstances." Around nine A.M., a burst of activity showed up on Mr. Easyrider's heretofore quiescent monitor. But even in the corner of his eye, Dr. Radhakrishnan could see that something was wrong. The signals coming in from the biochip showed no clear pattern in terms of intensity or duration.

"Glitches," Dr. Radhakrishnan said.

"But a whole hell of a lot of glitches," Zeldo said.

"Glitcherama," said one of the other Americans. Dr. Radhakrishnan bit his lip, knowing that for the rest of his career, this phenomenon, whenever it occurred, would be referred to as Glitcherama.

Sudden movement caught his eye. He looked over at the closed-circuit monitor for Mr. Easyrider and saw, instead of the patient, the backsides of several nurses who were standing around him, working feverishly.

By the time Dr. Radhakrishnan made it over to Building 2, Mr. Easyrider was dead. His heart had stopped beating. They wheeled out the defib cart and shocked him a couple of times, trying to get a stable rhythm back, but in the end they could get nothing but bad rhythms on the scope, and finally no rhythm at all.

When they were sure he was dead, when they had closed his eyes, rolled away the cart, and washed their hands, Dr. Radhakrishnan picked up the intercom to Building 1. "Are you getting any signals from the chip?" he said. He asked the question out of purely academic interest; supposedly there was a bit of random electrical activity in the brain after death.

"It's been dead for a couple of minutes," Zeldo said.

"Completely dead?"

"Completely dead. We didn't think to include a surge protector."

"Surge protector?"

"Yeah. To protect the chip from sparks and lightning bolts, you know."

"I haven't seen any lightning."

"You held the lightning in your hands. You shocked him, man. That jolt from the defibrillator blew our chip to kingdom come."

They did a postmortem more or less on the spot. A sterile environment was not required for an autopsy, so they partitioned off one corner of the room to prevent other patients from seeing what was happening, and Dr. Radhakrishnan took Mr. Easyrider apart, piece by piece, paying special attention to the head.

Building 2 was a distracting work environment because it was full of head cases—old ones dying of natural causes and new ones being wheeled in all the time, from all over the subcontinent. Brain injury sometimes left people as vegetables, but in some cases it could cause bizarre behavior, and over the brief course of this project they had already seen their quota of screechers and head-bangers. In the middle of Dr. Radhakrishnan's autopsy, they apparently brought in a new one. A loud, coarse voice began to echo off the tin ceiling:

"WUBBA WUBBA WUBBA WUBBA WUBBA WUBBA WUBBA WUBBA . . ."

It was no worse than a room full of excited baboons. He continued working, narrating his observations into a tape recorder, but he had to speak a little more loudly now because underneath his words was a constant background noise of WUBBA WUBBA WUBBA WUBBA WUBBA . . .

The cause of death was obvious enough. Mr. Easyrider's body had rejected the implant. Dr. Radhakrishnan tried to be clinical about it.

WUBBA WUBBA WUBBA WUBBA . . .

"The organic portion of the biochip shows pronounced atrophy . . ."

WUBBA WUBBA WUBBA WUBBA . . .

"The inorganic or silicon portion of the biochip is virtually rattling around loose inside the skull . . ." That was not very scientific. He took a deep breath.

WUBBA WUBBA WUBBA WUBBA WUBBA WUBBA WUBBA WUBBA . . .

"There is considerable scarring and atrophy in the portions of the brain adjacent to the implant." His head was spinning. He was tired. He just wanted to sit down and have a drink. "Conclusion: the host rejected the graft."

He was becoming conscious of another irrelevant sensory input besides the stream of WUBBAs: he was smelling perfume. It was not something that would really pass for perfume in India, where people knew as much about tastes and smells as Americans knew about heavy metal music. This was some kind of tedious lavender-and-roses concoction, something stupid and English.

"It appears that necrosis started at the site of the implant and spread to the brainstem—leading to the patient's demise."

WUBBA WUBBA WUBBA WUBBA . . .

"Doc?" someone said. Zeldo.

He looked up at Zeldo, feeling very tired. Zeldo had pulled the curtain aside and was now gaping at the bloody, dismembered corpse of Mr. Easyrider. He was not a medical person and was not inured to this kind of thing.

Dr. Radhakrishnan turned to face Zeldo, bumping the table with his hip. The hemisphere of Mr. Easyrider's skull rocked back and forth a little bit on the tabletop.

"Two things," Zeldo said.

"Yes?"

WUBBA WUBBA WUBBA WUBBA . . .

"There's a problem with Scatflinger. And there's a lady here to see you."

All of a sudden, the fact that he had gotten up at three in the morning was really getting to Dr. Radhakrishnan.

Maybe these were simple problems, easy to fix. He emerged from the autopsy room still wearing his rubber gloves, smeared with blood and gray matter. If this was just going to take a minute, there was no point in getting ungloved and then regloving later. "First things first," he said, and led Zeldo toward the room that, as of this morning, Mr. Scatflinger now had all to himself.

As he approached the door, the sound of WUBBA WUBBA WUBBA grew louder.

No. It couldn't be.

He opened the door. Half of his staff was gathered around the bed.

Mr. Scatflinger, who had been unable to do anything except lie in bed since his accident, was now sitting bolt upright in bed.

He had been totally aphasic as well, unable to make a sound. But now he was saying, "WUBBA WUBBA WUBBA WUBBA" as loudly as he could.

Everyone was looking at Dr. Radhakrishnan to see how he was going to react.

"Well," he said to his staff, "I think one can make the case that being able to say 'WUBBA WUBBA' is better than not being able to say anything at all, and that, at least in a limited sense, we have done Mr. Scatflinger here a great service."

"Excuse me! Are you the gentleman in charge?" someone said. It was a lady's voice. Not just a female voice, but really a *lady's* voice.

Dr. Radhakrishnan turned around slowly, half-paralyzed by an unexplainable sense of fear and loathing. The odor of lavender and roses was quite strong now.

He was looking directly into a bosom of Himalayan proportions, stoutly contained in some kind of undergarment and covered with a flowery print dress. His gaze traveled from the bottom to the top of the bosom, changing focus the whole way, and then encountered a soft, pale, yet sturdy neck. Above that was a face.

It was a nice English lady's face, but too big. It was like looking at the young Victoria through a big Fresnel lens. And on top, where custom would dictate some kind of a tightly curled, chemically induced permanent wave, was something altogether out of place, a short, simple, straight, and maybe just a bit shaggy kind of haircut. Certainly not an ugly way to wear one's hair, but just a little bit out of keeping with the social stature that was implied by her accent.

"Madam," he said, "I am Dr. Radhakrishnan." He extended his hand.

"Lady Wilburdon. How do you do," she said, shaking it.

"Oh, god," Zeldo said, and ran away, gagging audibly.

A gasp came from the staff. Dr. Radhakrishnan felt the back of his neck get hot. He was tired, he was stressed, and he had forgotten about the gloves. This Lady Wilburdon creature now had Mr. Easyrider's brains all over her hand.

There was a brief moment of utter despair as he tried to think of a way to draw this fact to her attention without making the breach of etiquette even worse than it already was.

"Oh, it's really quite all right," she said, fluttering her bloody hand dismissively. "I worked in the refugee camps of Kurdistan for a month, at the height of the insurrection, so a bit of a mess does not trouble me at all. And I wouldn't dream of having you interrupt your work just to shake hands with an interloper."

Dr. Radhakrishnan was looking around uneasily, hoping to make eye contact with someone who knew who this lady was, why she was here, how she had gotten in past all of those Sikh commandos at the front gate, all of those .50-caliber machine-gun nests.

Behind her he could see another woman, a smaller, auntish lady, conversing with Mr. Salvador. Mr. Salvador kept glancing at the backside of Lady Wilburdon; he wanted to be here, not there, but clearly was having trouble extricating himself from polite small talk with this other woman.

WUBBA WUBBA WUBBA WUBBA . . .

"You are . . . a guest of Mr. Salvador?" he said.

"Yes. My secretary, Miss Chapman, and I were passing through Delhi on an inspection tour and we thought we would pop in and see how Bucky's project was coming along."

"Bucky?"

"Yes. Bucky. Buckminster Salvador."

"His name is Bucky?"

"Buckminster. The boys at school used to call him B.M. for short, but we suppressed that. It was uncouth and cruel."

"School?"

"The Lady Wilburdon School for Spoiled Boys in Newcastle upon Tyne."

"I didn't know there was such a thing as a school for spoiled boys," Dr. Radhakrishnan said numbly.

"Oh, yes. There are a lot of them in England, you know. And all of their parents are desperate for an environment that will give them structure . . ."

"That's quite enough," Mr. Salvador said, interrupting. Dr. Radhakrishnan was shocked to see the look on his face; suddenly he was pale and sweating. His mask of total aplomb had been shattered, he was rolling his eyes, clearly out of control.

"Quite enough of what, Bucky?" Lady Wilburdon said, locking eyes with Mr. Salvador, who looked very short standing next to her.

"Quite enough of having you stand around in this unpleasant place when I should be treating you to a lavish dinner along Connaught Circus!" Mr. Salvador improvised. He was close to coming completely unhinged.

WUBBA WUBBA WUBBA WUBBA . . .

"Oh, but I can go into some restaurant and order a meal whenever I please. It's not every day I get the opportunity to tour an advanced neurological research facility," Lady Wilburdon said.

"Tour?" Dr. Radhakrishnan said.

She seemed taken aback. "Yes. Well, I thought, as long as I was here . . . "

"Naturally you can have a look around, Lady Wilburdon," Mr. Salvador said, shooting Dr. Radhakrishnan a panicky warning look. Clearly, resistance was out of the question.

Suddenly Lady Wilburdon was looking past Dr. Radhakrishnan, over his shoulder, and a completely new expression had come over her face. It was a wonderful, sweet, lovely, maternal expression, like a mother greeting her children home from school.

"Hello, sir, and how do you do? I am so sorry for intruding."

She was looking at Mr. Scatflinger.

Mr. Scatflinger was looking right back at her. Staring her straight in the eye. There was even a hint of a smile on his face. "Wubba wubba," he said.

"Very well, thank you. Perhaps Dr. Radhakrishnan would be so good as to introduce us?"

"Yes. Lady Wilburdon, this is, uh, Mr. Banerjee. Mr. Banerjee, Lady Wilburdon."

"It's so nice to make your acquaintance."

"Wubba wubba wubba."

Mr. Salvador was taking advantage of this break in the conversation to sit on the edge of an empty bed and clamp one hand over his face.

"I take it that Mr. Banerjee will soon be undergoing this miraculous new surgical procedure that Bucky was telling me about."

"Wubba wubba wubba."

"Actually, he has already undergone it," Dr. Radhakrishnan said. No point in dissembling.

She was just a trifle taken aback. "I see."

"Before the operation he could not sit up in bed or speak. Now, as you see, he can sit up for prolonged periods, and he has developed the ability to say 'wubba wubba.'"

"Wubba wubba wubba," Mr. Scatflinger said.

"Do you suppose that, as time goes on, he will develop the ability to say other sorts of things?"

"Absolutely. You see, the implant has not been patterned yet. There is a powerful computer inside his head. But right now, the connections are scrambled. The computer has no program. We will have to train him to speak over a period of weeks or months."

"I see. So after the operation, there is a prolonged period of rehabilitation."

"Exactly."

"And the new facility you are building will have such facilities, which, as I notice, are lacking here."

"Precisely."

"Wubba wubba wubba wubba," Mr. Scatflinger said.

"It was so nice to have met you, Mr. Banerjee," Lady Wilburdon said, "and I wish you the best of luck in the course of your therapy." She stepped back out of Mr. Scatflinger's room, which obliged Dr. Radhakrishnan to follow her.

"We have high hopes for him," he said.

"I am sure that you do," Lady Wilburdon said. "But I see that another one of your patients has not been as fortunate."

She was looking over at Mr. Easyrider, sprawled out on a bloody table with his brains spilling out of his head, the cup of his skull upended next to him.

Mr. Salvador was still collecting his wits, which had been blown all over the Indo-Gangetic plain. Dr. Radhakrishnan had to handle this himself.

The woman had to be important. He had never heard of her, but with some people, you could just tell that they were important.

"The name of Lady Wilburdon is famous throughout the world," he said.

"I am the seventh person to bear that title," she said, "and by far the least distinguished."

"You evidently travel quite a bit, inspecting things."

"Hundreds of institutions throughout the world, yes."

"Then you will appreciate, perhaps better than anyone, that the patients who come into this place are often in very grave condition."

"I see that very clearly."

"It is not unusual for them to pass away while they are under our care."

"Yes," Lady Wilburdon said, "but this poor gentleman passed away after you performed the operation, did he not?"

"Ha, ha!" Dr. Radhakrishnan said. "You are astonishingly perceptive." No point in denying it, now. "How could you possibly have known that?" Maybe this woman had deeper connections than he had supposed.

"I am not an anatomical expert," Lady Wilburdon said, "but as I cast my eye over the gentleman, I see that you have sawed off the top of his head and extracted a large gray sort of thing that I take to be his brain."

"Of course, you are right."

"And I have taken the liberty of assuming that the distinguished director of this institute would not bother personally to perform a detailed autopsy on a patient who had expired of causes that were merely incidental."

"Infection," Dr. Radhakrishnan said. "His surgical wounds became infected with a nosocomial microbe, which is to say, a bug that he picked up in the hospital."

"I am familiar with the terminology," Lady Wilburdon said, and exchanged an amused look with her female companion.

Finally Mr. Salvador had recovered sufficiently to weigh in. "Infections are always a terrible problem in brain surgery," he said.

"That is why we operate out of these buildings," Dr. Radhakrishnan lied. "Because they are not hospitals per se, the chance of nosocomial infections is greatly reduced."

"But we still must perform all of the surgical procedures at AIIMS," Mr. Salvador said.

"And this is where he picked up the fatal organism," Dr. Radhakrishnan concluded. He and Mr. Salvador exchanged a triumphal look, trying to shore each other up.

"Then I shall be extremely careful to wash up," Lady Wilburdon said, looking at her bloody hand, "now that I too have been infected with this very deadly pathogen."

"Yes. We should all probably do that," Dr. Radhakrishnan said, "before we spread the infection to Mr. Singh or any of the other patients." This phase of the lying process was known as backfilling.

The backfilling process continued as Dr. Radhakrishnan and Lady Wilburdon scrubbed themselves in the sink that had been set up at one end of the building. Mr. Salvador and the lady's companion, Miss Chapman, washed their hands too, for good measure, to ensure that the fatal infection did not spread through the ward. Lady Wilburdon obviously knew a thing or two about washing up and threw herself into the process at a frighteningly vigorous pitch, running a stiff plastic brush back and forth under her fingernails with the speed of an automatic paint shaker, spraying a fountain of pink suds into the air. She scrubbed herself all the way to the elbows, like a surgeon.

"You must forgive us for handling your visit so awkwardly and discourteously," Mr. Salvador ventured, "as this is the first time that anyone has ever come to visit any of our patients."

"Ooh, how terribly sad," said Miss Chapman.

"I shall relay news of this situation to the Lady Wilburdon Organisation for the Visitation of Destitute Invalids here in Delhi," Lady Wilburdon said. "Arrangements can be made—"

"Oh, we really couldn't ask—"

"Emotional factors are terribly important. Loneliness can kill just as surely as nosocomial infections."

"No," Dr. Radhakrishnan said. He had to draw the line somewhere. "You are very generous. But I must rule it out on medical grounds. Later, when we have the permanent facility constructed, perhaps we can arrange for routine visitation."

Mr. Salvador cringed visibly. Lady Wilburdon got just a bit sniffy. "Well," she said, "I count myself fortunate that I was able to come in and have a lovely visit before this very strict policy was imposed."

"As you will understand, we did not have to impose a policy until now."

Mr. Salvador was trying to patch it all up. "But if you can provide me with a forwarding address in England, I will keep you apprised of our progress."

"England?" Lady Wilburdon said. "Oh, no. We shall be here in India for another month at least."

"Oh. Well, that's delightful news. Delightful."

"Of course, we will be all over the subcontinent, but sooner or later we always come back to Delhi."

"Then I shall look forward to dinner with you on at least one occasion," Mr. Salvador said weakly.

"When does the next fellow, Mr. Singh, have his operation?"

"We have it scheduled for Wednesday."

"Four days from now," Miss Chapman said. She took an oversized appointment calendar, a desktop model, from her tote bag, and opened it up. "Mr. Singh has his brain work done," she mumbled to herself, penciling it in.

Meanwhile, Lady Wilburdon was reading over her companion's shoulder. "Tomorrow we leave for Calcutta, to inspect the Lady Wilburdon Institute for the Rehabilitation of Syphilitic Lepers."

Both men drew sharp breaths.

"*Can* they be rehabilitated?" Mr. Salvador said. He seemed astonished, verging on slightly amused.

"Syphilitic lepers are easy," Lady Wilburdon said, "compared to spoiled boys."

Mr. Salvador turned red and shut up, leaving Dr. Radhakrishnan all alone to terminate the conversation. "Feel free to phone when you return to Delhi," he said.

"Telephone?"

"Yes. No visitation, remember."

"But Mr. Singh will be having his operation in the new facility, will he not?"

"Oh. Yes, that's right. It should be ready by then."

"So he will recover in the new facility as well."

Dr. Radhakrishnan could only nod.

"See you in a few days," Miss Chapman said, snapping her appointment book shut and beaming at them cheerily. The two women bustled out and climbed into a waiting car.

Mr. Salvador spun on his heel, went straight across to Building 1, and pulled a bottle of gin out of his desk. He and Dr. Radhakrishnan sat down across from each other, wordlessly, and began to drink it, straight, from paper cups. After a minute or two, Zeldo came over and joined them. This was a little troubling in and of itself, because Zeldo was some kind of a puritanical health freak. Drinking straight gin from a paper cup was not his style at all.

"What was *that*?" Dr. Radhakrishnan finally said, when he and Mr. Salvador, or Bucky, or B.M. as he was called by his school chums, both had a few ounces of ethanol pumping through their systems.

Mr. Salvador threw up his hands. "What could I possibly say to you verbally that would add to the impression you have already received?"

"She knows you."

Mr. Salvador sighed. "My father was Argentine, of German and Italian ancestry. My mother was British. One of our homes was in England and that is where I went to school. Once or twice a year, *she* would come sweeping through the place to inspect it. She would sit in the back of a classroom for a few minutes and watch. Made all the teachers nervous as hell. Students too. She even made the *custodians* nervous."

"You had dealings with her then?"

"None. Never. How she could possibly remember my name is a complete mystery to me. She must have a photographic memory. She is a freak of nature," he finally concluded, belaboring the obvious.

Dr. Radhakrishnan said nothing. He had the feeling that Mr. Salvador lied to him quite a bit. But this seemed a particularly obvious lie. Mr. Salvador had been extremely upset. Lady Wilburdon was more than the titular head of his old school; she must have some power over him. And the idea of someone actually having power over the all-powerful Mr. Salvador was certainly interesting.

"What killed Mr. Easyrider is still mysterious," Dr. Radhakrishnan said, "but I have high hopes for Mr. Scatflinger."

"I don't," Zeldo said. It was the first time he had spoken since he had taken to drinking.

"Why not? Everything's going perfectly with him."

"Once we get his chip trained," Dr. Radhakrishnan said, "presumably he will become a bit more versatile."

"We can't train his chip. His chip is dead," Zeldo said.

"If it were really dead, he wouldn't even be able to say wubba wubba.'"

"It crashed. It's stuck. We ran afoul of that bug I was trying to warn you about."

"So what's it doing?"

"It got caught in an infinite loop."

"*An infinite loop?*" Dr. Radhakrishnan was flabbergasted. Infinity was a mathematical concept, very easy for a bithead like Zeldo to bandy about, but not something that biologists usually had to deal with.

"Yes."

"Meaning?" Mr. Salvador said.

"Meaning that he will keep saying wubba wubba until he dies," Zeldo said.

"Hmm. That's not going to make much of a favorable impression on Lady Wilburdon," Mr. Salvador said.

"We can send him back," Dr. Radhakrishnan said. "Send him off to the hinterlands. He can found his own religious sect."

## CHAPTER SIXTEEN

It was a creepy and surreal morning when they implanted the biochips in the mind of Mohinder Singh. Dr. Radhakrishnan got up early, as he always did on the morning of an operation. He went downstairs, eschewing room service, and watched the sun come up over Delhi from the café of the Imperial Hotel. The air pollution was especially bad this morning. Some kind of dire temperature inversion had clamped itself down over the city like a bell jar, trapping and concentrating the cocktail of dust, automobile exhaust, coal smoke, woodsmoke, manure smoke, and the ammoniated gases that rose up from the strewn excreta of millions of people and animals. This being winter, the air was relatively humid, or as humid as it was ever likely to get. The humidity condensed around the countless nuclei provided by all of that air pollution, so that when the sun rose, it had to force its way up through a thick cloacal fog, and turned a furious red color, the color of Elvis's face in his last moments on earth. When it finally burst free of the horizon, the sun simply disappeared and became a mere bright tendency in the burnt-orange sediment of the eastern sky.

Dr. Gangadhar V.R.J.V.V. Radhakrishnan sipped tea and ran over the whole project one more time, wondering if they had overlooked anything.

Mr. Salvador had been spending even more time than usual on the telephone recently. This was totally irrelevant to today's operation, but Dr. Radhakrishnan remained curious about the American side of this project. Old Bucky had to spend a certain amount of time every day at the Barracks. The phone would ring, he would answer it, and he would talk. For hours. And Dr. Radhakrishnan would stroll back and forth through the Barracks, tending to his own work, and occasionally cock an ear in old Bucky's direction, hoping to overhear something.

Most of what he overheard, he already knew; Mr. Salvador was just relaying information about the project to others. But on one occasion, wandering around near Mr. Salvador's desk, Dr. Radhakrishnan heard him involved in a very intense, and very loud, conversation about something called Super Tuesday.

Dr. Radhakrishnan was sure he had seen this phrase somewhere before, but he did not have the foggiest idea what it meant. Some kind of American thing. He kept meaning to ask Zeldo if he knew, but kept forgetting.

After a while, Zeldo came down, murmured a sleepy hello to him, occupied another table nearby, and began to read the *Times* of India.

Dr. Radhakrishnan had far too much on his mind to concern himself with politics, and rarely looked at the *Times*. But when Zeldo moved on to one of the interior pages, opening the paper and holding it up in the air, Dr. Radhakrishnan could clearly see a headline, down low on the first page:

U.S. CANDIDATES VIE IN "SUPER TUESDAY" ELECTIONS

"What is Super Tuesday?" he said.

Zeldo spoke to him through the paper. "It's today," he said. "A bunch of the states have their primaries on the same day."

"Primaries?"

"Yeah. You know. To select the presidential candidates."

Dr. Radhakrishnan didn't want to hear anything more about it. He knew it would cloud his mind. He sat there drinking his tea. Then it was time to go to work.

*It all went* smoothly there in the magnificent central operating theater of the Radhakrishnan Institute. He had never seen the place, except in his dreams, or in the computer simulations, until he walked in to begin the operation. The room was circular, huge, high-ceilinged, a cathedral of technology. The floors were white and mirror-smooth. The walls were white painted concrete. All the light was recessed halogen fixtures, painfully bright, and unnaturally pure in coloration compared to the tainted, smoky-yellow illumination provided by old-fashioned bulbs. It felt just the way it should: as though every technological system on earth converged on this one spot, on the operating table that stood in the middle of the room.

"Jeez," Zeldo said, walking into the place, "all we need is a skylight and some lightning rods."

They did it much better this time around. Everything was calm and quiet. Everyone knew their moves. All the equipment was brand new and worked perfectly.

They lowered the biochip down a shaft into the middle of Mohinder Singh's brain and nestled it into the space that had been cut away. This time it was a perfect fit. The incision had been made under the control of a computer, there were no gaps, the new cells would knit together with the old ones much more quickly.

The closing process took a couple of hours but Dr. Radhakrishnan stayed there through the whole thing, watching his assistants put Mr. Singh's head back together. Zeldo stood off to the side at a Calyx console, monitoring the signals from the chip.

By the time they were sewing Mr. Singh's scalp flap back down over the reassembled skull, lines of data had begun to scroll up the monitor screen. The biochip had already made contact. Zeldo was astonished by this, but Dr. Radhakrishnan wasn't. They had done it right this time.

*"What is it?"* Mr. Salvador said. He had just come in from the hotel. Clearly, he had been catching up on sleep, sex, drinking, or some other fundamental bodily function, and had been interrupted in the middle by Dr. Radhakrishnan's telephone call. Clearly he was not happy about it.

"Check this out," Dr. Radhakrishnan said, leading him into the room where Mohinder Singh had, for the last few days, been recovering from the operation.

"Is this going to be more wubba wubba?" Mr. Salvador said.

Mohinder Singh was sitting up in bed, as usual, and smoking, as usual. His scar was nearly obscured by the deepening shadow of his hair. He looked up as Dr. Radhakrishnan and Mr. Salvador came into the room, squinting at them impassively through cigarette smoke.

Dr. Radhakrishnan spoke to him briefly in Hindi, gesturing in the direction of an ashtray that rested on a table next to the bed on Mr. Singh's paralyzed left side.

Mr. Singh looked down at the hand and it began to twitch. Then it jumped into the air like a small animal spooked by a sudden noise, and came to a stop out in front of Mr. Singh's face. The hand began to move toward his mouth, a few inches at a time, in a zigzagging course, like a sailboat trying to tack upwind into a moorage. As it got closer the fingers began to vibrate nervously. They wanted to close over the cigarette but they didn't want to get burned.

Then, suddenly, he had gripped the cigarette. He yanked it out of his mouth and extended his arm out over the ashtray in one explosive movement, scattering ashes the whole way. His hand vibrated for a moment above the general vicinity of the ashtray, dumping a few more ashes from the end of the cigarette, some of which actually landed in the ashtray.

Dr. Radhakrishnan spoke another couple of words and Mr. Singh's hand dropped straight down into the ashtray, crushing the cigarette and mostly putting it out. Then he jerked his hand back into his lap, leaving the cigarette in the tray, spinning out a long tenuous line of smoke.

"Astonishing," Mr. Salvador said. He looked quite awake and considerably less grumpy.

Dr. Radhakrishnan spoke another few words. Then he said, to Mr. Salvador, "I have asked him his name."

Mr. Singh's mouth came open and then closed again, the lips coming together: "Mmmmmo—"

"Mo," Dr. Radhakrishnan echoed.

"Derrrrrr."

"—der. Mohinder."

"Ssssin."

"Mohinder Singh. Very good." Dr. Radhakrishnan spoke in Hindi again, then translated: "What kind of lorry were you driving at the time of your accident?"

"Ta . . . ta."

"That's right. A Tata 1210."

"Still no signs of tumor or rejection?"

"None."

"Right," Mr. Salvador said, "that's it, then." He spun on his heel and burst out of the room.

Dr. Radhakrishnan waited for a few moments, then followed him.

The offices were upstairs. He entered the stairwell and heard Mr. Salvador above him, taking the steps two or three at a time.

By the time he had followed Mr. Salvador, quietly, up to the office level, old Bucky had already got through to someone on the telephone:

"What? All right, I'll speak loudly. Can you hear me? Good. Listen carefully: we are go for launch. Yes. Yes. Unequivocally. Yes, you have a good day too."

## CHAPTER SEVENTEEN

158

Working out the politics of Mary Catherine's temporary leave of absence from her residency and arranging the trip to the various and far-flung organs of the Radhakrishnan Institute took a few weeks. The trip itself lasted a week and a half. When Mary Catherine flew home from California, Mel drove his sports car, a Mercedes 500 SL, down from Chicago and picked her up at the Champaign-Urbana Airport. He took U.S. 45 from there; it passed within two blocks of the Cozzano house and served almost as a private driveway connecting the family with the outside world. Mel preferred two-lane roads with lots of heavy trucks, because that way he had something to pass.

Mel tried to make small talk as they blasted along between the snowed-over cornfields. Mary Catherine was preoccupied and spent most of the time squinting out the window. Farm machinery threw spouts of black diesel straight up into the sky, visible from miles away. From time to time the tires of the Mercedes rumbled as they drove over a spot where mud and cornstalks had been tracked across the road by a tractor and then frozen down hard to the pavement. South of Pesotum it became possible to see the towers of CBAP heaving up over the linear horizon, kicking out silvery bubbles of steam that dissolved into the clouds.

"Something on your mind?" he asked.

"Just a lot of impressions in a short time," she said, shaking her head. "I want to be coherent when I talk to Dad."

Mel grinned, just a bit. So that was it. Even in his current condition, Dad continued to scare the hell out of Mary Catherine. "Just give your professional opinion," Mel said. "After that, we're all grownups."

He slowed the Mercedes and turned off the highway. The tires started to buzz as they drove down brick streets. A plywood sign marked the entrance to town:

WELCOME TO TUSCOLA
ATTEND OUR CHURCHES

*"It's small in* terms of staff. It is absolutely gigantic in terms of resources. Everything they own seems to be brand new," Mary Catherine said.

She was sitting on the sofa in the living room. Dad was sitting directly across the coffee table from her, watching her face. Mel was off to the side. Patricia was hovering, throwing logs on the fire, getting coffee.

"If you buy their basic scientific approach, then these guys are certainly equipped to move forward with it," Mary Catherine continued. "They have money to burn."

"Do you buy it?" Mel said.

"It works on baboons. It makes paralyzed baboons capable of moving, and even walking, again. That has been proved, I think, beyond a doubt."

"Does it work on femelhebbers?" Cozzano asked, using his new word for people.

"I asked them that question many times," Mary Catherine said, "and I might as well have been saying 'femelhebbers' for all the information I got."

Cozzano laughed and shook his head ruefully.

"I was skeptical going in. But what they have done is extremely impressive, and it seems to me that if they could produce one healthy person who has gone through this therapy, then we might actually have something."

"Tell me about your detailed impressions," Mel said.

"I saw the institute itself dead last—just this morning. These guys made up the whole itinerary for me, so I didn't have much flexibility."

"Did you feel you were getting the Potemkin Village treatment?" Mel asked.

"Yes. But that's normal."

"True," Mel said.

"First place I went was Genomics, in Seattle. It's south of downtown, near the Kingdome, in a big old warehouse that they gutted and redid. All pretty new and clean, as you'd expect. Most of the space is used for things unrelated to this project. They have one suite on the top floor where they do brain work for Radhakrishnan. When I was there they had several cell-culturing projects underway.

It's a typical lab with small glass containers all over the place with handwritten labels stuck to them, and by reading the labels I could pick up the names of some of the subjects they're working on. The names I saw were—" Mary Catherine leafed through her notes for a second, "Margaret Thatcher, Earl Strong, Easyrider, Scatflinger, and Mohinder Singh."

An uneasy laugh passed around the table. "I know who the first two are . . ." Mel said.

"That's what I thought. But later, when I went to Elton, I found out that Margaret Thatcher and Earl Strong are two of their baboons. They name all of the baboons after political figures."

"Did you also see baboons named Easyrider and Scatflinger?" Mel said. "Those sound more like animal names to me."

"No. And I have no ideas on Mohinder Singh, either."

"Mohinder Singh might be a baboon," Mel concluded, "named after some guy in India that Radhakrishnan doesn't like. But it's also possible that Mohinder Singh is a human being."

"They keep talking about their facilities in India," Mary Catherine said. "It may be a person they are experimenting on out there. Working on, I should say."

"Well, go on," Mel said.

"From Seattle I went to New Mexico for a couple of days. Very nice facility there—the Coover Biotech Pavilion."

Mel and Cozzano exchanged looks.

"Again, they obviously know what they're doing. I spent a long time going over detailed records of all of the baboons they've worked on. It's clear that they have learned a lot about this over the years. Their first subjects had rejection problems, or the biochips failed to take, et cetera. Over time they have solved those problems. Now they can do it almost routinely.

"Then I went to San Francisco and talked to some of the people working on the chips at Pacific Netware. These guys are really good —the best in the business. They were the only ones willing to talk about the human element."

"What do you mean by that?" Mel said.

"All of the biologist types are gun-shy about the idea of doing this with human beings. You can't get them to talk about it. It's clear that there are some potential ethical problems there that they have been trained to avoid. But the chipheads don't have any of those cultural inhibitions. They would probably volunteer to get these things implanted in their own heads."

"Why? Are they brain damaged?"

"No more so than anyone who works on computers for a living. But to them, see, it's not a therapy so much as it is a way of improving the human mind. That's what gets these guys psyched about it."

"You're joking," Cozzano said.

"The biologists won't even allow themselves to think about trying this on people—even severely brain-damaged volunteers. The computer people have already gone way beyond that point in their thinking. Half the guys I talked to firmly believed that in ten or twenty years they would be walking around with supercomputers stuck in their heads."

"This is getting weird," Mel said.

"I don't want to wash a duck," Cozzano said. "I just want to bring the trousers."

"Understood," Mary Catherine said, "but I'm here to talk about the credibility of this process. And the point I'm making here is that it is extremely credible as far as the people at Pacific Netware are concerned."

"Okay, we got that point," Mel said. "Tell me about the institute."

"Beautiful piece of real estate on the California coast. Very secluded. Has its own private airport. Lots of open space for recreation."

Once again, Mel Meyer and the Governor were exchanging significant looks. "A guy—even a famous guy—could get in and out of the place without being noticed?"

"Mel, you could fly in, go down the road to this institute, sun yourself in the courtyard, swim on the beach, and no one would ever see you."

"Read me the blueprints," Cozzano said.

"You want some information about the building?" Mary Catherine guessed.

"Yes."

"The building is nice and new, like everything else. Some parts of it aren't even finished yet. There's an incredible operating theater, which looked like it was finished, but there's no way to tell that without actually going in and trying to do brain surgery there. And the actual rooms are luxurious. All private rooms. Big windows with balconies over the ocean. The patients hang out on the balconies, watch TV, listen to CDs, or whatever."

"You actually saw patients there?" Mel said.

"Yes. But because of privacy considerations, I couldn't go to their rooms or talk to them. I saw one or two, from a distance, sitting out on the balconies in their wheelchairs, reading newspapers or just staring into the distance."

"You saw patients there. Which means they have actually done operations on human beings," Mel said.

"I guess that's the conclusion we are led to," Mary Catherine said.

"Well put. Well put," Mel said.

"You think we are being led to a false conclusion?" Mary Catherine said incredulously.

"No way to know, is there?"

"There's a couple of small things," she said, a little uncertain.

"Tell us everything," Mel said. "We'll decide what's small and what isn't."

"I went to the bathroom at one point and washed my hands. And when I turned on the faucet, it sort of coughed."

"Coughed?"

"Yeah. Sputtered for a few seconds. As if there was air trapped in the pipes. It used to happen here, whenever Dad worked on the plumbing."

At first, Mel shook his head, not getting it. Then his eyes widened with astonishment. Then they narrowed in fascination. "You were the first person ever to use the faucet in the ladies' room," Mel said.

"Goddamn it! I think you are wrong," Cozzano said to Mel.

"Since parts of the building were still under construction, it's possible that they had to alter some of the pipes after that sink had been in use for a while," Mary Catherine said, "and that this caused air bubbles to be introduced."

"Please continue," Mel said. He was acting like a lawyer in a courtroom now, interviewing a neutral witness.

"I wandered around the grounds a little bit. It's a nice place for a stroll. And on the bluff, overlooking the sea, a few hundred yards away from the building, behind a little rise, I found the remains of a fire. Someone had piled up a bunch of straw there and burned it."

"Straw?" Mel said.

Cozzano nodded. "It keeps the patio slippery."

"When we used to pour concrete on the farm, we would cover it up with damp straw. You have to keep concrete damp for several days, preferably a week or two, while it cures," Mary Catherine said. "So it's not surprising that they would have a bunch of straw lying around a place where they were building a big reinforced-concrete building. There are a lot of ranches nearby and it's a natural thing for them to use. When I walked back from the site of the fire to the building, I saw a lot of pieces of loose straw caught in the undergrowth, and many of them were stained white with concrete. Some of the straw was still damp."

"So when they were finished, they got rid of the straw by dragging it to this place and burning it," Mel said.

"Yeah. They burned it the night before," Mary Catherine said.

"How do you know that?" Cozzano said.

Mary Catherine held up the little finger on her right hand. The tip was cherry red. "I made the mistake of sticking my finger down into the bed of ashes."

Mel said, "They got rid of the straw right before you got there."

"It was lying around somewhere after they finished the building," Mary Catherine said. "They knew that I was coming and they wanted the place to look tidy, so they burned it."

"What about the goddamn patients? What about other potential contributors? Don't they want the place to look tidy for those people too?" Mel said. "What's so special about you?"

"It was just a coincidence," Cozzano said.

"I think they finished the building the day before you got there," Mel said.

Everyone except Mel burst out in nervous laughter.

"Bullshit," Cozzano said.

"Mel you showed me a photograph of the place two and a half, three weeks ago," Mary Catherine said. She said it kiddingly. She knew what Mel was up to here. It was just like him to state things in the most exaggerated, overstated way possible, just to shake people up.

"There was something funny about that photograph. It was too clean-looking. I think it was fake," Mel said.

Cozzano shook his head and twirled one finger around his ear. There was no point arguing with Mel when he had shifted into full combat mode.

"They have ways of faking that stuff now," Mel insisted.

"And the patients I saw?"

"Actors."

"What are you getting at, Mel?" Mary Catherine said. She said it with one eye on Dad; she was trying to anticipate the kinds of things he would say if he could. "I can't think of any logical explanation for what you are saying."

"I can. Here's how it goes: Coover runs into that guy from Pacific Netware. Kevin Tice. They run into each other golfing or something. And Coover tells Tice about this guy Radhakrishnan and his work with baboons. Coover is a tired old guy with a soft spot, he just thinks of it as a way to help stroke victims. But Tice is a big idea man, he reads too much science fiction, he's not satisfied with just being a billionaire, he wants to have a supercomputer in his head as well. Because if what you are saying is true, then this process of putting chips into people's heads will one day be huge. It's the kind of technology that Tice has to get a jump on right now so he can become the world's first trillionaire a couple of decades down the road.

"So Tice starts pumping money into it for his own purposes. They continue working with baboons, maybe even round up some untouchables in Calcutta or somewhere and do it to them so they can learn how to do it on humans. And then, all of a sudden, Governor Cozzano has a stroke. And Tice and Coover see a big opportunity. By fixing the brain of someone who is powerful and famous they can jump-start this new industry of theirs. So they go out and build this thing in California. I'll bet it was already under construction and they just hurried up the process a little bit. Just got it done yesterday in time to impress Dr. Mary Catherine Cozzano here. But she was a little too observant."

"Bullshit," Cozzano said.

"If what you say is true," Mary Catherine said, "then the worst conclusion we can come to is that they really want Dad as a client, and they've pushed their schedule up in order to make a good impression on him."

Mel thought that one over for a while. Cozzano, obviously amused, watched Mel's face. "I don't like the idea of them using Willy as a guinea pig," Mel said.

"Phooey," Cozzano said. "Better a dead pioneer than a live feeb."

"You want to pursue this?" Mary Catherine said.

"Yes, goddamn it," Cozzano said.

Mel just closed his eyes and shook his head in disbelief.

"There is a step we can take now, without committing ourselves," Mary Catherine said. "I don't know whether I like this. But I have to give you all the information. As you said, Mel, we're all adults."

"What is it?" Mel said warily.

"Dad has to go up to Champaign, to Burke Hospital, tomorrow for a routine checkup. While he's in there, we could arrange for a biopsy."

"Of what?"

"Brain cells."

"Why?"

"We could send them to Genomics. They could hang on to them there. That way, if Dad made the decision to go ahead with an implant, they could culture the cells and prepare the biochip at any time."

"Do it," Cozzano said.

"Oh, shit," Mel said.

"Do the biopsy?" Mary Catherine said. "Tomorrow?"

Cozzano just looked her in the eye and nodded. His eyes looked a little brighter. He smiled at Mary Catherine with the good side of his mouth, and a thin trickle of drool streamed down out of the other side.

"I'm tired of this," Cozzano said, wiping off the drool with his good hand. "This is bad."

"Yes, it's bad," Mel said, "but—"

"I want to be the Milhous," Cozzano said.

"And one day you will be," Mel said, "but—"

"Shut up, goddamnit!" Cozzano bellowed. Suddenly he ripped the blanket off his lap with his good hand. Then he pitched forward in his wheelchair so violently that he seemed to be falling out.

Everyone jumped up and converged on him. But he wasn't falling. He was trying to stand up. The momentum of his upper body carried him halfway to his feet and he used the powerful thrust of his good arm to push him up on one leg. Then he almost tottered over, but Mary Catherine had already danced around the coffee table and now she drove her shoulder up under her father's armpit, taking most of his weight.

Though no one but Mary Catherine would ever know it, this had taken a lot of guts on her part, because her impulse had been to shrink away. Suddenly back on his feet, Dad was massive, dark, and towering. Mary Catherine's love for her father had always been mingled with a judicious amount of fear, or maybe respect was a nicer word for it. He had never struck her or even threatened to, but he never needed to. The tornadic force of his personality made people cringe and scurry, especially when he was mad, and right now he was really pissed. He threw his entire weight on her body for a moment, nearly buckling her knees, and finally got his weight centered over his good leg again.

And then he started to hop. He was going somewhere. He had fixed a dark, unblinking gaze on the far wall of the den, and seeing this, Mary Catherine tried to help him along. They moved together one hop at a time across the shag carpet and into the den. Mel shuffled along behind them.

Cozzano was headed for a framed picture hung on the wall. It was a picture of Cozzano shaking George Bush's hand on the south lawn a few years ago. Barbara Bush stood off to the side, hands clasped together, beaming supportively. Behind them rose the columns of the White House.

Cozzano went straight across the floor and fell, crushing Mary Catherine into the wall with his bad shoulder and pinning her there. He reached across his body with his good hand and slammed the end of his index finger into the framed picture so hard that it whacked back into the wall and a couple of cracks appeared in the glass.

He wasn't pointing to himself or to the Bushes. He was pointing to the White House.

"This is mine," he said. "This is my barn." He slammed his index finger into the White House a couple of more times for emphasis. "I should have done it before."

"You have to get better first," Mary Catherine said in a strangled voice.

"Well, I guess I better print up a shitload of bumper stickers," Mel said morosely. "Femelhebbers for Cozzano."

Mary Catherine didn't say anything. She was feeling the hairs stand up on the back of her neck.

Her dad was running for president. Her dad was running for *president*. President of the United States. It was enough to make her forget about the stroke, to obliterate the fact that there was no way he could be elected in his condition.

She wanted to talk to her mother. She wished Mom was here. This would be a good time to have a mother.

But Mom wasn't here. She forced herself to open her eyes and stare at him.

He was looking right back at her with the frightening, soul-penetrating glare that made people want to leave the room.

Then it went away and was replaced by an idiotic grin. Mary Catherine had seen this grin a million times while examining neurology patients, and she had seen it on Dad's face a few times since the stroke, usually when it seemed like he was giving up. It was the drooling, clownlike, sheepish grin of a near vegetable. It was a lot more frightening than his intense glare.

"You are the quarterback now, peanut," he said. His eyes rolled back into his head and he went completely limp, as if his bones had turned to water. Mary Catherine let him down to the floor as gently as she could; Mel stepped in to support his head.

"He's just had another stroke," Mary Catherine said. "Forget about the phone, Tuscola doesn't have 911. Let's get him into that fast little car of yours. And then you need to drive it like a bat out of hell."

## CHAPTER EIGHTEEN

The South Platte River looked big and important on maps of Denver. It approached the city from the north-northeast. Its valley and flood plain were several miles wide and served as a corridor for a bundle of major transportation routes: state highways, an interstate, natural gas pipelines, major railways, and high-tension power lines. The first time Eleanor had seen it was shortly after she and Harmon had arrived in Denver and they were driving around looking for places to live. Harmon drove and Eleanor navigated, and she got them lost. She got them lost because she was trying to use the mighty South Platte as a landmark, and instead they kept crossing back and forth over a paltry creek or drainage ditch out in the middle of nowhere. Not until she actually saw the name of the thing on a sign by a bridge could she believe that this dried-up rill was all there was to it.

They had crossed the Platte again a couple of years ago on their way to the Commerce Vista Motel and Mobile Home Haven. In retrospect, Eleanor knew that Harmon had craftily plotted their trajectory so that they could reach the place without having to pass through any part of Commerce City proper. They'd come in from the northwest, from the middle-class suburbs where they had raised their family, past brand-new strip malls sitting totally empty with weathered FOR LEASE banners stretched across their fronts, across open grassland that was too close to the flood plain or too far from the highway to develop. At the edge of Commerce City they had passed quickly through a brief unpleasant flurry of franchise development and then come upon the Commerce Vista. Somehow Eleanor had failed to notice the WEEKLY RATES sign on the motel's marquee, and she hadn't even bothered to look across the highway, off to the eastern edge of the mobile home park. She hadn't looked that way because it was nothing but empty grassland stretching vastly under a white sky, and Eleanor didn't like to look east across that territory because it told her exactly how far she was from home. But if she had looked she would have seen that it was surrounded by a tall chain-link fence topped with barbed wire, with signs every few yards reading U.S. ARMY CORPS OF ENGINEERS—NO TRESPASS-ING. Tangles of plumbing stuck mysteriously out of the ground from place to place, and every few hundred yards was a white wooden box with a peaked roof, like an oversized birdhouse, containing instruments to monitor the air.

Prairie grass was the only thing that would grow in the yellow rock flour that passed for soil at the Commerce Vista. But the vegetation was all gone and so now it was just a hardpan mixed with broken glass so that it sparkled when the sun hit it right. There were no particular roads or streets, only the tracks left by the last vehicle. The only thing that kept it all from blowing away was the tamping action of car and truck tires, and the little waist-high fences that partitioned the land into tiny lots and gave each trailer a yard to call its own.

On their first visit to the place, Eleanor had noticed that the neighbor's gate had a little decoration on it. One of Doreen's kids had put it up. It was a jack-o-lantern: a circle of orange construction paper with three black triangles in it, one for each eye and one at the bottom that was apparently supposed to be the mouth. It hadn't struck her as odd that they had Halloween decorations up in June. Not until they'd moved in did Doreen explain that the symbol was, in fact, a copy of the radiation symbols that their kids saw across the highway at the arsenal.

She remembered all of these things one night as she reclined in the front seat of her old Datsun, trying to get some sleep. Eleanor tried not to think of the old Datsun as a car. She tried to think of it as a highly compact mobile home. She called it the Annex.

She could still remember walking down the street in D.C. with her mother when she was a kid and encountering dirty men who slept in parked cars. She could remember how frightened she was of those men and of the way they lived. She didn't want to be like that.

It was not really such a big deal, when you thought about it logically. She was living in a mobile-home park, for god's sake. What was a mobile home but a big boxy car without an engine? Her old beat-up Datsun, parked on four flat tires in front of the mobile home, was like a little annex, a mother-in-law apartment.

The seats did not exactly recline all the way, but they reclined quite a bit. The only hard part was trying to find a comfortable place to lay her head, because it tended to roll back and forth on the hard surface of the headrest as she relaxed. After a couple of hard nights she finally worked out an arrangement of pillows that held her head in place comfortably. That and a sleeping bag and she was all set. She knew that she might be sleeping this way for a while, so she safety-pinned clean sheets into the inside of the sleeping bag and took them out every week and laundered them.

The car's battery was run down but it still had enough juice to run the radio, so it could be said that the Annex had a home entertainment system. Sometimes Eleanor would sit there and listen to a little music, or to news of the presidential candidates. Looking out the windshield, she could see into her neighbor Doreen's trailer and see the candidates running around on Doreen's TV set on top of the fridge. When she watched TV in this way, from a great distance, through layers of dirty glass, unable to hear the sound, it had a weird, pixilated look to it. There were so many politicians going so many places, doing so many cute things to get the attention of the cameras. It was like a nursery school, she thought, full of lonely kids who were always punching each other, running with sharp objects, and sticking pencils up their noses—anything to draw attention to themselves. The TV producers, like overburdened nursery-school teachers, cut frantically from one three-second shot to another, trying to keep track of them, and all their little activities. Each cut made the image on Doreen's TV set jump, startling Eleanor a bit and making her eyes jerk involuntarily toward the screen.

So that was why kids couldn't stop watching television.

The candidates did not seem to have much of an attention span. As the weeks went on, most of them ran into trouble of one kind or another—a poor showing in a state primary, a scandal, or money woes—and dropped out. It always seemed momentous at the time of the actual announcement, and when Eleanor saw a candidate standing somberly in front of some blue curtains, she would turn on the Annex's radio and listen for news of his withdrawal. But a few days later she would realize that she could hardly even remember the candidate's name or what he stood for. And it got to the point that whenever one of the candidates made his little withdrawal speech, she would say, "Good riddance," and snap off the radio.

*Eleanor Richmond was* sleeping in her car because there was no room left in the mobile home. It only had two bedrooms. Until recently, she and Harmon had slept in one and their children Clarice and Harmon, Jr., had slept in the other.

Now everything was discombobulated. Harmon had killed himself. Harmon, Jr., had taken to staying out late. Clarice had remained stable and reliable, a good girl, for a few weeks following the suicide, and then one night she had not come home at all.

And then Eleanor's mother had moved back in with them. Eleanor spent about half of one night trying to sleep in the same bed with her mother before going out into the living room, where she found Harmon, Jr., sacked out on the couch. From there she had gone straight to the car.

Eleanor loved her mother, but her mother had died a long time ago. Only the body lived on. The Alzheimer's had started when she was in the first retirement community. The nice one. The expensive one. By the time they were forced to move her into the not-so-nice one, she had deteriorated to the point where she had no idea what was going on, which was a blessing for all concerned.

Now she was home with Eleanor. She was back in diapers. Mother didn't mind, but Eleanor certainly did—and the children couldn't handle it at all. Eleanor hadn't seen much of her children since Mother had moved in.

With other kids, that would have been worrisome. But Eleanor's kids weren't like that. She had raised them the way Mother had raised her. They had their heads on straight. Even when Clarice stayed out all night, Eleanor felt confident that she was using her head and not doing any of that stupid underclass behavior.

Harmon, Jr., was a case in point. He had been horrified that first morning when he found his mother sleeping in a car. He had tried to insist that he be the one to sleep outside. Eleanor had put her foot down. She was still a parent; Harmon, Jr., was still her child. It was the parent's duty to look out for her children. No son of hers was going to sleep outside, not while she could help it. Harmon, Jr., eventually backed down. But the next day he came home with some sheets of silvery plastic stuff that he had bought at an auto parts store. He went out to the Datsun and stuck this material up on the insides of all the windows, turning them into one-way mirrors. From inside the car, it just tinted the windows a little bit. But from the outside, no one could see in.

Eleanor really liked it. She liked to come out here and snuggle into her sleeping bag, lock the doors, and lie for a while, gazing out the windows. Usually when you went to bed, you were blind. If you heard a mysterious noise outside the window or in the house, you felt scared and helpless. You had to get out of bed and turn on all the lights to find out what was happening. Here in her silvered bubble she could see everything, but no one could see her. If she heard a noise, all she had to do was open her eyes, and she could see that it was a cat scratching in the dirt, or Doreen coming back from her evening shift at the 7-Eleven. And if it was anything more than that, she had Harmon's old officer's .45 sitting in the glove compartment right in front of her, practically in her lap. Eleanor had spent a few years in the Army herself and she knew how to use it. She knew exactly how to use it.

When money got short and times got hard, you stopped worrying about all the superficial nonsense of modern life and you got down to basics. The basic thing that a parent did was to protect her family. That is why Eleanor Richmond felt more comfortable, and slept much more soundly, in her silverized glass bubble with a loaded gun six inches away. Whatever else was going wrong, she knew that if anyone tried to get into her house and hurt her family, she would kill them. She had that one base covered. Everything else was details.

*Her eyes came* open in the middle of the night and she knew that something was wrong without even turning her head.

The Commerce Vista ran right up to the edge of the highway, and it didn't have any of this exit-ramp nonsense. One minute you were going sixty miles an hour and the next minute you were skidding across yellow dust and broken glass, trying to kill speed. Whenever someone performed this maneuver, Eleanor heard it and opened her eyes. The first thing she saw was always the white aluminum front of the mobile home. If the car then turned onto her particular lane, its headlights would sweep across that surface.

It had just happened a few seconds ago. And now she heard footsteps crunching in the gravel, right outside of the car.

She lifted her head slowly and quietly. A man was walking in front of her car. A beefy, bearded white man, young-looking but with the bulk of middle age, dressed in jeans and a dark windbreaker, wearing a baseball cap. He moved confidently, as if he belonged in her front yard, as if he belonged on her front step.

Which he definitely did not.

Eleanor had practiced this; she had been ready for it since the first night in the Annex. As the man was mounting the steps to their front door, his back turned to her, she rolled out the front door of the car, dropping to her knees, pulling the gun out of the glove compartment, and took cover behind the corner of the mobile home, sighting down the side of the house, drawing a bead on the center of the man's windbreaker. From here he looked exactly like a silhouette target at the firing range.

He hadn't heard her yet. She raised her head for a second and looked at his car. It was a beat-up old sedan with no one else in it. The man had come alone. His mistake.

"Freeze! I'm covering you with a .45," she said. "I'm an Army veteran and I have fired hundreds of rounds into targets that were a lot smaller and farther away than you are."

"Okay," the man said. "Can you see my hands? I'm holding them up."

"I see 'em. Why don't you lace them together on top of your head and then turn around to face me."

"Okay, I'll do that," the man said. He did.

"What are you doing here?" Eleanor said.

"My job."

"You a robber?"

"No. I'm a cop. Detective Larsen of the Commerce City Police Department."

"Can you prove that?"

"I can prove it by showing you my ID," Detective Larsen said.

"But in order to do that, ma'am, I'll have to take it out of my pocket, and it would be a shame if you misinterpreted that as reaching for a gun. So let's talk about this for just a second and see if we can negotiate a way for me to extract the ID from my pocket without giving you the wrong idea."

"Don't worry about it," Eleanor said, pointing the gun up at the sky and coming out from behind her cover. "Only a cop would talk like that."

"Well, let me show you my ID anyway," Larsen said. He turned sideways so that she could see his butt. He slowly reached around into his back pocket and took out a black wallet. He underhanded it twenty feet to Eleanor, then left his hands well away from his sides while she opened it up and looked at it.

"Okay," she said, tossing it back. "Sorry if I spooked you."

"Normally I'd be real pissed," he admitted. "But under the circumstances, ma'am, it's all right. You Eleanor Richmond?"

Larsen's face went all fuzzy and out of focus. Eleanor's eyes were filling up with tears. She didn't even know why, yet. "I got the feeling something real bad happened," she said.

"You're right. But it's going to be okay, considering."

"What happened?"

"Your son is in the hospital in serious but stable condition. He's going to be all right."

"Car crash?"

"No, ma'am. He was shot."

"Shot!?"

"Yes, ma'am. Shot in the back by a suspected gang member, in downtown Denver. But he's going to be okay. He was very lucky."

Suddenly Eleanor was seeing clearly again. The tears had gone away. It was so shocking that just for a minute, curiosity overwhelmed everything else.

This was terrible. She should have been freaking out and panicking. Instead, she felt eerily calm and alert, like a person who had just been sucked out of an airliner into a cold, scintillating blue sky. Her life was completely falling apart now. She felt the complete abandon of a person in free fall.

"My son was shot and you're saying he's lucky?"

"Yes, I am, Mrs. Richmond. I've seen a lot of people shot. I ought to know."

"Detective Larsen, is my son in a gang and I don't even know about it?"

"Not as far as we can tell."

"Then why did they shoot him?"

"He was using a pay telephone downtown. And they wanted to use it."

"They shot him over a pay phone?"

"As far as we can tell."

"What, my son wouldn't let them use it?"

"Well, no one uses a pay phone forever. But he didn't give it up as quickly as they wanted him to. They didn't want to wait. So they shot him."

She frowned. "Well, what kind of a person would do something like that?"

Detective Larsen shrugged. "There's a lot of people like that nowadays."

"Well, why are our presidential candidates running around having sex with bimbos and sticking pencils up their noses when we have people growing up in Denver, Colorado, with no values?"

Detective Larsen was looking progressively more bewildered. "Presidential politics aren't my specialty, ma'am."

"Well, maybe they ought to be."

A *few weeks* later, Eleanor found herself sitting on a rather nice, brand-new wrought-iron bench in front of the Boulevard Mall in downtown Denver. She was in no mood to be at a mall, but circumstances put her here a couple of times a day.

Her son was convalescing, and taking his sweet time about it, at Denver County Hospital, which was a mile or so down south of the state capitol and the high-rise district. This part of town included the hospital, various schools, and museums—all of the municipal stuff. It also included the old downtown shopping district, which had been badly in need of some really devastating urban renewal for quite some time.

Just recently the urban renewal had come in the form of the

Boulevard Mall, a brand-new pseudoadobe structure built on the bulldozed graves of more traditional retail outlets. It was near Speer Boulevard, only a few blocks from the hospital. A lot of bus lines converged there. Denver had hired some publicity genius who had come up with a catch phrase for the bus system: The Ride. This being the automotive West, where only tramps and criminals were thought to take public transit, the buses were slow, few, and far between, and so Eleanor had been spending a lot of time taking The Ride lately, or waiting for it, which was even more humiliating.

She consoled herself with the fact that it made sound financial sense. Sitting down with her calculator, like the banker she had once been, and weighing all the alternatives, she eventually figured out that the most logical way for her to spend her time was to take The Ride downtown twice a week, to this neighborhood. Along with all of its municipal buildings, it included a few big old main-line churches, several of which had gotten together and started up a food bank. Originally it was just to help Mexicans live through the Rocky Mountain winter, but in recent years it had started to attract a more diverse clientele. So while Eleanor was out of the house picking up cheese, powdered milk, oatmeal, and beans, Doreen was keeping an eye on Mother. In return, Eleanor gave Doreen some of the food and watched Doreen's kids for a couple of hours a day. This was known, among intellectuals, as the barter economy.

Since the shooting, she had added an additional stop: she would go out and visit Harmon, Jr., at Denver County Hospital. Harmon had learned, from his father, to hold his feelings inside and not complain about things, so sometimes it was hard to tell how he really felt. But he seemed to be doing okay psychologically, much better than Eleanor would have been if she had been shot in the back for no reason. As Harmon, Jr., came out from under the shock and the effects of the drugs, he got his old spark back, plus a little bit of a macho swagger that had not been there before. He had been shot and he had survived. That was one way to get a name for yourself in high school. The macho bit was cute, as long as he didn't take it too far.

Thinking of her son made Eleanor smile to herself as she sat on the bench in front of the Boulevard Mall. Across her lap was a large brick of orange cheese encased in a flimsy cardboard box, and several pounds of rolled oats and pinto beans in clear plastic bags. Above her head was a large sign in red metal saying THE RIDE.

All around her, people were strolling in from the parking lots, converging on the front entrance of the mall. These people had their very own rides, many with license plates from outlying counties. She got more than one dirty look from these people. This was not unusual in Denver, which now had its ghettos at the outskirts of town, but even for Denver it seemed like she was getting a lot of dirty looks. Then she realized that every other one of these people was wearing a T-shirt or a baseball cap emblazoned with the slogan EARL STRONG COMES ON STRONG.

Everybody knew that Earl Strong's real name was Erwin Dudley Strang, but no one seemed to care, and that was just one of the many things about the man that pissed Eleanor Richmond off.

Not that there was anything wrong with changing your name. But political candidates had been crucified in the press for doing far less significant things. Earl Strong/Erwin Dudley Strang seemed to get away with murder.

He could have picked something a little less obvious than Strong. To change your name, and then use the name's double meaning as part of a campaign slogan . . . it was a little much. As if he were nothing more than a new TV series. But even though people knew exactly what Erwin Dudley Strang was doing, they lapped it up like thirsty dogs.

Maybe one reason Eleanor felt bad when she heard of the man was that she had known of him from way back and she had never taken him seriously.

The first time she had ever seen the name Erwin Dudley Strang, it had been printed across the laminated face of a photo ID card. She had seen it through the distorting lens of the peephole on the front door of the house in Eldorado Highlands. She was on the inside of the house, by herself, waiting for the cable TV installer to show up; the cable company had promised that an installer would arrive between nine and five, and so she had spent the whole day waiting in an empty house. He had finally rung her doorbell at 4:54 P.M. and stood out on the front doorstep holding up his official cable

TV installer's ID card so that it was the only thing she could see through the peephole when she looked out.

She could at least pride herself on one thing: she had known, just from that one little gesture, that Erwin Dudley Strang was a creep.

*She opened her* front door. Erwin Dudley Strang lowered the badge to reveal a narrow, concave face, cratered like the surface of the moon. He looked Eleanor Richmond in the eye, and his jaw dropped open. He stared at her without saying anything for several seconds. It was the look that white people gave to black people to let the black people know that they didn't belong there. To remind them, just in case they'd somehow forgotten, that they were on the wrong continent.

"Can I help you?" Eleanor said.

"Is the lady of the house in?" he said.

"I am the owner. I am the lady of the house," she said.

Keeping that fixed stare on her face, Erwin Dudley Strang blinked a couple of times and shook his head melodramatically. But he never said anything. It almost wouldn't have been so bad if he had said, "Shit, I never thought I'd see a black person out here." But he didn't do that. He shook his head and blinked, and then he said, "Yes, hello, I'm here to install your cable TV."

In the course of installing the cable system he had to go in and out of the house half a dozen times. Each time, he was careful to stare her down while standing in the corner of her peripheral vision so that she would know that he was there. Each time, she felt herself getting hot under the collar and turned squarely toward him, and each time he glanced away just a moment before her eye met his, blinked, shook his head, and continued about his work.

He walked around the house brandishing a power drill with a preposterously elongated bit, which he used to drill holes all the way through the exterior walls wherever she told him she wanted a cable TV wire. Even the way that he handled this tool raised Eleanor's hackles; it seemed clear, somehow, that a large portion of Erwin Dudley Strang's ego was bound up in this tool, and that penetrating the walls of total strangers' homes was the really swell part of the job as far as he was concerned.

And consequently he always pushed on the drill a little bit too hard, tried to make it happen a little bit too fast, and ended up shoving the drill bit through the wall with brute force rather than waiting for it to cut cleanly; everywhere he poked a hole through the wall he managed to burst a sizable hole through the drywall, and every time he did it, he came back in and shook his head in astonishment as if this were the first time it had ever happened. As if defective drywall had been used to build the Richmonds' new house, the Richmonds had been foolish enough not to notice, and there was not a thing he could do about it.

He ran the cables along the outside of the house, not by stapling them but by tucking them between the pieces of vinyl siding. As a result they all fell out within the first couple of days, leaving gaps in the siding where it no longer interlocked properly. Harmon ended up spending an entire weekend fixing the holes in the drywall and reattaching the cable to the house and getting the siding popped back together. Harmon also noticed that Strang had neglected to ground the cable system properly, which put the whole family at risk of electrocution, and so he rigged up a way to ground it to a cold-water pipe down in the basement.

All of this was in defiance of Erwin Dudley Strang's statement, which he repeated to Eleanor several times, that the stuff was cable company property and they were not allowed to mess with it in any way.

"It's all hooked up," he said, at some point when he had arbitrarily decided that he was finished. "Now, if you'll show me your TV, I'll hook it up for you."

The Richmonds had not moved into the house yet. There was not a stick of furniture in the house, or for that matter in the whole development. Erwin Dudley Strang had passed through every room in the place and must have noticed this. Now he was asking to see their television set, staring at her blankly, with the forced innocent expression of a sixth-grade bad boy who has just nailed the teacher with a spitball.

She was just completely baffled by the man. Clearly, what he was saying had no relationship to what he was thinking. He was playing some kind of game. She had no idea what it was.

"It's not here. We haven't moved in yet," she finally said. Mother had taught her, when in doubt, to be polite.

"Well, then I can't show you how to hook it up."

"It's cable-ready," she said. "All we have to do is screw the cable into the back and turn it on."

"And plug it into the power outlet," he corrected her, just a hint of a smirk on his face.

"Yes, and plug it in. Good point," she said.

"Now, is it ready for all bands of cable? Because the bands here might be different from the bands there."

She had been expecting something like this. Telling Erwin Dudley Strang that their set was cable-ready was tantamount to making fun of his drill bit. He could not let it go unpunished. He would have to one-up her and display his technical mastery.

"From the bands where?" she asked.

His eyes darted back and forth. Clearly this was something of a curve ball. "Wherever y'all came from," he said, putting a long, drawling emphasis on the "y'all."

"If you don't know where we came from, how do you know that the bands are different?"

"Well, you came from back East, didn't you? From one of them big cities?"

"No. We were at Fitzsimons Army Medical Center for a couple of years. Before that we lived in Germany."

"Oooh, Germany," he said. Then, moving so suddenly that he made Eleanor startle, he stood up straight, clicked the heels of his work boots together, and jutted his right arm out in a Nazi salute. "*Sieg Heil!*" he hollered. He dropped his arm and a smile spread across his face as he watched Eleanor's reaction. "Lot of those kind of people there? You know, National Socialists?"

"You mean Nazis?"

"Well, that's kind of a slang term, but yeah, that's what I mean."

"Never saw one *there*," Eleanor said. "If you're finished, you can leave now."

Strang raised his eyebrows fastidiously. "Well, technically speaking, I'm not finished with the installation until I have hooked up the TV set and gotten it running to the satisfaction of the owner."

"My husband is an engineer. He'll get it running. If we're not satisfied, we'll call the cable company."

"But before I leave, I have to get your signature on this document," Strang said, holding up an aluminum clipboard, "which states that the installation is complete and you are satisfied with the quality of service."

"I'll sign anything, at this point."

"You sure?" Strang said, wiggling the clipboard just out of Eleanor's reach.

"Positive."

"We could test it right now if you could get a TV set."

"For the eight hundredth time, I do not have a TV."

"I'll bet you could get one, though."

"I have no idea what you're talking about."

Strang looked out the windows of the living room, down the block. "Must be some other houses around here that have TVs. I'll bet you could figure out a way to get your hands on someone else's TV set, if you really wanted it."

She just stared at him, narrowed her eyes, shook her head in amazement.

He continued, "Course now that *y'all* are out here in the nice part of town, I'll bet you don't do that kind of thing no more. But I'll bet you still got the skills. *Y'all* are just a little rusty."

"I'm going to call the cable TV company and they are going to fire your ass," she said.

"They can't," he said. "I don't work for them. I'm an independent contractor. Just a small-time entrepreneurial businessman struggling to make my way."

"Then I'll make sure they never hire you again."

"Your word against mine," he said, "and even if they believe you, there's plenty of other cable systems out here in Colorful Colorado that keep my services in high demand."

She knew it was crazy for her to be arguing this with him. She should just throw him out of the house. But her parents had raised her to talk things out. They had worked their fingers to the bone paying for an expensive Catholic education so that the nuns could teach her to be a rational, intelligent citizen. She could not get over the impulse to make Erwin Dudley Strang see reason. "Why shouldn't they believe me?" she said. "Why would I bother to call in such a complaint? It's not something I would do for fun."

"Hell hath no fury like a woman scorned," he said.

"What!?"

"I seen the way you been looking at me," he said. "If you want a taste, why don't you just ask for it?"

"Oh, Jesus," she said, "get out of my house. Get out now. Just get out."

"Upstairs bedroom has some nice carpet in it. Almost as good as a bed."

Then she astonished herself by kicking him in the nuts. Hard. A direct hit. His mouth formed into an O shape, his eyes got big, he stuck his arms down between his thighs, sank to the living room floor, and lay down on his side, sucking in quick, short breaths through his puckered lips.

She went right out to her car, rolled up the windows, locked the doors, and started the engine.

After a few minutes, Strang came out, walking in little tiny baby steps, climbed gingerly into his van, and after sitting there in the front seat for a few ominous minutes, backed out of the driveway and went away.

Later they found out that he had forged Eleanor's signature on the work order form. She didn't care.

*The next time* Eleanor saw Erwin Dudley Strang, he was on television, his name was Earl Strong, and his complexion was frighteningly, unnaturally smooth, as if he had been lovingly spackled, buffed, and polished. The white skin of his cheeks was luminous under the lights of the television studio, and almost fuzzy, like an off-focus beauty shot of an aging movie star. As if the camera could not find any feature or blemish to focus on.

She saw his face on the local public-access cable TV channel one night when she was flipping through the channels after Harmon and the children had gone to bed. It went without saying that the cable had never worked perfectly ever since Strang installed it. It was always a little snowy, with a bit of fuzz in the audio, and whenever the wind blew, the picture started to jump. But putting up with bad television was preferable to phoning the cable TV company and having them send *him* back to fix it.

It was creepy and ironic to be flipping through the channels, cursing the bad reception, cursing the man who had installed it, and suddenly to have *him* show up on screen, in a full talking head shot, wearing a business suit.

She looked at him for a moment and flipped on to the next channel. She didn't want to see the man. So he was wearing a business suit. He had found some other profession to give a bad name to. She didn't care.

But a few nights later she saw him again, and this time the letters EARL STRONG were superimposed on the bottom of the screen, and finally she had to stop right there and watch.

It was some kind of talk show. Not a slick network production by any means. Just a sheet-metal desk in front of a big piece of blue paper with a Goodwill sofa next to it where the guests sat.

But Earl Strong/Erwin Dudley Strang wasn't sitting on the sofa. He was sitting behind the desk, in a cheap folding sheet-metal chair that creaked whenever he shifted his weight. He was the host.

Eleanor had to go and dig up the little channel guide, the little slip of cardboard that Strang had given her years ago, to find out what channel she was watching. It said CH. 29—PUBLIC ACCESS CABLEVISION.

Earl Strong was talking politics with an assortment of off-brand philosophers who drifted across his little stage, seemingly following their own cues. The camera angle never varied. Clearly there was only one camera taping this thing, and it was sitting on a tripod, running on autopilot. It was comically inept, just the kind of thing that he would throw together.

The title of tonight's broadcast was "The Three-Fifths Compromise: Error or Inspiration?" Eleanor could only listen to about thirty seconds of it before she was overcome by an odd combination of boredom and fury.

The name of the show was *Coming on Strong*. Earl Strong kept coming on, week after week, year after year. It seemed that every time she happened to flip past his little program, he looked a little different: he did something about those crooked teeth. Got his chin lengthened. Fixed the nose. Bought a narrower and more conservative set of neckties. Played endlessly with his hairstyle until he found one—close-cropped but carefully sculpted—that worked. Bought himself a chair that did not creak. Moved to a better studio, got a two-camera setup, then a three-camera setup. Got commercial sponsorship from Ty (Buckaroo) Steele, a prominent local purveyor of cut-rate used cars, and made the jump from public-access cable to one of the local commercial stations.

And at each step of the process, Eleanor laughed and shook her head, remembering him curled up on the floor in her living room, sucking in short little breaths, and she wondered how long it would take for this man to be found out for the shabby little fraud he really was. Each time he attained a little more success, Eleanor was shocked for a moment, even a little frightened. Then she calmed herself down by reminding herself that the higher he got, the harder he would fall in the end.

Surely someone would take it upon themselves to expose this man.

But no one ever did.

And then, all of a sudden, Earl Strong was running for the United States Senate, he was ahead in the polls, and everyone loved him.

## CHAPTER NINETEEN

A white limousine pulled into the parking lot of the mall, swung past the line of waiting buses, and came to a stop in front of the main entrance. This limousine was far from elegant; it was a rolling billboard for Ty (Buckaroo) Steele's Pre-Owned and Remanufactured Vehicles Inc. The only time it ever came out of the garage was during parades, when Buckaroo himself would drive it down the street with some local beauty queen popping out of the sunroof to wave at the crowd and pelt the young 'uns with hard candy.

But Buckaroo had now found another way to use it. The doors opened up and several men in dark suits climbed out and walked, in a cluster, toward the entrance of the mall. In the middle of the group she could clearly make out the pre-owned and remanufactured face of Earl Strong, who in these parts was invariably described as "the next Senator from Colorado."

A few moments after he went into the mall, a big cheer rose up from inside. They were holding some kind of a campaign event inside there.

She shook her head, staring at a huge COMES ON STRONG poster stuck to the side of a bus directly in front of her.

Her bus wasn't due to leave for half an hour. There was really no reason for her to sit outside on this bench when she could go into the mall and kill time. It was just that she felt so trashy, walking through the nice mall in her clothes, rumpled from having been slept in, and her rumpled hair, carrying big hunks of generic bulk food that she had gotten for free.

Right next to her was a big pseudoadobe litter basket, nearly overflowing, and resting on the top layer, neatly folded and put away, was a thick glossy shopping bag from Nordstrom.

Eleanor pulled the bag out and unfolded it. It was clean and new.

She put her cheese and oatmeal inside the Nordstrom bag, got up, and walked toward the entrance of the shopping mall. She wanted to see what Erwin Dudley Strang was up to.

As she was approaching the entrance, she saw her reflection in the glass doors. She had thought it was a clever trick, hiding her welfare cheese in the Nordstrom bag, but when she saw herself, she recognized something about her silhouette, a shape she'd seen in many cities, on many park benches, and a realization came to her.

She had become a bag lady.

It was a spear through her heart. She lost her stride and stumbled to a complete halt. Tears flooded her eyes uncontrollably and her nose began to run. She sniffled, blinked, swallowed, and fought it back.

The Earl Strong supporters were veering around her, turning back to look at her face. She couldn't just stand there. She picked up her pace and punched through the glass doors and in so doing, transformed herself from a bag lady into a shopper.

In the central part of the mall, Earl Strong was standing up on a raised podium, coming on strong.

"Thank you all for coming today. I wanted to do this in January, but the mall wouldn't let me have the space because they said it was Martin Luther King, Jr., Day. And I said that I certainly wouldn't want to have my name associated with a man who plagiarized his dissertation and shacked up with women he wasn't married to."

Nervous but exultant laughter ran through the crowd: a lot of heavy middle-aged white men raising their eyebrows at each other to see if they dared laugh at Martin Luther King. They did.

"Then I wanted to do it in February, but they said it was President's Day. And I said that I liked the sound of that, but that I was only running for the Senate, and the presidency would have to wait for a few more years."

That line brought a round of applause and a slowly gathering chant of "Run! Run! Run!" from the crowd. Earl Strong, obviously pleased, let the chant build for a few seconds, long enough to be picked up by the TV cameras, then made a big show of quieting it down by waving his hands over the crowd.

"That left March or April. But in April, we've got Easter, when Christ rose from the dead, and that one is a little out of my scope. So I settled on March. March is a plain and simple month, raw and honest, not tricked up with any fancy holidays, and I decided that suited my style best. And another thing about the month of March: it comes on strong!"

That cued an outburst of cheering and chanting that went on for several minutes.

Below, Eleanor wandered through the crowd with her shopping bag, watching the Strong supporters cheering and jumping up and down and pumping their fists in the air. She was totally invisible. They had eyes only for Strong. The few who did notice her, got the same shocked look that Erwin Dudley Strang had gotten years ago when he had first seen a black woman standing in the doorway of a suburban house. Then they looked away. Guiltily.

People were so easy to understand, when you were a mom. Eleanor could see their guilt a mile away, see them trying to delude themselves, like kids who believed that they could make unpleasant things go away just by wishing.

The only thing they needed, she realized, was a good talking-to. Which was one thing that Earl Strong could never give them.

Eventually the cheering died away and Earl Strong stopped shaking his clasped hands over his head and returned to the podium, shot his cuffs, adjusted his collar just a bit. Eleanor had wandered rather close to him, was now looking up at him from just a few feet away. His face was thickly plastered with television makeup. In his perfect, stiff suit and his injection-molded haircut and his heavy pancake, he looked like a cardboard cutout.

"Now you might ask why I went to so much trouble, and waited so long, for the opportunity to speak here at the Boulevard Mall. After all, there are better places to hold a campaign event. But this mall has something that none of those places can provide. As I stand here in the crossroads of this beautiful mall I can look in all directions and see economic prosperity at work."

Applause.

"I don't see people standing in line for a handout. I don't see people going to court and suing other people for what they think the world owes them. I don't see people breaking into other people's homes and stealing things. I see people working hard in honest businesses, small businesses, and to me that is what makes America the greatest nation on earth."

Applause.

"And I have particular respect for the small businessmen, and women—let's not forget the women's libbers!—" laughter "—who built these businesses, because for a number of years, I was a small businessman myself, owning and operating my own enterprise as an independent contractor."

Eleanor could not restrain herself; standing now at the base of the podium, she spoke up. "Excuse me! Excuse me?"

Earl Strong looked down at her with a fixed, glazed smile. He noticed that she was black. Once again, he got that look on his face.

But he was older and, if not wiser, then smarter. He didn't let it throw him off. She could see the wheels turning beneath his artificial face. She could see him having an inspiration, making a quick command decision.

"I don't usually take questions from the audience at this point in the speech," he said, "but some people have been saying that I only appeal to one kind of person, and I'm glad to see that a racially diverse group is here today, and I see that one of them has a comment she wants to make, and I'm very interested in hearing what she has to say. Ma'am?"

Television sound men brandished their boom microphones like fishermen on a dock waving grotesque, furry lures, competing for the attention of the only fish in the pond.

"You were saying that you were a businessman," she said, and suddenly her voice was very loud through the amplifiers, and she realized that she didn't have to shout anymore.

"That I was," Strong said. But his voice didn't come through; Eleanor had the microphones.

"You were a cable TV installer," she said, in a normal tone of voice. She sounded good. Everyone had always said she had a good telephone voice.

"Yes, ma'am, that I was," Strong said, shouting toward the microphones now, his voice high and strained.

"Well, a cable TV installer isn't so much a businessman as he is a burglar with pretensions."

Most of the crowd gasped. But a lot of them actually laughed. Not the deep forced belly laughter with which they had responded to Earl Strong's canned jokes. It was nervous tittering, choked off in the middle, just this side of hysteria.

Earl Strong was cool. He was good. The smile on his face barely wavered. He was silent and calculating for a few moments, waiting for the laughter to die away, searching her up and down with his eyes.

"Well," he said, "I must say that's quite a disrespectful attitude for a woman who's carrying a big piece of cheese in her bag that was paid for by my tax dollars."

A smattering of belly laughs, and sparse applause. Most of the people were silent, nervously realizing that Earl Strong was verging on dangerous territory. And in the near vicinity of Eleanor, there was violent convection in the crowd. Die-hard Earl Strong supporters were stepping away from her as if she were going to give them AIDS, and minicam crews and news photographers were converging on her as if she were going to make them famous.

"Well," Eleanor said, "I would say that even showing yourself in public is pretty cheeky when you are nothing more than a pencil-neck Hitler wannabe with a face from Wal-Mart."

This time, there was utter silence, except for a few sharp intakes of breath.

Earl Strong had gone bright red under his pancake makeup.

"Besides," she added, "this cheese didn't come from your tax dollars. It was bought by churchgoers who give money to support a public food bank. Have you ever been to church, Mr. Strong? Before you started running for something, that is."

"I am a conservative Christian," he said. "I have no qualms about saying so."

"You have no qualms about saying anything that'll get you elected."

Another nervous titter from the crowd. But farther away, around the fringes, a cheer went up; passing shoppers had gathered, attracted by the noise, and now they were cheering her on.

"I saw you show up just now in that tacky limousine. Most of the people who ride around in that thing are used-car salesmen or silicone beauty queens. Which one are you?" she said.

"I resent the implication that there's something wrong with the used-car trade."

"It's not exactly a character reference for you, Erwin Dudley Strang or whatever your name is."

"My name is Earl Strong. And it's an *honest* business like any other."

"Oooh, Erwin Dudley Strang is giving me a lecture about how to be honest," Eleanor said. "I know you think all black people are dishonest. Well, the only dishonest thing I've ever done is tell myself I had a chance to make it in a white society."

"There we have it," Strong said, addressing the crowd again. "The defeatist attitude that is bringing our economy down and brainwashing many minority people into thinking that they have to have affirmative action programs in order to succeed. This is a classic example of the attitude problem that prevents black people from succeeding, even where no real impediments exist."

"I don't have a car," Eleanor said. "That's a real impediment. I don't have a job. My husband's dead. How many more impediments do I need?"

"None whatsoever," Strong said. "That's plenty. Why don't you just shut up now."

"I won't shut up because I'm hurting you on television, and you don't have the brains or the balls to stop me."

A big *whooo!* went up from the shoppers.

Strong laughed. "Lady, I represent a political ground swell in this country that is more powerful than you can imagine. And there is nothing you can do, on or off television, to hurt me. All you do is annoy me."

"I know that's what you think. Ever since you took that belt sander to your face you think you're the second coming of Ronald Reagan. You think you're made of teflon. Well, it takes more than a simple mind and a synthetic smile to be Ronald Reagan. You also have to be likable. And you aren't any more likable than you were when you showed up at my door at 4:54 P.M. and installed my cable like some kind of a trained monkey."

"Oh, so that's it," he said. "This is some kind of a vendetta." Strong looked up at the crowd, turning his face up into the light again. "This woman is upset because she gets static on her daytime soap operas."

"No," Eleanor said, turning around to face the crowd, "I'm upset because my son just got shot in the back for using a pay phone. And Earl Strong, this juvenile delinquent with a fifty-dollar haircut, is standing up tall and pretty telling me it's all because I don't have values. Well, I may be sleeping in a car and eating government surplus cheese but at least I haven't sunk low enough to become a politician who feeds happy lies to starving children."

"I am exactly the opposite of the kind of politician you think I am," Earl Strong said, "I am a man of the people. A populist."

"A populist? To you, a populist is someone who's popular . . . to you, a homecoming queen is a populist. To me, a populist is someone who serves the needs of the populace. And the only thing you've ever done for the populace is show up late, drill holes in their houses, and hand them a big fat bill. Which is exactly what I predict you'll do for us in the Senate."

A high, enthusiastic screeching arose from the predominantly female shoppers gathered around the edge, whose numbers had now swelled to exceed the Strong supporters. They rattled their shopping bags, waved their fists in the air, and stomped the floor with their stylish pumps.

## CHAPTER TWENTY

There were lots of empty offices on the upper floors of Cy Ogle's old Cadillac dealership. When the PIPER project got underway, Aaron requested some space for the West Coast headquarters of Green Biophysical Associates. Ogle just shrugged and told him to go upstairs and stake a claim. Aaron picked out an office on the third floor. As far as he could tell, he was the only other person in the whole building, which was kind of surprising in an election year.

But he was hardly the first. The building had the eroded, overused character of a subway station, with depressions worn into the thresholds and steps. Every time Aaron stepped through a doorway, through the sole of his tennis shoe he felt a gentle concavity in the floor, burnished down through several stacked layers of linoleum that left concentric ovals that looked like lines on a topographic map.

The offices were furnished with old steel desks and chairs done up in the colorless hues and unconvincing wood grain reserved for office furniture, but the walls were virtually papered with brightly colored bumper stickers and posters. Giant multiline telephone cables hung from rude holes in the plaster. Ogle was just in the process of computerizing his whole operation, buying big high-powered Calyx workstations from Pacific Netware, and those unsightly holes in the plaster made installation a snap. The vendor would haul the boxes into an office, uncrate the computers, and feed cables into the holes. They would emerge from ragged holes in other offices and plug into other workstations.

Aaron could only identify about 10 percent of the candidates hyped on the bumper stickers and posters that covered the walls, ceilings, doors, and even toilets. Most of them seemed to be for senatorial and gubernatorial races in states he wasn't familiar with. Many seemed to be from other countries. There were a few in Cyrillic and other alphabets that Aaron couldn't even recognize, much less read.

Aaron's life in the PIPER project was hectic but comfortable. He had discarded all pretense of being a serious businessman and gone back to basic R&D, and he was surprised to find how much happier he was. This was his natural way of life. He would meet with the Pacific Netware people, either here in Oakland or in Marin County, and identify a set of problems to work on. He would fly to Boston and solve those problems with his partners, then fly back here and repeat the cycle. He left his nice suit in Boston on his first trip and then returned to Oakland on the red-eye, checking a duffel bag stuffed with T-shirts and flannel shirts. He slept on the floor of the new office in Oakland, ate pizza, and was happy.

On many occasions he ran into people in the empty hallways or the empty stairwells, carrying sheafs of paper or videotapes from one bleak, empty office to another. So far he had not seen anyone twice. He did not know anyone well enough to say hello to them. A lot of people worked for Ogle, it seemed, but they didn't stay in one place for very long. So he was a little startled one evening when Ogle abruptly stuck his head into the doorway and said, "You want to see a hell of a thing?"

"What is it?" Aaron said.

"The first female president of the United States," Ogle said.

"I didn't realize they had held an election."

"Mark my words. I will lay money on it," Ogle said. "C'mon."

Aaron got up and followed Ogle down the stairs. He needed to stretch his legs anyway.

Ogle had a video editing studio set up on the first floor, back behind the "Oval Office" and all the other sets. Half a dozen small but good color monitors were mounted on racks, each hooked up to a different videotape machine, and all the machines were hooked up to each other, and to a Calyx workstation, with an incomprehensible web of thick black cables.

Two men and a woman were in the room, draped over the furniture in poses that suggested they had been there for quite a while. Aaron had seen a couple of them, here and there, around the building from time to time.

Ogle was a goofball. He was loose enough to seem positively loopy to most people. He spent a lot of time staring off into space with his rosebud mouth twisted in kind of an incredulous, sneering grin. But he was also a southerner and could suddenly turn on full charm-school etiquette when it was the appropriate thing to do. So as he led Aaron into the room, he pirouetted and held one hand out to gesture at these three people and properly introduce them.

"This is Aaron Green of Green Biophysical Systems, our head genius on PIPER," he said. "Aaron, I would like you to meet Tricia Gordon, who is the most talented time buyer on earth; she did the buying on the big Coke campaign last year."

Aaron did not have the slightest idea what Ogle was talking about. He smiled at Tricia Gordon, she held out her hand, he shook it. She was wearing a relatively formal blue knit dress, largish abstract jewelry, and had red hair that was done up in a fairly ambitious style. She was confident and pleasant.

"And this is Shane Schram, a clinical psychologist from Duke by way of Harvard. He does our FGIs, and can he ever dig down beneath the surface on an FGI!"

Aaron still had no idea what was happening. He shook the hand of Shane Schram, who did not stand up or say anything, just dropped the chopsticks he was using to eat with and held his hand up in the air for Aaron to shake. He was broad-shouldered, prematurely bald, rumpled, and smart.

Ogle was still laughing at Shane Schram. "When our FGI people come out of the room, they feel like they've been on the rack. Shane is the Savonarola of focus groups."

"I see, that's great," Aaron mumbled.

"And this is my old pal Myron Morris, who once said that the single most important political development of the last quarter century was the zoom lens. Myron's a filmmaker, in case you hadn't guessed. He did those cinema verité flood-damage spots for Representative Dixon down in Texas."

Aaron shook the hand of Myron Morris, who was a wide-faced, jolly but cynical type in his early fifties, wearing bits and pieces of a fairly nice suit.

"I just caught this off CNN," Ogle said, waggling a thick, three-quarter-inch video cassette in the air, "and I thought y'all might like to see it."

"Was this on Prime News?" Tricia Gordon said.

"It was indeed," Ogle said, shoving the cassette into a big professional videotape recorder. The VTR clunked loudly, like a big truck shifting into gear, and an image materialized on the screen above it.

The anchorman was introducing a segment; over his shoulder was a small head shot of Earl Strong, the scary populist who had been making waves in Colorado. Aaron couldn't hear much, because the sound was turned down. They cut to a shot of a shopping mall with the words DENVER, COLORADO supered across the bottom.

Everyone except Aaron laughed.

"Original choice of venue," Myron Morris said, apparently being facetious.

Reverse angle: as seen from near the entrance to the mall, a white limousine pulled up, festooned with flags and slogans, and a number of people climbed out, including Earl Strong.

"Jesus, what a putz," Myron Morris said. "It's deserted. What a waste."

Ogle must have noticed that Aaron looked confused. "They probably have a million supporters inside the mall, but none positioned outside to greet him. So he looks like a nobody," Ogle explained.

"They should have pulled a bus or something up as a backdrop. Something. Anything," Morris said.

"See, the parking lot behind is full of glare," Ogle explained. "Reflections of windshields and so on. But the entrance to the mall is in shade. So we can't see the guy's face at all—"

"Now watch! He's just going to disappear here," Morris said.

On the TV, Earl Strong crossed into the shadow of the mall and became a featureless silhouette. The camera zoomed in on his face, trying to compensate for the high contrast between the glare out in the parking lot and the dim light on Strong's face, but it looked terrible either way.

"He tried," Ogle said.

"Who tried?" Aaron said.

"The cameraman," Morris snapped.

On the TV, Earl Strong approached the doors of the mall and then there was another cut. Aaron still couldn't hear anything, but it sounded like a reporter was delivering a voice-over during all of this.

"Master race in skimmers," Morris said.

As if on cue, the screen was filled with a couple of big fat middle-aged white ladies in COMES ON STRONG T-shirts and EARL STRONG skimmers, clapping their hands to the beat of a campaign song.

"Good rhythm for Aryans," Shane Schram said.

"UFOs Ate My Brain," Tricia Gordon said.

"Now we'll go to some stumpage," Morris said.

Again, perfectly on cue, Earl Strong appeared on screen, delivering some prepared remarks.

"Have you seen this footage before?" Aaron asked Morris.

"Get out of here," Morris said.

"Nice lighting, huh?" Tricia Gordon said.

"I love it," Morris said.

Earl Strong was standing on a platform. The camera shooting this footage was down below him, aimed upward so that, as backdrop, Earl Strong had mostly the ceiling of the mall. But part of the ceiling consisted of skylights, and where it didn't have skylights, it had brilliant mercury-vapor lamps. The skylights made great patches of glare and the lamps made long wavy streaks across Earl Strong's face.

"Jesus. Television cameras should be outlawed in the Sun Belt," Morris said. "Film only. How many times do I have to say it?"

Everyone in the room was laughing at Morris. But Morris had eyes only for the TV set. "Whoa! Whoa! Hold up here! We have some real-life campaign drama!"

Everyone was suddenly totally silent, crowding in closer to the screen.

The camera was now aimed at a black woman who was apparently standing down below Earl Strong. She was slender, with high cheekbones, and at first glance she looked as if she might be in her late twenties. But on second thought, early forties was more like it.

For a woman in her early forties she was a knockout. Not in an overtly sexy way. She had a nice face, with big eyes. She was wearing an overcoat that was too big, but its bulk contrasted well with her relatively sharp and slender build, and its navy-blue color suited her skin tones. Her backdrop was a wall of Earl Strong supporters wearing colorful T-shirts, all of whom were hastily backing away from her; she stood in the center of an arena of fat, vivid Aryans, all facing inward, emphasizing her importance. As she spoke, she inclined her face up into the even, omnidirectional light streaming down from above; the same light that cast Earl Strong into shadow served as perfect illumination for her.

"The choreography blows my mind," Ogle said.

"I love her," Tricia Gordon said. "And she lights well."

"She's telling the truth," Schram said. "Whatever she's saying, I believe her."

"The drama of this thing is unreal," Myron Morris said. "One woman standing alone, all these trailer-park Nazis shrinking away like rats."

Cut back to Earl Strong, now looking straight down at her so that his face was completely obscured by a sinister shadow.

Myron Morris suddenly went nuts! He fell out of his chair, dropping to his knees below the television set, and clasped his hands together as if in prayer.

"Zoom in! Zoom in! Zoom in and his career is over!" he screamed.

The camera began to zoom. Earl Strong's face grew to fill the screen, grew into a devastating extreme closeup.

"Yes! Yes! Yesss!" Morris was screaming. "Slit the bastard's throat!"

Once the backlighting had been removed by zooming in tight, the camera's electronics were able to pick up every nuance of Earl Strong's face in clinical detail. A storm front of perspiration had burst through the powder and pancake on his forehead; individual drops of it began to run down. One of them made a beeline for the corner of his eye and that eye began to blink spastically. Earl Strong's mouth was half open and his tongue had come forward, sticking half out of his mouth as he tried to think of what to do next. A huge Caucasian blur burst up through the bottom of the frame: his hand, brushing the sweat away from his stricken eyeball, stopping on the way down to shove one thumb into a nostril and pick out something that had been troubling him there.

Morris suddenly jumped to his feet and thrust an accusing finger directly into Earl Strong's face on the screen. "Yes! You are dead! You are dead! You are dead! You are dead and buried, you inbred booger picking little shit! We gotta find the cameraman who did that and give him a medal."

"And a decent job," Ogle said.

Back to the black woman, still standing there. Her face was alert, her jaw set, her eyes burning, but she remained solid and still, a perfect subject for the camera. The camera zoomed in a little closer but still found no imperfections. There were a few wrinkles around the eyes. It just made her look even wiser than she already did, standing next to Earl Strong.

"Ronald Reagan eat your fucking heart out," Shane Schram said.

"There's something about her face, too," Ogle said.

"She's been through some heavy shit, you can tell. An American Pietá," Tricia Gordon said.

"Let's go down there and represent her," Shane Schram said.

"What's she running for?" Morris said.

"Nothing. She's a bag lady," Ogle said.

A look of ecstatic fulfillment came over Morris's face.

"No!" he said.

"Yes," Ogle said.

"It can't be. It's too perfect," Morris said. "It is just too fucking ideal."

"She's a bag lady, and according to our polls, she knocked twenty-five points off of Earl Strong's standings today."

Morris threw up his hands. "I quit," he said. "There's no need for me. Real life is too good."

"We have to run her for something," Tricia Gordon said, staring fixedly at the TV screen.

"Excuse me," Aaron said, "but aren't you all forgetting something?"

"What's that?" Ogle said. They were all staring at him, suddenly quiet.

"We haven't heard a word the woman's said," Aaron said. "I mean, she could be a raving lunatic."

They all burst into dismissive scoffing noises. "Screw that," Shane Schram said. "Look at her face. She's solid."

"Fuck that shit," Morris said. "That's what writers are for."

## CHAPTER TWENTY-ONE

Mary Catherine was expecting a car, not a limousine, so she didn't know that the shiny black behemoth was hers until the driver got out, walked around, and opened the door for her. By that time, the sight of the limousine was already drawing a crowd; not many of these showed up in this particular neighborhood of Chicago.

Her lunch date had told her that he would send a car around to pick her up at the hospital. Instead, he had dispatched a limousine. Which didn't make a lot of difference to Mary Catherine. Both of them were just vehicles to her, just ways of getting around town. She had been around enough not to be bowled over by the gesture. It was just another exercise in being William Cozzano's daughter and trying to keep things in perspective.

The limousine had a TV and a little bar inside of it. The driver offered to give her a hand mixing a drink. She laughed and shook her head no. She was going to have to come back from this lunch and keep working.

She knew that there was a certain kind of person—a certain kind of *man*, to be specific—for whom the back of this limousine was like a natural habitat, who felt as comfortable sitting on those leather seats and drinking Chivas in the middle of the day as Mary Catherine felt behind the wheel of her beat-up old car. During the time that Dad had been Governor, she had run into a lot of those people, gotten to know their peculiar rhythms and their particular view of life. They had always seemed completely alien to her, like cosmonauts or Eskimos.

Then Dad had proclaimed her the quarterback. As if her regular job wasn't enough responsibility. Now, she had to dash out of the neurology ward, filled with gunshot-paralyzed drug dealers and demented AIDS patients, and dash down the stairs and jump into the back of a limousine where the decisions were all different: what kind of drink to mix, what channel to view on the TV.

She had club soda and watched CNN, which was what the TV set was already showing when she climbed in. The timing was fortuitous: it was high noon, the beginning of a fresh news broadcast. The Illinois primary was tomorrow. The elections were still very much up in the air, not much else was happening in the world, and so the campaign was being covered pretty heavily.

The out-of-power party had their front-runner (Norman Fowler, Jr.), their runner-up (Nimrod T. ["Tip"] McLane), and their plucky underdog (the Reverend Doctor Billy Joe Sweigel). And just to make things interesting, they also had a popular favorite: Governor William A. Cozzano, who wasn't even running. But wildcat Cozzano petition drives were popping up all over the place and so the media had to treat him as a serious candidate.

All three of the legitimate candidates got roughly the same sort of coverage: shots of the great man flying or driving into a prefabricated campaign event, a rally at a high school or whatever. They shook hands, they smiled, and they all did something just a little bit wacky, hoping that it would gain them just a little more recognition among TV viewers.

Mary Catherine was tired and stressed and she quickly zoned out, found herself watching all of this stuff without really processing it. She had slumped way down in the soft leather seat of the limo, displaying posture that would have driven her late mother to hysterics, and was gazing through heavy lids at the colorful images on the screen, letting them pass directly into her brain without hindrance. Which was exactly the way you were supposed to watch TV.

As if on cue, there was her father.

CNN was showing her a wall of glass windows. The camera was aimed upward at the outside of a building. Ceiling lights could be seen in a few rooms, and many of the windows were festooned with mylar balloons, flowers, and children's artwork. Mary Catherine saw an IV bottle hanging from a rack and realized that she was looking at a hospital. The camera zoomed in on a particular window with lots of expensive flower arrangements. A man in a wheelchair was dimly visible peeking out between the bouquets.

Then it all snapped into place. This was Burke Hospital in Champaign, and they were zooming in on her father's private room. The TV crew must have gone to the roof of the parking ramp directly across the street, five stories high, and aimed the camera up and across to his window.

Dad was nothing more than a silhouette. The windows were all metallic and reflective; you could only see into them when it was dark outside. But sometimes when the sky was profoundly overcast in the middle of the day, it was possible to look in those windows and see dim shapes underneath the silvery reflections. And that was what some enterprising cameraman had captured on videotape: Dad, sitting in a wheelchair, looking out his window.

The image was gray and indistinct and so you couldn't tell that Dad was, in fact, strapped into the wheelchair to keep him from slumping over. He had been turned squarely toward the window and so you couldn't see the support that rose up behind his head to keep it from flopping around. He was lit from behind so you couldn't see the drool coming out of his mouth and the moronic expressions on his paralyzed face.

A couple of standing silhouettes were visible behind him: a nurse and a slender young man. James. James pushed the wheelchair closer to the window so that Dad could see out. Then he left Dad alone there and disappeared from the frame. The camera panned 180 degrees.

The parking ramp covered about half a square block. Parking was not hard to find in the area, so few cars ever made it all the way up to the rooftop level. Right now, half a dozen vehicles were scattered around. Most of the remainder of the roof was covered with people.

Hundreds of them. They were carrying signs and banners. They were all looking straight up in the air. Straight up toward Dad. And now that he had appeared in the window, they were all rising to their feet, reaching into the air, shoving their signs and banners up into space as if Dad could reach down and pluck them out of their hands. But it was a strangely silent demonstration.

Of course it was—they were in front of a hospital. They had to be quiet.

The camera zoomed in on a long, crudely fashioned banner, like the ones that fans hold up at football games: WE LOVE YOU WILLY! Others could be seen in the background: FIRST AND TEN FOR COZZANO! GET WELL SOON—THEN GET ELECTED!

There were a couple of shots of other hospital patients, in their flannel jammies and their walkers, looking out windows and pointing. Then back to the shot of Dad's silhouette, just visible from the chest up, in front of his window.

He waved out the window.

Which wasn't possible. Most of his body was paralyzed after the second stroke. But he was doing it. He was waving vigorously to the crowd.

Something looked funny: his hand and arm weren't big enough.

It was James. He must be down on his knees next to Dad, concealed behind the windowsill, holding up his hand and waving for him.

Cut back to the crowd, waving their banners hysterically, going nuts.

Cut back to the window. James was still waving, pretending to be Dad. Then his hand stopped waving and became a fist. Two fingers extended from the fist in a V sign.

Mary Catherine shot upright and spilled her club soda on the limousine's wool carpet. "You bastard," she said.

Back to the crowd. Finally they lost it, forgot they were in front of a hospital, started screaming and cheering. Hospital security cops jumped forward, waving their arms, telling them to keep it down. And then they cut back to network headquarters, where all of this was being watched by their afternoon anchorman. Pete Ledger. Former pro football player, turned sportscaster, turned newscaster. A well-respected, middle-aged black guy with a sharp, fast tongue who'd probably end up having his own talk show one of these days.

His eyes were red. He reached up with one hand just for an instant and wiped his runny nose with the back of one finger, sniffled audibly, took a big deep breath, forced himself to smile into the camera, and announced, in a cracking voice, that they were going to break for a commercial.

"My god," Mary Catherine said out loud to no one. "We're in deep shit."

She flinched as the door of the limousine came open, letting in bright unfiltered light. The car had stopped.

She'd lost track, but something about the light told her they were near downtown, hemmed in by skyscrapers. They were in a crowded little side street, just south and west of the Board of Trade, stopped in front of a brownstone with a first-floor restaurant. An awning extended from the front door, across the sidewalk, to a loading zone along the curb. A uniformed doorman had opened the door for her.

He reached in with one hand and helped her out, which was a nice, if superfluous, gesture. He was an older guy, a kindly white-haired doorman type, and as he was helping her out onto the sidewalk, he gave her hand an extra squeeze, nodded at her, looking at her in a way that was almost worshipful.

There was another man, a guy in a plain old dark suit, standing under the awning waiting for her. Dad had once told her that you could gauge the quality of a restaurant according to how many people you spoke to before you actually got around to ordering food. She wasn't even into the door of this place yet and she had already encountered two people.

"Howdy, Miz Cozzano," the man said, "I'm Cy Ogle."

"Oh, hello," she said, shaking his hand. "Did you just get here?"

"Nah, I nailed down a table for us," he said. "But I figured that since I drug you out of work like this on such an ugly day, least I could do was come out and say hi."

"Well, that's very nice," she said noncommitally.

So far, he didn't seem like the cynical, media-manipulating son of a bitch that he was supposed to be. But it was way, way too early to be jumping to conclusions.

Another guy in a suit, who clearly *did* work here, nearly killed himself bursting out the front door of the place, and met her half-way up the sidewalk, holding out one hand, bending his knees as he approached so that by the time he reached Mary Catherine he was practically duck-walking. Mary Catherine could see in his whole face and affect that he was Italian.

He was crying, for god's sake. He pumped her hand and grabbed her upper arm with his left, as if only all the willpower in his body prevented him from violently embracing her. He said nothing but merely shook his head. He was so overcome with emotion that he couldn't speak.

"We were just watching CNN over the bar," Ogle explained. "It was incredible."

Some kind of a huge commotion was going on inside the place. It got louder as Mary Catherine moved toward the door, led by the crying Italian and followed by Ogle, and as she crossed the threshold, it exploded.

The back of the restaurant was all quiet little tables, but the front of the place was a sizable bar, currently packed with bodies. They were all men in suits. This was an expensive place where people in the commodities business, and the lawyers and bankers who fed off them, gathered to fortify themselves with martinis and five-dollar mineral water.

And right now they were all on their feet, howling, applauding, stamping their feet, whistling, as if the Bears had just run back an interception for a touchdown. They were going nuts.

And they were all looking at Mary Catherine.

She came to a dead stop, shocked and intimidated by the noise. Ogle nearly rear-ended her. He put one hand lightly on top of her shoulder and bent toward her. "Pretend they don't exist," Ogle said, not shouting but projecting a deep actor's voice that cut through the noise. "You're the Queen of England and they're drunks in the gutter."

Mary Catherine stopped looking at them. She stopped making eye contact with any of them. She focused on the back of the maître d', who was plunging through the crowd of pinstripes, making an avenue for her, and she followed him straight through the thick of it and into the restaurant proper. The people at the bar were chanting now: COZZANO! COZZANO! COZZANO!

Half of the people dining in the restaurant area stood up as she came through. Nearly all of them applauded. The maître d' led them straight to a table at the very back of the place, behind a partition. At last, they had privacy. Just Mary Catherine and Ogle.

"I'm really, really sorry about that," Ogle said, after they had been seated, menued, watered, and breadsticked by a swirl of efficient, white-aproned young Italian men. "I should have arranged to bring you in the rear entrance."

"It's okay," she said.

"Well, I'm embarrassed," Ogle said. "This is my business, you see. It was unprofessional on my part. But they had CNN going above the bar, and I didn't reckon on that footage being shown just before you got here."

"Powerful stuff," she said.

"It was unbelievable," Ogle said. He stared off into space. His face went slack and his eyes went out of focus. He sat motionless for a few seconds, moving his lips ever so slightly, gradually beginning to shake his head from side to side, playing the whole thing back on the videotape recorder of his mind.

Finally he blinked, came awake, and looked at her. "The kicker was Pete Ledger getting choked up. I never thought I'd see that in a million years."

"Me neither," she said. "He's usually too smart for that kind of thing."

"Well," Ogle said, "this is some powerful stuff that's going on right now."

That led them into small talk about the primary campaign, the misguided petition drives that were trying to put her father's name on the ballots in several states, and eventually into a discussion of Dad's stroke and its aftermath. Mary Catherine kept the whole thing quite vague, and Ogle seemed content with that; whenever the conversation wandered close to Dad's medical condition, or his political prospects, his face reddened slightly and he grew visibly uncomfortable, as if these topics were way beyond the bounds of southern gentility and he didn't know how to handle it.

She had only rarely gotten a chance to watch Dad doing business. But she knew that this was how Dad operated: lots of small talk. It was an Italian thing. It meshed pretty well with Ogle's low-key southern approach.

In fact, Ogle seemed to have no desire to talk business at all, as if the near riot at the bar had embarrassed him so deeply that he couldn't bring himself to return to that subject. So, after an opportune pause in the conversation, Mary Catherine decided to open fire. "You manage political campaigns for a living. My dad's not running for anything and neither am I. Why are you buying me lunch?"

Ogle folded his hands in his lap, broke eye contact, and glanced around at the food on the table for a few moments, as if this were the first time he'd ever thought about it. "There's a bunch of people in my business. Most of the important ones are busy running primary campaigns, for various candidates, right now. But not me. So far I have not committed my resources to any one candidate."

"Is that a deliberate strategy?"

"Sort of," Ogle said, shrugging. "Sometimes it pays not to commit too early. You may end up backing some loser. In the process, you antagonize the guy who ends up being the nominee, and then you can't get any work during the general election, which is where the big money gets spent."

"So you're holding back until you find out who's likely to get nominated. Then you try to get them as a client."

Ogle frowned and stared at the ceiling as if something was not quite right. "Well, there's more to it. I have been doing this for a number of years now. And frankly, I'm getting tired of it."

"You're getting tired of your business?"

"Certain aspects of it, yeah."

"Which aspects?"

"Dealing with campaigns."

"I don't understand," Mary Catherine said. "I thought you *were* the campaign."

"I would *like* to be the campaign. Instead, I'm the media consultant *to* the campaign."

"Oh."

"The campaign proper consists of the party's national committee and all of its hierarchy; the individual candidate's campaign manager and all of his hierarchy; and all of the pressure groups to which they are beholden, and their hierarchies."

"Sounds like a mess."

"It's a hell of a mess. If I can just make an analogy to your business, Ms. Cozzano, running a campaign is like doing a heart-lung transplant on the body politic. It is a massively difficult and complicated process that requires great precision. It cannot be done by a committee, much less by a committee of committees, most of whom hate and fear each other. The political nonsense that I have to go through in order to produce a single thirty-second advertising spot makes the succession of the average Byzantine emperor seem simple and elegant by comparison."

"I find that kind of surprising," Mary Catherine said. "People have known about the value of media since the Kennedy-Nixon debate."

"Long before that," Ogle said. "Teddy Roosevelt staged the charge up San Juan Hill so it would look good for the newsreel cameras."

"Really?"

"Absolutely. And FDR manipulated the media like crazy. He was even better at it than Reagan. So media's been important for a long time."

"Well, you'd think that the major political parties would have figured out how to deal with it more efficiently by now."

Ogle shrugged. "Dukakis riding in the tank."

Mary Catherine grinned, remembering the ludicrous image from 1988.

"The Democratic candidates in the '92 debate, sitting in those little desks like game show contestants while Brokaw strode around on his feet, like a hero."

"Yeah, that was pretty silly looking."

"The fact is," Ogle said, "the major parties haven't learned how to handle media yet. And they never will."

"Why not?"

"Because of their constitution. The parties were formed in the days when media didn't matter, and formed wrong. Now they are like big old dinosaurs after the comet struck, thrashing around weakly on the ground. Big and powerful but pathetic and doomed at the same time."

"You think the parties are doomed?"

"Sure they are," Ogle said. "Look at Ross Perot. If Bush's psy-ops people hadn't figured out how to push his buttons and make him act loony, he'd be president now. Your father has everything going for him that Perot did—but none of the negatives."

"You really think so?"

"After the reception you got when you came through that door," Cy Ogle said, nodding toward the entrance, "I'm surprised you would even ask me such a question. Heck, your dad's already on the ballot in Washington state."

She was appalled. "Are you joking?"

"Not at all. That's just about the easiest state to do it in. Only takes a few thousand people."

Mary Catherine didn't answer, just sat there silently, staring across the restaurant. She had been watching this political business for a while, but she still couldn't believe that a few thousand total strangers in Seattle had taken it upon themselves to put her father on the ballot.

"This is kind of interesting, as an abstract discussion," Mary Catherine said. "I mean, I'm enjoying it and I guess I'm learning something. But how it relates to my dad isn't clear to me."

"You're going to be hearing from a certain major political party," Ogle said. "Medical situation permitting, they're going to try to draft your father at the convention."

"And if that happens, you want me to use whatever influence I've got to get them to hire you?"

Ogle shook his head. "They won't hire me. They don't work that way. They always form their own in-house agency so that the political hacks, with all their little ambitions and intrigues, can exert more control over the ad people, whom they see as unprincipled vermin."

"So beyond having interesting conversations, what use are you to me? And what use am I to you?"

Once again, Ogle broke eye contact, put his silverware down, stared off into the distance, thinking.

"Let me just state one ground rule first," he said. "This conversation is not a business thing."

"It's not?"

"Nope. But it's not a social thing either, because we are total strangers."

"So what is it, Mr. Ogle?"

"Two people talking to each other."

"And what exactly are we talking about?"

"Surfing."

"Surfing?"

"Media is like a wave," Ogle said. "It's powerful and uncontrollable. If you're good, you can surf on it for a little bit, get a boost from it. Gary Hart surfed on that wave for a few weeks in 1984, after he won New Hampshire from Mondale. But by the time the Illinois primary came around, he had fallen off the surfboard. The wave broke over him and swamped him. He tried again in 1988 but that time he just plain drowned. Perot rode the wave for a month or two in '92, then he lost his nerve."

Ogle turned in his chair and focused in on Mary Catherine now. "You and your family, you've been having a day at the beach. You've been out wading in the shallow waters where everything is warm and safe. But the currents are tricky and suddenly you find that you have been swept far out into the deep black water by a mysterious undertow. And now, great waves are cresting over your heads. You can get up and ride those waves wherever they take you, or you can pretend it's not happening. You can keep treading water, in which case the tsunami will break on top of you and slam you down onto the bottom."

Mary Catherine just kept her mouth shut and stared into her water glass. She was feeling several powerful emotions at once and she knew that if she opened her mouth she'd probably regret it.

There was fear. Fear because she knew that Ogle was exactly right. Resentment because this total stranger was presuming to give her advice. And there was a frightening sense of exhilaration, wild thrilling danger, almost sexual in its power.

Fear, resentment, and exhilaration. She knew that her brother, James, was experiencing the same feelings. And she knew that he was ignoring the fear, swallowing the resentment, and giving in to the exhilaration. Holding up his hand in the V sign, egging on the crowd. It was unforgivable. A hundred million people were going to see that.

She looked at Ogle. Ogle was looking back at her, a little bit sideways, not wanting to confront her directly.

"There's a third outcome you didn't mention," she said.

"What's that?" Ogle said, startled.

"You start riding the wave because you enjoy the thrill of it. But you don't know what you're doing. And you end up getting slammed into the rocks."

Ogle nodded. "Yes, the world is full of bad surfers."

"My brother, James, is a bad surfer. He's a *really bad surfer*," Mary Catherine said, "but he thinks he's good. And he seems to have located a really big wave."

Ogle nodded.

"Now, I have no idea, still, what it is that you want, or what you are proposing, or what you think you're going to get out of it," Mary Catherine said. "But I can tell you this. James is a problem. My father and our lawyer Mel and I would all agree on that. And without committing myself or my family to anything financial, let me say that if you can provide some advice in dealing with this problem, it would not be forgotten."

*"You did what!?"* Mel said.

She knew he was going to say it. "I asked him for advice," Mary Catherine said. She was in the back of the limousine, riding back to the hospital.

"You shouldn't have done that," Mel said. "You shouldn't even have met with the guy without my being there."

"I was very good. I'm not the sap you think I am, Mel. I didn't make any kind of financial commitment. It was just a couple of people having lunch together, talking. And I asked him for advice."

"About what?"

"About James."

Mel sounded disappointed, wounded. "Mary Catherine. Why would you ask a total stranger for advice in dealing with your own flesh and blood?"

"Because half of my family is dead, or nearly dead, you're away on business, and James is being a complete asshole."

"What do you mean? What's James doing?"

She explained it all to him: the wave, the V sign, the cheers of the crowd, the hysterical reaction of the businessmen inside the bar.

But Mel didn't get it. He listened, he understood, but he hadn't *seen* it. He hadn't seen the emotion on people's faces. He didn't understand the power of what was going on here. To him it was all TV, it was all Smurfs, and he couldn't bring himself to take it seriously. He didn't get it.

She was glad she had talked to Cy Ogle, who definitely did get it.

"What did this guy say?" Mel said.

"His name is Cy Ogle," Mary Catherine said, "and he said that he would think about it."

"What kind of a name is Ogle?"

"That's beside the point. But he said that it was originally Oglethorpe, which is a big name in Georgia. But somewhere along the line someone had a bastard child, who ended up with the name Ogle, and he's descended from that person."

"So he comes from a long line of bastards."

"Mel!"

"Don't Mel me. He charmed you with some kind of southern shit, didn't he? I can smell it from New York. Told you a bunch of wacky tales about his picturesque family down in the land of cotton, seemed like the nicest guy in the world."

"Mel. Be honest. You don't know anything about handling the media. Do you?"

"I happen to know a lot about it."

"Then how did that happen today? That thing with James? If you're so good at handling the media, then why is it that everyone in the country has the impression, today, that Dad is running for president?"

Mel didn't say anything. She knew she had him.

"Because of what happened today, we have to have a media person," Mary Catherine said. "It doesn't have to be Cy Ogle. But depending on what he does with James, it might very well be."

Mel sounded glum. "I hate the media."

"I know you do, Mel," she said. "That's why we're in deep shit now. We need someone who loves the media. And I can tell you that whatever imperfections Cy Ogle might have, he definitely loves his work."

## CHAPTER TWENTY-TWO

William A. Cozzano was a lousy patient. Mary Catherine had never understood this until she became a doctor in her own right, and got into the habit of judging people's ability to receive medical treatment.

Good patients were as close as possible to being laboratory rats. They were meek, docile, cooperative, and not very intelligent. The intelligent ones gave you fits because they were always asking questions. They knew full well that they were as smart as the doctor was. That if they were to go off and enroll in a medical school, they'd know as much as the doctor did within a few years.

Willam A. Cozzano was one of those patients who disputed everything the doctor said. Who forgot to take his medicine— deliberately. Who pushed his recovery schedule into the realm of the absurd. Partly it was a holdover from the war, where you had to keep going even when you were wounded, and partly it came from football, where the standard treatment for broken bones was a layer of athletic tape.

The stroke had been hell for him because it left him unable to argue with his doctors. Mary Catherine had seen it in his face. A doctor would come in and tell him to turn off CNN and get some rest, because he needed sleep. Dad would get a certain look on his face, the look that signaled the beginning of intellectual combat, the look that he got when he was marshaling his arguments and preparing to demolish an opponent. Then he would open his mouth and gibberish would come out. The doctor would turn off the TV, turn off the lights, and leave him there in the dark.

He had been much the same way during his four-day stay at the Radhakrishnan Institute in California. But there it wasn't quite so bad. It was a cross between a research institute and an exclusive private hospital. From the very first contacts the Cozzanos had with the Institute, it was made plain to them that here, the patient wasn't just a laboratory rat. Here, the patient was a partner in his own treatment and recovery. He was consulted on a number of major decisions. He sat in on the meetings where recovery strategy was discussed. These people weren't afraid of intelligent, questioning patients. They welcomed them. They preferred them.

"Neurology is a fascinating science, full of riddles and mysteries," Dr. Radhakrishnan had said during their first meeting, in the conference room on the high bluff over the Pacific Ocean.

Mary Catherine had stifled a smile. Radhakrishnan was a neurosurgeon, and uncharacteristically, he was talking about what a wonderful discipline neurology was. She wondered if it had anything to do with the fact that the patient's daughter was a neurologist.

"In your therapy," Radhakrishnan continued, "we will be exploring realms that have never been entered. We will watch the data streaming out of your biochip like the astronomers viewing the images from the *Voyager* spacecraft on its journey to the outer planets. Every day and every hour, we will see new and unexpected things. Enough new data will be generated to write a thousand articles and a hundred Ph.D. dissertations.

"But the information that we receive from the implanted biochip will be reaching us through a narrow bottleneck. You, the patient, will have access to a far broader spectrum of information and experience. This is why we welcome the opportunity to pursue this therapy with a highly intelligent and perceptive patient. We need your help, Governor Cozzano. We need your partnership in this scientific venture."

Dad hadn't spoken a word, just gazed out the big windows at the pounding surf. But Mary Catherine knew that he was hearing and understanding every word. He knew exactly what was going on. And she knew he was excited about it. Two months of being treated like a child by Patricia had left him ravenous for this kind of thing.

She had gone over every inch of the Radhakrishnan Institute. Reviewed the records of their baboon experiments and of their work on an Indian truck driver named Mohinder Singh, who had been miraculously cured using the same therapy. Viewed many hours of videotapes of Singh, taken before the implant and over the course of his subsequent therapy. The results would have been impressive to anyone; to a professional neurologist, they were uncanny.

She had interviewed Dr. Radhakrishnan and some of his top staff members for hours, asking them a lot of hard questions about what could go wrong with this procedure and what steps they had taken to avoid it. She always got good answers to her questions. Answers that seemed to have been prepared in advance, as though they had anticipated all of her thoughts.

But this was a paranoid attitude. She couldn't find anything wrong. The only bad thing that could be said about the Radhakrishnan Institue was that they had made the transition from baboons to humans rather hastily. They had taken big chances. If it had failed, it would have meant that they were rash and foolish. But it had worked, so they were brilliant and daring.

It would have been better—a lot better—if they could have trotted out a dozen or so Mohinder Singhs, at various stages of recovery. Because this one Punjabi truck driver did not make for a track record. He was not a trend. He might just be a fluke.

But William A. Cozzano had taught his daughter to be scrupulously egalitarian, and so at this point in the argument she always caught herself short. Because it wasn't fair to adopt that attitude. The only way to test this thing was by doing it on humans. Sure it would be nice to see a dozen Mohinder Singhs. It'd be nice for the Cozzanos. But what about the second Singh, and the third? They'd be taking a big chance with not much to go on. And their lives were worth just as much as William Cozzano's.

*It wasn't fair.* That's what Dad would say. It wasn't fair to have other people take all the risk, then reap the benefits after it had become a sure thing.

Besides, this way it was more of an adventure. And she just knew that he'd be thrilled by that idea. Dad was a wild man at heart; he'd always wanted to go out and do crazy things. But his position as the head of the Cozzano clan had forced him to behave conservatively all his life. The stroke had freed him of that oppressive responsibility. He had nothing to lose now.

So she signed the papers. Since the stroke, Mary Catherine had been in charge of her father's body. She sent him into that operating room with many doubts about the operation—but in the full confidence that it was what he wanted.

They shaved his head and rolled him into the operating theater

at 7:45 A.M. on the morning of March 25, a little more than two
months after his initial stroke. Mary Catherine gave him a last kiss
on his burnished scalp before they scrubbed him for surgery. Then
she pulled on a jacket and went for a long walk along the edge of
the bluff, letting the pure Pacific wind blow through her hair. They
had said that she could watch the operation if she wanted, but if it
turned out to be fatal, she didn't want that to be the last memory of
her father.

She found a high rocky outcropping, climbed to the top, and
sat down. Below her, half a mile out to sea, a huge, beautiful ketch
was tacking upwind. Farther out, she could barely make out the
silhouettes of big freighters cruising up and down the California
coast.

God, I need a vacation, she thought. Then she thought: this is it.
This is my vacation. So she enjoyed her vacation for a few minutes.

Then, hearing a noise behind her, she looked over to see James
approaching, fresh from the airport, a big grin on his face.

So much for the vacation. Dealing with James had developed
into business.

*"You're right,"* Cy Ogle had said to her on the telephone the day
of the Illinois primary. "Your brother's a terrible surfer."

"How'd you find that out?"

"Remember that lunch you and I had?"

"Sure."

"I did the same thing with your brother. Brought him in from
South Bend on a chopper. Bought him lunch at the same place."

"And?"

"The way he handled it was totally different."

"Different how?"

Ogle had chuckled. "You weren't impressed. You weren't impressed by any old limousine. You weren't impressed by a fancy
lunch or by my reputation, or by people cheering at you because
your last name's Cozzano."

"And he was impressed?"

"Oh, yes. Profoundly impressed. You could see it in his face."

"Stop," she had said. "Don't even describe it to me. I know exactly how he must have looked."

"Well, we had a nice little chat, anyway."

"What did you talk about?"

Ogle had laughed. "Not anything even remotely similar to what you and I talked about. See, you are interested in relationships. James is interested in power. So we talked about power for a while."

This had left Mary Catherine feeling slightly queasy, because she knew that Ogle was exactly right.

It was a testosterone thing. She knew it was. James had been suppressed by Dad. James was small, weak, had a low pain threshold, couldn't throw or catch a football, didn't like getting dirty. Dad had been enough of a good father to swallow his disappointment. But everyone knew it was present, just under the surface. James just hadn't developed. And as soon as Dad had been removed from the picture, all those pent-up hormones had come flooding out and he had started developing too fast. Developing in the wrong direction, without any guidance from Dad.

He needed a trellis to grow on. He needed it now, before he started any more trouble for the family. But Mary Catherine knew there wasn't a damn thing she could do; in James's current state of testosterone overdrive, he was incapable of taking direction, or even advice, from a big sister.

Mel couldn't do it either. Mel and James had never had much to say to each other, they had never had the simpatico that Mel and Mary Catherine did. Mel was a street fighter and James was coddled and naive, despite all of Dad's efforts to toughen him up. The two of them just didn't connect on any level.

This was a case in point. Dad had gone under the knife an hour and a half ago. James should have been there to kiss him good-bye. Mary Catherine knew damn well that people died in surgery and that you had to be there when they went under, because they might never open their eyes again. And she had explained all of this to James. Stated, over and over again, the importance of his being there before the surgery. And he had missed the boat.

"Hey, sis. How you doing?"

He didn't even realize that he had screwed up. That was the frightening part. No self-awareness.

"You're late," she said.

He was shocked, shocked to find that she was mad at him. He

shrugged and held his palms up. "My flight was delayed. You know
how O'Hare is."

"So do you," Mary Catherine said, "and a Ph.D. candidate at
Notre Dame should have the brains to allow for it."

"Jesus," he said, now sounding wounded, "this whole thing has
turned you into quite the dragon lady."

"You can say 'bitch' if you want."

"Suit yourself."

She turned away from him and looked out over the ocean again,
watching the big ketch come about. Its booms swung across the
deck, its jibs went limp and fluttered for a moment, then reinflated
and snapped tight again as the boat settled into a new course.

It didn't bother her at all. They were dealing with some heavy-
duty shit here. And now, all of a sudden, she understood a lot of
things about Dad that she hadn't understood before. Why he was
such a tough guy. Why he could be so calculating.

"There's plenty of flights. I thought maybe you would come out
last night," Mary Catherine said, trying not to sound quite so harsh.

"I was busy. I had business to take care of."

These words terrified her. She looked into his face. "What kind
of business?"

"Take it easy," he said reassuringly. "I'm not running around doing
stuff behind your back."

"I've never accused you of doing so," she said. "This is the first
time that notion's come up."

He blushed, looked away, got real clumsy for a few seconds.
"Well, this thing is my own gig," he said. "Nothing to do with you or
the family."

"What thing?"

"I got a job," he said, beaming with pride.

"Well, that's great," she said, "but isn't that going to interfere with
your Ph.D. work?"

"No, that's just the thing," he said. "It's part of my Ph.D. work.
I'm double dipping. I get paid to do this job, and I get my regular
stipend as a grad student, and I'll probably get a book contract out
of it too." James had a devilish look on his face, as if he had just
outmaneuvered Satan himself.

"Well, James, that's wonderful!" she said. "What kind of job is this?"

"I'm doing a study of the presidential campaign. All of the politicking that's been going on during the primary season. With emphasis on media strategy. And if I play my cards right, I'm pretty sure this could turn into a book eventually."

"That's great. How'd you get on to this idea?"

"It just hit me the other day. I was talking to this guy. He's a big-time campaign media consultant. You might not have heard of him."

"What's his name?"

"Cy. Cyrus Rutherford Ogle."

"Oh. How'd you get hooked up with him?"

"He just invited me out to lunch," James said nonchalantly. "I'm not sure exactly why. But I think that, obviously, because of my family connections, combined with my poli sci expertise, he thought maybe I'd be a good person to know."

"Yes, I should think so," Mary Catherine said, sounding terribly impressed.

"We engaged in small talk for a while, nothing specific. Then he started asking me a lot of questions about my dissertation. He seemed to be fascinated with the topic."

"I'll bet he was."

"I was asking him about some of the work he does and it occurred to me that, since he seemed to be so interested in my work, a mutual back-scratching arrangement might be possible. So we hammered this whole thing out, right there at the lunch table. He's giving me access to a number of campaigns—he has friends and protégés working in virtually every important campaign right now. So I get lots of material I wouldn't otherwise have access to."

"Well," Mary Catherine said, "it sounds like you just made a brilliant career move." It was taking a lot of effort to keep from smiling at her brother. He had the same proud, beaming look on his face that he'd had at the age of six, when he caught a big toad in the backyard.

James shrugged. "Yeah. But Jesus, it's a lot of work."

"It is?"

"Oh, yeah. Suddenly I've got all these contacts. Dozens of major sources. All these people to keep track of. I've spent the last few days just talking to people on the phone, setting up a database to keep track of all the information I'll be taking in. I'm going to be running flat-out until Election Day."

"Uh-huh."

"But if there's one thing that I learned from Dad, it's that when you see an opportunity you have to go for it in a big way."

"Well," Mary Catherine said, "I hope you're not biting off too much."

This was manipulation in its purest form. He would have found it patronizing to be congratulated. Better to fret and worry about what a big, manly job James was undertaking.

"What's that supposed to mean?" he said. He was irked, and rapidly getting more so, building up a nice crescendo of self-important rage. "You think I can't handle a big job?"

Mary Catherine shrugged. "I have a lot of respect for you, James," she said noncommittally.

"No, you don't. You still think I'm a little kid. But I'm not. I'm an adult. And maybe you don't want to admit that fact, now that you've become the self-appointed capo of this family and you think you know what's best for everyone."

"Fine. It's your choice," she said.

"I've done big jobs before. And I'm going to do this one. I'm going to succeed."

"Good. I wish you the best of luck."

James shut up for a moment, calming himself down. "It's been hard, being the son of the Great Man."

"I know it has been," she said. "I know it's been really rough."

"There've been a lot of times when I felt like the idiot son, you know. A lot of Dad's old cronies treat me like a little kid."

By this, Mary Catherine knew that he was referring to Mel.

"But Cy is totally different," he continued. "He treated me with respect. As an equal. He had no doubts whatsoever that I could handle this job. And I'm grateful to him for that."

*So am I,* Mary Catherine thought.

"You should meet this guy sometime," James said.

"Maybe I should."

An interesting thought had occurred to Mary Catherine. Maybe Cy Ogle had manipulated her just as brilliantly as he had James.

Or maybe not. She had handed him something close to a quid pro quo: help me out with James, this loose cannon on the deck of the good ship Cozzano, and then we'll talk some more. And he had delivered. He had done it in less than a week. He had solved a big problem for them.

Cy Ogle might be a person that they could use.

## CHAPTER TWENTY-THREE

Eleanor's first hint that anything funny was going on was when she heard Doreen, in the next trailer over, going, "Whoo-ee! Look at this, baby!" in the singsong falsetto that she used to attract the attention of her children. Meanwhile, Eleanor could hear the sound of tires grinding and popping on gravel, right outside of her trailer.

Eleanor looked out the window. Mobile homes, like jet airplanes, offered great views off to the sides but you couldn't see what was directly in front or behind. All she could see was the side of Doreen's trailer, and Doreen's big hairdo in one of the windows, flanked by the faces of her three kids, their eyes and mouths wide open to accept new input. They were all looking at something that was going on in front of Eleanor's trailer.

It must be the Nazis. They were coming to get her. Eleanor ran up to the front of the trailer, slapping the chain onto her door as she went by it. She got up to the front where two tiny little windows looked forward, and she peeled the windowshade back just a little.

It was a big old Lincoln Town Car, navy blue, freshly polished, the cleanest and prettiest car within several miles of this trailer park. You could back it into an empty slot here and make it pass for a mobile home.

All the doors were open. Several men were getting out. They

were all young men. They were all wearing sunglasses. At least two of them had walkie-talkies as well, and they were using them. And they were looking around, scanning all points of the compass through their dark glasses, swiveling their heads back and forth like searchlights on a guard tower. One of them went up to the Datsun, put his face up close to the silvered glass, and cupped his hands around his eyes.

For the first few moments, Eleanor was convinced that they were Nazi hit men who had come to blow her away. But that was just paranoia. The followers of Earl Dudley Strang were not affluent men in suits and Lincoln Town Cars; they were greasy-haired Roto-rooter operators. And if they wished to do away with her, they would come in the middle of the night like the jackals they were. Not in broad daylight, in a big car, like this.

Besides, they didn't act like hit men, or how she thought hit men would act. They had gotten out of the car immediately on arrival, but then they just stopped. They made no move to enter Eleanor's trailer.

Eleanor raised her windowshade a little more, feeling bolder, and noticed that there was still one man inside the Lincoln Town Car. He was sitting in the middle of the backseat and he was talking on the telephone.

He finished his conversation, hung up, and scooted down to the end of the seat. He climbed up out of the car, assisted by one of the young men in the dark glasses, and stood up on the gravel. He squinted into the unfiltered sunlight, his face wrinkling up tremendously, like a High Plains arroyo.

She would have recognized him on the dark side of the moon: it was Senator Caleb Roosevelt Marshall, Republican of Colorado. He was so old that he was actually named after Teddy, not Franklin, Roosevelt. And he was so conservative that, during the thirties, when a lot of his idealistic young peers were going to Spain to fight on behalf of the revolutionaries there, he had volunteered to fight for the Fascists.

He had been virulently opposed to America's participation in World War II. A strong supporter of General MacArthur and a fierce advocate of "nuking the evil Chinks" (his words) in Korea. He had spent most of the fifties rooting out "Comsymps" from Capitol Hill and the media. He had called Goldwater a pinko. He had seen both the Berlin crisis and the Cuban Missile Crisis as golden opportunities for a first nuclear strike against the Soviet Union, and had stood side-by-side with Curtis LeMay in the recommendation that North Vietnam be bombed back into the Stone Age.

He had run abortively for president in four decades, from the fifties through the eighties, whenever he felt that the frontrunning Republican candidate was not gloomy, threatening, and violent enough. Consistently voted against affirmative action. Though Eleanor knew her civil rights history well enough to know that he had astonished just about everyone by voting in favor of the Civil Rights Act of 1964.

He was like that: he was fringy enough to teeter on the edge of becoming a one-dimensional stereotype, but once or twice a year he would do something freakish and astonishing. He had gained the grudging affection of some people by consistently hating Richard Nixon's guts from the very beginning. He had come down on the side of Anita Hill during the Clarence Thomas confirmation hearings, and delivered a lengthy and profane speech in her defense on the Senate floor, using it as an occasion to lament the total implosion of American values.

Just when his image seemed on the verge of being rehabilitated, he would do something reactionary. For the last several years, he had celebrated Animal Rights Day by going out to his family ranch in southeastern Colorado and branding a few calves in front of the TV cameras. It got him tons of publicity, reinforced his caveman image, and made him wildly popular among farmers, westerners, and anyone else who made money from animals. The man knew how to get a campaign contribution.

Now this weathered, deathless, inexplicable gnome was standing in front of her trailer, surrounded by men that, she now realized, were Secret Service agents. She did not know if she should run away and hide, or welcome him.

Soon enough he was pounding on her front door and she had to make up her mind. She pulled her hair back and wrapped a scrunchie around it, went to the door, and opened it. But it was still chained shut and so it only came open a few inches. She found herself staring through the chain at Caleb Roosevelt Marshall. They were of roughly the same height.

"Take it easy, woman," he said, glancing at the chain. "I'm not here to burn a cross on your goddamn lawn."

She closed the door, unchained it, and opened it all the way. "Senator Marshall?" she said.

"Eleanor Boxwood Richmond?"

"Yes."

"Slayer of Erwin Dudley Strang?"

"Well . . ."

"Fastest tongue in the West?"

She laughed.

"If you would invite me in, I would have a few things to discuss with you."

"Come in."

"You don't have to invite any of these people in," Marshall said. He turned around and slammed the door in the face of an agent.

"Can I offer you anything to drink?" she said.

"I am in suspended animation. The only things I am allowed to drink are strange concoctions brewed up by pharmacists. You would not be able to afford them, and I can only do so by taking honoraria," he said. He talked like a guy who was used to having his voice heard by a million people.

"Well, then, please sit down anywhere you like."

"Whenever I lower myself to a seated or reclining position, it occurs to me that I may never stand on my feet again," he said. "To a man of my age, even sitting down becomes a morbid thing. So I hope it will not make you feel awkward if I stand up."

"Not at all." Eleanor pulled up a tall bar stool, one of the artifacts that they had salvaged from the wreck of their middle-class lifestyle, and sat down on it without losing any altitude. This way she could still talk to him face-to-face.

"I know that this conversation has already gotten off on the wrong foot because you think that I am an evil vicious old man who hates persons of your race," Senator Marshall said.

"The thought had occurred to me."

"But in fact, the only thing I hate is bullshit. I hate bullshit because I grew up on a ranch and I spent the first three decades of my life shoveling it. I went into politics largely because it was a desk job and naturally I thought that in a desk job I would not have to shovel any more bullshit. Of course nothing could have been further from the truth. So you see I have spent my whole life up to my nostrils in bullshit and consequently know more about it, and hate it more, than anyone else on the face of the earth.

"Now, the reason that a lot of Negroes think I hate them is simple: there is a whole lot of bullshit in racial politics, even more than in other aspects of politics, and when I react against that bullshit, they think I'm reacting against them. But I'm not. I'm just reacting against their bullshit politics. Like affirmative action. That's bullshit. But civil rights isn't bullshit at all. I voted for that."

"I know you did."

"And all these different terms—colored, Negro, black, Afro-American—that's all bullshit too. They're always willing to come up with new words for Negroes, but never to actually do something that will help them, and that's bullshit. The basic fact is that all people should be treated the same, as specified in the goddamn Constitution, and everything else is bullshit."

"Well, Senator, I am aware that you are not a totally one-dimensional person, and so I am willing to give you the benefit of the doubt as long as you are a guest in my home."

"I thought you would. A lot of Negroes hate my guts and start jumping up and down and organizing protest rallies as soon as I come over the horizon, but I figured you would be able to see things a little more clearly. You know why?"

"Why?"

"Because you have a bullshit detector as good as mine, and that is a rare quality."

"Well, thank you, Senator."

"And you're not afraid to use it."

"Well, that was a somewhat unusual thing for me to do. I was very upset at the time and not thinking clearly."

Senator Marshall was peeved and disappointed. "Bullshit! You were thinking as clearly as the human mind has ever thought. What do you mean, you weren't thinking clearly?"

"I mean that I was raised to have good manners and be diplomatic, and I would not have violated those standards if I had not been at the end of my rope emotionally."

"Well, you and I have different interpretations of this. Shit, I've been at the end of my rope emotionally since I was five years old."

"This fact has been widely commented upon," Eleanor said.

"You were perfectly justified in saying everything you said," Senator Marshall said. "Do you realize that Earl Strong may never recover, politically, from what you did to him?"

"I think you are being very optimistic to say that."

"Bullshit. This is your polite upbringing talking, isn't it?"

"Possibly."

"I got a stack of poll results an inch thick. We have been watching this thing. Hell, I wanted to come over here and congratulate you the same night you did it. But instead I waited a few days for the poll results. And lady, you blew that son of a bitch to smithereens. You ripped that little tick's head off. You deserve a medal."

Eleanor laughed. "A medal? I'd rather have a job."

Senator Marshall stuck out his right hand and looked at Eleanor expectantly.

She didn't know what to do. The man was so weird. He was weird, he knew he was weird, he knew that she knew it, and he didn't care.

Finally politeness took over and she reached out and shook his hand. He seized hers, not with the perfunctory squeeze of a politician, but with the powerful grip of a man who has to pull himself up out of chairs and beds. He didn't let go.

"Done," he said, "you're hired."

Eleanor laughed wildly. "You're crazy!" she said, "what are you talking about?"

"I don't know."

"So you're just kidding."

"Oh, no. I sure as hell ain't kidding. You're definitely hired. I just haven't worked through all the bullshit yet."

"The bullshit?"

"Job title, GSA level, what kind of desk to get you, what kind of goddamn picture to hang on the wall of your office. See, one of the things you learn, when you've hired a lot of people, and then fired most of them, is that when you find a quality person, you hire them right away and work out the details later. And I just hired you."

"Just on the strength of the fact that I said some nasty things to Earl Strong."

"You said some true things," Caleb Roosevelt Marshall said, "which is something that few people in Washington are capable of doing. And you said them well, which is just as unusual."

He still hadn't let go of her hand.

"I would have expected you to like Earl Strong."

"Ha! You think I'll support anyone who comes along and spouts a few positions similar to mine. What do you think I am, a senile old moron?"

"Isn't that how it works?"

"Positions change. People don't. Earl Strong may or may not always be a so-called conservative populist. But he will definitely always be a pencil-neck Hitler wannabe with a face from Wal-Mart, as you pegged him. I don't want to serve with him in the Senate. And you may have saved me from that fate. So I owe you a job."

"Well, I'm not sure I want to work with you."

"Because of my politics?"

"Well, yes. Because of your politics."

"Eleanor Boxwood Richmond," he said, "you and I got exactly the same politics. Only thing is, you don't know it yet."

"How can you say that? I've been a liberal Democrat all my life."

Still gripping her hand, Senator Marshall shook his head dismissively. "All that Democrat/Republican stuff is bullshit," he said. "And as far as liberal versus conservative, well, people are very promiscuous in the way they use those words. They don't really mean anything. Within those two camps there are very wide divisions. And between those two camps, there is a lot more overlap than you think. None of that bullshit really matters. The only thing that matters is values."

"Values?"

"Values. I've got 'em. You've got 'em. Earl Strong doesn't. That means you and I are on the same side. We have to stick together, you and I."

"And that means you're going to give me a job."

"I already figured it out. Took me a few minutes, but I figured it out. I need a health and human services liaison for my Denver office. We can start you on Monday. You'll work your ass off and make forty-five thousand plus full medical. Interested?"

"What can I say?" Indeed, what could she say? "Sure. I'll take it. What do I have to do?"

"Answer irate phone calls from parasites who want to know what became of their welfare checks."

"Okay. I can do that."

"Done," the Senator said, and let go of her hand finally.

"One question."

"Yeah?"

"Do you expect me to blow these people off, or to actually help them? Because if someone calls me wanting to find their welfare check, I intend to help them out."

"None of them vote," the Senator said, "so they can all go to hell as far as I'm concerned. You can handle it any way you want."

## CHAPTER TWENTY-FOUR

The Ride took her in slowly through Commerce City and north Denver, the attic of the West: square miles of warehouses, stacks of empty cargo pallets that must have consumed whole forests, entire blocks of businesses devoted to truck clutches. Eleanor had seen it too many times to count, but sitting on The Ride in her one and only decent dress, on her way to work—*work*—she saw it all from a new perspective, like a queen surveying her domain.

The sky was always sapphire blue when Eleanor looked straight up, but as she tracked it down toward the horizon it faded to a hot yellowish brown as if something had singed it around the edges. Eleanor was never sure if the stuff in the air was pollution or airborne topsoil, but it usually gave her a bad feeling about wherever she was going. She was tired of being able to see so far, and wanted to be hemmed in a little bit.

Downtown Denver fit that bill. It always looked clean because it was built-up, and so you couldn't see far enough to notice how dirty the air was. Eleanor sat on a bench for a while, waiting for another Ride, and marveled at the place. When you were used to the dusty flatlands out by the arsenal, the smallest things—a freshly painted GODS drop box sitting on a street corner, a young woman wearing white stockings, a Volvo with water beaded up on its hood from the car wash—looked impossibly clean and new, like images from a Kodak or Polaroid advertisement.

This was the world where a lot of people lived their whole lives. A world where Eleanor had lived for many years but that now looked like an alien planet to her dusty bloodshot eyes, and where she had just been given the tiniest of handholds.

Tree-lined Pennsylvania Street ran north-south behind the state capitol. At some point in Denver's early boom years it had been the fashionable place for barons to construct their mansions—not just homes, but seats of political and social influence. The architecture was diverse, and exuberant bordering on eccentric, including huge Victorian homes, plantation-style classical structures, arched-and-turreted Romanesques, and one especially large and bizarre structure, a red sandstone mission building that bore more than a passing resemblance to the Alamo.

Senator Caleb Roosevelt Marshall used that building as his home office, and he referred to it as the Alamo, which was not a popular joke among his Mexican-American constituents, but then he was not the type to care.

Like any big rambling eccentric old building, it had good offices and bad ones. The office assigned to Eleanor Richmond was especially bad, but that was a fact that wouldn't even occur to her until she had been working there for a while. When she showed up for her first day as Health and Human Services Liaison, all she cared about was that she had a job. And a damn good job, as these things went.

She was wearing her interview dress. She wasn't sure why. She had worn it to all of her job interviews in the past several years and it hadn't done a thing for her. She had interviewed for her job with Senator Marshall in a Towson State University sweatshirt and nonmatching Army sweatpants. But this was the one dress that she had been at pains to take care of through all the turbulence in her life. She had somehow thought that she could never become a true bag lady if she owned one clean, decent dress. So now she was wearing it to work. When the paychecks started coming in, she could go back to the Boulevard Mall, this time as a paying customer, and cut a swath through Nordstrom, like General Sherman plowing through Dixie.

The first thing that anyone said to her was a sound effect: "Foop-foop-foop."

She had been walking down a hallway in her interview dress, carrying a box full of photos and other personal effects in her arms, looking into each door as she went by, trying to find the one that belonged to her. And when she finally found it, walked into the small windowless room (later she learned it had been the walk-in closet of a railway baroness), and set her box down on the cratered and elbow-worn formica of the desktop, she heard it. She turned around. A man was standing in her office doorway. She didn't like him.

He was in his mid-to-late twenties, or maybe he was an older guy who just looked young. He was wearing a pinstriped suit with cowboy boots. His comb had left visible, parallel grooves through his heavily gelled brown hair, like the tracks of fleeing dinosaurs in a fresh volcanic mudflow. He had sparkly gray eyes and high mischievous eyebrows that could have made him look wild and fun, if he could have ditched the suit and the gel for, say, a pair of shorts and a long outdoorsman's mane. But instead he struck Eleanor as unnaturally pinned back.

When she first saw him, he was leaning into her office doorway, holding one index finger straight up in the air, rotating his hand around in a circle, saying, "Foop-foop-foop."

"Excuse me?" she said.

"Somebody ought to put a revolving door on this office," he said. "Seems like I get a new neighbor in here every week—Hello," he said, segueing in midsentence like a game show host, and turning the rotating index finger into an outstretched right hand, "Shad Harper. You'd be Eleanor."

Eleanor took half a step toward him and began to extend her right hand. He dove in, grabbed her hand too soon, seized the very tips of her fingers, squeezed them together hard, and pumped for a few seconds.

"Eleanor *Richmond*," she said, but this hint was completely lost on him, as she knew it would be.

"Good to know you, Eleanor."

"You have the next office, *Mr. Harper?*"

"Yeah. Come on over any time you want to have a look at the courtyard," he said, widening his eyes just a bit and staring significantly at the blank wall behind Eleanor's desk. The office of Shad Harper was a big old master bedroom or something, and she could already see that he had lots of windows.

These were all things that would bother her later. At the moment, nothing could penetrate the endorphin buzz that she had from actually being on a payroll.

"Thank you," she said, "you're very kind."

"Saw you on TV. That was quite a little tantrum you threw in front of Earl Strong there."

"And what do you do for the Senator?" she said.

"Oh," he said, as if he were surprised that she didn't already know, "I'm the BLM liaison."

"BLM?"

"Bureau of Land Management," he recited, with calculated nonchalance.

Looking over his shoulder across the hallway, Eleanor could see a bleached longhorn skull hanging on one of the rare parts of Harper's office wall that did not consist of windows. That, and the cowboy boots, told the story of Shad Harper.

Bureau of Land Management. Colorado had a lot of land that needed to be managed. A lot of voters lived on or near that land. When the land did get managed, it was through federal programs. Shad Harper must be keeping tabs on a lot of money.

He was very young. Which was not a problem in and of itself; Eleanor had known a lot of bright young things who were a pleasure to be around. But Shad Harper didn't seem to realize that he was still a young man. He ought to be out riding a mountain bike around

Boulder. Any man of his age who was not out goofing off was difficult to trust.

He raised his eyebrows, showing exaggerated concern, and puckered his lips into a silent O shape. "I think your phone's ringing, Eleanor," he said.

Eleanor turned around and looked at her phone, an elaborate, high-tech, multiline model with lots of tiny little buttons on it. Each button had tiny little red and green lights next to it. Some buttons had red lights going. Some had green lights going. Some had both. Some of the lights were blinking, others were not. It looked like a Christmas decoration.

"Well, thank you," she said, "but I don't hear anything."

"I took the liberty of turning the ringer off while this office was vacant," he said. "It was driving me crazy. I gotta get back. I'll see you later, Eleanor."

He dodged out the door and across the hallway and made a diving grab at his own telephone, then burst into a good-natured, booming, masculine welcome. Whomever Shad Harper was talking to, if he had been there in person, Shad would have been pounding him on the back and possibly even giving him noogies.

Eleanor set her box of stuff down on her desk, went around behind it, and looked at the silently ringing telephone. She wanted to sit down, but there was no chair in the office, just a desk.

She knew the deal here. Shad Harper, being a boy, had figured out how to turn off the telephone's ringer. And she, being a girl, was supposed to sit helplessly for a while, and then go across the hallway and meekly ask him to turn it back on for her. Ten minutes into her job, she would already owe him one.

She already knew that she would rather shove a freshly sharpened pencil into her eye than ask Shad Harper for a favor. So she picked up the telephone, clamping the handset down into its cradle with her thumb, and rotated it around, looking at all the tiny little switches and jacks and plugs and connectors. It took some looking and some experimenting, but eventually she found it. She flicked a switch. The phone rang.

She picked it up. But before it even reached her ear she could hear a conversation, already in progress. It was Shad Harper listening to a crusty old rancher somewhere complaining about the cultural and genetic deficiencies of the Mexican race. He was doing this by listing all of the ways that, in his view, they were similar to "niggers." After the man made each point, Shad Harper would say, "Uh-huh," in a chuckling and indulgent tone of voice.

Her phone was still ringing. She pushed another button.

It was Senator Marshall himself, now in D.C., talking to someone about polls. Her phone was still ringing; she pushed another button.

It was a young black woman who apparently worked here in this office, talking trash with another young black woman who apparently worked in someone else's office. Her phone was still ringing; she pushed another button.

"Hello?" a voice said. White female. Screaming kids in background.

"Hello, Senator Marshall's office," Eleanor said.

"I know I already reached the Senator's goddamn office," the woman said, "but who am I talking to?"

"Mrs. Richmond. Health and Human Services Liaison."

"Finally. Jeezus, I been on hold for a quarter of an hour and my kids are going nuts here. Kin you hear 'em?"

The sound of the kids got louder for a few moments and Eleanor realized that this woman must be holding the phone out toward them, waving it around a motel room or trailer full of screeching and fighting rug rats like a rock star pointing his microphone at the crowd. Another Commerce City resident, no doubt.

"Yes, I believe I can, ma'am," Eleanor said. "How may I help you?"

A brief moment of stunned silence on the other end of the line. "Well, didn't I already just explain that about three times?" Then, her voice farther away: "Brittany! Ashley! You stay away from your goddamn brother or I'll tan your hides!"

"I don't know, ma'am," Eleanor said, "you never explained it to me."

"Well, I explained it to the other gal."

"Well, ma'am, I'm not quite sure who the other gal is. But I'd be happy to listen if you'd care to explain it again."

Another silence. Eleanor couldn't figure out why this woman was being so quiet until her voice came back on again, and it was obvious that she had begun to cry. "Well, I ain't going through the whole goddamn thing again! But let me tell you, bitch, that if it don't get taken care of today, I'll—"

"You'll what, ma'am?"

"I'll go out and find wherever it is that I'm s'posed to register and get myself registered to vote and go out and vote against that old fuck that you work for next time he comes up for reelection! Bitch!" Then the woman slammed the phone down.

The phone began ringing immediately. Eleanor was starting to get the hang of this now; she pushed the button with the blinking light next to it.

"Hello, Senator Marshall's office," she said.

"Finally!" someone said. Black female. Then, away from the phone: "Hey, I finally got through!" Then, back into the phone: "You have any idea how long I been waiting on the line?"

"A quarter of an hour or so?"

"Shit, I been waiting all day."

"It's only 9:13—but I'm sorry for the delay, ma'am. How can I assist you?"

"I took my little daughters to a unlicensed day-care at my neighbor's house down the street and when I come home from work, her boyfriend had come in during the day and molested 'em, and I want to know if I can force him to take an AIDS test."

"Did you call the police?"

"Shit no. Why would I want to call them?"

"Because a very serious crime has been committed."

"Shit. I called you for serious advice, girl."

"I'm giving it to you. Call the cops. Tell them what happened. Send the bastard to jail."

"This G done already told me if I call the cops he come kill me."

"Ma'am, how could being killed possibly be any worse than having your daughters raped?"

Stunned silence. "What kind of an attitude is that?"

"It's a reasonable attitude. It's the kind of attitude that any parent should have."

"Well, who are you to be telling me this?"

"I'm a woman who was raised right by her parents and who's been trying to raise her two kids right."

"What are you saying, that I ain't been raised right?"

"That's exactly what I'm saying, if you care so little for those two precious daughters of yours that you won't even seek justice for them. If anyone in my family ever got raped, nobody would rest until the perpetrator was dead or behind bars."

"Well, I didn't call you up so you could give me abuse."

"Girlfriend," Eleanor said, "I'm gonna tell you something *real* important right now and you better listen."

"I'm listening," the woman said. She sounded cowed and meek now.

"This that I am saying to you is not abuse. It's the truth. It's just that sometimes the truth is so harsh that when people hear it spoken, it sounds like abuse. And one of the problems we got in this country, not just among black people but with everyone, is that everyone is so easy to offend nowadays that no one is willing to say the things that are true. Now, I just told you what to do. You go and do it. And if you have to go out and get a gun to protect you from that son of a bitch that raped your daughters, you damn well better do it, because that's your responsibility, and if you can't handle it, then you don't deserve to have those two little angels that are a precious gift from God."

Eleanor slammed the phone down. It started ringing.

"Senator Marshall's office."

The creaky voice of a very old man said, "Help! I've fallen and I can't get up!"

"Good morning, Senator Marshall, how are you?"

"Wide awake and full of inspiration, after that!"

"After what?"

"Your motivational talk to that young woman. Well done!"

"You were listening to that?"

"I always listen in on my liaison staff," Senator Marshall said. "It's an essential part of the job. And if I had managed to get through to you before you actually swung into action, I would have given you fair warning. But now you know."

"Well, I don't normally shoot my mouth off this early in the morning, but—"

"You weren't shooting your mouth off. You were doing just fine. All those people out there are crying for more welfare checks when what they really need is to have someone like you pound some common sense into their heads."

"I don't necessarily agree with that," Eleanor said, mortified.

"Anyway, nice to see you changed your position on gun control. You're going to fit right in at the Alamo!"

"Who said anything about gun control?"

"You did," Senator Marshall said. "You were pro-gun control, weren't you?"

"In theory, yes," Eleanor said, "but I have a gun, and I know how to use it."

"Well, tell me something. If that woman you were just talking to had to fill out a bunch of forms and get permission from the government to have a gun, she wouldn't be able to take the advice you just gave her, would she?"

Eleanor shook her head in exasperation. "You are just full of piss and vinegar, aren't you?"

"No, I just like a good discussion, is all."

"I have important people to talk to," Eleanor said, and hung up on him. Her phone rang immediately.

## CHAPTER TWENTY-FIVE

Aaron Green put his feet up on his desk at Green Biophysical Systems in Lexington, Massachusetts, enjoying the first lull in the action since his big conversation with Cy Ogle back in January. They had ironed out all of the problems that they could think of having to do with the PIPER miniaturization project. Responsibility had been transferred to the shoulders of the Pacific Netware people. Aaron had brought in a *New York Times* and a *Boston Globe*, and was reading some astonishing results from the Illinois primary, which had taken place the day before.

Several members of the party in power had challenged the incumbent President. Usually such efforts were purely symbolic, but the President's policy on the national debt had provided fodder for a more serious challenge this time around, and these candidates had racked up some surprisingly high numbers.

The situation in the other party was even more interesting. There were two announced candidates—three, if you counted the Reverend William Joseph Sweigel, which almost no one did. Everyone knew, and had known since Super Tuesday, that the real race was between Tip McLane and Norman Fowler, Jr., the boy billionaire of Grosse Pointe.

But apparently in the last week before the Illinois primary, unspecified persons had initiated a write-in campaign for William A. Cozzano, the Governor of Illinois, who was in the hospital recovering from a stroke. It seemed to be a genuine, spontaneous ground swell. People had begun showing up in T-shirt stores and asking to have COZZANO printed on shirts and hats. Crudely fashioned, xeroxed COZZANO posters had begun showing up on mailboxes and in car windows.

In yesterday's primary, a lot of people had written in the Governor's name. *A lot* of people. So many that the counting of the ballots had been delayed. But the results available as of the middle of the night before, when the newspapers had gone to press, suggested that Cozzano had actually won a number of precincts, made a strong showing overall, and might actually come in second to Norman Fowler, Jr. He had been so strong, in fact, that he had actually gotten several thousand write-in votes in the *other party's* primary.

When Aaron saw the preliminary numbers printed in the paper, he turned on the TV in his office to see if he could get some up-to-date numbers. He never used to pay attention to this stuff, but since he had started hanging out with Ogle he had become very election conscious.

The news networks were full of Cozzano. Cozzano in Vietnam. Cozzano being carried around on the shoulders of fellow Bears. Cozzano raking leaves in front of his big house in some backwater town in Illinois. Cozzano waving from the window of his hospital room in Champaign. And the name COZZANO, crudely printed on T-shirts and homemade yard signs.

He was startled to realize that someone was standing in his office doorway. It was Marina, the office manager, word processing and desktop publishing genius, fixer, diplomat, you name it. She looked a little dreamy. If this had been a Warner Brothers cartoon, she would have had stars and birds circling around her head.

"I just got the weirdest phone call," she said.

"Tell me about it," Aaron said.

"This guy called up. A guy with a southern accent. I think it's that guy you've been dealing with out in California."

"Cy Ogle."

"Yeah."

"Well, what did Mr. Ogle have to say?"

"That I was fired."

"He said what?"

"That I was fired. That the corporation was undergoing a restructuring and that I could apply for reemployment later."

Aaron was more nonplussed than he was angry. It had to be Ogle's weird sense of humor at work. "Well, who the hell is Ogle to be saying stuff like that?"

"Exactly what I asked him. He said he was the chairman of the board of directors."

"I'm the chairman," Aaron said.

"I know that."

Another person appeared in the hallway, standing behind Marina. It was Greg. College buddy of Aaron's. Cofounder of the corporation. Chief biologist. "I have just been informed that I'm fired too," he said. "But maybe it's not so bad since our stock is selling for twice its normal value today. So I'm worth twice as much."

"Good," Marina said, "so am I." Marina had lots of stock too.

"Selling?" Aaron said. "None of our stock has changed hands in months."

"Get with it," Greg said. "Fifty-five percent of it changed hands at 9:05 this morning."

"What you're saying is that our venture capitalists sold us to someone else."

"That's what it amounts to."

"And Cy Ogle claims to be that someone," Marina said.

The telephone on Aaron's desk began to purr. Aaron picked it up, indicating with a hand gesture that it was okay for Greg and Marina to stay in the room.

"You're probably pissed because I just fired half of your company," Ogle said. "Which is understandable. It's hard to run a tight ship based on emotion and personal loyalty. Damn hard."

"Who's next? Me?"

"Nope. You're staying on, along with your two electronics guys. We can use them. Everyone else has served their purpose."

"How am I supposed to run an office without Marina?"

"You don't have to worry about running an office anymore. We have plenty of room down here in Falls Church."

"But I don't live in Falls Church, Virginia. I live in Arlington, Massachusetts."

"Then you better get used to a hell of a long commute," Ogle said, "because a moving truck is showing up at your office door in five minutes to pick up all your equipment and drive it down here."

"Now, wait just a second," Aaron finally said. He had been fighting the impulse to get pissed off ever since this weirdness started. "This is just totally unacceptable. You can't just uproot our lives like this. Hell, I don't even know for sure that you're the real chairman!"

"I am," Ogle said, "but there's no point in your getting pissed off at me."

"There certainly is," Aaron said, "if you're the chairman."

"I'm the chairman of Green Biophysical Systems as of 9:05 A.M.," Ogle said, "but as of 9:03 A.M. I was no longer the chairman of Ogle Data Research."

"Huh?"

"I got bought out too."

"By whom?"

"A whole bunch of folks. MacIntyre Engineering. The Coover Fund. Gale Aerospace. Pacific Netware. They own me now. And the first thing they did was tell me to buy you. So I did. And then they told me to initiate a radical downsizing program. So I did. And part of that is closing the Lexington office and moving it down here to Falls Church."

"And all of these events took place during the first five minutes of the business day."

"Yup."

"Gee," Aaron said, "a guy could almost get the impression that the groundwork for this whole thing had been laid well in advance."

"Draw your own conclusions. Throw a tantrum. Call me names. Just don't be late for the meeting."

Aaron rolled his eyes. "What meeting would that be?"

"Emergency board meeting for Ogle Data Research, which you're invited to sit in on, to be followed immediately by an emergency board meeting for Green Biophysics."

"When and where?"

"Right here at Seven Corners, at two o'clock this afternoon. That should give you time to grab a pair of shuttle flights. Oh, and Aaron?"

"Yes?"

"We bought you out at twice your book value."

"So I heard."

"We'll double that figure again if any of your existing stockholders want to sell out. But they have to do it today."

"I'll pass that along."

"See you at two o'clock."

Aaron hung up his phone. Cy Ogle's phone. MacIntyre's, Gale's, Coover's, and Tice's phone.

"The bad news is, we just got hit by the financial equivalent of Desert Storm," he said, "and we lost. The good news is that we all just quadrupled our net worth."

Marina laughed, verging on hysteria.

"Not bad for an hour's work," Greg said, looking at his watch. It was ten o'clock.

A big, handsome head shot of Governor William A. Cozzano flashed up on the television screen. Roaring white noise came out of the speaker, the sound of a wildly cheering multitude.

*Aaron sold his* stock. There was no point in hanging on to the stuff when he knew that it would drop to one-quarter of its current value by the end of the day. He took a taxi to Logan, hopped the shuttle to LaGuardia, walked across the concourse and hopped another shuttle to National Airport in Washington.

As the shuttle twisted and veered down the lower Potomac, Aaron looked out the window and saw the Washington Monument, the Mall, which seemed prematurely green to a person used to New England winters, and the dome of the Capitol. He realized, somewhat to his own astonishment, that this was the first time he had been to Washington, D.C., since his high-school band trip fifteen years before.

It was thirty degrees warmer here, humid, green, with flowers coming out all over the place. Spring, which hadn't even started in Boston, was a memory here. It gave him a feeling of being out of it, of being way behind the times. He got on a little bus that inched its way through the airport's pathetically constricted traffic pattern and finally let him off at Avis. There, he climbed into a brand-new navy-blue Taurus. It was about a hundred and twenty degrees inside the car, and the controls for the air conditioner were already set to MAX.

D.C. was going to take some getting used to. His car in Boston didn't even have air-conditioning. He was going to have to buy a new goddamn car.

He went right out and got badly lost. That was okay, he had plenty of time, and he felt like driving around lost for a while. Eventually he pulled into a 7-Eleven and bought a big oversized street map atlas for northern Virginia and figured out where Falls Church was: just a few miles due west of D.C. Right in the middle of that was a place called Seven Corners, where a whole lot of roads came together. It was difficult to miss. From its folksy name, Aaron was expecting it to be sort of a quaint, woodsy crossroads.

It wasn't. It was a place where seven different franchise ghettos intersected and piled their congestion on top of each other, a universe of asphalt parking lots stewing in the Virginia sun. And most of it was a couple of decades old, and showing its age. It had been superseded by newer and nicer competitors farther away from the center of the metropolis.

And because Aaron Green had come to know and appreciate the style of Cyrus Rutherford Ogle, he knew where to look. He eventually found his way into the vast, mostly empty parking lot of a big old shopping center at the heart of Seven Corners. It was a ghost mall. The anchor store, the behemoth at the dead center of the mall, was a windowless monolith, sheathed in a sort of white-gravel substance that had probably been sparkling and clean back in the fifties but which had now gone dull gray and become stained with long vertical streaks of rust. A constellation of rusty, decapitated bolts projected from the wall way up high, and Aaron could see that it had once been a major department store. But now the sign was torn down and the row of plate-glass display windows and double doors that stretched along the entire front of the building at side-walk level had been replaced by particle board, painted black. Aaron walked into the place without hesitation.

It was just like the Cadillac dealership, except bigger. And, at the moment, it was somewhat noisier and more crowded than Ogle's operations tended to be when he was between campaigns. More colorful, too. A lot of people were working here right now, mostly young people, mostly female, mostly black. Most of them were wearing bright new T-shirts. And all of the T-shirts had the word COZZANO printed on them. They were operating T-shirt printing machines. Printing up more of them.

But they weren't fancy. The insignia going onto those shirts (and hats and sweatshirts and windbreakers) was not a nifty logo, like a national campaign would use. Everything was being done in simple block letters, with no graphics. It was exactly what you would get if you went into a seedy discount T-shirt printing place at a carnival midway and asked them to print the word COZZANO onto a T-shirt.

The same could be said of the crude 8 1/2-by-11 campaign post-ers floating out of the xerox machines, and of the campaign signs, being stapled together from fence pickets and refrigerator boxes and hand-lettered by more women in cheap COZZANO T-shirts.

One corner was given over to folding tables with many tele-phones on them. Young people sat behind the tables talking on the phones. There were also a dozen desks with older people, suit-wearing people, sitting behind them, and these people were talking on the phones too. On the wall behind all of this was a large map of the fifty states, nearly obscured with little colored pins, streamers, flags, and yellow notes.

"That right there," said the familiar voice of Cy Ogle, "is the spontaneous ground-swell department."

Aaron ignored him. Ogle walked around until he was standing in Aaron's peripheral vision. He had pulled a bright yellow COZZANO T-shirt over his dress shirt and donned a COZZANO skimmer.

"See, the problem with spontaneous ground swells is they are so damn disorganized," Ogle said. "And that don't cut it, because the ballot rules in the various states are just unbelievably complicated. For example, in New York—"

"Spare me," Aaron said. "Spare me."

"Anyway, welcome to the metacampaign," Ogle said.

"Okay, I'll bite. What is the metacampaign?"

"Y'know how, after the New Hampshire primaries, the commentators always concentrate on the runner-up? They never seem to give a shit about who actually won the damn thing. All they want to talk about is who came in second. Who's got momentum. Big Mo. That's the metacampaign. The struggle for the hearts and minds of the media, and of big contributors."

*When Aaron first* came into the Pentagon Towers offices of Ogle Data Research, carrying half a dozen PIPER prototypes in a box, he knew that Ogle must be serious about something, because he had never known his new boss to own, rent, or come anywhere near real estate that was so civilized.

This particular nice new office building was rooted in a big shopping mall called Pentagon Plaza. It was one of the nicest malls in the D.C. metro area, which was saying something. It was a self-contained metropolis; in addition to the mall it had a parking ramp, movie theaters, a Westin, a Metro station, and office space. From the suite that Ogle had rented, on the eleventh floor, you could look out over the vast geometry of the Pentagon itself, across the Potomac, and into Washington. Or, if you looked in the other direction, you could stare straight down through the spectacular glass roof of the mall, down through its atrium, and into the food court, half-full of tired shoppers, half-full of lunching brass from the Pentagon.

The office had been professionally decorated by someone with a serious thing about sleek. It was sleek from top to bottom and end to end, the kind of place where any man who didn't have his hair slicked back felt like some kind of a shit-kicking redneck. A sleek receptionist sat at the polished-granite cyclorama of the front desk, ensconced beneath the ODR logo, answering phone calls and routing nearly all of them to the shabby department store in Falls Church or the shabby Cadillac dealership in Oakland. Behind her was all windows, chrome and glass—beautiful offices that no one ever used except, apparently, when they had some kind of an important meeting with someone fatuous enough to be impressed by this kind of thing. Which probably included 99 percent of all politicians.

But Ogle hadn't chosen this building because it was new, sleek, or convenient. As he told Aaron repeatedly, he liked it for one reason and one reason only: you got into the place by walking through a mall. The point was not that Ogle liked shopping malls. The point was all in the symbolism of the thing. Rooted in a goddamn shopping mall. The ultimate symbol of the American middle class. The very people that Ogle made his money and staked his reputation on.

It was also practical at times like this, when Ogle wanted to do what was known as focus group interviews. The idea behind an FGI was that you got a few people together who represented a cross section of America and you interviewed them, maybe showed them a few proposed campaign commercials, and got their reactions.

Finding a cross section of America was pretty easy at Pentagon Plaza. Take the elevator down to the mall level, wait for the doors to open, fling out a lasso, and you could reel in a complete focus group before they even knew what was happening.

People who assembled focus groups for Ogle were very good at wandering through the mall and sizing people up. By watching a person's clothing, hair, jewelry, the way they walked, the things they looked at, the stores they were fascinated by and the stores they ignored, the kind of food they selected at the food court and how they ate it, these observers could peg a person's income bracket to within about ten thousand bucks and make some pretty accurate guesses about what part of the country they were from, whether they came from a big city or a small town, and even what sorts of political views they were likely to hold.

These Ogle employees were officially called Focus Group Analysts, but in the corporate parlance they were simply referred to as ropers. The ropers had a parlance all their own, a system of classifying the American population. It was a vast field of expertise and

Aaron didn't have more than a foggy idea of how it worked. He didn't need to. They assembled the focus groups. Aaron ran the equipment.

They attached half a dozen PIPER prototypes to the backs of chairs. Each one had a cuff dangling from it. The chairs were arranged in a cozy semicircle in a nice little carpeted room in a nice, proper office in the Pentagon Towers offices.

When they had gotten their little room all hooked up with the prototypes and some video stuff, Shane Schram, the burly, rumpled, prematurely bald, tough-guy psychologist, materialized from some other part of the country and sent a couple of ropers down into the mall. Within a few minutes, sample Americans began to drift out of the elevators.

Schram met them right there in the elevator lobby with a hearty hello and a thank-you for having agreed to participate. The receptionist showed them into the interview room, where they filled out little information cards, drank coffee, and ate doughnuts. Pretty soon, they had a full complement of half a dozen. Schram came into the room, shut the door, thanked them all one more time, and launched into his spiel.

Each of the six subjects was being paid a hundred dollars for this. Ogle was spending a total of six hundred bucks to test a system that cost millions. It was a heck of a deal.

CHAPTER TWENTY-SIX

"This is our office," Schram said, "and we're paying you our money. But this time is all *yours*. You haven't heard of us. But we are a public opinion research company with a lot of big clients in politics and corporate America. A lot of people are listening to what we say about American opinion. And the way we learn about that is by talking to people like you. And that's why I say that this time is all yours—because the whole idea is for you to unload on us. To tell us exactly what you're thinking. I want you to be brutally frank and honest about it. You can say anything you want in this room, because I'm from New York City and you can't hurt my feelings. And if you don't bare your true opinions to me, then I can't tell my clients what is going on in the minds of America."

Aaron wasn't in the room. He was in the next room, watching all of this on television. Or hearing it, rather. None of the cameras was pointed at Schram. They had half a dozen cameras in that room, each pointed at one of the subjects. Their faces appeared on half a dozen television monitors, lined up in a nice neat row, and underneath each TV monitor was a computer monitor providing a direct readout from the PIPER prototype attached to their chair.

The PIPER readout consisted of several windows arranged on a computer screen, each window containing an animated graph or diagram. Right now, all of these were dead and inactive. On the monitor speaker, Schram could be heard explaining to the subjects how to put on the cuffs: roll up your sleeve, remove jewelry, et cetera.

One of the ropers, a young woman named Theresa, came into the monitor room. She was carrying a stack of cards, one for each of the subjects. She took a seat behind a table, where she could watch the monitors, and began to arrange the cards in front of her.

"Got a pretty wide spread today, considering," she mumbled. She shuffled through the deck, pulled out a card, and laid it out on the left side of the desk, looking up at the TV monitor on the far left. The monitor was showing a woman in her fifties, frosted blond hair in a complicated set, big jewelry, shiny lipstick, harshly penciled eyebrows. "Classic MHCC, which we get too many of in this mall."

"MHCC?"

"Mall-hopping corporate concubine," Theresa mumbled. "Though to really find them in their pure form you need to go somewhere like Stamford, Connecticut. Here they aren't really corporate, they're more government. Generals' wives."

"Oh."

Theresa put another card on the desk. This one apparently belonged to the person on the second TV monitor, a slightly portly man in his mid-thirties, with a receding hairline and a somewhat nervous affect. "This guy is a debt-hounded wage slave. In its purest form," she said.

"Is that a pretty common one?"

"Oh, yeah. There's millions of debt-hounded wage slaves." Theresa put down a third card. The third TV monitor depicted an older black woman, gray hair in a bun, thick-rimmed glasses, with a wary look on her face. "Bible-slinging porch monkey."

Number four, another black woman, this one in her late thirties, wearing the uniform of a major in the Air Force: "First-generation beltway black."

Number five, a pleasingly plump middle-aged white woman with a big hairdo, who seemed excited by the whole thing, eager to please: "This dame is a frosty-haired coupon snipper right now. Later in life, depending on the economy, she'll probably develop into either a depression-haunted can stacker or a mid-American knickknack queen."

Number six, an older white gentleman with a gaunt face, very alert and skeptical: "Activist tube feeder. These guys are really important. There's millions of these and they vote like crazy."

"How many of these categories do you have?" Aaron said.

"Lots of 'em. Hundreds. But we don't use all of them at once," Theresa said. "We tailor the list to the job. Like, if we're trying to sell athletic shoes, we don't pay attention to the tube feeders, porch monkeys, Winnebago jockeys, or can stackers. On the other hand, if it's an election thing, we can ignore groups who don't vote very much, like trade school metal heads and stone-faced urban homeboys."

"I see."

"Also there's a lot of overlap between groups, which makes the stats a little gloppy sometimes."

"Gloppy stats?"

"Yeah, it's hard to interpret the statistics because things get confused. Like, you've got your 400-pound Tab drinkers. That's an adjective, pertaining to their lifestyle. You could treat 400-pound Tab drinkers as a group unto themselves. Or you could narrow things down by looking at the ones who have no worthwhile job skills. In that case, you'd have a new group called 400-pound Tab-drinking economic roadkill."

"What good would that do you?"

"Say you wanted to market a new diet system that was really el cheapo. You decide to market this thing by aiming for fat jobless individuals. You come up with a marketing strategy where you say that losing weight improves your chances of getting a job. Then you zero in on the 400-pound Tab-drinking economic roadkill and market it to them as directly as possible."

As the members of the focus group snapped the cuffs into place around their wrists, the computer screens came alive with data. The windows on the monitor screens, which had been blank and inert, sprang to life with colorful, rapidly fluctuating graphics. The cuffs contained sensors that tracked various bodily responses and sent them down the cable to the prototypes; here, the information coming in from the cuff was converted to digital form and transmitted to a receiving station in this room.

Aaron had spent much of the last month writing software to run on a Calyx workstation. This software would scan the incoming stream of data and present it in a graphical form so that Ogle, or anyone else, could glance at the computer screen and get an immediate snapshot of what the subject was feeling.

Several times, Aaron had been on the verge of asking why it was that such quick analysis was needed. He couldn't understand what the big rush was. But before he asked this question, he always remembered what Ogle had told him during their meeting in Oakland: *You can't understand everything. Only I, Cyrus Rutherford Ogle, can understand everything.*

*Shane Schram's voice* continued to drone from the speaker. When he had greeted these people as they came from the elevators, he was bouncy and exuberant. But now that they were cuffed to the chairs, he had gone back to speaking in a knowing, New York tone. Everything he said, he said as if he were resigned to it, tired of it, and as if it should be fairly obvious to anyone who wasn't stupid. If you listened to it long enough you began to think that you and Schram were in together on a number of secrets that were hidden from ordinary saps.

"Now, the subject of today's little get-together is the wonderful world of politics."

Up on the TV screens, six faces nodded and winked knowingly. You could get a rise out of just about anyone by referring to politics in this tone of voice.

"Since we can't bring any politicians in here, we're going to show you a bunch of television instead. All I'm asking you to do is to watch this TV program—it'll run to about a quarter of an hour—and then afterwards, we'll sit and talk about it."

In the hallway outside the monitor room, Aaron heard a shuffling noise. Then a loud metallic clank. Then another shuffling noise. Then another loud metallic clank.

"I'm pushing the button that says PLAY," Schram said, jabbing at a button on the VCR, "but it's not playing. Another wonderful product from our sneaky little Jap friends."

Intense movement and color blossomed on all six of the monitors. This crack about the Japanese had produced the strongest emotional response of anything he had said today.

The only problem was how to translate the physical data coming over the wires into information about their emotional state. That was still an inexact science. Seeing the vivid responses on the computer monitors, Aaron glanced up at the television screens, trying to read faces.

To some extent, all of them were smiling at Schram's little joke. But most of the smiles did not look very sincere. They knew he had made a racist remark at the expense of the Japanese, and they knew that they were supposed to find it funny, but none of them was sincerely amused. They were faking it.

Which still didn't tell Aaron what they were *really* thinking. Were they angered by Schram's display of racism? Did they feel humiliated to be reminded of Japan's economic success?

"Oh, no wonder," Schram said, "there's no videotape in the machine. My secretary must have taken it out. That fucking cunt."

Another burst of color and activity hit the computer monitors. The faces all looked shocked and nervous. But not all of them were responding in the same way. In particular, the women responded completely differently from the men.

Schram left the room, leaving the subjects alone with each other.

Once again, Aaron heard the shuffling and clunking noise out in the hallway. He stuck his head out the door. It was a janitor empty-ing metal wastebaskets into a rolling dumpster. The janitor was some kind of an astonishing carnival freak; he was hunched over and he dragged one leg as he walked, and something didn't look entirely right about his complexion.

"Jesus," Aaron mumbled under his breath.

The janitor turned to look at him. He must have been some kind of a burn victim. His skin was rough, mottled, striated, like a pizza. He had no neck per se; his chin seemed to be welded directly to his chest by a long sheet of skin that had contracted as it healed.

He turned into the room where the subjects were seated, drag-ging his dumpster behind him. Aaron ducked back into the monitor room to see all of the computer screens going wild. The six faces reacted almost in unison: they glanced up, their eyes widened, they gaped and stared for an instant, then manners got the better of them and they pretended not to notice. But Aaron could see the emo-tional impact of this spectacle continuing to simmer away beneath the surface. He could see them sneaking quick glances at the janitor, then looking away, ashamed by their own curiosity.

Within a few seconds, the janitor had finished emptying the wastebaskets and moved on down the hallway. The subjects sat quietly, shooting looks back and forth, daring one another to say something.

Schram came back into the room. "Well, my fucking secretary took an unauthorized break. She obviously thinks she can use the bathroom any time she feels like it."

This brought up lots of interesting stuff on the computer screens, particularly among the women.

"But I rummaged through her desk and I found this videotape in her bottom drawer. It's unlabeled, but I think it's the right one."

Aaron's monitor room had a seventh TV screen showing him the same program that the subjects were watching. Until now it had just been showing static. At this point, the static was replaced by a moving image.

It was a videotape of a woman sucking a man's penis.

"Whoops," Schram said. "How do you stop this thing?"

The image changed. Now it was a woman sandwiched between

two men on a large, heart-shaped waterbed, having simultaneous anal and vaginal sex.

"Goddamn new VCR. I'm not familiar with the controls," Schram said. "Hang on a second, I think I heard my secretary coming in, she knows how to work this thing. I'm really sorry about this."

Schram left the room for a minute or so, long enough for the woman on the heart-shaped waterbed to reach an electrifying climax. Both of her lovers withdrew and reached a simultaneous, on-screen orgasm. Then a new sequence began: a man tied to an overhead pipe being whipped by a woman in black leather.

About this time, Schram and his secretary got back into the room.

"Oh, jesus," the secretary said, "where did you get this? Where did this come from? Turn this thing off."

The pornography stopped rolling and was replaced by static. Aaron could hear the sound of the videotape being ejected from the VCR.

"I found it in your desk," Schram said. "I was trying to find the political spots, which you so brilliantly lost."

"Oh. And that gives you the right to go through my personal things?"

"Hey. What you do on your own time is your own goddamn business. If this kind of stuff turns you on, you're welcome to have it around your home. But when you bring it to work—"

"You *bastard!*" the secretary screamed. "You *bastard!* Just because you couldn't get it up with me! That's why you did this!" Then she burst into sobs and ran out of the room, screaming in humiliation.

"I couldn't get it up with you because you were such a frigid bitch!" Schram yelled down the hallway.

Aaron had long since stopped paying attention to any of the monitors. He was just staring at the wall, listening to the speaker, as if it were some kind of intense radio play.

"I'm sorry about that, folks," Schram said. "To tell you the truth, I've always harbored a suspicion that she was one of those Anita Hill types. You know, comes on real sexy and then turns around ten years later and says you've been harassing her."

Out in the hallway, Aaron could hear the secretary's high heeled shoes clacking and popping as she returned. He stuck his head out the door.

She was storming back toward the interview room, her face a ghoulish vision of streaked mascara. And she was carrying a gun. Aaron withdrew his head and slammed the door.

"This is what you deserve, you son of a bitch!" she screamed, and then three quick explosions overwhelmed the speaker system.

"I should kill you all, because you're witnesses!" the secretary said. "Don't anybody move from your chairs!"

The only thing Aaron could do now was look at the TV monitors. The subjects' faces had turned into sweating, distorted fright masks. Their eyes were wide open, darting back and forth, they were blinking rapidly, their jaws trembled, several held their hands over their faces, trying not to scream.

One of them—the debt-hounded wage slave—suddenly held both of his hands straight out in front of his face and turned his head to one side, bracing for the impact of a bullet.

A metallic click sounded from the monitor speaker.

"Shit!" the secretary said. "I'm out of bullets."

This revelation triggered a burst of emotions on the computer screens that was more vivid than anything seen yet.

"Freeze!" another voice shouted, a deep male voice. "Nobody move! Put that weapon on the floor, ma'am."

Aaron couldn't see what was happening, but he could see the relieved expressions on the subjects' faces, he could see the emotional response on the computer monitors. On the speaker, he heard the litany of the Cop Show Bust: "Lie down on your stomach and lace your fingers together behind your head. Don't move and nobody will get hurt."

It sounded safe. Aaron decided to go out and see what was going on. He walked down the hall to the interview room.

The secretary was lying on the floor. A large black cop was in the process of handcuffing her. Schram was half-sitting, half-lying on the floor, crumpled against the far wall of the room, covered with blood. Huge bursts of his blood had splattered onto the wall from the impact of the bullets and what looked like a gallon of the stuff had run out of his wounds and puddled on the floor all around him.

"My god," Aaron said. "I'll call an ambulance."

"I already done it," the cop said. "Go to the elevators and wait for 'em."

Aaron did exactly that. And he didn't have to wait for very long; the crew arrived with astonishing speed, four men rolling in a big gurney and carrying their equipment in bags and boxes. They didn't do much work on Schram, just lifted him directly onto the gurney and wheeled him out of the room. And down the hallway. Down the hallway to the bathroom.

The bathroom? Aaron followed them in there.

Schram had already climbed to his feet and was in the process of stripping out of his bloodstained clothes. Underneath his shirt, several small packets had been taped onto his body, electrical wires running into them. All of these things were soaked with blood and appeared to have been blown open from within. As Aaron watched, Schram ripped them off his body, exposing clean, unblemished flesh, and tossed them into the garbage.

"Squibs," he said. "Do you think they bought it?"

Aaron was still just standing there, his jaw flopped open like the hood of an abandoned car.

"You bought it, obviously," Schram said, "so they probably did. Why don't you go back in there and I'll meet you in a couple of minutes, after I get cleaned up." Schram stripped off the last of his clothes and walked, buck naked, into a shower stall, leaving a trail of bloody footprints on the polished white marble floor.

The secretary had been hauled off in chains. Several more "cops" had arrived and begun to interrogate the six witnesses. One of the cops was blustery and bullying and seemed to be treating the six as though they were all potential suspects in the crime. One of them was soothing and sympathetic. As they took turns talking to the six subjects, the readouts on the screen fluctuated back and forth from one extreme to the other.

Within a minute or two, Schram had joined Aaron in the monitor room, wearing a fresh set of clothes. "Can't you get in trouble for doing this?" Aaron said. He knew it was sappy even as he was saying it. But he couldn't help himself.

"For doing what?" Schram asked, sounding perfectly innocent.

"For—for what you just did."

"What did I just do?" Schram said.

"You—I don't know, you scared those people."

"So?"

"Well, isn't that a little extreme?"

"Life is extreme," Schram said.

"But isn't it illegal to do that, or something?"

"They all signed releases. Why do you think we're paying them money?"

"Did the releases give you permission to do *that?!*"

"The releases say that these people are willingly taking part in a psychological experiment," Schram said, "which is certainly the case."

"But aren't you going to tell them it was fake?"

"Of course I will. Of course I'll tell them," Schram said. "How else are we going to get them pissed off?"

"You want them to be pissed off?"

"Before they get out of that room," Schram said, "I want to run them through every emotion in the book."

"Oh. Well, which emotion are they being put through now?"

"Boredom. Which is going to take a while. And in the meantime, I want to go back over our results so far."

Everything that had happened to this point—the six feeds from the six video cameras, the audio track coming over the speaker, and the streams of data coming from the PIPER prototypes—had all been recorded by the computers. By entering some commands into the Calyx system that controlled the whole thing, they were able to go back and replay portions of the experiment, seeing everything, on the dozen or so screens, just as Aaron had seen it the first time it had happened.

The door opened and the hunchbacked janitor dragged himself into the room. He fixed his one good eye on Schram, slouched over to him, and gave him a high five.

"Oscar-winning performance," the janitor said.

"You get best supporting actor, Cy," Schram said.

"Nah, it's all special effects," Ogle said, reaching up to grab the curtain of tortured flesh that ran from his jawbone down to his chest. He pulled on it, and most of it peeled away in a single piece, leaving a few strips and patches of burnt-looking skin adhering to his face and neck. With a few minutes of additional peeling and scrubbing, Ogle managed to get loose from most of the makeup, though a few fragments of it still stuck to him here and there, like bits of tissue paper left over from a bad shave, and the part of his face that hadn't been covered still had colored greasepaint on it. Ogle didn't care; he was too busy staring at the monitors.

He loved it. His eyes were virtually popping out of his head. His mouth was wide open and frozen in an expression of boyish glee, like a farm boy getting his first look at Disney World. His eyes darted back and forth from one screen to the next; he couldn't decide what to look at.

"Days. Weeks," Ogle said. "I'm gonna be looking at this thing for weeks."

"Check out the look on that can stacker's face when you dragged your sorry ass into the room," Schram said.

"She's not a can stacker," Aaron said, "she's a coupon snipper."

They ran through the whole thing a couple of times. The computer allowed them to run it like a videotape, with fast-forward, rewind, freeze-frame, the whole bit. As they went through it, Schram jotted down notes on a yellow legal pad. Finally they shunted the screens back over to a real-time display of what was happening, right now, in the interview room.

Nothing was happening. The six faces were a picture of terminal boredom. The good cop and the bad cop had gone away and been replaced by a droning, monotonous voice that was going on and on in some kind of pseudolegal jargon.

"That's an actor claiming to be a lawyer for Ogle Data Research," Ogle explained. "He's been lecturing them for half an hour while we dicked around with all this stuff."

"Let's see what self-righteous indignation looks like," Schram said, rising to his feet and heading for the interview room.

"Ten-four on that," Ogle said.

Schram walked into the interview room a moment later and the monitors all went ballistic. Ogle howled like a dog.

"All the same," he said, "they all react the same. The hunchback, the shooting, the pornography, and they all reacted differently. But when they're pissed off, they all look alike. And that's why self-righteousness is the most powerful force in politics."

## CHAPTER TWENTY-SEVEN

The first thing he learned how to move was his right thumb. It wasn't a fluke, either. It was something that William Cozzano worked on constantly from the first moment that he came awake after the implantation.

Within a day, he was able to make the thumb jerk spasmodically from time to time. By the time they loaded him on the plane and flew him back to Tuscola, two days after the implantation, he was able to jerk it whenever he wanted to.

Then he learned how to move it both ways, straightening the thumb and then curling it into the palm of his hand. Once he got that down, he repeated it several thousand times, sixteen hours a day, until they gave him sedatives to make him sleep. Eight hours later he would wake up and begin exercising his thumb again.

For the first few days, neither Mary Catherine nor anyone else could figure out why he was concentrating on the thumb. They had assumed that he would want to work on his speech skills. And he did, from time to time; within a week after the operation, it was possible to watch him playing with muscles in his face. The under-side of his jaw throbbed in and out as he moved his tongue around inside his mouth, and his lips began to move, on both sides, jerkily at first and then smoothly. Within five days he had learned to pucker up so that he could give Mary Catherine a kiss when she bent down to offer her cheek.

But the whole time he was doing these things, his thumb was active. It became a subject of concern among Cozzano's therapy team—the half-dozen physical therapists, neurologists, and com-puter people who had moved into some of the unused bedrooms in the Tuscola house to monitor the Governor's recovery. They had meetings about that thumb, worried about whether the movement was voluntary or involuntary, discussed the idea of taping it down so it wouldn't get worn out and arthritic over time.

It all became clear the first time they put a remote control into his hand. By that time, his fingers had developed enough coordination to wrap around the underside of the remote and hold it in place, giving that thumb, now highly coordinated, the freedom to roam around on its top surface, punching buttons. Changing channels. Moving the volume up and down. Activating the VCR to tape certain programs, then playing them back later.

They decided to give him a test. They arranged a dinner party on a Thursday evening at seven o'clock, knowing that it would interfere with Cozzano's favorite TV show, a satirical cartoon. He passed that test with flying colors; without any hints or prompting from the therapy team, he used his thumb to program his VCR.

"He still knows how to do it," said the head computer person, Peter (Zeldo) Zeldovich. He was awed. "I mean, I wrote half of the Calyx operating system. But I can't program a VCR."

"His memory seems pretty good," Mary Catherine said. She had driven down from Chicago to attend the dinner, then snuck up to the hallway outside the master bedroom to see Dad rewind the videotape and play back his favorite program.

The other bedrooms had been turned into a high-tech wonderland. Zeldo filled Mary Catherine's old bedroom with computers and James's with communications gear. Mom's sewing room was full of medical stuff. The two guest bedrooms were set up with bunk beds and mattresses on the floor so that the nurses and therapists could alternate between sleeping and working without leaving the house.

Everything that Dad did now—every tiny motion of his thumb, every twitch of his lips—had huge informational ramifications that Zeldo could plot and graph on his computer screens. Thousands of connections had now grown into place between Dad's neurons and the biochip, and hundreds of new ones were still being made every day. All of the impulses passing from his brain outward into his body and back passed through these connections, and could be monitored by the biochip. Even when Dad was sleeping, it amounted to an overwhelming flow of information, like all of the telephone calls being made into or out of Manhattan at a given time.

There was no way to understand all of it. No way to keep track. The best that Zeldo could do was keep a running tab on what was happening, build up a statistical database, maybe get some sense of which connections were being used for the thumb and which for the left eyebrow. Still, it was fascinating to watch.

That all of these things worked was no news. The chip had worked in the baboons and it had worked in Mohinder Singh, after all. The real question on their minds was: how much damage had the strokes done to other parts of Cozzano's mind, for example, memory, personality, cognitive skills?

The fact that he still wanted to watch the same TV show, still thought it was funny, and still knew how to program his VCR answered several questions. It was good news on all fronts.

But mostly Cozzano watched the news and public affairs programs about the presidential campaign. They would pin the latest newspapers and magazines up on a reading stand in front of his face and he would pore over them, his eyes flicking back and forth between the coverage on the television and the printed page.

Only then—after he had got control of the TV channels and had caught up on the newspapers—only then did he start working on speech.

They set an ambitious schedule for him, worrying that they might stress him out and overwork him, and he left that schedule in the dust. First thing in the morning, the physical therapists came in, at first helping him move his limbs, later, when he got the hang of that, running him through exercises. Then the speech therapist came in and got him to put his tongue and lips in certain positions, got him to make certain sounds, and then to string those sounds together into syllables and words. Following an afternoon nap, the physical therapists would come back in and work on the parts of his body that they had missed in the morning. During the evenings he could relax, watch TV, read.

He exercised his speech during physical therapy and he exercised his body during speech therapy. He also exercised both of them while he was pretending to take his afternoon nap, and then he exercised them all evening long when he was supposed to be taking it easy. He even woke up in the middle of the night and exercised.

Getting up out of the wheelchair was an ambitious goal that he wouldn't attempt for a few weeks. In the meantime there were a few things he couldn't do for himself, such as going to the toilet, taking baths, carrying in wood for the fireplace, and swapping tapes in and out of the VCR. Nurses, aides, and family members had to do these things for him.

Almost two weeks after the implant, Mary Catherine came down for another visit. She had been doing so much driving that they had gone to the trouble of leasing a car, a brand-new Acura luxury sedan, so that she could make the trip in comfort and safety. The evening she arrived, she had a conversation with Dad.

"Vee . . . Cee . . . Arrr," he said.

"VCR. You want me to do something with the VCR?"

"Yes."

"Okay. What do you want me to do?"

Dad aimed the remote shakily toward the TV cabinet and hit the EJECT button. The VCR spat out a tape.

"You want me to take this out?"

"Yes."

"You want me to put a different tape in?"

"Yes."

The TV cabinet had a shelf along the top with a few dozen videotapes in it, mostly old family tapes or favorite movies. Mary Catherine began running her finger along the line of tapes.

"New!" Dad blurted.

"You want a new tape?"

"Blank."

"You want a blank tape."

"Yes."

Mary Catherine rummaged around in the cabinet until she found a six-pack of fresh blank videocassettes. Dad always bought them half a dozen at a time at Wal-Mart. He always bought everything in vast, bulk quantities, dirt cheap, in huge drafty warehouselike stores out in the middle of the prairie.

She unwrapped one and stuck it into the machine. "Okay, what should I do with this old one?" she asked, wiggling the tape she had just removed.

"Label."

The fresh videotape had come shipped with a number of blank labels. She peeled a couple of them back and stuck them onto the black shell of the cassette. Then she dug a small felt-tipped marker out of her purse. "What do you want to call this?"

Dad rolled his eyes as if to indicate that this was not important, he would remember what it was. Mary Catherine grinned and looked him in the eye, pen poised over the tape, challenging him.

He looked her right back in the eye. "Eee . . . lack . . . sun."

"Election."

"One," Dad said. The fingers of his hand trembled and jerked uncertainly. Finally the index finger extended, while the other fingers clenched into a loose, jittering fist.

"Election One," Mary Catherine repeated, writing it onto the top and side of the tape. "Does this imply that it's the first in a series?"

Dad rolled his eyes again.

Later, after he had gone to sleep, Mary Catherine curled up on the living room sofa with a bag of microwave popcorn, rewound "Election One," and watched it.

It was outtakes from election-related news coverage from the past week or week and a half, ever since Dad's thumb had gotten nimble enough to control the machine. Most of it had to do with the peculiar, stereotyped behavior patterns of men competing in state primary elections. It made good training for a neurologist. Hours and hours of men walking around under bright lights, moving with the spasmodic gait of candidates. A candidate walked on two legs like a normal man, but every time he sensed that he was in a position that would make a good photograph, he would stop and freeze for a moment as if suffering a petit mal seizure, and turn toward the nearest battery of cameras. No candidate could climb on board a vehicle or enter a building without freezing for a moment and giving the thumbs-up. Handshakes all lasted for hours, and the candidate never looked at the person whose hand he was shaking; he looked toward the audience.

Super Tuesday, Illinois, and New York were history. California wouldn't happen for weeks. By this point in the campaign, the nominations were usually settled. But there was nothing settled about them this year. Both parties were running several candidates. The flakes, the paupers, and the weaklings had long since been weeded out. The remaining strong contenders had been beating one another mercilessly. By the time the real campaign began on Labor Day, neither of the two surviving candidates would have any reputation left.

Maybe the GOP would try to draft Cozzano. But she had to ask herself—Dad had to be asking himself—what was the point of parties anyway? All they did was get in the way. Ogle was right.

*The film crew* showed up in Tuscola a few days later. It consisted of a producer, a cameraman, and an audio person who happened to be female. They rented a couple of rooms at the Super 8 Motel on the edge of town, out near I-57, a short drive from the Cozzano residence.

The producer was named Myron Morris. He came with the personal recommendation of Cyrus Rutherford Ogle, who continued to phone Mary Catherine at work from time to time, just keeping in touch. She had a series of conversations with him: Ogle on a plane or in a car or hotel room somewhere, and Mary Catherine standing in the hallway at the hospital, usually in the neurology ward, where the comings and goings of various paralyzed, epileptic, senile, psychotic, or demented patients provided a useful reality check.

Ogle had first brought up the idea of a film crew just a few days after the implant. He had gone about this in a typically diplomatic fashion, in a late round of the conversation, after greetings, small talk, chitchat about politics, and a little bit of gentle probing into the Governor's condition.

"This is like your baby learning how to walk: it's only going to happen once," he pointed out. "And consequently, you're going to want it on film. It might seem like a weird idea now, but believe me, sooner or later, maybe ten years down the road, you and the Governor are going to wish that you could go back and watch him saying his first words and taking his first steps."

"We have a camcorder stashed back in the garage," Mary Catherine said. "I'll get it out."

"That's an excellent idea," Ogle said encouragingly, "and make sure that when you're finished, you break off the little plastic tab on the videocassette so you can't record over it by accident."

"I'll do that," Mary Catherine said, trying to hide the smile in her voice.

A week later they spoke again. It was the same routine: small talk, chitchat, and all the rest.

"Did you dig up that long-lost camcorder?" Ogle said knowingly.

"Yes," Mary Catherine said.

"But it doesn't work."

"How'd you know?"

"Old ones never do," Ogle said. "The first time you put them away in the garage, you lose half the pieces."

"There's a little black box that is supposed to charge up the battery," Mary Catherine said. "I can't find it anywhere. Dad knows where it is, but he can't tell me at this point in his recovery. So maybe I'll go buy a new one."

"Don't do that," Ogle said. "There's too many camcorders floating around the world not being used for you to go spend money on a new one."

"I sense that you have a scheme on your mind."

"As usual you are right. I know some people. People who are very good working with film and videotape. Who would be glad to come in to Tuscola and spend some time videotaping your father's recovery."

"Is that right."

"Yes, it is. We could send out a three-person crew as soon as you give the okay."

Mary Catherine laughed. "Well, I must say that is an *exceedingly* generous offer. To think that three people who presumably have jobs and families could come all the way out to Tuscola and donate their time and expertise to making some home movies for the Cozzano family."

"Isn't it a remarkable thing?" Ogle said.

"You realize that this recovery process is going to stretch out over a period of several weeks. Possibly months."

"Yes, I know that."

"Don't these people have anything better to do during this part of their lives?"

"Nope. They sure don't," Ogle said.

Mary Catherine let a long pause go by. "What's going on here?"

"I'll tell you," Ogle said. "Your dad's gonna get better. I know he is."

"I appreciate that confidence."

"At that point he'll be a healthy, strong, middle-aged man with a great deal of popularity, in Illinois and in the rest of the country. And based on his past behavior I have this feeling he's not ready to retire yet."

"I couldn't say."

"And I don't know what he'll choose to do with the remaining, best years of his life. But would it be fair to say it's not out of the question that he might continue with his current career in politics?"

"Who knows?"

"Well, if he does continue in politics—even if he just wants to run for mayor of Tuscola—I would very much like to serve as his media consultant."

"I'm looking at my watch," Mary Catherine said, "and noting the time. I think you just set a new record."

"For what?"

"For beating around the bush. You've been talking to me for a month and this is the first time you've come out and said that."

"Well, I hate to be direct," Ogle said. "It's just the way I am."

"Please continue." She sighed.

"If he were to make that choice, and if he were to hire me, I would want to make campaign ads explaining to the voters who William A. Cozzano is and why he would be a good man to vote for. And as a man who understands the media, I cannot think of anything that would tell voters more about the character of your father than some footage—discreet, dignified—showing his slow and difficult recovery from the terrible, terrible tragedy that overcame him. And, because it is my job to think ahead, it has occurred to me that, if all these things were to come to pass, I would not be able to make such advertisements unless I had footage of the real thing."

"So you're willing to spend, what, tens of thousands of bucks to put a film crew in Tuscola full-time, just on the off chance that he will recover fully, choose to continue a career in politics, and choose to hire you as his media consultant."

"What can I say," Ogle said. "I'm an optimist."

Ogle was up to something. That was no surprise. Mary Catherine wasn't a professional politician but she wasn't a complete moron either and she had known from the beginning that Ogle must have some kind of agenda.

Her first reaction was not to trust him, not to get herself entangled in anything. To play it safe, in other words. She had been noncommital when Ogle had suggested that Dad might want to continue his career in politics. The fact was, of course, that Dad very much did want to continue it. She had something of a duty to help him. Not to close off any options that he might want kept open. And if she failed to accept Ogle's suggestion, she'd be blowing an opportunity. Being the overprotective daughter.

Besides, she still wasn't committing the Cozzanos to anything. There couldn't be any harm in letting some people hang around and film Dad. Later, when he had recovered more fully, then he'd be able to make the command decision. If he didn't like Ogle, those people would be out on their asses.

Mel wasn't crazy about this. But he had changed his tactics. He no longer challenged Mary Catherine on every little point, just grumbled and simmered a lot in the background. Just to give him something to do, she had him deal with Ogle's lawyers. They drew up an agreement that gave the Cozzanos absolute, permanent, unequivocal control over any films, videotapes, audiotapes, or other media that Ogle's people created on Cozzano property. Mel was good, Mel knew how to make the agreement airtight, and by the time Myron Morris and his two assistants pulled into Tuscola in their four-wheel-drive Suburban, Mel was as satisfied as he could ever be that this thing was above board. There was no way they could pull anything sneaky.

*Mary Catherine was* astonished the first time she saw the crew in action. Myron Morris himself wasn't there; he had hung around quite a bit for the first day or two, then excused himself. That left the cameraman and the sound woman. The sound woman was carrying some heavy-duty gear: a big reel-to-reel machine slung over a shoulder strap, with an assortment of microphones. But the cameraman was packing a cheap piece of junk: a home-style VHS camcorder not much different from the one that was rusting away in the Cozzanos' garage.

"Why are you using a home camcorder?" Mary Catherine asked him, when he wasn't actively filming Dad.

He shrugged. "That's what Myron said to use. I don't get it either."

"Where's Myron?"

"Scouting."

"Scouting?"

"Locations. He's looking around the area."

"Why? Is he planning on producing a movie in Tuscola?"

The cameraman shrugged. "I'm just repeating his words."

*She found him* outside of town, at the old Cozzano farm. His giant Suburban was parked along the shoulder of the country road, looking as if it might roll over into the ditch. Morris had jumped a fence into a cornfield and was walking down one of the freshly plowed rows, his shoes sinking into the soft black earth. Every few paces he would stop walking and turn toward the farmhouse, which had been rebuilt by Dad and his cousins after the tornado destroyed it in the early fifties. He would lift a short, stubby black telescope to one eye and peer through it for a few seconds. Two or three of these devices were hung on ropes around his neck, clacking into one another as he walked.

Mary Catherine parked behind his Suburban, jumped the ditch, and vaulted the fence. Fence-vaulting was something she had known how to do, expertly, since an early age; in the extended Cozzano family, kids who couldn't vault fences got left behind and never had any fun. In her fancy grownup clothes it was slightly more complicated, but nowadays she had the advantage of height. Half a mile away she could see her second cousin Tim out plowing the field on one of the old tractors.

Myron Morris noticed her approaching. He stopped, waved, and stood there for a few moments, hands in pockets, watching her approach. Then he picked up one of the short stubby telescopes and used it to peer at her. He dropped that one and looked at her through another. Then another.

"What are those things?" she asked as she got closer.

"They simulate what I would see looking through the viewfinder of a camera with a particular lens on it. It's just a visual device that makes it easier to frame one's shots, figure out where to put the camera."

"I've been following you around town," she said. "People said they've seen you out at the park, the high-school playing field, the old train station."

"I don't get out to Tuscola very often," he said. "So as long as I'm here I thought I'd get to know the place."

"Don't you think you're getting ahead of the game? Dad's staying at home."

"I won't bullshit you," he said. "Cy Ogle wants to work for your dad. This is important stuff to him. If anything happens, we'll need to know where are the best places to shoot. And that's what I'm finding out. Is that okay?"

Mary Catherine nodded at the little telescopes. "Do any of those things work with a video camcorder?"

"Nah. These are all for professional film cameras."

"I'm confused," she said. "In some ways, you guys are taking this thing way too seriously. In other ways, you're goofing off."

"You want to know why we're using that Kmart special to video-tape the Governor."

"Yeah."

"The whole point here is that these things are supposed to be home movies. If the Governor chooses not to use our services, then you end up with home movies in a format you can use. But if he does hire us, we can make them into ads."

"Ads that look like shitty home movies."

"A-ha!" Myron Morris said, holding up one finger. "You were expecting something a little slicker."

"If there's one adjective that's most commonly used in connection with Cy Ogle, it is slick," Mary Catherine said.

"Which is why we want to go with the opposite of slick."

"I don't follow."

"Imagine it. A television ad showing big moments in the life of William Anthony Cozzano. We see him horsing around this very farm as a child. Scoring a touchdown in the Rose Bowl. We see him in Vietnam. We see him playing for the Bears. Raising his kids. All of this is going to be trashy, grainy, antiquated film stock. Home-movie stuff. And then we see his recovery from the stroke—some private moments at home—and all of a sudden it looks slick. It's shot on 35-millimeter film stock, the lighting is perfect, he's wearing makeup, all of a sudden it looks like goddamn Lawrence of Arabia. You think people aren't going to notice that?"

Mary Catherine didn't have an answer for that one.

"Americans may be undereducated, lazy, and disorganized, but they do one thing better than any people on the face of the earth, and that is watch television. The average eight-year-old American has absorbed more about media technology than a goddamn film student in most other countries. You can tell lies to them and they'll never know. But if you try to lie to them *with the camera*, they'll crucify you. Which is why, when we shoot home movies of your father, we use exactly the same machine that Joe Sixpack uses when he sends a tape of his dancing Dalmatian to *America's Funniest Home Videos*. And to tell you the truth, we may actually have to go through and process that videotape and make it look worse than it does now."

"Are you sure about this?"

"Reagan did it in '80. I believe he made out okay."

"But everyone will know that Ogle's working for Dad."

Myron shook his head dismissively. "That's a verbal thing. Nobody gives a shit about that, as long as the ads don't look slick. Believe me, as long as we stick with half-inch videotape, and as long as we avoid releasing any images of your Dad standing with one arm around Cy Ogle, nobody who matters will think that he's ever been near a slick media man."

## CHAPTER TWENTY-EIGHT

As Mary Catherine trudged back across the field to where she had parked her car behind Morris's Suburban, a third car cruised up the road and pulled onto the shoulder behind hers. It was Mel's Mercedes.

Mel set the hand brake, climbed out, waved to her, and then ambled around on the shoulder for a minute or two, squinting off into the distance, taking in the vista. Views in this part of Illinois were not exciting, but they were vast, and a person like Mel, who spent much time pent up in a city, could come out here and stare at the horizon in the same way that a vacationer in New York or L.A. might go to the ocean and gaze off into emptiness.

Mel had given up cigarettes by the trick of switching to cigars, which were so noxious that, like nuclear weapons, they could not be used except in remote, desolate environments. He did not smoke them in his Mercedes for fear of imparting an eternal reek to the leather and the carpets. Now that he was out on the road, he fished the extinct butt of a fat stogie from the pocket of his trench coat and stoked it into life with a wooden safety match. Bubbles of silver smoke blew out from the corners of his mouth, elongated in the wind, and whipped off across the prairie, picking up almost palpable momentum as they headed for the Indiana border.

After a minute or so, Mel's gaze settled on the farmhouse, which he had helped to rebuild. The concept of a Jew learning to use a claw hammer had been considered revolutionary by both the Meyers and the Cozzanos, and had met with some resistance from both groups. But the young Mel enjoyed his trips out of town and had insisted on riding the train down at least once a week during the summers to pound nails. Three volumes of the library of Cozzano family photo albums were devoted to the reconstruction of the house, and Mel showed up in a number of pictures, pale, skinny, and bent as a peeled banana, kneeling on the bare plywood of the new roof among burly, copper-hued Cozzanos, nailing down the shingles one strip at a time.

Since then, Mel had always felt a proprietary interest in the Cozzano farmhouse. He had only a distant relationship with the Cozzanos who lived there now, but he liked to drive out from time to time and look at it, as he was doing now. Mary Catherine did not know whether he did this from pure nostalgia or from curiosity about the durability of his handiwork or both. She did know that photographs of the completed farmhouse had circulated widely among the Meyer family, as far away as Israel, as evidence of the wonders that a Meyer could achieve if he was not afraid to brave unknown fields of endeavor.

"When I was pounding in all those damn nails, *whack whack whack,* day after day, I had this terrible fear that I didn't really know what I was doing," Mel said, as Mary Catherine was vaulting the fence again. "I would have nightmares that all of the nails I had pounded in to that house would suddenly pop loose and all of Willy's nails would hold fast, and everyone would blame me for the house falling down."

"Well, it's still standing," Mary Catherine said.

"That it is," Mel said with satisfaction and finality, as if his sole purpose in driving down from Chicago had been to make sure that the house was still there.

"Have you seen Dad?"

"Yeah, Willy and I saw each other," Mel said. "So the social aspect of today's visit has been consummated."

"Oh. You don't want to socialize with me?"

Mel looked around them. A farm truck blasted down the road, kicking up dust and rocks with its windblast, inflating Mel's trench coat and Mary Catherine's hair for a moment. The red coal on the end of Mel's cigar flared bright orange and caught his eye. He stared into it as though mesmerized. "This is no place," he said, "to social-ize with a lady."

She smiled. Mel was old enough, and good enough, to talk this way without seeming stilted or weird. "You didn't come down to socialize with me anyway."

Mel took one last draw on his cigar and then examined it regret-fully. He pinched it carefully between the ball of his thumb and the nail of his arched forefinger, straightened his arm, aimed it into the ditch, and snapped the butt into a swampy patch. It died with a quick sizzling burst. Mel stood still for a moment, staring at it, and then expelled the last of the smoke from his mouth.

"Get in," he said. "Let's go get some coffee at the Dixie Truckers' Home."

She grinned. The Dixie Truckers' Home was right out on I-57. Mel had driven by it a million times but never been there; for him it was an object of morbid, sick fascination. Mary Catherine opened the passenger door and climbed in. Normally Mel would have gone all the way around the car and opened the door for her, but his mind was elsewhere today. As he had implied, this was business, not a social visit, and he wasn't thinking about the niceties.

The Mercedes was perfect for two, crowded for anyone else. It was ideal for Mel, who was unmarried and childless and presumed by many to be gay. He started up the engine and pulled out onto the road and gave the car a tremendous long burst of acceleration that took it all the way up past a hundred.

Mary Catherine's heart melted. Mel had always enjoyed thrilling her and James with the power of his fancy European cars, ever since they had been children. She knew that when he put the pedal down and squealed the tires on this country road, he was evoking a memory, for his own benefit as much as for Mary Catherine's.

"You know that the relationship between our families has been strong and will continue to be," Mel said, "even though, over time, it has gone through a lot of different shapes."

"What's going on?" she said.

Mel slowed the car down and looked sideways at Mary Catherine for a moment. He seemed a little surprised by her impatience.

"Just take it easy," he said, "this is hard for me."

"Okay," she said. Her vision got a little blurry and her nose started to run. She drew a deep silent breath and got the impulse under control.

"The reason our families have gotten along together is that the leaders—the patriarchs—have always been wise men who took the long view of things. And who were willing to do what made sense in the long run. Other people have looked at the strategies of the

Cozzanos and the Meyers and scratched their heads, but we have always had reasons for what we did."

"What are we doing now?" Mary Catherine said.

"Willy doesn't know this, because I didn't want to stress him out," Mel said, "but the shit is finally hitting the fan on what happened in February."

"What shit? What fan?"

Mel cocked his head back and forth from side to side, weighing his thoughts. "Well, you know that we could have just hauled Willie down the front steps of the capitol and the whole thing would have been splashed all over the evening news. Instead we took a more old-fashioned approach. Like when FDR was in a wheelchair, but hardly anyone in America was aware of that fact because his media coverage was manipulated so well."

"We concealed the extent of his illness," Mary Catherine said.

"Right. We let his organization run the state government for a while instead of just abdicating and turning things over to that putz, the Lieutenant Governor, as we were technically supposed to do." Mel spoke the last phrase in a screwed-up, Mickey Mouse tone of voice, as if the question of succession were a finicky bit of fine print, a mere debater's point. "Well, it might be possible to make the claim that what we did—what I did—was not, strictly speaking, ethical. Or in some cases, even legal. And sooner or later this was bound to come out."

"Let me ask you something," Mary Catherine said. "Did you know, at the time you were doing this, that it might come out?"

Mel was pained. "Of course I knew it, girl! But it's like dragging a man out of a burning car. You have to act, you can't think about the possibility that he'll later sue you for spraining his shoulder. I did what I had to do. I did it well." Mel turned and looked at her, a dry grin coming to his lips. "I was awesome, frankly."

"Well, what are you getting at?"

"You know who Markene Caldicott is?"

"Of course I do!" She was surprised that Mel would even ask this question.

"Oh, that's right. You're probably the type who listens to RNA all the time."

Mary Catherine grinned and shook her head. Most people considered Radio North America to be the height of journalistic sophistication, but Mel still had it lumped together with MTV and Arena Football. He got his radio news via shortwave, from the BBC.

"What about Markene Caldicott?" she said.

"Well, apparently she's some hotshot reporter," Mel said skeptically.

"You could say that."

"She's after my ass. And I don't mean that in the sexual sense," Mel said. "She's called every single person I've ever worked with. I can read this woman's mind like a fucking cereal box."

"What's she doing?"

"She'd really like to shoot down your father," Mel said, "but she can't, because Willy is without flaw, and was incapacitated for the last couple of months besides. So instead, she is going to do a big exposé where she makes me out to be this sort of Richelieu with a yarmulke. The shadowy power who pulled the strings while Cozzano drooled down his chin. You know the kind of thing."

"Your basic overinflated election-year scandal."

"Yeah. She probably figures that Willy is going to get into the race and she wants to be the first to take shots at him. So I'm going to head her off at the pass."

"How are you going to do that?"

"I'm going to drive back up to Daley," Mel said. He and Mary Catherine had both fallen into the habit of using Cozzano's poststroke jargon. "And have dinner with Mark McCabe. A political reporter from the *Trib*. And I'm going to spill my guts. Going to lay the whole thing out."

Mary Catherine was shocked. "You're going to tell him everything?"

Mel looked at her with an expression that was somewhere between fatherly disappointment and pity. "Are you nuts? Of course I'm not going to tell him everything. I'm just going to make it look like I'm telling him everything."

"Oh."

"So McCabe will get a big front-page story. We will release the information in the form most favorable to us. Markene Caldicott will have been scooped, and her story, if she even bothers to air the damn thing, will have virtually no impact. And the Cozzano family and administration will be totally exonerated, because I, the runty Jew lawyer, will take all the heat."

"That's very good of you," Mary Catherine said.

Mel laughed and slapped the steering wheel. "Ha! Good of me. I like that. You downstaters just kill me. 'Very good of you,'" he mimicked her, not unkindly, and laughed again. Mary Catherine could feel her face radiating warmth. "Look, kid, this is not about good. This is not a good and evil thing. This is about being smart and taking our losses in the way that is least disadvantageous to us. That's what I am trying to set up here."

"Okay."

"I'm going to great lengths to be clever and set this whole thing up the way that is best for us," Mel continued, now starting to sound almost a little peeved, "and it just kills me when you try to characterize it as some kind of church-social altruism. It's like you're failing to see and appreciate the full artistry that is involved here."

"Sorry. I think it's very devious," she said, now getting a little peeved herself.

"Thank you. That's a compliment I can handle. Now we are on the same wavelength."

"Good."

"We're both listening to the same station," Mel said, extending the metaphor. "Both listening to the BBC instead of that RNA crap." He spoke the final word with a resounding, sardonic whiplash that made them both laugh, albeit nervously. "So let's stay away from this weepy sentimental shit and do what is best for our families over the next several generations," Mel said.

"Okay."

"What is best, for right now, is that I, Mel Meyer, get out of Dodge."

"What do you mean?"

Mel sighed, a little defeated, as if he'd been hoping that Mary Catherine would simply get it. "Jesus, girl, I'm going public tonight. Telling the whole world that I did something unethical. I'm going to take the heat for the decisions that I made in January and February.

Which were good decisions—but sooner or later, the karma comes back and hits you. Now, once I've made myself out to be the evil, scheming homunculus that I am, how can I possibly continue to be a close adviser and confidante of the Cozzano clan? The whole point is that everyone throws shit at me, it all sticks, and then I run away and take all the shit with me. If I stick around you guys, some of it's bound to rub off."

As Mel explained all of this, the whole situation became clear to Mary Catherine, and the cloud of emotion that had obscured the beginning of this conversation lifted away. She felt calm and relaxed.

"How far away are you going to run?"

"Oh, pretty far, at least for a while," Mel said. "I'm formally severing my relationship with your father, as his attorney, and sending his files over to Ty Addison at Norton Addison Goldberg Green. Ty'll take good care of you guys. I will stay in touch by phone, but this is the last time I'll show my face in Tuscola for a while. It's okay for us to see each other when you come up to Chicago, as long as it's something casual, like lunch. Anything more than that, and someone in the media will notice it, and make it out to look like I'm still lurking in the shadows, pulling strings."

"What about the long term you were talking about?"

"Long term, nothing has changed. This is a blip on the screen of history."

During the conversation he had been steering the Mercedes randomly around the gridwork of roads that covered the area, occasionally zigzagging his way back toward the Cozzano farmhouse. Myron Morris's Suburban passed them going the other way and they waved at each other. Finally Mel stopped next to Mary Catherine's car, parked along the shoulder, and she realized that he meant for her to get out.

"Do I get a hug?" she asked. "Or is that too sinister for Markene Caldicott?"

Mel just sat there passively, as though suddenly stunned by what he was doing.

Mary Catherine unfastened her seat belt, leaned over the gap between the seats, and encircled Mel's neck in her arms, nearly lying down sideways across the front of the car. Mel wrapped his arms around her body and held her tight for at least a minute. Then he let go, all of a sudden.

"Okay, I want to be alone now," he said.

Mary Catherine pecked him once on the cheek and climbed rapidly out of the car without looking back. She slammed the door behind her. Mel's car was moving forward before the door was even shut. The tires broke loose from the pavement, spun, and squealed, kicking back twin spurts of blue smoke, and the Mercedes shot down the road past the old farmhouse, just like in the old days. In the windows of the farmhouse, the faces of young Cozzanos appeared, drawn by the noise, then drifted away as they saw that it was just Mel Meyer, the old lawyer from Chicago who liked to drive fast.

*William A. Cozzano* was out for his morning constitutional: out his back door, through the gate and into the alley, half a block down, through a break in the hedge, and into the Thorsen's driveway. Down the edge of their side yard, waving to ninety-year-old Mrs. Thorsen, who was invariably standing at her kitchen window washing dishes, then into the street, another half block up, through a gap in the chain-link fence around Tuscola City Park, and from there, wherever he wanted to go. It was a route he had been following since he had learned to walk the first time, and it was one of the first things he had done when he learned to walk the second time.

Nowadays, of course, he was usually accompanied by half a dozen support personnel when he did it. Mrs. Thorsen didn't seem to mind all those people traipsing through her yard. She lived alone now. It was a mystery how she could have so many dishes to wash, but she was always there washing them.

The trip to the park was a tricky, twisting affair that Cozzano's entourage had to accomplish in single file. Once they reached the broad open spaces of the park proper, they were able to spread out and walk in a group. Usually the entourage consisted of a couple of nurses, Myron Morris's home-movie crew, and someone from the Radhakrishnan Institute, connected back to a bedroom in the Cozzano house by a radio headset. On this particular day, Zeldo came along for the walk.

"You're walking. You're talking. Congratulations," he said.

"Thanks. It's nice," Cozzano said.

"If you keep improving the way you have been, then by some-time in mid-June you should be essentially back to normal."

"Excellent."

"I'd like to know if you would have any interest in developing some capabilities that are *better* than normal."

This was a bizarre suggestion and Zeldo knew it; he was visibly nervous as he spoke the words. He watched Cozzano's face carefully for a reaction.

For a long time, Cozzano didn't react at all. He kept walking as if he hadn't heard. But he was no longer looking around. He was staring down at the grass in front of his feet, trying to scorch a hole in the ground with his eyes.

After a minute or so, he seemed to reach a conclusion. He looked up again. But he still didn't speak for another minute or so. He was apparently formulating a response. Finally he looked at Zeldo and said, nonchalantly, "I have always been a strong believer in self-improvement."

*"I'm seeing my* aunt Mary taking an apple pie out of the oven," Cozzano said. "It is Thanksgiving Day of 1954 at 2:15 P.M. A football game is going on the television in the next room. My father and some uncles and cousins are watching it. They are all smoking pipes and the smoke stings my nose. The Lions have the ball on their own thirty-five, second down and four yards to go. But I'm concentrating on the pie."

"Okay, that's good," Zeldo said, typing all of this furiously into the computer. "Now, what happens when I stimulate this link?" He swiveled around to another keyboard and typed a command into another computer.

Cozzano's eyes narrowed. He was staring into the distance, unfocused.

"Just a very fleeting image of Christina at the age of about thirty-five," Cozzano said. "She's in the living room, wearing a yellow dress. I can't remember much more than that. Now it's fading."

"Okay, how about this one?" Zeldo said, typing in another command.

Cozzano drew a sharp breath into his nostrils and began to smack his lips and swallow. "A very intense odor. Some kind of chemical odor that I was exposed to at the plant. Possibly a pesticide."

"But you're not getting any visuals?"

"None whatsoever."

"Okay, how about this one?"

"Jesus!" Cozzano shouted. Genuine fright and astonishment had come over his face. He half-slid, half-rolled out of his chair and dropped to the floor of the bedroom, landing on his belly, and crawled on his elbows so that he was half-hidden under a bed.

"Let me guess," Zeldo said. "Something from Vietnam."

Cozzano went limp and dropped his face down onto his arms, staring directly into the floor. His back and shoulders were heaving and sweat was visible along his hairline.

"Sorry about that," Zeldo said.

"It was unbelievably realistic," Cozzano said. "My god, I actually heard the sound of a bullet whizzing past my head." He sat up and held up one hand, just above and to one side of his right temple. "It was from an AK-47. It came from this direction, right out of the jungle, and shot past me. Missed me by a couple of inches, I'd say."

"Is that a specific memory of something that happened to you?" Zeldo said.

Cozzano's eyes became distant. He was staring at the wall, but he wasn't seeing it. "Hard to say. Hard to say."

"When you saw the apple pie, it seemed very specific."

"It was specific. It really happened. This was more of a fleeting glimpse of something. Almost like a reconstruction of a generic type of event."

"Interesting," Zeldo said. "Would you like to take a break?"

"Yeah, I wouldn't mind," Cozzano said. "That one really shook me up. How many more do we have to do?"

Zeldo laughed. "We've done three dozen so far," he said, "and we could potentially do a couple of thousand. It's up to you."

By the end of the day, Zeldo had stimulated more than a hundred separate connections into Cozzano's brain. Each one elicited a completely different response.

AN ENTIRE PASSAGE FROM MARK TWAIN MATERIALIZED IN HIS HEAD.

HE SMELLED THE ROOT CELLAR AT THE OLD FARMHOUSE OUTSIDE OF TOWN.

HE FELT AN OVERPOWERING SENSE OF GRIEF AND LOSS, FOR NO REASON AT ALL.

A COLD FOOTBALL SLAMMED INTO HIS HANDS DURING A SCRIMMAGE IN CHAM-
PAIGN.

HE BIT INTO A THICKLY FROSTED CHOCOLATE CAKE.

A B-52 STREAKED OVERHEAD.

HE SAW A FULL PAGE FROM HIS WEEKLY APPOINTMENT CALENDAR, MARCH 25–
31, 1991.

SNOWFLAKES DRIFTED ONTO HIS OUTSTRETCHED TONGUE AND MELTED.

HE BECAME SEXUALLY AROUSED FOR NO DISCERNIBLE REASON.

AN OLD BARRY MANILOW SONG PLAYED IN HIS HEAD.

HIS CAR SKIDDED OFF AN ICY ROAD IN WINTER 1960 AND HIT A TELEPHONE
POLE; HIS FOREHEAD SLAMMED INTO THE WINDSHIELD AND CRACKED IT.

THE TINKLING SOUND OF ICE CUBES IN A GLASS PITCHER OF ICED TEA BEING
STIRRED BY ONE OF HIS AUNTS.

HE TRIMMED HIS FINGERNAILS IN A TOKYO HOTEL ROOM.

MARY CATHERINE DID SOMETHING THAT MADE HIM VERY ANGRY; HE WASN'T SURE
EXACTLY WHAT.

"I have to quit," Zeldo said. "I can't type any more. My fingers are dead."

"I want to keep going," Cozzano said. "This is incredible."

Zeldo thought about it. "It *is* incredible. But I'm not sure if it's useful."

"Useful for what?"

"The whole point of this exercise was to figure out a way to use this chip in your head for communication," Zeldo said.

Cozzano laughed. "You're right. I had forgotten about that."

"I'm not sure how we use all of this stuff to communicate," Zeldo said. "It's all impressionistic stuff. Nothing rational."

"Well," Cozzano said, "it's a new communications medium. What is necessary is to develop a grammar and syntax."

Zeldo laughed and shook his head. "You lost me."

"It's like film," Cozzano said. "When film was invented, no one knew how to use it. But gradually, a visual grammar was developed. Filmgoers began to understand how the grammar was used to communicate certain things. We have to do the same thing with this."

"I should get you together with Ogle," Zeldo said.

"You should have studied more liberal arts," Cozzano said.

## CHAPTER TWENTY-NINE

Eleanor made the mistake of giving out her full name. Since her name was listed in the telephone book, she was now reachable by everyone, all the time. She had the impression that her phone number must have been spray-painted in digits ten feet tall on the wall of every public housing project in greater Denver. And somehow they had all heard that Eleanor Richmond was a nice lady who would help you out with your problems.

She began to get calls from constituents in the middle of the night. When some unemployed mother of three phoned her at one o'clock one night and asked her for a personal loan of a hundred dollars, Eleanor came to her senses and decided that this had to stop. She could not be unofficial mom to all of Denver. She soon got into the habit of turning off the ringer on her phone when she went to bed.

This was a difficult step for a mother of two teenagers to take, because once she turned off that ringer, she knew that her kids would not be able to wake her up in the middle of the night and ask her advice, or request help, apologize, or simply burst into tears whenever they got themselves into a Situation. And although Eleanor's kids were reasonably smart and fairly responsible and kind of prudent, they still had an amazing talent for finding their way into Situations.

But by this point in her mothering career, Eleanor had seen enough Situations that she had begun to suspect that her kids were more apt to get into them when they knew that Mom would be there at the other end of the phone line to bail them out. And sure enough, when she got in the habit of turning her phone off at night, the incidence of Situations dropped. Or maybe she just stopped hearing about them. Either way it was fine with her.

It didn't help her sleep, though. Turning off the phones prevented them from ringing. But she could still hear the mechanical parts inside her answering machine clunking and whirring all night long, as people left messages for her. She put the answering machine in the far corner of her trailer and buried it under a pillow, but that didn't help. She still lay awake at night wondering, Why the hell are these people calling me?

She had never called anyone. It had never even occurred to her, when she was broke, and her husband had gone on the lam to the Afterlife, and her mother was soiling her pants in the middle of the night, and Clarice and Harmon, Jr., were out getting into Situations, to pick up the phone and contact the office of the Senator. It would not have occurred to her in a million years.

Where had these people gotten the weird idea that the government was going to take care of their problems?

The answer to that one was pretty simple: the government had told them as much. And they had been dumb enough to believe it. When it turned out to be a lie (or at least a hell of an exaggeration) they didn't go out and help themselves. Instead they stewed in their own problems and they got self-righteous about it and started calling Eleanor Richmond in the wee hours to vent their outrage.

She had to stop thinking this way. She was thinking exactly like Earl Strong. Blaming everything on the welfare mothers. As if the welfare mothers had caused the savings and loan crisis, the budget deficit, the decline of the schools, and El Niño all at once.

She would lie awake every night for hours, sensing the distant clunking of her answering machine under the pillow in the next room, and run through this series of thoughts over and over again, like a rat on a treadmill, exhausting herself but never going anywhere.

One morning in the middle of April she got up, turned on her coffee maker, took the pillow off her answering machine, and played back the messages, as she did every morning. Today there were only four of them. The people who had Eleanor's phone number written on the walls of their trailers and project flats had begun to learn that she never responded to messages and, bit by bit, weren't bothering to call anymore.

One of the messages was from someone speaking a language that Eleanor had never heard before. He rambled on until the machine cut him off. Then there were a couple of irate voters. And then there came a voice she recognized: it was one of Senator Marshall's political aides, calling from Washington.

"Hi, this is Roger calling from D.C. at nine A.M. local time."

Eleanor glanced at her clock. It was 7:15. This message had just come in while she was showering.

"We have a major problem that's up your alley. Please call me as soon as you can."

Eleanor picked up her phone and started punching numbers. She got through to Roger in D.C. During her month of working for Senator Marshall she had spoken briefly to this man once previously, and seen his name on a lot of memos.

Senators were too important to do anything personally. They were like sultans being carried around on sedan chairs, their feet never actually touching the ground. They showed up at the Capitol to make speeches and cast votes, and they made a lot of essentially social appearances, but most of the actual grunge work was delegated to a few key aides. This Roger character was one of those aides. He was a highly media-conscious, touchy-feely sort who spent a lot of time worrying about Senator Marshall's image with the folks at home. When a high-school band made a trip to Washington, D.C., it was Roger who made sure that they got in to the Senator's office for a photograph and a brief chat.

"Hi, Eleanor, I'm glad you called back," he said. "Look, I got a call this morning from Roberto Cuahtemoc at the Aztlan Center over in Rosslyn."

Rosslyn was part of Arlington, Virginia, right across the bridge from Eleanor's hometown. Aztlan was a Hispanic advocacy group. Roberto Cuahtemoc had formerly been Roberto something-else and had switched to a Nahuatl last name during his college years. He was obscure to northeastern Hispanics, but in the Southwest, particularly among migrant workers, he was revered.

Naturally, he and Senator Marshall hated each other. At least, they did in public. In private they had apparently reached some kind of an arrangement. When Roberto Cuahtemoc phoned the Senator first thing in the morning it probably meant he was pissed about something.

"He's really pissed," Roger said. "He got a call from Ray del Valle this morning at seven A.M. our time, which means that our buddy Ray was up and at 'em at five A.M. in Denver."

Ray del Valle was a Denver-based activist and protégé of Cuahtemoc. He was young, smart, and, considering the intensity of his convictions, Eleanor had found him easy to get along with.

"What's Ray up to?" she said.

"He's convinced that some migrant family is getting screwed over by Arapahoe Highlands Medical Center. There's a little kid involved. It's the kind of thing where he could really beat our brains out in the media, and believe me, if anyone understands that fact, it's Ray. So before he makes the Senator out to look like Francisco fucking Pizarro or something, please get over there and show the flag and tell everyone how concerned the Senator is. Are you ready to write down this address?"

"Shoot," she said.

Fifteen minutes later she was there. It was a straight shot. She'd used most of her first paycheck to fix up the Volvo. She crept up to the edge of Highway 2, looked both ways, and punched the gas, spraying dust and rocks back into the Commerce Vista, screaming a wild left-hand turn onto the highway, headed southwest toward Denver. She weaved her way through heavy truck traffic, passing one trailer park after another, eventually getting into the heavy industrial zone of southern Commerce City—all the stuff that Harmon had avoided when he'd first taken her to look at the Commerce Vista. Passing out of the refinery zone, over and under freeways and railway lines, she entered a flat, hot warehouse region of north Denver that catered entirely to semitrailer rigs and the men who drove them. One parking lot had been turned into a makeshift bus station where you could catch a bus straight to Chihuahua. Finally she passed under Interstate 70 and into the area she was looking for.

Her destination was a tiny brick bungalow in a neighborhood of tiny brick bungalows. The neighborhood was entirely Mexican-

American and it seemed like 90 percent of its population was clustered around this particular house. She had to park her car a couple of blocks away and excuse her way through the crowd until she reached the epicenter.

The center of attention wasn't the house itself; it was a pickup truck parked in its driveway. A yellow Chevy pickup, at least twenty years old, rusted in many places, with a white fiberglass camper cap attached to the back, held on to the box by means of four C-clamps. The truck's tailgate and the rear window of the camper cap were spread open like a pair of jaws to provide a view inside: a couple of bulging Hefty bags filled with clothes, and a flannel sleeping bag, zipped open to expose its colorful lining (mallards in flight over a northern wetland) and spread out flat on the rusted steel floor to soften its corrugations. There were a couple of pillows shoved into the corners and some wadded-up sheets and blankets.

And there were a lot of flowers too. A number of bouquets had been tossed in on top of the sleeping bag. More bunches were leaning against the side of the truck or resting on the roof of the fiberglass cap.

At the very center of the action were two men whom Eleanor recognized. One of them was a tall, good-looking young man in jeans and a blazer. With his black ponytail he could have passed for a full-blooded Apache. This was Ray del Valle. He was talking to a local newspaper reporter who covered the Chicano affairs beat.

Eleanor didn't pay much attention to them. She just made her way through the crowd, trying to suppress a gag reflex that was gradually rising in her throat. She got close enough that she was practically standing in between the two men, staring into the maw of the pickup truck.

Last night, the four children of Carlos and Anna Ramirez had lain down on that sleeping bag to sleep while their parents, sitting up front in the truck's cab, had driven them across the high plains southeast of Denver. They had gone to sleep quickly, and slept well, not because it was cozy but because the back of the truck was full of carbon monoxide leaking from the truck's exhaust. Three of the children had died. One was in the hospital in critical condition, with irreparable brain damage. Carlos and Anna Ramirez had not known what was going on until they had arrived here, early this morning, at the home of Anna's sister.

She knew all these things from her phone conversation with Roger. He had run through the story quickly and tersely and she had listened in much the same spirit, looking at it as a political problem to be solved. But now that she was here in the middle of a sniffling and wailing crowd, looking into the bed where the innocents had died, the emotional impact suddenly hit her like a truck. Eleanor put her hand over her mouth, closed her eyes, and tried to suppress the urge to become physically ill.

"Eleanor," Ray del Valle said, "come on, let's talk somewhere else. You don't want to dwell on this." Eleanor felt Ray's arm tightening around her shoulders. He led her around the truck and into the backyard, gently but surely, like a ballroom dancer leading his date around the floor.

She took the opportunity to rest her head on his chest for just a moment. She didn't exactly cry, though tears were in her eyes.

"It's a hard thing for a parent to look at, isn't it?" Ray said. "It's our worst nightmare come to life. Like an image from the Holocaust."

Eleanor took a half step away from Ray and drew a few deep breaths. "Are the parents inside?" she said.

"Yes. Anna has been sedated. Carlos is drinking a lot and vowing to kill himself. Anna's family is trying to keep him on an even keel. It's very difficult."

"I heard that there is a problem with the surviving child's medical care and I am here to inform the Ramirez family that Senator Marshall is at their service in whatever capacity is needed. Do you think that you could go in and relay that message to them?"

Ray snorted with just the tiniest hint of amusement and glanced down at his wristwatch. "The Senator runs a tight ship. As always."

Ray went into the house and came out a couple of minutes later with Anna's sister Pilar. From a distance Pilar seemed utterly stonefaced, but from arm's length her eyes were swollen and red and she looked stunned, rather than impassive.

"I told her what you said," Ray said. "She has authorized me to explain the child's medical situation."

"Okay."

"When they arrived this morning and found their four children unresponsive, they called the ambulance. Three children were pronounced dead at the scene. The fourth, the eight-year-old girl Bianca, still had a pulse. The ambulance took her straight to Arapahoe Highlands Medical Center."

"Why there?" Highlands was a private hospital, well endowed, certainly not the closest to this bungalow. Not the kind of place where migrant workers ended up.

"Carbon monoxide poisoning was obviously the culprit here. And Highlands has a hyperbaric oxygen chamber. It is the best treatment. So that's where they went. The emergency room staff at Highlands treated Bianca but they refused to admit her for hyperbaric oxygen treatment. Instead they dumped her back to Denver County, where she is now."

"How can they justify that?"

Ray just shrugged. "As we say in the Third World, *Quién sabe?*"

Something clicked in the back of Eleanor's head. Maybe it was her temper breaking. She squared her shoulders and flared her nostrils. "Would you please come with me, Ray?" she said.

"Okay. Where we going?"

Eleanor realized that she didn't even know. "We're just going to take care of a few things, that's all."

The two of them got into Eleanor's car and headed in the direction of Denver County Hospital, where Ray knew some doctors.

"This happens hundreds of times every year," Ray said. "All over North America."

"What happens?"

"Exactly this situation. Remember what a migrant worker is: someone who migrates. These people cover a lot of territory and the vehicle of choice is a pickup truck. It's always the same: the parents sit up front in the cab and the kids lie down in the back and try to sleep. The exhaust comes up through holes in the floor, or else it leaks through the crack under the tailgate. In warm weather they open the windows and survive. But if it's chilly, like it was last night, they close the cab up and suffocate."

"You'd think that they would have gotten some indication before. That their kids would have gotten headaches or felt woozy."

Ray snorted. "If you drove for eight or ten hours in the back of a truck, you'd feel that way even without carbon monoxide."

At the county hospital, Ray tracked down Dr. Escobedo, a young internist who was looking after Bianca. They all sat around a table in the corner of the cafeteria.

"Should Bianca be here, or at Arapahoe Highlands?" Eleanor said.

"At Highlands," Dr. Escobedo said without hesitation, and without rancor.

"Why?"

"They have a hyperbaric oxygen chamber."

"And that is the standard treatment for this kind of thing?"

"Not exactly," he said. "That's the problem."

"What do you mean, not exactly?"

"Well, for example, there are a lot of migrant workers up in Washington State, and this kind of thing has happened up there on a fairly regular basis. Now, there is a hospital in Seattle that has a hyperbaric oxygen chamber, which is basically used to decompress divers with the bends. When you put a patient with carbon monoxide poisoning into such a chamber, it helps get oxygen into their tissues, which is what such a patient needs. So people up there have learned that when an unconscious kid is pulled out of the back of a pickup truck, you send them straight to the one hospital with the hyperbaric chamber. But this is kind of a new practice, and in the eyes of some, it's experimental."

"And that's what the people at Highlands think."

"Exactly. If this treatment were standard medical practice, they'd have no excuse not to admit Bianca. But because they can label it experimental, there's no way they'll admit her. Because they know they'll lose money."

"Why does Denver have a chamber like this?" Ray said. "We don't have many scuba divers around here."

"It's used for diabetics and other people with poor circulation," Escobedo said. "So it's popular in areas with a large middle-aged and elderly population that's well insured. It's an expensive treatment with a high profit margin for the hospital. Which is why they don't want to tie up the chamber with a charity case."

"Okay, I get the picture," Eleanor said. "Now, who is in charge of Arapahoe Highlands Medical Center?"

"The chief administrator is Dr. Morgan," Escobedo said.

Eleanor stood up and yanked her jacket off the back of the chair. "Let's go kick his white ass," she said.

Ray and Escobedo looked astonished and glanced at each other, a bit nervously. "You might want to call ahead and find out where he is first," Ray suggested.

"I'm sure that an important man like Dr. Morgan has a secretary who is very good at putting people like me off—over the phone," Eleanor said. "The more I get in that secretary's face, the more helpful she'll be."

"*This may not* be an appropriate time for me to get political," Ray said, after they had all been driving in silence for a few minutes, humming down Broadway toward the rolling, prosperous southern suburbs. "But this is going to be a long drive and I can't help myself."

"Shoot," Eleanor said. "It would be unlike you not to get political."

"Okay. Well, there is one question you have forgotten to ask me about this whole affair."

"What question is that?"

"Why did the Ramirezes suddenly jump into their truck and take a six-hour drive across the prairie in the middle of the night?"

Eleanor thought that one over, feeling slightly embarrassed. "I thought you said this is what migrant workers do. They migrate."

"They're human beings," Ray said.

"I know that," Eleanor said, somewhat testily. Ray had a tendency to be a little obnoxious in his political correctness.

"So they have to sleep. They generally do it at night. And they drive during the daytime, like everyone else."

"Okay. So tell me, Ray, why did the Ramirezes suddenly get it into their heads to jump into their truck and go on a long night drive?"

"Because a couple of months ago, after the State of the Union address, there was a stock market crash."

Eleanor looked over at Ray. He was smiling back at her mysteriously.

"I'll bite," she said.

"The capital markets crashed. People sold their stocks and

needed somewhere else to put their money. In times of economic uncertainty, people tend to invest in commodities. So, on the Chicago Board of Trade, the price of beef went up. Raising cattle became a money-making proposition. But it takes time to raise cattle, you don't make a full-grown steer overnight. So cattlemen in this state began to raise a larger number of calves than usual."

"In the expectation that they'd be able to make more money off them when they were full-grown," Eleanor said. She did not know the first thing about ranching but this concept seemed simple enough.

"Right. Well, by now, these calves are starting to get big and starting to need more food—you know how growing children are. In this part of the country, cattle graze—they eat grass out on the range. Much of the range land is owned by the federal government, and cattlemen are allowed to graze their cattle on that land.

"There is a nice patch of BLM land I know of about six hours from here. It's in the basin of the Arkansas River, so it always has plenty of green grass, but unlike a lot of the other land around there it hasn't been converted to truck farming yet."

"Truck farming . . . that means vegetables and so on?"

"There's a lot of that stuff down there along the Arkansas," Ray said. "Migrants work there, picking vegetables for shipment to Oklahoma and Texas."

"Okay. Go on."

"Last year, when the price of beef was low, no one wanted to use this land and so a number of migrant workers—including the Ramirezes—went there and parked their trucks and trailers on it and started living there. Set up a little community. Planted some little gardens and so on. Waiting for the next harvest to come in."

"But last week, a cattleman in that area found that he was running out of land on which to graze all of those calves that he started when the price of beef got high. And now, in place of the community of migrant workers that used to be on that land, this man's cattle are there, eating the lush green grass."

"You're saying that the Ramirezes were kicked off the land."

"They and all the other people living there were evicted yesterday," Ray said. "The closest place for the Ramirez family to stay was

Anna's sister's house, here in Denver. So they put the kids in the back of the truck and came here."

"Oh."

"Hundreds of people are on the road today, all over the High Plains, because some cattle got hungry," Ray said. "And I wouldn't be at all surprised if there were several more cases of carbon monoxide poisoning in the backs of pickup trucks that we haven't heard about yet."

"If I am a cattleman," Eleanor said, "and I want to use a piece of BLM land, and some migrant workers happen to be living on it, then what is the mechanism? How do I make those workers go away? Call the cops?"

"No, you don't call the cops. There are a number of approaches one could take," Ray said, "but if I had the right connections, my first choice would be to make a phone call to the Alamo."

Eleanor thought that one over for a minute.

"Ray, if nothing else, you just guaranteed Bianca Ramirez a spot in the hyperbaric chamber," she said.

Eleanor was right. Dr. Morgan did have a very capable secretary. She could tell just by looking at the woman that she knew her business.

"Good morning, my name is Eleanor Richmond and I just got off the phone from talking to my boss, Senator Marshall," she lied, "and based on the results of that conversation I think I can promise you that the single most important thing that your boss Dr. Morgan will do this whole month, possibly this whole year, will be to have a conversation with me right now."

Out of the corner of her eye, she could see Ray and Dr. Escobedo grinning at each other. This was like a carnival ride for them.

Dr. Morgan's secretary was cheerful enough about it. If she was pissed off, she was good enough not to show it in front of Eleanor. She reached Dr. Morgan on his car phone; he was on his way in.

Within fifteen minutes, Dr. Morgan, Eleanor, Ray, and Dr. Escobedo were all sitting around a table in Morgan's office. They made small talk about what kind of additives they wanted in their coffee and what a nice day it was. Then things got quiet, and Eleanor found that everyone was looking at her expectantly. She folded her hands in her lap and composed herself for a moment.

"I'm not very good at this kind of thing," she said, "so maybe the best way for me to proceed is to just come out and say something."

"Shoot," Dr. Morgan said.

"This is an exercise in raw political brute force. You will give Bianca Ramirez treatment in the hyperbaric oxygen chamber or else the Senator, I'm sure, will make it his mission in life to turn this medical center into a smoking hole in the ground."

"Consider it done," Dr. Morgan said cheerfully. "Dr. Escobedo, you'll make the arrangements to send Bianca over?"

"Yes."

"Excellent," Dr. Morgan said. He seemed pleased and cheerful, as if he woke up every morning of his life and got slapped around by a U.S. Senator. "Now, is there anything else on the agenda?"

*"God," Eleanor said,* an hour later, over breakfast with Ray, "I really overdid it. I'm so embarrassed."

Ray shrugged. Significantly, he didn't try to disagree with her. "Don't worry about it," he said. "You got what we wanted."

After she had dropped Escobedo off at the county hospital, it had come to their attention that neither one of them had had any breakfast. So now they were at a little family place not far from the Alamo. Eleanor was having huevos rancheros. Ray was licking his lips over a huge steaming bowl of tripe.

"I tend to forget how powerful a senator is," Eleanor said. "I probably could have just made a phone call and gotten the same result. Instead I came in like Rambo. Used a flamethrower where I could have flicked a Bic."

"Hey, if nothing else it was great theater," Ray said. "That's your genius, you know."

"Huh?"

Ray was studying her face interestedly. "You don't know, do you?" he said. "You just do it on instinct."

"Do what on instinct?"

Ray shook his head flirtatiously. "I don't want to make you self-conscious and ruin it."

"What are you talking about?"

"I really admire what you did to Earl Strong, you know," he said, changing the subject none too subtly.

"Yeah, you tell me that every time we see each other."

"Now what we need to do is get that flamethrower aimed at the right target."

"Aha," she said. "The hidden agenda comes out."

"I told you I was paying for breakfast. What did you think?"

"And an excellent breakfast it is," she mumbled, chewing her first mouthful. They ate in silence for a minute. Both of them were ravenous. Emotion burns calories.

"I talked to Jane Osborne," Ray said. "I was all ready to be pissed at her, but she's nice."

"Here's the part where I ask who Jane Osborne is."

"She's a forest ranger out in La Junta."

"A forest ranger? In the prairie?"

"Funny, that's exactly what she said when she was assigned there," Ray said. "She likes forests. She went into the Forest Service hoping she would end up in one."

"Logical enough."

"She didn't count on the fact that the Forest Service owns a lot of grassland. Including the piece of land where the Ramirez family was living until yesterday. And they need people to look after that land. These people are called forest rangers. They wear Smokey Bear hats and everything. So Jane Osborne is stuck out there, not a single tree, much less a forest, for a hundred miles, in this shitty, dead-end GS-12 position, driving around in a pickup truck chasing dirt bikers and replacing signs that have been shotgun-blasted by the local intellectuals."

"Must be disappointing."

"Yeah. But it's not as bad as what comes next."

"And what's that?"

"She's about ready to turn in for the evening when she gets a call from On High and she is ordered to personally evict about a hundred migrant workers from this patch of grazing land."

"How does a single woman do that?"

"She called in a few other rangers and brought in some federal marshalls too, as a show of force."

"Who gave the order?"

"Her boss. Who got it from Denver. And they got it from Washington, I'm sure."

"Correct me if I'm wrong," Eleanor said, "but I'm sure that this wasn't the only patch of federal land in Colorado that was housing squatters."

Ray smiled. "You got that right."

"Have any other such communities been evicted?"

Ray shook his head.

"Just this one," Eleanor said.

"Just this one."

"So this wasn't a blanket order from Washington. It was targeted at this one piece of land."

"Sure looks that way."

"And why," Eleanor said, "do you suppose that some bureaucrat in D.C. would suddenly take an interest in this one parcel?"

Ray shrugged. "I can only speculate."

"Please do."

"This bureaucrat probably went to law school with one of Senator Marshall's aides. Or was his college roommate. Or their kids go to the same day care. Something like that."

Eleanor waggled a finger at Ray. "There you go making assumptions. How do you know there's a connection to Caleb Roosevelt Marshall?"

"The piece of land in question adjoins the Lazy Z Ranch," Ray said, "and the cattle grazing on it now all wear the Lazy Z brand."

"Say no more." Eleanor sighed. "You win."

The Lazy Z Ranch was owned by Sam Wyatt. Sam Wyatt was Caleb Roosevelt Marshall's biggest private contributor. And the president of Senator Marshall's PAC. Sam Wyatt was one of a dozen or so constituents who could get through to the Senator on the phone whenever he wanted to.

But in this case, he probably hadn't. This was too much of a dirty detail for the Senator to mess around with personally. He had probably just called one of the Senator's aides. He had probably called Shad Harper, that underaged son of a bitch who had the office across the hallway from Eleanor's.

Ray was watching her in fascination. "You have this look on your face like you're plotting an assassination," he joked.

"Something like that," she said.

## CHAPTER THIRTY

When little Bianca Ramirez was finally released from Arapahoe Highlands Medical Center after one week of hyperbaric oxygen treatment, a dozen television camera crews, four satellite uplink trucks, one Academy Award–winning documentary filmmaker, thirty print reporters, a hundred supportive protesters, the Mayor of Denver, staffers from all of the local senators' and representatives' offices, and a few lean and hungry lawyers were waiting for her. The only question was whether or not her parents, Carlos and Anna Ramirez, would actually show up to collect her.

Her progress from nameless refugee to media star could be tracked by checking the headlines on a local newspaper, which had been sliding in the direction of out-and-out tabloid journalism for a number of years, and which had been driven completely beyond the pale by the Bianca Ramirez story.

"TRUCK OF DEATH"

had been the first headline concerning the Ramirez family. Slightly less hysterical coverage of the tragedy had actually made it on to a couple of national network newscasts, which was unusual to say the least; plenty of Chicano kids had suffocated in the backs of trucks without even being mentioned in local newspapers. But this time around, several national Hispanic organizations got into the act and managed to stir up some interest on a national level. The case of the Ramirez family was a good one for TV. The truck of death per se was sitting in a driveway in Denver and anyone could go and videotape it. There had been one survivor, who happened to be an adorable little girl, and although this didn't get reported right away, there was, as the saying goes, more to the story: a failure of responsibility by a major, rich, private hospital, and hints of potential scandal involving one Sam Wyatt, wealthy cattleman, golf partner of senators and CEOs.

"LET HER DIE!"

was the headline on Day 2. The story about Highlands' refusal to treat Bianca had been leaked to the press by Ray del Valle. *Leaked* was a deceptive term. A leak was a tiny seeping crevice. In this case, *blowout* might have been more accurate. Ray made sure that everyone with a minicam, laptop, pen, or pencil knew about the story. More sober journalists just viewed it as another example of "dumping," the refusal of some hospitals to treat indigent patients. If they knew their business at all, it was an issue that they had already covered. Much more melodramatic examples of it had happened in other cities.

"HANG ON, BIANCA!"

was the headline for Day 3. This was somewhat meaningless. Day 3 was a Sunday and not much was going on. And Bianca's ability to hang on had never really been in question. The fact that she was still breathing when she was pulled from the Truck of Death, and when the ambulance crew had taken her to Highlands, where they had been told Let Her Die, meant that the parts of her brain that controlled breathing and heartbeat still worked. She was, in other words, stable, albeit in a coma. There was nothing to hang on to. But it made for a great headline, and it gave the tabloid (and the television journalists who functioned at the same journalistic level) a bit of breathing room. For a couple of days they had been accumulating a great mass of basically irrelevant human-interest material: pictures of the big-eyed Bianca, testimonials from family and playmates, descriptions of her favorite foods and toys. Sunday gave them a chance to unload all of that stuff on the public. If nothing else, Sunday was the day that Bianca became an official public figure, someone who could be referred to by her first name in a tabloid or on a TV broadcast, like Madonna or Di. As such, she represented a money factory to the tabloid; for at least the next couple of weeks, whenever they needed to goose their circulation figures they just printed any headline containing the name Bianca.

But Sunday was not a day of rest for everyone. A bleary-eyed Ray del Valle led a caravan of half a dozen journalist-laden vehicles on a drive across the prairie, headed for the patch of Forest Service grazing land where the Ramirez children had played their last game of soccer. The reason that Ray was bleary-eyed, even though the caravan departed at the civilized hour of ten A.M., was that he had spent the entire night driving from Denver to the site and back. On his drive out to the site, his car had been full of used toys and housewares, which he had purchased for a few dollars at Goodwill. On his drive back to Denver, his car had been empty.

When the caravan of journalists arrived at the site in mid-afternoon they were treated to the blindingly photogenic sight of cattle grazing over the remains of a hastily evacuated migrant settlement. Remains of the human tragedy were strewn everywhere: Raggedy Andy dolls, overturned cooking pots, baby clothes, a battered, well-loved Malibu Barbie or two.

None of it had been there the day before; the migrant workers had had plenty of time to pick up their things before they'd evacuated the site, and were not so wasteful as to leave perfectly good pots and toys strewn around. But it looked great, especially when the handsome, pony-tailed Ray del Valle squatted down in the grass to ponder an abandoned soccer ball as fat cattle emblazoned with the Lazy Z brand grazed contentedly nearby. So it was no big surprise when a photograph along those lines took up most of the front page of the next morning's tabloid, accompanied by the headline:

"WYATT: 'THROW 'EM OUT!' "

It would be an understatement to say that Sam Wyatt, his very close friends in Senator Marshall's offices, and most of the Denver medical establishment were, so far, not amused by the way the Ramirez situation had been covered in the media. And although Ray del Valle had begun the new week with a crushing sucker punch, afterward it became the Week of the Backlash. The "THROW 'EM OUT!" headline had been on the newsstands for less than six hours when two cars full of INS agents pulled up in front of the home of Pilar de la Cruz, née Ramirez, and came to the door with the intention of arresting Carlos and Anna Ramirez, who both happened to be illegal aliens. If these agents had been reading their tabloids, they would not even have stopped; they would have known that Carlos and Anna were not there by the fact that the TRUCK OF DEATH was not parked in the driveway. But they made the mistake of going to the door anyway. Pilar, alerted to the fact that Immigration was after her sister and brother-in-law, telephoned Arapahoe Highlands Medical Center, where they were visiting Bianca, and warned them. They cut their visit short, jumped into the Truck of Death, and vanished from the face of the earth.

"MOMMY HAS TO GO, BIANCA!"

graced the newsstands the next morning, accompanied by a photo of the tearful Anna bidding farewell to her daughter, who was bottled up inside the giant pressurized chamber where she had been receiving her treatment. A photographer had been present in the room when Anna and Carlos received the warning from Pilar and had snapped pictures of them bidding a hasty farewell.

None of which made the Powers That Be look especially good to the public. Which is why social workers from Health and Human Services started paying very close attention to Bianca at about the same time, and a motion was filed in court for the state of Colorado to become Bianca's legal guardian. The gist of this legal document was that Carlos and Anna Ramirez, by driving their kids around in a truck full of lethal gases and killing three of them, had clearly demonstrated their unfitness as parents and should not be allowed to take care of Bianca anymore. The district attorney let it be known that his staff was actually investigating the possibility of filing charges against the Ramirezes and that, with every fiber of his being, he was refraining himself from issuing an arrest warrant for Carlos and Anna. It was all well and good to put public service announcements on TV begging people not to drive their kids around in the back of pickup trucks, but what would really put a stop to this sort of thing was punitive legal action against parents who did it. So the headline for Wednesday morning was

"STATE: BIANCA IS OURS!"

But all of this legal squalor was obscuring an interesting medical story. When Bianca arrived in the hyperbaric chamber she had been in a deep coma and totally unresponsive. But in the photo accompanying the "BIANCA IS OURS" story, a state social worker stood outside the hyperbaric chamber, smiling and waving through its thick pressure-proof window at the unseen Bianca inside. And there wasn't much point in smiling and waving to a vegetable. It seemed that Bianca had staged a miraculous recovery. She was far from being back to normal, but she was awake, alert, responsive to verbal communication, and mumbling a few words.

This gave Arapahoe Highlands Medical Center's new PR director the ammunition he needed to thunder into the media fray. His predecessor and former boss had been sacked with astonishing dispatch as soon as "LET HER DIE!" had hit the streets. The new man had spent the first few days just trying to get on his feet. By the time Wednesday rolled around, he was ready. He brought in a select troop of journalists to videotape and photograph Bianca through the window of the chamber; she obliged by smiling and waving to them. Since she had all but been written off as a vegetable a few days earlier, this was certainly going to have an electrifying effect on the public.

There followed a news conference in a hospital meeting room, where all of Bianca's doctors, nurses, therapists, and court-appointed guardians stepped up to the microphone to deliver a few bright, upbeat sound bites praising Bianca's plucky nature and emphasizing the incredible nature of her recovery. A few cynical journalists tried to spoil the day by asking difficult questions, e.g.: "Does Bianca know that the INS is trying to deport her parents?" But the new PR director was standing by the mike at all times, trying to anticipate any line of questioning that might lead to another headline along the lines of "LET HER DIE!," and whenever these issues came up he would mumble something about protecting the patient's privacy and then point to some other journalist with a less acute critical faculty. In general, the PR director was finding that bald, middle-aged print journalists with nicotine stains on their fingers were troublesome, and beautiful twenty-five-year-old TV journalists who had arrived at the hospital carrying stuffed bunnies for Bianca were good people to call on. So the headline for Thursday morning was:

"BIANCA: MIRACLE GIRL!"

accompanied by a picture of her smiling her gap-toothed kid's grin through the window of the chamber, cuddling a bunny to her chest.

Anyone who bothered to read a complete news story about Bianca, all the way to the end, could find out that her treatment in the chamber was essentially complete, and that Arapahoe Highlands was going to release her the following day, on Friday.

Which meant that by the time the "MIRACLE GIRL" headline began to circulate on Thursday morning, all of the participants in the Ramirez Affair, from Denver to the Lazy Z Ranch to Washington, D.C., were gearing up for the endgame.

Most of Friday would be taken up with logistics: getting all the players to the hospital on time and keeping in touch with everyone on the phone. So Thursday was the last day for actually making moves. Ray del Valle kicked off the final round by arranging a press conference, in a "safe house" somewhere in greater Denver, in which Carlos and Anna Ramirez stepped before the Court of Public Opinion to defend themselves from charges that they were illegal aliens and bad parents.

The illegal alien part was difficult, because they were, in fact, illegal aliens. But in America, no issue was so clear-cut that it could not be obfuscated beyond recognition by a talented lawyer. The Ramirezes now had one: a nationally famous hell-raising San Francisco lawyer who liked to do pro bono work if lots of TV cameras were present; he insisted that he was going to get these people green cards real soon.

The part about being bad parents was different. The Ramirezes were actually known in their community as very good parents. Carlos was a teetotaler who spent every minute of his free time with his children, and Anna was a domestic saint. Ray had arranged for character witnesses to show up at the safe house and say as much.

Eleanor Richmond's part in the endgame was a different matter. She snuck into, and ransacked, the office of her young colleague Shad Harper. This was easily enough to get her fired and possibly enough to get her thrown into jail. She understood this clearly and had already typed up a letter of resignation to Senator Marshall. She had been working at this job for exactly one month and had received exactly one paycheck.

It was completely insane for her to be doing this. If she had been looking for snippets of information that she could have kept to herself and used discreetly, that would have been one thing. But her entire goal was to dig up some dirt that she could turn around and release to the media. Eleanor Richmond had gone native. She was out of control.

She had lost it sometime over the weekend. The realization that Sam Wyatt, her boss's main man, had triggered this whole chain of events was bad enough by itself. For a day or two she had wavered, mostly because she was turned off by Ray's tactic of planting toys in the grass for the photographers. When the INS had come around looking for Carlos and Anna, she had been annoyed. But when the state had tried to take Bianca away from her parents, Eleanor Richmond had gone nuts. That was no fair. She'd rather be a bag lady than a coconspirator in an affair that involved breaking apart a family.

So on Thursday, whenever Shad Harper left his office for more than about ten minutes, Eleanor went in and made herself at home. It would be worth destroying her own career if she could find anything to bring Shad down along with her. It would have been nice to find something on Sam Wyatt, or on the aide in D.C. who had made the fateful phone call to the Forest Service, or even on Senator Marshall himself. But she was willing to settle for Shad Harper's head on a platter.

Somewhat to her own astonishment, she didn't get caught. Once or twice, someone poked their head into Shad's office while she was there, and she explained that she was looking for a stapler that Shad had borrowed. This explanation worked because Shad was always borrowing stuff, including money, and not returning it. Shad himself spent most of the day out of the office, deeply enmeshed in some kind of plot involving the Ramirez family.

By the time the sun rose on Friday morning, illuminating the new headline:

"BIANCA: I WANT MY MAMA!"

nothing had really changed. Arapahoe Highlands Medical Center was going to release Bianca at 6:05 P.M. By an astonishing coincidence, this put her release just a few minutes into the local evening news programs, making it an ideal candidate for live TV coverage. Their new PR director, who had been on the job for five days and had already received a raise and a bonus, insisted that this was just a coincidence and that the time of the release had been set for purely medical reasons.

He deserved his raise. From a media/PR standpoint, Highlands had started out the week gut-shot and had made a miracle recovery of their own until they now looked like archangels in white coats, their arms brimming over with fuzzy stuffed animals. At 6:05, they would roll Bianca Ramirez out into the horseshoe drive where their uniformed valet parking attendants stood guard twenty-four hours a day, and release her into the world. This would be good for two reasons: it would cement their reputation as medical geniuses and it would clear out the hyperbaric chamber so that heavily insured middle-aged diabetics could get into it again.

The question was: who was going to take charge of Bianca when her wheelchair reached the curb? The fact that no one knew the answer to this question turned the entire scenario into a certified Real-Life Drama and insured vast, saturating media coverage.

Colorado was still trying to get a court order making Bianca a ward of the state, but the Ramirezes' high-profile lawyer and his team of young legal ninjas had thrown this action into a procedural snafu that would take weeks to untangle. Barring any last-minute action by the judicial branch, Carlos and Anna would still be Bianca's legal guardians as of 6:05.

But Carlos and Anna were illegal aliens and the INS was looking for them. As a matter of fact, the INS was right there at the hospital, and had been for three days, waiting for them to show up. So if Bianca's parents actually showed up at 6:05 to take custody of their daughter, they would immediately be taken off to the slammer and someone else would have to step in anyway to take care of Bianca. This would probably end up being Anna's sister Pilar, but there had been rumors that the state might use the arrest of Carlos and Anna as a pretext to seize Bianca, in which case the media could look forward to a tearful three-way Solomonic showdown right there in the horseshoe drive.

All the networks showed up, and as early as six o'clock on Friday morning, twelve hours before the Big Event, Highlands' new PR man was already out in the horseshoe drive with a thick piece of blue chalk, marking out camera positions: ABC, CBS, NBC, CNN, CHAN 4, CHAN 5, CHAN 7, and more.

As one journalist could be overheard remarking to another journalist while they waited in the car-rental line at Stapleton Airport: "It's got a coma baby. It's got a miracle recovery. Weepy parents. A crooked senator. And it's even got a fucking cowboy!"

By itself, the story was plenty, but things got even better, if that was possible, in the middle of the day, when rumors began to circulate that one of Senator Marshall's staff members had documents incriminating another staff member in the Lazy Z Ranch grazing scandal that had triggered this whole mess, and that she was going to be there this evening to lay the whole thing out before the massed forces of the national press. And when this rumor was embellished a little, to the effect that the woman in question was the famous bag lady who had recently cut Earl Strong's nuts off in public, journalists all over Denver had to put their drinks down and breathe into paper sacks for a while.

*Eleanor Richmond strode* like a gunslinger into the horseshoe drive at 5:55 P.M. cradling a three-inch-thick stack of xeroxed handouts. Before she said a word, she held one of the handouts up next to her face and stood motionless for a few seconds. She had learned this from watching the pros in action. It gave the video people a chance to adjust the white balance on their cameras so that she, and everyone who followed her into the center of the maelstrom, would not look pink or green on television. At the same time, it was a great pose for the still photographers. Dozens of motor drives whined, clearly audible in the astonishing silence that had suddenly fallen over this makeshift technological amphitheater.

If the Four Horsemen of the Apocalypse had chosen this moment to gallop through the horseshoe drive on their fiery mounts, the journalists would have chased them out of the shot with verbal abuse, and possibly interviewed them later, after the main event. The only figure who dared to break into the frame was a helpful reporter from the *Washington Post* who scurried up to Eleanor, relieved her of the stack of handouts, and frisbeed them wildly into the crowd.

"My name is Eleanor Richmond. I am the Denver health and human services liaison for Senator Caleb Roosevelt Marshall. I have held that position for one month.

"When I began working for the Senator I was convinced, based on his past record and statements, that he was a racist. I am now convinced that he does not have a racist bone in his body. I have never met a man more willing to judge people on their individual merits, or lack thereof.

"However even the most perceptive judge of human nature can occasionally be fooled by ambitious persons who practice to deceive. It is my unpleasant duty to report to you that several such people have risen to positions of influence on the Senator's staff and, unbeknownst to Senator Marshall, have abused the power of his office for private gain.

"Going direct to the media is not the best way to handle this situation. I should have met with the Senator first. I have made repeated efforts to reach him but he has been unavailable. Unfortunately I cannot wait any longer to release this information, because it has a bearing on the matter of Bianca Ramirez, and if, by my inaction, I were to cause damage to her family, I could never forgive myself. So I am releasing the information now and I am also offering my resignation to Senator Marshall at the same time."

"Eleanor!" shouted all of the journalists at once, raising their hands.

"Excuse me, excuse me, but I think that I should be given an opportunity to speak," someone said, coming up behind Eleanor.

She turned around and looked directly into the face of Shad Harper.

And then she hesitated. She had her back to the lights and cameras now; he was facing them, every pore in his face exposed to their pitiless illumination. She felt like an interrogator as she stood there staring into his face, weighing the situation, trying to make up her mind.

He didn't look good. Shad was just a boy, after all, not very well seasoned, and although he had a few on-camera skills, he was hardly a master of the game. And right now, he was really, really upset.

She knew that if she let Shad talk, he'd cut his own throat. He'd do it because he was a man and he had been conditioned, all his life, to deny his fear, to act before thinking, to get in over his head. A woman, or an older man, would have backed off, thought it over, chosen the right time. Not Shad; Shad had to confront her right now; he couldn't let her win even a single skirmish.

"Be my guest," she said, and stepped away from the microphone.

"I'm Shad Harper," he said, his voice cracking. "BLM liaison for Senator Marshall. And since I'm still on his staff, unlike Eleanor here, who has apparently resigned—and if she hasn't resigned— which I can't say for sure either way, since I have not seen and do not have any independent knowledge of any letter by which she might have resigned—if she hasn't resigned then she will probably be fired, and in any case no longer speaks for Senator Marshall, if indeed she ever did—I do speak for Senator Marshall and so, since it appears that very damnable allegations are being made about him that I should step up and say something."

"She's not making allegations about the Senator," one of the journalists shouted, glancing through the handout. "She's making allegations about you personally, Mr. Harper."

Harper's mouth fell open. "Well, I haven't seen these alleged allegations yet, but—"

"Is this your handwriting?" said another journalist, a woman from the L.A. Times, holding up one page of the handout.

It was a photocopy of a sheet of stationery printed, at the top, with the words FROM THE DESK OF SHAD HARPER. It was covered with hand-written notes.

"I'd have to take a better look—"

"Let me just read you some of this and maybe you can explain why you were writing some of these things down," the woman said. " 'State of Washington versus Garcia 1990.' That sounds like a court case."

"I don't remember," Shad said.

"I looked it up," Eleanor said. "It was a case in which some children died of carbon monoxide poisoning in the back of a pickup truck and the state of Washington successfully took custody of the surviving children on grounds that their parents had neglected them."

"Why were you looking up that case, Shad?" the woman from the *L.A. Times* said. "How does that relate to your job as BLM liaison for the Senator?"

"First and foremost, I am a servant of the people," Shad said. The protesters gathered off to one side hooted derisively. The sound threw Shad off balance and he stumbled for a moment. "Uh, I'm entitled to look up court cases in the privacy of my own office."

"You were trying to assemble material with which to blackmail Anna and Carlos Ramirez," Eleanor said. "By threatening them with the loss of their only remaining child, you could coerce them into silence, and reduce the intensity of the spotlight on the cozy arrangement between you and Sam Wyatt—which never drew any public attention until a freak accident exposed it to public view."

"That is just, just—a terrible thing that you are saying."

"What is terrible is to live in a time when saying things is considered to be worse than doing them," Eleanor said.

"You seem to be forgetting here that people in this state, and in this country are damn tired of these unemployed welfare mother illegal aliens coming into this country and stirring things up!"

"Why don't you call them spics and wetbacks, the way you do when you're speaking on the telephone to Sam Wyatt?"

"That is a totally unprovable allegation!" Shad yelped. He looked shocked, horrified, to hear these words spoken in public, as if he and Sam Wyatt had invented the words for their personal use. "Listen. I am not a person with any kind of ethnic bias or bigotry. I limit my concern to those people, of whatever ethnic group, who take advantage of the system. Who are like parasites on the prosperous economic system that has been built up over the years by the hard work of productive citizens the likes of Sam Wyatt."

"Sam Wyatt," Eleanor said. "Sam Wyatt, who grazes his cattle on government-owned land. Land that was occupied by Native Americans until the government paid soldiers to come out here and kill them. Sam Wyatt, who irrigates his ranch with water from a government-built dam. And you think that Anna Ramirez is a welfare queen? I've got news for you, cowboy. Everyone in the state of Colorado is a welfare queen. We all live and feed off the largesse of taxpayers in other parts of the country. It's just that some of us, like

Sam Wyatt, have been here longer than others, and have had time to pile up more government welfare checks in their bank accounts and funnel more of that money back into big campaign contributions. So don't stand here in Denver, a metropolis built on a creek, the capital of Colorado, a state that would dry up and turn back into a prairie without the continuing help of the government, and bray about the bad moral qualities of welfare queens. Because these people who come north across the border may not have gel in their hair and they may not have ostrich-hide cowboy boots, but unlike you, they have something a lot more important. They have values."

The hospital doors slid open and Bianca Ramirez rolled out in a wheelchair, pushed along by a smiling nurse, escorted by her entire medical team.

A disturbance moved through protesters and suddenly Carlos and Anna Ramirez emerged from the crowd, smiles on their faces, tears streaming down their cheeks. They moved across the horseshoe drive, unhindered by journalists or INS agents or Shad Harper or anyone else, and engulfed their daughter in their arms. And were engulfed, in turn, by hundreds of their supporters.

The whole thing was a lot warmer and calmer than anyone had expected. The only real disturbance was off to the side, where an INS van, a paddywagon with steel grilles over all the windows, had begun rocking from side to side. The driver jumped out, leaving the van empty, and a broad open space suddenly appeared in the crowd. Then a dozen men, their arms and backs burly from stooping in Arkansas Valley truck farms, rolled it all the way over onto its roof and left it there like a turtle upended on a highway.

## CHAPTER THIRTY-ONE

Eleanor was in the middle of cleaning out her office. This wasn't much of a job since she had barely moved into it and the empty boxes were still stacked conveniently in the corner. Bent over with both hands in a file drawer, she didn't notice Caleb Roosevelt

Marshall coming into her office until he got her attention by tossing a keychain onto her vacant desktop.

"I'm taking you on a ride, lady," he said.

She straightened up, startled to see him standing right in front of her, dressed in a blue work shirt and chinos, leaning on a cane. "I have my best conversations when I'm driving flat out into the mountains," he said, nodding at the keychain. Eleanor picked it up; it was a set of keys to a rented Cadillac. "But now I'm getting too old to drive. Can't even see the goddamn hood ornament."

"Allow me, then," Eleanor said.

It was a nice Cadillac, a convertible, parked in the Senator's private space in back of the Alamo. The Senator had apparently dismissed his security detail, so Eleanor offered her arm and helped him out of the building and into the passenger seat. Then she got in and cranked it up. The car had a nice sound system with a tape player, and although the Senator complained that he wanted to get going, Eleanor decided to rummage around in the hollow center armrest for one of his tapes.

"What are you going to play? Rap music?" he said as she popped a tape out of its case and shoved it into the dashboard.

"Resurrection Symphony," Eleanor said, as the opening bars came from speakers hidden all over the car.

"Good," Marshall said. "I been listening to it a lot. Figure I'd better become expert in the subject. Now let's get going, damn it."

The Senator had a particular, highly detailed route he wanted to follow through Denver and up into the mountains. He eschewed the newfangled foolishness of freeways in favor of a devious route that took them down alleys, through parks, along curvy residential streets. For a while, as she followed his barked and seemingly improvised instructions, she was afraid that he had gone completely off his rocker and was getting them hopelessly lost. But they never got stuck at a slow stoplight, never had to make an impossible left turn, and in time the city began to spread out and undulate as the landscape awoke from the thousand-mile slumber of the prairie.

"Thanks for saving my ass," Senator Marshall said, when he wasn't giving directions.

She smiled. "I was wondering whether you'd see it that way."

"Course I do. I'm not senile," he said. "Sooner or later a senator has to rely on someone like you."

"How do you figure?"

"A senator has a big staff. He has to, in order to carry out the basic functions of his office, and to get reelected. Normal people don't take those kinds of jobs. If I could take people off the street, I would. That's how I got you. But normally I gotta hire the kinds of people who angle and maneuver for such work, which means weasels like Shad Harper. And almost the moment they get into the job, they start spinning their own goddamn agenda. Some of them know what they're doing and some are just complete assholes. And when the assholes get themselves into trouble, like Shad did, then a senator has to have some way to get rid of them without bringing down his whole career. And you served that purpose admirably in the affair of Shad Harper."

"Did you get my letter?"

"What letter? The resignation?"

"Yes."

"Yeah, I got that damn letter. I don't accept your resignation. I want you working for me. Hell, woman, you're like a pit bull trained to attack white men. I want you on my side."

Eleanor laughed. "I don't attack anyone."

"Well you sure do leave a lot of corpses in your wake."

The smile fell away from Eleanor's face and she drove in silence for a while.

She and Harmon hadn't spent a lot of time driving into the mountains. She was not really a mountain person. They looked dangerous to her. For years she'd felt trapped, in a way, between the mountain wall on one side and the endless plains on the other. The devil and the deep blue sea. Now that they were getting close to the first real range of mountains, a ridge of red stone that swept smoothly up out of the grassland and broke off jaggedly hundreds of feet above their heads, she was beginning to remember that the mountains had their attractions, that they were a lot more interesting when you got up close instead of viewing them through miles of brown Denver smog.

"Sorry," Caleb said, "that was a real stupid thing for me to say."

Clearly, the Senator was not a man who apologized very often, and he found it difficult.

"It's okay," she said. "I know what you meant."

"If I intended to run for another term, I'd have to sack you," he said, after they had drawn closer to the base of the first ridge and turned parallel to it along a rolling and winding road. They were now completely out in the country.

"You don't say."

"When one of my staffers steps up in front of the single largest collection of journalists ever assembled in Denver and announces that everyone in the state of Colorado is a welfare queen, it makes things a little awkward for me."

This time Eleanor didn't laugh. She smiled, but it was a sheepish kind of grin. This was a Monday morning. She had spent yesterday morning reading scathing editorials and rebuttals in the editorial sections of the newspapers. To say that she had hit a nerve didn't do justice to the level of indignation.

"How many death threats have you gotten?" Senator Marshall asked.

"I stopped listening to my messages after the third one," Eleanor said.

"They actually put them on tape? They must have been really pissed."

"Yeah."

"I can have the Secret Service check them out."

"It just sounds to me like a bunch of ranchers blowing off steam," she said.

"It ain't just Colorado. You're the most hated woman in the West," Senator Marshall said. "A lightning rod."

"I know it."

"People wouldn't be so vehement unless your words were largely true," Senator Marshall said.

She gave him a searching look. "What's your opinion?"

The Senator winced, as if he wished she hadn't asked this question. He looked out the window for a while, appalled.

"Well, of course you're right," he finally said. "The economy of this whole region is built on subsidies and federal programs. But people refuse to admit that because they want to believe in the cowboy myth. That their ancestors came out and made the desert bloom solely through their own hard work and pluck.

"Now, they were plucky, and they did work hard. But there are a lot of plucky, hard-working people in other places who have gone down the toilet anyway just because they were pursuing a fool's errand, economically speaking. The people who came here sort of lucked into a situation of cowboy socialism. Without federal programs they'd go broke—no matter how hard they worked."

"Federal programs that are kept alive by senators."

"Yeah. Colorado's a small state population-wise. Our delegation in the House can't do diddly. But in the Senate, every state is equal. When one senator, like me, gets some seniority, works his way up into a few key committee chairmanships, then some states are more equal than others. My job—my *raison d'être*—is to keep certain federal programs alive that prevent this region from turning back into the buffalo farm God intended it to be.

"It's a feedback loop. This is high-tech lingo that I picked up in the sixties when some goddamn ecologist was raving to me. I keep the programs alive. The economy thrives. People move to Colorado and vote for me. The cycle begins again.

"As long as those programs continue to exist, no one notices. They are part of the landscape. They are forces of nature, like the wind and the rain. The people who live off them, people like Sam Wyatt, have come to think of them as natural and divinely ordained. To them, living off of federal largesse is no different in principle than, say, fishing salmon from the Gulf of Alaska or tapping maple syrup from trees in Maine. So, when someone like you steps in front of the TV cameras and points out the obvious—that these people are no different in principle from people who live off of welfare checks—it just drives them crazy. It strikes at the heart of who they are."

Eleanor listened to this numbly. She couldn't believe that Senator Marshall was saying these things. "So, why aren't you going to accept my resignation?" she said.

"My whole career I've been doing things because I had to. Now that I'm in my last term, I get to do all the things I always wished I could do but was afraid to."

"Well, the press should have a field day with that."

"The press can fuck themselves. Now I can say that. Take a right here."

Eleanor turned right onto a road that cut due west, straight into the mountains. Finally she understood what Caleb had been doing: steering them toward a cut through the mountain wall, the only place within miles you could get through it. The sight of it made her want to go fast and she punched the gas and surged toward it. It was a narrow gap with almost vertical sides that revealed a cross section of the ridge, normally hidden under grass and sage, its pink and peach and salmon and maroon strata fluorescing in the late afternoon sun.

"You must be getting a lot of pressure to sack me."

"To hell with that. They'll forget all about it in a week, believe me. What I'll do is give you an internal transfer."

"Oh. So I'm getting a new job?"

"Yeah. You're getting a new job. I'm getting you out of Colorado before someone lynches your ass. Or mine."

"Oh, my god."

"That's right. You are going to Washington, D.C., lady. Back to your hometown. And if you thought that Denver was a nest of vipers, you just wait."

They both shut up for a moment driving through the gap. Caleb groped out with his left hand and turned the Resurrection Symphony up to the point where it was loud even to his leathery ears, and they cut through and suddenly found themselves in the heart of the Rocky Mountains. Once it passed through the gap, the road split off in three or four directions, and none of the signs meant anything to Eleanor. "Which way do I go now?" she said.

"I got you here," Caleb said. "Now you're on your own."

# vox populi

If, though unjust, I acquire the reputation of justice, a heavenly life is promised to me. Since then, as philosophers prove, appearance tyrannizes over truth and is lord of happiness, to appearance I must devote myself. I will describe around me a picture and shadow of virtue to be the vestibule and exterior of my house; behind I will trail the subtle and crafty fox . . .

But I hear someone exclaiming that the concealment of wickedness is often difficult; to which I answer, nothing great is easy. . . . With a view to concealment we will establish secret brotherhoods and political clubs. And there are professors of rhetoric who teach the art of persuading courts and assemblies; and so, partly by persuasion and partly by force, I shall make unlawful gains and not be punished.

Plato, *Republic*

## CHAPTER THIRTY-TWO

On a gentle summer evening back during the Eisenhower administration, Nimrod T. ("Tip") McLane had once watched his uncle Purvis beat a man up with a sharpened motorcycle chain. It happened outside of a very inexpensive and dangerous bar in north central California that catered to agricultural laborers. Okies.

Nimrod's grandfather, James McLane, had obtained a piece of land in Oklahoma during one of the land runs in the late 1800s. He commenced to work that soil literally within the hour, scooping out shallow graves along the Cimarron River in which to place the bodies of the previous occupants, who had arrived shortly before he had, with faster horses but not quite so many guns.

A few decades later, that stream dried up and all the topsoil blew away to Arkansas. James had long since died, and so had his eldest son Marvis, who had gotten into an altercation with a piece of newfangled farm machinery and spectacularly lost. James's surviving sons, Elvis and Purvis, abandoned the land and went to California, following a rumor of jobs. Elvis married another Okie—actually, an Arkie—named Sheila White, and they started to have kids. Purvis joined the Navy and came back from World War II full of lies, liquor, and shrapnel. Half of him was covered with tattoos and the other half with burn scars. For the next few years of life, until he discovered some exciting new career openings in the benzedrine trade, he shuttled back and forth between short-term, low-paying jobs on the waterfront in Oakland and in the vegetable fields of the Valley. Purvis later obtained a sinecure of sorts, as a founding member of the Hell's Angels.

Elvis and Sheila, by contrast, were stay-at-home types. Elvis stuck to the one thing he had talent for, which was stoop labor, and over the years, more because of his reliability than because of brains or skill, he managed to work his way up into a position as foreman for Karl Fort Enterprises, Inc.

Karl Fort was also an Okie who had gone west in the 1930s, but he was different: he was from Tulsa, and he had gone west with money in his pocket and connections in Washington. His money bought him land. The money went a long way because at the time he bought the land, it was worthless. His connections in Washington knew that the federal government was soon to establish huge irrigation projects in the area. As soon as water reached Karl Fort's land, it became worth a hundred times what he had paid for it. Fort established agricultural Gulags where his fellow Okies labored under the watchdog gaze of Fort guards, occasionally getting enough of a paycheck to keep them and their families alive.

Elvis McLane was not really cut out for management. He didn't understand that when you made the cut and moved up to the next rank, you had to stop drinking next to the people you were giving orders to, hiring, and firing. His brother Purvis sat him down and talked to him about it. Purvis had been in the military and understood the concept of fraternization and why it was a bad idea. But he never really got through to Elvis, who (it was rumored) had, while still in the womb, lost a wrestling match with his own umbilical cord.

It was only a matter of time before Elvis went into a bar and ran into someone he had fired, yelled at, or otherwise humiliated, and trouble broke out. Actually, it happened several times, but the most memorable case involved a sullen, dangerous broccoli picker named Odessa Jones. He was named after the city in Texas where he had been abandoned by his mother.

*Nimrod McLane, who* among other distinctions had a Ph.D. in philosophy from Notre Dame, despised liberal hand-wringing types who were always whining about America being a violent society. These people had read too many poorly written accounts of bar fights that turned grisly.

The standard newspaper account of a grisly bar fight contained a deeply buried assumption: that people participated in bar fights because they were stupid. Some minor slight, such as looking at another man's girl or jumping the line for the pool table, would degenerate into meaningless, pointless violence. Liberals would read about it in the paper the next morning, wring their hands, and advocate better education and gun control.

Nimrod McLane had seen a lot of these altercations as a child. After his voice changed he participated in a few. He had a pretty clear understanding of how bar fights started and why they turned ugly. Americans participated in bar fights for exactly the same reason they had joined, with such gusto, in the Civil War: because they had values and considered violence and mayhem a small price to pay.

Odessa Jones was a case in point. He was a proud, hard-working man who had been fired by Elvis McLane because of what amounted to a personality conflict. So when he walked up to Elvis in that bar and went upside his head with a glass beer pitcher, he wasn't doing it because he was a stupid low-class drunk. He was doing it because his honor had been violated and because honor was more important to him than temporal, earthly considerations, such as keeping his front teeth or staying out of jail. Odessa Jones probably had ancestors who, like him, were rootless white trash, but who had picked up rifles and gone North to fight the Yankees anyway, not because they believed in slavery but because they were incensed that the Northerners refused to stay at home and mind their own business. They were willing to have their legs shot off in Pennsylvania because principle, to them, was more important than flesh. This was what made America such an ethereal society.

Sprawling out on the floor of the bar, Elvis's eyes fell on the underside of a nearby table, and he realized that he could probably rip one of its legs off and use it as a cudgel. Which is what he did; but the much larger Odessa Jones beat the shit out of him anyway, or at least continued to until both of them were thrown out of the bar, and he ran afoul of Purvis McLane and his motorcycle chain.

Years after this event, when Nimrod was pursuing his philosophy degree, he spent a lot of time contemplating the following question: if Odessa Jones was fighting for a principle, and Elvis McLane was fighting out of a defensive reflex, then what was Purvis McLane up to?

Purvis McLane was engaged in long-range strategic thinking. He acted calmly and dispassionately. Uncle Purvis, Navy veteran and cofounder of the Hell's Angels, simply did what was needed to look out for the overall welfare of his family unit. Nimrod McLane had come to believe that all persons could be divided into Odessas, Elvises, and Purvises, and he considered himself a Purvis all the way.

Representative Nimrod T. ("Tip") McLane values. He went to church, he studied the Bible, he read Aquinas. All his life he had despised materialistic people who could only think about money. He had made himself famous and got on the cover of *Time* by becoming The Conservative Who Hated Yuppies. Which was why he wanted to become president: so he could clean up America.

*Tip McLane watched* his chief rival for the nomination, Norman Fowler, Jr., sign his own political death warrant, with a flourish, at precisely twelve o'clock noon on the day after Memorial Day. Norman Fowler, like Dan Quayle and a few others, belonged to a fourth category of humanity: he was a Marvis.

McLane was late for a luncheon in Bel Air and had stopped by his hotel suite in downtown L.A. for a quick change of clothing when he happened to notice the digital clock turning over 12:00. Reflexively he turned on his television, which was already set to one of the local network affiliates, and was treated to the never-to-be forgotten sight of Norman Fowler, Jr., at Disneyland, shaking hands with Goofy.

"My god," said his media consultant Ezekiel ("Zeke") Zorn.

"Is this something from *Saturday Night Live?*" asked his campaign manager Marcus Drasher.

"He's a dead man," was the only comment Tip McLane would make.

"Jesus, the man is worth billions," Drasher said. "He can afford to hire the best. And what do they do? They send him to Disneyland. And they let Goofy shake his hand!"

"This has got to be Cy Ogle's work. Ogle has a Goofy fetish. It's a known fact," Zorn said suspiciously.

"Are you crazy?" Tip McLane said.

Zeke Zorn was a high-intensity sort of guy. He was an Elvis—he reacted but he didn't think much. For all this, he had a basically sunny, open, California personality, and it was unusual to hear this kind of paranoia coming from him. This was the third time he had brought up the subject of Cy Ogle, apropos of nothing, in the last week.

"I would bet you money," Zorn said glaring suspiciously at the screen, "that the man in that Goofy suit is none other than Cy Ogle himself. It's just what he would do."

"You're off your rocker," McLane said.

"Well, let me just say that if this campaign ever went to Disneyland—which it never would—I would have half a dozen snipers following you around with orders to blow Goofy's head off if he came within half a mile. Because this is just the kind of thing that Ogle would cook up."

Drasher watched this startling performance and then burst out laughing. Drasher was a Purvis. Like McLane, he had grown up poor and become a highly educated conservative. He was black and had grown up in Mississippi; but he and McLane had much more in common with each other than they did with Zeke Zorn, a man who dressed so finely that they did not even know the names of many of the articles of clothing that Zorn wore every single day.

"You're serious," Drasher said in wonderment. "You think that Cy Ogle sent Goofy in to do a political hit on Fowler."

"It's just too perfect," Zorn said. "When these perfect things happen, you have to look for a guiding hand somewhere. It's like Dukakis and the tank helmet in '88. I suppose you think that *just happened*." Zorn said these words almost contemptuously. "*Someone* noticed that Dukakis looked like Snoopy. *Someone* put the Snoopy helmet in his hands. Mark my words—somewhere out there is a cartoon character with your name on it, Nimrod McLane."

"Yosemite Sam," Drasher suggested.

"Sounds paranoid to me," McLane said.

"Hey," Zorn said, throwing up his hands, "once Norman Fowler has shaken hands with Goofy, no force in the universe can stop us. But"—he shook his finger accusingly at the television, "once the presidential campaign gets underway, this is the kind of thing that we have to look out for."

"Let's not get cocky," Drasher said. "There is still one force in the universe that can keep us from the nomination."

"What's that?" McLane said.

Drasher suddenly raised his voice into a polished baritone with a white southern accent, rendering a flawless imitation of the Reverend Doctor William Joseph Sweigel. "The power of JEEEEE - zuss!" he said.

"Good point," Zorn said. "Let's get our butts over to that damn picnic."

## CHAPTER THIRTY-THREE

"I was spreading some of this fancy gourmet mustard on my frankfurter just now," the Reverend Doctor Billy Joe Sweigel said, holding a jar of the savory condiment up so that all the people at the luncheon could see it, "when I noticed that there were some small flecks of material mixed in with the mustard. Now, in the part of the country where I come from, mustard is bright yellow and perfectly smooth and homogeneous in its composition. But since I have come to California . . ." Having telegraphed the joke, he paused briefly to allow laughter to build, and then subside. Then, as only a politician could, he went ahead and delivered it anyway. "Let's just say that I have spread some things on my frankfurters here in Southern California that were labeled as mustard, but in my part of the country probably would have been confiscated and analyzed in a police laboratory." The crowd laughed dutifully, for the second time, but Rev. Sweigel would not let go of the theme. "I engaged one of my staff in a lighthearted conversation about this mustard, or MOO-tard as it says on the jar, and he informed me that these flecks of material that I had alluded to were, in fact, actual seeds of the mustard plant. Mustard seeds."

The crowd went dead silent, like Sunday school children who know that they are about to be told that they stand a high chance of burning in Hell. All of the people here at the Southern California

Rightist Coalition who had been brought up Christian (which was most of them) knew what was coming. The non-Christians were already so alienated by the heavily pork-oriented meal that they weren't talking much anyway.

Sweigel continued. "Now our lord JEEE-zuss once spoke of mustard seeds. He said that all one needed in order to perform miracles was to have faith the size of a mustard seed.

"This is a piece of Scripture that I have known since I was just a little boy. But I never really understood what it meant until today. You see, in all of my life, this is the first time that I have ever actually seen a mustard seed. My mustard has always been the bright yellow substance to which I earlier alluded. So I did not know, frankly, whether a mustard seed was a very small thing, like a poppy seed, or a very large thing, like a coconut. So when I read these words of our lord JEEE-zuss, I did not know whether he was saying that we needed just a tiny little bit of faith, or a whole lot of faith.

"But today the LORD has seen fit to educate me in these matters and I have had my first taste of expensive Southern California MOO-tard, and I have seen actual mustard seeds. And I can report to you that they are neither extremely small, as seeds go, nor are they extremely large."

Ten feet away from the lectern, Nimrod T. ("Tip") McLane was sitting with his hands folded in his lap, trying to resist the temptation to order another hot dog. He knew exactly where this was going and he had to keep his wits about him.

The Reverend Doctor Sweigel was an Odessa. He did things out of pure, dumb principle, and for that reason he was about to go upside Tip McLane's head with a little bit of JEEE-zuss, as he had been doing for about the last couple of weeks—ever since William A. Cozzano had begun to make television appearances.

The media had given Sweigel a free ride all the way through Super Tuesday. They liked having a goofball in the campaign; it put variety in their tedious, ink-stained lives. When he had done well on Super Tuesday, they had turned on him in Illinois.

McLane had turned on him too. As part of their Illinois campaigns, all of the candidates had made ritual visits to the bedside of

William A. Cozzano, who was still hospitalized at that point. McLane, like the others, had been shocked to see how bad Cozzano looked.

Billy Joe Sweigel had become a wealthy and powerful TV evangelist by claiming to heal people through the power of faith. He would heal anyone of any disease in return for a ten-dollar contribution. So the question had naturally arisen: as long as he'd been in the room, why hadn't he just healed William A. Cozzano? It seemed like a fair enough question to Tip McLane and he had repeatedly raised the issue in public, and during debates. It seemed safe as anything, like asking Sweigel to heal the craters on the moon.

Then Cozzano had put on a miraculous recovery.

Sweigel continued, "So what our lord JEEE-zuss was saying was that in order to move mountains, one need not have a great deal of faith—one need not be some kind of a paragon—but a teeny little bit of faith won't do it either. We have to have a reasonable amount of faith. A sort of in-between amount of faith.

"Now, some people have more faith than others. I don't think that it's unfair to say that. And I can remember a night a couple of months ago, in an auditorium in Illinois, when one of my opponents didn't seem to have very much faith at all."

A stir ran through the crowd. In the corner of his eye, McLane could see long lenses swinging in his direction, zeroing in on his face for reaction shots.

"And a certain candidate who shall go unnamed expressed skepticism that I could, through the divine power of JEEE-zuss, heal the terrible affliction that had descended upon a certain prominent Illinoisan. And I will admit that on the night of that debate, my faith was much smaller than a mustard seed. I went back to my hotel room and asked, as JEEE-zuss did on the cross, 'God, why hast thou forsaken me.' But it came to me that it was not God who had forsaken me, but the other way around. Gradually my faith returned and waxed until it was the size, not just of a mustard seed, but of a sunflower seed, or maybe even a Brazil nut. And just a few short weeks later I was astonished to turn on my television set and see this prominent Illinoisan suddenly looking the very picture of health. Praise the Lord!"

About three people in the audience, widely spaced, shouted, "Praise the Lord!" Everyone else just looked embarrassed.

"Truly doth the Lord work in mysterious ways," Sweigel said.

*That's for sure,* McLane said to himself, thinking of Goofy.

Norman Fowler, Jr., the Goofmeister himself, the reincarnation of Marvis, had not been invited to this little get-together, in the football-field-sized backyard of the Markham estate in Bel Air. The Southern California Rightist Coalition was not the kind of outfit that would let a moderate like Fowler anywhere near their campaign events, or their coffers. Tip McLane was a shoo-in, and the group had a large enough evangelical Christian wing that Sweigel had gotten an invite too.

After the debacle in Illinois, followed by severe drubbings in the northeastern states where television evangelists had a bit of an image problem, Sweigel had stayed in the race anyway, as a broker for the evangelical vote. He was a political vampire. His broadcasting network in the Bible Belt served as an inexhaustible source of funds, and in every city he had a hard core of supporters who could be relied on to sustain his campaign.

The incredible recovery of William A. Cozzano had caused a sudden surge in Sweigel's popularity. Because of the number of people who believed that Sweigel had cured Cozzano, his numbers were now climbing up into double digits, and he was starting to become a major annoyance to McLane.

But nothing more than an annoyance. Sweigel was frightening enough that he served as his own worst enemy, his own personal Goofy. Whenever he rose in the polls, he started to get more television coverage, people started having bad dreams about him, and he sank again.

*The hot dogs* said everything about this luncheon. Hollywood people would not have served hot dogs. They would have served caviar, fine wines, California cuisine and all that, to show how rich and tasteful they were. But this luncheon was full of people who had come to California and staked claims to real estate prior to the invention of the movie camera, which was to say that they tended to be very old and endowed with a level of wealth that far transcended the petty plane of movie stars. Much of this wealth was not in liquid assets; all together, the territory owned by the people at this luncheon probably composed an area larger than many northeastern states. But however you looked at it, they were loaded, and this was one invitation you did not turn down.

The man who had invited McLane to speak was none other than Karl Fort himself. Fort was now in his nineties. He had long since cashed in his agricultural holdings. Those original investments had made him a rich man, but they only produced steady dividends as long as Fort was right there on the ground, personally dispatching thugs with ax handles. This kind of micromanagement had grown wearisome, and so Fort had moved into less earthy forms of investment.

This had left him with a great deal of free time, only some of which could be taken up on the golf course. Karl Fort had begun dabbling in politics during the sixties, supporting the likes of Caleb Roosevelt Marshall, Goldwater, and Wallace. He had been a major player in the California conservative movement of the seventies and eighties. He had given lots of money to the conservative think tanks that had provided Tip McLane with his first few jobs.

And when the Markhams had begun making plans to host this luncheon, Karl Fort had called Tip McLane personally and actually reminisced about the good old days back in the Depression, and Tip McLane had actually called him "sir."

*Sweigel eventually concluded* his sermon with a prayer. A few people clenched their hands and bowed their heads fervently. Everyone else just looked restless or embarrassed. And then it was Tip McLane's turn to speak.

They applauded generously. The nervous silence that had reigned during Sweigel's performance was finally broken. McLane got up from his seat at the high table in the front and waved and nodded to the crowd: a hundred and fifty of the richest people in the West, seated at a few long tables with their paper plates and plastic wineglasses. To one side, the press corps was corralled behind a red plastic ribbon, like wild animals.

This was going to be a piece of cake. These people loved him; he could do no wrong here. "Thank you very much. And thanks to Mr. and Mrs. Markham for making the backyard of their magnificent home available for this event. In a few months I hope to return the invitation—though I'm afraid that you'll have to fly all the way to Washington, D.C."

A few men in the crowd barked out laughter and there was a smattering of applause.

"I have a dirty little secret for you: I'm sick to death of campaigning. I think everyone in America has heard my message by now. Most people who have heard it seem to agree with it. My opponents don't, but, excepting Reverend Sweigel here, I've always found my opponents to be just a little bit on the goofy side."

About half a dozen people—those who had already seen the Fowler/Goofy image on TV—laughed loudly at this. Everyone else tittered uncertainly. The line wasn't intended for them. It was intended to be used on the evening newscasts, at the appropriate moment.

"So I'm not going to harangue you with my usual stump speech. Instead I'd like to speak, very briefly, about some of the ideas that I intend to put into action once I get settled into the White House next January."

At this point McLane paused for a moment and pretended to fiddle with his note cards. He was doing this because some kind of a distraction had arisen at one of the tables, and he didn't want to try and shout his way through it. He assumed it was something minor, like a glass of lemonade that had spilled into someone's lap. But it didn't die away. It kept building.

Several people had stood up now. They were all facing inward, looking at an elderly man who was leaning way back in his chair, almost lying down, pressing one fist into his breastbone. His mouth was open, he was gasping for breath.

"Are there any doctors present here? This man is in distress," McLane said.

Something caught his eye: Zeke Zorn, standing up, waving him away from the lectern with both hands, like one of those guys at the airport directing the jetliners. McLane moved quickly away from the lectern. Only later would he understand that this had been good advice. There were very few things a man could say into a microphone at such a time that would make him look as though he had handled the situation presidentially. There were many ways to screw up.

No one had responded to the call for a doctor. All of the lenses and microphones in the makeshift press gallery had swung over and brought themselves to bear on the man in distress.

People were doing the normal sorts of folksy first-aid things. A couple of men cleared off a table in one instant by yanking at the tablecloth, sweeping all the plates and glasses off onto the ground, and then four people gathered around the stricken man and lifted him up onto the table's clean surface. They loosened his tie. Someone offered him a glass of water. None of it was doing anything for his life expectancy, which clearly was measurable in seconds or minutes.

Mr. Markham approached the lectern, pulled down the microphone, and spoke into it. "I'd like to ask everyone to please remain in their seats for now. Give Karl some air."

The stricken man was Karl Fort.

McLane couldn't keep his eyes off the man. Fort had ruled over the McLanes' portion of California like a demon king. McLane had known the man's name and face since he had been a toddler. He had been fearsome and omnipresent to those Okies who worked for him, who suffered beatings from his goons and who wondered, each week, if Fort would see fit to sign their paycheck. Uncle Purvis had, for a period of three or four decades, personally vowed to kill Karl Fort with his bare hands at least once a day. And now, after all that, Karl Fort was dying right in front of Nimrod McLane's eyes. If only Purvis could have been here to see it.

There was sudden motion off to McLane's left. Someone had vaulted the high table and now was striding confidently across the lawn toward Karl Fort. Tip glanced over and realized that it was the Reverend Doctor William Joseph Sweigel.

In the same instant, the entire press corps realized it too.

Karl Fort's attack had been an unfortunate coincidence. But when Rev. Sweigel stepped in to lay on his hands, it became something else: a campaign event. The plastic ribbon snapped. It was like a dam breaking. The journalists charged toward Karl Fort.

There were three long rows of tables. Karl Fort was in the middle row. The first row formed a low barrier standing in the way of the journalists. The vanguard—nimble print reporters—made an end run. The second wave—burdened by minicams—simply rolled directly over the top of it, their knees nearly buckling from the weight as they jumped to the grass on the far side, and headed the print reporters off in the narrow pass between the first and middle rows.

Three minicam operators, with their instinct for seizing the high ground, jumped to the top of the middle row. One of these three planted his foot in the midst of a paper plate heaped with baked beans and slipped; his boot shot off to the side and slammed into the chest of the fifth richest man in California so hard that it sent him toppling backward onto the ground. The cameraman slithered to his knees and then his feet, trashing a few more plates of food as he tried to accelerate in pursuit of the two other minicam operators who were now well ahead of him. His boots got traction on the tablecloth but the tablecloth slipped over the table, and so for the first few moments he actually ran in place, like a cartoon character, his feet churning madly and his body going nowhere as the tablecloth, with its burden of plates and cups, accordioned down to one end of the table, depositing a slippery obstacle course of beans, ketchup, MOO-tard, and ice cubes as it went.

Finally he got traction and pursued the others, who had run into an obstacle of their own. Between them and Karl Fort was an ice sculpture, an intricately carved bowl of ice filled with pink lemonade. It had gone unnoticed by the cameraman who had momentarily taken the lead. His only concern was getting Karl Fort and Billy Joe Sweigel into his viewfinder as quickly as possible, and so he was running with one eye squinted shut and the other eye pressed into the neoprene cup of his eyepiece. Seeing the world in out-of-focus, black-and-white tunnel vision, he missed the ice sculpture entirely and slammed into it at a full sprint, catching it with both knees. The impact knocked his legs backward. The weight of the minicam on his shoulder jerked his body forward. He spun in midair, appeared to become completely horizontal, and then fell straight down on top of the ice sculpture. Half of the lemonade went up in the air and then all of it burst down and sideways as the cameraman's body crushed the sculpture into convenient bite-sized fragments. Nearby luncheon-goers caught the tsunami of ice and lemonade full in the face.

The second cameraman was only a pace or two behind the first; he tried to stop, his feet got ahead of his body, and he landed on his ass in the midst of the ice storm, sliding to a halt and then careening off the edge of the table and landing full-length in the laps of three consecutive luncheon-goers.

The third cameraman, also suffering from video tunnel vision, planted one foot in the small of the first cameraman's back. That leg buckled. He caught his full weight on the other leg, hopped on it three times like a wide receiver trying not to go out of bounds, planted that foot on some ice, and skidded on one rigid leg for a distance of several feet, now looking perfectly like a figure skater. He finally got the other foot down on the edge of a serving platter, catapulting a dozen freshly grilled burgers into the chest of a prominent comedian-turned-real-estate magnate.

At which point he realized, finally, that he was about to run over Karl Fort's body. He planted both feet and once again created an accordion effect on a tablecloth. This carried him forward until he reached the edge of Fort's table, where his rubber-soled boots contacted solid, clean, dry formica, and stopped dead. This slammed him forward onto his knees, which was perfect: he stopped in a kneeling position with the lens of his camera about four feet away from Karl Fort, looking straight down on his body.

Unfortunately, from a strictly media-conscious point of view, Fort's face wasn't visible; the view was blocked by the beefy arms of a young man, possibly a security person, who had the heels of both hands in the middle of Fort's naked breastbone and was rhythmically shoving on it, compressing his entire ribcage, making his bony thorax bulge outward around the sides like a stepped-on balloon. Even if this man had not been there, Fort's face still would have been obscured by another man who was gripping Fort's chin in one hand and his temples in the other, holding his mouth open in a yawn, bending forward to fasten his mouth over Fort's.

The Reverend had just arrived by Fort's side; despite all of the above-mentioned hindrances, most of the journalistic corps had actually beaten Sweigel to the scene of the action.

"Please step aside, please make way," Sweigel was saying, in the rising, chantlike intonation of a preacher quoting Scripture. Since most of the people in his way were journalists who had come specifically to see what Sweigel was going to do, they made way willingly.

Sweigel stood belly-up to the table, only inches away from Fort, and clasped his hands together for a moment, praying with his eyes tightly clenched shut. Then he held out both hands, palms downward, and laid them gently on Fort's bare skin: one on the shoulder, one down on the belly, where they didn't interfere with the CPR. Billy Joe Sweigel knew how to hedge his bets.

Twenty feet away, Tip McLane stood numb with horror.

He had been fighting the primary campaign for almost a year. It had been very much like an Okie bar fight: desperate men wielding brass knuckles, ice picks, and broken bottles in a dark back lot. In Iowa, New Hampshire, Super Tuesday, New York, he had taken on all comers. He had not made many friends, but, with Drasher providing the strategy and Zorn providing the media kidney punches, he had thrashed all of his adversaries into bloody, inert sides of meat. Norman Fowler had hung on all the way to California and then taken his own political life. He had come here, to safe, comfortable ground, to celebrate victory.

And now he was being dry-gulched. Sweigel was going to nail him right between the eyes.

If the CPR worked, if the ambulances got here in time, if the doctors arrived to deliver their miraculous clot-dissolving miracle drugs, then Sweigel would be two for two on national TV: first Cozzano, and now Karl Fort.

Between his memories of Fort in the old days, and the prospect that the old son of a bitch might, by surviving, now torpedo his political career, Tip McLane had never wanted anyone to die quite so badly.

"It's fake," Zorn said, standing very close to him and muttering into his ear. "Fort's not really having a heart attack. Cy Ogle set this whole thing up."

"You're a lunatic," McLane said. But Zorn's words had made him nervous anyway.

"Lord, hear our prayer," Sweigel said. "This man has been stricken. We pray that, in the name of JEEE-zuss, he may be healed, and walk among us once again."

Then he prayed silently, while the two men continued with CPR and mouth-to-mouth, until the ambulance showed up and the EMTs took over the job.

McLane was a little surprised. He had expected that the EMTs would bundle Fort up and whisk him straight back to the ambulance as fast as possible. But instead they set up some equipment and worked on him for a few minutes, right there on the table, doing CPR with a sort of large plungerlike object and squeezing air into his lungs with a resuscitator.

The attention of the guests, of the media, and especially of Billy Joe Sweigel could hardly have been more focused on Karl Fort. Standing at the periphery of the crowd, Tip McLane realized that, for once, absolutely no one was paying attention to him.

From a media standpoint he was just like Gyges, ancestor of Croesus, who was able to become invisible. This was a story mentioned in Plato's *Republic*. Gyges, being invisible, could get away with anything. If he used his power to do evil, but no one saw him, and he was thought to be a just man, then did he ever suffer for his crimes? Tip McLane decided to ponder this issue as he went for a bit of a stroll around the Markham estate.

They were in the backyard, hemmed in between a sheer cliff wall on one side and the almost equally massive Markham mansion on the other. Perfectly manicured gardens wrapped around the mansion on both sides—neat paths winding between trellises of roses. Mrs. Markham adored her roses. Tip McLane walked into the fragrant and colorful jungle, quietly at first, then with longer strides as he became confident that his departure had gone unnoticed.

Within a few seconds he had worked his way around the side of the house to the front. He stood for a moment, framed in an arched trellis groaning with peach-colored roses, and took in a broad view of the horseshoe drive, which was paved with little interlocking geometric tiles.

A few minutes ago this drive had been clogged with limousines and media vans. When the ambulance had been called, all of the drivers had pulled out of the horseshoe, down the long driveway, through the twelve-foot-high gate, and parked on the road. Now the whole front of the house was empty except for the ambulance, square in the middle of the horseshoe, doors open, engine running.

Representative Nimrod T. ("Tip") McLane sauntered out of the rose garden and into the horseshoe, trying to look like a man who was just out for a stroll, trying to clear his head and get away from the chaos out back. He looked carefully in all directions: into the garden, into the windows of the mansion, into the front seat of the ambulance itself. He saw no one. Everyone was out back.

He had one or two irreducible habits that he had picked up when he was just a boy, working in the broccoli fields, and that had remained unbroken through years of parochial education, Ph.D. study, conservative theorizing at various think tanks, White House dinners, and service in the House of Representatives. One habit was that he always carried a pocketknife. It was amazing how often a pocketknife came in handy.

He squatted down against the left front tire of the ambulance, unfolded the small blade of his pocketknife, which he always kept sharp as a scalpel, and paused for a moment to ponder his next move.

As Socrates had pointed out, the highest reach of injustice was, like Gyges, to be deemed just when you were not. Karl Fort was Gyges. He went to White House dinners, gave money to charities, spent half his life at various testimonial dinners where the most important people in the country stood in line to gush about what a wonderful man he was. No one ever said a word about the ax handles.

But did that justify slashing the tires of his ambulance? McLane continued to thumb his way mentally through Plato's *Republic*, looking for guidance.

Plato advocated dividing the republic into three categories: rulers, warriors, and tradesmen. Tradesmen were allowed to become rich. Rulers and warriors were to live simply and to receive the best possible education, in the hopes of producing philosopher kings.

Tip McLane was a philosopher king. Karl Fort was a tradesman. And according to Plato, the worst form of injustice occurred when people tried to force their way into a class where they did not belong—e.g., when warriors tried to seize political power (the Soviet coup), or politicians meddled in military campaigns (Vietnam War), or in the affairs of private enterprise (burdensome government regulation).

Or when tradesmen tried to use their wealth to gain political power, which could lead to the degenerate form of government known as oligarchy.

Representative Nimrod T. ("Tip") McLane inserted the blade of his pocketknife deep into one of the treads. The rubber was tough, but so was Tip McLane, and eventually it gave way and he felt the blade penetrate into the tire. Then all he had to do was twist, and air began to hiss out, feeling cold and wet as it flowed over his hand.

The ambulance settled, almost as if it were going to roll over on top of him. He was startled by a popping noise that came from the flaccid tire as its bead popped loose from the rim. That was extra good; it would make the tire much more difficult to reinflate.

He withdrew the knife, folded it back into his pocket, and then strolled back through the roses to the backyard.

The EMTs transferred Karl Fort onto a gurney and wheeled him across the yard, through the Markhams' house, and out to the ambulance, chased the whole way by journalists who left a trail of baked-bean footprints across the polished-granite floors and the oriental rugs. The ambulance traveled about ten feet down the drive, veering uncontrollably to the left, and then stopped.

Someone ran inside and called another ambulance. Two of the EMTs jumped out and began to change the tire. Shooting through the rear windows of the van, the media were able to get beautiful shots of another EMT, on his knees next to Fort, holding up the electric paddles, preparing to administer the sacrament of defibrillation.

*Karl Fort lingered* in the hospital for five days. According to tracking polls commissioned by the McLane campaign, the Rev. Sweigel's support climbed all the way up to the 20 percent mark when Fort's condition was upgraded from critical to serious. But when Fort's kidneys went, on the Saturday before the big vote, the voters began to show disillusionment, and when he finally died on Sunday evening, just in time for the eleven p.m. news, the Reverend's standing collapsed like a popped balloon.

Tip McLane and his crew had already gotten the news, through private channels. He and Zorn and Drasher went down to their hotel bar for a drink and watched the coverage of Fort's death, and then of the day's campaign events. They were joined by a couple of writers for major East Coast newspapers, men who had been assigned to the McLane campaign for the last few months and whom they had gotten to know well. They bought each other drinks and talked off the record late into the night. Though no one came out and said it, they all knew that the primary campaign was over.

CHAPTER THIRTY-FOUR

Eleanor Richmond rented a town house in the Rosemont neighborhood of Alexandria. It had actually been part of D.C. at one point and had been ceded back to the state of Virginia in 1846, so she could weakly maintain that she was back living in her hometown once more.

This historical argument was completely lost on all of her relatives in the District, who had been delighted when she announced she was coming home, and then hurt and angry when she chose to live in Virginia. But Eleanor had already seen her son get shot in the back, and as far as she was concerned, D.C. didn't have anything to offer her kids except for a few museums and a whole lot of ways to get shot.

She was in a nice, mixed-race neighborhood near Alexandria's eighteenth-century waterfront. If she went uphill she got into an aristocratic neighborhood of big houses, bordering on mansions. If she went downhill, toward the Potomac, she got to the proverbial other side of the tracks in just a few minutes. Straddling the boundary, on the tracks themselves, was the Braddock Metro station, from which she could ride into D.C. in about ten minutes. Braddock's modest parking lot was ringed by nice new yuppie condos, shops, and office buildings. Beyond that was a floodplain between the tracks and the river, filled with dingy town houses and projects, bounded by the outskirts of National Airport on the north and the swank cobblestones of Old Town on the south. Compared to the bad parts of D.C., it didn't deserve the description of ghetto; it was just a lower-middle-class neighborhood. It was something that Eleanor could point to when her relatives in D.C. made catty remarks to the effect that she had sold out and fled to white suburbia.

She still hadn't gotten used to being respectable again. When she looked at real estate, she kept expecting people to glare at her suspiciously and say, "Have you ever been a bag lady?" But all she had to do was say that she was senate staff and all the doors were open to her: nice new apartments, charge accounts at Pentagon Plaza, auto loans. It astounded her when she was able to go into a Toyota dealership and drive out an hour later with a brand-new Camry.

Harmon, Jr., and Clarice stayed behind in Denver long enough to finish out the school year and then followed her out to Alexandria. In the fall they would go to T. C. Williams High School, just a mile or two up the street. In the meantime, over the summer, there was a lot for them to do. The nearby Metro station meant that they could get around town easily (which they liked) and safely (which Eleanor liked). And, after a bit of looking around, Eleanor found a nice extended-care facility (what used to be called a nursing home) where she could put Mother.

Mother had no idea, really, that she was back home, but as she looked out the windows of the car on her way in from the airport and smelled the air of the late Virginia spring, Eleanor imagined that, at some level, she knew where she was, and that she was glad to be back where she belonged, not out in the middle of Colorado sharing a room with some rancher's widow. Whether or not Mother knew what was going on, bringing her back here was good for Eleanor's heart, and made her feel that she was doing right by her mom.

When Eleanor showed up for her first day of work, a week before Memorial Day, she had no idea what she was doing; Senator Marshall still had not defined her responsibilities or even provided her with a job title. She was both excited and intensely curious. She walked to the Braddock Metro station at seven. Her neighborhood's sidewalks were filled with commuters headed for the Metro station. As Eleanor entered this stream of suit-and-tie-wearing, newspaper-reading professionals, carrying her very proper attaché case, wearing her Reeboks, and holding on to her *Washington Post* she felt like a spy testing out a new undercover identity.

From the raised platform of the Metro station she looked across the public housing toward National Airport, the 727s plunging in at forty-second intervals, and across the Potomac to D.C. The pleasant, scented spring air was still cool, and as she looked through the haze, she could see the monumental structures that were now part of her world. The Metro glided into the station, eerily clean and high-tech compared to The Ride. She boarded, found a place to stand where she could look out the window, and watched the progression through Crystal City, Pentagon City, Pentagon, and then out into daylight across the Potomac. She saw the National Cathedral drawing the light of the sun, peeked in at Thomas Jefferson, and got to L'Enfant Plaza, where she transferred to the Orange Line for two stops over to the Capitol. Since she was a few minutes early, she chose to be a tourist, and strolled through the Capitol on her way over to the Russell Senate Office Building.

She was greeted at the gate of the Russell Building by a handsome, very young-looking black man from Senate Security. "If you'll follow me, Mrs. Richmond, we'll get your credentials in order."

Eleanor was still new enough at this that she was surprised when people recognized her. "Thank you," she said. "I didn't expect someone to meet me at the door. I thought I'd be standing in lines all day."

"When Senator Marshall speaks, we move," the man said. "We're taught that all senators are equal, but we love Senator Marshall. He's not one of your blow-dry wonders, if you get my drift."

They took an elevator down two levels and entered an office where Eleanor was photographed, finger-printed, asked to sign her official signature, and then take the oath as an employee of the United States. A petite, perhaps sixty-year-old woman read the oath.

She proceeded into the next office and was given her holographic badge, complete with innumerable codes implanted in the strips on the back of the badge. She wondered what she was going to do with a Top-Secret Alpha clearance.

"That's it," her guide said. "Now you have one very cranky senator waiting to put you to work."

*The Russell was* the oldest and most prestigious of the three senate office buildings. It had the aura of fine old wood, penetrated by decades of good tobacco smoke. It was the building of choice and Marshall had the office of choice, with a commanding view of the Capitol out one window and down the Mall and Constitution Avenue down the other. Entering the office, Eleanor was struck by the profusion of Native American art, mission decor, and numerous watercolors painted by Marshall before his arthritis had made it impossible for him to hold a brush. His secretary of thirty years, Patty McCormick, turned and said, "Hello darlin', welcome to the last frontier."

From around the corner, the familiar husky voice shouted, "Goddamn it Patty, don't scare her away. Come on in, Eleanor."

Eleanor edged into the Senator's office and found him working his way through a breakfast sent up from the cafeteria. "Have a seat," he said, waving at one of the heavy leather chairs.

"Good morning, Senator, how are you feeling?"

"Shitty, as usual, but that's nothing new. I'll be goddamned if I'll take pain medication. I haven't got an awful lot of brain cells left and I want them to work."

They made a little small talk about her move to Alexandria. Caleb seemed surprisingly unhurried, for a senator. Eleanor kept wondering when he was going to tell her why she'd been hired. Finally she came out and asked.

"Should we talk about what you want me to do?"

"Sure, why not. What do you want to do?"

"I don't know, I'm still slightly overwhelmed to be here."

"How'd you like to be my spokesperson?"

Eleanor couldn't help laughing. At first she chuckled politely because she assumed it was a joke. Then she laughed out loud in shock, realizing he was serious. "Senator, you are one crazy fool."

"You ever see one of those stupid old Westerns where the bad guys come riding into town and they just start shooting at everything? They shoot out all the windows, they shoot holes in the water barrels, they pick off people on the balconies. I always thought that looked like fun. Well, I'm out of here soon and I have a lot to say and I want to have somebody to say it who will make an impression, not one of these generic press mavens who keep massaging messages and doing sound bites. You and I, young lady, are going to shoot a few holes in this goddamn town before I end this ride."

As he talked, Marshall was unable to hide his extreme pain. He became so angry about the pain and so intense in his conversation that he accidentally knocked over his coffee, spilling the contents all over the top of the desk. "Goddamned son of a bitch," he screamed.

Patty poked her head around the corner and said, "Did it again, Your Grace?"

"Bitch," he said, throwing the coffee drenched *Washington Times* at her. Then he grimaced, doubled over in his chair, and rested his forehead against the desktop for a moment, his shoulders heaving.

Eleanor, horrified, looked at Patty for a cue. Patty didn't seem to notice. She winked at Eleanor and said, "We have a very formal office."

While Patty cleaned up the mess, Eleanor helped Caleb to a small conference room next door and let him collapse in a chair. Then she sat down across the table from him.

Marshall, slumped down low in his chair, said, "In all seriousness, Eleanor, I thought long and hard about this appointment. I have very little time left. My problem is not arthritis. It's galloping bone cancer. I have, maximum, three months of useful activity left."

"Oh, god, Senator, I'm so sorry—"

"Spare me. And call me Caleb."

"Is there anything—"

"Yes. Shut up and listen for a second."

"Okay," Eleanor said.

"I'm stuck in a party that was once for the individual, and now it's dedicated to controlling the individual. The Bible thumpers and the single-issue people and all of those other control freaks have no idea of what the United States is all about. And they are going to win. But I will make my contribution. And here it is."

Resting on the table was a book, bound in leather, Western-style. Imprinted on the cover in gold leaf was:

POLITICAL WILL AND TESTAMENT
SEN. CALEB ROOSEVELT MARSHALL

Marshall put his hand on the book and shoved it across the table at Eleanor. She caught it before it tumbled into her lap. "I have a press secretary, of course," Marshall said. "And he has a whole god-damn staff of flacks. I'll continue to use them for the run-of-the-mill announcements and contacts with local bubble heads. I want you to work on this and wait for the phone to ring."

"Senator, I thought you were going to bury me in a corner of your staff somewhere."

"Well, I'm not."

"But your constituents are going to hate you."

"Eleanor, I don't give a good fuck. Get to work."

Eleanor carried the book into an adjoining office, a small but nice one with a view of the Capitol. Patty was already in there, straightening a few things up. Eleanor's stuff had been moved in and unpacked. Her personal things all looked humble and shabby in the magnificent building.

Patty was sniffling. "I love that man, Eleanor," she said. "He's the most decent person in this town, and he's dying."

"How many people know?"

"Most of the Hill."

Eleanor settled into her leather chair behind the immense wooden desk and looked at the walls, decorated with Hopi and Navajo art. On one corner of the desk was a recent photo of both her kids, and on the other corner, from Ray del Valle, a dozen roses with the note, "Knock 'em dead, tiger."

Before she could open the Senator's book, the phone rang. It was Patty.

"Dr. Hunter P. Lawrence on the line for you, Eleanor."

"Okay, put him through."

Eleanor heartily disliked the professor. He was one of the new breed of talking heads who had turned civilized shows like *Meet the Press* into the intellectual equivalent of the World Wrestling Federation. The format of Lawrence's show was simple: a victim would be invited to sit in the center chair and then two commentators from the alleged left wing and two from the alleged right wing would abuse them. If they weren't abusive enough, the Professor would step in and stir them up. It got great ratings.

"Hello?" she said.

"Ms. Richmond, this is Dr. Lawrence of *Washington Hot Seat*. Welcome to town."

It was strange to hear that famous voice coming out of her telephone. She felt as if she knew the man, even though she didn't. "Thank you Dr. Lawrence. How may I be of service to you?"

"We'd like you to appear on our show next week," he said cheerily.

"Oh, that's very flattering, but I'm sure that I wouldn't be of much interest."

"Oh, on the contrary. You gained great visibility when you took the neo-Nazi apart. Your advocacy for the Hispanics also was impressive. Your relationship with that troglodyte Marshall is a subject of conversation. And let's be blunt, there aren't that many highly visible black women. We're so tired of the usual suspects."

Eleanor had come to work in a state of new-job euphoria. If Dr. Lawrence had reached her a few minutes earlier, she might not have taken offense. But hearing about the bone cancer had changed her mood. She hadn't even had time to process the bad news yet; she felt edgy and deranged.

"What's the matter, Dr. Lawrence? Did Aunt Jemima cancel at the last minute?"

A long silence. "Uh—"

"If all you want is a black female, why don't you just go east of Rock Creek Park for once in your life, and just pick one off the street? Some of those girls clean up real nice."

"We don't really want just anyone."

"I could recommend a few nuns from my old school who might be able to give you some pointers on treating other people with common courtesy. Once you've learned all about that, why don't

you call my token black female ass back up and talk to me again."
Eleanor hung up so hard that the telephone bounced.

Marshall, in the conference room next door, howled and
wheezed with agonized laughter.

"You have a problem, Caleb?" Eleanor shouted.

"You're some P.R. whiz," he shouted. "He even called you personally—he usually has one of his munchkins do the scheduling."

"You got me in a bad mood."

"It was perfect. This story will spread all over town and you'll be
even more in demand than you are now. You couldn't have done
better."

"Whom should I be nice to?"

Marshall hooted, "Not one of those cold-blooded, cock-sucking
sons a bitches. They crank out these talking-heads programs like
bad sausage. They have to fill air time every night. Their Rolodexes
are full of white men and everyone nags them about it. If they put
you on TV, then they can point to you and prove how racially
diverse they are."

"Oh. I thought it was because of my cogent analysis."

"That too," Senator Marshall said.

The phone rang again a few minutes later. This time it was Anita
Ross of the Style section of the *Post*. "Ms. Richmond, we've heard
how you stiffed Dr. Lawrence. We'd like to do a feature on you for
the Style section."

Marshall was still sitting within earshot, apparently having nothing better to do with his time, so Eleanor hit the mute button and
shouted, "It's the *Post*."

"Fuck 'em."

"Ms. Ross," Eleanor said, "why not call me in a couple of weeks,
when I've had the chance to get settled in. Why, the ink on my
badge is hardly dry."

"You'd better know that by taking on the Professor, you could
become an instant culture hero. But only if the story gets published."

"A culture hero in five minutes? Not bad."

"Some have come and gone here in fifteen minutes," Ms. Ross
said pointedly.

"Well, its been nice talking to you," Eleanor said. "Call back in
twenty minutes and see if I'm still around."

"Nicely done," Marshall said. "What do you think of my thoughts?"

Eleanor realized that Marshall was waiting for her to look into the book. "I really can't say. I haven't had a chance to open it up yet."

Marshall tottered into her office, audibly grinding his teeth from pain. "Go ahead, have a look, I'll just stretch out here on this couch."

Eleanor picked up the book and opened it. The first page was blank, and the second, and the third. She riffled through the pages. They were all blank.

"Senator, what is this?"

"It is my *tabula rasa*. A work in progress. You're going to ghost-write it for me. Just like the old song says, 'Ghost writers in the sky.'"

"What do you want me to write?"

"Don't trouble me with details, woman. I don't have much time left."

"But I can't just go out and write it."

"Listen to me. When you made the 'Colorado is a welfare queen state' speech you set me to thinking. I am as much a part of the problems as Jesse is or Ted Kennedy or for that matter that poor little Shad Harper son of a bitch you nailed in Denver. You know, I love this country. I never had much trouble with money because my dad left me a lot of property and I had the privilege of being a maverick. The one thing I noticed in forty-eight years of public service, forty-four up here, is that the rarest thing in life is a person who speaks the truth. The most dangerous thing in life is a person who constantly refers to 'values.' If I was going to write down my testament, that is it. None of us has the right to tell anyone else how to live. None of us has the right to hold back anybody else for any reason—race, religion, income, or what have you. The rest of life is an open field, a crap shoot. The role of government is to make it an equal crap shoot for everybody. Not real profound, but real effective."

"So what do you want me to do?"

"If you feel able to adhere to the general message I just laid out—"

"I do."

"Feel your way through this P.R. maze, go out and represent me on TV, and keep writing your best thoughts down in this goddamn book. Represent freedom and honesty—whoops, there I go talking about values again."

"You really think that someone like me is the person to represent a card-carrying member of the power structure, like you."

"You're goddamned right. I never got co-opted by nobody. Nobody is ever going to co-opt you. And in this auto-erotic, kill to stay in the Beltway town, that's a huge advantage."

"When I go public, how do I identify myself?"

"Why, as Eleanor Richmond."

"Do I say I'm your spokesperson?"

"If you want to. Lady, you're my last gift to the country."

By the end of the day, Eleanor's calendar had been filled for the summer. One major interview show a week, and two print journalists a week. Her first interview would be with the *Alexandria Gazette* on Friday. Even Dr. Lawrence called up, full of contrition about his lack of sensitivity, and tried to take Eleanor out on a date to the Maison Blanche. Eleanor was a hot topic for the rest of May and June.

It didn't take her long to figure out why: she was close to Senator Marshall, and everyone in town had heard rumors that Senator Marshall was dying. They would pump her for information about the Senator, in more or less subtle ways. She would ward off their questions and then talk about whatever she wanted—which is what Washington people always did with the press anyway.

## CHAPTER THIRTY-FIVE

"Floyd Wayne Vishniak," said the digitized voice from the computer, and an array of fresh windows popped into life on Aaron Green's high-resolution video screen. One of the windows was a photograph, a head shot of a white man with lank blond hair, not short enough to be short and not long enough to be long, sticking out from beneath a blue baseball cap turned around backward on his head. He had pale blue eyes that were turned down at the corners, giving him a sad and bedraggled appearance, and his skin was flushed and glossy under the blaze of an electronic flash. This was not a posed shot. It had been taken from a low angle as Floyd Wayne Vishniak rode down an escalator at a shopping mall somewhere. He was staring down into the camera with a blank and baffled expression that had not yet developed into surprise. He was wearing a tighly stretched, inside-out, navy blue T-shirt with a couple of holes in it and he had the ropy muscles of a man who got them by doing physical labor and not by working out at any health club.

This image was not the only window on the computer screen. There was a smaller one next to it, this one showing a brief video clip that kept looping back and replaying. It showed Floyd Wayne Vishniak sitting in the cheap seats at a sports arena somewhere, leaping to his feet along with all of the other people in his vicinity to shout abuse at some miscreant down below. In this clip, Vishniak was wearing a tremendously oversized, bright yellow foam rubber hand over his real hand. The long finger of the hand was extended. Just in case this message was not clear, it had been printed with the words FUCK THE REF. And in case the ref did not happen to be looking in his direction, Vishniak could clearly be seen mouthing the same words—chanting them over and over—in unison with all of the other sports fans in his section. In Vishniak's other hand he was holding a plastic beer cup the size of the Louvre. While he was waving his giant yellow digit in the air, beer sloshed over the rim and splashed down on the shoulders of the fan in front of him, who reacted, but either did not care or was afraid to make a big deal out of it. Floyd Wayne Vishniak was not a person that most people would consider picking a fight with. He was not especially big, but he was tightly wound in the extreme.

Other people were waving giant foam rubber hockey sticks and other hockey-related paraphernalia. Though the action below—the source of the controversy—was not shown on this video clip, it was evidently a hockey game, and at least one of the teams was apparently named the Quad Cities Whiplash.

Another window, below the video loop, showed a map of the fifty states with a blinking red X superimposed on the Mississippi River, between western Illinois and eastern Iowa. Under the blinking X was the label DAVENPORT, IOWA (QUAD CITIES).

There were two other windows on the screen, both of them carrying textual information. One of them was a brief c.v. of Floyd Wayne Vishniak. He had grown up in the Quad Cities, straddling the Illinois-Iowa border, dropped out of high school to get a job in a tractor factory, and been laid off and rehired six times in the intervening fifteen years. During the past year he had barely managed to earn his weight in dollars.

The remaining window was a tall narrow one that ran down the side of the computer screen. It was a list containing exactly one hundred items. Each item consisted of a phrase describing a subset of the American population, followed by a person's name.

As this presentation—this computerized dossier—proceeded from one name to the next, the corresponding item on the list was highlighted, a bright purple box drawn over it so that the user could see which category he was dealing with at the moment. The hundred categories and names on the list were as follows:

IRRELEVANT MOUTH BREATHER

400-POUND TAB DRINKER

STONE-FACED URBAN HOMEBOY

BURGER-FLIPPING HISTORY MAJOR

SQUIRRELLY WINNEBAGO JOCKEY

BIBLE-SLINGING PORCH MONKEY

ECONOMIC ROADKILL

PENT-UP CORPORATE LICKSPITTLE

HIGH-METABOLISM WORLD DOMINATOR

MIDAMERICAN KNICKKNACK QUEEN

SNUFF-HAWKING BASEMENT DWELLER

POSTADOLESCENT ROAD WARRIOR

DEPRESSION-HAUNTED CAN STACKER

PRETENTIOUS URBAN-LIFESTYLE SLAVE

FORMERLY RESPECTABLE BANKRUPTCY SURVIVOR

FROSTY-HAIRED COUPON SNIPPER

CYNICAL MEDIA MANIPULATOR

RETICENT GUN NUT

UFOS ATE MY BRAIN

MALL-HOPPING CORPORATE CONCUBINE

HIGH-FIBER DUCK SQUEEZER

POST-CONFEDERATE GRAVY EATER

MANIC THIRD-WORLD ENTREPRENEUR

OVEREXTENDED YOUNG PROFESSIONAL

APARTMENT-DWELLING MALL STAFF

TRADE SCHOOL METAL HEAD

ORANGE COUNTY BOOK BURNER

FIRST-GENERATION BELTWAY BLACK

80'S JUNK-BOND PARVENUE

DEBT-HOUNDED WAGE SLAVE

ACTIVIST TUBE FEEDER

TOILET-SCRUBBING EX-STEELWORKER

NEO-OKIE

SHIT-KICKING WRESTLEMANIAC

SUNBELT CONDO COMMANDO

RUST-BELT LUMPENPAOL

and others . . .

Aaron hit the space bar on the Calyx workstation's keyboard. All of the windows disappeared except for the long skinny one with the list of categories. The next item on the list was highlighted and spoken aloud by the digitized computer voice: RETICENT GUN NUT—JIM HANSON, N. PLATTE, NEBRASKA.

Another set of windows appeared, just like the last set but carrying different images and information. The photo was in black and white this time, reproduced from a newspaper, showing Jim Hanson, a lean-faced man of about fifty, wearing an adult Boy Scout uniform and standing out in the woods somewhere. As before, there was a short loop of videotape. It showed him standing by a picnic table in a backyard somewhere, tending a barbecue and acting as éminence grise to a crowd of small children, presumably his grandkids. The map window was the same except that now the red

X had moved to the middle of one of those states in the middle of the country; apparently this was Nebraska.

Jim Hanson didn't look very interesting. Aaron hit the space bar again, moving on to the next item on the list: HIGH-METABOLISM WORLD DOMINATOR—CHASE MERRIAM, BRIARCLIFF MANOR, N.Y. This time, the photo was a glossy color studio shot. The video clip showed Chase Merriam teeing off at a very nice golf course somewhere along with three other high-metabolism world dominators.

Aaron started whacking the space bar, paging through the list, flashing up the hundred photos one at a time. When it worked its way down to the bottom, it cycled back up to the top again, so he could keep it up forever if he wanted to. The red X on the map hopped back and forth across the country, tracing out a perfectly balanced demographic profile of the United States.

*Floyd Wayne Vishniak* was sitting in his trailer, watching *Wheel*, when he heard the sound of tires on gravel. He went to the front door, glancing over to make sure that his sawed-off shotgun was sitting in its secret place; it was there all right, craftily concealed in the narrow gap behind three stacked cases of beer, right next to the door. Having thus established his parameters, he looked out the window to see who had come all the way out here to pay him a visit. If it was another bill collector, he was not going to get a very friendly reception.

From initial appearances, it could very well be a bill collector. It was a little skinny dark-haired man with glasses and he got out of the car wearing a button-up shirt and a tie. First thing he did was open the back door of his gray Ford LTD Crown Victoria and unhook his suit jacket from the little hook that was above the back door.

Floyd Wayne Vishniak had been driving around in cars since he was tiny, of course, and he had seen those little hook thingies above the doors and someone had told him a long time ago that they were to hang coats off of. But this very moment was the first time in his entire life that he had actually seen one used.

A seed of resentment was germinated in his mind. Garment hooks in the back seats of cars. Always there, never used. A mysterious vestige of other times and places, like spittoons. Nobody used them, that's how it was. Nobody wore suits to begin with, unless they were going to a wedding or a funeral. When they did wear suits, if they absolutely had to take off the jacket for some reason, they would toss it out flat on the backseat. To hang it up that way— what was this little geek trying to say, exactly? That the lint or whatever on the backseat of his fancy luxury car (which was spotless) could not be allowed to touch the fabric of his fancy suit jacket?

It was a nice car all right, brand new and probably costing in excess of fifteen thousand bucks. Its beautiful gray finish had been streaked, below the beltline, with dark brown mud thrown up by the wheels as it had come up the gravel road from the highway. Floyd had been kicked out of his apartment in Davenport so that the landlord could rent it out to a big family of African-Americans come from Chicago to steal away a few more of Davenport's nonexistent jobs. Fortunately he knew someone who had this farm just outside of town, and was willing to let him live here in this trailer.

The man put his suit jacket on. The satin lining flashed in the horizontal sunlight of the early evening. He shrugged his shoulders a couple of times so that the jacket would fall into place and look pretty on him. The jacket had padding in the shoulders that made the man look bigger than he really was. He reached into the backseat and pulled out a briefcase.

As soon as he saw that briefcase, Floyd opened the door of his trailer and stood there leaning against the doorframe and smoking his cigarette and looking down the full height of the jury-rigged, mud-tracked staircase at this little man.

"Hello, Mr. Vishniak," the man said, looking up at him.

"That's funny, I ain't introduced myself yet. How'd you know my name? I don't know you. I don't know anyone like you. All my friends drive pickup trucks with a lot of rust on 'em. Who the hell are you?"

The visitor seemed taken aback. "My name's Aaron Green," he said. He looked like he really didn't want to be here. That actually made Floyd more sympathetic to the man because Floyd didn't want him to be there either. So that was a start anyway.

"What do you want?" Floyd said.

"I want to give you ten thousand dollars."

"You got it with you?"

"No, but I have a down payment of one thousand."

Floyd stood there in the doorway for a while and smoked his cigarette and pondered this unusual situation. A man, very likely a Jew from Chicago, had just driven up to his trailer and offered him ten thousand dollars.

"This a Publishers Clearinghouse thing? You a friend of Ed Mc-Mahon or something?"

"No, it's not a sweepstakes. I represent ODR, which is a poll-taking organization based in Virginia. We've identified you as being a typical representative of a particular part of the United States population."

Floyd snorted derisively. He could just imagine.

"We would like to keep track of your reactions to the current presidential campaign. What you think of the different candidates and issues."

"So you want me to go to Virginia?"

"No. Not at all. We want you to change your lifestyle as little as possible. That's crucial to the system."

"So you're going to call me up every couple days and ask me questions."

"It's even easier than that," Green said. "Can I step inside and show you?"

Floyd snorted again. "My little abode ain't much to look at."

"That's okay. I'll only take ten or fifteen minutes of your time."

"Come on in then."

Aaron Green and Floyd sat down in front of the TV. Floyd turned the volume down a little bit and offered his visitor a beer, which he declined. "I have to drive to Nebraska tonight," he said, "and if I have a beer now I'll be pulling over to urinate all night long."

"Nebraska? What, you taking one guy from each state?"

"Something like that," Aaron Green said. Obviously he did not believe that Floyd Wayne Vishniak, a dumb uneducated factory worker, would ever be smart enough to understand the details.

"You ever read Dick Tracy comics?" Aaron Green asked.

"They don't have it in the paper here," Floyd said. "You ever read Prince Valiant?"

Again, Aaron Green stumbled. He was having a hard time building up his momentum. "Well, you might have heard of the wristwatch television set."

"Yeah, I heard of that."

"Well, here's your chance to have a look at one." Aaron Green pulled something out of his briefcase.

It looked like a super high-tech watch or something. Like some kind of secret military thing that a commando in a movie would wear.

The band of the watch was not just a strip of leather or anything like that. It was made of hard black plastic ventilated with lots of holes. It was huge, about three inches wide. It consisted of several plates of this hard black plastic stuff hinged together so that it would curve around the wrist.

Instead of having just one clockface on the top surface, it had a whole little screen type of thing, just like on a digital watch except that it wasn't showing anything right now, just gray and blank. And in addition to that there were a few other raised black containers molded to the outer surface of the watchband, but they didn't have any screens or buttons or anything like that, they were just blank, and must have contained batteries or something.

"Shit," Floyd said, "what the hell is it?"

"Most of the time it's a digital watch. Part of the time, it's a television set, complete with a little speaker for sound."

"Can I get Whiplash games on it?"

"I'm afraid not. The TV will only show one type of program and one type only, and that is political programming having to do with the election."

"Shit, I knew there was a catch."

"That's why we're offering you the money. Because this is not all fun and games. Some responsibility falls on your shoulders as part of this deal."

Floyd Wayne Vishniak thought that if Aaron Green were not trying to pay him ten thousand dollars, he might throw him down the stairs and jump on him out in the yard and mess him up a little bit. He did not appreciate the fact that this little man, who was about the same age as him, and maybe a bit younger, was lecturing him about responsibility. It was the kind of thing his dad used to say to him.

But for now he was going to be cool. He put his feet up on the table next to the briefcase, sat back, raised his eyebrows, peered at Aaron Green through the smoke of his cigarette. "Well, for ten thousand bucks I guess I could be responsible."

"Think of it as a part-time job. It'll take maybe ten minutes of your time every day. It doesn't prevent you from having other jobs. And it pays very, very well."

"What do I got to do in this job?"

"Watch TV."

Floyd laughed. "Watch TV? On this little wristwatch thing?"

"Exactly. Now, most of the time, it'll just act like a digital watch." Green pressed a button on the face of the wristwatch and the screen began to show black numerals on a gray background, giving the current time and date. "This is just a convenience for you," he explained. "But from time to time, something like this will happen."

The watch emitted a piercing beep. The numerals on the tiny screen disappeared and were replaced by a color-bar test pattern.

"Whoa, it's in color!" Floyd said.

"Yeah. Of course, you can't see any color when it's pretending to be a wristwatch. But in TV mode, it's just like a small color television set."

After a couple of seconds, the test pattern was replaced by a videotape of John F. Kennedy giving his "Ask not what your country can do for you" speech.

"This is just a little canned demonstration. Once the program gets underway, it'll show you coverage of campaign events. Debates, news conferences, and so on."

"Why don't I just watch 'em on my own TV set?"

"Because we're going to pipe our own coverage directly to you, through this watch. We might want you to see some events that the networks wouldn't cover, so we have to generate the programming ourselves. Besides, we think we'll get better compliance this way."

"Compliance?"

"Suppose you're out of the house. Like maybe going to a Whiplash game. You wouldn't be able to watch normal TV. But with this PIPER watch, you can watch it wherever you are."

"PIPER?"

"That's the name of this program."

"How much of this stuff do I have to watch?"

"Many days there won't be anything at all. We might show you fifteen minutes or half an hour of programming a few times a week. Sometimes it'll be a little more intense. The only time when we'll really give you a lot of stuff to watch will be during the conventions in July and August."

"What else do I gotta do? You call me up and ask me questions about this stuff, or what?"

"That's it. Just watch the TV programs."

"That's it?"

"Yes."

"Then how do you know what my opinion is? I thought the whole idea was to get my opinion."

"It is. But we can do that electronically."

"How?"

"Through the PIPER watch." Green reached into his briefcase and pulled out a videotape. "I see you have a VCR in here. You should watch this tape. It'll explain how everything works."

"I don't get it."

"The PIPER watch does more than just show you campaign events. It also monitors your reactions. You ever go to a mall or an amusement park and see one of those machines where you drop in a quarter and it gives you your biorhythms, or your emotional state, or something like that?"

"There's one down at Duke's Tavern that gives you your sex rating."

"Oh." Green seemed embarrassed. "How does that work?"

"You grab this big rod sticking out of the top and it measures your sex quotient and flashes it up on the screen. I always get a real high score."

"Okay, it's probably a galvanic skin response device."

"Say what?"

"This PIPER watch has the same kind of thing built into it as your sex quotient machine. So it could provide a twenty-four hour a day readout of your sex quotient, if that was what we wanted."

"Why would you want my sex quotient?"

"We probably wouldn't, to tell you the truth—no offense!" Green laughed nervously. "But by using the same type of detectors, we can get a sense of how you are reacting to the programming shown on the TV screen. That information is piped directly back to us over the radio."

"So, it gives you my emotions. Tells you what my body's thinking."

Green smiled. "That's a good way to describe it. What your body is thinking. I like that."

"What about my opinions, though?"

Green shook his head and frowned. "I'm not sure quite what you mean."

"Well, this tells you how my emotions respond, right?"

"Yes."

"But that's not the same as an opinion, is it?"

Green seemed to be baffled, lost. "It's not? I'm not sure what you're getting at."

"Well, maybe I watch some guy giving a speech. Maybe he's real good at giving speeches and so my emotions are good. Then, I'm lying awake in bed in the middle of the night, thinking about what he said, and suddenly it doesn't seem so logical any more, and I can see all kind of holes in his argument and I change my mind and decide he's just another pencil-neck, media-slick son of a bitch out to take my money and send the jobs to Borneo. So my final opinion of the guy is that he's a bastard. But all you know is that I had a good emotional response to his speech."

Floyd knew that he had Green now. Clearly Green, the big-city, high-paid intellectual, had never thought about this. He had never anticipated that someone might make this objection. He did not know what to say. "We don't have the technology to read that sort of thing," he finally said, speaking very slowly and carefully. "We don't have any way to read your mind in the middle of the night and find out that you think Senator So-and-so is going to send your job to Borneo."

"Humph," Floyd said, shaking his head.

"But PIPER is just one way we have of getting information," Green said, picking up momentum now. Floyd had the distinct impression that he was just trying to talk his way out of the tight corner that Floyd had backed him into. "Needless to say, we are receptive to any kind of input that you might want to give us. So if you have these thoughts in the middle of the night—"

"I do," Floyd affirmed, "all the time. They come to me like a thief in the night."

"—in that case, you would be more than welcome to provide those to us."

"My phone service got cut off," Floyd said. "But I could write you letters."

"That would be absolutely fine," Green said. "Our address is printed right there on the videotape. You go ahead and send us as many letters as you like. We'd like to hear your opinions on any subject."

"So I gotta wear this thing twenty-four hours a day?"

Green shrugged. "Just when you're awake."

"And what else do I gotta do to get this ten thousand bucks?"

"Absolutely nothing."

"Absolutely nothing?"

"Just get up in the morning and put it on, every day from now until Election Day. If you agree to this, I give you a thousand dollars right here and now. We'll be able to tell, by monitoring the signals from the watch, whether you're wearing it or not. As long as you keep it on during all of the programming segments that we broadcast, we will continue to send you a thousand dollars a month. On Election Day, we send you the remainder of the ten thousand."

Floyd grabbed the PIPER watch. The two halves of the watchband were spread wide apart. He put it on his wrist, wrapped his other hand around it, and the watchband tightened down firmly but comfortably.

"To take it off, just push that little button right there and the ratchet will be released," Green said.

"We got a deal," Floyd said. "Where's my thousand?"

## CHAPTER THIRTY-SIX

"This is it, baby," Cyrus Rutherford Ogle said, sitting in the big chair and twiddling the joysticks. "This is the moon shot. T minus half an hour and counting." That is what Aaron Green saw as he was climbing into the back of the big GODS truck out in back of the Decatur Civic Center in Decatur, Illinois. It was 7:30 P.M. on Flag Day.

"My god," Aaron said. That was all he could force past his lips for the first several minutes.

It looked just like a plain flatbed semitrailer truck with a shipping container on the back. The shipping container, a steel box about the size of a mobile home, was brand new and slickly painted with the three-colored logo of Global Omnipresent Delivery Services. These days, as the U.S. Postal Service continued to go the way of Greyhound, the logo had become as ubiquitous as a mailbox. Most people wouldn't notice this thing unless it was parked in their driveway. Out behind the Decatur Civic Center, sandwiched in between a food delivery truck and a video truck from Television North America, it was invisible. The only indications that it carried something other than mail were a soft humming noise and a glassy twist of heat waves coming from a small opening on its top. It carried its own power plant.

Aaron entered through a door in the rear, passing directly into a narrow aisle, some ten feet in length, between racks of electronics and heavier equipment that stretched from floor to ceiling. Nuclear submarines must be like this, Aaron thought, as he peered into the racks, picking out the familiar shapes and logos of various top-of-the-line Pacific Netware computer systems.

The aisle finally opened up into sort of an office and communications center. Countertops ran along both walls for several yards and a couple of desks sat in the middle. These surfaces were strewn with telephones, scrawled yellow notes, staplers, laptop computers, a miniature photocopier. Higher up, at head level, heavy shelves and racks were mounted to the walls, loaded with video stuff: three-quarter-inch and half-inch tape machines, monitors, and other rack-mounted goodies that Aaron recognized as being parts of a television editing suite.

The front third of the trailer belonged to Cy Ogle. It looked totally different. The other parts of it were nice, high-tech, expensive, but they hadn't even started to spend money until they'd reached this part.

The trailer was eight feet wide. They had built a hollow sphere eight feet in diameter, put Cy's big chair in the center, and then paneled the inner surface of the sphere with monitors. Each monitor was about the size of the ones used in notebook computers. They were in full color and they were very sharp. The only feature that broke this sweep of tiny little color monitors was a twelve-inch television screen, dead center, right in the middle of everything.

"Welcome to the Eye," Ogle said. "Welcome to the Eye of Cy."

Now that he mentioned it, it did look as though Cy Ogle were sitting in the center of an eight-foot eyeball, lined with computer monitors, with the TV screen in the middle serving as the pupil.

Aaron already knew the answer, but he had to do it anyway: he started counting the monitors. There were exactly one hundred of them. Each one of those monitors was running the software that Aaron Green had spent the last couple of months developing. All of the experience they had gathered from all of those focus groups at Pentagon Towers—all of the mock shootings, fire drills, movie clips, hunchbacked janitors, staged marital disputes, and every other scenario that had come from the fevered imagination of Shane Schram —had been distilled into the animated graphs and charts and colored bars on those hundred screens.

By examining those graphs in detail, Ogle could assess the emotional status of any one of the PIPER 100. But they provided more detail than Ogle could really handle during the real-time stress of a major campaign event. So Aaron had come up with a very simple, general color-coding scheme. The background color of each screen fluctuated according to the subject's general emotional state. Red denoted fear, stress, anger, anxiety. Blue denoted negative emotions centered in higher parts of the brain: disagreement, hostility, a general lack of receptiveness. And green meant that the subject liked what they saw. Green was good. Regardless of color, the brightness went up with the intensity of the emotion.

Stepping a little closer and scanning the screens, Aaron could see that a good eighty or ninety of the PIPER 100 were wearing their wristwatches, as per their agreement with Ogle Data Research. There were a few stragglers. Almost all of them were women. One of the problems that had come up with the PIPER program was that the bulky watches looked clumsy on a woman's wrist, and most women didn't want to wear them all the time. Hopefully, they were carrying them around in their purses, and would take them out and put them on as soon as the program started.

If they didn't, they'd forfeit the rest of their money, and their wristwatches would be given to someone a little more reliable. For this, the first test of PIPER, a 90 percent compliance rate would be pretty decent.

"So, what's the mood of America?" Aaron said. He couldn't resist asking. He stepped as far forward as he could and stood right next to Ogle's chair, so that the panorama of screens completely filled his peripheral vision. The effect was like hanging in outer space, in the center of a dynamic young galaxy: against a backdrop of velvety black, bursts of colored light flared unpredictably in every direction, in hues of red, green, blue, and mixtures thereof.

"Hard to say, since we don't know what any of these people are reacting to," Ogle said. "I been keeping an eye on this poor guy right here." He pointed to a screen that had been consistently red ever since Aaron had come into the room. "I think this guy must be right in the middle of a bar fight or something."

Aaron leaned closer to the red screen and squinted to read the label at the bottom. It read, TRADE SCHOOL METAL HEAD/KENT NISSAN, MT. HOLLY, N.J.

"His blood pressure is through the roof," Aaron said. "Maybe you're right."

He couldn't help checking out his five participants. Floyd Wayne Vishniak seemed to be in a quiescent state, probably sacked out on his couch watching television. Chase Merriam was in an excellent mood, probably getting lubricated at a cocktail party in the Hamptons.

"Hey, this looks *great!*" another voice exclaimed. "Jesus! Look at this thing! It's virtual reality, man!"

It was a tall man in early middle age, with a neatly trimmed beard and a ponytail: the controlled hippie look. He was wearing shorts and sandals and a Hawaiian shirt, and was just tossing a weather-beaten leather satchel onto one of the counters.

"Evening, Zeldo," Ogle said.

Zeldo's gaze was fastened upon the Eye of Cy. "This thing is *killer,*" he said. "Does it work?"

"The input side works," Ogle said, "as you can see for yourself. Now that you're here, we can run some tests on the output side."

"What's the output side?" Aaron said.

"Okay, I'm up for it," Zeldo said. He ran over to the nearest Calyx workstation and started to sign in. "I just came over from Argus's dressing room. He's waiting."

"Who's Argus?" Aaron said.

A faint beeping noise sounded from the direction of Cy Ogle. His big chair, in the middle of the Eye of Cy, had a telephone built into it, and he was punching in a number.

"Good evening, this is Cy Ogle," he said. "Is there any possibility that I could speak to the Governor? Thank you so very much." Ogle was actually capable of delivering this kind of dialogue as though he meant it.

"I have acquired Argus," Zeldo said. The screen of his Calyx system had come alive with a multiple-window display showing the status of some incredibly complicated system.

"Evening, Governor. You mind if I put you on the speaker-phone?"

One of the windows on Zeldo's screen was a rapidly fluctuating bar graph. It had been dead for a little while, but now it put on a burst of colorful activity.

"Okay," Ogle said, and punched a button on his phone.

"I hate these speakerphones," said a deep voice. When he spoke, the bar graph on Zeldo's screen came alive.

"They make me feel like I'm in a box," the voice continued. Aaron had finally recognized it: it was the voice of Governor William A. Cozzano.

"We want to test our communications link," Ogle said.

"That's what Zeldo told me," Cozzano said. "Go ahead and do something."

The armrests of Ogle's chair were huge, like the captain's chair on the bridge of the *Enterprise*. The right one was covered with small keys, like on a computer keyboard. Each key was labeled in small letters.

The left armrest contained a row of several joysticks or sliders that could individually be moved back and forth, left to right, between two extremes. Aaron stepped forward, leaned over Ogle's shoulder, and read the labels on the joysticks:

| | | |
|---|---|---|
| LIBERAL | 1 2 3 4 5 6 7 8 9 10 | CONSERVATIVE |
| LIBERTARIAN | 1 2 3 4 5 6 7 8 9 10 | AUTHORITARIAN |
| POPULIST | 1 2 3 4 5 6 7 8 9 10 | ELITIST |
| GENERAL | 1 2 3 4 5 6 7 8 9 10 | SPECIFIC |
| SECULAR | 1 2 3 4 5 6 7 8 9 10 | RELIGIOUS |
| MATERIAL | 1 2 3 4 5 6 7 8 9 10 | ETHEREAL |
| KIND/GENTLE | 1 2 3 4 5 6 7 8 9 10 | BELLIGERENT |

Right now, all of the joysticks were set close to the middle except for GENERAL/SPECIFIC which had been set to 1 (GENERAL) and stuck in place with a piece of duct tape.

Ogle punched a button on his armrest.

"Bullet whizzing past my head," Cozzano said.

"Correct," Ogle said. "That means that you're under attack and you'd better take cover and defend yourself."

"Got it," Cozzano said. "Do another one."

Ogle punched another button.

"Apple pie," Cozzano said. "Which means American values."

Ogle punched another button.

"Ice cubes. Which means I should cool it."

Ogle punched another one.

"A B-52. A strong national defense."

They went on in this vein for several minutes. Ogle had a few dozen buttons on his armrest.

"Argus is Cozzano," Aaron said.

"Right," Zeldo said. "Argus was the mythological figure who had a hundred eyes. With Ogle's help, and with the PIPER 100 feeding him their emotions, Cozzano becomes the new Argus."

*At first, Floyd* Wayne Vishniak didn't know what it was: a burst of tinny music with sort of a patriotic brass-band sound to it. It sure wasn't coming from his TV set, which was tuned to a fishing program. Finally a flash of red-white-and-blue color caught his eye. It was coming from his wrist. From the big fancy wristwatch that he was being paid to wear. It was showing a logo, a computerized American flag image.

Finally they were doing something. He'd been wearing the damn thing for two weeks and hadn't seen anything on it except for occasional test patterns. He turned off the TV—the fish didn't seem to be biting anyway—cracked open a beer, and sat down to watch.

*Chase Merriam was* out on the lawn of his brother-in-law's house in East Hampton, Long Island, savoring a mint julep and enjoying the cool night air, when his watch came to life. It didn't much bother him, since this was a dull party anyway. The sound of the music attracted the attention of several other partygoers, and by the time the program got underway, he was in the center of half a dozen people, standing on tiptoe, staring at his wrist in fascination.

"This is ridiculous," he said. "Why don't we all just watch it on C-SPAN."

*Dr. Hunter P.* Lawrence, pundit extraordinaire, moderator of the *Washington Hot Seat*, and nemesis of Eleanor Richmond, was a veteran of the Kennedy glory days. He had come down from Harvard to serve as an Undersecretary of State for Cultural Affairs, "liaising" with Ed Murrow's USIA. After putting in his three years, he had returned to Harvard to take a joint appointment in the Political Science Department and as an administrator at the Kennedy School. He had a Savile Row tattered professorial elegance with a hint of dandruff around the shoulders of his dark gray pinstriped suit. His graying hair, cut long in the back to compensate for its gradual retreat in front, defied the best efforts of spray and gel to get it to lie down, and the backlights of the set turned them into silvery scratches against the dark blue background. As the house filled up and the media consultants fussed over their candidates and the technicians ran around barking into their headsets, he sat in his chair, legs crossed, flipping listlessly through some papers.

In a normal debate, tickets would have been distributed equally among supporters of each of the three candidates. But William A. Cozzano was not technically a candidate at all, even though a spontaneous ground swell had put his name on the ballot in forty-two states. The President of the United States was continuing to pursue his Rose Garden strategy and would not be in attendance tonight, though some of his handlers were already cruising the press room, buttonholing journalists and trying to apply some prespin to the event. The only "real" candidate was Nimrod T. ("Tip") McLane. A reasonable number of tickets had therefore been handed out to the McLane campaign. Other than that, it was open seating; but given that the event was happening thirty miles away from Tuscola, the place was dominated by Cozzano supporters. Tip McLane was coming into the lion's den tonight, which was exactly the kind of situation in which he excelled.

Most politicians were soulless tools, windup dolls, but these two guys, Cozzano and McLane, could more than hold their own in intellectual combat. This was going to be a hell of a confrontation, and Dr. Hunter P. Lawrence was just the man to act as ringmaster and lion tamer.

As Dr. Lawrence was engaged in this rather self-satisfying series of ruminations, the voice of the set director scratched from his earplug, "One minute to air." Lawrence set his papers down, sipped some water, did a phlegm check, walked unhurriedly to each of the debaters and shook their hands warmly and firmly. At times like this, he had to consciously resist his normal tendency to apply what an overly honest colleague had referred to as his "fish kiss" handshake.

The theme of "Campaign '96" rose in the earplug, unheard by the audience, and on the monitors he could see the nifty computer graphics in which the globe segued into the United States which in turn segued into the flag which in turn blended into a rather nice establishing shot of the Decatur Civic Center, still brightly illuminated by the late evening sun of midsummer. The building was surrounded by buses and cars. People were streaming into the entrances. Most of them were students who had been bused in from local colleges and high schools.

Superimposed over these images were some credits. The logos of various sponsoring corporations were flashed up as the godlike voice of an announcer, prerecorded weeks ago in New York, intoned: "Tonight's debate is brought to you by MacIntyre Engineering, bringing American technological excellence to the world. Global Omnipresent Delivery Systems, the world leader in physical communications technology. Pacific Netware, creator of the industry-leading Calyx computer system. Gale Aerospace, providing new solutions for a changing world. And the Coover Fund, investing in America for a prosperous tomorrow.

"Tonight, from Decatur, Illinois, the presidential town forum. Joining our moderator, Dr. Hunter P. Lawrence, will be Representative Nimrod T. ("Tip") McLane of California and Governor William A. Cozzano of Illinois."

Dr. Lawrence was enough of a self-consciously stodgy eccentric that he had actually armed himself with a gavel. As the voice-over began, he started to whack it. Audience members moved toward their seats and the buzzing clouds of aides and well-wishers that had surrounded the two debaters began to disperse. The noise level dropped and the house lights came down, leaving the three men down below in pools of halogen light, TV-bright. As backdrops they had tall floor-to-ceiling banners—colorized images of turn-of-the-century politicians: Teddy Roosevelt, William Jennings Bryan, and William McKinley.

Dr. Lawrence loved this moment, loved the notion that millions of people were watching, loved the fact that, unlike so many other people, he performed without notes or a teleprompter, in short, he loved his own glibness—what open field running was for Barry Sanders of the Lions, extemporaneous and clever speech was for the professor. It was his chance to go and say "in your face" to the tongue-tied masses. It was as good as the first fuck with a new graduate student.

"I will be blunt: this country is on the verge of disaster."

That was good; that shut them up. Dr. Lawrence cleared his throat unnecessarily and took another sip of water.

"This may be our last free presidential election. I make this alarming statement for the following reasons:

"Our national debt has now reached the level of ten trillion dollars, the surest sign of a society in disequilibrium, even free-fall.

"Our political leaders in the past few decades have shown no ability to address the problems facing our aging, failing democracy.

"Our federal leadership works only in response to pollsters and spin doctors; the sheer mediocrity at the executive, legislative, and judicial levels has driven away the most talented civil servants.

"The only sign of life is at the level of state government, and these officials are burdened to the point of paralysis by the albatross of Washington.

"The values that made this country what it once was—hard work and honesty, or as Emerson put it, 'self-reliance'—have, like our finances, gone to hell."

Dr. Lawrence paused to allow his words to sink in. "Are any of you in this audience convinced that the picture is anything but bleak for the future? I am sorry to be so blunt, but a lifetime of study of and love for this country compels me to set the stage for this debate with these thoughts.

"One century ago, a candidate looking back on events of the last decade would have seen feverish activity in the realms of technology, art, and politics. During that period, men with names such as Diesel, Benz, and Ford had been hard at work perfecting a new device called the automobile. The first telephone switchboard had been installed, the first subway system was under construction in Boston, and Thomas Edison had opened something called a kineto-scope parlor—the first movie theater. The gramophone, the rocket engine, the radio, and X rays had all just been invented. And, as if these innovations were not important enough, the first professional football game had been played in Latrobe, Pennsylvania."

A murmur ran through the crowd and gradually bloomed into laughter. Cozzano and Dr. Lawrence exchanged smiles. This was

typical for Dr. Lawrence: a subtle jibe that could have been inter-
preted as either a dig or a compliment. Cozzano chose to treat it as
the latter.

"But despite this rapid technological progress, the political picture a hundred years ago was far from rosy. Foreign interests controlled our economy; an unfeeling business class brutally exploited
the people of the United States; the political structure of this country was shot through with the most shocking corruption from top to
bottom; divisiveness characterized the relationship between sections
of this country, and between races; foreigners newly arriving to
work in our country suffered attack simply for wanting to come to
this blessed land to improve themselves. Beginning in the late 1880s
the poorest farmers and workers in the West and South united to
form the Populist movement. They failed to reach the middle
classes and the cities; their message became shrill. But out of that
movement came the Progressive movement, one of whose most
eloquent spokesmen was William Jennings Bryan, who spoke in this
town a century or so ago. His message was simple: government is
for the people. The effect was profound. The Progressive movement
spread across this part of the country with the speed and fury of a
prairie fire. Progressivism blended the skills of the best of this country with the ambitions of the middle 70 percent—the middle classes
—to remake the system and allow this country to endure through
the twentieth century.

"We need a new populism and a new progressivism and a new
way to remake the system so that the values of honesty and hard
work can once again have a nurturing environment in which to
grow, and self-reliance can once again take its place.

"Tonight we will discuss these problems from many different
directions. But I would like to begin by discussing a concrete issue:
the trade imbalance.

"It is January of next year and you have just taken the oath of
office. The economy remains uncertain. It seems as though the Japanese lead in the automotive sector has become insurmountable.
How do you, as President, tackle that problem? Representative Mc-
Lane?"

## CHAPTER THIRTY-SEVEN

Tip McLane had already adopted his characteristic pose, leaning forward toward the camera, head down, staring intently into the lens. As soon as the red light came on, he unloaded: "First of all, Dr. Lawrence, let me say that I would like to thank you, and the people of Decatur, for the opportunity to come here and participate in this forum."

A few hundred yards away, Cy Ogle was crowing. He had thrown his head back and broken into triumphant, falsetto laughter. All around him, the Eye of Cy had gone into various shades of blue. It had happened the moment the phrase "first of all" escaped from Tip McLane's lips.

"Lemme just jot that one down," Ogle said, making a note. "Never begin with 'first of all.' "

Ogle was also happy because only three of the screens were blank. They were getting 97 percent compliance. Back in Falls Church, Virginia, three ropers were on the phones, trying to get through to the three delinquent members of the PIPER 100. Over the next few minutes, two more screens came to life.

Almost thirty seconds had gone by, and Tip McLane still hadn't begun to answer the question: ". . . people who say that presidential campaigns are all style over substance obviously haven't been paying attention to fine, substantial programs like the one that we are participating in tonight."

"Thank you, Tip," Ogle said, "I did my very best."

"Now, as far as the auto industry. There are a lot of so-called conservatives who would disagree with me on this and say that we should just let the Japanese come in and walk all over us. That somehow, this constitutes free trade. Well, it's not free trade. It's an economic Pearl Harbor, is what it is. And I'll be damned if I'm going to stand by and let it happen to America on my watch. And that is why, when I am President—"

"—thank you, Congressman McLane, your time has expired," Dr. Lawrence said, amused but firm.

"—we should deal with this in a tough, but not protectionist way—"

"—thank you, Congressman McLane."

"—and even out this trade balance—"

"—your time has expired and we must now move on to Governor Cozzano."

The verbal duel between Representative McLane and Dr. Lawrence petered out gradually. By that point, the screens were largely bluish and reddish. "Well, that just makes them all look like assholes," Ogle said. "I can't tell if they're reacting to McLane or Lawrence." He turned and caught Aaron's eye. "Can you give me a breakdown by economic bracket?"

Aaron grabbed the mouse attached to his Calyx workstation and chose a couple of items from menus. A graphic flashed up on his screen and he bounced a copy of it to one of Ogle's screens.

"What this tells me is that everyone dislikes Tip McLane just about equally," Ogle said.

"That's about right. Which is interesting, coming from the upper income brackets."

"Yeah," Ogle said. He held one index finger up in the air. "I am about to make a prediction," he said.

"Shoot," Aaron said.

"I predict that we are going to see a whole lot more data to the effect that people think Tip McLane is too rough. Too coarse to dance with the Queen of England."

The Eye of Cy grew brighter and took on a decidedly greenish tinge. "Hot damn," Ogle said. "Now just hold it, baby, don't squander this." As he spoke, he was pressing a couple of buttons on the pad that he used to communicate with Cozzano.

Cozzano looked great on TV. The stroke had aged him somewhat. He had lost some weight without becoming gaunt. It had brought out his features, which were worth bringing out. He had a serious, thoughtful, rock-solid look about him now. He could probably win a lot of votes simply by doing what he was doing now: sitting in front of a camera and not saying anything.

This was new behavior for him. Cozzano loved to argue. He loved competition in any form. He had always been the first to show up for football practice. Whenever he appeared in one of these debates he always leapt into the fray as soon as his turn came up.

But you didn't become president by seeming eager. Ogle understood this perfectly well, and so, as soon as Cozzano's name came up, he began to stroke that keyboard, sending calm, solid, quiet images into Cozzano's brain. Cozzano just sat there, quiet, solid, contemplative. The longer he sat there, the brighter, and greener, the Eye of Cy became.

"Getting good results here," Zeldo said, looking at the readouts of Cozzano's blood pressure. "He's calming down. He was a little nervous before."

"Perfect," Ogle said. "I just invented a new form of political rhetoric: don't say a damn thing."

It was perfect, Aaron realized, sitting there staring at Cozzano on the TV. He had seen a lot of these debates. The candidates always came off as high-strung, bickering game show contestants. But Cozzano had a solid dignity that was way above all that. He gave the impression of a man who had been deeply absorbed in thinking profound thoughts, not paying any attention to his surroundings, who had suddenly been interrupted by the nervous, carping moderator of the debate. Who was now giving the matter some serious thought before he blurted anything out.

Aaron felt as though he should jump to his feet and salute Cozzano. He felt that way even though he was sitting ten feet away from Ogle and knew damn well this was a manipulated image.

"I have certain values that I am not willing to play games with," Cozzano said. Then he paused for quite a while, thinking. The audience was dead silent. Even the inside of Ogle's trailer was dead silent. The whole universe seemed to be revolving around Cozzano. "One of the things I value is dignity and self-respect. These things are our birthrights. Some squander them. Once you have lost them, you can't get them back. And one way to squander your dignity and self-respect is to whine and carp and beg." Cozzano pronounced these words with almost palpable disgust. "My attitude is that I don't care how unlevel the playing field is. I'm going to play by the rules anyway." At this point Cozzano seemed to become visibly pissed off. He leveled his gaze directly into the camera for the first time, held up his meaty right hand, pointed into the lens. "I will never crawl on my knees to Japan or any other country and cry uncle, the way George Bush did in 1992. I'd rather die." Cozzano sat back in his chair, held his gaze on the lens for a few more seconds, then looked away.

The Eye of Cy had become blindingly bright: America was feeling strong, conflicting emotions.

There was silence and then confusion. He had only used up a small portion of his allotted time. Dr. Lawrence wasn't sure what he should do. The TV feed cut uncertainly back and forth between Governor Cozzano and Dr. Lawrence.

"You still have thirty seconds," Dr. Lawrence said. "Would you like to elaborate?"

"What's to elaborate?" Cozzano said.

A definite pattern was now noticeable when the feed cut between Dr. Lawrence and Cozzano. People had generally made up their minds that Dr. Lawrence was a jerk.

"That was wild," Ogle said. He sounded a bit uncertain. He grabbed the POPULIST/ELITIST joystick and shoved it a little closer to POPULIST. "That took balls. Aaron, don't we have a toilet-scrubbing ex-autoworker?"

"Yeah," Aaron said, choosing a line of the same name from a menu on the computer screen. A graphic came up summarizing the way that this particular member of the PIPER 100 had reacted to Cozzano's speech.

It was all jaggedy contrasts and mood swings. Clearly this man's feelings had been hurt. But it wasn't all negative either. Toward the end of Cozzano's statement, the ex-autoworker's emotional state had swung sharply upward.

"Huh. That's interesting," Ogle said. "The appeal to pride seems to work. But it's not old-fashioned jingoism. It's a question of personal, individual pride. Core values."

On TV, Dr. Hunter P. Lawrence was explaining that the candidates could now rebut each other's statements.

McLane flashed up on the screen with a bit of a stunned, nervous, beady-eyed look, as if he wanted to stare at Cozzano but couldn't. "Well, it seems to me that, uh, the best ticket to self-esteem and dignity is to have a steady job. Everything else follows from that. Under my administration, I'll be pursuing policies that will stimulate the vigor of our free enterprise system and lead to job growth in general. After all, it's hard to be dignified when you're living on welfare."

The Eye of Cy pinkened briefly as the word "welfare" was spoken. "Cheap shot," Ogle mumbled.

"It's easy to scoff at the concept of the unlevel playing field when you have been born into an affluent family and haven't suffered from massive layoffs the way our auto workers have," McLane continued. "But for those people in Detroit —"

The Eye of Cy displayed a few brief flashes of green as several people took pleasure in McLane's personal attack on Cozzano. But most people didn't like it. They didn't like it at all.

Cozzano had turned slightly in McLane's direction. He looked like a great man, alone in his study, busy with important matters, who has to get up and discipline a puppy who has just piddled on the rug.

"My family is affluent because we love each other and we work hard," Cozzano said. "And I can promise you, Tip, that if you seek to gain the esteem of the American public by running my family into the ground, I will make you regret it on many levels. When a man makes cracks about my family, my natural response is to invite him to step outside. And I'm not above doing that here and now."

Ogle rocketed half out of his chair and started screaming. "CUT TO TIP! CUT TO TIP! CUT TO TIP!" Aaron could hardly see anything; the Eye of Cy had become blindingly intense, like a parabolic dish pointed directly into the sun. But the image in the middle changed and Tip came on the screen; his mouth was half open, his eyebrows somewhere up in the middle of his forehead, his eyes darting back and forth nervously. The Eye of Cy turned blue (people who, as of three seconds ago, hated Tip McLane), with a few angry red screens (people who wanted Cozzano to punch McLane right here and now).

"Knockout punch," Ogle said. "Tip's out of the race." But just in

case, he shoved the KIND/GENTLE-BELLIGERENT joystick toward
KIND/GENTLE. Then he moved the MATERIAL-ETHEREAL joystick
a lot closer to ETHEREAL.

It was almost possible to see the wheels turning in McLane's
head. The look of surprise gradually faded, until he looked impassive, then calm and almost coldly defiant. "It wouldn't be the first
time I had settled an argument that way," McLane said.

"Ouch," Ogle said.

"But one of the first things a president has to learn is to separate
his personal feelings from the affairs of the nation, and—"

Colors shifted all over the Eye. "Damage control!" Ogle said, and
slammed one of the buttons on the armrest.

"—as for the issue of the auto industry," Cozzano said, continuing his own sentence as if McLane had never opened his mouth, and
blithely running him off the road, "it is simply wrong to say that
people get jobs first and then feel good about themselves. That is a
shallow view of human nature. Dignity can't be bought with a paycheck. Your student deferments kept you out of Vietnam, Tip, so
you never saw what I saw: stooped peasants in the rice paddies who
never made a dime in their lives but who had more dignity in the
last joint of their little finger than a lot of highly paid lawyers and
chief executives I can name. It goes the other way: if you have
dignity, if you respect yourself, you will find a job. I don't care how
bad the economy is. When my great-grandfather came to this part
of the country, there weren't any jobs. So he came up with his own
job. He had only been in America for a few weeks, but in that time
he had become thoroughly American. He had come to believe that
he could change his own life. That he could take charge of his own
destiny."

"Very inspiring. But when my family came to California—" Mc-
Lane began.

"Some think that unemployment hurts because of *money*," Cozzano said. "Because you can't afford to buy Nintendo games and
fancy sneakers. That is shallow and cheap. Americans are not pure,
money-grubbing materialists. Unemployment hurts people's feelings
far more than their pocketbooks."

In the past few seconds all the graphs had veered downward, the colors turned bluish. "I fucked *that* up!" Ogle said, whacking keys and sliding joysticks furiously. "Bad move!"

Suddenly Tip McLane was on the screen. It was too late for Cozzano to dig himself out.

"Shit!" Ogle hissed. "Where does he get off saying that Americans are not shallow materialists?"

McLane was amused. He knew he had Cozzano. "Apparently the Governor of Illinois thinks that we'd all be happier being fully employed . . . in rice paddies!"

The audience laughed. The Eye warmed suddenly to Tip McLane.

"Damn!" Ogle said. "Why'd he have to get profound on us?" He scratched his chin nervously, thinking hard, and fussed with the controls. "We have to suppress that urge to philosophize."

"Maybe the Governor hasn't been seeing a full cross section of the American public from his backyard in Tuscola," McLane said. "But I have, because I've visited all fifty states during the long primary campaign—even smaller states that my campaign manager begged me not to visit because he said they weren't important. I have talked to a lot of people. And over and over again, I get the impression that the people of America don't like being talked down to by politicians."

"That's for damn sure," Ogle said, punching a key that caused a hallucinatory bullet to whiz past Cozzano's head.

"They know what they want: jobs. Good jobs," McLane said. "What they don't need is vague talk about how to feel more dignified."

Ogle groaned. The PIPER 100 were showing strong support for McLane now. "They're killing us," he said, and slammed a big red button that said, simply, FLIP FLOP.

"When the forces of freedom and democracy stormed Hitler's Fortress Europe on D day," Cozzano said, "the elite spearhead of that invasion rained down out of the sky on parachutes. Parachutes made of nylon that was manufactured about half a mile away from my house in Tuscola, by my family. The nervous paratroopers, standing in the open doorways of those airplanes, looking down at the landscape of France thousands of feet below them, were putting a lot of trust in those folds of nylon."

"What does this have to do with anything?" Aaron said, mirroring the feelings displayed on the Eye of Cy: a state of chaotic flux.

"Shut up," Ogle mumbled. "This is good material. Reaganesque in its cloying nostalgia—with the metaphorical punch of Ross Perot before he went batshit."

"When you jump out of an airplane flying over a war zone, you need more than self-esteem to get you safely to the ground," Cozzano said. "You need a solid, well-made parachute. Young people leaving high school and college within the last few weeks have a lot in common with those troopers jumping out of that airplane. And if you think that William A. Cozzano intends to send them out that door with nothing more than some feel-good talk, you're dead wrong."

"But that's the opposite of what he just said," Aaron said.

"Just shut up," Ogle said. "I think he's got them going." As Cozzano's analogy started to become clearer, the monitor screens had stopped fluctuating and begun settling down into a dim greenish pattern. "We need to get Anecdote Development working on that D day thing."

Cozzano continued. "Just as nylon replaced silk in parachutes, new technologies have to replace the old ones in our job market. And I can promise you that no country in the world is better than America when it comes to inventing new technologies."

McLane interrupted him. "And no country is better capitalizing on those inventions than Japan," he said, "which is why I'm going to make sure that America, not Japan, reaps the benefit of her creative powers, unique among all the nations of the world."

Ogle slapped his face and groaned. "That McLane son of a bitch is a vampire. Give me a projection."

Aaron worked at his computer for a minute, running some statistical routines. "Based on the reactions of the PIPER 100, allowing for a typical seventy-two-hour debate bounce, correcting for their likelihood to actually cast a ballot, we get 27 electoral votes for the President, 206 for Cozzano, and 302 for Tip McLane."

"We have a long way to go," Ogle said.

"Seems pretty good to me," Aaron said, "considering he's not even running for president."

"Details!" Ogle scoffed.

## CHAPTER THIRTY-EIGHT

It took William A. Cozzano nearly an hour to fight his way from the dressing room, where his TV makeup had been sponged off, to his car in the parking lot of the Decatur Civic Center. Along the way he had to shake what seemed like every hand in downstate Illinois, and kiss a fair percentage of the babies. His car, a four-wheel-drive sport/utility vehicle with every luxury feature and antenna known to science, showed up regularly on downstate television (every time he changed the oil in his driveway) and so everyone knew where he was going. Meanwhile, Tip McLane skulked from an obscure fire exit into his waiting Secret Service motorcade.

The Decatur Civic Center was equipped with loading docks and ramps that would have enabled Cozzano's driver to pull straight into the building and pick him up, but it looked a lot better for him to fight his way through a crowd of supporters. Ogle's men had set up a double rope line to hold them back, providing a clear corridor across the asphalt from the building to Cozzano's car. Cy Ogle had personally walked the length of this corridor with a tape measure, making sure it was just narrow enough to allow the crowd to nearly surge in on Cozzano as they bent over the ropes and waved babies and pens and papers in his face. Banks of lights had been erected on mobile jackstands, illuminating the scene like a high-school football field on a Friday night, and network camera crews gladly availed themselves of the platforms Ogle had set up for their use.

"It was not half-bad," Cozzano said. He was sitting in the backseat of his car, next to Zeldo. His driver and an Illinois State Patrolman were in the front. They were driving down a two-lane blacktop road at eighty miles an hour, accompanied by one of Ogle's vehicles, a Secret Service car, and a few Highway Patrol cruisers. It had taken them several hours to get to Decatur this morning because they'd taken a circuitous route through Champaign and Springfield. But on the direct route, at this speed, Tuscola was minutes away.

Zeldo's brain was practically overloaded by everything that had just happened, but to him the most marvelous thing about the whole night was that they were driving eighty miles an hour—with a state patrolman right there *in the car* with them.

He shook his head and tried to concentrate on matters at hand. Cozzano had turned on a little courtesy light that shone a pool of golden light into his lap, and was jotting down some notes. Zeldo watched the Governor's right hand, gripping the thick barrel of an expensive fountain pen so tightly it looked like it might burst and spray ink all over the car. He wrote in shaky block letters, one at a time, like a first grader. His recovery had far exceeded their wildest hopes, and a person who did not know of his stroke would never notice anything was wrong—except when he tried to write. Cozzano knew this, it infuriated him, and he spent a lot of time practicing his penmanship, trying to erase this last vestige of weakness.

"We've got a lot of data to crank through. We're going to do a core dump on this whole night," Zeldo said. "Analyze it every which way. Then we'll go over the results with you."

"Good," Cozzano said, thinking about something else.

"I just have one question," Zeldo said. Cozzano looked up at him expectantly, and Zeldo hesitated for a moment.

Even after all the time they'd spent together, Cozzano made him nervous. Zeldo always got thick-tongued and self-conscious when he was about to ask the Governor something personal, something he suspected that Cozzano might not appreciate. Like a lot of powerful men—like Zeldo's boss, Kevin Tice—Cozzano didn't suffer fools gladly.

"What was it like?" Zeldo said.

"What was *what* like?" Cozzano said.

"You're the only person in history who's ever done this, so I don't know how to ask. I know it's a vague question. But someday I'd like to get an implant of my own, you know."

"So you've said," Cozzano said.

"So I'm trying to get some sense of what it's like to communicate in that way—transmissions from outside, bypassing all the sensory subsystems, going directly into the brain's neural net."

"I'm still not sure if I follow," Cozzano said.

Zeldo started to grope. "Normally we get input through our

senses. Information comes down the optic nerve, or through the nerves in our skin or whatever. Those nerves are hooked up to parts of the brain that act like filters between ourselves and our environment."

Cozzano nodded slightly, more out of politeness than anything else. He was still nonplussed. But one good thing about Cozzano was that he was always game for an intellectual discussion.

"Ever see an optical illusion?" Zeldo said, trying a new tack.

"Of course."

"An optical illusion is what we computer people would call a hack—an ingenious trick that takes advantage of a defect in our brain, a bug if you will, to make us see something that's not really there. Normally our brains are too smart for that. Like, when you watch something on television, you understand that it's not really happening—it's just an image on a screen."

"I think I'm following you now," Cozzano said.

"The inputs you were getting from Ogle tonight didn't pass through any of your normal filters—they went straight into your brain, kind of like an optical illusion does. What's that like?"

"I'm not sure what you mean by inputs," Cozzano said.

"The signals he was sending you from his chair."

Suddenly Cozzano's face crinkled up in amusement and he chuckled. "Oh, that business," he said. Then he shook his head indulgently. "I know you guys have a lot of fun with that stuff. It's all just parlor tricks. Was Cy doing any of that nonsense tonight?"

"He was doing it more or less constantly," Zeldo said.

"Well, then you can tell him to stop wasting his time," Cozzano said, "because it didn't have any effect. I didn't notice a thing. Zeldo, have you ever been in a situation like that? Debating on live television before millions of people?"

"I can't say that I have," Zeldo said.

"You get into a sort of zone, as the football players like to say. Every minute seems to last an hour. You forget about all the lights and cameras and audience and become totally focused on the event itself, the exchange of ideas, the rhetorical counterplay. I can assure you that if Cy Ogle were to walk onto the set during one of those debates and throw a bucket of ice water over my head, I wouldn't even notice it. So none of that silly business with the buttons and joysticks has any effect."

"Didn't it stimulate memories and images?"

Cozzano grinned paternally. "Son, the mind is a complicated bit of business. It is a churning sea of memories and images and everything else. My mind is always filled with competing ideas. If Cy wants to toss in one or two extras, then he's welcome to do so, but it's kind of like pissing in the ocean."

Cozzano stopped talking and got a distant look in his eyes.

"What's going on?" Zeldo said.

"For example, right now my mind is full of images, an overwhelming flood of memories and ideas—you have any idea how many memories are buried in the mind? Fishing for bluegill on Lake Argyle with my father, the hook caught in his thumb, forcing it through the other side and cutting it off with wirecutters the severed barb flying dangerously into the air spinning its cut facet gleaming in the sun and I jerking back for fear it would plunge into my eye, squinting protectively, opening my eyes again it is mud, all mud, a universe of mud and the mortar shell has just taken flight, my fingers jammed into my ears, the smell of the explosion penetrating my sinuses making them clench up and bleed, the shell exploding in the trees, a puff of white smoke but the trees are still there and the gunfire still raining down like hailstones on the cellar door on the day that the tornado wrecked our farmhouse and we packed into my aunt's fruit cellar and I looked up at the stacked mason jars of rhubarb and tomatoes and wondered what would happen to us when the glass shattered and flew through the air like the horizontal sleet of Soldier Field on the day that I caught five for eighty-seven yards and put such a hit on Cornelius Hayes that he took five minutes to get up. God, I can see my entire life! Stop the car! Stop the car!"

Then William A. Cozzano froze up entirely, except for his eyes which were jittering back and forth in their sockets, irises opening and closing sporadically, focus changing in and out as they tried to lock on to things that weren't actually there.

They pulled onto the shoulder, opened the back doors of the car, and laid Cozzano out full-length on the backseat. But then he sprang back up, slid out the open door into the roadside ditch, and began to march into a field of eight-foot-high corn, bellowing in Italian. At first it was just inchoate noise, but then it settled down into a passable rendition of an aria from Verdi, baritone stuff, a bad-guy role. The state patrolmen did not know what to do, whether or not they should try to restrain him, so they did what cops do when they feel uncertain: they shone lights on him. He had thoughtfully removed his suit jacket and so his white shirt, neatly trisected by suspenders, stood out brilliantly among the cornstalks. He was walking across the field, leaving trampled stalks in his wake, followed at a respectful distance by a couple of the patrolmen. His course zigged and zagged, but he seemed to be settling on one particular direction. He was headed for the only landmark in the vicinity: a tall narrow tower that rose from the field several hundred feet from the road, with blinking red lights.

"The red lights," one of the patrolmen said. "He's attracted by the lights!"

But Zeldo just shook his head. Right now his brain was almost as overloaded as Cozzano's, and it was all he could do to force an explanatory word out: "Microwaves."

Cozzano finally collapsed a stone's throw from the microwave relay tower. The patrolmen rushed inward, converged on him, hoisted him into the air, and began to hustle him back.

By the time they got him back to the car he was thrashing around again, but the spittle and blood around his mouth told Zeldo that he'd had a seizure and probably bitten his tongue. "Let's get out of here!" Zeldo said.

Zeldo had already folded down the rear seat of Cozzano's sport/utility vehicle and opened the tailgate. They threw him in back like a heavy roll of carpet. "Go! Go!" Zeldo shouted, and the driver pulled off the shoulder and down the road, all four tires burning rubber.

Cozzano relaxed and, apropos of nothing, quoted a lengthy passage, verbatim, from the General Agreement on Tariffs and Trades. Then he was silent for a while.

Then he said, "Why the hell is the tailgate open? You want us to end up like Bianca Ramirez?"

. . .

*Floyd Wayne Vishniak* wanted to sleep but his thoughts would not let him. He lay on his mattress having an imaginary discussion inside of his head, moving his lips and gesturing with his hands in the air as he debated politics with William A. Cozzano and Tip McLane. The more he went over the discussion in his head, the clearer his thoughts became, and he kept finding new ways to explain them. Finally he decided that he would write them down.

The light over the kitchen table hurt his eyes. He held one hand over his face as a visor and tripped around the kitchen looking for something to write with. Eventually he located the stub of a pencil on top of the fridge. Back next to his mattress was his weight bench and underneath that was a box full of weights and dumbell parts. In the bottom of that, under all the weights, was an old spiral notebook with half the pages missing, which he had used to record his progress when he was sticking to his weight-lifting program. He turned it to a fresh page and tossed it onto the kitchen table; directly under the light, the white page was very bright and made him squint. He grabbed a beer from the fridge and sat down to collect his thoughts.

He took the address from the videotape, as Aaron Green had told him to do.

Floyd Wayne Vishniak
RR. 6 Box 895
Davenport, Iowa

Aaron Green
Ogle Data Research
Pentagon Towers
Arlington, Virginia

Dear Mr. Green:
I am writing this letter to you to express my additional thoughts and opinions, which you said you wanted to hear all about. Maybe you have already forgotten about me since I am just a nobody who lives in a trailer. But we have seen each other face-

to-face once, and maybe we will again. This is about the Debate that was tonight in Decatur, Illinois, not so very far from where I live.

It is real interesting that one hundred years ago people were thinking the same things they are now about the Wall Street financial kingpins running the country. How ironic that still nothing has changed. I wonder why that is. Maybe it is because all of the politicians run on money, money, money.

McLane is power-grubbing scum and you can see it in his face and in how he acts, like a stiff. That is because if he acts natural and tells the truth he will probably offend someone who is feeding him money.

But Cozzano is an honest man and he tells it straight. He is the only honest man up there because he is the only one who is not running for anything. To me, the favorite part of the debate was when he invited McLane to step outside. I felt good when I heard Cozzano speak those words of righteousness, like out of the Bible, and I truly wanted to see his fist smashing into McLane's face.

I bet that you got some good reactions off my wristwatch at that moment. I bet the readings all went off the scale. Now you probably think that I am some kind of a violent person.

But in my heart that is not the real truth. When I lay in bed I felt ashamed to think that I had felt such violent thoughts. Even if Tip McLane is a shithead it would not be OK to punch him out because that is not the basis of our democratic system. So I think that I would not vote for Cozzano after tonight's debate, no matter what your computer system said about me. Please make a note of it.

You will be hearing again from me soon, I am sure.

Sincerely, Floyd Wayne Vishniak

Dr. Mary Catherine Cozzano finished her neurology residency during the last week of June. She spent a couple of days in Chicago celebrating with her fellow graduates, but during the past four years they had forgotten how to goof off, and it took a positive effort to have fun. Then she moved back into her old bedroom in Tuscola. She wasn't crazy about moving back home at the age of thirty, but she needed a quiet place in which to study for the board exams. She didn't have a job lined up yet, and probably wouldn't, at least until things settled down, which would not be until Election Day.

Besides, the house was still partly occupied by technical personnel from the Radhakrishnan Institute, their computers were all over the place, and so she could almost convince herself that she was actually living in an advanced neurological research center. She spent an hour or two each day going over the records of Dad's recovery, learning about the therapy and how it worked. As Dad had gotten the basic rehab out of the way—learning to walk, learning to talk—his staff of therapists had withered away to a handful who helped him with things like writing. In the same way, the hard-tech people had dwindled, going back to the Radhakrishnan Institute and leaving high-bandwidth communications links in their place, so that they could monitor the biochip from the other side of the country. Zeldo had told her at the beginning of June that he too would be leaving soon, but he was still here, sleeping on the floor of James's old bedroom, which had become a weird mixture of James's adolescent decor (ILLINI pennants and Michael Jordan posters) with appallingly pricey, high-powered computer gear. When Mary Catherine asked Zeldo why he was still here, he broke eye contact and muttered some hacker aphorism about how hard it was to chase down the last few bugs.

She wasn't sure what to make of the fact that her father was now right-handed.

On the night of the State of the Union address, the blood clot had shot up Dad's aortal arch, the giant superhighway that carried almost all of the heart's output. It had spun off into two separate fragments. One had gone up each of the carotid arteries, left and right. The one on the right had caused paralysis on the left side of his body, and the one on the left had nailed that hemisphere's speech centers, causing aphasia.

Then, a couple of months later, in the den, the second stroke had caused more damage to the left side of his brain, causing paralysis on the right side of his body.

Dad's soul could make the decision to move, and his brain could issue the order to his arm or leg, but the order never got there because the links had been severed by the stroke. Dr. Radhakrishnan had implanted two chips, one on each side of the brain. Their function was to replace those broken links so that the orders to move could get out to his body again. Now that the chips had been trained to convey messages to the correct body parts, Dad's paralysis was gone.

But aphasia was a different thing. It wasn't just paralysis of the tongue. It went deeper than that. And you couldn't simulate it with baboons. It was uncanny that this therapy had worked so well the first time out. Dad sounded like Dad, and said the things that Dad would say, but sometimes when he was talking, she suddenly became disoriented, stopped listening to him, and began to wonder where his words were coming from, whether they were passing through the biochip. Dad could tell when Mary Catherine was doing this; he called it "going neurologist" and it drove him crazy.

*She felt flaccid* and out of shape after four years of residency. Every morning she would rise at five and go for a run. Any later in the day, and it would get so warm and sticky that she couldn't really get a good workout. Besides, she had done much worse things to her sleep schedule during residency and so she didn't mind getting up early to do something she felt good about.

Her usual route took her down the street to the city park, where she would take a couple of laps around the softball diamond and do some stretching on the infield. Then she would head out of town, crossing U.S. 45 and the Illinois Central, and run along one of the farm roads, measuring her distance by counting the crossroads, which came at one-mile intervals. Central Illinois in July was stiflingly humid, and as often as not she found herself running through fog and mist. The early morning sunlight, shining in low, threw a clammy metallic haze over the landscape.

On the morning of the Fourth of July, a shape materialized in front of Mary Catherine as she jogged down the country road. At first she thought it was a car coming toward her in the wrong lane, but then she realized that it was not moving. She thought it must be a car that had broken down. As she got closer she could see a dark shape standing next to the car, motionless, waiting. She unzipped her belt pack and reached into it, making sure that the stun gun was in there.

It was a small car, low to the ground. A sporty little Mercedes. A big hand-lettered sign was leaning against the rear bumper, printed on a square of poster board. It said, MARY CATHERINE—DON'T MAKE A SOUND!

The figure leaning against the car was Mel Meyer. As Mary Catherine approached, Mel straightened up and turned to face her, holding one finger up to his lips, shushing her.

It was not exactly a warm and affectionate reunion. Mel pulled a small black box from the pocket of his black raincoat. He walked toward Mary Catherine, clicked a switch on the box, and then waved it up and down the length of her body, watching an LED graph built into its top. Every time the box passed near her midsection, the graph shot up to its peak level. Mel moved the little box in a narrowing orbit until he finally zeroed in on her belt pack.

The pack was still unzipped. Mel pulled it open and peered into it, his bald head grazing Mary Catherine's bosom. He nudged the stun gun out of the way and carefully pulled her keychain out. The world's largest keychain had shed a couple of pounds since Mary Catherine had left the hospital, but it was still formidable. Mel turned it over in his hand, waving his little black box over it, and finally zeroed in on the miniature Swiss Army knife.

He disconnected it from the keychain and held it right up next to his black box. The LED graph was pinned at its highest reading.

Then he walked across the road, wound up, and flung the knife off into the middle of a cornfield. He made one more pass over Mary Catherine's body with the little black box. This time the LED meter did not flicker.

"Okay," Mel finally said. He spoke quietly, but it was easy to hear him in the absolute silence of predawn. "You're clean."

"What—"

"If anyone asks, tell them that, uh—" Mel closed his eyes and stood motionless for a few seconds, "you noticed a dog that had broken away and gotten its collar tangled up in a barbed wire fence and you had to take out your knife and cut through his collar to get him loose. In the process you dropped your knife on the ground and forgot to pick it up."

"Hardly plausible."

"It doesn't have to be plausible. Just good enough that no one can call bullshit on you without bringing down the wrath of the Governor."

"What was in the knife?"

"A listening device."

"Must have been a small one."

Mel was disappointed. "Are you kidding? Don't be a sap. They can make them the size of fleas now."

"Oh. Sorry."

"Mary Catherine, some heavy shit is going on, and we need to talk. What time you usually get back to the house?"

"Around six."

"Okay, I'll drop you off by the park about then," Mel said. "Hop in."

The passenger door of the Mercedes was already ajar. Mary Catherine, a little shell-shocked, climbed into it. Mel sat down behind the wheel, started the engine, drove thirty feet up the road and turned onto a gravel farm road, a tunnel into the corn. He drove for a quarter of a mile, until the main road was shrouded in the mist.

"Where are we going?"

"Partly we're just getting off the road so people won't see us," Mel said. "Partly I want to show you something." Mel let the Mercedes coast to a stop, set the hand brake, and popped his door open.

A short distance away from the lane was a tree, one of the

magnificent, solitary oaks that sprouted from the cornfields every few miles and that was allowed to remain there by the farmers, just because it was beautiful.

"Now I'm totally lost," Mary Catherine said, getting out of the car. She faced Mel over the hood. "You're acting kind of paranoid, Mel, if I can offer a professional opinion."

"I'm fully aware of that," Mel said. "Now, check this out. You might be surprised to know that I have become quite the observer of nature on my little drives down here."

"Nature? I didn't know there was any nature left in downstate."

"Well, you have to look for it, but it's there. Watch the tree." Mel turned toward the oak, cupped his hands around his face like a megaphone, and then did something incredibly un-Mel-like: he made a high-pitched screeching sound, three sharp falsetto cries.

The tree rose into the sky. That's what it looked like, for a moment. A thousand black birds rose from its branches in unison and soared across the cornfield, holding for a moment the shape of the tree, then forming into a tightly organized cloud that twisted around itself, turned inside out, changing directions and leaders but always staying together.

Mel was grinning at her. "You didn't know those birds were there, did you?"

Mary Catherine shook her head no.

"Look at 'em," Mel said. "I've been watching them from my car. Watch how the flock can vanish."

Every bird in the flock snapped into exactly the same banking turn. At a certain point they were all coming directly toward Mel and Mary Catherine, and the flock became nearly invisible as each bird was viewed edge-on. Then Mel made his screeching noise again and they all turned sideways, the hidden flock snapping back into existence, much closer to them, almost merging into a solid wall.

"You know, Mary Catherine, that I have spent my career as an integral part of the military-industrial complex. Whatever the hell that is." Mel waved his arm toward a patch of mist at about three o'clock. "Right over there is Willy's nylon factory, where they made parachutes for the Army. You can't get much more military, or industrial, than that. So I have always scoffed at people who blamed all the world's troubles on the military-industrial complex. But I can't escape the idea that something very big is going on involving our Willy. Something that involves spending an ungodly amount of money."

"The biochip implant is definitely a big deal," Mary Catherine said. She was still mystified by the business with Mel's little black box, and the bird thing made no sense at all, but she decided to play along for now. "The Radhakrishnan Institute definitely has a lot of money behind it. We knew that from the beginning. And we've always been realistic enough to understand that there's an economic dimension to this therapy. If it goes well, the institute and its backers will have a gold mine on their hands."

"Yeah, yeah, yeah," Mel said, waving his hand dimissively, "that is all a given. That's the Invisible Hand argument—that we're seeing free enterprise in action here. I've been thinking about that argument ever since you came back from your inspection trip. It doesn't hold up under scrutiny."

"Why not?"

"Sure, a lot of people have brain damage. But there are a million diseases. Cancer, muscular dystrophy, car crashes. Now, there's a good example—car crashes. For decades, a ridiculous number of people died in car crashes. Still do. But even simple things like seat belts took a long time to develop. The car makers had to be dragged kicking and screaming into air bags. The Invisible Hand didn't work then."

"What other possible reason could there be?"

"That this therapy was developed specifically for one patient—William A. Cozzano."

"But you're talking about a vast expenditure," Mary Catherine said. "Billions of dollars."

"Right," Mel said, "which means two things: first of all, the people who did this are loaded. In fact, it can't be a single entity. It has to be a group of separate entities working in tight formation—like that flock of birds. And secondly, they expect to get a huge return on their investment."

"What could possibly be worth that much money?"

"Only one thing I can think of. The presidency of the United States," Mel said.

At the intellectual level, Mary Catherine thought this whole conversation was ridiculous. But at some deeper level she was coming down with a severe case of the creeps. She had cooled off from her running now and the sweat on her limbs was suddenly replaced by goosebumps. She said, "And you think that this explanation is actually more believable than the Invisible Hand theory?"

"I have insufficient data to answer that," Mel said, "but as long as it's a possibility, I have to consider it. Maybe you can help gather more information for me, so that I can rule out this ridiculous theory and buy into a more respectable explanation."

"What should I do?" Mary Catherine said.

"First of all, assume it could be true," Mel said. "Assume that you might be enmeshed in a very large conspiracy. Assume that you are being listened to and watched, all the time. I already found a bug in my car, and I just found one on you," Mel said.

Mary Catherine was stunned. "Are you sure?"

Mel clenched his jaw and actually looked a little peeved. "Don't ask me if I'm sure when I say something like this. Of course I'm fucking sure. I have connections you don't know about, kid. My whole life is not this fucking corncob business."

"Sorry."

"I went out of town for a couple of days. Came back. Got in my car. Pushed the button for WGN and got some Jesus station from DeKalb. All my station presets were screwed up. So I took it to a friend of a friend who used to work in the Agency, and he found a bug. Then we did a full sweep and found bugs in my house too."

"My god," Mary Catherine said. If Mel was telling the truth, then there really was some heavy shit going on. If he wasn't, he was demented. Either way, this was starting to get serious.

"They weren't Radio Shack specials either," Mel said, "they were very good bugs. KGB-level technology."

"Okay, I'll assume I'm bugged. Then what?"

Mel sighed. "Hell, I don't know. The problem with you downstaters is that everything has to be spelled out."

"Sorry."

"Just keep your eyes open. Is that too general? You want a specific question from me? I can't provide you with a specific question."

"I'll keep my eyes peeled for signs of the military-industrial complex," Mary Catherine said.

"It's not that. It's something else," Mel said. He turned to look at the flock of birds, which was still careening across the fields, turning this way and that according to some plan that Mel and Mary Catherine couldn't puzzle out, vanishing and then snapping back into full view, each bird somehow knowing what all the other birds were doing. "Let's call it the Network."

This discussion was crystallizing a number of vague ideas and perceptions that had been floating around in Mary Catherine's mind for a few months. The outlines of an idea were beginning to emerge, much as Mel and his car had materialized from the fog.

"There is something going on, now that you mention it," she said.

"What can you tell me about it?" Mel asked. He had suddenly relaxed and softened.

"I don't know. It's just that the same few names keep coming up. Gale Aerospace, Pacific Netware, GODS, Genomics, Ogle Data Research, MacIntyre Engineering. They're independent, yet they act in a coordinated fashion."

"Can you give me names of any people who work for the Network?"

Mary Catherine leaned her forearms on the roof of the car, watching the birds, trying to bring things into focus. "A lot of people work *for* the Network. Including me, I guess, in a way. Cy Ogle, Dr. Radhakrishnan, Pete Zeldovich, are all in that category. But I've only seen one person who seems to be *of* the Network. Does that make any sense?"

"Sure. Who is this person?"

"He is called Mr. Salvador," Mary Catherine said. "He stops in from time to time. Like he's on an inspection tour or something. From the way people act around him, I'd say he's definitely the one in charge."

"Of the whole Network?"

"No."

"How do you know?"

"Just a feeling. He acts like a guy who has a boss. I think he's in charge of everything pertaining to Dad."

"So Salvador is an ops man," Mel said. "He manages one of the Network's projects—Willy. Who is this boss of Salvador's?"

"I don't know," Mary Catherine said. "I've had a bare minimum of contact with Salvador. His boss doesn't even enter the picture."

"Can you give me any clues at all? Does he make phone calls when he's there?"

"Yeah. But he uses the phone in his car."

"Does he get phone calls, or letters, at the house?"

Mary Catherine suddenly remembered something. She stood up straight and stared intently at nothing in particular, her eyes jumping back and forth as she tried to reconstruct the memory. "Yesterday morning when I was coming back from my run, a GODS van pulled up in front of the house. The driver had an envelope for Mr. Salvador. But he wasn't in; he was due to show up a few hours later. So I signed for the envelope. Salvador showed up later and ripped it open. And threw it away."

"You're saying that the envelope is still in the garbage?"

"They're too security-conscious to throw things in the garbage. They only throw away things like McDonald's wrappers. Everything else goes into a burn bag, or straight to a shredder."

"My god, it's just like the Agency," Mel said.

"I think that they shred the *contents* of envelopes. But the envelopes *themselves* go into the burn bag—and those only get collected once or twice a week. So I may be able to dig it out."

"I need that envelope. It has tracking codes and stuff on it," Mel said.

"I'll do some looking around later," Mary Catherine said.

Mel looked ever so slightly crestfallen. Apparently she had not shown enough enthusiasm for this cloak-and-dagger assignment.

He had a Bruckner symphony going on the CD player in the

trunk of the Mercedes. He climbed back into the driver's seat and turned it up. Mary Catherine climbed in too. They sat in the car and listened to it for a few minutes.

"Listen to me," Mel said, turning it down again, "I'm way behind the curve in dealing with this thing."

"How's that?"

Mel laughed. In another man it would have been a laugh devoid of humor. But Mel had a talent for finding humor in strange places and he seemed genuinely amused, though he was not exactly happy. "I'm supposed to be Willy's trusted adviser. I'm supposed to tell him whether it's a good idea to run for president. And now look. He's announcing in a few hours. And I'm still trying to figure out what the hell's going on."

Mary Catherine had nothing to say to that. She waited for Mel to continue.

"I take my job very seriously and right now I'm failing at it," Mel said. "I have to get my ass in gear. I have to do stuff. To take steps. Some of what I do may not make me very popular with the Network. So let me ask you something: do you want to work with me? Or not? Either way is fine."

It was Mary Catherine's turn to laugh. "Either way is *not* fine," she said. "We're talking about Dad."

"No, we're not," Mel said gently, "we're talking about what your dad became when that chip went into his head. And I'm not sure it's the same thing."

This was such a disturbing comment that Mary Catherine decided not to let it sink in just now. "Well, even if he were just another presidential candidate—one way I'm doing good and one way I'm doing evil."

"Leave it to a farmer to see things in those terms," Mel said. "Okay, are you going to do good or evil?"

"Good," Mary Catherine said.

"That's a nice girl," Mel said.

"I think that Dad wants to do good also—whatever you might think," Mary Catherine said.

Mel turned and looked at her face. "What's that supposed to mean?"

"You know," she said, "there are many cases of people who have had strokes and recovered from them."

"I thought the brain tissue was dead. How can you recover from being dead?"

"The dead tissue doesn't recover. But in some cases, other parts of the brain can take over for the parts that died. It takes a lot of work. A lot of therapy. And some luck. But it's been known to happen. There are people who had half of their brains blown out in Vietnam who are walking and talking normally today."

"You don't say. Why didn't you try this with Willy?"

"We did," Mary Catherine said, "but when the chance of a quick fix arose, he opted for that. There's no telling where he would have gone with normal therapy."

"You think he might have come back?"

"The chances are very low," she said. "But remember, he's mixed-brain dominant. People like that have a knack for recovering from these injuries."

"So what are you saying exactly—about Willy wanting to do good?"

"I'm saying that the Network may be able to exert great influence over him through the biochip," she said, "but that underneath, his brain may be struggling to reassert control. And that if he pursues the proper therapy, we can increase the chances that this will eventually happen."

"What kind of therapy?" Mel said.

"He just has to use his head. That's all," Mary Catherine said. "He has to exercise his brain and his body, in a lot of different ways, and retrain his neural pathways."

"Hell," Mel said, "a presidential campaign's not exactly the place for that."

"Granted," she said, "unless the candidate travels with, dines with, and rooms with a neurologist."

She and Mel locked eyes for a moment.

"You sure?" Mel said.

"Of course I'm sure."

## CHAPTER FORTY

"Last year at about this time I accepted an invitation from the chairman of my party to deliver the keynote speech at their convention, a couple of weeks from today," William A. Cozzano said. "Last night, I telephoned him from my home here in Tuscola and expressed my regrets that I would be unable to participate in that convention in any way, shape, or form—as a keynote speaker, a delegate, or a nominee. And he was gracious enough to accept my apology for this sudden change of plans."

Cozzano finally paused long enough to allow the crowd to detonate—something that they were primed to do, since they had been practicing it under the eye of Cy Ogle's crowd handlers for the last hour and a half. When he finally paused for breath, the freshly painted bleachers surrounding the Tuscola High School football field suddenly bloomed with signs, banners, balloons, confetti, and all the other bright insubstantialities of a political campaign.

"It's not that I bear a grudge against my party, because I don't. In fact, I am still a card-carrying member and expect to remain one, assuming they'll still have me after today."

This line triggered a laugh that developed into a cheer, which built into another flag-waving crescendo.

It looked great. It looked great to Cozzano, to his close friends and family seated around him on the field, and to the three dozen camera crews that had come in from all the networks, major urban markets, and several European and Asian networks.

Until about a month ago, this field had only had one rank of low-rising bleachers, on one side of the field. That was adequate for just about any crowd that the Tuscola Warriors were likely to draw. Then a big donation had come in from the Cozzano family and the bleacher space had been quadrupled, with brand-new ranks installed on both sides of the field. The lighting system had been beefed up to the point where it lit up half the town. Tuscola now boasted the best football field of any town of its size in Illinois.

For today's festivities, a huge podium had been built straddling the fifty-yard line, raised about six feet off the ground. There was enough space for a couple of hundred folding chairs, heavy media support, and one great big red-white-and-blue lectern, massively constructed but nevertheless groaning under the weight of nearly a hundred microphones. Amazingly enough, most of those mikes had arrived preattached to the lectern, were not actually connected to anything, and bore the logos of networks and TV stations that were imaginary or defunct.

Mary Catherine was especially interested to note that Dad now rated a Secret Service detail. Half a dozen of them were clearly visible on and around the podium, which probably meant more circulating through the crowd.

Ogle had arranged the thing in concentric circles. The inner circle consisted of VIPs, friends and family in the folding chairs up on the podium. A few select camera crews and photographers had also been allowed to circulate up here, getting closeup shots. Surrounding the podium was an inner circle of especially hysterical Cozzano fans, sort of an all-American cross section, spiced with a few dozen astonishingly beautiful young women who were not wearing very much in the way of clothing but who were careful to hold up their Cozzano signs and point to their Cozzano skimmers whenever photographers and cameramen pointed lenses in their direction, which was constantly. Banks of high-powered bluish-white floodlights, similar to stadium lights but only a couple of yards off the ground, had been erected on the edges of this crowd, pointed inward so that their light grazed the heads of the Cozzano supporters. At first Mary Catherine had thought that this must be a mistake, and that the technicians would turn the lights toward the podium. But then the Cozzano supporters had held their white COZZANO FOR PRESIDENT signs up above their heads and the light had caught them brilliantly, making them glow like snowflakes in a car's headlights.

Beyond was a broad sweep of open turf where most of the media were stationed, including a raised platform for the TV crews, arranged so that every time they aimed their cameras at the lectern they had to shoot over the unnaturally brilliant field of waving signs, flags, soaring skimmers, mylar balloons, and pumping fists.

The outermost circle, surrounding everything, was a vast sweaty crowd consisting of all the population of Tuscola and then some. Their function here was to hurl up a barrage of noise whenever Cozzano said something mildly interesting, and to provide a colorful backdrop rising up behind him. In fact, the geometry of the bleachers, the lectern, and the main media area was such that it was impossible to get a shot of Cozzano without taking in several hundred supporters in the bleachers behind him, all waving hankies and signs, just like fans seated behind the goalposts at a football game. To make sure that the level of enthusiasm never dropped, the Tuscola High School cheerleading squad had been deployed, in full uniform, in front of one set of bleachers, and the squad from Rantoul was egging on the opposite set of bleachers. Cy Ogle had promised a free set of new uniforms to whichever squad elicited the most noise from their half of the crowd. The Tuscola High School marching band was lined up behind the podium, primed to burst into music whenever the mood seemed right. All of this, combined with the reckless Cozzano supporters setting off strings of firecrackers amid the crowd; the giant vertical COZZANO banner hanging from the soaring sign of the Dixie Truckers' Home; the circling airplanes trailing more banners; the hovering choppers; the team of three precision skydivers who had skimmed over the podium in formation just before Cozzano was introduced, trailing plumes of red-white-and-blue smoke; and the appearance of William A. Cozzano himself, landing in the home team's end zone in a National Guard chopper and jogging—*jogging*—across the field, through a tunnel of supporters, slapping hands on either side the whole way— it all added up to a show the likes of which had never been seen in downstate Illinois, and which Guillermo Cozzano could not have imagined when he first came down here to toil in the coal mines.

*Mary Catherine had* the seat closest to the lectern. She was wearing brand new clothes purchased for her by her personal shopper at Marshall Field. The personal shopper and the clothes were both paid for by Cy Ogle. The personal shopper was a fifty-five-year-old Sunday school teacher and had chosen the clothing accordingly. Except, that is, for the underwear, which Mary Catherine had picked out herself, and which probably would have gotten her in big trouble if she got into a car accident.

It had already become obvious that for purposes of the campaign, Mary Catherine would serve as a kind of surrogate wife. This was an awkward notion, to say the least, and as she sat there broiling and sweating under the July sun she made up her mind that she was going to have to have a talk with Ogle about it. The fact that she was now acting as a secret agent for Mel Meyer made it a little more palatable.

James was next to her, very handsome in a new suit that had obviously been chosen by a personal shopper of his own. She hadn't seen much of him lately, which was probably a good thing. His book project seemed to have added years to his age—in a good sense. Somehow he looked taller, leaner, more confident. He looked like a grown-up.

The remainder of the front two rows was completely occupied with family. The Cozzano family, after a dodgy first couple of generations during which a lot of people had fallen victim to war or influenza, had begun to multiply ferociously during the last twenty years. The distribution of ages up here on the podium—a few oldsters, a few more middle-agers, and half a million kids—was a visible demonstration of the exponential growth concept. In addition, her mother's family, a prosperous clan of blue-eyed midwestern engineers, had shown up in division strength. The Cozzanos still had deep roots in the Chicago Italian community. A lot of them were here. And so were a bunch of Meyers.

It was the biggest family reunion ever. She had kissed a hundred people on her way to her seat. She must have half an inch of powder caked up on each cheek from bussing all those old ladies. Roughly one thousand people had come up to her and told her that she looked beautiful.

Mary Catherine was glad that this campaign hadn't yet gotten so slick and controlled that kids had been banished from these big events. The podium was an absolute riot. A little toddler girl wandered around behind Cozzano with her diaper peeking out from under her dress. A Domenici boy and a Meyer boy, both wearing suits that were a size too small, jumped and ducked around the rows of chairs, sniping at each other with squirt guns, occasionally picking off an old lady by mistake. Some of the mothers with young kids had folded up a bunch of the chairs, tossed them off the platform, spread out blankets, and set up an impromptu day-care center. With their wide-brimmed hats and their spreading skirts, all in light hues of yellow and white, they looked like a field of daffodils, the toddlers running around from one to the other like fat little bees. Inspired by the bleacher crowd, the extended family up here on the podium had become rowdy. A dozen ex-Bears had showed up and were seated in a massive phalanx at the very back of the podium, where their shoulders wouldn't block anyone else's view; they had started passing a hip flask very early and were now beginning to lead the podium crowd in cheers.

It was a blast. Mary Catherine was having a great time. She could hardly hear a word Dad was saying. All of the kids in all of those extended families looked up to her, she was like a goddess, role model, and honorary big sister to dozens. She had the special status accorded to big girls who know how to drive, are skilled at kissing owies, and aren't afraid to throw and catch a football. Consequently she was visited by a never-ending stream of perfectly dressed-up little kids who came up to her to pay homage, admire her dress, show her their owies, give her presents, have their shoes tied, display important baseball cards, and ask for directions back to their mommies.

Consequently she had no idea what was going on when, suddenly, the entire crowd—bleachers, podium, everywhere—suddenly jumped to its feet and burst forth in wild exaltation. Ten thousand helium balloons launched themselves from the end zone and headed for Mars. Tremendous barrages of firecrackers went off all over the place, releasing skeins of acrid smoke into the air. Boat horns screeched all over the place as if all the world's seagulls were dying at once, the podium reverberated with the thumping bass drums of the marching band, and from somewhere—a helicopter, maybe?—a thunderhead of confetti descended upon the scene, so dense that for a few moments you could hardly see your own hand. Mary Catherine instinctively looked to her father, who was just visible through the confetti as a glowing outline, limned by the television lights, blurred by the red-white-and-blue blizzard.

It seemed like he was a thousand miles away from her. Not a human being, but an electronic figment conjured up from the computers of a media laboratory. Ronald Reagan had been an actor. At times, William A. Cozzano had begun to seem like a special effect.

Then the blizzard of confetti cleared and he was just standing there, letting the waves of sound roll over him, and he turned toward her, his eye searching through the faces, the smoke, the streamers and balloons, and he found her, caught her eye, and smiled a smile that was for her and for her alone.

She smiled back. She knew that both of them were thinking about Mom.

She wasn't sure what she was supposed to do. She didn't even know what was going on, really. But she wanted to be with Dad, and so she walked across the podium and climbed the steps to the raised lectern. He caught her up with one arm around her waist as she reached the top step and crushed her to his side. The noise level went up by another few decibels, if that was possible, and she did what she was supposed to do: she looked not at her father, but out into the crowd, into the battery of lenses, and waved. She felt terrified and forlorn, but with Dad holding her up she knew she'd get through it. It was so good to have him back.

A huge banner had unfurled from the top of the bleachers and it said, COZZANO FOR PRESIDENT. This was not the first time that Mary Catherine had seen those words, but when she saw them up there, ten feet high, on the Tuscola High School bleachers, she knew it was for real. And she finally realized what had touched off all of this tumult: Dad had done it. He had announced. He was running for president.

The rest of the day was completely out of control. It was like being stuck in the middle of a riot in which no one got hurt. It was like the biggest, rowdiest, most drunken wedding of all time, to the tenth power; and instead of a single photographer telling everyone what to do, there was an army of photographers. So many flashes went off in Mary Catherine's eyes that she began to see things that weren't there, as if the electronic flash was a gateway to a hidden dimension. The rally devolved into an open-air hugging, kissing, handshaking, and sweating festival and, assisted by shuttle buses, gradually migrated across town to the Tuscola City Park, where half of the pigs in the Midwest were revolving on spits inside giant, rusted, smoking, portable barbecue pits. Green fiberglass portable toilets were lined up in ranks at one end of the park, like ceremonial guards at a coronation. A linear mile of picnic tables had been set up with red-white-and-blue tablecloths and loaded up with lemonade, iced tea, punch, water, coffee, and beer.

Mary Catherine made her way through all of this one step at a time, stopping every yard or so to greet someone new. After the first thousand or so people, she completely lost her ability to remember faces. A nice lady came up and shook her hand and chatted with her for a while; Mary Catherine had her pegged as her old Sunday School teacher until she realized that this woman was, in fact, the wife of a Supreme Court justice. She said hello to Althea Coover, DeWayne Coover's granddaughter and an old college mate of hers. As the hours went on, she saw a great many people whom she recognized, but oddly enough they were people she had never met before. They were movie stars, professional athletes, senators, and musicians. She knew their faces as well as she knew the faces of her own aunts and uncles, and so it didn't seem strange at all to see them wandering around Tuscola, to see the Senator from Wyoming swapping jokes with the coach of the Bulls.

At one point she even ran into Cy Ogle and had the presence of mind to tell him that she wanted to talk to him when he got a chance. He couldn't talk to her right away because he was addressing the two squads of cheerleaders, Tuscola and Rantoul, who had all gotten a chance to take showers and get pretty. He was confessing his total inability to choose which squad had done better, and promising to buy new uniforms for both squads. Consequently he didn't talk to Mary Catherine until about an hour later, when he finally tracked her down on the edge of the festival.

She was standing at home plate on the softball diamond. She had hung her blazer up on a nail sticking out of the wooden backstop. She had an aluminum bat in her hands and she was knocking fly balls and grounders to half a dozen preadolescent boys, arrayed throughout the infield and outfield, playing a game called five hundred. In honor of her high birth, superior muscles, and pinpoint place-hitting ability, they had named her All-Time Batter. She punched the balls out. They caught them, keeping track of their own scores, and threw them back. By hitting the balls in the right places, she was able to keep their scores pretty closely bunched together. After a while, a Japanese TV crew showed up and began to film her. She didn't mind.

"I detect some bias here," someone drawled, just after she hit an easy grounder to a small boy who had just entered the game.

She turned around. It was Ogle, watching her through the backstop. "How long have you been watching?" she said.

"Couple minutes. I was going to come out and catch for you. But that'd spoil the visual," he said, nodding toward the Japanese video crew. She could not tell, from the way he said this, whether he was serious or making fun of himself.

"They've got their visual," she said. "Why don't you come out and catch before I break a nail and spoil that visual."

"Okay, kids!" Ogle shouted, emerging from behind the backstop, "now y'all got an all-time catcher too! First one who bops me in the head gets two hundred points!"

A ball came sailing from left field, directly toward Ogle's head. He pretended not to notice until it was nearly there, then suddenly held up his hands and grabbed it inches away from his face. "Wow!" he said, looking frightened and shaking his head in astonishment. The kids went nuts.

Ogle underhanded the ball gently to Mary Catherine. She one-handed it, then turned to survey the field. All the kids jumped up and down and punched their gloves. Little Peter Domenici was currently trailing the field, so she tossed the ball lightly up in the air and punched a pop fly to him. He didn't even have to move in order to catch it, but he dropped it anyway.

"We need to talk about a couple of things," she said.

"I'm all ears," Ogle said, pulling on his ears ridiculously. They were prominent ears at the best of times. A hard pitch from Peter Domenici was sailing directly toward his right temple and at the last minute he let go of his ear and clawed the ball out of the air. A moan of disappointment went up from the fielders.

"This whole thing is so vast that I don't know where to begin," she said. "I have so many questions."

"There's no way you can understand everything," Ogle said, tossing the ball to her. "That's my job. Why don't you just tell me your main concerns."

Mary Catherine knocked a difficult grounder out to one of her Tuscola cousins. "Whose idea was it to have Dad jog from the helicopter to the podium?"

Ogle squinted into the sun, thinking that one over. "I'd be hard put to remember who came up with that one first. But your dad enjoyed doing it. And I didn't try to discourage him."

"Do you think it's advisable, given his medical problems?"

"Well, he's been jogging three miles a day."

"Yeah, but wearing a suit, under all that stress, and in front of all those cameras—what if he had some kind of a problem? Even healthy people like Bush and Carter have had problems while jogging."

"Exactly," Ogle said "that's exactly why it works."

"What's that supposed to mean?"

"You know and I know, and your dad knows, that it's perfectly okay for him to run that short distance. My god, the man is like a human steam locomotive. But most people don't know that. All they know is that Cozzano is supposed to have been sick. They have developed this image of him as a frail, faltering invalid. When they see him jog across that football field, they see vivid evidence that this is a wrong impression, and they watch very carefully, because there's an element of danger."

"Could you run that last part by me again?" Mary Catherine said. She and Ogle had gotten into a smooth rhythm now, knocking hit after hit out to the little kids with their baseball gloves.

"The skydivers," he said. "We had three skydivers come in low over the podium and land on the grass. Now, why on earth did we do that?" Ogle sounded mystified.

"I don't know. Why did you?"

"Because everyone knows that sometimes skydivers break legs. They can't help watching. Same deal with those idiots who were setting off firecrackers."

"They worked for you?"

"Sure they did. Oh, those were just tiny little ladyfingers. You could set one off in the palm of your hand and you'd be fine. But it sure looked dangerous. So people watched. And that's why it was a great visual when your dad ran across the field."

Mary Catherine sighed. "I don't know how I feel about that."

Ogle shrugged. "Everyone's entitled to feelings."

"Speaking of that whole safety issue," she said, "when did the Secret Service start following Dad around? I didn't know he had a Secret Service detail."

"He doesn't," Ogle said. "Those were just actors."

She dropped the tip of the bat down onto home plate and stared at him. "What did you say?"

"They were actors dressed up like Secret Service."

"Hired by you."

"Of course."

She shook her head uncomprehendingly. "Why?"

"For the same reason that we built extra bleachers, and put extra microphones on the lectern."

"And what reason is that?"

"Being a third-party candidate has big, big advantages," Ogle said. "But it has some disadvantages too. One of the disadvantages, as Perot found out, is that people may not take you seriously. That is the single most dangerous thing we have to worry about. So at every step along the way, we need to surround your father with the visible trappings of presidentiality. Chief among those is the Secret Service detail."

Mary Catherine just shook her head. "I can't believe you," she said.

"Sometimes I can hardly believe myself," he said, turning to face her. A soft, arcing throw was headed toward Ogle from a five-year-old stationed on the pitcher's mound. Ogle deliberately took it in the back of the head and went into a staggering pantomime of a silly man with a mild concussion, wobbling around home plate, rolling his eyes, bouncing drunkenly off the backstop. The kids went completely out of their gourds and a couple of them actually fell down on the grass, tossing their gloves up in the air, screaming with uncontrollable laughter. Mary Catherine shook her head, smiling in spite of herself. She looked at the kids who were still strong enough to remain on their feet and twirled her finger around her ear.

"When you've recovered," she said, "I have one or two more things."

"I think I feel a little better now," Ogle said. "Shoot."

"I feel like I'm being set up as some kind of a surrogate wife. It's creepy."

"Yes, it is," Ogle said.

"It borders on the perverse. I'm not going to do it anymore."

"You don't have to," Ogle said. "The only reason it happened today was that this is a formal event, kind of like a wedding. In a wedding, you know, the father is supposed to give away the bride. But if the father of the bride is dead, or if he hit the road twenty years ago with some white trash floozy and a fifth of Jack and never was heard from again, then that place must be filled by some other individual—it doesn't matter who—anyone with a Y chromosome. Could be a brother, an uncle, even the bride's high-school basketball coach. It just don't matter. Well, a campaign announcement is the same deal except that normally the wife is there in her silly hat and her sensible shoes. You performed that role today; it's just that you happened to look a hell of a lot better."

"Thanks," she snapped, rolling her eyes.

"Now that the ceremony is over, you can go back to being who you are. No more creepy stuff at least until he gets inaugurated."

"One more thing."

"What's that?"

"I'm the campaign physician."

Ogle was a bit startled. "We already hired—"

"I'm the campaign physician."

"We need you for other—"

"I'm the campaign physician," she said.

This time it sunk in. Ogle shrugged and nodded. "You're obviously the best person for the job."

The direct hit to Ogle's head had put the little kid on the pitcher's mound over the five-hundred-point mark. Mary Catherine thought about starting another game, but her attention had been drawn by a great deal of cheering and hilarity from one of the other playing fields. She headed in that direction.

A football game was in progress. Two teams of at least fifteen players each had taken the field. The ex-Bears were evenly divided between those two teams. Cozzano was, of course, the quarterback of one team. The opposing quarterback wore two Super Bowl rings. The ages of the teams ranged from ten years old up to the early seventies. Some of the players were farmers and some ran major corporations. Mary Catherine recognized Kevin Tice, the founder of Pacific Netware, serving as a wide receiver; in person, he was bigger and more athletic than his nerdy image would lead one to believe. Zeldo was in the trenches on the defensive line, being blocked by none other than Hugh MacIntyre, CEO of MacIntyre Engineering, who must have been in his early sixties but looked as strong and healthy as Dad.

The game was an extremely loose and goofy affair, with players of both teams constantly circulating on and off the field to get refreshments or visit the portable toilets. It was too hot to play hard. Still, each team had a hard core of adult men with highly competitive natures, and as the game wore on, all the little kids and the dilettantes dropped out and left behind half a dozen or so guys on each side, playing football that verged on serious. They didn't have a formal timekeeper, but they did have a deadline: a formal reception was taking place later at the Cozzano residence and they all had to quit playing at six o'clock.

At the end, the game actually got exciting. Cozzano's team was down by three points with time left for only one play. They came out in shotgun formation; the ball was expertly snapped by a Nobel laureate from the University of Chicago and Cozzano dropped back to pass, faking repeatedly in the direction of a very tall retired Celtic who was running toward the end zone, waving his arms frantically. The defense shouted in unison "ONE MISSISSIPPI TWO MISSISSIPPI THREE MISSISSIPPI!" giving Cozzano a little bit of time, and then they attacked. Zeldo defeated the blocking efforts of Hugh MacIntyre, despite the fact that MacIntyre illegally held on to his belt and began to chase Cozzano around the backfield. Cozzano scrambled expertly and wildly, evading tackle after tackle; he was older and slower than Zeldo, but he was wearing shoes with rubber soles. Finally, Zeldo managed to bring Cozzano down near the forty-yard line, just as Cozzano launched a desperation pass known as a Hail Mary. To no one's surprise, the ex-Celtic grabbed the ball out of the air high over the outstretched hands of the defenders and then fell into the end zone, winning the game.

Mary Catherine applauded and cheered along with the rest of the crowd, then looked back up the field at her father and Zeldo. They were lying on the grass next to each other, propped up on their elbows, watching the action, laughing the deep, booming laughter of men completely out of their mind on a potent cocktail of dirt, football, male bonding, and testosterone.

## CHAPTER FORTY-ONE

Mary Catherine extricated herself from the reception around midnight and snuck upstairs to her room. Once inside, she stuck a bent paper clip into the keyhole of the old door hardware and shot the bolt, a skill she had picked up through long practice at the age of eight. Now that most of the techies and therapists had left, she had her room back the way it was supposed to be, with her old single bed with the handmade quilt on it, family pictures, her own little TV set on a table at the foot of the bed. She kicked her shoes off and stretched out full length on top of the old quilt. For the first time she realized how completely exhausted she was.

The red digits of the bedside clock flipped over to 12:00. A barrage of firecrackers went off all over town, ringing out the Fourth of July. "God forgive me for this," Mary Catherine said, reaching for the remote control on her bedside table, "but I have to see how this looked on TV."

It was the top story on CNN. And it looked fantastic. Mary Catherine had always known, vaguely, that things looked different on TV than they did in reality. But she didn't understand that well enough to predict how something would turn out on the small screen.

Ogle, obviously, had the knack. The rally had been impressive enough in person. But on television, you didn't see any of the boring, grungy stuff around the edges. All you saw was the good stuff. They covered the smoke divers. They showed most of Cozzano's run across the football field, and even a brief glimpse of a string of firecrackers being set off. The shower of confetti looked incredible.

And *she* looked incredible. She almost didn't recognize herself, but was embarrassed anyway. Could it be that she was destined to wear this sort of clothes?

The CNN report didn't last long. They hit all the high points of the rally, airing all of the shots that Ogle had handed them on a silver platter, and then tossed in a few shots of the picnic, including some great footage of Cozzano throwing the Hail Mary.

CNN moved on to other topics. Mary Catherine picked up the remote control again and wandered up and down the electromagnetic spectrum, catching glimpses of fishing shows, Home Shopping Network, Weather Channel, and *Star Trek* before finally locating C-SPAN, which was playing Dad's speech back in its entirety. For the first time, she got a chance to hear what he had being saying while she was looking around and chatting with all the little kids.

"About half a mile from here there's a factory that my father built, largely with his own capital and with the sweat of his brow, during the 1940s. The Army wouldn't let him fight—his mother had already lost one son to a German torpedo—but he was determined to get into the war one way or the other."

This was not true. He didn't build it with his own capital. The Meyers raised most of the money.

On the TV, Dad continued. "That factory made a new product known as nylon, which was an inexpensive replacement for silk— the main ingredient in parachutes. When the D day invasion was finally launched, my father couldn't be there. But the parachutes that he manufactured right here in Tuscola were strapped to the backs of every paratrooper who ventured into the skies of France on that fateful day."

He didn't make the chutes. Just the nylon fiber. The Army bought nylon from a whole bunch of suppliers.

"After V-E Day, a young man showed up in my father's factory one beautiful spring morning, asking to see Mr. Cozzano. Well, in a lot of places he would have gotten the brushoff from the receptionists and the PR people but in my father's company you could always go straight to the top. So in short order this man was ushered into John Cozzano's office. And when he finally came face-to-face with my father, this strapping young lad became positively choked up with emotion and couldn't bring himself to speak for a few moments. And he explained that he was a paratrooper who had been in the very spearhead of the D day invasion. A hundred men had parachuted down from his unit and a hundred of them landed safely and took their objective with a minimum loss of life. Well, it seemed that these troopers had noticed the Cozzano label printed onto their chutes and decided that they liked that name and they had begun to call themselves the Cozzano gang. That became their rallying cry when they would jump out of the airplane. And at that point, my dad, who never shed tears in my presence in his entire life, well, he just burst out crying, you see, because that meant more to him than any of the money or anything else that he had gotten out of his factory—"

The TV set went dark. Mary Catherine was sitting up in bed, holding the remote control, aiming it at the screen like a gun. She was frozen in place.

The man she had been watching on the TV set wasn't her dad. Everything he'd just said was an out-and-out fabrication. And Dad would never tell a lie. It wasn't her father. Mel was right.

A familiar feeling came back. It was the clammy fear that had gripped her on the night of her father's first stroke. For weeks she had thought it would never go away. Then it had begun to relax its hold over her mind and her heart, and as Dad had recovered after the operation, it had gone away completely. She had thought that she and her family were out of the woods.

She'd been wrong. They weren't out of the woods. They had just walked through a little clearing. Now she found herself in the heart of a deeper and vaster forest than she'd ever imagined.

The party noise downstairs had faded to a low murmur. She could hear a new sound from the next room. James's old room. It was the sound of fingers whacking a keyboard with the speed and power of a drumroll.

Zeldo was sitting at his workstation. He had turned off the lights and inverted the screen so that it was showing white letters on a black background. He had a huge high-resolution monitor with at least a dozen windows open on it, each one filled with long snaking lines of text that Mary Catherine recognized, vaguely, as computer code.

"Hi," she said, and he almost jumped out of his skin. "Sorry to startle you."

"That's okay," Zeldo said, taking a deep breath and spinning his chair around to face her. "Too much Jolt. You can turn on a light if you want."

"It's okay," she said. She grabbed another swivel chair and sat down.

"Thanks. I'm running in blackout mode here," Zeldo said, "been on this damn machine too long and my eyes won't focus anymore."

"What's going on?" she said. She had to assume, from what Mel had told her, that they were probably being listened to right now. For that matter, Zeldo himself was presumably part of the Network, though he seemed like a nice enough guy. And today, in the football game, she had seen a side of Zeldo that he didn't normally show. She could tell that, whatever devious schemes Zeldo might be involved in, he genuinely liked William A. Cozzano.

"We've had interference problems when your father goes near microwave relay stations," Zeldo said. "We're going to keep him away from those things, maybe work up some kind of a hat with EM shielding in it."

"But TV trucks use microwaves, don't they?"

"Exactly. And he spends a lot of time around TV trucks. So as a last line of defense, I'm building some safeguards into the software so that when the chip starts getting stray signals, it'll be smart enough to realize that there's a problem."

"Then what?"

"It'll go into Helen Keller mode until the interference goes away."

"What happens then? Dad goes into a coma?"

"Not at all," Zeldo said. "The chip will keep doing what it's supposed to do, filling in for the damaged parts of his brain. It's just that it won't be able to send or receive data anymore."

"That's not an important function anyway, is it?" Mary Catherine said. "You only send signals into his brain when you are fixing a bug in the software. Right?"

There was a long pause, and Mary Catherine wished that she had turned on the room lights. She suspected that she might be able to read some interesting things on Zeldo's face right now.

"As we mentioned before the implant," Zeldo finally said, "the biochips do more than just restore his normal capabilities."

This struck Mary Catherine as evasive. "You hackers aren't very good at playing these kinds of games, are you?" she said.

"No comment," Zeldo said. "I didn't spend half my life learning what I know so that I could get tangled up in politics."

The snappy technical patter had been replaced by a completely different sort of conversation. Both of them were now speaking elliptically with long pauses between sentences. Suddenly, Mary Catherine realized why: both of them knew that they were being listened to. Both of them had things to hide.

She had said something to Mel earlier in the day: Zeldo was in the Network but not of the Network. His fear of speaking freely in the bugged room was confirmation.

"As Ogle may have told you, I'm the campaign physician," she said.

"Yes," Zeldo said. "Congratulations. It's going to be a grind."

"Nothing like residency, I'm sure," Mary Catherine said.

"Because of . . . because of these pesky bugs and glitches," Zeldo said, framing the words carefully, "I've been assigned to travel with the campaign, at least for a while. So let me know if there's anything I can do to help you out."

"For starters you could tell me exactly what happens when he goes near a microwave relay station."

Zeldo answered without hesitation. Now that they had gotten away from dangerous topics he had relaxed again. "He has a seizure."

"That's all?"

"Well . . . before that there are other symptoms. Disorientation. A flood of memories and sensations."

"When these memories and sensations enter his mind, can he tell that they are just hallucinations from the chip?"

This question made Zeldo pause for a long time.

"You shouldn't grind your teeth. Bad for the enamel," Mary Catherine said, after at least sixty seconds had gone by.

"That's a profound question," Zeldo said. "It gets us into some heavy philosophical shit: if everything we think and feel is just a pattern of signals in our brain, then is there an objective reality? If the signals in Argus's brain happen to include radio transmissions, then does that mean that reality is a different thing for him?"

Mary Catherine held her tongue, for once, and did not ask why Zeldo was referring to her father as Argus. It was most definitely a slip of the tongue, a glimpse into something that Mary Catherine hadn't been allowed to see yet. If she got inquisitive, Zeldo would just clam up again.

Another, more interesting, possibility occurred to her: maybe Zeldo had slipped the word in deliberately.

"And if so," Zeldo continued, "who are we to say that one form of reality is preferable to another form?"

"Well, if he says things that simply aren't true, and seems to believe them, I would say that that was a problem," Mary Catherine said.

"Memory is a funny thing," Zeldo said. "None of our memories are really accurate to begin with. So if he's got a memory that works a little differently from ours, and is otherwise healthy and happy, is that better than being aphasic in a wheelchair? Who's to say?"

"I guess it's up to Dad," Mary Catherine said.

*Clearly she had* to find the GODS envelope. The events of the day had convinced her beyond doubt that Mel was right: there was a Network, and it was up to something. Mary Catherine went back to her room, changed out of her daughter costume, put on a bathrobe, and walked downstairs. The caterers were at work in the kitchen, cleaning up the aftermath of the party; all of the guests had gone home except for a few old Vietnam buddies of Cozzano's, who sat around the coffee table in the living room having a few drinks and reminiscing about the war, alternately laughing and crying.

404

Mary Catherine avoided them and went out onto the back porch. A row of black plastic garbage bags were lined up against the wall, waiting to be collected. She opened one of the bags, sorted through a few loose pieces of paper, and found the brightly colored envelope, still intact except for the broken seal. The mailing label was a bewildering panoply of numbers, code words, and bar codes: the inscrutable mutterings of the Network. Mary Catherine folded the envelope, stuffed it into her bathrobe, closed up the burn bag, and called it a day.

Floyd Wayne Vishniak
R.R. 6 Box 895
Davenport, Iowa


Aaron Green
Ogle Data Research
Pentagon Towers
Arlington, Virginia


Dear Mr. Green:
Just for starters, I figured out your game that you are playing. When you came here you gave me some shit about working for that Ogle Data Research. Like you were some scientist writing a dissertation. But now I have figured out what you really are: you are working for William A. Cozzano. He must be paying you money to work on his campaign.

How did I figure it out? By just noticing what things you put on the little TV set on my wrist. You always show Cozzano but you don't show the other candidates as much.

Well, I watched Cozzano announcing that he would run for president this afternoon. I did not watch it on the little wrist-watch. I went down to Dale's, which is a bar, and watched it on the big-screen TV there with some other guys. And I can tell you for your information that just about all the guys who were in that place thought it was real impressive.

I thought it was impressive too. But now it is two

o'clock A.M. and I can not get to sleep. Because I am thinking about some of the things that Cozzano said and it troubles me.

When he was in that debate in Decatur, Illinois, he spoke about his dad's parachute factory and how important it was to the men on D day standing in the open door of the plane. But today, he told a whole story about a bunch of paratroopers and how one of them came to personally thank his dad. This is a strange discrepancy, don't you think?

My opinion: something got scrambled up inside Cozzano's head when he had those troubles. And now, either he has memory troubles or else he can't tell right from wrong. So don't expect me to vote for him.

You will be hearing again from me soon, I am sure.

Sincerely, Floyd Wayne Vishniak

CHAPTER FORTY-TWO

Mel Meyer drove into Miami, Oklahoma, in his black Mercedes 500    SL at 4:30 on a hot mid-July afternoon. The sky was a sickening, yellowing white. He stopped at the Texaco station to fill up with gas and check his oil. He checked his oil religiously—though the car used none to speak of—because thirty years ago the Cozzanos had made fun of him for not knowing how.

He also needed to ask for directions. As he opened the window to talk to the attendant, the 103-degree heat poured in on him like boiling water. He ordered ultrapremium from the Texaco pump and popped the hood for the oil check. "How far to Cacher," he asked the grease-streaked, acne-ridden kid smearing his windshield with an equally appetizing-looking rag.

The kid had never seen anything like Mel Meyer—dapper, intense, clad in a perfect black silk suit—nor had he seen many 500 SLs. "Why d'ya wanna go to Cacher? Nobody lives in Cacher except some crazy old farts," he said. He went to the front of the car, could not figure out how to raise the hood, looked pleadingly at Mel.

Mel did not like the kid, did not like Miami, Oklahoma, and would have given anything to avoid being there. But this was the closest thing to a lead he had come across in four months of investigating the Network. He could have hired a private investigator in Tulsa or Little Rock and had him drive out to the place and look around. But he knew that, whatever this Network might be, it was good at hiding itself. A private investigator, who made his living watching unsubtle people commit marital infidelities in cheap motels, could not be trusted to pick up the nearly invisible spoor of the Network. In the end Mel would have to come out and look around himself. He might as well get it over with.

"Why do you think people in Cacher are crazy?" Mel asked, thinking to himself that he had no right to ask that question, sitting in a black silk suit in a black car in July in Oklahoma.

He had found precious little in absolute terms as he chased down lead after lead: the institutional roots of the Radhakrishnan Institute; the fascinating pattern of stock trades surrounding the takeover of Ogle Data Research and Green Biophysical Systems in March; the interlocking directorates of Gale Aerospace, MacIntyre Engineering, Pacific Netware, and the Coover Fund; and the even more shadowy group of very private investment funds that held majority shares in them.

He had even placed intercepts on the lines and numbers of various people, hiring monitors placed in vans near microwave relay towers. Nothing had come up. He had gone through financial reports, he had gone to friends in the FBI, he had tried everything, but he could not find the Network. He had hired private detectives, he had hired investigative accountants. He had spent a whole month pulling strings and working various connections in order to get his hands on some IRS data that he thought would be promising. It had turned out to be worthless.

The one lead that he had was the GODS envelope that Mary Catherine had pulled from the Cozzanos' burn bag on the night of July fourth. Mary Catherine was the one to blame for his being here.

The envelope did not bear anything as obvious as a return address. It had code numbers instead. GODS was a well-run company,
highly centralized, and was not interested in helping Mel decipher
those codes. He had provided some financial aid to a financially
troubled GODS delivery man in Chicago and eventually gotten the
information that the envelope appeared to have been routed
through the Joplin Regional Airport in extreme southwest Missouri,
near where that state came together with Kansas and Oklahoma.

Mel had spent four days living at a Super 8 Motel on Airport
Drive outside of Joplin. He claimed to be a businessman from Saint
Louis, working on a big project of some kind. He spent several
hundred dollars express-mailing empty packages to an address in
Saint Louis, and quickly became a familiar sight to the three people
who worked at the Joplin GODS depot.

One of them had informed Mel that he was now their biggest
customer. Mel pursued this line of conversation doggedly and got
the man to say that they had another fellow across the border in
Oklahoma who mailed almost as much as Mel did. Finally, yesterday afternoon, Mel had gotten them to specify a town: Cacher,
Oklahoma.

He snapped back to the steamy reality of Miami. The gas station
kid was peering at him. "You okay, mister?"

"Yeah. How's the oil?"

"Fine." Then, continuing to pursue his endemic insanity theory,
he said, "It's the lead."

"Lead?"

"Yeah. Even though the lead mines are shut down, Cacher is
soaked through with lead pollution, and like we learned in school,
that will make you crazy."

Mel muttered genially, as if this information were fascinating,
and handed over his credit card. The kid took it into the battered
old station and swiped it through the electronic slot. Their building
didn't look like much but they had the latest point-of-purchase
electronics.

"You got something else, buddy?" asked the kid with a satisfied
leer on his face, waggling the card in the air. "You've got to pay your
bills from time to time, you know . . . just kiddin'."

Mel was too surprised to be embarrassed. He compulsively paid every bill within twenty-four hours of receipt, especially the national ones. You didn't let bills get overdue. Unlike the people who ran Washington, Mel understood that an overdue bill was a club that other people could wave over your head.

"It's a mistake," he said, "but why don't you try this one." He handed the kid another credit card. Once again, it was rejected.

"Shit buddy, don't you ever pay your bills? What about cash?"

Mel looked in his wallet. It contained several hundred-dollar bills, a ten, and a five. The bill was $16.34.

"Can you break a hundred?" Mel asked, already feeling he knew the answer.

The kid yukked it up for a little bit. "I can't remember the last time I saw a C-note. We never got more than a few bucks in change."

Down the street, set anachronistically into the sandstone facade of an old bank, was an ATM machine with a familiar logo. Mel took off his jacket, ambled slowly down the street, trying not to get hotter than he was, and stuck his bank card into the slot.

The video screen said PLEASE WAIT.

An alarm bell began ringing on the side of the bank.

A siren began to sound from the direction of the police station in downtown Miami, two blocks away.

Mel lurched back down the street, got to the car, and turned on the ignition.

"Hold it right there, hot shot," said the kid. Mel looked over and was astounded to see a twelve-gauge pump shotgun cradled in the kid's hands. "You might as well wait for Harold to come."

The Miami P.D. patrol car, an aging Caprice, swung around the corner. Mel knew that he could easily outrun it. But it wouldn't be a good idea. Instead he shut off the ignition, and, as a good faith gesture, took the keys out of the ignition and tossed them up on the dashboard, in plain sight. He rolled the window back down and put both hands on the steering wheel.

A lean, small, pox-faced cop emerged reluctantly from the Caprice, winced from the heat, and walked over toward Mel, moving with exaggerated slowness.

"Harold, I presume," Mel said, when he got close enough.

"What we got here li'l buddy?" Harold said to the kid.

"Looks like it's credit card fraud to me," said the kid.

"Come on out of there fellow," said Harold, shooting a mean, judgmental look at Mel. "Don't make a bad thing worse for you."

Mel was pissed off, hopelessly out of any chance to control things. He eased out of the car, frustrated, frightened, feeling helpless for the first time in years, and said, "I don't know what the hell has happened."

"Nothing yet, and nothing will, unless you do something stupid."

"All I want is to pay for my gas and go to Cacher."

Harold looked at the kid and said, "Why in the name of God would anybody want to go to Cacher?" Mel knew what was coming next; Harold said it anyway. "Ain't nobody there, but a bunch of loony-tunes."

Mel said, "Let me talk to you straight." He had spent enough time downstate to know that this attitude might be appreciated. "I'm not trying to pull a fast one, and I don't know why none of my cards don't work. Look, take the AMEX, call the eight hundred number and you'll see I've got a huge line of credit, and Texaco's been all paid up, and I don't know why the ATM went crazy."

Harold looked at him and then at the kid. "He broke any laws?"

"Not exactly."

"Fella, you look decent enough. Let's go rescue your bank card and send you on your way out of town."

They strolled down to the bank, which had closed at three o'clock. Harold banged on the front door, and a Big Hair Girl peered out the door.

"Honey, your machine's done eaten this man's card. Think you could dig it out so's he could leave to go to"—and here Harold could not keep a straight face—"Cacher."

"Cacher," she shrieked, "who the hell would want to go there?" Mel by this time had heard all he wanted to about the deficiencies of Cacher and simply said, "I've got some relatives out there."

Honey retreated into the bank, opened up the machine from the back side, and retrieved Mel's card. "Before I can let you have this, mister, I got to make sure you're who you say you are," she said. She sat down at a desk, called Chicago, asked a few questions, whistled, shook her head in wonderment.

"Buddy," she said, handing the card over, "I'm going to treat you with a lot more respect. You're one rich sucker."

Mel relaxed, realizing for the first time that he was probably going to get out of Miami alive. "Could I get change for a hundred so I can pay off boy wonder over at the Texaco?"

Harold didn't like that. "Now slick, you just be careful. That's my nephew over there, and you bad-mouth any of my kin, you might be spending a night in jail."

Mel fumed at his own stupidity, considered a number of replies, and decided to shut up.

Honey gave him his change. Mel thanked her and resolved to get out of Miami as quickly as he could, saying as little as possible. He handed boy wonder a twenty.

"Seriously mister," the kid said, getting Mel's change, "take care of yourself. We had people go out there and not come back. Those shafts go down a couple of miles, and those crazy people are not accountable."

Mel got back in the Mercedes and drove carefully out of town, accompanied by Harold and his radar gun. That's all I need, he thought, to fall into one of Harold's speed traps. As soon as he got out of radar range, he turned the car toward Cacher and put the hammer down.

As he drove, the vegetation thinned away and vanished, and the rolling hills took on a steep, foreboding quality. The road itself was potholed asphalt that shook the Mercedes' frame. In the distance he could see the malevolent tips of the mine tailings, looking much like the Welsh coal tips that periodically unloaded and covered small villages in sad valleys. There were no farms, no ranches, only ancient weather-beaten abandoned shacks, a legacy of the thirties. Running along the road was a single telephone line. There was no evidence of electricity. On the road was regional roadkill: armadillos, 'possums, the occasional dead cat. As the evening approached, the whole scene made Mel want to turn around and go back home.

And as he approached the scattered buildings of the town, he did

just that. He stopped half a mile short of Cacher, turned directly
north onto a section line road, and drove north at a hundred miles
an hour, turning up a roostertail of yellowish lead-saturated dust.
Mel prided himself on being a rational man. Usually that meant
controlling his fear. Today it meant giving into it.

The faster he drove, the more frightened he became, and as the
crossroads flashed by every six miles, he did not look either way. He
was convinced that he was being pursued, and not until he crossed
the Kansas line did he begin to slow down. His heart was pounding
dangerously and his forehead was stiff from sweat, which poured
out of his body and was dried to a crust by the air conditioner
running full blast.

*Cacher was made* up of an old two-story brick school tilted at a
precipitous angle, undermined by a mine shaft that went too close,
or a water table that was drained. There was no sign of life, no dogs,
no cats, no lights. Gas stations were boarded up. The only inhabited
building was a shabby general store, the paint long since blistered
away from its rough, knotty wooden siding. In front was a set of
thirties-style, manually powered gas pumps, and, as an afterthought,
a U.S. post office zip code sign bearing the WE DELIVER FOR YOU
emblem.

Inside the store, it was as dry and hot as a sauna. The heat
strengthened the smell of stale urine that emanated from Otho
Simpson, who was sitting in an old wooden swivel rocker with the
canes busted out. His son, Otis, was standing by the entrance holding a small 9 mm automatic weapon with a long clip. It was a crude
and awkward device, almost as clumsy as Otis himself, but he had
gotten good at using it. He would take it out among the mine
tailings and fire clip after clip, lead thudding into lead. No one was
around to complain about the noise.

If Mel Meyer had pulled into Cacher, the gun would have turned
his Mercedes into scrap metal in seconds. Otis would have pushed
the car down a mine shaft. It would have fallen a mile or two into
the earth and never been seen again.

"Looks like the little Jew got scared," Otis said. "Got some sense
in his head. Won't have much more trouble with him."

Otho said nothing. A couple of decades ago he would have sighed hopelessly at the racial slur, but he had long since reconciled himself to the fact that his son was a product of his environment and would never be as cosmopolitan as Otho was, with his fancy education at the Lady Wilburdon School for Mathematical Geniuses on the Isle of Rhum. "He's good," Otho said. "He's gotten closer to us than anyone."

Otho was shaken. No one had ever come to Cacher before. The very fact that Otis had been placed in this position—standing in the door of the old general store with a machine gun, locked and loaded —was disastrous. If the Network knew that they had been reduced to such methods, they would probably be cut off, and Otho's responsibilities transferred to someone else. Otho knew that there were others—like Mr. Salvador—waiting to take his place as soon as he slipped up.

"Should we kill him?" Otis said. It was a painfully stupid question, but it was good that Otis had come out and asked it. Otis had spent an unhealthy amount of time watching spy movies and thrillers on HBO. Since he had become aware of the nature of the current undertaking, he had let his imagination run away with him, thinking that they were in the middle of some asinine James Bond movie.

"That's not what this is about," Otho said. "This is not violence, son. It's not war. It's not espionage. The whole point here is to get this country back to basics: contracts, markets, keeping your promises, meeting your responsibilities. Meyer's an honorable man and if we killed him we'd cut the ground out from under our feet." Otho paused for a moment and stared through a dusty windowpane. "If we were killers, I'd kill Mr. Salvador."

"How come?" Otis said, astonished. "I thought he was doing a real good job."

"If he was doing a real good job," Otho said, "Mel Meyer never would have come here. He wouldn't even have known that anything was going on."

## CHAPTER FORTY-THREE

William A. Cozzano's National Town Meeting, which took place in Chicago in August, was the equivalent of a political convention. But because it was a pure media event, with no procedural nonsense to gum up the works, it was a lot more entertaining.

The opening event was held in Grant Park, a green swath that ran between the towering center of downtown Chicago and the lake. At the cost of permanently alienating the animal-rights and anticombustion constituencies, Cozzano's campaign managers had set up a huge Sunday evening barbecue. The ten thousand participants in the town meeting had been streaming into Chicago all weekend, checking into the big downtown hotels and getting themselves settled in the rooms where they would spend the next week. The Grant Park barbecue was an informal way for everyone to get together and goof around before the scheduled events got underway at the convention center on Monday morning.

From the balcony of her hotel suite along Congress Plaza overlooking the heart of Grant Park, Mary Catherine could see the barbecue developing through most of the day. Around five P.M., when the afternoon heat was starting to subside, the smoke rising up from all of those barbecue pits began to look appetizing, and so she put on a sundress. It was rather prim by the standards of an urban beach on a hot summer day, but racy by the standards of candidates' wives and daughters. Furthermore, it was light and loose enough that she could play softball in it, though sliding into base would be out of the question. Since her display of place-hitting acumen in Tuscola on the Fourth of July, being spunky and athletic had become part of her job description.

She took the elevator down to the street and strolled through the park. Mary Catherine could now stroll anywhere in Chicago, wearing any clothing she wanted, at any time of the day or night, because she was always followed by Secret Service agents. She had decided that armed guards were a great thing and that every girl should have a few.

The barbecue couldn't just be a plain old barbecue. It had to be built around some kind of a central media concept. In this case, the concept was that all of the various regions of the United States were competing to see where the best barbecuing was done. Mary Catherine strolled among the smoking beef pits, from Texas, North Carolina, Kansas City, and decided that, beyond providing her with a quick take-out dinner, comparative barbecue was not very interesting to her.

Flocks of black birds, just like the ones Mel had raved about, swirled around the grassy areas scavenging the ends of french fries. One of Dad's favorite sixties rock bands was playing in the bandshell to the north, but she found their songs just one step above Muzak. To the south, on Hutchinson Field, a number of impromptu games were underway: touch football, frisbee, softball, volleyball. She didn't feel like getting sweaty just yet, and stayed close to the footpaths, which were lined with double rows of shade trees.

Across Lakeshore Drive, along the border of the yacht basin, things were much quieter and several degrees cooler. The basin was dotted with numbered white-and-blue buoys where recreational boats could tie up. There was no beach here, just a stone seawall with one or two depressed platforms where boats could take on or discharge passengers. A couple of big tour boats were circulating between these sites and the open lake, taking people on free rides so that they could appreciate the splendor of the Loop as seen from Lake Michigan. That looked cool and relaxing, so Mary Catherine climbed on board one of the boats, sat down in a deck chair, and took her freshly barbecued hamburger out of its wrapper. She and her Secret Service agents were the last persons to cross the gangplank; within a few moments the boat was motoring out through a broad avenue between the white buoys, headed for a gap in the breakwater.

As she was polishing off the last of her hamburger, a woman separated herself from the crowd of people standing along the railing of the boat and approached her. She was black, nicely dressed, probably in her forties but capable of looking younger. She moved with unusual confidence through the loose picket fence of Secret Service agents, giving each of the guards a knowing smile and a nod. She had a nice face and a nice smile. "Hello," she said, gesturing to an empty deck chair next to Mary Catherine. "Is this taken?"

"Go ahead," Mary Catherine said. "You're not from around here, are you?"

The woman laughed. "Eleanor Richmond. It's nice to meet you, Ms. Cozzano," she said, extending her hand.

"Nice to meet you," Mary Catherine said, shaking it. "I'm sorry I didn't recognize you right away—I've seen you several times on TV."

"Several times. Well, you are one attentive TV watcher. I haven't been on that many times."

"I watch Dr. Lawrence's program pretty regularly," Mary Catherine said, "and he seems to like you."

"He hates me," Eleanor said, "but I do wonders for his ratings. And, I suspect, for his fantasy life."

"I was so sorry to hear about Senator Marshall," Mary Catherine said.

"Thank you," Eleanor said graciously.

*Caleb Roosevelt Marshall* had gone back to his ranch in southeastern Colorado "to clear some brush" in the third week of July. The doctors, aides, and bodyguards who traveled with him all the time had arisen early one morning to find his bed empty. Eventually they had found him on the top of a mesa. He had ridden up there before dawn, watched the sun rise over the prairie, and then blown his heart out with a double-barrelled shotgun.

He left letters addressed to several people: his staff, various senate colleagues, old friends, old enemies, and the President. Most of the contents of these letters were never revealed, partly because they were private and partly because many of them were unprintable. The President read his letter—two lines scrawled over a piece of senate stationery—threw it into the fire, and ordered a double Scotch from the White House bar.

Eleanor's note said, "You know what to do—Caleb. P.S. Watch your back."

They flew his body back to the Rotunda, where it lay in state for twenty-four hours, and then they flew him back to Colorado, where he was cremated and his ashes spread over his ranch. As per Marshall's written instructions, Eleanor ran the office for the next two weeks, while the Governor of Colorado debated whom to appoint to replace Marshall.

He ended up appointing himself. The polls indicated that many Coloradans took a dim view of this, seeing it as naked opportunism. But his first official act was to fire Eleanor Richmond. That announcement sent his approval rating sky-high.

"*I hope you* get a good job," Mary Catherine said, "you deserve one."

"Thanks," Eleanor said. "I've had some feelers. Don't worry about me."

"You know, as a person who was raised Catholic, I have to take a dim view of suicide," Mary Catherine said, "but I think that what the Senator did was incredibly noble. It's hard to imagine any Washington person having that much backbone."

Eleanor smiled. "Caleb felt the same way. And apparently he said so in some of the notes he left behind."

Mary Catherine threw back her head and laughed. "Are you kidding? He taunted people—"

"—for not having the guts to commit suicide," Eleanor said, "which would be the only decent way out for some people in D.C."

"Are you here as an observer," Mary Catherine said, "or are you a participant?"

"This whole thing is so slick I'm not sure there's a difference," Eleanor said.

"I hear you," Mary Catherine said.

"But to answer your question, I was invited here for the debate."

"Debate?"

"Yes. Thursday night. After *The Simpsons* and before *L.A. Law*. All of the potential running mates are going to fight it out."

"He's considering you as a running mate?" Mary Catherine asked. She was embarrassed to have been so surprised. Eleanor was looking at her knowingly and indulgently. "I mean, don't get me wrong, you'd be great," Mary Catherine said. "You'd be fantastic. But I hadn't heard any of this."

"Honey, remember how this works," Eleanor said. "Neither your dad nor any other candidate is going to pick a black woman as a running mate anytime soon—and if they did, they'd never pick me. But he does get some brownie points—as it were—for putting one in the final four. And that's why I'm invited."

"Well, I'll definitely look forward to the debate."

"How about you? What's your role in all this?" Eleanor said, sweeping her hand across the smoking panorama of the barbecue.

Mary Catherine looked at the view and considered this question. She knew now why she had chosen to go on the boat ride: to get away, to stand back from things, to look at her life from a distance. The same impulse had probably struck most of the people on the boat. This conversation with Eleanor was just what she had been looking for.

She trusted Eleanor instinctively and wanted to tell her the truth: that something was wrong with her father. That during the last couple of months she had watched his every move, listened to his every utterance, used every scrap of her neurological training to piece together the puzzle of what was happening inside his brain. That she was spending a couple of hours a day with him in intensive, private therapy, trying to bring him back. And that the further she got into this thing, the lonelier she got, the more scared she became.

But she couldn't quite say that yet. So she had to play the airhead. "Who the hell knows?" she said.

Eleanor put one hand over her mouth, in a gesture that was incongruous and cute in a tough middle-aged woman, and laughed.

Mary Catherine continued, "My role is to be pretty, but not too pretty; smart, but not too; athletic, but not too. I think what they really wanted was a nice college girl. You know, the kind of girl who could go to college campuses in jeans and a sweater and sit cross-legged on the floor in dorm lounges and rap with her peers. They got a neurologist instead. And there's only so many AIDS babies I can kiss before that gets kind of old. So my life is on hold for a while until things settle down."

"Well, we all go through transitions," Eleanor said. "This sort of thing—a big campaign—is a kind of upheaval that can be useful."

"Useful how?"

"It shakes everything up. Everything's in flux for a moment, you have the chance to go off in new directions, fix old problems in your life. Believe me on this."

Mary Catherine smiled. "I believe you," she said.

*Ever since the* beginning of William A. Cozzano's National Town Meeting, the high-tech wristwatch strapped to Floyd Wayne Vishniak's arm had been flaring into action several times a day, confronting him with live coverage of the events that were taking place only a couple of hundred miles away. He welcomed the free entertainment, which took his mind off the stupid work he was doing.

He had lived for quite some time now on a meager unemployment check, and had long since given up trying to find himself a job. But now, Floyd Wayne Vishniak, by virtue of the PIPER watch on his arm, had become, in effect, a personal adviser to Governor Cozzano. It was a weighty responsibility. He was not going to sit around in his trailer drinking beer and acting like some kind of a buffoon. He was going to educate himself. He was going to start paying attention to the presidential campaign and learn about all of the candidates and the issues.

A week or two after he had first donned the PIPER watch, back in June, Vishniak had been in downtown Davenport to take care of a bit of business, and he had seen a cluster of newspaper machines on a street corner. In addition to the Quad Cities paper and *The Des Moines Register*, these included the *Chicago Tribune, USA Today, The New York Times,* and *The Wall Street Journal.* As it happened, his pockets were heavy with quarters, and so he bought a copy of each, blowing two and a half dollars. He took them all back to his trailer and read them. There was some interesting stuff in there.

Since then it had become a habit. Two and a half bucks a day, six days a week, added up to fifteen bucks, plus an additional five bucks on Sunday made twenty bucks a week. Eighty dollars a month. On Floyd Wayne Vishniak's budget it was a lot of money. He had cut back on his beer consumption, and, as the summer wore on and the tassels began to sprout from the corn, he had taken a job detasseling.

Detasseling was a common practice in Iowa; it was the mass

castration of corn plants by the forcible removal of their tassels. The actual yanking was done by hand, by individual detasselers walking up and down the rows, endlessly, beneath the hot August sun.

Floyd Wayne Vishniak would drive out to the fields early each morning to put in a couple of hours before the sun became hot, go back into Davenport to feed rolls of quarters into the newspaper machines, read the papers and drink Mountain Dew all day, then drive back out to the fields in the cool of the evening to continue his work. For the first couple of weeks of the detasseling season, the evening shift had been rather dull, but things perked up when Cozzano's National Town Meeting finally got started, and he began to get coverage two or three hours a night.

The Town Meeting had seemed a little bit hokey when they announced it, but in practice it turned out to be damn impressive. Some very important people were showing up at this thing. They had a couple of so-called surprise appearances every evening, as movie stars, ex-football heroes, captains of industry, and even a few renegade politicians began to show up at the Meeting and throw their support behind Cozzano.

By the third or fourth evening, a clear pattern emerged in the coverage. At seven P.M. the PIPER watch would come on, with the familiar logo and theme music. For fifteen minutes or so it would show an edited broadcast of that day's events at McCormick Place, Chicago's huge lakeside convention center, the site of the National Town Meeting. Then there would be fifteen minutes of analysis from a team of pundits, some pro-Cozzano, some anti-. Then half an hour of taped stuff, like a speech by Cozzano from earlier in the day. Then the program would cut to a hotel suite somewhere, a living-room-type environment, and Cozzano would sit down with various groups of Americans who wanted to bitch about their problems: unemployment, lack of health insurance, shitty public schools, and so on. Cozzano would sit there and listen to them ventilate, jot down the occasional note, ask the occasional question, and then he would usually deliver some kind of a little sermon that was intended to calm them down and make them believe that he cared about their problems and would certainly do something about them at the White House.

The PIPER watch beamed out these little images as he made his way across a vast flat cornfield, completely alone, the only thing moving within several miles. His hands bobbed up and down rhythmically as he shuffled down the mile-long rows, reaching out with both arms to grip and yank the tassels, and when something especially interesting came on the screen—a surprise appearance by a major star, for example—he would stop for a minute and stand motionless, staring at his wrist. At the beginning of these evening shifts, the images on the little screen were pale and washed-out, but as he inched his way across the field, and the sun sank into the flat horizon, the light from the watch became brighter, its colors purer, until finally the moon and the stars came out and Vishniak was groping his way across the field in darkness, the images of the National Town Meeting radiating in pure intense colors as though the wristwatch were a bracelet of rubies, emeralds, and sapphires.

*Tonight, Governor Cozzano* was meeting with a group of black persons who had organized themselves out of the undifferentiated mass of Americans gathered together for the National Town Meeting. They had got together and formed their own little organization which had then promptly splintered into little groups who all hated each other. Now, the leaders of all the little factions were meeting with Governor Cozzano over a nice dinner in his hotel suite. They were eating tiny little miniature chickens and drinking wine.

One of the black people was using an analogy to explain why black people were not becoming successful executives in large enough numbers. In the game of football, he pointed out, black people were often valued as wide receivers and running backs, but coaches were resistant to making them quarterbacks. Governor William A. Cozzano listened to this analogy soberly and thoughtfully, chewing on a morsel of the miniature chicken and nodding his head from time to time, never taking his gaze off the face of the man who was speaking. When the man was done, Cozzano sat back in his chair, took a sip of wine, and went on a little stroll down memory lane.

"You know, that business about quarterbacks really hits home to me. I can remember back in about 1963 when I was on the Illinois team, and we traveled to Iowa City to play a game against the

Hawkeyes. They had a starting quarterback and two others on the bench, all of them white, and they also had a few black players recruited from across the river, here in Illinois. In particular they had a young man named Lucullus Campbell, who had been the starting quarterback for his high-school team in Quincy, Illinois, a river town. He had been splendid in that role—an incredible passer who could also run the ball. Well, before the game even started, the Hawkeyes' starting quarterback was out with the stomach flu. They started their second-string quarterback, and sometime in the second quarter of the game, he took a very serious hit and went down with a knee injury that knocked him out of the game. And so they put in their third-string quarterback.

"And let me tell you, that young man—with all due respect to him—was just no good as a quarterback. He dropped the ball. He threw interceptions. He tried to hand off the ball to people who weren't even there." Cozzano paused for a moment and dabbed at his mouth with his napkin while the people around the table laughed. "Now, I was an offensive player, and so, when their offense was on the field—while this poor fellow was making all of these mistakes—I was on the sidelines, looking straight across the field at poor Lucullus Campbell. He was watching this third-string quarterback in disbelief. I could clearly read the frustration on his face. Finally he got up and approached the coach and spoke to him. I couldn't hear his words, but I knew what he was saying. It's a universal plea: 'Put me in, Coach. I can do it.' And you know what? That coach didn't even look up at him. He wouldn't look Lucullus Campbell in the eye. He just shook his head no and kept going through his clipboard. And I remember thinking that that was just about the most unfair thing I had ever seen. I went up to him after the game and I told him so, and I'd like to think that he took a bit of comfort in my words." Cozzano had delivered the first part of this story with kind of a wry humorous tone, then turned sad. But at this point he became angry at the memory, sat up straight in his chair, and began pounding his index finger into the dinner table. His guests sat riveted. Cozzano, pissed off, was a formidable presence. "Ever since that day, I have found it heartrending to see talented, ambitious black people, willing and able to compete in whatever field, held back by tired old white men who don't want to give them a chance. And I vow to you that I will never become one of those tired old white men—and I won't allow any of them to serve under me either."

The dinner guests broke into spontaneous applause. Floyd Wayne Vishniak, standing two hundred miles away in a cornfield, who did not give a damn about black persons, got a lump in his throat.

*The next day*, after he had bought all of his newspapers and read them over a bottomless cup of coffee in a diner, he went to the public library and, with some assistance from a librarian, looked up the microfilms for *The Des Moines Register* during the fall of 1963. He searched back and forth, the photographed pages zooming across the screen of the microfilm reader, until he found the account of the Illini-Hawkeye game.

An hour later he was out on the road in his truck, headed south along the river, toward the town of Quincy.

After he returned from his night detasseling shift, he sat down at his kitchen table with a beer and a fresh white piece of paper and relayed the results of his research activities to the one man who could make the best use of the information.

Floyd Wayne Vishniak
R.R. 6 Box 895
Davenport, Iowa

Aaron Green
Ogle Data Research
Pentagon Towers
Arlington, Virginia

Dear Mr. Green:
Yesterday night your friend and mine Governor Cozzano told a very interesting dinnertime story about the 1963 Illini-Hawkeye football game and one Lucullus Campbell. This story put a lump in my throat and so I went down to the public library to read more about it, as they often encourage us to do at the end of important TV shows.

Imagine my surprise to discover that the young William A. Cozzano did not even participate in the 1963 game because he was suffering from the stomach flu. He did not even set foot in Iowa City on that day.

Perhaps he just got the year wrong. Well, I checked 1962, '61, and '60 also. In '60 and '62, the game was held in Champaign. In '61, it was held in Iowa City. Cozzano was there all right, but according to the *Des Moines Register*, the starting quarterback played the whole game.

Perhaps it happened in Champaign? Well, in '60, the starting quarterback for the Hawkeyes got hurt and the second-string quarterback played very well for the entire game. And in '63, the starting quarterback played the entire game.

There was no Lucullus Campbell playing for Iowa ever.

I took a little drive down to Quincy and found out that there was a Lucullus Campbell who played for their high school and who was on the 1959 Illinois All-Star team. That was the same year Cozzano was an All-Star. He was a halfback. He never played college ball because he got killed in a car crash on the night of his graduation from high school.

So a person might think that William A. Cozzano is making up lies. That he is a dishonest politician like all the others.

But I do not agree with this idea because I believe in Cozzano and I could see the strong emotion on his face when he told that story. No doubt, he believed in the sincerity of his own words.

Then how to explain it? Is Cozzano crazy?

No, I do not think so. But it is a well-known fact that Cozzano had a stroke earlier this year and that his Jew lawyer covered it up and secretly ran the state of Illinois for some time.

Then Cozzano went and had him a special high-tech operation and got better. OR SO THEY SAY. But maybe things aren't completely fixed inside of his head. Maybe his brain's memory banks have been scrambled. Maybe that new chip or whatever that they used to fix up his brain is actually playing tricks with his memory!

I trust that you will provide this info to Governor Cozzano as soon as possible so that he can take steps to have the problem fixed before he becomes President and begins to run the entire country with his faulty brain. This is a matter of total importance.

I cannot sleep anymore.

You will be hearing again from me soon, I am sure.

Sincerely, Floyd Wayne Vishniak

## CHAPTER FORTY-FOUR

Chase Merriam, the High-Metabolism World Dominator and squire of Briarcliff Manor, New York, actually knew some people who seriously thought that the way to beat the crime problem in New York was to drive a junky old car. Most of these misguided people were rather young—kids who had come up in the eighties and had a lot of cleverness but no real intelligence, when it came to money. At a certain point along their sharply rising income curves, they had all gone out and bought BMWs or the equivalent. Not top-of-the-line BMWs, but mediocre ones. Sports sedans. And, inevitably, within a couple of weeks, someone smashed out a window, the alarm went off, they had to get up in the middle of the night, sweep up the glass, call the insurance company—the whole ritual.

Then they pontificated. It was easy enough to understand the psychology of it: all of these people were still young enough to think that life was terribly meaningful, that every little event had some role to play in the tightly written plotline of the universe. You were supposed to learn from these things. Smash went the window, *whoop-whoop-whoop* went the car alarm, and then the yuppie came out of his brownstone, put his chin in his hand, and thought deep thoughts. The conclusion they always came to was that, by buying a nice car, they had somehow offended God with their dirty material-ism, and now they were being punished. As if the dumpster colo-nists who roamed the streets at three A.M., punching out windows and scooping up people's tollbooth change to buy crack, were righ-teous angels dispatched by an avenging God.

Chase Merriam drove a Mercedes-Benz the size of an aircraft

carrier and he made no apologies for it. It had a built-in alarm system, but he had no idea how to work it. He never used it. In fact, he never even bothered to take the keys from the ignition or lock the doors, because he never parked it more than fifty feet away from a good man with a gun. His parking space in Manhattan cost more than a three-bedroom split-level in the upper Midwest and was probably a better investment.

A really, really expensive car emitted a powerful psychological force field of its own. Smashing out the driver's-side window of a BMW 535i was a routine and insignificant New York gesture, on the level of vaulting a turnstile. Chase Merriam himself was often tempted to give it a try, to wrap his jacket around his hand and poke it through the glass just to see the little blue diamonds spray. But people were still awed by a big Mercedes sedan, Rolls-Royce, or Ferrari. They respected these things intuitively. Maybe they harbored just a bit of fear, deep inside their hearts, that such cars were owned by Mob bosses or Colombian drug lords. But Chase Merriam liked to think that it wasn't just the fear of retribution. He liked to think that deep inside their battered, blackened hearts, people still harbored a respect for Quality.

Merriam had seen the Mercedes-Benz side-impact simulator in action on the promotional videotape that the Mercedes dealership had given to him. It was a naked automobile chassis with a huge block of concrete projecting out the front end, painted with dangerous black-and-yellow diagonal stripes. Like a rifle bullet, exploding balloon, or hummingbird's wings, it was a thing never seen by the naked eye; it was visible only in high-speed movie films, drifting in from the side with ghostly clarity, utterly silent, seeming to move only at a snail's pace. But when it drifted into the side of the big Mercedes-Benz sedan, like a cloud scudding across the summer sky, the side of the car caved in and the head of the dummy snapped sideways and you realized, for the first time, just how fast that black-and-yellow juggernaut was moving.

Those side impacts could be vicious. It didn't take many viewings of the side-impact videotape to figure that out. The side of your head always whacked into something. And that's where all of the good stuff was. The front of your head held your personality, and if the rim of the steering wheel happened to punch through it at sixty miles per hour, the worst you could expect was maybe a divorce and then you had to throw out your ties and buy new ones. Big deal. A personality change, after all these years of having the same old one, would be kind of interesting. But the side of your brain held all the good stuff. That's where you did your thinking. The left side, which was the one at risk during a side impact, contained your logical, rational, spatial capabilities, and if you got a hunk of imploding door frame jammed into that, you'd be out of a job. You would have to start taking pottery classes.

The Mercedes people were intelligent enough to realize this and so they had plowed their big black-and-yellow slab of concrete through a few million dollars' worth of rolling stock, gone over the creepily silent high-speed films, and made a few changes. Which meant that the left hemisphere of Chase Merriam's cerebral cortex was about as safe as it could ever be inside of a moving car.

These factors put together—the guarded parking space; his safe haven up in Westchester, where crime was still illegal; the mysterious psychological force field; and the high-speed films—all combined to give Chase Merriam a feeling of invulnerability. Which was a good thing, because he liked to work late, long past the dinner hour in his office in lower Manhattan. And he wouldn't have been able to do that if he drove a Subaru and parked it on the street. He would have been too terrified to venture out after dark, he would have slept on the leather couch in his office and scurried out at daybreak to find that his Subaru was now a stripped frame.

He did some of his best work late at night. Which, in any given month, more than paid back the cost of the big car. The one drawback to working late was that, lately, his damn wristwatch kept interrupting him. But in a way, he didn't mind all that much. He enjoyed keeping up with political events. This thing on his wrist only came to life once or twice a day, and it was always with something important. It was like having a personal assistant who did nothing but screen the political coverage for him, letting him know when to tune in.

Cozzano's National Town Meeting was about halfway through its one-week life span when Chase Merriam worked rather late one night, watched the eleven o'clock news just long enough to get the baseball scores, and then headed down to the parking space where his Mercedes-Benz awaited, keys in the ignition, gleaming and polished under the brilliant homeboy-chasing lights in his private parking ramp. The guards washed and polished the car during the day. They didn't have much else to do.

Chase Merriam thought that his car looked especially clean and nice tonight and so he slipped a few greenbacks to the guard as he opened the driver's-side door for him. He sank into the ergonomic leather and twisted the key and the tachometer needle lifted off the pin and settled in at a comfortable idle. Short of getting down on your hands and knees behind the car and sticking your tongue into the tailpipe, this was the only way to tell that the engine was running. He was out on the West Side Highway, northbound, almost instantly.

The West Side Highway was not much of a highway at all until you got a little bit farther north and it became a proper limited-access affair with on-ramps and so on. At this hour it was always surprisingly free from traffic. The only people out tonight were a few nocturnal taxi drivers and one or two heavily burdened third-worldish vehicles, the lifeblood of the New Economy, out running errands.

Columbia Presbyterian Medical Center towered above the highway on concrete buttresses, like a hydroelectric project accidently constructed in the wrong place, appallingly large. Chase Merriam weaved through some complicated ramps and lanes under the George Washington Bridge, almost out of Manhattan now, and pulled up short behind a rickety, windowless gray-and-rust-colored van, bouncing along on bald tires and dead shocks, with a whole lot of shit piled on top of the roof. The driver was badly confused by all of those lanes, splitting and converging inexplicably under the distracting sight of the mighty bridge. Chase Merriam could have roared past him to one side or the other, but the driver of the van kept changing his mind as to which lane he should be in, making violent changes in his course, and each time he jerked the wheel toward this lane or that, his van, top-heavy with scrap metal, rocked dangerously on its overmatched suspension.

The gloom-slicing headlights of the Mercedes-Benz illuminated the rear bumper of the van, some kind of a homemade number welded together from diamond-tread steel plate. The owner, who was quite obviously in the scrap business, had manufactured the bumper himself. It was hardly less imposing than the black-and-yellow ram of the sideways impact simulator, and so Chase Merriam resolved to keep the gleaming perfection of his Mercedes far away from it.

The maker, upon finishing the structural part of the bumper, had turned his torch to decorative purposes. He had laid down a thick bead of molten iron on the back surface of the bumper, inscribing the following message on it in careening, heavy-metal cursive: SOLO DIOS SABE HACIA DONDE VOY.

Chase Merriam, who did not speak Spanish but who had developed a basic level of skill in Romance languages during his prep years, was mentally translating this phrase (ONLY GOD KNOWS something . . . ) when a sleek aluminum-alloy wheel rim, freshly stripped from a hapless Acura Legend somewhere on the streets of the naked city, slid off the roof of the van, bounced once on the pavement, and plunged directly through his windshield, catching him in the forehead.

In the instant that the rim had taken its fateful bounce, glittering in his headlights like a meteor, the whole world had become a Mercedes-Benz crash-testing laboratory. Chase Merriam, of course, was the dummy. But he experienced it with the eerie clarity of the white-coated Teutonic engineers in the safety of their screening room, going over the silent videotapes. It all happened silently and very, very slowly, and when the car, at some point several minutes into the crash, slammed into some sort of a momentous object—he wasn't sure exactly what, but he had the sense that he was a great distance from the roadway proper at this point, and that the car hadn't been properly horizontal for a long, long time—he actually saw the air bag unfurl before him, fluttering like a white flag raised in a hurricane.

The car kept skidding and rolling and plowing through things for a long time, repeatedly changing direction, like the Magic Bullet meandering through Kennedy and Connally. Each little scrape and secondary impact probably did about five thousand dollars' worth of damage. After a while, it almost got boring; he must be leaving a trail of torn-up sod and flattened road signs all the way to Yonkers. But eventually, he stopped. His inner ear still told him he was riding the Tilt-a-Whirl, but by now his left arm had flopped outward, through the place where the double-glazed window was supposed to be, and was resting limply on some kind of a surface—hard-packed, inorganic New York dirt—and that surface sure wasn't moving.

So far he had not experienced even the smallest bit of physical pain, but something about the car just didn't feel right. Because his eyes got smeary with blood and then swelled shut pretty quickly, he had to figure it out using other sensory inputs. But the upshot seemed to be that his Mercedes-Benz was upside-down now and he was hanging by the safety belt and the shoulder harness, his legs supported by the steering wheel, his knees poked uncomfortably by the turn-signal levers.

The phone was right there, he could find it by groping for it, he knew which button turned it on. Then all he had to do was dial 911. But he couldn't see the number buttons. He punched one of the presets, the one that dialed his home number. He would tell Elizabeth to call the NYPD. But it was now past eleven thirty and Elizabeth had turned off the ringer on the phone and gone to bed; all he got was his own answering machine.

He considered dictating a last message to the world. Elizabeth would find the light blinking on the machine tomorrow and listen to it; she would call the NYPD and they would at last find him, dead from boredom. They would play the tape at his memorial service. It would be dry, calm, witty, noble, and brave.

But he could always call back later and do that. So he hung up to consider his options. All the other presets were business numbers. No one would answer them at this time of the night. Dialing 911 was harder than it sounded, because the phone had too many buttons and they all felt the same.

"You okay?" a voice said. A man's voice.

"Hello?" Chase Merriam said.

"Shit, man, that was incredible," the man said. "I can't believe you alive. That is a bitchin' car, man!"

He couldn't seem to move his left arm, which was still dangling on the ground. He reached across his body with his right hand and stuck the phone out the window. "Would you please dial 911?"

"Sure," the man said. Chase Merriam heard him shuffling the

phone around in his hands, figuring out which way was up, then he heard the three electronic beeps.

"Hello, Officer," the man said, "I would like to report a car crash in Fort Washington Park. Down by the river. This car jumped the guardrail on the highway and now it's upside down. And I think you better get here real quick, because this dude is stuck inside the car, and this is a real bad area. It's full of bad criminals man, people who would cut this guy's heart out for a dollar, and they are all gathering around the vehicle right now, like jackals around a wounded beast, waiting for the right moment to strike. Huh? No, I'm sorry, I won't give you my name. Okay. Bye."

"Thank you," Chase Merriam said.

"No problem."

"That business about the jackals—that wasn't for real was it?"

"Shit, man, where do you think you are? Cape May?" the man said. "We are, like, just a couple blocks from the biggest homeless shelter in New York City. The only ones here are the people they wouldn't let into the shelter because we're too big and bad and scary."

"Take whatever you want," Chase Merriam said. "I don't care."

"Okay. We'll begin with the watch," the man said. He picked up Merriam's arm, which instantly began to hurt, and after a little bit of fiddling around, figured out how to detach the watch. "What kind of watch is this, anyway? Looks like some cheap piece of digital shit."

"It's a long story."

"Well, if a guy was going to look for your wallet—"

"Beats me," Chase Merriam said. "I have to assume it fell out."

The man reached in the window and patted Merriam down, finding no wallets in the usual places. "Does this thing have a dome light?" he asked.

"I believe a dome light is standard on the big Mercedes. It's probably broken."

"Yeah," the man said, crestfallen. "I guess I'll just have to grope around."

He picked up Merriam's left arm and moved it out of the way, gently and firmly. Then he lay down on his belly and crawled forward, shoving his arms, head, and shoulders in through the crumpled window frame, shoving Merriam back against the seat, and began to feel around on the ceiling of the car, now the floor.

"Damn!" he said. "It ain't anywhere. You sure you had a wallet?"

"Positive. Maybe it was thrown out of the car."

"Shit!" the guy said. He crawled into the car even farther, all the way up to his waist, the bulk of his body pinning Merriam tightly back. To judge from his breath, it had been a few decades since this guy had laid hands on dental floss.

The insides of Chase Merriam's eyelids glowed a warm pinkish-orange color.

"Shit!" the guy said again, and began to thrash around wildly, trying to extricate himself from the car. In the process he did a little bit more damage to Chase Merriam, but by now it was all kind of superfluous. "They never come this fast!"

"Freeze!" shouted a nearby voice that could only belong to a cop. "You are under arrest!"

After that it was all footsteps. The man ran away. A cop followed him; they crashed into some brush and then receded into the distance. And then another set of footsteps approached the overturned car. Slowly, calmly.

"Nice car," the cop said. "Didn't know these babies were four-wheel-drive."

*The debate would* be starting in less than five minutes. In addition to the cavernous exhibition space where most of the Town Meeting was happening, McCormick Place had its own theater, which was currently filling up with audience members chosen at random from Ogle's ten thousand typical Americans.

Eleanor Richmond, sitting in a dressing room backstage, having her face fixed by a professional makeup artist, was startled to realize that she wasn't nervous at all.

That was strange because she was about to go on national television. She had been on national television quite a bit recently, but this time she was going to engage in verbal combat with three other people who were better at this kind of thing than she was. Had she become so jaded that she didn't even care anymore?

Someone knocked on the door and pushed it open before Eleanor could tell them to get lost. It was Mary Catherine Cozzano. She slipped quickly into the room, glancing nervously behind her, and leaned back against the door, pushing it shut. She was carrying a bouquet of blue flowers.

"Sorry, I didn't want to be seen coming in here," she said. "People would say I was playing favorites."

"Did you get those from a boyfriend, or just some political weasel?" Eleanor said, eyeing the flowers. "They're nice."

"I got them from a florist," Mary Catherine said. "They're for you."

"Well, how nice! Thank you!"

"I got blue ones, to symbolize the truth," Mary Catherine said, "because you always tell the truth."

"Well, not always," Eleanor said, "but often enough to give people the willies."

"You look great," Mary Catherine said. "I hope you knock 'em dead."

Eleanor didn't figure out the real reason for her lack of nervousness until she went out and sat down on the set. She was the last one to get there. The other debaters were a white man; a somewhat Anglicized Hispanic man; and a middle-aged woman, blond and blue-eyed. And all of them were perfect. They were good-looking, with large, clear features that looked good on television. They were poised, coiffed, made-up, dressed, prepped. She felt like she had blundered into the Academy Awards.

She was here as a token. Nothing more. She didn't have a chance of becoming William A. Cozzano's vice-presidential candidate, even if she and Mary Catherine did have a mutual admiration society. That's why she wasn't nervous.

*Less than a* hundred yards away from the debate set, Cyrus Rutherford Ogle was settling into the comfy swivel chair at the center of the Eye of Cy. For purposes of the National Town Meeting, the GODS container had been driven into the very heart of McCormick Place and everything else constructed around it; the platform where Cozzano and his guests stood every night was directly above his head.

Compliance was good tonight. Ninety-eight of the hundred screens were lit up. The PIPER 100 had started out as a somewhat disorganized and unreliable group and, through practice, had now become steady and disciplined.

That was comforting, because Cy Ogle was scared. The v.p. thing was the hardest of all. Practically everyone screwed this up. For the last week, Ogle had not been able to close his eyes at night without seeing the ghostly faces hanging before him: Nixon, Agnew, Eagleton, Bush, Quayle, Stockdale.

The best that Ogle could do was round up the four best people he knew of—that is, the four people who made the best impression on television—put them up on the tube, side by side, and chart people's reactions to them. Of course, he would have to bring in a moderator to ask them some questions. What kinds of questions didn't really matter. Neither did the answers. The important thing was just to get their faces up on the tube, get their voices working. The hard part was going to be interpreting the data. Because the deeper he got into this, the more weird little angles he began to notice inside the minds of the PIPER 100.

*Mae Hunter was* sitting not far from the banks of the Hudson River, applying lipstick and watching the sun go down on New Jersey. She had discovered the lipstick earlier today, in a wastebasket in the women's room at the New York Public Library, and decided that it was a good shade for her. It was a pretty nice one, and brand new; some fickle shopper must have picked it up in one of the nice stores on Fifth Avenue, ducked into the library to touch herself up, and decided that under that light, it didn't look so hot.

Mae Hunter admired that decisiveness, the ability to fire a brand-new lipstick directly into the wastebasket because it was the wrong shade. Most women would have taken it home and put it on their dresser and left it there for the next twenty years. But here in New York, you met all kinds. People had higher standards. They did not tolerate imperfections quite so easily. This lipstick had obviously been thrown away by a woman of breeding.

She had found a lot of interesting things in the restrooms of the New York Public Library. They didn't let you bring food into the building, so the wastebaskets were cleaner. Almost everything that was in there was paper. Actual merchandise like the lipstick stood out prominently.

Mae Hunter spent a great deal of time in the library because she didn't have a job, family, or home to distract her from her real mission in life, which was to improve her mind. For the past few months she had been working her way through Gibbon's *Decline and Fall of the Roman Empire*. She was halfway through the fifth of seven volumes.

Reading was the most important thing in her life. She had found, over the year and a half since her husband died, that she could handle sleeping out of doors and dumpster-diving for food. She could handle the uncertainty and fear. She had been raped twice and she could even handle that. But the one thing that drove her nuts was the ignorance. She saw these people all around her, sleeping in the parks, spare-changing at Port Authority, checking themselves in to those awful homeless shelters, and none of them made any effort to improve their minds. You could hardly walk ten paces in New York City without coming across a discarded copy of *The New York Times*, the world's finest newspaper, but none of these people bothered to avail themselves. As a former elementary-school teacher, she found that this really irked her. All that wasted brainpower.

Another thing that annoyed her was people's failure to take care of themselves, which is why she was being so exquisitely careful to get this lipstick on correctly. That done, she found a comfortable place and settled in against the base of a small embankment with some shrubs growing on top of it.

She jumped as a burst of music sounded from nearby. Someone was listening to a transistor radio behind her, back in the bushes. "Hello?" she said. "Is someone back there?" But there was no answer.

There was still barely enough light to see. She stood up and peered into the bushes. "Hello?"

The music faded out and was replaced by the sound of an announcer. "From the National Town Meeting, four contenders for the vice presidency debate the issues . . . "

She was almost positive that no one was back there. She walked back and forth in front of the bushes, peering in through gaps between the leaves, trying to see. Something was glowing back there. It looked like a little TV set. And no one was anywhere near it. She found a sort of gap through the little thicket where it looked as though someone had charged through it, flattening down the branches. She followed it in and picked up the source of the noise and light: a Dick Tracy watch.

She debated whether to take it. It had obviously been stolen and dropped here by some criminal who might come back later to look for it.

She looked at the screen. It was showing a TV program: a debate featuring four people who wanted to be William Cozzano's vice-presidential candidate. One by one, the announcer introduced them as they nodded into the camera.

"Brandon F. Doyle, former U.S. Representative from Massachusetts, currently on the faculty of Georgetown University . . ." This was a handsome, youngish man, probably in his late forties but young-looking for that age. He smiled a tight little smile into the camera and nodded. She didn't like him.

"Marco Gutierrez, Mayor of Brownsville, Texas, and a founding member of the international environmental group Toxic Borders . . ." This was a burly Latino man with a mustache and large, intense black eyes. He was leaning back in his chair, stroking his mustache with one finger. He raised his hand away from his face as his name was called and waved at the camera.

Mae Hunter snapped the Dick Tracy watch into place around her wrist. She wanted to see at least this one program.

The TV image cut to a blond, blue-eyed woman with one of those professional-looking haircuts that Mae always saw on the young women in midtown. She stared directly, and almost coldly, into the camera. "Laura Thibodeaux-Green, founder and CEO of Santa Fe Software, who, two years ago, came within a thousand votes of being elected senator from New Mexico."

Finally, to Mae Hunter's surprise and delight, *she* appeared on the screen!

"And Eleanor Richmond of Alexandria, Virginia, assistant to the late Senator Caleb Marshall."

The woman was so cool. She didn't even look at the camera, didn't react to the introduction at all. She was looking at some papers in her lap. Then she glanced up and looked around a little bit, calm, alert, but not paying any attention to the announcer or the TV cameras. She was so like a princess.

What a terrible introduction that was! It didn't do justice to the life and times of Eleanor Richmond at all. Mae Hunter knew all about her, she had followed her career in the discarded pages of *The New York Times*. She was a modern-day hero. Mae pushed her way out through the bushes and went onto the broad open bank of the Hudson to watch her girlfriend Eleanor.

*The moderator was* Marcus Hale, a grizzled ex-anchorman who had gotten to the place in his career where he could write his own job description. He did a lot of work for TV North America now, because there, he didn't have to keep stopping in midparagraph to pimp hemorrhoid remedies to the American public. And now that the candidacy of William A. Cozzano had developed into a media-certified Important Phenomenon, he had been all too eager to serve as the moderator of this vice-presidential showdown. He opened things up, in typical Marcus Hale style, with a lengthy editorial, though he probably would have preferred to call it analysis. Eventually he worked his way around to asking a question.

And it was a doozy. "All of you are young people, in your forties. Chances are you'll be around for at least another twenty-five years. One or more of you may even become president during that time. By then, people who are being born today will just be coming into the adult job market, and their success in that market will depend largely on the economic and educational initiatives that are taken during the next decade. These will be most important to the poorest people, who today face the most restricted opportunities. And without putting too fine a point on it, you know and I know that what I'm really talking about here is inner-city blacks. My question is: twenty-five years from now, what will life be like for these people, and what will you have done to make that life better?"

Brandon F. Doyle of Massachusetts went first, and he looked scared. It was easy enough for an old man like Marcus Hale to drag these scary and difficult issues into the limelight. It was a lot harder for someone like Doyle to deal with the resulting mess, especially considering that he was sharing the stage with a black person who could shoot him down whenever she wanted.

"Well, first of all, Marcus, let me say that opportunity—for all people, white or black—is a function of education. This is a message that we have always taken to heart in Massachusetts, which has a long heritage of brilliant institutions of higher learning. It's my hope —and my intention—that twenty-five years from now, a lot of the people you're talking about will be entering graduate school, or law school, or medical school, and they'll be doing it with the full assistance and support of a government that takes these things with the utmost seriousness. Which is not to support big-spending government programs. I prefer to think of education as an investment, not an expense."

Next came Marco Gutierrez, who had a heavy, stolid, calm affect. That and his hair and his clothes had all been developed to make him seem like a cool norteamericano, not the jumpy, emotional Mexican that blue-eyed Duluth voters were afraid of. "Well, I would second a lot of what my friend Brandon said, but where we differ is at the end. Look. Government has a moral duty to educate its children. No matter what it costs. To say that education is a good investment misses the point. Even if it cost every penny in the Treasury, we should educate our kids to the best of our ability, because it's the right thing to do."

It was Laura Thibodeaux-Green's turn. "Kids spend seven hours a day in front of the television. Seven hours a day. Just think about that for a second. That's a lot more time than they spend in the classroom. Well, my opinion is that TV doesn't have to be mindrotting garbage. It has the ability to educate. And the digital, highdefinition TV that's just starting to be introduced to the living rooms of America can be the most potent educational tool ever devised. I advocate a massive program to develop educational software that can run on these TV sets of the future, so that those seven hours a day spent in front of the TV can turn our little kids into little Shakespeares and Einsteins instead of illiterate couch potatoes."

Finally, Eleanor Richmond got her chance. "Look," she said, "Abe

Lincoln learned his lessons by writing on the back of a shovel. During slavery times, a lot of black people learned to read and write even though they weren't allowed to go to school. And nowadays, Indochinese refugee kids do great in school even though they got no money at all and their folks don't speak English. The fact that many black people nowadays aren't getting educated has nothing to do with how much money we spend on schools. Spending more money won't help. Neither will writing educational software to run on your home TV set. It's just a question of values. If your family places a high value on being educated, you'll get educated, even if you have to do your homework on the back of a shovel. And if your family doesn't give a damn about developing your mind, you'll grow up stupid and ignorant even if you go to the fanciest private school in America.

"Now, unfortunately, I can't give you a program to help develop people's values. Personally, I'm starting to think that the fewer programs we have, the better off we are."

For the first time, the live audience broke into applause.

"*Amen to that!*" Mae Hunter shouted, her voice echoing out across the gray Hudson. A couple of passing joggers glanced at her, then looked away quickly and pretended not to notice the crazy lady.

Cy Ogle saw a screen flare bright green in the corner of his eye, and turned to look. The name at the bottom of the screen was CHASE MERRIAM.

It was amazing. Out of all these candidates, Merriam's clear favorite, so far, was Eleanor Richmond. Between the poor people and minorities on the bottom, and the women and people like Chase Merriam on the top, an astonishing number of people liked Eleanor Richmond.

But on second thought, Ogle reflected, maybe it wasn't so surprising after all. Months ago, when she had confronted Earl Strong in the shopping mall, he had pointed his finger at her image on the screen and pronounced her the first female president of the United States.

## CHAPTER FORTY-FIVE

Eleanor went straight to her hotel room after the debate, talked to her kids in Alexandria, watched some TV, went to bed, and slept until ten Friday morning. When she opened her eyes, she knew without looking at the clock that she had lost control of herself and overslept massively. The red light on her phone was flashing like a police car, the blackout curtains on her hotel room windows were limned with the hot, hysterical white light of midday. She felt wizened and dehydrated and headachy.

She opened her curtains about six inches, letting a slab of arid light into the room, ordered some room service (yogurt, a large infusion of juice, and lots of coffee), and took a shower. The yogurt arrived with a stack of message slips from various journalists, most of whom had deadlines that had already expired. She was still sitting on her bed in her hotel bathrobe, trying to get the coffee into her system as fast as possible, sorting these messages into stacks, when someone knocked at her door. Shave and a haircut, two bits.

It was her girlfriend Mary Catherine Cozzano, turned out in a smashingly professional navy blue ensemble. Mary Catherine was doing some major grinning, showing some serious dimple action this morning.

"I'm not worthy," Eleanor said, placing one hand to the breast of her white terrycloth bathrobe.

"My daughter costume," Mary Catherine explained.

"Well, I knew I overslept," Eleanor said, ushering her into the room, "but looking at you I feel like I am *way* behind the curve."

"You don't know how right you are," Mary Catherine said provocatively. She groped for the curtain pull and yanked it decisively, flooding the room with light. Then she turned around and sat down on the unmade bed, facing Eleanor, who was squinting between her fingers.

"You have this look on your face like you are in possession of important state secrets that you can't wait to blab," Eleanor said. "So let me assure you that I have a Top-Secret Alpha clearance. Coffee?"

"No, thanks," Mary Catherine said. "I had breakfast four hours ago."

Eleanor laughed and pretended to be ashamed of herself. "In Alexandria my neighbor's dog starts barking at five A.M. sharp," she said, "so I never get the opportunity to sleep in."

"Well," Mary Catherine said, "I think you'll find that the accommodations are much quieter on the grounds of the Naval Observatory."

"Naval Observatory?"

"Yeah," Mary Catherine said innocently.

The Naval Observatory was a circular patch of land along Massachusetts Avenue, northwest of downtown D.C., in a part of town that Eleanor had rarely visited while growing up there. Its function was to provide very nice housing to a few important Navy types who needed quick access to the White House. And it contained the official residence of the Vice President of the United States.

She inhaled sharply and looked at Mary Catherine's face. Mary Catherine was sucking in her cheeks, trying not to break out laughing.

"I'm going to be made an admiral?" Eleanor said.

Mary Catherine shook her head.

The idea was too stunning. Eleanor couldn't speak. It couldn't be.

If Cozzano were a fringe candidate, she'd understand it. A purely symbolic candidacy, like the Libertarians or the Socialists, might pick someone like her as a running mate. But Cozzano was no fringe candidate.

Hell, Cozzano was the *leader*. All the polls had him out in front. It was impossible.

"You're playing with me, girl," Eleanor said.

Mary Catherine just shook her head. She put one hand over her mouth, trying to contain herself.

That one gesture finally brought it home to Eleanor. This wasn't just some nice young lady she had made friends with at a convention, after all. This was the daughter of the candidate himself. And the way she was dressed—

"You came here to do some serious business," Eleanor said.

Mary Catherine nodded.

"You came here to *NOTIFY ME!*" Eleanor said, and finally she couldn't hold back any longer; she slid forward out of her chair, onto her knees, put both hands over her face, and started screaming. Mary Catherine, laughing hysterically, wrapped Eleanor up in her arms and held her tight.

In some deep, remote part of her soul, Eleanor knew that she was acting just like the winning contestants on the game shows that she used to watch when she was unemployed. But she didn't care. Come to think of it, it wasn't a bad analogy. She had gone on the biggest quiz show of all time and won the penultimate prize.

*The results were* so odd and yet so important that Cyrus Rutherford Ogle ran one more test, shortly before the announcement. They were starting off the broadcast with a round-table discussion among the four metapundits whom Ogle had handpicked from Central Casting.

One of them was a gruff, grandfatherly old man who projected traditional American family values. He had made a comfortable living playing a cowboy patriarch in various Westerns and an admiral on *Star Trek: The Next Generation.* Another was a tweedy academic (lab-coat wearing pseudoscientist on a couple of drug commercials). Then there was a middle-aged, professional-looking young woman whose role was to puncture the egos of the two men (occasional lawyer on *L.A. Law*). Finally, they had a stylish, younger black woman with a Hispanic surname and generically progressive politics (roommate/best friend to better-known actresses in various films). All four of the metapundits would gather every evening and engage in a spirited discussion of political issues that had come up during the day's events at the National Town Meeting. All four of them had, at one time, worked in soap operas and had the ability to memorize dialogue rapidly, which came in handy since Ogle and his staff scripted the discussions.

During tonight's discussion, the tweedy academic metapundit delivered a bombshell several minutes into the program by announcing that he had spoken with a high-level Cozzano operative minutes before the program and that this person had confirmed that Eleanor Richmond would be the vice-presidential candidate.

Cy Ogle was ensconced in the Eye of Cy at the moment his line was delivered, and the results were intense and striking. There were a few discrepancies between the new information and last night's debate results, but they were not big discrepancies. Richmond had a hard core of support that would never change. There was also a smaller but strong anti-Richmond segment, led by Byron Jeff-cote (Trailer-Park Nazi, Ocala, Florida) and by a few others like the Post-Confederate Gravy Eater and the Orange County Book Burner.

But reaction among more moderately conservative whites was not half-bad. And the big surprise was still there: Chase Merriam loved Eleanor Richmond. Cy Ogle picked up the phone and got his press secretary.

"Go ahead and announce it," he said. "The demographics are perfect."

"Richmond?" the secretary said, still a little uncertain about this whole idea.

"Eleanor Richmond," Ogle said.

On the other end of the line, he heard keys whacking on a computer keyboard. The press release was now being transmitted digitally to the wire services, computer-faxed to every press outlet in the Western world. Cozzano's state and local campaign managers, in all fifty states, were receiving information packets on Eleanor Richmond—pictures, videotapes, and canned sound bites for them to toss off to the local media. It all happened in an instant.

"It's done," his press secretary said.

"Good," Ogle said. "White House, here we come. I gotta go," he concluded. "I have a call on another line."

It wasn't just any old phone line. This was a special line that Ogle had agreed to keep open. The only person who had this phone number was Buckminster Salvador. Cy Ogle's boss. Rarely heard from, rarely seen, but always there.

"Ogle," Ogle said.

"Hold everything!" said the voice of Mr. Salvador, which was barely recognizable; his throat was tense to the point of strangulation. "Don't move! Don't push any buttons or make any phone calls or let anyone do anything!"

"I am alone. Alone and powerless," Ogle said. "You have my undivided attention."

"Thank god I reached you in time," Salvador said. "I knew there was something wrong with that whole Eleanor Richmond thing."

"What do you mean?"

Salvador spent most of his time hanging out in ODR's fake headquarters in the office tower above Pentagon Plaza, so that he could monitor all of the PIPER 100 data at the same time as Ogle did. And he did so constantly, as Ogle had learned; scarcely a single campaign event went by that Bucky Salvador didn't phone him up right in the middle of it and provide his own commentary on how the PIPER 100 were reacting. He fancied himself something of an expert. And, dilettante that he was, he completely failed to grasp the mediagenic advantages of Eleanor Richmond.

"Chase Merriam called me just a few minutes ago. He just got out of the hospital."

Ogle laughed. "Haw, haw, haw," he said, "don't tell me. He had an operation. He was on laughing gas or something during the debate."

"Worse than that. He was in a car crash Wednesday night. Some hoodlum stole his watch. We have no idea who's wearing that thing!"

"A late-middle-aged black female homeless person with good education and traditionalist values," Ogle said.

Salvador was caught off guard. "Oh. You've found the watch, then?"

"Nope," Ogle said, "just an educated guess."

"Well," Salvador said. "Well."

"Well what?"

"This changes everything!" Salvador said, shocked by Ogle's seeming indifference. "The statistics are completely fouled up!"

"If all the PIPER 100 got together and traded watches, that would foul up the statistics," Ogle said. "One person doesn't foul them up too bad."

Deep in his heart, Ogle knew Salvador had a point. But he didn't want to agree with him. He did not really get along with Salvador very well.

"That's ridiculous!" Salvador said. "You told me yourself last night that the single strongest thing in Richmond's favor was the fact that Chase Merriam loved her. You said it was a key factor in making your decision."

"Hey," Ogle said, "try to keep this in perspective. We're talking about the goddamn vice presidency here. It just doesn't matter."

"So you admit that Richmond is the wrong choice," Salvador said triumphantly.

"From here on out, she's the right choice. She's a brilliant choice. A daring, incisive, masterstroke of leadership on Cozzano's part," Ogle said, "because she's a choice we already made."

"Not true," Salvador said, "the formal announcement doesn't happen for another hour."

"The formal announcement doesn't mean diddly," Ogle said. "We already unleashed the cascade. Stories have already been filed. Hell," Ogle said, grabbing a remote control and clicking channels on a nearby TV monitor, "I got Koppel on screen right now with a picture of Eleanor Richmond over his shoulder. And when Eleanor's peering over Ted Koppel's shoulder on national TV, and Koppel's got that smirky know-it-all look on his face, it's just too goddamn late."

"Good lord." Salvador sighed, sounding quiet and defeated. "When I got into this thing, I never realized how complicated it was going to be."

"Cheer up," Ogle said, turning his attention back toward the Eye of Cy. "Look at the screens. I am seeing a generally green color this evening. The electorate is mellow and satisfied. If Richmond turns out to be a wrong choice, we'll just send her to kiss babies in Guam."

"I see a case of measles," Salvador said. "I see a lot of red screens. Look at Economic Roadkill! Economic Roadkill is a key bloc. And tonight, Economic Roadkill is frightened."

Ogle looked at the screen labeled FLOYD WAYNE VISHNIAK. As Salvador had pointed out, it was bright red. "It's nothing," Ogle said. "He does that all the time. He's in another bar fight."

Suddenly, Vishniak's screen turned bright green. Ogle and Salvador both laughed. "Ha ha!" Salvador said, "I'll wager his opponent is out cold on a barroom floor in Davenport, Iowa!"

## CHAPTER FORTY-SIX

Floyd Wayne Vishniak strode into McCormick Place and heaved a tremendous sigh of relief. A cascade of sweat fell out of his hair and showered his face. He had made it through the metal detectors!

The Fleischacker had performed as advertised. It was a ceramic-and-plastic gun, made in Austria, that didn't trigger metal detectors. After cashing in his latest check from Ogle Data Research, picking up his paycheck from detasseling, and pawning all of his other weapons, he had finally raised the capital he needed to purchase the Fleischacker at a gun store in Davenport and to top his truck's fuel tanks. That done, he had made the trip across northern Illinois in two hours flat, blasting across the nearly empty pavement of I-88 at an average velocity of eighty-five miles per hour. He had wanted to leave himself an adequate time cushion upon reaching Chicago, because he wasn't sure how to locate McCormick Place. But that turned out to be a snap. He just took the interstate into town and, to his astonishment, began to see signs for the damn place. A whole series of big signs that took him straight where he wanted to go.

This kind of thing did not happen to Floyd Wayne Vishniak very often, because usually he went places where no one else wanted to go: cornfields that needed detasseling, riverfront bars, and defunct factories. He had been forced to develop a certain amount of navigational cunning over the years. He had assumed that once he trespassed upon the borders of Chicago, he would, as usual, spend a considerable amount of time idling on the shoulder of various roads and in the parking lots of convenience stores, poring over his Chicago map collection.

But it wasn't like that. All he had to do was pay the tolls and follow the signs. And as he was doing so, it dawned on him that this was natural and logical, because if he had the correct understanding of it, a convention was a thing where a whole lot of people came together at once for a purpose. Which meant that a whole lot of people were having to find their ways to McCormick Place all the time, every day.

Like most of the other new ideas that entered Floyd Wayne Vishniak's head, this one came in the form of a pang of bitter resentment. It hit him straight between the eyes and made him grind his teeth and mumble indistinct profanities.

The whole world was set up for the benefit of the rich folks. That interstate, four beautiful lanes of pavement cutting straight across the state of Illinois, had been put there just to ferry the wealthy and privileged into Chicago so that they could go to conventions and meet with others of their kind and plot new conspiracies to keep the common man in his place: on the bottom. Far be it from these people to find their own way to McCormick Place. Oh no, these people were too busy and dignified and important to actually buy maps and find their own way. No, they had to have special signs.

It was easy enough to reach the convention center, but difficult to park in its vicinity; the lots were jammed. Not making it any easier was Vishniak's own extreme nervousness. He was afraid to slow down, so he just orbited the target zone like an Indian circling a wagon train. He shot right past a few perfectly good spots. McCormick Place was the southern end of a whole chain of big civic projects, including Soldier Field, some museums, and Grant Park, and parking lots were strung for several miles up the shore of the lake. Vishniak ended up parking way the hell and gone up in the vicinity of Grant Park and then walking for half an hour, which was fine because it helped him burn off adrenaline.

Grant Park, he realized, must be named after General Grant. As in Grant and Sherman. Vishniak had learned all about those two guys on TV. One was drunk and one was crazy, he could never remember which, but the thing was that both of them kicked ass for their country. When the war started Grant was living in Galena, which was just a few miles up the river from where Vishniak lived. And he was working in a livery stable, which was equivalent to working in a car wash nowadays, or detasseling.

He walked south past Soldier Field, where William A. Cozzano had attained glory in an earlier life, and then took a pedestrian overpass across Lakeshore Drive into the extreme northern end of the McCormick Place parking lots. The first thing he encountered was a line of portable toilets. On the theory that you should never pass up a chance to make water or take water, he went into one of these, wiped the seat with a wad of toilet paper, and sat down. All he really had to do was take a leak—the series of thirty-two-ounce coffees he had picked up at various Chicagoland 7-Elevens was having an effect—but as long as he was here he flicked his Bic and had one last good look at the Fleischacker. He popped the magazine loose from the grip, checked it, shoved it in.

Someone pounded on the fiberglass door of the portable toilet. "Is anyone in there?"

"Fuck you," said Floyd Wayne Vishniak reflexively. His heart was pounding; he was afraid it was a cop. But it wasn't. Just another Cozzano supporter. Vishniak reholstered his gun under his windbreaker and started getting himself together, wondering whether this rude person had any friends, whether he was big, whether he would be worth picking a fight with. But when he came out he saw it was just a little man in a suit, accompanied by a little kid who was holding his crotch and jumping up and down.

Fuck it anyway, Vishniak realized. He had abandoned his trailer and hit the road with a pocket of cash, a pickup truck, and a plastic gun. He had to get used to the idea that he was a different kind of man now, a man who had risen above the common crowd, who could not trouble himself with meaningless hassles over toilet access.

McCormick Place was a huge rectangular black thing with a much larger black slab of a roof that overhung the building quite a bit on all sides. As Vishniak walked toward it through the parking lot, Lakeshore Drive was on his right and a little backwater of Lake Michigan on his left; beyond that was a peninsula with a private airport on it, small planes taking off and landing and taxiing. The yachts of the rich and powerful were tied up in the water only yards away from the private jets of the even more rich and powerful, and Vishniak could plainly see that if you were the right kind of person, you didn't have to waste your time with parking lots, or even cars.

All the way from Grant Park southward, the pedestrian traffic had been getting heavier. At the southern end of the parking lot, all the people were funneled down a wide staircase and into McCormick Place's subterranean entrance. The flow was backed up a little

Stephen Bury

bit, the crowd milled rather than streamed down the stairs. Working his way slowly down the steps, Vishniak was able to get a clear view of the metal detectors bracketing the doors.

He immediately got scared shitless. His heart was going so fast it was more of a vibration, like an idling truck engine, than a beat, and he was sweating like a pig. But it was a warm humid night and he was wearing a windbreaker, so he had every excuse to sweat.

Looking up, he could see into the underside of McCormick Place's huge flat overhanging roof, which was supported and stiffened by a latticework of black girders. Laced through the structural members was a barely perceptible network of thin red lines—a system of pipes carrying water to the automatic sprinkler system. As Vishniak worked his way down the steps, swept along by the eager Cozzano supporters, he wondered whether anyone else ever bothered to look up in the air and take notice of these things, these hidden connections and networks that were laced imperceptibly through the structure of everything.

Then he was there, confronted with the metal detector, people pushing him from behind, and all he could do was give himself up to the force of the crowd, the pressure of history, and walk on through.

Nothing happened. As he kept on walking with the crowd now filling the main floor of William A. Cozzano's National Town Meeting, becoming invisible and anonymous, he was overcome with relief, which showed up as a vivid green on the monitors in the Eye of Cy and at ODR headquarters in Pentagon City.

*The National Town* Meeting was a political convention in all but name, and it followed some of the same protocols. One of these was the hierarchy of introductions. It wouldn't do just to have the nominee stroll out on stage and start talking. He had to be introduced by someone. Preferably by someone very, very important. And anyone who was important enough to make that introduction was, likewise, too important to step out in front of an ice-cold audience and just start talking. He would have to be introduced by someone else. That person had to be important enough that his role as introducer did not seem to belittle the stature of the introduced . . .

Suffice it to say that the first person who stepped out in front of the microphones that evening was as completely anonymous as any person could be. His job was to get the attention of the crowd. To sever all of the conversations that had sprung up among the people standing shoulder to shoulder on the convention floor. Then he introduced an alderman, who introduced a former mayor of Chicago, who introduced a former Governor of New York, who introduced a movie star, who introduced a former Secretary of State, who introduced Governor William A. Cozzano. At each stage of the hierarchy, the dull roar of bored conversation diminished and the excitement of the crowd built.

Twenty thousand people were in the hall. The original roster of the National Town Meeting had been ten thousand, but these people were just statistical abstracts who had been snatched off the streets and transported into town to spout their opinions and represent their demographic groups. Many of them supported Cozzano, many didn't, and the ones that did, did so in the same moderate, reasonable way that most average people supported political candidates. Which was to say that, while they might vote for Cozzano, they would not be willing to paint his name across their foreheads and jump up and down screaming at every mention of his name.

Consequently, Cy Ogle had brought in an additional ten thousand people who would do exactly that. They tended to stand closer to the dais, crowding the National Town Meeting participants into the back of the hall. The fact that these riotous supporters were not the same as the ten thousand average Americans who had been appearing on TV all week was not, of course, explained to the nationwide television audience, which was watching on no fewer than eight networks.

This was a good thing for Floyd Wayne Vishniak, because, until tonight, you couldn't have gotten into the convention center without a special National Town Meeting photo ID. Vishniak didn't have one. But neither did any of the other ten thousand fanatical Cozzano supporters who had packed the hall tonight.

Tables had been set up at the back of the hall and piled high with Cozzano paraphernalia: signs, bumper stickers, skimmers, buttons. Vishniak scored an armful of stuff and festooned himself like the hard-core Cozzano supporter that he, in fact, was. He even filled out a little COZZANO FOR PRESIDENT stick-on name tag: HELLO, MY NAME IS Sherman Grant. He was amid relatively glum, drab National Town Meeting participants who had now been relegated to the outer darkness. As the hierachy of introductions rose toward its peak, he shouldered his way through them, working toward center stage.

*Like a lot* of other secretaries of state, the one who introduced Cozzano had not been allowed to die a natural political death. He had resigned or been forced out, or something like that, in the middle of a term. Everyone concerned had agreed that it was over a question of principle on which reasonable people could honestly disagree, which gave this man the image of a person who was willing to stake his job on a matter of principle. As such, he was exactly the right guy to introduce Cozzano.

He delivered a lengthy and somewhat less than thrilling address about his career in big-time Washington politics and how disgusted he had been by the decadence and corruption of it all. He talked about the need for change. Finally, his voice began to rise in pitch, he started to pump the crowd back up out of the comatose state into which he himself had placed them, to pull them back in from the lines at the rest rooms, and by the time he bent forward to shout the name of William A. Cozzano into his microphone, he was completely inaudible, even to himself: thousands of people were screaming the name.

Cozzano appeared on the stage, holding hands with Eleanor Richmond. Behind them were four younger people: Mary Catherine and James Cozzano, and Clarice and Harmon Richmond, Jr., all holding hands.

The screaming, and the sound of the air horns, seemed loud enough to split the molecules in the hot sweaty air of the convention hall. The candidates and their families stood in a pool of blue carbon-arc light that set them apart from everthing else, which now looked dim and yellowish by comparison, like a TV screen blaring in the middle of an antique living room.

It was just like when the Quad Cities Whiplash scored a winning goal with one second remaining in a playoff game, thought Floyd

Wayne Vishniak, standing just below the dais, a stone's throw from William A. Cozzano.

He had a clear shot from here. But shooting him was not really part of the plan. The idea was not to hurt Cozzano, but to protect him.

Cozzano was a great man. A hero. The only honest politician in the United States. But even a great man could be led astray by the forces of evil, and Vishniak had been forced to the conclusion that it was happening to Cozzano right now.

Why couldn't anyone else figure it out? It was so obvious. They were all stupid. The world was full of morons. In all of the United States, only a tiny number were capable of seeing the truth.

They knew, of course. The people who were manipulating Cozzano had access to all kinds of secret FBI and CIA files. They could use their computers and satellites to pry into people's school records, police records, and bank accounts. They had figured out that Floyd Wayne Vishniak, and a few other people around the country, would see through the charade and would represent a threat to their conspiracy.

They couldn't just send out hit men to kill Vishniak and the others. No, that was just a little too obvious. Instead they were taking the subtle approach. All the way across Illinois, Vishniak had been laughing at himself. To think he had actually believed the ridiculous story that the little Jew had told him! "We're doing research on public opinion and we want you to wear this Dick Tracy watch."

Research on Floyd Wayne Vishniak's brain waves was more like it. They were watching him. Waiting for him to figure out the conspiracy and make his move. And he had played into their hands. He had worn the watch. He had even sent them letters, explaining his opinions in detail, and in these letters, he had made the incredibly stupid mistake of tipping them off to the fact that he was suspicious.

He could have just taken the watch off his wrist and been free of it, but he was a little smarter than that. To take the watch off his wrist at this point would probably mean certain death. They would send out a hit man to get him.

To hell with a hit man. The watch probably was booby-trapped.

It probably had a little needle coated with shellfish toxin, and if he tried to take it off now, that needle, activated by a satellite transmission from ODR headquarters, would jab into the underside of his wrist and shoot the poison straight into his vein. But as long as he kept wearing the watch, they'd think he had still been duped. He could continue his careful reconaissance of the Cozzano campaign.

This was the first step: to get close to Cozzano, to get a good look at his security apparatus, and so memorize the faces of the people who were close to him. Not the obvious ones like Eleanor Richmond and Mary Catherine—they were just pawns too—but the men in suits who hovered around the edges, just out of reach of the arc light's rainbow-tinged border.

The platform was huge, as big. as the stage for a major rock concert, and it was hollow, and all of the mysterious men in suits had special access to the cleverly concealed doors and stairways that led beneath. All the doors were guarded by uniformed cops who would only let certain people through; you had to have a special backstage pass around your neck. But from time to time when some bigshot went in or out, a door would swing open for a few seconds, giving Vishniak a glimpse into the hidden world under Cozzano's feet. What he saw confirmed everything he'd been thinking: thick black cables snaking everywhere, and banks of television monitors, men wearing radio headsets, talking on phones and typing on computers. And in the center of it all, hard to glimpse through the tangle of technicians and cables and structural supports, sitting right in the middle of the web, was a semitrailer rig, a nice new one. He couldn't see enough of it to read the words on its side, but he didn't have to; you could recognize it from its color scheme; it was a GODS truck.

He took a good look at the people under the platform whenever those doors opened up. These were the ones who were controlling Cozzano's mind. The ones who, sometime between now and Election Day, were going to be taking nine-millimeter bullets between the eyes, fired from Floyd Wayne Vishniak's plastic gun.

Vishniak jumped up and down and screamed along with the crowd. "I'll save you, Governor Cozzano! I'll get you out of this conspiracy or die trying!" But his words of encouragement were lost in the tumult.

## CHAPTER FORTY-SEVEN

Eleanor didn't get a real chance to talk to William A. Cozzano until several hours after the announcement. She had met him once, briefly, prior to the debate, and spoken with him in formal circumstances, in a conference room full of flacks and advisers, before the announcement. After the announcement they had spent most of their time partying in the ballroom of Cozzano's hotel. This had not been a real party, of course, any more than a talk show appearance was a real conversation; it had been a staged event, and she had had to stay on her toes the entire time. She knew, without being told, that she was going to have to get in the habit of holding her tongue more than she was used to, and try to avoid making gaffes.

Finally, shortly before midnight, she and Cozzano and Mary Catherine got together in Cozzano's hotel suite, on the top floor of the hotel, naturally. The women changed out of their party dresses and into comfortable, casual clothes, and they had a nightcap up on the balcony.

She had known about William A. Cozzano for many years and she had always been a bit put off by the hyper-macho foundations of his image: war and football. He had always seemed like the type who'd be great for smoking cigars and shooting wild game with corporate CEOs, but who wouldn't be able to handle the subtle nuances of national politics, who wouldn't really grasp women's issues.

After about five minutes on the balcony with him, she decided she was wrong. He wasn't a macho shithead at all. He was courtly in an almost European way and he had a fine, self-deprecating sense of humor. He had an easy rapport with his daughter that told Eleanor everything about what kind of man he was.

They ended up conversing for more than an hour. Cozzano had a penchant for anecdotes and he told several of them. Toward the end of the evening, Eleanor could tell that this was beginning to make Mary Catherine slightly uneasy. She would shift in her chair and say, "Oh, Dad!" when he was beginning to launch into a story.

And as he was telling these stories, she would watch his face intently and occasionally frown or bite her lip.

Eleanor wasn't quite sure why. Cozzano liked to talk, but this was not senile rambling by any means. It didn't make Eleanor uncomfortable. He told his stories concisely and they always had a point that was germane to the conversation. But all they did was make Mary Catherine agitated.

It looked to Eleanor as though father and daughter had some talking to do, and so finally, a little after one in the morning, she excused herself, insisting that she could find her own way down to the lobby and back to her own hotel. She wanted to enjoy her last evening of freedom before her full-time Secret Service contingent kicked in the following morning.

The elevator came quickly—demand was low at this time of the morning—and she climbed on and punched the button for the lobby. When the doors closed, she found herself alone in a room for the first time since Mary Catherine had come to see her earlier that day. She was exhausted. She dropped her tote bag on the floor, sagged against the wall of the elevator, closed her eyes, and heaved an enormous sigh.

This was a type of pressure she'd never known before. Since her first meeting with Cozzano earlier today, not a second had gone by without her photograph being taken. It boggled the mind to think about a lifestyle in which you could never pick your nose, never allow your hair or your face to get messy.

The elevator slowed. Eleanor opened one eye a crack and saw that they were pausing on the tenth floor. She closed her eye again, content to spend another few minutes relaxing before she exited back into public life again—no doubt, photographers would be waiting on the sidewalk.

The doors opened and Eleanor sensed someone climbing on board. Remembering that she was now a role model, she forced herself to open her eyes and stand up straight. It was a thin man in a suit. He had very short hair and burning, hyperactive eyes. He was staring at her. His eyes dropped to her tote bag.

"Whatcha got there?" he said, brusquely.

"My stuff," she said, unable to come up with anything more eloquent at this time of the morning.

"What's this?" he said, bending over and reaching for it.

The tote bag was just a cheap freebie given out by her travel agent in Alexandria. Eleanor had brought it along precisely because it was so flimsy that it could be wadded up and stuffed into other luggage. Tonight it had come in handy for carrying a change of clothes. Right now she was wearing jeans and an old sweatshirt with TOWSON STATE printed across the front. Her party dress, jewelry, and purse were all in the tote bag. The purse was on top. As the man in the suit bent down, she followed his gaze, and saw that the strap of the purse—a heavy gold-plated chain, a la Chanel—was dangling out. His hand reached out, quick as a snake, grabbed the chain, and yanked, taking the purse out with it.

"Hey!" she said, and grabbed at the chain. But he yanked the purse away as her hand was closing around it, ripping it out of her hand and bending a couple of nails back.

She'd heard of these guys: well-dressed thieves who wandered around in posh hotels late at night, snatching purses and picking pockets. They'd be in the lobby any second and then this guy would be in trouble. "Goddamn it," she said, and kicked him in the knee.

"You bitch," he said. He bent down, got one shoulder into her solar plexus, and used the thrust of both legs to body-slam her into the wall of the elevator. Her head snapped backward against the wall, which didn't cause any serious damage but did leave her disoriented; she slid down the wall and collapsed to the floor with her legs sprawling, and realized that she could not draw a breath.

The man loomed in front of the elevator's control panel. He had pulled out a huge keychain, the kind that's attached to a spring-loaded reel on the belt, and shoved a tubular key into the switch at the base of the panel. He rotated the switch one notch and then pressed the button beneath the one for the lobby.

The door opened a moment later. This was not the lobby of the hotel: she saw barren concrete walls, harshly illuminated with cheap industrial lights, and steel doors with numbers painted on them. The man turned the key switch one more time and the elevator froze in position with the doors open. She still couldn't breathe. This was the first time she'd had the wind knocked out of her since the second grade.

"Get out," the man said, reaching down to grab her wrist. He yanked hard and trudged out into the corridor. He wasn't so much helping her to her feet as he was dragging her over the floor. Eleanor hardly cared; the lack of oxygen was a more immediate concern than this guy's bad manners. She ended up tumbled in a heap on the floor next to a steel door in the corridor, close to the elevator. The keychain jingled once again, the door swung open on a big room with a few people in it.

Finally she drew in a breath. Her lungs had constricted, her airway was clenched shut, and the air passing through it made an ugly sobbing noise. But it felt good. She forced that breath out and drew in another one. Color vision returned. Her panic subsided.

In the meantime, a couple of other men in suits had stepped to the door, grabbed her arms, hauled her up off the floor, and dragged her into the room. They sat her down on a chair. The room contained four cheap steel desks, chairs to go with them, a couch, and a table with a coffee machine. In the corner was some kind of a communications setup: a phone switchboard and a two-way radio.

Eleanor closed her eyes and just concentrated on breathing for a while. But when she closed her eyes, her head began to swim around; she was still dizzy from having it slammed into the wall. She kept her eyes open just enough to get a strong visual fix on one object: a cheesy pinup of a woman with huge breasts, dressed half in a cop uniform and half in sexy lingerie, a pistol stuck into the band of her fishnet stocking, dangling a set of handcuffs from her finger.

Finally she recovered enough to get pissed. "What the hell is going on here!?" she said, and rose from her chair. But someone gripped the collar of her sweatshirt from behind, twisted it tight around her neck, and jerked her back down into the chair. "Shut up, sister," a voice said. "You should know better than to make trouble."

Then they grabbed her arms and pulled them around behind her back, behind the back of the chair. She heard a high zipping noise and felt something go tight around her wrists: plastic handcuffs. She couldn't move her arms.

"Would you guys mind telling me who the hell you are?" she said.

They ignored her. The man in the suit who had confronted her in the elevator went over to the telephone, punched a couple of buttons, and spoke: "Yeah, this is Moore in Security. We have apprehended a black female carrying a bag with someone's purse and some jewelry. She is intoxicated, violent, and disorderly. Have you had any complaints of missing property from any of the guests tonight?"

He listened for a moment. "Okay. Well, it's possible she hit one of the other hotels on the block and just got here. You want to phone some of the others and see if they've had any problems?"

By now, the entire contents of Eleanor's tote bag had been spread out across a table, and the hotel dicks were pawing through them, making lewd comments about her underwear and appraising her jewelry.

Eleanor knew she should have been chewing them out. She should have been calling down the retribution of heaven above. But she was so stunned that it was almost more interesting to stand back and observe.

A television set was going on the coffee table, showing a late-night news program. Her face flashed up on the screen right next to Cozzano's. What happened next was the most gratifying moment she had experienced since the birth of her last child. "Look at the TV," she said.

*Mr. Salvador reached* Cy Ogle by sky phone the next day. Ogle was on one of the Cozzano campaign planes. *Cozzano 1* carried the candidate, his Secret Service detail, staff, and immediate hangers-on; *Cozzano 2*, was a press plane; and *Cozzano 3*, which hardly anyone knew about, was a GODS cargo plane. It carried a GODS shipping container, the Eye of Cy. Ogle was on *Cozzano 1* when he got the call from Mr. Salvador, who was upset. "Did you see the morning papers?"

"Of course I did," Ogle said.

"It's exactly as I predicted. Eleanor Richmond is a loose cannon."

"Now, why would you say that?"

"Are you kidding? The first thing she does is go out and get herself arrested."

"Detained. Not arrested."

"And then, immediately, without consulting you, she begins to run her mouth. Yap yap yap, racists here, racists there, lynch mob mentality, all the usual radical Afro-American buzzwords."

"You can't blame her for being pissed."

"I can blame her for being strident. Did you see her on TV this morning? In front of the hotel?"

"Yes."

"Who authorized her to throw a street rally?"

"I don't think she threw it, per se," Ogle said. "It just sort of happened. A bunch of people came up from the South Side and wanted to burn the hotel down. She came out and cooled them off."

"Well, it *looked* like a rally."

"I know it did."

"And the last thing we need is some kind of an outspoken radical black woman running through the streets with a megaphone."

"Mr. Salvador," Ogle said, quietly and forbearingly, "Eleanor Richmond, as we speak, is on a plane to Cashmere, Washington, to pick apples with migrant farm workers. Then she's going to go white-water rafting and read a scripted speech about the importance of wild rivers. Then she's going to fly to San Diego to mend fences with those Mexican people who run up the centerlines of highways. Then—"

"Okay, I get the picture," Mr. Salvador said.

"So does she, I think," Ogle said.

---

## CHAPTER FORTY-EIGHT

Presidential campaigns had their own calendar: a series of special days, sprinkled throughout the year, determined by certain arcane astrological formulae. Chief among these was Election Day itself, which was the first Tuesday after the first Monday in November. Another such occasion was Labor Day, which, to most people, marked the end of summer, but which to politicians marked the formal beginning of the presidential campaign—a complete surprise to almost everyone in America.

So television viewers across the land, who for the last year had not been able to settle into their recliners without being exposed to a scene of red-white-and-blue balloons and flawlessly coiffed candidates standing in front of blue curtains in hotel ballrooms, were generally befuddled when they checked the evening news on Labor Day and were informed, by solemn anchorpersons, that Tip McLane, the President, and William A. Cozzano had all kicked off their campaigns today.

The shortest point between a camera and a backdrop is a straight line passing through the candidate's head. Who these three candidates were, and how they would run their campaigns, could be inferred from the things they stood in front of.

The President stood in front of an empty Buick plant in Flint, Michigan. This informed the viewing public that he was a serious, taking-care-of-business type who cared about the downtrodden (unlike, for example, Tip McLane) and that he intended to renew America.

Nimrod T. ("Tip") McLane stood in a lettuce field in California where he and his parents had once stooped at menial labor; behind him rose a mountain vista. This backdrop told the viewing public that Tip McLane had not forgotten his humble roots, that he was a grass-roots, back-to-basics conservative who was not afraid to roll up his sleeves and get his hands dirty.

William A. Cozzano and his running mate Eleanor Richmond kicked off their independent campaign on the runway of a municipal airport south of Seattle. This was a fairly complicated bit of multileveled background engineering. The immediate background consisted of a runway, outlined in colored lights and streaked with tire marks, conveying a strong sense of motion (Cozzano is taking off!). The next thing down the line was a vast Boeing airplane factory; brand-new 767s were lined up on the apron, each tail fin freshly and brightly painted in the color scheme of a different airline somewhere around the world. Finally, in the deep background, Mount Rainier heaved itself up out of a low, dark line of foothills. It was so vast that it looked like a telephoto lens shot, even through a normal lens, and when the cameramen enhanced it with their telephotos (as none of them could resist doing) it looked like a giant ice-covered asteroid looming over the shoulders of William A. Cozzano and Eleanor Richmond.

Boeing had nothing to do with the Cozzano campaign, of course, or so they said. This whole event was being held on municipal property. The presence of a Boeing facility next door was a convenient accident.

Cozzano looked snappy in his homburg, the sort of old-fashioned men's hat that had gone out of fashion when JFK had refused to wear one, and that Cozzano was now singlehandedly bringing back into fashion. In the middle of his campaign-kickoff address, a new 767, painted with the logo of Japan Airlines, taxied onto the runway. Its tail fin momentarily came between Cozzano and the glaciated slopes of Rainier, then narrowed into a vertical blade as the plane turned onto the runway, revealing the mountain, illuminated by a peach-colored sunrise. The icy clarity of Rainier was muddled by the heat waves rising from the jet's engines. Then those engines glowed bluish-white, the plane accelerated down the runway, directly toward Rainier, shot into the air, banked into a climbing turn, and headed west, bound for Japan. It happened just as Cozzano was making a point about the trade deficit; and as the roar of the jet engines died away, it was almost possible to hear a dim cacophony of whacking noises from the directions of California and of Flint, Michigan, as Cozzano's competitors and their campaign managers smacked their foreheads in anguish.

*Floyd Wayne Vishniak* watched this lovely spectacle in a cool, dark hollow set in the folds of the Monongahela National Forest in West Virginia. He was not much more than a hundred miles outside of Washington, D.C., and yet the location could scarcely have been more remote.

He had been camping out here for a couple of days, just lying low for a time, watching Cozzano on his wristwatch TV-cum-brain-control device, tossing the occasional lure into the stream that ran past his little campsite, draining cans of beer and then shooting them full of big starburst holes with his nimble Fleischacker. His truck was stopped on a gravelly floodplain, the floor of a ravine with nearly vertical sides that made a perfect backstop for shooting. He had brought two cases of inexpensive beer with him, going out of

his way to obtain cans rather than bottles. You could only shoot a
bottle once, but you could shoot a can over and over again until not
much was left of it; this was how a man had to pinch his pennies
nowadays.

Out here in the Eastern time zone, the sun had already been up
for a few hours and so the peach-colored light on the slopes of
Rainier looked strange and faky. Vishniak was sure that the lumber-
ing jetliner and the ice-covered volcano looked great on the kind of
thirty-nine-inch Trinitron that rich people would own, but on his
postage-stamp wristwatch it didn't really look so hot.

That was okay. Images were all fakery and manipulation cobbled
together by the evil gnomes of Ogle Data Research, who had their
secret headquarters just a short distance away, in the mysterious
place called Pentagon Towers. What counted was words. So when
Cozzano stepped up to the microphones to make the formal campaign kickoff speech, Vishniak emptied his Fleischacker into a hapless beer can, set the safety, put the gun into the shoulder holster
under his QUAD CITIES WHIPLASH windbreaker, and sat down on
the tailgate of his pickup to listen to the murmuring of the stream
and the speech that William A. Cozzano was delivering to him and
the rest of the American people. As the introductions were being
made, Vishniak pulled a small reporter's notebook out of his pocket.
The last page read:

COZZANO'S HATS (CONTD.)

| SUN AUG 25 | CHICAGO CUBS BASEBALL CAP |
| MON AUG 26 | HARD HAT (STEEL MILL VISIT) |
| TUE AUG 27 | NO HAT — BUT HE STAYED INDOORS!!! |
| WED AUG 28 | THE HOMBURG |
| THU AUG 29 | U.S. FLAG BASEBALL CAP |
| FRI AUG 30 | BIKE HELMET (ORLANDO BIKE-A-THON) |
| SAT AUG 31 | THE HOMBURG |
| SUN SEP 1 | NO HAT — WENT TO CHURCH |

and now he added a new line:

| SUN SEP 2 | THE HOMBURG AGAIN |

Some kind of spooky shit was definitely going on with those hats. They were all saying now that the homburg was some kind of a Fashion Statement, but William A. Cozzano had never felt any need to make such statements until he had gotten that chip stuck into his brain. It obviously had something to do with brain waves.

In his speech, Cozzano covered the usual bases: the corruption of big-party politics, the need for change. Change not only in the political system but in the values system of the entire country. Change that would renew our commitment to education and to long-term investment in the future. This topic led, inevitably, to the subject of the economy, at which point Vishniak finally started to pay attention. The economy was the only thing that mattered to him.

"There are those who say that we are doomed to be a second-rate power, subjugated to the Japanese," Cozzano said, just as the big Boeing jet was beginning its takeoff run. Vishniak clenched his teeth and became enraged, as he always did when people said this kind of thing.

"To those people," Cozzano continued, "I have only one thing to say: BEHOLD!" He turned aside and swept out one arm toward the jet, then watched it take off. To shout above the scream of its turbofans would have been futile, would have made him look tiny and weak by comparison. As Vishniak watched the miniature figure of the jet take off on his little screen, saw it bank into its turn, exposing the Rising Sun logo painted on its tail fin, his anger was replaced by a surge of defiant pride. Sure the economic situation looked bleak, but a country that could make airplanes like that could accomplish anything if it just set its mind to it.

Cozzano turned to the microphones and said, "No matter how bleak the economists and the pundits say our situation is, I think that any country that can make airplanes like that one can, with hard work and determination, accomplish anything."

Vishniak felt relieved that a great man like Cozzano felt the same as he did, that his feelings weren't just stupid, blind patriotism. But he was a jittery and suspicious fellow by nature and could not be satisfied with this kind of happy talk for long.

"Now, I would be lying if I stopped there, and left you with the impression that happy talk is going to close the trade deficit," Cozzano said. "Uplifting speeches and slick media images do not an economy make. What we need is to educate our children. But not just to cram their heads with facts and figures—to teach them values as well, values of hard, steady work."

That was a little better. Cozzano was talking some sense there. Although Vishniak was beginning to get a little skeptical about politicians who always spouted this easy talk about education. Education was great but it wouldn't really help the economy for another twenty years. And it wouldn't help the likes of Floyd Wayne Vishniak at all.

"People think that when I speak of education I mean kindergarten, elementary school, and high school," Cozzano said, "but education is more than that. Education is a lifelong process. An unemployed, down-and-out factory worker in the Midwest can benefit from education just as much as a five-year-old child."

"Wait just a goddamn minute," Floyd Wayne Vishniak said, out loud.

It was just a little too much—that bit about the down-and-out midwestern factory worker. He rewound his mental tape of the last few minutes and played it back inside his head, ignoring the rest of Cozzano's speech (Cozzano had now gone on to talk about the need for corporate America to shape up and restructure itself).

Vishniak held the Dick Tracy watch up to his eye and scrutinized the scene carefully. Cozzano didn't have any notes up there on the lectern. And it didn't seem like he was using a TelePrompTer. He was looking around naturally, seemingly speaking off-the-cuff, making everything up as he went along. This was a habit that had been noticed and remarked upon by all the papers that Vishniak had been reading over the summer: Cozzano, who in years past had written his own speeches and read them back, hewing closely to a fixed script, had, in the last few months, taken to speaking extemporaneously.

Floyd Wayne Vishniak was beginning to understand why. William A. Cozzano was reading his mind. He was reading Vishniak's brain waves and telling him exactly what he wanted to hear! How was he doing it? Through the wristwatch, no doubt. That was the key to the whole thing.

Vishniak rotated his forearm, the palm of his hand facing upward, to expose the little button that would release the ratchet and pop the watch off his wrist. All he had to do was take it off and then he would be a free man again, and William A. Cozzano would no longer be able to read his brain waves. He had been wearing it continuously for a couple of weeks, and underneath it his skin was itching fiercely. But he couldn't take it off, no matter what. He had to trust his instincts. He knew that they were watching him and that to remove the wristwatch meant certain death, a nice dose of shellfish poison straight into his arm. He'd never get that thing off. He was on a suicide mission.

He jumped off the tailgate, climbed into the cab of his truck, dug his road atlas out from under the seat, and began to contemplate possible approach vectors to the seat of all evil in the world.

## CHAPTER FORTY-NINE

Shortly after Floyd Wayne Vishniak entered the greater Washington metropolitan area, something completely shocking and unprecedented happened to him: he got a job.

It happened in Pentagon Plaza, of all places. He had gone there expecting to stage a bloodbath and ended up filling out job applications. The unpredictability of life in America was a constant source of amusement to him.

He had spent half a day doing recon. Pentagon Plaza, he concluded after driving around it at high speed several dozen times, was a single building that just happened to look like a whole bunch of different buildings very close together. There was a parking ramp (the rich and powerful had to have their parking spaces!) and a low, squat, enormous structure mostly concealed behind that, and rising up from it were a couple of skyscrapers—Pentagon Towers. But they were all part of the same complex. The fortress of darkness owned and operated by Ogle Data Research.

How best to make his approach? His maps told him that there was a Metro stop beneath Pentagon Plaza. That would be a good way to get in close. But in the end he decided against it. He had no idea what was going to happen. If he didn't get killed, he would want to get out of there fast, and taking the subway wasn't the way to do it. Better to have his truck handy.

He could park outside and walk in or—daring idea—he could actually drive onto the parking ramp. This latter idea, while it might seem impossibly audacious, held major advantages. It was worth checking out. He drove past the entrances to the parking ramp several times, going very slowly, his window rolled down, and observed people driving into the place. Everyone got in without hassle. They pulled up to a little machine, slammed a button, and pulled out a ticket. The gate rose up and they drove on in. No one inspected them. You didn't have to show any kind of ID.

It was worth a try. The worst thing that could happen was that he'd have to crash through the gate. He pulled into the chute. So much adrenaline was pumping through his system now that his teeth hurt and his gums felt hot and swollen.

He stopped by the little machine, and, trying to look nonchalant, like he did this every day, he reached out and punched the button. A cardboard ticket spat out of the machine. He jerked it out. The gate rose up.

Calmly, like he belonged here, Floyd Wayne Vishniak piloted his pickup truck into the bowels of Pentagon Plaza.

The parking ramp held no secrets. He found a space and backed into it. This unorthodox maneuver caused consternation and horn-honking among several other would-be parkers, but (a) they could all fuck themselves, (b) he had a gun, and (c) he needed to park this way so he could pull out rapidly when the time came.

The Fleischacker was hanging in his armpit. He had purchased several overly long thirty-round magazines for it. Loaded with teflon armor-piercing bullets, these were secreted in the long cargo pockets built into the thighs of his trousers. By reaching down and unsnapping the flaps on the tops of those pockets, he could whip out a new magazine in a fraction of a second. One magazine was already stuck into the handle of his Fleischacker, making the gun huge, unwieldy, and L-shaped. His QUAD CITIES WHIPLASH windbreaker hid the weapon adequately as long as he kept it zipped up most of the way, and kept his arm down to his side.

He locked up his truck (wouldn't do for his getaway vehicle to get ripped off while he was busying himself inside) and then followed a few other people toward a sky bridge and a set of glass doors that joined the parking ramp to the huge, squat building next to it.

The headquarters of Ogle Data Research was cleverly disguised as a fancy department store!

Vishniak forced himself to keep calm. He walked through the middle of a huge display of women's shoes, trying to act just as cool as all the other people, like he came through here all the time. He did this on the assumption that the department store was just a false-front operation like the ones on *Mission: Impossible* and that it would be all of about thirty feet deep. Once he passed through this shoe display he would begin to see the brain-wave monitors and satellite dishes. Then the Fleischacker would come out and Ogle's evil operation would come to an end. Vishniak would die, probably, and Cozzano would be released from electronic bondage.

But when he made it through the shoe display, he came to a section full of purses. Then more women's clothes. Perfume. Cosmetics. He went up an escalator (Keep walking! Don't stop and look!) and found a display of television sets, then a little gourmet restaurant. It went on and on and on.

He kept walking. His brain was reeling. He went up and down the escalators several times and eventually walked out through a huge doorway and into something that looked very much like a shopping mall. But not like any shopping mall that Vishniak had seen in the Quad Cities. For him, a mall was a single narrow concourse, one story, lined with tiny shops, a few benches, and maybe a fountain in the middle.

Compared to the malls he was used to, this place was like—well, like Washington, D.C., compared to Davenport, Iowa. It was four stories high. The floors were gleaming white marble. A central atrium was filled with light streaming down through a glass ceiling; looking up through it, Vishniak could see the sky, and airplanes taking off from the airport, and the office skyscrapers towering overhead.

It went on forever. Thousands of people were here, visiting hundreds of stores. Some of the stores were tiny rinky-dink ones, but a lot of them were huge and fancy. It was no longer possible to support the belief that this was all a false-front operation for Ogle Data Research. This was a real, honest-to-god shopping mall, albeit an incomprehensibly vast and rich one.

He kept walking. On the one hand, he was confused and a bit disappointed that he had failed to locate Ogle Data Research. On the other hand, he was relieved, and breathing easily for the first time since he had entered the city. This business was clearly much more complicated than he'd thought at first. He was going to have to settle in and put a lot more thought into the intelligence-gathering phase of the operation.

Before long, he came to a big electric sign: a color-coded directory of the Pentagon Plaza Mall. It contained floor plans of each of the four levels, each store identified by number, with a listing of all the stores by category.

It was almost too much to hope for that he could find ODR in this way, but he gave it a shot. The stores were arranged by category: WOMEN'S APPAREL, MEN'S APPAREL, RESTAURANTS, JEWELRY, GIFTS, and so on. Vishniak was unclear about which category described Ogle Data Research, and so he just began at the beginning and read through the names of every single business in the mall, which took several minutes. There was no Ogle Data Research listed.

Inspiration came in the form of a HELP WANTED sign in the window of one of the stores. Applying for jobs was one good excuse to get into a store and check it out without actually spending money. And—unthinkable as it might seem—if he could actually get a job here at Pentagon Plaza, he would be able to spend all his time here, and recon the place in detail. An inside job was always the best way to do a crime.

He had filled out enough job applications in his day to know that you had to have an address. So he exited the mall the way he had come, paid an outrageous fee for parking, and, under the name Sherman Grant, rented a room at a motel near National Airport, only a mile or two from Pentagon Plaza. Then he found a post office where he was able to rent a box, giving him that all-important mailing address. By this point his money was beginning to run low, but he had spent the summer accumulating credit cards that had been mailed to him unasked-for, by fatuous banks in places like Delaware and South Dakota, and these went a long way.

Thus did Floyd Wayne Vishniak set up his own little base of operations in the nation's capital, joining every other person, company, pressure group, trade association, and maniac with a national agenda. A second trip to Pentagon Plaza that evening (this time via the less expensive Metro) netted a dozen more job applications. He stayed up until one in the morning filling them out in his best sixth-grade penmanship, and was down at the mall bright and early the next morning, as soon as the stores opened up, to hand them all in. And on this, his third trip to the mall, he didn't even bother to bring his gun.

Success came surprisingly quickly; the mall management offered Sherman Grant a job working in the food court, clearing and wiping down tables. A yuppie bastard interviewed him for the job, just to make sure that he, who had formerly assembled giant tractor transmissions for a living, was intelligent enough to pick garbage off of tables and wipe them with a damp rag. Vishniak swallowed his resentment and averred that he would try his very best to handle the unprecedented challenges of the job.

He considered holding out to see if any other jobs were offered to him, but decided to take the first one that came along. He had to keep his eye on the ball here. The purpose of this trip was not to develop new career paths. The purpose was to put bullets in the heads of the top management stratum of Ogle Data Research and then destroy as much of their high-tech brain-wave equipment as he could get into his gunsights before he himself was gunned down by the SWAT teams that showed up, so inevitably, at these kinds of events.

He started immediately. They issued him an apron and a hat. The training period lasted for about ten seconds and then he was working. The food court at Pentagon Plaza was on the ground floor, filling up a big open space in the floor plan that, in higher stories, was occupied by a hole with a railing around it: a huge atrium that looked down on the sea of tables and chairs shared by all of the fast-food places lining the food court. The atrium and the court were vaulted by a huge glass ceiling that let in so much light that Vishniak often wore sunglasses.

At first he was humiliated to take the job. He was the only English-speaking person doing it. He never felt good about the job itself, but after a short while he began to understand that, from a reconaissance standpoint, it could hardly have been more perfect. Vishniak ambled across a large territory all day long, sizing up thousands of people, overhearing snatches of their conversations, learning where they worked and what they did. It was exactly the job he needed.

One day, after he'd been there for about a week and scanned tens of thousands of faces, he actually saw one he recognized: Aaron Green. Green was all by himself at one of the stand-up tables, eating raw fish—sushi, they called it—and reading a computer magazine. He was wearing a suit. On the floor, a briefcase stood up between his legs. Vishniak circled around him once or twice, watching his face, and confirmed the ID.

Vishniak got that adrenalized feeling again for the first time since he'd made his first approach to Pentagon Plaza. If Aaron Green looked up and recognized him, he was as good as dead. Fortunately, he was wearing his sunglasses. And since he had begun working here he had taken the precaution of wrapping an Ace bandage around his wrist every morning to conceal the wristwatch Green had given him.

Vishniak watched Green through his sunglasses the same way that he watched babes down along the river on hot summer days: his head turned sideways to the target, his eyes swiveled in their sockets so the women didn't know they were being watched. Eventually Green finished eating his sushi, flipped through the last few pages of his computer magazine, and picked up his briefcase. He maneuvered through the crowded floor of the food court and climbed on the up escalator. Vishniak followed him, climbing onto the bottom of the escalator just as Green was getting off at the top.

Green went up a couple of floors and then began to walk through the mall, skirting the edge of the atrium. Vishniak followed him at a distance. Finally Green stopped at a pair of elevator doors set unobtrusively into the wall, between a leather store and an electronics place. He took a key out of his pocket and shoved it into a wall switch. The elevator doors opened and Green climbed on board and disappeared.

Vishniak gave the elevator doors a closer inspection, cursing himself for having been so dense. He had walked past these doors a hundred times and never really noticed them. He had assumed that they were a freight elevator or something else—not a secret entrance to Ogle Data Research.

This discovery did not help him much; you had to have a key to get on the elevator. But still, a lead was a lead. That day, Vishniak took an early lunch, went to a haircutting place in the mall, and spent his day's salary getting his long hair cut short and his beard shaved off. He couldn't risk being recognized by Aaron Green. With the new hair and the sunglasses, he was unrecognizable.

Not far from the elevator doors was a bench where tired shoppers could rest their legs. During his off hours, Vishniak took to spending a lot of time on that bench, watching the elevator doors.

Most of the people who went in and out of the elevator were typical office workers, all nicely dressed. But very soon, Vishniak began to notice a pattern: certain of these office workers would habitually come out of the elevators, always in pairs. One of them would stand by the elevator doors with a key. The other would go off into the mall. Within a few minutes, unfamiliar people would begin to gravitate toward the elevator doors—plain, old, off-the-street types. The person stationed by the elevator doors would use the key to open the doors and dispatch them up to the eleventh floor. An hour or two later, these people would emerge again and then go their separate ways.

Vishniak was curious as to what was being done to these regular people during the hour or two that they spent up on the eleventh floor. Was it some kind of brain surgery? Were they all being turned into robots like Cozzano?

After a while he came to recognize the people who went into the mall to rope these people in, and he took to following them around to see what they were doing. They always carried clipboards; the clipboards always had lists on them, and as they persuaded different people to come up to the eleventh floor they would cross an item off the list. And they did not go up to people at random; they would go to particular stores, or busy intersections in the mall, and scan the faces of the shoppers, looking for particular types.

Vishniak overheard an interesting bit of conversation on one occasion, as he was trailing a young woman with a clipboard. She happened to run into another clipboard-toting woman who was out in the mall trolling for subjects.

"Marcie! Hi!"

"Oh, hi, Sherry. What are you looking for?"

"The usual—a mall concubine and a porch monkey. How about you?"

"I've got everything on my list except for a Post-Confederate Gravy Eater."

"Oh. You know what you should do? See that newsstand over there?"

Sherry gave some instructions to Marcie. Marcie thanked her and went to the newsstand, where she found a long-haired young man, wearing a T-shirt with a confederate flag on the back, leafing through a copy of *Guns & Ammo*. After a short conversation, this young man nodded, put the magazine back on the rack, and followed Marcie out of the store.

*Pentagon Plaza was* not the kind of mall where you could come by Confederate flags easily, but there were many such places in the less affluent stretches of northern Virginia, and that night, Floyd Wayne Vishniak hit a few of them. He also stopped in at a newsstand and bought a few gun magazines—a subject that interested him anyway.

The next day, after finishing his shift wiping tables, he went to the men's room, locked himself into a stall, and took off his apron and his hat. He pulled on a Confederate T-shirt. Over that he put on his shoulder holster. He was wearing his cargo pants with the ammo clips in them. Finally he pulled on a bright red windbreaker with the Confederate flag on the back and zipped it up just enough to hide the gun. Then he went upstairs and sat on the bench near the elevators and settled in comfortably to read his gun magazines. He was going to have to come up with a new name—Lee Jackson or something.

In the end, he read those magazines pretty thoroughly, and got to know everthing a man could know about the latest in weapons technology, because he ended up spending three solid eight-hour shifts on that bench before he was finally noticed.

"Excuse me, sir?" a young woman said.

Vishniak looked up. It was Marcie. She had her clipboard.

"I work for an opinion research company called Ogle Data Research," she continued, "and I was wondering if you'd mind if I asked you a few questions. Are you in the twenty-six to thirty-five age group?"

"Yes, I am," he said.

"Are you from the South, and do you consider yourself to be a Southerner?"

"Proud of it too," he said.

"And would you consider yourself unemployed or underemployed?"

"Absolutely."

"Well, how would you like to make fifty dollars? It'll take about an hour."

"Fifty bucks in an hour?" Vishniak said. "Well, yee-ha! This is my lucky day."

## CHAPTER FIFTY

This was where he'd have to be careful. He still had no idea what the Ogle Data Research people were actually doing to their test subjects up there on the eleventh floor. If it was some kind of brain surgery, then Vishniak would have to open fire before they could get him under anaesthesia. Otherwise he would become one of the living dead, a robot slave like Cozzano.

To outward appearances, everything seemed real nice. They had a big lobby by the elevators. It was all decorated. A nice young woman, whom Vishniak recognized from his reconnaissance, greeted him and led him around past the big curving desk where the receptionist sat with her space-age headset. Two security guards stood by, shifting their weight from one tired foot to the other; one of them was about ninety years old and the other one was overweight. Vishniak considered picking them off right here and now but decided against it; as long as they kept leading him deeper into the bowels of ODR, there was no reason to get feisty.

The girl offered him coffee but he refused; maybe that was how they knocked people out. She ushered him into a room with half a dozen chairs, all facing a big fancy TV set. Made in Japan, naturally. Three other people were already sitting there, and Vishniak recognized them as the sort of typical mall-cruising Americans that the ODR agents were always trying to recruit. A couple of them were drinking coffee but seemed to be suffering no ill effects so far.

Vishniak took a seat and waited for the usher gal to leave the room. Then he stood up, ambled over to the door, and stuck his head out into the hallway, trying to get a sense of the layout. They were not far from the receptionist's station. In the other direction, the hallway led past a line of offices. All the offices had big picture windows to let in the light, and so Vishniak could tell from a distance which doors were open and which were closed. Glancing back the other way he saw that the fat security guard was eyeballing him. He withdrew into the room and went over to the windows.

They had an incredible view. A fellow could probably make money, Vishniak reflected, by renting out an office in this building and charging mall shoppers a quarter to ride the elevators up and look out the windows. They were so close to the Pentagon that you could probably hawk a loogie into its central courtyard. Off to the left of the Pentagon was a huge cemetery with millions of white gravestones. This juxtaposition made good horse sense in that the Pentagon had to do with killing people. Beyond these landmarks was a river, and on the far shore of that river, Vishniak looked right into the heart of Washington. He didn't recognize it at first because, compared to Chicago, it was sparse and low-slung, like a farm or a park.

A long, narrow strip of grass ran off into the distance and it was lined with white buildings. In the middle of it was a tall spiky thing. At the far end of it was a dome that Vishniak recognized as being the Capitol. Beyond that, he could not really tell one building from another: there were a million of them, they were all white, they had lots of columns and the occasional squat dome. The only other one that looked familiar was located on the far side of the strip of grass, off the main drag: he thought it was the White House.

But it didn't look exactly right. He had seen the White House on TV a million times, always with a TV reporter standing in front of it, and thought it had a simple crackerbox shape with a veranda bulging out from the long side of it. But from this vantage point he could see that this thing he had always thought of as the White House was just the central unit in a sprawling, far-flung affair. The thing had wings sticking out to both sides, and the wings had additions tacked onto them. It was like a simple crackerbox house that the owner kept adding rooms to, until it rambled crazily all over the lot.

Seeing this, Vishniak felt betrayed. He had been raised to believe that the White House was just the President's house. His family lived there and his kids hunted easter eggs on the lawn. It was big and nice by house standards, but still a house. But now he could see that the White House wasn't a real house at all. It was a false front for a rambling complex of sinister-looking additions that were cleverly concealed behind trees and bushes. And a fellow had to ask himself what happened in those additions, and what kind of people worked there, that their existence was so carefully kept hidden from the American public.

"Excuse me, sir?" someone was saying. He felt a hand placed gently on his arm, and startled away from it. It was one of the ODR gals. "Would you like to have a seat? We're about to get started."

"Sure," he said, and took a seat, one that had a good view of the door. While he had been standing at the window analyzing the structure of the U.S. Government, two other mall folk had come into the room, making a total complement of six.

What happened next was kind of amusing: they passed out wrist cuffs, one per customer. They were just like the one that Vishniak was already wearing, except that these didn't have the built-in TV screens. Playing dumb, Vishniak watched the gal explain how to put them on your arm, and followed her instructions with artificial clumsiness. Now he had one on each wrist.

Then she closed the blinds, turned off the lights, and showed them about fifteen minutes of television. Most of it consisted of advertisements but there were a few news stories in there too. All of it had to do, one way or another, with William A. Cozzano. Some of the ads were fuzzy-warm, touchy-feely numbers showing past events in Cozzano's life, including some grainy home videos of Cozzano recovering from his stroke that made Vishniak get choked up. Some of the ads were attacks on the President or Tip McLane. And then there were news stories—excerpts from what looked like network broadcasts. But the anchormen were unfamiliar to Vishniak. And the news events being reported had not actually happened.

Watching the anchorman read the stories, Vishniak sensed, somehow, that he was familiar. But not as an anchorman. As something else. Then it came to him: this man had played the captain of a starship—not the *Enterprise*—in an episode of *Star Trek: The Next Generation*. He was an actor. And this news story was fake. It hadn't really happened. It was just a *potential* news story.

*"Huh. Getting some* interesting reactions from our Post-Confederate Gravy Eater," Aaron Green said. He was sitting in the next room, looking at half a dozen monitor screens. Next to him was Shane Schram.

"What's this guy's problem?" Shane Schram said. He looked at a TV monitor showing the face of the Post-Confederate Gravy Eater, who was staring fixedly at the screen, jaw muscles throbbing.

"Incredible cortex activity," Aaron said, scrutinizing the readout.

"What does that mean?"

"It means his mental gears are spinning at a million rpm. He's thinking way too hard about everything."

"Can't have that. We'll just throw out his results," Schram said.

The videotape came to an end. Schram got up, walked next door, and turned on the lights in the focus group room. Then he delivered his usual self-introduction, which Aaron Green had now listened to a million times.

The door opened and Mr. Salvador came into the room, joining Aaron. Everyone called him Mr. Salvador because he had a kind of intercontinental breeding that inspired un-American levels of formality and because he was their boss. Even Cy Ogle's boss. But he wasn't just some figurehead who golfed and went to the occasional board meeting. He was very much a hands-on type. He spent days at a time holed up in the room where they had set up all of the monitors for the PIPER 100.

"We're doing a PIPER broadcast in a couple of minutes," Mr. Salvador said. "I'd like you to join me and give me your analysis."

"What's up?"

"Cozzano's giving an address to a convention of gun nuts in Tulsa," Salvador said. "It's going to be his major statement on the gun control issue. Which, in this country, seems to be hysterically emotional."

"That's for sure."

*"I'm just sick* of all this gutter politics," the lady said. She was a solidly built, bifocal-wearing woman with a conservative midwestern haircut, wearing a lavender jogging suit. Fresh off a tour bus from Indiana, no doubt. "I just don't want to see any more of this trash."

"I think you *do* want to see it," Schram said, "I think you are fascinated by this kind of thing. I think that, when you go to the grocery stores, you deliberately stand in the longest checkout line so that you will have time to pull the tabloids off the racks and leaf through them. And then you put them back on the racks, because you're not the kind of person who would read sleazy tabloids—are you?"

The woman was utterly dumbfounded. "How—how did you know that? Have you been following me around or something?"

"Stop messing with her brain waves!" said the Post-Confederate Gravy Eater. Contrary to his assigned stereotype, he did not have a southern accent. More midwestern.

"How's that again?" Schram asked.

"You get into people's brains, I know you do. Can't you see you're bothering that woman?"

Schram shrugged innocently and held up his hands, palms up. "Hey. I'm just here having a conversation with her. I don't know anything about brain waves."

"Oh, yeah?" the man said, yanking the cuff off his wrist. "Then what's this?"

"That's already been explained," Schram said.

"Your explanations are all lies and cover-ups," the man said.

"Look," Schram said, "let me be honest. We're done with your interview, sir. Why don't you go ahead and take off. You can pick up your fifty dollars at the desk."

"What about these others?"

"I'd like to talk to them a little bit more."

"Why don't you want to talk to me? Isn't my opinion important?"

"We had a bug in our equipment," Schram said. "It didn't work in your case. So to keep you here any longer would be a waste of time. Thank you for coming in."

The man stood up out of his chair, facing the door, and then hesitated. He had grabbed the zipper pull on his red Confederate flag windbreaker with his left hand and was nervously zipping it up and down. He seemed to be deep in thought.

"Sir? That's all we need from you," Schram said. "You can go home now. Thanks for coming in."

"Okay," the man said, finally zipping his zipper all the way up to his neck. "Okay, I think I'll go back home now. Thanks. It was real interesting. I learned a lot."

"You're welcome," Schram said.

The man started for the exit. Then music began to come out of him, as if he were carrying a transistor radio in his pocket. He stopped and froze for a moment.

The music was tinny and compressed, as if coming from a very small speaker. It was a patriotic fifes-and-drums number. Shane Schram stared in astonishment.

The man took his hands out of his pockets. One wrist had an Ace bandage wrapped around it. The music became louder. He ripped the Ace bandage off. The sound of applause was now coming from his wrist.

*William A. Cozzano* stepped to the lectern and waved down the applause and cheers of the attendees at the Tulsa Gun and Knife Show.

"My Secret Service people wanted to provide additional security for me today," he said, "because I was addressing a bunch of gun owners, and for some reason that made them nervous. Well, I have one thing to say to you gun owners: if any one of you really wants to take a shot at me, *here I am!*"

Cozzano stepped back from the lectern and held his arms out wide. The hall was filled with stunned murmuring for a few moments. Then the gun owners exploded. Peals of cheers, applause, and foot-stomping overwhelmed the sound system on the PIPER watch.

*Floyd Wayne Vishniak* was staring into Shane Schram's face, sizing him up. Schram's eyes were jumping back and forth between the little TV and his face.

"You're Economic Roadkill," Schram said. "You're Floyd Wayne Vishniak!"

Floyd Wayne Vishniak unzipped his windbreaker and reached inside. "That was a really stupid thing for you to say," he said. Then he pulled out a handgun and pointed it at Schram. Everyone else in the room collapsed out of their chairs.

"I can see that you're very upset," Schram said.

"How many times do I have to tell you," Vishniak said, "to stay the hell out of my brain waves!" Then he fired a single round that entered Schram's head through the bridge of his nose and left through an exit wound, in the back of his skull, that would have accommodated a grapefruit.

"Don't worry," Vishniak said to the five people on the floor, who could scarcely hear a word he was saying because their ears were ringing from the incredible blast of the handgun. "You don't have to worry about these bastards anymore!"

*"What the hell* was that?" Mr. Salvador said. He and Green were in the PIPER monitor room, watching Cozzano shake his hands together above his head, basking in waves of applause.

"Nothing," Green said. "Another one of Schram's psychological experiments."

"I thought we were finished with the calibration phase," Mr. Salvador said.

"Believe me," Green said, "this place is like Dodge City sometimes. It's all fake."

*Vishniak popped his* head into the hallway and withdrew it before anyone could get off a shot. But the precaution was unnecessary. No one was there.

He chanced a second look and saw the fat security guard in the lobby, looking back at him with only mild concern, as if highranking executives at ODR got their brains blown against the walls every day. Vishniak drew back into the room, his back to the doorway. He gripped the Fleischacker in both hands, spun around into the hall while bringing the gun downward, steadied his arm against the door frame for a second, and fired three quick shots. The first two hit the guard in the chest and the last one was high.

Now he had to move fast. He ran toward the lobby, spun through the doorway, and took aim at the old guard, who was in the act of unsnapping his holster. He fired two rounds into the man's head and upper body from a distance of about six feet. Then he spun toward the receptionist's desk.

She had already vaulted her desk and was cowering and screaming on the far side. That was okay, she was just a gnome. The key was to take out the switchboard. Vishniak fired a spread of some half-dozen bullets into her computer and her telephone switchboard.

He turned back into the hallway, reached down with one hand, and unsnapped the flaps on the tops of his cargo pockets. He tucked the flaps down into the pockets, as he had practiced many times, so that they would not get in the way when he reached down to pull out more clips.

Then it hit him: though it was a bit early in the day to be getting cocky, he was doing an incredibly good job so far. He had wiped out their pathetic security detail and blown their communications to shreds. Now he'd be able to clean out the remainder of the eleventh floor in a thorough and methodical way.

. . .

*"Generally good results* so far," Mr. Salvador said. "Of course, the gun control advocates will never like this kind of thing."

"Yeah. But check out some of our gun owners," Green said. "Look at Vishniak."

"Who?"

"Economic Roadkill," Green said, tapping a screen that had suddenly gone brilliant emerald. "He's one of my guys. And you can see how happy he is with the speech so far."

*He had gone* almost completely deaf from the blasts of the Fleischacker and could barely hear the voice of William A. Cozzano coming from his PIPER watch: ". . . would go out in the fields with my father, each of us with a shotgun tucked under his arm, and look for the pheasants that would go through the harvested fields for loose corn. Our retriever Lover would accompany us, often staying well back because he had learned that the blasts of the shotgun hurt his ears."

At this point Cozzano paused in his speech as the audience laughed indulgently. It wasn't really that funny, but he had delivered it in the cadence of a joke, and they knew their cues.

Vishniak kicked open an office door and saw nothing but a desk, and the knees and elbows of a man in a suit who was cowering behind it. This was not much to go on, but he was able to use his mind's eye to reconstruct the approximate shape and position of the owner of those knees and elbows, and pumped several rounds into the probable locations of his vital organs. When he saw what looked like an appropriate quantity of blood on the floor, he left the office, leaving the door ajar as a reminder that he had already visited this particular room.

*"This is a* bit excessive, wouldn't you say?" Mr. Salvador said. "I shall have to speak with Dr. Schram about this. It's too late in the campaign for these distractions."

"There is an incredible amount of gunfire," Green said, a little nervous.

On the central TV screen, Cozzano continued: "On one of my first such trips, after Lover had flushed a pheasant, I swung my gun in its direction, as I had practiced so many times with clay pigeons. But suddenly the barrel swung up in the air and I held my fire. My father had suddenly reached out and pushed the barrels up in the air, ruining my aim, and I was very upset.

"By way of explanation, he pointed to our neighbor's house, which had been directly in my line of fire—almost a mile away from us! I protested that there was no way that birdshot could travel for such a distance. 'Better safe than sorry,' he said."

*Vishniak moved on* to the next room. This one contained half a dozen TV screens and an equal number of computer monitors. One of the computer monitors was dead and the other five were glowing a brilliant red color. He put a bullet into each. This clip was running low, so as long as he was in a safe room, he ejected it, put it in his trouser pocket, and put in a fresh one. Cozzano's voice was still coming from his wristwatch. "When I first learned that there were some people in Washington who wanted to take our guns away from us, I was more astonished than offended. The idea seemed ludicrous. My father—and all of the other gun owners I knew—practiced firearm safety, and were at pains to pass those practices on to their children. The notion that some person in Washington could come out to Tuscola, Illinois, and take our guns away from us, because we were not, in their view, fit to own them, was completely baffling to me. And it still is."

The audience laughed; the laugh deepened into a cheer.

*"Something's definitely going* on out there," Aaron Green said. "I'm going to lock the door."

"Good idea," Mr. Salvador said, picking up the phone, holding it to his ear. "It's dead. The phone's dead."

Aaron had almost reached the door when the knob rotated and it opened. A man with a gun was standing in the hallway looking him in the eye.

The man's eye was drawn to the enormous racks of computer monitors that covered every wall of the room, the banks of computer systems. His jaw dropped open as he took it all in. While the man was gaping, Green had time to recognize him: it was Floyd Wayne Vishniak with a haircut.

Vishniak's gaze finally returned to Aaron's face. And it was clear that the presence of Aaron Green, here in this room, was the final piece in some kind of mental puzzle that Vishniak had been assembling in his head. "This is it," Vishniak said, talking way too loud, as if he were deaf. "Isn't it?"

Never argue with a man with a gun. "Yes," Green said, "this is it." He turned to Mr. Salvador for support. "Isn't it?"

"Yes, this is it," Mr. Salvador said, climbing very gingerly out of his chair, holding his hands together in front of his chest, fingertip to fingertip, in an attitude halfway between contemplation and prayer. He had the presence of mind to look over at Vishniak's monitor screen; it had gone pale and colorless.

Then it turned brilliant green.

"You're the Big Boss of it all!" Vishniak said. He stepped forward, shoved Aaron out of the way, leveled the gun at Mr. Salvador, and began to pull the trigger. He pulled it over and over again and the muzzle flashed like a strobe. Mr. Salvador was backing across the room with his hands dangling numbly at his sides, and before long he collapsed against a window.

But the window wasn't there anymore; it had long since been blown out of its frame, and the only thing there was a closed venetian blind with a lot of holes in it, flopping outward into the wind, betraying the warm Virginia sunshine. Suddenly, Mr. Salvador was no longer in the room.

"Jesus, where'd he go?" Vishniak said. He stepped forward into the room, looking around suspiciously. He went over to the window, pushed the blind out with one hand, and looked down.

But by that point, Aaron Green was already in the elevator.

*The lunchtime crowd* in the food court at Pentagon Plaza had first been alerted by a loud rattling noise on the glass overhead. The roar of conversation mostly drowned this out, but a few perceptive diners looked up to see fragments of broken glass sparkling in the sun as they bounced on the greenhouse roof.

Then the body came toward them in a smooth silent arc and

punched through the ceiling without any perceptible loss in speed. When it hit the glass it lost its sharply edged silhouette as a lot of stuff was forced out of it by the impact. It continued through the central atrium of the mall, now more a cloud of loosely organized remains than a corpse, and burst across four separate tables. A couple of seconds later, the broken glass came down in a hailstorm.

Floyd Wayne Vishniak, esq.
Parts Unknown
United States of America

Letters to the Editor
*Washington Post*
Washington, D.C.

Dear Mr. (or Miss, Mrs., or Ms.) Editor:
I have a bone to pick with you. Your coverage of my shooting spree (your way of describing it, not mine!) was the most biased and inaccurate piece of newspaper reporting I ever saw. All this year I have been reading a lot of newspapers (more than $300 spent so far) so that I could be an informed voter come November. But when I read a piece of garbage like your articles of 14, 15, and 16 September it makes me wonder if I have been informing myself at all. Or was I just filling up my head with all kinds of trash that your reporters just made up when they decided it was too much work to just go out and find out the Real Truth?

1. It was not a "bloodbath," as you have called it over and over. Only five people got killed. And the injuries to the diners in the food court do not count as this part was an accident. Just today you had an article about a car accident on the Beltway where five people got killed, but you never said it was a bloodbath.

2. You said I "roamed through the office suite firing indiscriminately." This is totally biased. I was not roaming. And I was not firing indiscriminately, or else why didn't I kill the five people who were in the brainwashing room with me? I will tell you why: because these five were average all-American citizens who I was trying to protect, not kill.

3. The part about the "spray of gunfire" really made my blood boil. There was no spraying. I decided what to shoot and I shot it.

4. Then in the article of 16 Sept. you said that I calmly and methodically went through the office suite executing people. If I was so calm and methodical then why did you write all that stuff about roaming, spraying, firing indiscriminately, etc. This shows the bias that is in your writing.

5. I am not a reclusive loner. As you would understand if you had to WORK for a living, it is cheaper to live out in the middle of nowhere. This does not make me a loner, just a poor honest working man.

6. Finally (this is the BIG POINT of my letter), every single word of your coverage makes me out to be a psycho. Like you would never even consider the idea that I might ACTUALLY BE RIGHT!

WAKE UP AMERICA! The so-called election of the president is a SHAM controlled by the MEDIA MANIPULATORS who have turned Cozzano into a ROBOT by planting a CHIP IN HIS HEAD that receives secret coded transmissions from SATEL-LITES. These same MEDIA MANIPULATORS have also put BRAIN WAVE MONITORS on average people's wrists disguised as DICK TRACY WRISTWATCHES.

One day I will be recognized as the hero I am for uncovering this secret conspiracy. Then you, the *Washington Post*, will be exposed for what you are: A TOOL OF THE CONSPIRACY that helps to control people's brains by putting out BIASED SO-CALLED NEWS.

You will be hearing from me again soon, I am sure.

Sincerely,
Floyd Wayne Vishniak

## CHAPTER FIFTY ONE

The Cozzano campaign was a third-party effort, which meant that it had to fight for every voter and every state. It had gotten off to a relatively late start in July and hadn't really gotten rolling until August; then Cozzano had suffered in the polls for a couple of weeks from his surprising choice of Eleanor Richmond as running mate.

Since then, Cozzano had crushed everything in his path. In city after city he strode up to the microphones, utterly relaxed and confident, shrugging off his aides, ignoring the notes and tele-prompters, and spoke. The words poured out of him effortlessly. He wasn't speaking to the journalists; he seemed to be speaking directly to the American people. In his homburg he looked like a figure from the middle of the century, like one of the men who had defeated Hitler and charted the course of empires and alliances. Compared to the sniping, weasely sons of bitches who had been leading America for the last few decades, he seemed like a throwback to the days when leaders were leaders, when there was such a thing as a great man. He looked as if he would have been right at home at the Yalta Conference, sitting with Roosevelt, Churchill, and Stalin. Whether he was meeting with foreign leaders or tipping a hotel doorman, he conducted himself with surefooted dignity and gentlemanly grace mixed with a kind of earthy, scab-knuckled vigor.

He did not seem to be running for anything at all. He seemed to be going around the country just being himself.

Mary Catherine didn't know a lot about presidential politics, but she knew it was significant when they ended up in Boston for an overnight stay. Massachusetts never went to anyone except Demo-crats; the fact that Cozzano was there meant that it was now up for grabs. It meant that her father was heading for a fifty-state sweep.

They stayed at a magnificent hotel along the waterfront with a huge arch that opened up like a gateway on Boston Harbor. This was, of course, Ogle's choice; the arch made a great backdrop for television appearances, and the proximity to the harbor made it easier to bash the Democrats on environmental issues.

The campaign had rented out a floor of suites. Mary Catherine and William A. Cozzano shared a two-bedroom suite, which was normal. She came straight from the airport and got settled in while her father hit a number of campaign stops, including tours of some high-tech firms in Cambridge.

The Cozzanos traveled with a lot of luggage, which was an easy thing to do when you never had to carry it yourself, and you had your own airplane. Not all of it was clothing. Some of it was equipment that Mary Catherine had bought for use in her father's therapy. Early in the campaign this had been simple stuff, like wads of stiff putty that Cozzano would squeeze in his left hand to develop strength and dexterity. By this point in the campaign, late in September, he was way beyond the putty-squeezing stage. He was now almost completely ambidextrous. In fact, he could sign his name with both hands at the same time. The left-hand signature looked similar to the prestroke version, albeit bigger and lazier. The right-hand signature was completely unfamiliar, though she had to admit it looked more presidential.

They had just flown into Boston's Logan Airport from a string of campaign appearances in Arizona. Mary Catherine had insisted that since it was going to be a long flight, Dad should write her a letter, and he should do it with his left hand. He had grumbled at this suggestion and tried to find ways to avoid it, but she had insisted, and finally he had buckled down to the job, ejecting all journalists and aides from his private cabin and sitting down with the big fountain pen gripped securely in his left hand and a pad of lined paper on his lap, writing the letters carefully, in block capitals, one at a time, like a schoolboy.

She had left him alone to the task. But when she came back an hour later, he was typing on a laptop computer.

"Dad!"

"Peanut," he said, "it was driving me crazy. I thought my head was going to split open."

"But you need to work on your right-hemisphere—"

"Spare me the neurobabble," he said. "Please observe that I am typing. I am typing a letter to you. And I am using both hands."

.    .    .

*Now, alone in* the hotel, she turned on Dad's laptop and opened up the file named "Letter to MC."

> Ddeeaarrest 3Maarryee Ccaattheerine,
> 3As eyqowuals claentter s1e3e my therapy is progressing well. I have you to thank
> wfaovres rtahveage gdraedast sbter1ifdreese I have made since you signed onto the
> tcearmapfaeiegn. wIrtcs whea1s1 been a constant joy having you with me. As you
> hdaavde pfreoabrasbly naovteirceeed Ibad carmew having some involuntary twitches in the
> fdiandgers aodfres emwye left hand, but under your supervision I have no doubt
> tgheatt stchriasbb1e small problem will clear up sooner or later and then I can
> tgeo11 b3aec1k to my old southpaw ways. I hope that this letter is long
> cenroausgeh 1feotrter me to receive at least a gentleman's C.
> 
> 　　　　　　　　　　　　Yxoxuxrs affectionately,
> 　　　　　　　　　　　　ydoaudr Father

She spent a while looking it over. The letter consisted of eleven lines. The first few words of each line were garbled, but she could usually puzzle them out from the context. For example, the word *campaign* at the beginning of line 4 was spelled *tcearmapfaeiegn*. It had been contaminated by several extra letters. Mary Catherine opened up a new window on the computer's screen and teased out the extra letters: they spelled terafee.

Terafee didn't mean anything. If you said it fast, it almost sounded like therapy. While Mary Catherine was typing it into the new window, she noticed that all of its letters were on the left side of the keyboard.

The letter complained of involuntary twitches in the fingers of the left hand. As he was typing, Dad must have noticed his left fingers pounding out a few unwanted letters and been unable to control it.

It was interesting that the twitches only occurred toward the beginning of each line. Mary Catherine went through the letter line by line, teasing out the left-hand letters and leaving behind only the ones that made sense. The letter her father had intended to write went like this:

Dear[est] Mary Catherine,
As you can see my therapy is progressing well. I have you to thank for the great strides I have made since you signed onto the campaign. It has been a constant joy having you with me. As you have probably noticed I am having some involuntary twitches in the fingers of my left hand, but under your supervision I have no doubt that this small problem will clear up sooner or later and then I can go back to my old southpaw ways. I hope that this letter is long enough for me to receive at least a gentleman's C.

> Yours affectionately,
> your Father

The letters that had been typed by the "involuntary twitches" of William A. Cozzano's left hand read as follows:

DEAREST 3AREE CATE
3 EQWA1S 1ETTER 13
WAVES RAVAGE DADS BE1FREE
TERAFEE WRCS WE11
DAD FEARS A VEREE BAD CREW
DAD ADRES EWE
GET SCRABB1E
TE11 3E1
ERASE 1ETTER
XXX
DAD

Someone knocked on the door of the suite. Mary Catherine jumped.

It had to be someone in the campaign, or else they would have been stopped by the Secret Service. Unless it was Floyd Wayne Vishniak, of course. But the famous spree killer of Pentagon Plaza probably would have made a lot more noise.

She went to the door and peered through the peephole. Then she opened it up.

"Hello, Zeldo," she said. "I thought you'd be with Dad."

He rolled his eyes. "Touring high-tech firms," he said, "is not my idea of an interesting time."

"Would you like to come in?"

He seemed uncertain. Maybe a little wistful. "I have to catch a plane," he said. He nodded toward the window of the suite. "Going to take the water taxi over to Logan and fly back to the Left Coast."

"You're done with the campaign, then?"

"For now," he said. "I've been called back. Your dad's been perfect for the last couple of weeks, there's no point in my tagging along anymore . . . we have other patients to work on in California." Zeldo reached into his satchel and pulled out an unmarked manila envelope, half an inch thick. "I've put together some data that is relevant to your efforts," he said, "and I thought you might like a hard copy."

"Thanks," she said, taking the envelope.

She sensed that something was going on. Something in Zeldo's tone of voice, his careful and vague phrasing, reminded her of the conversation in James's bedroom on the Fourth of July.

"Well, stay in touch," she said.

He seemed inordinately pleased by this offer. "Thank you," he said. "I will. I respect your activities very much and I respect you too. I can hardly say how much," he added, looking significantly over his shoulder. "Tell your dad I'm going to take a few liberal arts courses, as per his suggestion. Good-bye." Then he turned around, slowly and decisively, as if forcing himself to do it, and walked toward the elevators.

*The envelope was* full of laser printer output. Almost all of it was graphs and charts tracking various new developments in William A. Cozzano's brain. There was a cover letter, as follows:

Dear Mary Catherine,
Burn this letter and stir up the ashes when you are finished with it.
Your suite has a working fireplace that will be suitable.
Let me just make a few general statements first.

490

Politics is shit. Power is shit. Money is shit. I became a scientist because I wanted to study things that weren't shit. I got involved with the Radhakrishnan Institute because I was excited to take part in a project that was at the leading edge of everything, where neurology and electronics and information theory and philosophy all came together.

Then I learned that you can't escape politics and power and money even at the leading edge. I was about to resign when you came back to Tuscola and insisted on being made the campaign physician. This did not make Salvador happy but they had no choice but to let you in.

I knew what you were up to before you even started: you were putting your father through therapies designed to create new pathways in his brain that bypassed the biochips. I volunteered to stay on and follow you and your father on the campaign because I knew that otherwise Salvador would put someone else in my place, and he would eventually figure out your plan, and tip off the bad guys.

For the last three months I have been tracking your work, following developments in your father's brain through the biochip. I have not said anything because I didn't want to tip them off, so I will say it now: you are on the right track. Keep it up. In another four months (Inauguration Day) he should be able to function without the biochip, not perfectly, but good enough.

I have enclosed a schematic for a small device you can solder together using parts from Radio Shack. It will emit noise in the microwave band over small ranges (<100 ft.). This noise will cause your dad's biochips to put themselves in Helen Keller mode. You might find it useful.

Let me know if I can be of further use. I am fond of you and I hope, perhaps fatuously, that one day if we cross paths again you will allow me to take you out to dinner or something.

Pete (Zeldo) Zeldovich

Mary Catherine wandered out onto the suite's balcony. The harbor view was magnificent. Immediately to the north she could see the skyscrapers of downtown Boston's financial district standing out against the brilliant blue sky of the New England autumn. Logan

Airport was just a couple of miles away, directly across the harbor, and beyond that she could see the Atlantic stretching away so far that the curvature of the earth was almost visible.

The airport water taxi was just pulling away from the hotel wharf. Zeldo was standing in the back, his Hawaiian shirt blazing among dark business suits. He had his legs planted wide against the rolling of the small boat, and he was looking directly up at her.

She waved to him. He raised his fist over his head in a gesture of solidarity, drawing stares from the men in suits. Then he turned away.

Mary Catherine went back into the suite, burned the letter from Zeldo in the fireplace, and erased the files on her dad's computer.

The schematic for Zeldo's microwave transmitter was buried in the middle of a stack of graphs. He had hand-drawn it in ballpoint pen on a sheet of hotel stationery. It was a network of inscrutable electronic hieroglyphs: zigzags, helices, stacks of parallel lines, each one neatly labeled with Radio Shack part numbers. Mary Catherine folded it up and put it in her wallet.

## CHAPTER FIFTY-TWO

Eleanor's motorcade steamed across the Woodrow Wilson Bridge, and then immediately on the Maryland side, took the exit to the Inner Loop. To the left was the sewage plant, Bolling Air Force Base, the Defense Intelligence Agency, the Navy Yards. To the right, wooded hills, and then the projects, and then the decay of Southeast—one of the great free fire zones in urban America. Eleanor had been to three funerals of friends and relatives who had been shot to death there, and on her way to the third one she had almost been run off the road by a careening SWAT van.

D.C. was a great, historically black city that had been colonized, in a few places, by rich whites. Lacking a traditional organized crime network, it had become the battleground of a drug war among competing groups: Jamaicans, Haitians, New York elements, and home-grown Washingtonians competing for the lucrative trade to service the insatiable demand of the Beltway professionals. The police could only wait until the "market worked itself out," as one police official put it. Once turfs and boundary lines had been established, the murder, it was thought, would stop.

Instead the violence had infected a whole new generation with the notion of the cheapness of human life, and the flow of weapons into the region had made semiautomatics available to even preteens. The doctors who worked emergency rooms in the District had become some of the world's leading experts on the treatment of gunshot wounds. During the Gulf War they had been sent straight to the front lines, where they felt right at home.

Awaiting Eleanor was the Lady Wilburdon Gunshot Wound Institute, an ugly, brand-new, fortresslike structure built on the bulldozed foundations of the first of the War Against Poverty projects. Its architecture reflected its function, which was to treat people involved in deadly combat. The place had been made secure and bulletproof to discourage shooters from coming by to finish off their victims while they were being worked on by the doctors.

The only shooters here now were carrying cameras. Eleanor got out of her limo and followed her advance person through a wall of photographers and cameramen. She made her way, along with her Secret Service escort, to a small auditorium in the institute. Already present on the stage were the Mayor of D.C.; the medical director of the institute, who was a young black Gulf War veteran named Dr. Cornelius Gary; and the founder and namesake, an imposing Englishwoman named Lady Guenevere Wilburdon. An empty seat awaited Eleanor.

"Ms. Richmond," Lady Wilburdon said, extending her hand, "it's a pleasure to meet you. I look forward to your inauguration."

"Thank you so much, Lady Wilburdon, but we do have to go through the election."

"Pfft," Lady Wilburdon said, and waved her hand as if shooing flies away.

Eleanor repressed an urge to laugh. This was exactly the kind of attitude that she had sported, back before she was a candidate.

They were not able to converse anymore before the ceremony began. It opened with a presentation of songs by the massed choirs of several local churches, a lengthy, involved oratory-cum-prayer by the Mayor, and the presentation of Dr. Cornelius Gary, the executive director of the institute. Who in turned presented Lady Wilburdon, who said nothing except to introduce Eleanor, who dedicated the institute.

"*It was nice* to have met you, Lady Wilburdon," Eleanor said after it was over.

"Not so fast, Ms. Richmond," Lady Wilburdon said. "We are going to have a chat."

"I would like nothing better, but my schedule—"

"Arrangements have been made," Lady Wilburdon said firmly.

On their way out the front doors they had to jump out of the way of an incoming gurney: the institute's first patient, a thirteen-year-old boy who had been gutshot with a .357 Magnum.

Eleanor's advance person explained it to her in the motorcade. Eleanor's next two engagements had both been cancelled at the last minute. She had a couple of free hours. Nature abhors a vacuum and Lady Wilburdon had rushed in to plug the gap. They would be having lunch at the Willard.

It was a small lunch too—just Eleanor, Lady Wilburdon, and her secretary, Miss Chapman. Lady Wilburdon used both force of personality and sheer physical bulk to eject all of Eleanor's hangers-on from the room. Then they sat at the table together and lunched on tiny sandwiches.

"I should explain that I knew Bucky," Lady Wilburdon said.

"Bucky?"

"Salvador. The fellow who was shot by the madman across the river and exploded in front of the sushi bar. It is tasteless, I know, but I have become inured."

"I didn't know him myself," Eleanor said. "All I know is that he ran the company that does media consulting for our campaign. And that Cy Ogle has taken over for him."

"Bucky was the very embodiment of low cunning," Lady Wilburdon said. "Impressive in a superficial way. But flashy." She said this word with the same intonation she might have used if she were calling him a child molester. "In a way it is surprising that the Network hired him. Normally we have higher standards. But we are in an age when high standards are no longer fashionable."

"Network? He worked for one of the television networks?"

Lady Wilburdon rolled her eyes. "Certainly not. Not even Bucky would do that. You need to know about this, as you will be spending the next eight years—possibly the next sixteen—in a position of great responsibility."

"We have to win the election."

"You will," Lady Wilburdon said. "We have solved the problem of elections."

*It was somewhat* later in the afternoon. Lady Wilburdon had dipped into a bottle of sherry and held forth at some length on the subjects of Bucky, Ogle, Cozzano, and the functioning of the PIPER 100. Eleanor listened politely, soaked it all up, and made up her mind that she would not try to figure out until later whether this woman was completely out of her mind or telling the truth.

It would be easy enough to pass her off as a dingbat. But her words explained a lot. From time to time Eleanor would feel an uncomfortable shock of recognition as Lady Wilburdon's explanations matched up perfectly with what she herself had noticed. Consciously she kept an open mind. Subconsciously she had long ago decided that everything Lady Wilburdon said was true.

"If what you're saying is true," Eleanor said, "an unbelievable amount of money has been spent."

"It's all relative," Lady Wilburdon said. "It's all part of a long-range strategy."

"How long-range?"

"Centuries."

*"Centuries?"*

"There are only five entities in the world with sufficient wisdom to pursue consistent strategies over periods of several centuries," Lady Wilburdon said. "These entities are not national or governmental in nature—even the best governments are dangerously unstable and short-lived. Such an entity is self-preserving and self-perpetuating. A world war, or the rise and fall of an empire or an alliance such as the USSR or NATO, is no more serious, to it, than a gust of wind buffeting the sails of a clipper ship."

"What are these entities?" Eleanor said.

"In no particular order, one is the Catholic Church. One is Japan —which is nothing more than a group of *zaibatsus*, or major industrial combines. The third is a loose network of shtetls. After the expulsion from Spain in 1492, they forcibly realized the importance of long-range planning, and in the intervening years have accumulated formidable assets. The fourth one we don't know much about; it seems to connect many of the recalcitrantly traditional cultures of the Third and Fourth Worlds and to be headquartered somewhere in Central Asia. And the fifth is the Network. It is an alliance of large investors, both individual and institutional, predominantly European and American. You might think of it as the legacy, the residue, of the East India Company, the Hudson's Bay Company, the American railway companies, Standard Oil, and the technological empires of our time. It is the most decentralized of the five entities—really just an effort to pursue investments, and certain other activities, in a coordinated fashion. Before the war its funds were managed by a lovely Scottish gentleman who lived in an old castle near Chichester. Afterward it was moved to the interior of the States and placed in the hands of an American fellow, a mathematical prodigy who attended the Lady Wilburdon School for Geniuses on the Isle of Rhum."

"The Network owns Ogle Data Research?"

"Yes."

"And by implication, Cozzano?"

"Yes."

"So you're saying that the Network is going to take over the United States?"

"The Network wouldn't want it," Lady Wilburdon said. "Governments, as I mentioned, are dodgy. All the Network wants is to stabilize the return on its investment in the national debt."

"Wait a minute. You're saying that the Network would put together this incredible conspiracy just to get a couple of extra points on a loan?"

The idea did not seem troubling to Lady Wilburdon. She seemed a bit surprised that Eleanor didn't accept it. "My dear lady," she said, "do you have any idea how much money your government has borrowed?"

"A lot," Eleanor said. "Ten trillion dollars." It was a figure she had to cite regularly during campaign debates.

"Well, you certainly can't expect to borrow that much money from someone without incurring certain obligations, can you?" Lady Wilburdon said, as if it were all perfectly obvious. And it was, in fact, perfectly obvious.

"Of course not," Eleanor said, "you're right."

"When a business borrows money from a bank, and does so irresponsibly, and is profligate and incompetent, what happens?"

"It goes bankrupt. And the bank takes it over."

"Yes. The bank simply wants what is best for the business. It gets rid of the dead wood, fires the miscreants who drove the business to ruin, cleans it out, and sets everything right, so that the business is once again able to meet its obligations."

"And I'm one of the people who is supposed to set everything right."

"You and Mr. Cozzano, yes. And I'm sure you'll do a splendid job of it."

"You are? Are you kidding?"

"Of course not. I've been following your career, Ms. Richmond. Everything you've been saying in the last year about the failure of American politics is correct," Lady Wilburdon said. "Without going round and talking to them personally, I daresay that most of the people in the Network consider you something of a folk hero."

Eleanor's mind was whirling, and not just because she had taken two glasses of sherry. She had to see Mary Catherine. And providentially, one of her assistants broke through and signaled it was time to go. Eleanor had been listening with such rapt attention that she had not moved for an hour. One of her legs had gone to sleep, and the sherry also had reduced her coordination. When she stood up, it showed.

"You need to do some stretching exercises," Lady Wilburdon said. "Take it from me—I travel even more than a presidential candidate."

"I'll keep that in mind, Lady Wilburdon. Thank you for an illuminating chat."

"It was my pleasure, I assure you," Lady Wilburdon said, seeing her to the elevators. Eleanor had now been enveloped by her campaign staff.

"Good-bye," Lady Wilburdon said, as the elevator arrived, "I should enjoy paying a call on you at the Naval Observatory, if you would have me. I love telescopes."

## CHAPTER FIFTY-THREE

The Prince of Darkness arrived at Dulles Airport at one P.M. on the ninth of October, in a chartered Learjet with the windows painted black. He was met on the end of the runway by a black limousine that gave the terminal building a wide berth as it swung onto the Dulles Access Road. The limousine made its way into the stream of traffic, headed directly in toward the District of Columbia, trailed by a dark sedan full of men in sunglasses and suits.

Within half a mile the limousine had changed lanes all the way over to the left edge of the roadway and was traveling in excess of ninety miles per hour. In the back of that limousine, an astonishingly loud, grating voice was egging on the driver, like a hot poker shoving him in the ass. There were only two men in the vehicle, the driver and the passenger, they had been together for less than sixty seconds, and the driver was already fighting a nearly uncontrollable urge to pull onto the shoulder, vault the seat, and wrap his fingers around the Prince of Darkness's neck.

They were less than a mile from the airport when the limousine's brake lights flared and it suddenly veered onto the shoulder. The black sedan grumbled to an emergency stop directly behind it, spraying gravel. The high-speed traffic in the left lane of the roadway veered, screeched, and honked, nearly rear-ending this strange little caravan.

The door of the limousine had been flung open before the limo had come to a full stop. Jeremiah Freel, the Prince of Darkness, climbed out and jerked the driver's side door open before the driver even had time to set the parking brake.

"Out out out out!" he screeched in his terrible, grinding voice. People who had run afoul of the Prince of Darkness vied for ways to describe the sound of his voice: "like a cattle prod in the armpit," one had said. Like snorting pure Mace from the can. Like putting a single crystal of Drano in the corner of each eye. Having a killer bee stuck in each ear.

"Get out, you nigger!" Jeremiah Freel screamed at the driver, which was an interesting choice of words since the driver was a white boy.

He was a white boy with a southern accent. A rural, uneducated southern accent. And as Freel had obviously figured out, simply by listening to this man say, "Good afternoon, sir," the single most insulting thing you could call him was nigger. So he got out of that driver's seat in a big hurry and drew himself up face-to-face with Freel, or chest-to-face, actually, since Freel was short enough to sleep comfortably on an ironing board.

"You—" the driver began, but before he could get anything else out, one of the burly suits from the trailing vehicle had come up behind him, grabbed both of his elbows, and swung him away, shoving and dragging him into the median strip.

Which was fine with Jeremiah Freel. With the driver removed from his path, he made a direct line for the steering wheel of the limousine.

He was blocked by three other men who had jumped out of the dark sedan and who were now standing on tiptoe, as close to him as they could get, spreading their jackets wide open like wings to form a pinstriped curtain that blocked all view of his face from the cars screaming down the roadway. It was imperative that no one recognize the face of Jeremiah Freel, which stared out from so many wanted posters in so many post offices that it had actually been made into a poster, popular in the dorm rooms of cynical college students.

"Mr. Freel—" one of these men said, moving into position to block the door. The sentence ended there because Freel, taking advantage of the man's spreadeagled posture, reached up with both hands, gripped the tips of the man's nipples through his white linen shirt, twisted, and pulled. The man screamed, collapsed in on himself, and fell back against the side of the limousine. Instantly, Freel was sitting in the driver's seat, the doors all closed and electrically locked. The rear tires of the limousine began to spin wildly in the gravel. One of the other guys in suits lunged forward, grabbed his stunned comrade by the necktie, and jerked him away from the side of the car as it peeled out, fishtailing, onto the road, nearly causing a chain reaction smashup in the three leftmost lanes.

"Shit!" everyone was saying. Two of them ran back, jumped into the sedan, and took off, stranding the limo driver, the man who was trying to calm him down, and the man who had made the mistake of getting in Jeremiah Freel's way, who now had a pair of symmetrically placed two-inch bloodstains soaking through his white shirt.

"*So that's what* tertiary syphilis does to a man," said the driver of the sedan, screaming down the Dulles Access Road at ninety miles per hour in hot pursuit of the limousine. "They said he was an asshole but I had no *idea*."

"Shut up and drive," said the one in the passenger seat. "You have any idea how badly we screwed this up? Anybody catches sight of his face and we're finished."

They drove very fast, but they had a hard time catching up with Jeremiah Freel in his limousine. In theory the big limo was supposed to be the slower vehicle. The difference between them, though, was this: the Prince of Darkness was not afraid to ram. Not only was he not afraid to ram; he was practiced. Any vehicle in his lane not going as fast as he was got rear-ended and that was that. Lane changes were accomplished by *force majeure*. They passed at least three vehicles that had veered into the ditch or the median strip. In the end, the only way to catch up with Jeremiah Freel was to pull onto the shoulder and floor it. Which is pretty much what they did, though by the time they actually caught up with him, he was screaming across the Potomac River on the Theodore Roosevelt Bridge, vectored into the heart of the Capital like a poisoned dumdum from a sniper's rifle.

"You know what he's doing?" the driver said. "He's going to the goddamn Watergate!"

"Head him off," the passenger said.

Once they realized where Freel was going, they were able to do a bit of deft curb-hopping, lawn-driving, and zooming down oncoming lanes, and pull their sedan directly across Freel's path just a few yards short of the entrance to the Watergate. Freel rammed them anyway, caving in the side of the sedan, but both of the occupants saw it coming and dove and rolled out of the other side of the car just before impact.

The suit who had been sitting in the passenger seat pulled a gun out of his armpit and used the butt of the weapon to smash the driver's-side window of the limousine. The black glass dissolved into tempered fragments held together by the plastic sheet that had been used to blacken the window. When this debris was pulled out of the way, Jeremiah Freel was exposed, slumped against the steering wheel with a big laceration across his forehead, blood streaming out and dripping off the horn button into his lap. He was barely conscious, mumbling deliriously.

"Drive much?" he said. "Where'd you get your fucking license? K mart? Get the fuck out of my way, asshole, I got an equalizer in the glove compartment and more lawyers than you've got friends."

They shoved Freel across the seat onto the passenger side and then climbed in after him. The driver backed the limousine away from the wrecked sedan. A steady wisp of steam was piping from its radiator but it was still drivable. The passenger wiggled his hands into a pair of latex gloves and then set about tying Jeremiah Freel up with plastic handcuffs. Only when he was finished with that did he begin applying direct pressure to Freel's forehead.

Waiting at a stoplight, the two men in suits exchanged looks and rolled their eyes at each other. "Campaign consultants," the driver said, "gotta love 'em."

"Oh, *this is* a good one," said the chairman of the Republican National Committee, inspecting a sheet of paper he had just pulled from a file folder marked FREEL. "During a campaign visit to Minot, North Dakota, you ran a school bus off a road, causing thirty-six injuries, ten of them serious. The parents sued you for a hundred million dollars and won."

"Fuck you," Jeremiah Freel said. "Fuck your mother too." Freel had a nice dark line of stitches across his forehead, tracing a long welt that perfectly matched the curve of the limousine's steering wheel.

"When we add that to the libel and slander judgments from the last three presidential campaigns—let me see, those alone add up to almost another hundred million dollars, which you owe to a dozen and a half different people, including, by the way, myself. You owe me four million."

"Eat my shit," Jeremiah Freel said.

Several other distinguished-looking and well-dressed men were sitting around the conference table. They were in a suite in a very private hotel a few blocks north of the White House. They had rented a whole floor, covered the windows with black stuff, disabled the elevators, and posted guards with submachine guns by all the stairwells. Jeremiah Freel was sitting in a luxurious padded leather chair in the middle of the table. Standing behind him were two men with a combined weight of six hundred pounds, wearing latex gloves and clear plastic face shields.

The other men sitting around the table were all glaring coldly at Freel. One by one, they began to raise their hands and speak up.

"You owe me three million plus legal fees," said the chairman of the Democratic National Committee.

"One point five," said another man, holding up his hand.

"Eight hundred thousand," barked another man.

"One point one."

"Half a mil and a printed apology in *The Miami Herald*."

"What the hell is this, a fucking star chamber?" Jeremiah Freel said. "Why don't you just tell me what the hell you're after?"

"We're after Cozzano," the GOP chairman said.

"Fine. You got him. He's a dead man," Freel said. "By the time I'm finished with that wop son of a bitch, he'll curse his mother for ever having given birth to him. He won't be able to cash a check north of the Equator. Children will spit on his knees. His dog will climb onto his bed in the middle of the night and try to tear his face off and he'll beg for it to happen."

There was an awed silence in the room.

"Don't you want to hear what we are prepared to offer you in exchange for your services?" the Democratic chairman said uncertainly.

"Fuck that," Freel said. "You guys have no imagination. You think I do this shit to make money. But that's not true. I been sitting down there in Rio waiting for something like this. I do it for the pure joy of a job well done. Now, did you assemble my A-Team, or not?"

"We got 'em."

"All of 'em?"

"All the ones who aren't dead, in prison, or running other campaigns," said the Republican chairman.

## CHAPTER FIFTY-FOUR

A bit less than a month before Election Day, a flatbed truck carrying a GODS shipping container could be seen fighting its way through the bewildering vortex of Boston's Kenmore Square, on the eastern fringe of Boston University. The truck eventually broke through by asserting the divine right of semitrailer rigs to go anywhere they wanted, and entered the campus.

This area swarmed with Boston cops, campus police, men in dark suits, and nicely dressed young persons wearing COZZANO FOR PRESIDENT buttons. An impressive minority carried walkie-talkies. These people had been seizing parking spaces for the better part of the day. They did it by the power vested in them by various higher authorities; by sheer chutzpah; and in some cases by the brutally simple expedient of placing their bodies in those places and refusing to move when motorists tried to bluff them out. When the big GODS truck arrived, it found nine consecutive parking spaces waiting for it, which in Boston happened about as often as a Grand Alignment of the planets, or, for that matter, a World Series victory.

Not long afterward, a motorcade sliced through the Gordian knot of Kenmore Square and pulled up near Morse Auditorium, a squat, domed synagogue-turned-lecture-hall that was already about half full of media personnel and politically conscious students.

William A. Cozzano emerged from one of the cars, waved cheerily to a number of supporters who had gathered in back for a brief sight of the Great Man, and followed an advance person into the back of the hall. A dressing room had already been staked out behind the stage. He changed to a fresh shirt and had his hair and makeup fixed by trained professionals.

Then he walked onto the stage. From here he could see a wall of television lights and, dimly, a dark auditorium beyond it. The auditorium was full of students who applauded him when he emerged from the wings. Two chairs had been set up in the middle of the stage, angled toward each other, a table between them set with a glass water pitcher and two tumblers.

William A. Cozzano was going to talk politics with the chairman of the Political Science Department, a long-time Washington figure who had taken an academic appointment that gave him the freedom to do pretty much whatever he wanted with his time; in return, he lent prestige to the university. The whole idea was that the discussion would be loose and unscripted, and Cozzano would be open to questions, both from the audience (mostly students) and the local media. This was a daring maneuver, exactly the kind of thing that Tip McLane probably couldn't pull off without offending half of the ethnic groups in the United States.

Cozzano ascended the stage a few minutes before air time, unbuttoned his jacket, and sat down in his chair. A technician assisted him in clipping a microphone to his lapel, and asked him to say a few words so that they could adjust their sound levels. Cozzano quoted the "To be or not to be" soliloquy from Hamlet, which raised a smattering of applause from the students and even from a few of the TV people.

The host, looking professorial, sat in his chair and went through a sound check of his own. At five seconds before eight P.M., a man in a headset gave them a digital countdown (he used his fingers) and then the host delivered some prepared remarks, reading them from a TelePrompTer. Then he turned toward Cozzano and asked him a question about Middle East policy.

This was a hard pitch. The politics of the Israeli/Palestinian question had been dissected and analyzed to an impossibly minute degree, over decades, by persons whose sole function in life was to know everything about these issues. Every squiggle and jog in the contour of Israel's border had its experts, who knew about everything that had happened in that place since the time of the pharaoh. West Bank settlement and the status of the PLO had become more arcane than the concept of the Trinity in the early church: every conceivable idea had already been come up with, and its ramifications worked out and analyzed. Of all the millions of possible opinions one could have on these subjects, there were only a few that a presidential candidate could get away with having, and in order merely to explain these opinions the candidate had to master a new vocabulary and even a new form of logic that did not really apply anywhere else. The best way to trip up a governor who was running for president was to ask him a seemingly simple, innocuous question about the Middle East and then wait for him to hang himself.

Cozzano maneuvered through it perfectly, delivering an answer that was seemingly erudite; that hit all the key buzzwords that would prevent him from being vilified by Jewish organizations; and yet was so vague and imprecise that it said practically nothing at all. Like a compulsory figure in an ice-skating competition, it was devoid of content and not much fun to look at, but to the initiate, it was an extremely impressive display of technical skill.

By the time he was finished, it was time to break for a commercial. The host made a witty, self-deprecating remark about how dull the show had been up to this point and then promised that the rest would be more lively. The students applauded. The director, staring at a monitor, turned to the performers and said, "You're clear."

Cozzano turned toward the table and poured himself half a glass of water. He was just about to jump into some small talk with the host when a voice came out of the darkness behind the television lights.

"Governor Cozzano, Frank Boyle from *The Boston Globe*. I'm sorry to be the one to tell you this, but I just got a call on my portable phone here from our correspondent who's following your daughter in Minnesota. He called from the lobby of the hotel where she is staying in Minneapolis. Apparently Mary Catherine was late for an appearance at Macalester College. All the press went back to her hotel, and the floor where her room was is swarming with cops and detectives. Our correspondent talked to one of these detectives on background, and he said that apparently she was assaulted in the hallway by Floyd Wayne Vishniak. He managed to get past her Secret Service men and put a bullet into her heart and Mary Catherine bled to death right there in the hallway."

*A hundred feet* away, Cy Ogle, perched in the Eye of Cy, sat and watched William A. Cozzano's bio readouts go ballistic.

The television monitor in the Eye of Cy was patched into the pool feed from the cameras in the auditorium, and Ogle couldn't help watching it. Cozzano's face had turned deathly pale as Frank Boyle of the *Globe* told his story, and had now gone red. His eyes had become red and glistening too. And Ogle could see from the bio monitors that Cozzano's heart rate had gone up to 172, almost three times the norm. His blood pressure was explosively high.

"Jesus Christ," Ogle said out loud, "this could only be the work of Jeremiah Freel!"

He looked back at the television monitor, but Cozzano wasn't there anymore. Just an empty chair. Then the camera wheeled around, spinning past the host and then past an array of lights, cameras, technicians, and other stuff that was never supposed to be on camera. Finally the camera centered itself on the back of William A. Cozzano, who was striding into the crowd of TV people, print reporters, campaign aides, and Secret Service who filled the space between the stage and the front row of seats. Most of these people jumped out of his way instinctively. But a couple of men in suits, displaying considerable physical bravery, closed ranks in front of Cozzano and prevented him from charging into the auditorium.

In the background, a disturbance was making its way up the aisle as a man shoved his way toward the exit. Apparently this was Frank Boyle of the *Globe*. Cozzano had gone after him, and he had decided to get out of the building.

Throughout the campaign, Ogle had prided himself on being ready for anything. But he hadn't been ready for the return of Freel. Ogle took a deep breath, tried to still his own heart, and then put his hands on the control panel and set about calming Cozzano.

Cozzano was in front of the stage having a conversation with his

Secret Service men. They were all talking into their shirt cuffs and holding their hands over their earpieces, trying to hear each other over the murmur of the shocked and scared students.

A woman with press credentials stepped close to Cozzano. "Governor? I'm with the *Globe*. And we don't have anyone there named Frank Boyle."

The head of the Secret Service detail, listening to his earplug, shook his head conclusively and caught Cozzano's eye. "It was a total fabrication," he said. "Mary Catherine showed up at Macalester College on time and is speaking at this moment."

Cozzano, suddenly, was calm and collected. He shook his head, seemed to forget that anything had ever happened, and returned to his seat on the stage.

"Would you like to delay—" the host said, as the sound man was fixing Cozzano's microphone.

"No," Cozzano said. "Let's continue as planned."

"Are you sure? You must be very upset."

"I'm fine," Cozzano said. "Why should I be upset?"

*The headline of* the next day's edition of the *New York Post* read, "WHY SHOULD I BE UPSET?"

COZZANO NOT BOTHERED BY "MURDER" OF HIS OWN DAUGHTER.

*The President, delivering* off-the-cuff remarks in the aisle of *Air Force One*, said that he was shocked and disgusted by the impostor who had delivered the fake news to Cozzano.

At the same time, though, he could not help but find it strange, and just a bit disturbing, that a man who, to all appearances, had just lost his own daughter, would agree to continue with what was, after all, nothing more than a campaign event, the sole purpose of which was to scrape up more votes. Surely, he said, there were limits that should be observed, for the sake of decency.

Nimrod T. ("Tip") McLane made a surprise appearance in a hotel bar where a number of reporters had gathered—not just to drink, but because they had received a tip from McLane staffers that Tip might feel a bit thirsty around eleven o'clock.

Coincidentally, the evening news happened to be running on the big projection TV over the bar at the time. A football game had been on until a few minutes previously, but money had changed hands between Marcus Drasher and the bartender, and now the news was on—to the chagrin of several fans along the bar who had not brought nearly as much cash as Drasher.

McLane and the reporters engaged in some friendly banter, but everyone turned toward the television set when the image of William A. Cozzano appeared on the screen. The cameras had caught the entire thing and the feed had gone out all over the country. They watched Cozzano going into shock as he heard the false story about his daughter. They watched him jumping out of his chair in a blind rage, and they watched him sitting back down a minute later, calm and collected. The actual content of the two-hour discussion received no coverage whatsoever.

All of the reporters looked at McLane. McLane turned away from the TV and looked nonchalant. Finally a reporter asked him what he thought of the whole thing.

"Well, I don't really want to talk about it," he said, "the whole episode is really distasteful. But now I can see that the media have grabbed on to this whole thing—in the typical way that they do—looking for the sensational and paying no attention to content . . . and I can see that now the media are trying to take this event and turn it into some kind of a test of Cozzano's psychological fitness to be president."

"Do you think he looked presidential?" asked a reporter from a rabidly conservative Catholic magazine.

McLane shrugged. "People say I'm a hothead," he said. "People say I'm out of control and that I can't handle the pressure of the campaign. So maybe I shouldn't be the one to talk. But I've learned that the world is full of crackpots who will shout crazy stuff at you. I mean, they are everywhere. And you can't let them get under your skin. If you're going to physically assault every lunatic who babbles some nonsense to you, then you're not going to make much of a president—and if that's how you handle a nut case, then how are you going to deal with foreign leaders?"

## CHAPTER FIFTY-FIVE

Tuesday, October 22, two weeks before Election Day, the standings looked like this:

| | |
|---|---|
| COZZANO | 59% |
| PRESIDENT | 8% |
| MCLANE | 18% |
| UNDECIDED | 10% |
| OTHER | 5% |

An obscure Washington, D.C.–based organization called the American Association of Physicians, Surgeons, and Osteopaths staged a press conference at which a videotape was shown to the press and then disseminated to all of the networks. The videotape was a series of outtakes from Cozzano's campaign, a blooper film if you will. It started out with some excerpts from an interview in which he was still suffering from some speech impediments. From there it moved onward through the campaign, showing Cozzano during commercial breaks, bantering with reporters on airport runways, walking down the aisle of his campaign plane to the bathroom, doing sound checks before debates, and so on. The one thing that all of these takes had in common was that, in each of them, Cozzano did something wrong: slurred some words or tripped over his own feet. One particularly striking clip showed Cozzano working a crowd at a rally in Newark. A woman handed her baby to Cozzano for a kiss and he nearly dropped it, seemingly overcome by a temporary seizure. "I-I-I-I'm sorry," he stuttered, and handed it back to her. The conclusion reached by the experts of the American Association of Physicians, Surgeons, and Osteopaths was that Cozzano was still suffering from "severe neurological deficits" and was not fit to be president.

Excerpts from the videotape were broadcast repeatedly on virtually every television news program in the United States, in many cases as the evening's top story.

Wednesday, October 23:

| | |
|---|---|
| COZZANO | 51% |
| PRESIDENT | 10% |
| MCLANE | 21% |
| UNDECIDED | 13% |
| OTHER | 5% |

In Chicago, a press conference was held by Tommy Markovich, a venerable Chicago sportscaster who had been well known to sports fans in that city during the late sixties and early seventies. He had retired in 1980. Markovich said that his conscience had been troubling him about something. He showed an excerpt of a Bears-Vikings game from the year 1972. Late in the game, the Vikings were leading by ten points and the Bears were driving from their own thirty with only one minute left in the game. William A. Cozzano, who was a tight end, went out on a screen pass, caught the ball, and found himself out in the open with nothing between him and the goal line except for hard-frozen turf. He ran unobstructed all the way to the Viking ten, where, inexplicably, the ball squirted loose from his arms and dribbled back upfield for a few yards, where a pursuing Viking fell on it. It had been a famous gaffe at the time, not so much because it was significant to the outcome of the game (it wasn't), but because Cozzano was known for being a steady and reliable sort of player who didn't make mental mistakes.

Now, a couple of decades later, the shriveled old man who had called that game on TV wanted to point something out: the Vikings had been favored to win that game by ten points. By dropping the ball, Cozzano had preserved the point spread.

Thursday, October 24:

| | |
|---|---|
| COZZANO | 45% |
| PRESIDENT | 12% |
| MCLANE | 25% |
| UNDECIDED | 14% |
| OTHER | 4% |

In an exclusive interview with CBS Sports, a noted author of books on the Mob said that Nicodemo ("Nicky Freckles") Costanza, an important Chicago Mob figure who ran a huge illegal sports betting operation during the sixties and seventies, had made something like twenty million dollars off the 1972 Bears-Vikings game— money he would have forfeited if William A. Cozzano had simply held on to the ball long enough to reach the goal line.

A local TV reporter for one of the network affiliates in Chicago released the results of a two-month investigation into connections between the Cozzano family and the Mafia. The centerpiece was a vast family tree—actually, several family trees intertwined into a thicket—so big that it had been drawn, in minute letters and lines, on a four-by-eight foot sheet of plywood. The extended Cozzano family was shown in blue. Mob families were shown in red. The family trees went all the way back to twelfth-century Genoa and showed that William A. Cozzano, John Gotti, Al Capone, and Benito Mussolini were all distantly related.

*The Cozzano campaign* issued a press release stating that the American Association of Physicians, Surgeons, and Osteopaths had not existed until some two weeks previously, and appeared to have a membership of three, all of whom had shown up at the press conference two days ago as experts urging Cozzano to withdraw from the race. One of these three was a former Army doctor who had been discharged under other than honorable circumstances. One of them no longer practiced because he could no longer obtain malpractice insurance. The third had declared bankruptcy after fifty of his patients filed a class-action suit against him complaining of botched breast implants.

The Cozzano campaign also issued a blooper reel of its own, showing the incumbent President and Tip McLane tripping over their shoelaces and slurring words, and suggested that these two might want to have neurological exams of their own.

Finally, a video expert was trotted out to state that the videotape of Cozzano nearly dropping the baby in Newark had evidently been doctored; other videotapes made of the same event did not show him doing anything unusual.

Friday, October 25:

| COZZANO | 40% |
| PRESIDENT | 14% |

| | |
|---|---|
| MCLANE | 29% |
| UNDECIDED | 13% |
| OTHER | 4% |

Acting on an anonymous tip, a reporter for a Chicago network affiliate tracked down Alberto ("Stitches") Barone, ninety-six years of age, who was living in a dingy convalescent home on Chicago's south side. Stitches agreed to have the nurses unbutton his shirt so that he could display the numerous scars that he had received during an epochal knife duel with John Cozzano, William's father, some sixty years earlier, for the hand of the fair Francesca Domenici. Over time, these scars had contracted and become even more grotesque than they had been to begin with. Stitches Barone, fortified with a few injections, managed to sit up in bed and deliver an unrehearsed, four-hour statement to the TV cameras, telling the entire story of his ten-decade life and times. Of these four hours, one hour was devoted to his childhood in Italy, one hour to his heyday in the Al Capone organization, one hour to his physical ailments, and one hour to recounting the antics of his favorite dog, Bozo, who had died of vehicular trauma in 1953. The reporter took the videotape home and culled the one sentence devoted to the subject of John Cozzano: "he was a vicious man who would stop at nothing to get what he wanted, and I was afraid of him."

*William A. Cozzano* appeared at a press conference in New York with a number of leading Italian-Americans, including the daughter of Nicodemo ("Nicky Freckles") Costanza. The Italian-American leaders blasted the media for defaming Cozzano, and Costanza's daughter, in particular, stated that there had never been any connection between her father and Cozzano. A family tree was brought out to show that Cozzano was also related to Leonardo da Vinci and Joe Dimaggio.

Saturday, October 26:

| | |
|---|---|
| COZZANO | 36% |
| PRESIDENT | 14% |
| MCLANE | 31% |

UNDECIDED    14%

OTHER    5%

Campaigning in the state of Washington, William A. Cozzano visited Seattle's Pike Place Market, where a number of Southeast Asian immigrants had been able to set up thriving businesses selling produce that they raised on truck farms outside of the city. Making his way down the center of the market, surrounded by a huge cloud of media, Cozzano stopped at one stand and bought an apple from the attractive young Laotian-American woman on the other side of the counter.

Just as he was biting into the apple, he was assaulted, and nearly knocked down, by a tiny, rabid, screaming person who had charged in underneath the radar of the Secret Service men. It was an old woman, not much more than four feet tall, wearing a conical hat, screaming hysterically in Vietnamese, pummeling and clawing at Cozzano with both hands.

By the time the Secret Service dragged her off of the shocked Cozzano, roughly a hundred dollars' worth of assorted produce had been destroyed by the feet of video cameramen and still photographers who leapt up onto the high ground as soon as they heard trouble, running back and forth along the tables looking for a camera angle, churning the opulent displays of fresh strawberries, asparagus, basil, chanterelles, blackberries, and sweet corn into succotash. Most of them just barely had time to zero their cameras in on the contorted face of the old Vietnamese woman before she began to scream, in English: "You killed my baby! You killed my baby! You are an evil man!"

Sunday, October 27:

COZZANO    35%

PRESIDENT    15%

MCLANE    34%

UNDECIDED    12%

OTHER    4%

A front-page exclusive in the Sunday edition of *The Dallas Morning News* told an interesting story about Cozzano's son, James. James

Cozzano had spent most of the spring and summer following the primary campaigns as part of a research project for his doctoral dissertation. During this period he had made contacts with Lawrence Barnes, a wealthy Dallas businessman who was a big supporter of the candidacy of the Reverend Doctor William Joseph Sweigel. After Sweigel's loss to Tip McLane, Lawrence Barnes had approached James Cozzano and offered him a position on the board of directors of an import-export business, based in Houston, in which Barnes held a majority interest. The business dealt mostly in equipment related to oil exploration and drilling.

It was now revealed that this company did most of its business with Iraq and Libya, and that minority interests were owned by shady offshore companies that were known to be controlled by the governments of those countries.

Monday, October 28:

| | |
|---|---|
| COZZANO | 32% |
| PRESIDENT | 16% |
| MCLANE | 34% |
| UNDECIDED | 13% |
| OTHER | 5% |

Fifty newspapers across the United States ran the same photograph on the front page, a wire service photo taken on a small lake a few miles south of Tuscola, Illinois. The photo showed a local farmer out on a little rowboat, examining the surface of the lake, which was covered with dead fish. The farmer said that the fish kill was almost certainly caused by a spill of toxic waste originating from the CBAP plant in Tuscola—the economic foundation of the Cozzano family fortune.

*The Cozzano campaign* held a press conference in Seattle, in which leaders of the local Vietnamese-American community stated that no one had ever seen, or heard of, the little Vietnamese lady who had accused Cozzano of war crimes. The woman herself had gone into seclusion after having been released by the police, and was no longer speaking to the press; but her family insisted that Cozzano had rolled a hand grenade into their hut in Vietnam and blown up three small children.

Tuesday, October 29:

| | |
|---|---|
| COZZANO | 30% |
| PRESIDENT | 17% |
| MCLANE | 38% |
| UNDECIDED | 11% |
| OTHER | 4% |

A retired nurse who had once been hired to work in the Cozzano home, during the prolonged illness of Christina Cozzano, said that during the last few weeks of her life, Cozzano's late wife had become addicted to painkilling drugs.

The wife of Tip McLane's vice-presidential candidate, during a speech to a conservative Christian group, stated that Eleanor Richmond's overbearing and "unusually aggressive" personality had played a significant role in driving her husband to suicide.

James Cozzano resigned from the board of directors of the import-export company in Texas and stated that he had been taken for a ride.

Wednesday, October 30:

| | |
|---|---|
| COZZANO | 29% |
| PRESIDENT | 18% |
| MCLANE | 38% |
| UNDECIDED | 12% |
| OTHER | 3% |

The farmer who had accused CBAP of polluting the water and killing the fish retracted his statement, saying it had been based upon information given to him by an unknown "expert" who had since disappeared. Chemical analysis of the bodies of the fish showed that they had been killed by a common agricultural pesticide, which was available at any farm supply business, and which was not produced at CBAP.

The retired nurse who had told the story about Christina Cozzano's drug addiction was found dead in her garage in Peoria; she had committed suicide by breathing car exhaust.

The wife of Tip McLane's running mate stated in an interview that she had not meant, in any way, to say negative things about Eleanor Richmond.

William A. Cozzano canceled all of his campaign appearances for the rest of the week, saying that he needed to prepare for the big debate on Friday night.

Nimrod T. ("Tip") McLane, in an informal interview with Markene Caldicott on his campaign plane, deplored the way the presidential campaign had gone negative.

The President of the United States, addressing a Boy Scout jamboree in Arizona, said that he didn't blame young people for sometimes losing faith in politics, and promised that, when reelected, he would appoint a presidential commission to look into the state of America's elections.

The anchorman of the CBS *Evening News*, in a rare editorial, said that the presidential campaign had reached new depths this year, and stated that his organization was taking steps to make sure that it would not happen again.

*At the private* hotel that served as Jeremiah Freel's headquarters, security remained tight. The elevators were turned off except when someone very important was expected, or three times a day when room service was brought up from the kitchen.

For the fourth morning in a row, the waitress named Louella brought Jeremiah Freel his dish of stewed prunes. This did not go unnoticed by Freel. Louella was a hard woman not to notice. It was almost inconceivable that any woman, clad in the dowdy uniform of a hotel waitress, could appear sexy. But Louella managed. She must have taken her uniform home and modified it somehow, dropped the neckline, raised the hem. Every day, she was showing a little more cleavage, and every day, when she placed the breakfast tray on the table in front of Jeremiah Freel, she bent down a little bit lower, gave him a longer and deeper look down into the front of her dress.

Today he could no longer restrain himself. His hand darted down into her blouse, quick as a striking cobra, and caught her nipple. Not hard enough to hurt. But hard enough to keep her where she was.

"Mr. Freel," said one of his minders. One of the hated men in suits who surrounded him at all times.

"Shut up, asswipe!" Freel said.

Louella was staring straight into Freel's eyes. She wasn't angry at all. She was almost amused. She was interested. She licked her lips and said, "I'm sorry, Mr. Freel, but fresh fruit isn't on today's menu." Her face was about four inches from Freel's. She was wearing a lot of perfume and Freel could smell it wafting up from the middle of her hot cleavage.

"Then what do I have here?" Freel said, squeezing her nipple.

"You don't have a damn thing," Louella said, "unless you can get us a little bit of privacy." She looked around accusingly at all of the men in suits: four of them in this room alone.

"Get the fuck out!" Freel shouted.

"I'm sorry, Mr. Freel, you know we can't allow that!" said the head honcho, a guy who would only identify himself as Al. Al was clearly getting a little nervous. "Ma'am," he said to Louella, "I'm afraid you'll have to leave."

"But I can't," Louella said, "until Mr. Freel lets go of me. And I can tell he's not the kind of man who lets go until he gets what he wants."

"Get the fuck out," Freel said, "or this whole campaign goes up in flames. Can't you see I need to get laid?"

This appeal to simple, basic human needs got through to Al. He broke eye contact and thought about it for a second. "Well, okay," he finally said. "Come on guys, let's leave them alone."

All of Freel's minders got up and backed out of the room staring fixedly at Louella's backside. Louella turned around and yelled at them on their way out: "And I don't want you standing outside the door listening, either. You get back to your own rooms and watch TV or something."

Al, and the rest of the minders, left the room and closed the door.

They were still standing there, nervously, a minute later, when Louella stuck her head out the door. "I knew it!" she said. "You guys are all perverts. Get back to your rooms!"

Al posted one of his men by the elevators, just down the hall, and then the rest of the men retreated to their rooms, leaving the doors open.

A minute later, the guard by the elevators heard the little bell chime. The down arrow lit up. The elevator door opened to reveal a pair of brawny men, both wearing gas masks and ear protectors, who were just in the perfectly timed act of bursting out the doors; one of them grabbed the guard by the collar and jammed a thick wad of cloth over his mouth as the other reached out with a small but dense blunt object and took it upside of his head.

Louella emerged from Freel's room, stark naked, pursued closely by Freel himself. She was laughing and screaming; he was shouting, "You dirty bitch! Get back here!"

Louella made for the elevator. She reached it, and hit the lobby button, just as Al and the rest of Freel's guards were emerging into the corridor. They saw nothing but Jeremiah Freel diving into the elevator, and two large, unfamiliar men strewing stun grenades up and down the length of the hallway.

Twenty seconds later, staff and guests in the lobby were treated to the sight of Louella, a former Miss April, sprinting out of the elevator doors stark naked, still laughing and giggling, and running toward the front entrance, pursued the entire way by an old man with his erect penis sticking out of his fly.

A doorman, reflexes honed by years of practice, cleared the way. Louella ran through the open door, into the horseshoe drive, and jumped into the back of a windowless van. The doors slammed shut, the van burned rubber and shot forward out of the drive, revealing something that had been hiding on the other side of it: Cyrus Rutherford Ogle, flanked by two dozen TV cameramen and still photographers, all of whom were busily recording the quickly changing facial expression of Jeremiah Freel, and his vanishing penis.

"Come back to lose another election, Jeremiah?" Ogle said.

Freel's mouth dropped open and his nose wrinkled into a snarl. His eyes jumped back and forth between Ogle and the cameramen.

Then he charged.

Cy Ogle stood his ground, hands in the pockets of his trench coat.

Freel dove the last six feet, wrapped his arms around Ogle's thighs, and bent his head back, mouth open to bite into Ogle's genitals.

Ogle took his hand from his pocket, holding a small cylindrical object. His index finger twitched and fired a long stream of Mace directly into Freel's open mouth. Freel went into violent convulsions and fell to the horseshoe drive, thrashing, foaming, and howling like a wounded animal.

"Welcome to public relations hell," Ogle said, and then climbed into a waiting car. As it drove away, he was able to look back and watch Freel convulsing on the drive in front of the hotel, surrounded now by photographers and cameramen who were all aiming their lenses downward.

CHAPTER FIFTY-SIX

The final, and by far the most important, debate of the presidential campaign was held on the evening of Friday, November 1, four days before Election Day, in a lecture hall at Columbia University. The participants were the President of the United States, William Anthony Cozzano, and Nimrod T. ("Tip") McLane. The moderator was the president of the hosting university. He fielded questions among the three presidential candidates and a panel of four journalists, who were all of the first rank.

All three of the candidates had spent the last couple of days mostly in seclusion, honing their skills in mock debates. McLane and the President had both brought in mimics to simulate the other two candidates, and spent hours in exhausting practice sessions, during which simulated journalists would throw out the most difficult, vicious, twisted questions imaginable.

The advance people had been at the auditorium for a solid day. Lecterns had to be arranged on the stage. Lights had to be focused and adjusted. Camera placement had to be worked out. All of these were subject to intensive negotiation. A wrongly placed spotlight in

'84 had emphasized the bags under Mondale's eyes and made him look older than Reagan. The height of each lectern had to be adjusted relative to the height of the candidate. The color of the set and the color of the lights affected what kind of suits would look best; stand-ins had to be brought onstage, wearing different suits, in order to decide which looked best. Makeup had to be tried out; makeup artists had to have rooms in which to work, and no one candidate's room could be bigger, better equipped, or closer to the stage than any other's.

Though an audience was going to be present in the hall, its only real function was to provide a bit of ambient noise: applause (to be kept under control as much as possible) and possibly the occasional outburst of laughter, though using humor in these circumstances was probably too risky to be considered. In the current political climate, humor was a zero-sum game. The impression that the candidates made on the live audience was unimportant. A huge video screen was erected above the stage so that the people and the journalists in the hall could see the TV feed, which was the only thing that mattered.

The same feed was piped into a large, low-ceilinged room beneath the auditorium and displayed on a couple of dozen monitors. This room was filled with long tables where journalists could set up their laptop computers, plug into telephone lines, and file their stories. This was the room where the spin doctors from the three campaigns would circulate before, during, and after the debate, explaining to the reporters what was happening.

It was the single largest gathering of explosively tense people on the face of the earth. Tense people don't like surprises. Therefore, there was a great deal of shock and unhappiness in that hall when, ten minutes before air time, just as the President and Tip McLane were emerging from their makeup rooms and taking their positions on the stage, Cyrus Rutherford Ogle appeared, walked up to the moderator, and informed him that William A. Cozzano would not be participating in tonight's debate because he had more important things to do.

*Pandemonium* was a term coined by Milton to refer to the capital of Hell, where all of the demons were together in one place. From this it naturally came to mean any central headquarters of wickedness. Over time, though, as happens with many good words, its meaning had been diluted to mean any place that was noisy and chaotic. Nowadays, a person could speak of pandemonium at a birthday party full of two-year-olds.

Cy Ogle preferred the old definition of the word. No other word could possibly have described the situation in the auditorium after he strolled onto the stage and made his announcement. There was no doubt in his mind that if not for the presence of witnesses, the campaign staffs of the President, Tip McLane, the panel of journalists, and the organizers of the debate would drag him outside and hang him from a stately tree on the Columbia campus. Outside of an actual lynching, never had so much hostility been directed against one man by so many people for so many reasons. Consequently he could scarcely prevent himself from grinning through the whole thing.

There was an initial phase during which people merely screamed at him, then ran off into the wings to spread the news to other people, who ran out to scream at him some more. This probably would have gone on for quite some time if not for the fact that air time was rapidly approaching. So it got compressed into a very intense couple of minutes. A tone of emotional restraint was imposed by the technical types, who had a show to put on.

"Well, I can't give you Cozzano in person," Ogle said, "and I'm deeply sorry for that. But to make amends, we did blow quite a bundle buying some satellite time. We can bring you Cozzano live from his home in Tuscola."

This announcement brought all of Pandemonium into a state of stunned silence. Cozzano could participate via TV? And Ogle was paying for the satellite time? We can live with that.

"Only thing is," Ogle said, after they had bit on that, "that we will need to make one small change in the format. Cozzano has an important announcement to make. A very, very important announcement. And with your forbearance, we would like to have a minute or two at the beginning of this program for him to make that announcement."

Absolute silence reigned on the stage.

Pandemonium had relocated downstairs, into the press room, where a couple of hundred reporters were screaming into their telephones. Most of them were screaming the same thing: *Cozzano is withdrawing from the race!*

They managed to launch the program on time. The moderator took these last-minute changes calmly, made a few changes to his notes, and sat down in his throne, unruffled. McLane and the President met in the middle of the stage and shook hands (this encounter had been choreographed during an hour-long summit conference between their campaign staffs) and Cozzano's lectern remained unoccupied.

Out in the parking lot behind the auditorium, several semitrailer rigs were parked in parallel slots. There were some satellite uplink trucks, one GODS container on a flatbed rig, and a mobile studio from one of the networks, which was the nerve center of the whole debate: this was where the pool feed originated. Feeds from all of the cameras on the stage converged on this vehicle and showed up on small monitors. A director sat in front of them and decided which camera was going on the air. Now, the director had a new feed patched into his system, which came directly from a satellite downlink. This feed originated in Tuscola, Illinois.

When he had learned about the business with Cozzano, the director had been expecting just a simple, live, one-camera feed, probably Cozzano sitting in his living room by the fire, or something. It would be there all night long, and whenever Cozzano's turn came up, he would push the appropriate button and the image of Cozzano would go out.

Naturally, it turned out to be a lot more complicated than that. The feed from Tuscola, when he first saw it, consisted of a long shot of Cozzano's house as seen from the street. Obviously Cozzano's house wasn't going to participate in the debate. They would have to have at least one more camera, inside the house. Which meant that somewhere in Tuscola there was another director who was sitting in another studio like this one—a director who worked for Cy Ogle and William A. Cozzano. That director was managing feeds from at least two cameras, deciding which one was going to be fed up to the satellite.

The director, in his trailer behind the auditorium, was the first person in the United States to figure out that Ogle had taken them for a ride. The choreography of this debate, which had been hammered out through many hours of negotiations, over a period of weeks, had just been torn to shreds and replaced by something totally new, entirely Ogle's.

*The moderator began* the debate with a few introductory remarks. On TV, you always had to explain the obvious, over and over again: "In four days, Americans go to the polls to select the man who will be their next president. This is a profoundly significant choice . . ."

". . . this debate was originally intended to include all three major candidates. Tonight, we have two of them. The President of the United States. And Representative Tip McLane of California."

As the moderator introduced the two men, the director, outside in the trailer, caused their faces to appear on the air. Neither one of them seemed to be ready for it. Ever since Ogle's announcement, no one had really known what the hell was going on, what would happen when, who would be introduced in what order. McLane and the President had both spent a lot of time in front of television cameras in the last few days, in the privacy of their campaign headquarters, practicing what they would do at the moment they were introduced; now, neither one of them did the right thing. They looked agitated, sweaty, shifty-eyed, and when they realized they were on TV, they both looked surprised.

"The third candidate, William A. Cozzano, Governor of Illinois, announced a few minutes ago that he could not participate."

The director cut to a camera that had been set up to show all three of the candidates' lecterns in a single shot. McLane and the President looked stiff and self-conscious. The empty lectern made both of them look foolish.

"Instead, he will be addressing us from his home in Tuscola, Illinois."

Cut to the shot of Cozzano's house with the sun setting behind it. It looked inviting and refreshing compared to the stale tense atmosphere of the auditorium.

"Now, the format of this debate has been established in advance, by consensus between the campaign staffs and the sponsoring organizations, and I intend to adhere strictly to that format. But there is one deviation that needs to be made, and we will do that right now and get it out of the way. I understand that Governor Cozzano has an important announcement that he needs to make, and that he is going to make it now. So I will offer the floor to him at this time. Governor Cozzano, are you there?"

"Here goes nothing," said the director, out in his trailer, and cut from the image of the moderator back to the feed from Tuscola.

The feed remained steady on the image of the house for a minute. Lights were coming on inside as the sun set spectacularly behind it. It looked cheery and welcoming. And it broke the rigid, lockstep schedule of the debate. Then the Tuscola feed cut to a shot of William A. Cozzano. But it was not the expected picture of Cozzano in a suit, sitting by the fire reading a book and smoking a pipe.

It was totally different. For a few moments, it was difficult to make out. Cozzano appeared to be lying on his back in a cramped space, staring upward, reaching up above him with one arm. "Good evening," he said, "I'll be with you momentarily."

Cut to another angle on the same thing. Whatever Cozzano was doing, and wherever he was, they had at least two cameras on him.

This angle was a closeup of Cozzano's hand. It was dirty and greasy and flecked with a small drop of blood where he had torn one of his knuckles. He was spinning some small metal object around between his fingers. Then he yanked his hand away and a stream of black fluid shot out of an opening and into a metal tray beneath.

Cut to yet another angle, this one showing Cozzano's legs sticking out from beneath a car. He was lying on the floor of his garage.

Actually, he was lying on a mechanic's creeper. He slid out from underneath the car, sat up, and rose lightly to his feet. He picked up an old rag and began to wipe oil from his hands, addressing the camera. "My apologies. I wanted to participate in tonight's debate, but I've been very busy lately. A few days ago I stopped flying around the country for the first time in a couple of months and came back here to my home, the house that my father bought back during the Depression to impress a young woman named Francesca Domenici, who became his wife, and my mother.

"And, you know, I decided that I liked it here. And looking around the place I saw that there was a lot to do here that I had left undone." Cozzano nodded at his car. "For example, changing the oil in my car. I just took it out for a quick drive through the cornfields, out to the old family farm and back, to warm up the engine so that the oil would flow out. It was a nice drive. Some people think that the landscape here is boring, but I think it's beautiful."

Cozzano had begun to walk toward the camera, which backed away from him. It backed out of the garage door and into Cozzano's yard. Nearby was a large garden.

"This garden was in disgraceful shape. Hadn't been weeded in quite some time, and the weeds were bigger than the vegetables. So I took care of that. You can see it looks a little better now." Cozzano plucked a ripe red tomato from a vine and bit into it like an apple. Juice ran down his chin and he wiped it with the sleeve of his mechanic's coverall. "Of course, home is more than just doing chores. Home means being with your family too."

Cozzano had now reached a patio, which was illuminated. A picnic table had been spread with a nice tablecloth and set with fresh vegetables from the garden and a platter of hamburgers. Sitting at the table was Mary Catherine Cozzano, pouring iced tea from a pitcher into three glasses. At the end of the table, James was manning a sizzling barbecue, flipping burger patties and hot dogs.

"This is my daughter, Mary Catherine. You may have heard of her recently, as media manipulators hired by my opponents have made strenuous efforts to assassinate her character. She has been nothing short of noble in the face of this mudslinging." Mary Catherine smiled and nodded at the camera.

"And this young man at the barbecue is my son, James, who has been working his tail off all year long, writing a book about this year's presidential campaign. He has just signed a deal with a major publisher in New York, and that book is going to be published on Inauguration Day."

Mary Catherine stood up, threw one arm around her brother's shoulders, and kissed him on the cheek.

In the auditorium, the audience went, "Ahhhh."

Tip McLane did not. He stepped away from the lectern and began to shout at the moderator: "I demand that this be stopped! This is no announcement! This is a free campaign commercial!"

The moderator looked at Cy Ogle, who was standing in the wings. "I have to agree. Mr. Ogle? I'm going to have to pull the plug."

"This ain't no campaign commercial," Ogle said, "because there ain't no campaign."

On the giant TV screen above their heads, Cozzano was beaming delightedly at his daughter and son. He turned back toward the camera. "When I came back here a few days ago, my intention was to prepare for the debate. But the home and family that I rediscovered here delighted me so much that I could not bring myself to look at the huge briefing books and the endless position papers that my campaign staff had prepared for me. I found that I would rather dig potatoes in the garden or sit on the front porch swing reading Mark Twain.

"Now, these are perfectly good things to do. But in a modern political campaign, it's regarded as improper, somehow, to act like a normal human being. And this brought me to the realization that there is something evil and twisted about the campaign process: the traveling, the speechifying, the television spots. The mudslinging. Wearing makeup sixteen hours a day. And most of all, the debates, with their false and pompous trappings."

In the production trailer, the director could not restrain himself from punching the button that cut away to a long shot of the auditorium stage. At the moment, it consisted of a number of stuffed shirts, arguing, consulting with aides, and staring in shock at television monitors.

"And I made up my mind," Cozzano said, "that the entire thing was corrupt. Only a scoundrel can participate in such a campaign; only a cipher can win. I am neither. So I have decided that I am no longer interested in campaigning for president of the United States.

"Earlier today, I drove my car down to Sterling Texaco, down on the corner. It's a place I've been buying gas and tires ever since I bought my first car back in high school. And old Mr. Sterling came out to fill up my tank, wash my windshield, check my oil. This is kind of an old-fashioned town, and that's still how we do things here.

"Well, Mr. Sterling, who sold me my very first tank of gas back in the early sixties, took one look at my dipstick and he told me to get out of the car and come have a look. I did so. And sure enough, the end of that dipstick was coated with the darkest, grimiest, sludgiest coat of oil I have ever seen. It was disgraceful, and Mr. Sterling didn't have to say so. I knew it. I knew I'd gone too long without changing my oil. So I bought five quarts of fresh oil along with my tank of gas, and drove them home."

As Cozzano told this story, he was strolling back into his garage, where his car was angled up on a pair of ramps. He kneeled beside the car, reached underneath with one arm, and slid out the metal basin, which was now filled with black oil.

"Just a few minutes ago, as I was crawling under the car to let that old sludge out of the system, I realized that there was a powerful metaphor for politics. Our political system is basically sound, but over the years it has gotten all fouled with dirt and sludge."

Cozzano carried the basin over to a counter, where an empty plastic milk jug sat with a funnel stuck into the top. He held the basin up and tipped it, pouring the oil down the funnel and into the plastic jug.

"Of course, that kind of thing rubs off. It permeates everything after a while. And I realized that being a presidential candidate had fouled and stained my life in many ways, some obvious, some a little more subtle."

Cozzano set the basin down. He took a metal oil spout off a pegboard on the wall, then picked up a fresh can of oil. He shoved the spout into the can, piercing its top, then tilted it just a bit and spilled a few drops of clean, clear, golden oil into the palm of his hand. "Now, that's more like it," he said. "This is how my life used to be. And this"—he set the oil can down and slapped the milk jug full of sludge—"is how my life was after a few months of presidential politics. Of course, the President and Tip McLane have been in the same game for much longer than I have. I don't know how they do it."

Cozzano pulled the rag out of his pocket and wiped his hands. "Well, I've got some burgers to eat. A son and daughter to get reacquainted with. Some new oil to put in the car. Then I think we'll go for a stroll around town, maybe take in a movie. And I know that the President and Tip have got important things to do also. So I'll let you attend to those things. Best of luck to you all, and good night."

The Tuscola feed cut back to the long shot of Cozzano's house, now just a silhouette against an indigo sky, lights shining warmly from every window.

*In the press* room, Zeke Zorn was standing on a table shouting. Important blood vessels were showing on his forehead, which, like the rest of his face had turned red.

"This is an absolute disgrace!" he screamed. Then he took a deep breath and got himself under control. "This is the most dirty, underhanded, filthy campaign trick ever devised."

Al Lefkowitz, the President's chief spin doctor, was calmer, paler, seemingly almost distracted, like a man who has been hit on the head with a two-by-four and whose consciousness has withdrawn into a deeper neurological realm. He was speaking more quietly than Zorn, with the result that reporters, fleeing in fear of being struck by a loose drop of saliva ejected from Zorn's mouth, had clustered around him. "It's very disappointing. It's an act of political vandalism, really. If he just wanted to withdraw from the race, that would be one thing. But he went beyond that and attacked the candidates. And more importantly, he attacked the American electoral process itself. It's very sad that his career has to end this way."

Zeke Zorn suddenly grabbed the floor by howling, "THERE HE IS!" and pointing toward the entrance. Cy Ogle had just strolled into the room and was now blinking and looking around himself curiously, as if he had wandered in while searching for the men's room, and could not understand all the commotion.

Zorn continued, "Maybe you would like to explain how you're going to get Cozzano's name off the ballots in all fifty states in just four days!"

Ogle looked perplexed. "Who said anything about ballots?"

"Cozzano did. He claims he's withdrawing from the race."

"Oh, no," Ogle said, shaking his head, and looking a little shocked. "He never said anything about withdrawing from the race. He just said he didn't want to do any more *campaigning*."

Zorn was speechless.

Lefkowitz was not. "Excuse me, Cy, but I think we have a problem here. We negotiated the terms of this debate in good faith. Then you came in with a last-minute change. You said you wanted some free time for Cozzano to speak from Tuscola. And your excuse was that he wanted to make an important announcement. Am I right?"

"Yes, you're right. Those were my words," Ogle said.

"The only reason that Cozzano was granted that free time was because of this important announcement. He wouldn't have been given that time if all he wanted was to make editorial comments."

"True," Ogle said.

"So we all construed his words to mean that he was dropping out of the race."

"Oh, I'm sorry," Ogle said, "he didn't mean to say that."

"But if he wasn't dropping out of the race," Lefkowitz said, "then he wasn't making any important announcement—which means that you obtained that free air time under false pretenses. You committed a fraud against the American people! And I am sure that this fraud will be covered extensively by those here in the press room, and that you and Cozzano will be judged for it by the American people, who have grown sick of dirty campaigning."

"But he did make an important announcement. Just as I said he would. There's no deception here," Ogle said. "Just a misunderstanding."

"What are you talking about!?" Zorn shouted.

"You heard him," Ogle said, "he announced that his son was publishing a book. Doesn't that seem like an important announcement to y'all?"

# resurrection symphony

## CHAPTER FIFTY-SEVEN

Four days after Cozzano's landslide victory, the Speaker of the House suffered a stroke during a party in a private Washington club, while sitting on the toilet in the men's room. On the recommendation of the President-elect, the Speaker's family sent him to the Radhakrishnan Institute for therapy.

The house across the street from the Cozzano residence in Tuscola had become vacant a couple of months previously, and the Cozzanos had bought it. Cy Ogle and some of his best people now moved into it and made it into the headquarters for the transition. If the Cozzano house was the Tuscola White House, then the place across the street was the Tuscola Executive Office building.

Cy Ogle had a big leather La-Z-Boy set up in the living room and spent much of mid-November lying in it "like a sack of shit," as he put it, recovering from a cold, watching TV, and enjoying his first chance to relax in the better part of a year. It was a wonderful time for him. He had devastated not only the opposition candidates, but also his competitors in the election business. Even the fearsome Jeremiah Freel was in jail. And besides, he was a sucker for Christmas.

After Election Day, Ogle, as leader of the transition team, declared a three-week moratorium on all official activities for the President-elect. Eleanor Richmond likewise stuck close to home— her Alexandria apartment—attending a couple of T. C. Williams football games (Harmon, Jr., had become a star punter) and shopping for inaugural clothes with her daughter, Clarice.

At the beginning of December, Ogle issued a press release listing the members of the Cozzano transition team. Ogle claimed, of course, that he had hand-picked these men, but nothing could have been further from the truth. Whoever *had* chosen them had done an excellent job: they were professional, experienced, nonpartisan, and classy in a nonintimidating way. They had impeccable credentials and were universally regarded as ethical and trustworthy. It was claimed that these people had spent the last year behind the scenes, working on position papers for the Cozzano campaign. This was patently untrue, but Ogle had to admit that it sounded great. All of the serious press agreed, and praised the skills of the Cozzano team. The rest of the media was content with photo-ops of Cozzano and his family and entourage shoveling snow in Tuscola.

Ogle knew that the people, whose consciousness he had pummeled and abused so relentlessly for the previous year, needed a rest. They needed to concentrate on the NFL, sitcoms, and Christmas. They needed to recharge their batteries because what was to come in the Cozzano administration would be tough. A quick glance at the aforementioned position papers proved that much. The waffling and pathetic efforts of the previous administration were to be replaced by calm, cool decisiveness. No one knew what the plan was, beyond the endless evocation of the return to values, and its fiscal corollaries: cut the deficit, pay back every penny of the debt.

Ogle also knew that his role in this operation would end as of January 20. He had two major tasks left to organize, and this was the kind of thing he liked best—public displays without elections. Spectacles. On December 1 he gathered his staff together to launch the final push on the Cozzano Family Christmas Special. The buildup for the special would run until December 21. He would drop names out in the media like lures for hungry trout. Names for potential cabinet officers, names for White House staff. Names for possible judicial appointments. The idea was partly to show what fine people would be working for Cozzano, partly to build up suspense for the Christmas Special, and partly to avoid the tedious and demeaning sight of wannabes trudging back and forth between the Champaign-Urbana airport and Tuscola.

Instead he had a parade of foreign dignitaries make the same trip. It looked more impressive, and the sight of Brazilians and Saudis making snowmen on the front lawn was great television. Ogle toyed endlessly with the sequence of their arrivals. He also found ways to make use of the soaring stock market, inspired by the Cozzano victory, the knowledge that the debt would not be forgiven, and all of the feel-good symbolism that was radiating from Tuscola like heat from an old-fashioned wood stove.

Starting on the twenty-first he would begin to throw more logs on the fire. Mary Catherine had taken a job at Brigham and

Women's Hospital in Boston, and Dad was giving her a cozy brown-stone apartment to move into; while its exact location was not mentioned, *Today* show viewers were given a video tour of the place, complete with blazing fires, oriental rugs, and antique furniture.

On the twenty-second an affirmation of Cozzano's strength would be made: he would do a guest shot on a special live edition of a popular woodworking show. The pipe-smoking, suspender-wearing host would interview Cozzano working in his shop, steam coming out of his mouth, as the President-elect fixed a busted chest of drawers.

Scheduled for the twenty-third was the official launch of James Cozzano's new book, Kingmakers: The Inside Stories of Ogle, Zorn, and Lefkowitz and How They Created a President. The publisher was throwing a launch party at the Hay-Adams Hotel, across the park from the White House. Rich and powerful people would be present. So would TV cameras. The rave reviews had already been written.

The twenty-fourth would feature the Cozzanos at midnight mass. And the twenty-fifth would make the country feel good. *Real* good.

*The seven weeks* after the election were glorious for Mary Catherine. No more travel. Minimum of interviews, speeches, and other campaign hassles. Maximum of time with Dad. Most of this time was strictly business, though. As she had been doing for the last six months, she spent several hours a day putting him through therapeutic exercises, mostly concentrating on the left hand.

She had a lot of free time. Part of it she spent hanging around with her old high-school friends and driving up to Champaign or over to Decatur for Christmas shopping. She also took up a new hobby: electronics.

She had purchased a book on the subject months ago in Boston and had been reading it in free moments, learning about all the mysterious hieroglyphs that made up a circuit diagram: resistors, capacitors, and inductors. She didn't reckon she could design her own circuits now, but she could certainly put one together from a diagram.

The week before Christmas she made a stop at the Tuscola Radio

Shack, which doubled as an Ace Hardware store. She picked up a set of gloves and some tools for her father, and then she went into the little nook where all of the resistors, capacitors, and inductors hung in bubble packs. Reading part numbers from a wrinkled sheet of paper she'd taken from her wallet, she selected a couple of dozen items and paid for everything with cash.

Her father already had a soldering iron, of course; he had every tool known to the industrialized world. Mary Catherine let it be known that she was going into Dad's workshop to assemble a secret Christmas present and that her privacy had better not be disturbed. She locked the door, pulled down the windowshades, and cranked up the cast-iron stove that Dad used to heat the place up. When it was warm enough that her fingers worked again, she plugged in the soldering iron and went to work, soldering the little bits and pieces from Radio Shack onto a breadboard—a slab of plastic with holes punched through it. When it was finished the whole thing fit into a black plastic box about the size of a paperback book. A toggle switch and a red light protruded from one end.

President-elect Cozzano himself seemed to blossom under the period of rest and relaxation. Aside from receiving his daily CIA briefing and eyes-only presidential briefing, he was basically on vacation. He evinced no desire to have a hand in collecting names for his cabinet, being content to work with the same corps of advisers that had brought him here. Football season blended into basketball season at Tuscola High School, and periodically Cozzano would slip out to the football field or into the gym to watch the town's young student-athletes compete.

Cozzano had developed a new passion in the last months of the campaign: Scrabble. It had been his idea that they start playing the game, but Mary Catherine encouraged it because (as she explained to her father's curious handlers) it was a great form of therapy. Because it was a word game, it helped to exercise the parts of Cozzano's brain that handled verbal communication. But because no speech was involved, it bypassed the speech centers of the brain— which were now partly silicon. Mary Catherine insisted that Cozzano play it with his left hand. At first, Cozzano had found it surprisingly difficult to persuade his left hand to spell words; the necessary neural connections had been severed by the stroke.

Mary Catherine mocked him for being so inept. That was all Cozzano needed. He started playing to win. He was tenacious, and over the months, became good. He played once a day with Mary Catherine. He played it so often that even the Secret Service folks and the people at control stopped noticing it.

*Cozzano's cabinet members* were announced. They were mostly youthful and in good physical shape, their names indicated a pleasing and politically correct distribution of ethnic groups and genders, they had gone to the best schools, they had outstanding records. They were all perfect.

A day later, Mary Catherine got a Christmas card from Zeldo. It included several photos: a couple of Zeldo riding his mountain bike on the bluffs above the Pacific and a few of Zeldo at work.

One of the photos showed Zeldo sitting in the courtyard of the Radhakrishnan Insitute, enjoying *caffè latte* and typing away on his laptop. In the background, seated at another table, was one of the institute's patients. Mary Catherine recognized the man: he was the secretary-designate of Defense.

She went through the other photos very carefully, and saw three more patients "accidentally" caught in the background: the secretaries-designate of State, Treasury, and Commerce, and the Speaker of the U.S. House of Representatives.

*Early on the* afternoon of December eighteenth, Mary Catherine went cross-country skiing. Three inches of new snow had fallen the night before. By the standards of post-greenhouse effect Illinois, it was a winter wonderland. She tossed her skis and poles into the back of the family's four-wheel-drive pickup truck, checked her arsenal of waxes, and took off. A few minutes' drive took her to the old Cozzano farm. She got out, locked the front hubs, shifted into four-wheel-drive, pulled onto a dirt lane between fields, and drove for half a mile or so. Then she put her skis on and took off.

After a mile or so she was able to coast down into the gentle cleft of a river valley, lightly forested with skinny ironwood trees. She followed the river for another half mile until she came upon a beat-up, ramshackle old cabin, really more of a glorified duck blind than a dwelling. Parked beside it was a big Chevy pickup truck, and as she approached from downwind she could smell cigar smoke and hear subdued conversation.

Mel Meyer, ludicrously clad in a heavy insulated farmer's coverall, emerged from the building, walked up to Mary Catherine, and ran a bug detector over her body. This time he got a faint radio signal from one of the buttons on her shirt. Mary Catherine skiied a couple of hundred feet away from the shack and left the button under a log. Then she came back and gave Mel a long hug.

Inside the shack were a bulky, round-shouldered black man in his fifties, and a huge white guy with bushy eyebrows and a salt-and-pepper hair and beard. Mary Catherine knew them both already. Respectively, they were Rufus Bell, USMC Retired, and Craig ("the Crag") Addison, Chicago Bears, Retired.

"How's he doing?" Bell said.

"He's doing great," Mary Catherine said, "this is all boy adventure stuff. Just the kind of thing he likes."

Mel, Rufus, and Craig ("the Crag") all looked slightly embarrassed.

"Okay," Mel said, "now listen carefully, because I'm freezing my ass off, and because this is important. These two guys Rufus and Crag, can provide the bodies we need. With a little help from some of Eleanor's friends and supporters in D.C., we can even make it legal. And I can provide the paperwork. Mary Catherine?"

"I've got the black box ready. And I've got some information for you. The secretaries-designate of Defense, Treasury, Commerce, and State, and the Speaker of the House, have all spent time at the Radhakrishnan Institute in the last few months."

Mel shook his head. "Tragic," he said. "A tragic epidemic of strokes. Anyone else?"

"Not that I know of."

"Well, that will be useful knowledge," Mel said. "Now, Mary Catherine, there's only one thing we need from you."

"My father," Mary Catherine said.

"Right. Can you give me Willy?"

"I have a plan, Mel," she said. "I have a scam."

That night after supper, Cozzano called Mary Catherine in for another game of Scrabble. She'd had two or three glasses of Chianti, she was in a good mood, and she spoke without restraint. "Dad, it's the most boring game ever invented."

"If only you would play it right," he groused, "and not cheat."

They went to the study and sat down at the desk in front of the works of Mark Twain.

Mary Catherine always started the same way: she reached into the heap of tiles and spelled out ARE YOU STILL THERE. They had a fancy Scrabble board mounted on a turntable and so when she was done, she spun it around so he could read it.

Cozzano frowned. "Stop playing around," he said. "You know the rules." Both of his hands were active. It was a bizarre sight: with his left hand he was breaking up the sequence that she had spelled out, rearranging the letters, plucking more of them out of the overturned box top. With his right hand, he was picking seven tiles at random and placing them neatly on his little rack. He continued to speak at the same time. He seemed genuinely annoyed and appeared not to notice what his own left hand was doing. "You have to pick seven tiles. And you can only spell one word at once. Why do I have to explain this to you every time? Are you teasing me, girl?"

Mary Catherine was accustomed to strange neurological tics because of her work, and she had grown accustomed to her father's peculiarities over the months that she had been putting him through daily therapy. She had to remind herself just how bizarre this would look to anyone else.

Cozzano's left hand spun the board around so that Mary Catherine could read the words DID YOU SEE MEL.

She looked up into his eyes. He was frowning, staring down at the Scrabble board, befuddled. "How did those letters get there?" he asked.

Mary Catherine messed them up with her hand before his eyes could read them. Then she combed some more tiles out of the heap and spelled out the word YES.

He got the same look on his face as when she had come home from school with Bs on her report card. "Is that the best you could do? A three-letter word?"

"Sorry," she said, "I got bad letters."

"Thanks for giving me that big fat Y," he said. "That's four easy points for me. You need to think harder about strategy." As he was talking, both hands were again active on the Scrabble board. His right hand was turning her Y into the word YTTRIUM. His left hand was spelling out HOW IS HE on the bottom left corner of the board.

Mary Catherine spun the board around. Again, Cozzano's eyes picked out the letters that had been laid down by his left hand. "How did those letters get on there?" he said. "For god's sake, peanut, we need to make sure the board is clear before we start. Get rid of those."

She had already read them, so she swept them away. Then she used the I in YTTRIUM to spell out the word PLANNING. In order to do it, she had to rummage through the box top for some more letters. Cozzano frowned and grumbled about this cheating.

The conversation went back and forth like that for several more rounds, the Scrabble board spinning round and around.

Cozzano: FOR WHAT

Mary Catherine: INAUGDAY

"I defy you to find that word in any dictionary," Cozzano said.

*DuLafayette Webster, Heisman* trophy winner for the Elton State Comanches, scored three touchdowns singlehandedly in the first half of the Fujitsu Guacamole Bowl on Christmas Night. As soon as the first half clock ticked down to zero, the broadcast cut away to the cheerful theme music of the Cozzano Family Christmas Special.

A live shot from a hovering chopper zoomed down on the twinkling Christmas lights of Tuscola, which had begun billing itself as "America's hometown." The Christmas decorations had been heavily enhanced by the largesse of Ogle, and coordinated by his designers. The camera panned across church steeples, small businesses, and the city park, all decked with boughs of electric holly, and then settled on the now-familiar Cozzano residence. A street level camera peered through the large front window to view the roaring fire and the happy, smiling group gathered around the eggnog. "Good evening, ladies and gentlemen. From Tuscola, Illinois, America's hometown, we bring you an address by the President-elect, William Anthony Cozzano. Governor Cozzano."

Cut to a shot of Cozzano, James, and Mary Catherine sitting

together on the sofa. Zoom in to a talking-head shot of Cozzano alone.

The President-elect made a heartfelt statement of thanks to the American people, expressed his happiness with his daughter's career plans and his son's excellent book, and incidentally, announced his cabinet nominees.

Then he stood up and introduced them personally. The cabinet-to-be were all gathered around the huge dining room table, dressed in cozy sweaters, drinking cider. They interrupted the convivial routine for a moment as Cozzano introduced them, one by one, to the American people. They were good-looking, confident, bipartisan, and multicultural.

Finally, Cozzano returned to his seat by the fire to address a few last words of greeting and holiday cheer to the American people. Cozzano had developed a sense of timing that was positively eerie. He brought his little speech to a close just in time to cut back to the scoreboard clock at the bowl game.

On the eighteenth of January, the Cozzanos climbed onto a chartered plane and flew to Washington, D.C. Journalists from around the world were converging there at the same time. So were members of the incoming administration and transition team, all of Cy Ogle's top people, several big GODS trucks full of electronics, Floyd Wayne Vishniak, and an irregular caravan of buses, cars, and airplanes carrying old teammates and Marine comrades-in-arms of William A. Cozzano.

<hr/>

## CHAPTER FIFTY-EIGHT

At eight o'clock on the morning of Inauguration Day, a cluster of Secret Service agents burst from the elevators and into the lobby of the Georgetown Four Seasons Hotel, striding calmly but implacably across hardwood floors, green oriental carpets, and weathered brick. At the same time, a motorcade of three dark cars was spiraling out of a parking garage down the street. The motorcade pulled into the brick driveway at the front entrance just as the cluster of agents, and the dignitaries hidden among them, was bursting through the brass front doors. Within a few seconds, the cars and the people were gone, trailed by a few journalists who had been quick enough to notice that the President-elect was on the move.

At the same time, William A. Cozzano himself was emerging quietly from an elevator tucked into a dimly lit corner near the restaurant on the next floor down. He was accompanied by his son and daughter and two Secret Service agents. The Cozzanos were dressed in running clothes. They padded down a gray-carpeted stairway and exited onto a brick patio behind the hotel, two stories below street level, which led directly onto a herringbone-brick jogging path. Beyond the path was the C&O Canal, a narrow trench of stagnant water lined with massive, moss-covered masonry blocks.

The President-elect wanted to go for a damn jog with his family. Was that too much to ask? It would be his last opportunity to do so as a private citizen. He wanted to do it in Rock Creek Park, which was where he normally jogged when he was in D.C., but the Secret Service didn't like that idea. They had gotten positively jumpy about Floyd Wayne Vishniak, who was still at large. During his escapade at Ogle Data Research, Vishniak had displayed cunning and well-developed marksmanship skills. He was still firing off demented manifestoes to various newspapers and magazines. Everyone knew that Cozzano liked to jog in Rock Creek Park, and with its dense vegetation and myriad ways in and out, it would be like the happy hunting grounds for Vishniak.

Cozzano was a demanding sort. He didn't merely want to go jogging in an incredibly dangerous place: he was insisting on privacy too. He wanted to stage a diversion and send the journalists on a wild goose chase so that he could just run with his son and daughter.

The Secret Service agreed to a compromise. If Cozzano would go running in Arlington—in an area that was not quite so Floyd-friendly—then the Secret Service would stage the diversion for him. So far it was working perfectly.

Fifty feet away, the canal passed underneath the Rock Creek Parkway and joined up with Rock Creek itself. Three more Secret

Service cars were idling on the side of the Parkway, wheels up on the curb, waiting for them with doors open. This little motorcade would spirit them away to Arlington, where they could go jogging on the flawlessly groomed parade grounds of Fort Myer, next to the National Cemetery, under the protection of military police and Secret Service.

Cozzano had been talking football with the Secret Service men all the way down the stairs. As they crossed the brick patio, Mary Catherine drew close to her brother and said, "James, this is important. Remember when we were kids? Remember Follow the Leader?"

"Sure," James said sunnily, mistaking this for idle nostalgia.

"We're about to play the world's most important game of Follow the Leader. Don't screw it up," Mary Catherine said.

"Huh?"

They were stepping onto the jogging path. Mary Catherine reached into the open top of her belt pack and flipped the toggle switch on the end of her black plastic Radio Shack contraption.

William A. Cozzano stopped dead for a moment and shouted, "Hey!"

He was staring off into the distance, focusing on something that wasn't there.

"Dad?" James said. "Are you okay?"

Cozzano shook his head and snapped out of it. He looked at James and Mary Catherine for a moment, thinking about something. Then he glanced at the Secret Service men as if noticing them for the first time. "Nothing," he said. "I just remembered something. Déjà vu, I guess."

The family, trailed by the two agents, began to jog down the path, which angled up and away from the canal toward the edge of the parkway. A few yards short of the waiting cars, Mary Catherine broke sharply to the right, thrashed through some brush, and skittered down the jumbled pile of boulders that made up the creek's bank. She was followed by her father and, somewhat uncertainly, by James.

"Sir?" one of the Secret Service men said. They had fallen well behind the Cozzanos and were watching them pick their way toward the confluence of the canal and Rock Creek.

"Just stay there," Cozzano said. "We're going to pick up some of this litter. It's a national disgrace."

The whole family disappeared beneath the parkway. The Secret Service men stood dumbfounded for a few moments, then ran down the bank, awkward in their suits and trench coats and leather shoes, trying to regain sight of the Cozzanos. But all they saw was the creek.

Three of them charged under the bridge, but ran into an obstacle: several homeless men. They had apparently been awakened by the Cozzanos. Now they were up on their feet and feeling frisky. These men occupied a bottleneck: a rocky stretch of bank between the buttress of the bridge and the bank of the creek. One of them was even standing in the water, thigh-deep.

There were harsh words and some shoving. The Secret Service men did not fare well in the shoving match, because, as they had started to notice, all of the homeless men were astoundingly large, and, considering their lifestyle, inhumanly strong. By the time the Secret Service got around to pulling guns, and the homeless men held up their hands apologetically and let them pass, they had completely lost track of the Cozzanos.

Above them, tires were squealing out on the Rock Creek Parkway. The noise was made by half a dozen large rental cars skidding sideways, across both sets of lanes, blocking all traffic.

The drivers of these vehicles, an unexceptional lot of reasonably well dressed, middle-aged men, seemed to be the least excited people in all of Washington. They ignored the honking horns and shouted obscenities from the instant traffic jam that had materialized behind their roadblock. With the calm self-possession of a combat veteran, each driver strolled around his vehicle and jabbed a knife into each of the four tires before turning his back on his crippled vehicle and sauntering into the park.

If any of the furious drivers in the traffic jam had bothered to look up at the Four Seasons, which stood at the intersection of M and Pennsylvania like the cornerstone of the whole neighborhood, they would have seen Cy Ogle looking back at them from the window of his suite.

He had just received a telephone call from the man on duty in the closest GODS truck, informing him that a sudden burst of microwave noise had broken their link with Cozzano, and that they were unable to reestablish the connection. "Argus is not receiving any inputs," the man said. "Repeat: Argus is on his own."

*The stream channel* was shallow and lined with large blocks of brown rock. As soon as they got past the "homeless" men, the Cozzanos plunged into it, picking up their knees as they ran, Walter Payton style, to keep them up out of the icy water, and forded Rock Creek. Far above their heads was another bridge, much larger and higher: Pennsylvania Avenue. As soon as they got past the buttresses of the bridge they scrambled up onto the eastern bank, which even in winter was covered with a mixture of bamboo, ivy, and reeds. This was difficult territory, but William and Mary Catherine had been training hard for this and they didn't object to getting wet. Mary Catherine had been using all the slings and arrows of sibling rivalry to get James to whip himself into shape; he couldn't really keep up with them, but he had the minor advantage of being in a state of shock.

Rock Creek now ran between them and the parkway. This side of the park was more heavily wooded and had no road or bicycle path, just a little footpath paralleling the bank. All of them were still running as hard as they could, Mary Catherine leading the way, James bringing up the rear, still trying to gasp out questions when he wasn't sucking wind. His confusion was only deepened when he noticed that his father and sister had begun to rip off their clothes as they ran, dropping a trail of sweatshirts and tank tops in his path. Mary Catherine looked over her shoulder, into his eyes, and he knew that he was supposed to do the same. The world had gone crazy anyhow, why not run around Washington, D.C., stark naked?

They paused somewhere between N and P streets. Mary Catherine and William had gotten all the way down to gym shorts and running shoes, and James was able to catch up as soon as they stopped running.

William crashed down the bank. A cube of solid masonry projected from the bank and into the stream, carrying a storm sewer outfall a couple of feet in diameter. William A. Cozzano, thigh-deep in icy water, leaned into it for a moment with his left arm and shoulder, and emerged carrying a couple of plastic garbage bags weighted with stones. He threw them up onto the bank and then climbed up after them.

Mary Catherine was stark naked by this point. She ripped open one of the bags to expose folds of dark green cloth, and a few pairs of running shoes. The shoes were labeled in magic marker: WILLY, M.C., and JAMES. She tossed the appropriate pairs to James and William, then hauled the clothing out: three identical sweatsuits.

The change of clothes ate up about thirty seconds and then they were running down the footpath again. Mary Catherine was carrying a small black plastic box in her hand; the blazing red light on one end danced up and down as she pumped her arms. She had dropped to a slower, sustainable pace. They passed under several more towering stone bridges, at one point fording the creek again in order to keep it between them and the Parkway.

The path dead-ended at the fence of Oak Hill Cemetery, which ran downhill from Georgetown and all the way to the creek's edge. They made a left and ran parallel to the fence, following a footpath in the red, rocky soil, terraced by innumerable exposed tree roots. A few stray gravestones poked askew from the carpet of ivy.

Cemetery gates loomed on their right and they had emerged into the city again. They were in Montrose Park. It was two blocks long and a couple of hundred feet wide, bordered on one side by the woods and on the other by an alley that ran behind a row of old four-story red brick apartments. This was a bad stretch of blacktop, patches on top of older patches, covered with mud, leaf litter, and parked cars with the usual odd D.C. mixture of license plates. A delivery van, painted with the logo of a ubiquitous local diaper service, was sitting there with its motor running.

Mary Catherine ran up to it, hauled open the back doors, and motioned James and William in. They climbed in the back and she followed, pulling the doors shut behind them. They all collapsed, unable to do much more than suck in oxygen. But Mary Catherine was laughing, James was sputtering and starting to ask questions, and William's mind was elsewhere.

Mary Catherine was thinking that, no matter what else happened today, they had all gone out for a vigorous run together, just like the old days, and they had gotten wet and messy and enjoyed themselves. Now she was ready for all hell to break loose. She caught her father's eye for a moment and realized he was thinking the same thing.

They drove for fifteen or twenty minutes, not really knowing where they were, and then the truck stopped, and they could hear a garage door grinding shut behind them.

They staggered upstairs and found themselves in an old town house with plywood windowpanes. Mattresses and a few pieces of junk furniture were scattered around. But it had a few touches that made them feel at home: a coffeemaker on the floor, its red light shining cheerfully, and a sack of bagels next to a stack of paper plates, and, sitting on the floor in the middle of the room, chewing on a bagel and going over some papers, one Mel Meyer.

"Willy, if you can hear me, get your left hand over here and grab this pen. You have a hell of a lot of papers to sign before we get you dressed," Mel said.

"James," Mary Catherine said, "grab some coffee. I have a few things to tell you."

## CHAPTER FIFTY-NINE

In downtown Rosslyn, Virginia, a man in a nice suit and a trench coat, wearing a neatly trimmed beard, and hair so short that his scalp almost showed through, emerged from a Metro station and walked up the street to a mailbox. He removed a standard legal-sized envelope from his breast pocket, held it between his hands, and contemplated it for a few moments. Then he dropped it into the mailbox. He continued down the street, turned a corner, and walked downhill toward Key Bridge. Ahead of him, on the far side of the Potomac, he could see Dixie Liquors, which was on M Street, which would take him through the center of Georgetown and onto Pennsylvania. You could fire a bullet straight down the centerline of

Pennsylvania and it would pass through the middle of the White House and continue down to the presidential lectern on the reviewing stand on the Capitol steps.

Unfortunately Floyd Wayne Vishniak's Fleischacker was not quite powerful or accurate enough for that. He would have to follow much the same route on foot. But that was okay. He had planned this thing pretty well, had left himself plenty of time to get there. As he walked across Key Bridge, pounded by a cold crosswind that found every leak in his trench coat, he mentally reviewed the contents of the letter, which he had written at one o'clock this morning in the front seat of his pickup truck, parked in the holler in West Virginia.

> Floyd Wayne Vishniak, esq.
> Parts Unknown
> United States of America
>
> Letters to the Editor
> *Washington Post*
> Washington, D.C.
>
> Dear Mr. (or Miss, Mrs., or Ms.) Editor:
> As of yesterday A.M. I have spent, or maybe the right word is wasted, a total of $89.50 on your worthless rag, and this is not counting money spent on the other papers and magazines I had to buy just to cross-check all of the so-called facts you printed and find out which were true and which were false.
>
> So I know full well that you will screw everything up. So here is some information. The name is spelled V-I-S-H-N-I-A-K (see top of page). I am not a psycho. Just a concerned American citizen.
>
> And please don't screw this up: I—me—Floyd—did this ALL BY MYSELF. I did not get help from anyone—no co-conspirators, foreign governments, terrorist groups, or anyone else.
>
> Yes, as hard as it might be for you smug East Coast bastards to comprehend, a hick from the sticks is actually capable of doing something ALL BY HIMSELF.

See you in Hell—where we can look forward to many interesting conversations.

You will be hearing from me again soon, I am sure.

Sincerely,
Floyd Wayne Vishniak

By the time he had made it across Key Bridge he had decided that it was a good letter. He turned right underneath the red neon sign of Dixie Liquors and headed for the center of Washington.

*On the southeastern* fringe of Capitol Hill, just beyond the boundary between the yuppified zone and the ghetto, a tour bus made a difficult turn into a narrow alley running through the center of a block. Facing on the alley was a long, low, one-story cinderblock building, a former box-printing plant. Air burst from its brakes and the bus settled to a stop in the alley. The door opened up and men began to climb off. They walked in single file around the front of the bus and entered the building through a wide steel door, which was flanked on the inside and the outside by middle-aged men with nervous eyes and guns in their armpits.

Most, but not all, of the men were enormous. They ranged in age from their early thirties to their mid-fifties. Some of them were wearing dark suits already and some were carrying them in garment bags. They filed into the building, which was a single huge room. It was mostly empty; its concrete floor was scarred where huge pieces of machinery had been uprooted and dragged away. Most of the illumination was provided by skylights. But when all of the men had come inside, the door had been closed, more lights were turned on.

Already in the room was a busload of more men matching the same general description, drinking coffee from a couple of big industrial percolaters set up on a folding table, eating vast quantities of doughnuts. A lot of these men knew each other and so in some ways the atmosphere was like that of an old class reunion. But they were generally subdued and serious. This was especially true of those men who weren't huge.

The huge ones were former professional football players. The others were Vietnam veterans. They instinctively formed up into two separate groups, on opposite ends of the room. The Vietnam veterans had served with Cozzano in the mid- to late sixties and were, for the most part, older than the football players, and from a wider economic range: this group included corporate presidents, highly paid lawyers, janitors, auto mechanics, and homeless people. But today they were all dressed more or less the same, and they greeted each other wordlessly, with hugs and long, intense, two-handed handshakes.

A few minutes after the second bus had arrived, one of the veterans, a big, round-headed, round-shouldered black man, walked to the center of the room, whistled through his fingers, and shouted, "Listen up!"

The conversation rapidly dropped to zero. All of the men moved to the edges of the room, facing inward. "My name is Rufus Bell. For today, you can call me Sarge," said the man. "I have three people to introduce. First of all, the woman who will be our new Vice President in an hour and a half: Eleanor Richmond."

She had been standing by the coffee table. Now she walked into the center of the room. Scattered applause started up and rapidly exploded into an ovation. Rufus Bell whistled again.

"Shut up!" he yelled. "We don't want to bother the neighbors."

"Thank you all," Eleanor said.

Bell continued, "I would also like to introduce Mel Meyer, who will be the acting Attorney General of the United States."

Mel acknowledged by removing the cigar from his mouth momentarily.

"Finally," Bell said, "the Chief of the District of Columbia Police, who's going to swear you all in."

The Chief was snappy in full-dress uniform. He walked to the middle of the room and got no applause at all; his appearance, and his bearing, radiated no-nonsense authority. He turned to face the men around the edges of the room and examined them closely for several moments, making individual eye contact with every man in the room.

"This is some serious shit," the Chief said, "not some kind of a fun little field trip. If you're not willing to lay down your life in the defense of the Constitution of the United States, right now, then stay in this building for the next three hours and you'll be fine."

He stopped for a while to let that sink in, and surveyed the men's faces again. They all stared back at him, like statues. A couple of them couldn't hold the eye contact, and glanced away.

"If you are willing to take that risk," the Chief said, "then repeat after me." He held up his right hand, palm facing forward.

All of the men in the room did the same. Then the Chief swore them all in as deputies of the District of Columbia Police Department.

In the meantime, Mel had taken Eleanor aside and was talking to her in a corner of the room. "You ever bought a house?" he asked.

"Once or twice," she said, surprised and mildly amused.

"Remember all those fucking documents they pulled out for you to sign?"

"I remember them well."

"That's nothing compared to what we're doing today," he said. He opened up a time-worn leather satchel that was resting on the floor. "I have two sets of documents for you," he said, "depending on what happens. I have spent the last several months holed up in the middle of nowhere with a word processor, a laser printer, and a whole lot of law books, drawing these things up. Some of them you need to sign. Some of them Willy has already signed. It's all organized."

Mel pulled a white nine-by-fifteen envelope out of the satchel. "This is in case we're lucky," he said. "In that case, there's not that much for you to do—most of your duties will pertain to your role as President of the Senate."

Mel reached back into the satchel and pulled out a black envelope. This one was the expanding type, with bellows on the sides. It was two inches thick. "And this," he said, "is in case we're not so lucky."

"I see," Eleanor said. "White is good and black is bad."

"No," Mel said. "White is Willy and black is Eleanor."

The Chief had finished deputizing the men by now, and Rufus Bell was beginning to stride up and down the room, perusing a list of names, ordering men this way and that, forming them up into several groups of various sizes.

Eleanor opened up the envelopes, took a black ball-point pen (SKILCRAFT U.S. GOVERNMENT) out of her purse, and started signing her name to documents. All of the documents in the white envelope said:

Eleanor Richmond
Vice President, United States of America

All of the documents in the black envelope said:

Eleanor Richmond
President

Rufus Bell and Mel Meyer were dragging cardboard boxes across the floor and shoving them across the concrete in the direction of the various platoons that Bell had organized. The men began to rip the boxes open and pull out T-shirts. They were all black, 100 percent cotton, extra large. On the front was a white star and the words DEPUTY—D.C. POLICE. And on the back of each shirt were the words

## DEPT. OF
# JUSTICE

CHAPTER SIXTY

Lines of authority were never especially clear in Washington, D.C., where the jurisdictions of a dozen different law-enforcement agencies all overlapped. The presence of so many people with guns and badges made it impossible to figure out who was in charge of what. So when men with guns and badges had gone to several locations in the District of Columbia during the last few days and laid claim to numerous parking spaces—some on the street, some in parking lots of federal buildings—there had been disputes, arguments, even threats. But the issues raised could not have been untangled short of calling a convention of Constitutional scholars and locking them all in a room until they made up their minds. The people who had the parking spaces won the argument. The decision was sealed when those parking spaces were occupied by flatbed semitrailer rigs with big GODS shipping containers on their backs.

One of them took up a position in front of the headquarters of the Teamsters Union on Louisiana Avenue, only a block north of the Capitol Building. From there, it had a direct line of sight across Taft Park and Constitution Avenue onto the Capitol grounds; a person could climb onto the roof of the truck and get a clear, side-on view of President Cozzano delivering his inaugural address, not much more than a thousand feet away.

Another GODS truck seized a position along Lafayette Park, across the street from the White House. Others parked on Fourteenth Street, in the shadow of the Commerce Department; on C Street, in front of the State Department; in front of the Treasury Department on Fifteenth Street; and in the parking lot of the Pentagon.

Once the trucks were in place, they weren't likely to move. The owners—and the mysterious people who went in and out of the containers on their backs—seemed to have an infinite fund of bewildering paperwork, from various D.C. and federal agencies, justifying their presence. Any authority figure, at any level, who tried to move those GODS trucks, would soon find that each one had a lawyer living in the back, on call twenty-four hours a day, complete with cellular phone and portable fax machine. These were not just plain old lawyers either; they were asshole lawyers, ready and willing to issue threats and talk about their friends in high places at the slightest provocation.

And if things escalated beyond that level, each truck also had a couple of imposing plainclothes security guards who would emerge, crack their knuckles, flex their muscles, and glare threateningly when anyone tried to get them to move. The only people in the world who had the guts to confront these people were D.C. meter maids, and so the GODS trucks stayed where they were, accumulating stacks of D.C. parking tickets under their windshield wipers but incurring no further retribution.

At eleven o'clock on the morning of Inauguration Day, Cyrus Rutherford Ogle could be found in the truck that was parked in front of the Teamsters Building, a thousand feet from the inaugural podium. He was seated in the Eye of Cy, keeping tabs on the PIPER 100, and trying to reestablish radio contact with the chips in Governor Cozzano's head.

The radio transmissions were short-range, line-of-sight affairs and so they were used to breaking contact whenever Cozzano strayed more than a couple of thousand feet from the truck. But Cozzano had gone out of his way to be elusive this morning. The listening devices secreted in his clothing and in that of his children were not transmitting any sounds other than the soothing burble of running water. The Secret Service had converged on Rock Creek Park, hindered by a nightmare traffic jam, and found no sign of the Cozzanos other than the abandoned clothes.

It looked a hell of a lot like a kidnapping. But the outgoing President, and several news outlets, had received brief, untraceable telephone calls from Mary Catherine Cozzano, assuring them that everything was okay. She promised that her father would show up for the inauguration.

Ogle had been planning to reinstate contact with Cozzano's biochip from the truck in Lafayette Square when he paid a call at the White House, which was traditionally what an incoming president did on inauguration morning. Then, as the outgoing and incoming presidents made their way down Pennsylvania for the inaugural parade, control would be relayed to the truck at Treasury and then at Commerce. Then there would be a blackout of several minutes as the motorcade proceeded down Pennsylvania.

But those moments of freedom were useless to Cozzano. He would have to come to the Capitol eventually. As the motorcade emerged from the shadow of the U.S. Courthouse, the truck at Teamsters—Cy Ogle's truck—would be able to establish contact with the biochip. From that point onward, Cy Ogle would have full control through the inauguration.

William A., James, and Mary Catherine Cozzano emerged from the Farragut West Metro station at eleven o'clock. They had reached Pennsylvania Avenue before anyone recognized them.

The person who did was a well-dressed man in a trench coat, with a neatly trimmed beard and very short hair, proceeding west on Pennsylvania. He was standing at a streetcorner waiting for the light to change when he saw the Cozzanos coming toward him. "Good morning, President-elect Cozzano," he said.

The light changed and all of them crossed Seventeenth Street together. The Old Executive Office Building was on their right, the White House a stone's throw away.

"Good morning. How are you today?" Cozzano said.

"Just fine, sir, and you?"

"I'm great, thank you," Cozzano said.

"How's your head?" the man asked, as they reached the east side of Seventeenth Street. They stopped at the corner and waited for the light to change. Across Pennsylvania, in front of the White House gates, was a mob of cops and Secret Service. One of them noticed the Cozzanos. Binoculars swiveled in their direction. A Secret Service detail broke from the gates and ran toward them, plunging directly into traffic.

Cozzano looked at the man quizzically. "My head's fine," he said, "why do you ask?"

"I need to know if they're controlling your brain with radio waves," the man said, as the WALK light came on. "It's very important for me to know this."

Mary Catherine's and James's faces fell into expressionless masks. Crossing the street, they got between Cozzano and the man in the trench coat, and stared at the man coldly. But Cozzano laughed indulgently. "You know, there was a movie that I saw, at the Tuscola Main Street Theater, when I was a kid, about mind control. Some mad scientist had taken over people's brains and turned them into zombies . . ."

"Don't tell me another anecdote!" the man said. "I don't want to hear any of your stupid anecdotes!"

"I'm just trying to answer your question," Cozzano said cheerfully.

"Ever since they started controlling your brain, you can't think any more—all you do is tell those heart-warming stories!" the man in the trench coat said.

They were approaching the south side of Pennsylvania. James pulled up close to the man and stared at him coldly. "You're out of line," he said.

The man in the trench coat stared back at James, not intimidated in the slightest. "I'm out of line, huh?" he said. His total lack of fear unnerved James a little bit. James almost tripped over the curb.

Suddenly, the Cozzanos were surrounded by men in suits and trench coats. Mary Catherine was startled for a moment before she realized that they were Secret Service men.

Then she looked back at the strange man. But he was gone. "That was really weird," she said. "That man didn't show any of the external symptoms of an active psychotic. But he sure talked like one."

*The presidential motorcade* pulled out of the White House gates onto Pennsylvania Avenue at 11:30 A.M., hung a right, and headed for the Capitol. Inside, distributed among several cars, were the outgoing President, his wife, the outgoing Vice President and his wife, Cozzano, Mary Catherine, James, Eleanor Richmond, and her two children Clarice and Harmon, Jr. Eleanor's mother was already in her place at the Capitol, attended by a couple of nurses.

The outgoing and incoming presidents sat across from each other in the back of the presidential limousine and made small talk. The motorcade wound around a couple of corners, getting past the Treasury and Western Plaza, and finally pulled onto the long uninterrupted stretch of Pennsylvania Avenue that ran straight to the Capitol. William A. Cozzano bent down and peered through the window, across the front seat, through the windshield, and down to the Capitol, where the temporary podium was clearly visible. Federal Triangle was on the right; half a block ahead rose the towering spire of the Old Post Office.

Cozzano reached across his body with his left hand, grabbed the limousine's door handle and popped the door open.

"What are you doing?" the outgoing President said.

"Quite frankly, I have no idea," Cozzano said. He jumped out of the limousine, which was traveling at a slow jogger's pace. The driver, seeing what was happening, braked the limousine to a stop.

"But—"

Cozzano leaned into the open door. "Don't worry," he said, "I think everything's going to be okay." Then he slammed the door and strode southward across the intersection.

By now the entire motorcade had come to a halt. Mary Catherine and James had jumped out of their limousine and run forward to join Cozzano, who plunged directly into the crowd lining the parade route. He was followed by a number of Secret Service agents; but although the crowd opened wide to accept the Cozzanos, it closed ranks behind them, forming a dense wall of bodies.

Large bodies. It seemed that this entire section of the parade route was lined with men no shorter than six foot six, and no lighter than two hundred and seventy-five pounds. The Secret Service men tried to elbow their way through, but elbows had no effect on these guys.

Eventually they got through by drawing guns. By that time, the Cozzanos had disappeared. Again.

The Federal Triangle Metro station was half a block away on Twelfth Street. Like all of the stations in the D.C. Metro system, it included an elevator for wheelchair users. Rufus Bell was standing in that elevator, leaning against the door to keep it from closing, and he had an empty wheelchair with him.

The Cozzanos arrived at a dead sprint, pursued only by a few autograph seekers. James and Mary Catherine got on first, then Cozzano followed, spinning around as he came through the door and slamming down ass-first into the wheelchair. Bell let the door slide closed and then the elevator began to drop.

Mary Catherine was standing to the left of the wheelchair, a heavy purse slung over her shoulder. She unclasped it and opened it up.

"Here goes nothing," Cozzano said.

His left hand reached into Mary Catherine's purse, rummaged around, and pulled out a black box with four metal prongs on the end. He squeezed the trigger once, testing it, and a purple lightning bolt snapped between the prongs.

"I already tested it, Dad," Mary Catherine said affectionately, her voice already getting thick with emotion.

"I know you did, peanut," Cozzano said.

Then he shoved the prongs into the side of his head and pulled the trigger.

His body convulsed so violently that it threw him half out of the wheelchair. James and Mary Catherine stood well away until the high-voltage current had stopped blasting through Cozzano's body. His arm snapped out into a stiff-arm position, as though fending off a linebacker from Arcola or Rantoul, and the stun gun flew across the elevator car, bounced off the wall, and clattered to the floor. Rufus Bell picked it up and shoved it back into Mary Catherine's purse.

Mary Catherine had gone into an unemotional, doctorly mode. She grabbed one of her father's arms and got James to take the other one, and they righted his limp body in the wheelchair, then buckled the lap belt.

The elevator doors opened; they were on the platform of the Metro station. A Blue Line train bound for Addison Road was sitting on the tracks, waiting for them; the doors had been physically blocked open by more members of the Cozzano crew, and the D.C. Chief of Police himself, still resplendent in his full dress uniform, was standing at the head of the train, talking to the conductor.

Bell wheeled Cozzano out of the elevator, across the platform, and onto the train. The doors closed behind them and the train began to move. They had a whole car to themselves; sheets of newsprint had already been taped up along the insides of the windows so that none of the shocked tourists on the platform could capture an image of the unconscious President-elect on film or video.

Mary Catherine pulled a stethoscope out of her purse, stuck it in her ears, and held it up to her father's chest. "He's got a normal rhythm," she said. "It sounds good."

Cozzano was not unconscious, just dazed. Mary Catherine pulled a small white tube out of her pocket, snapped it in half, and held it up under Cozzano's nose. Cozzano's brow furrowed, his eyes rolled around in their sockets, and he snapped his head away from the smell.

Lights flashed by, illuminating the papered-over windows. They had rolled through the Smithsonian station without stopping and were now swinging through the broad curve that would take them eastward into L'Enfant Plaza.

Two Yellow Line trains, pointed in opposite directions, were being held for them at L'Enfant Plaza. One of them was a northbound train that could take them straight back up to the Archives station, right along the parade route. They could reemerge at that point and continue on to the Capitol as if nothing had happened.

The other train was southbound. It could take them to National Airport, where a private jet was waiting for them. It would take them far, far away, if that was necessary. Hopefully, it would take them somewhere with good hospitals.

The train doors opened to reveal L'Enfant Plaza. Their way out onto the platform was lined with large and serious-looking men. Standing right in the middle was Mel Meyer.

Bell wheeled Cozzano out onto the platform and right up to Mel, who kneeled down and looked Cozzano in the face. He grabbed one of Cozzano's limp hands and squeezed it, then reached up and patted his friend gently on the cheek. His face was tight, a study in controlled intensity. "Willy," he said, "Willy, do you feel like being President today? Or do you feel like going to a nice rehab center in Switzerland? You have to give me some indication either way."

Cozzano's head had been rolling around loosely. Finally, with some effort, he raised it up and looked Mel in the eye.

"Let's take this thing downtown," he said.

Mel stood up. His eyes were glistening. He turned toward one of the crew. "You heard the President," he said, "tell the guys at the airport we won't be needing them."

The escalator at Archives brought the Cozzanos up into the sunlight only a few minutes after the presidential motorcade had gone by. A phalanx of some thirty-six ex-NFL players, hand-picked by Rufus Bell for their height and bulk, materialized around them. Cozzano was on his feet now, still a little unsteady, supported on either side by ex-Bears. The phalanx got itself organized and then accelerated to a slow jog, moving en masse into the middle of Pennsylvania Avenue and heading straight for the Capitol, two-thirds of a mile away. The crowd along Pennsylvania had begun to disperse, believing that all of the important people had already gone past them, and none of them knew what to make of the solid bloc of beefy men—some of them quite famous in their own right—who ran down the center of the avenue in tight formation, headed straight for the Inauguration, surrounded by M-16–toting outriders on foot, car, and motorcycles.

But it was a strange enough sight that it was picked up by the television cameras. The media were on their toes. They were aware that Cozzano had done something highly unusual during his morning jog, that he had arrived at the White House on foot—contrary to the planned itinerary—and that he had abandoned the motorcade at Twelfth Street. When their cameras on the parade route picked up the phalanx, it went out over the networks. Nothing interesting was going on anyway; the outgoing President had already reached the Capitol, and was now in the Rotunda, awaiting the change of power.

*Cy Ogle, seated* in his truck in front of the Teamsters Building, saw Cozzano's Praetorian Guard jogging down Pennsylvania and had a pretty good idea of what it meant. He had watched on television as the motorcade had passed in front of the U.S. Courthouse—the point at which radio signals from his truck should have been able to reach Cozzano's biochip. It hadn't worked. Nothing was there. He'd known then that Cozzano wasn't in the motorcade.

He was still telling himself that it didn't matter. By one route or another, Cozzano had to show up at the Capitol. Sooner or later they would reacquire the chip. The only question was when.

The appearance of the phalanx moving down Pennsylvania answered that question. The cameras were kind enough to track it all the way through its slow, thundering, five-minute march on the Capitol. When it passed in front of the U.S. Courthouse, Ogle tried once more to reestablish the radio link.

Nothing. Cozzano wasn't in the phalanx; it was just a diversion. Either that, or the biochip wasn't responding anymore. Which was impossible. Cozzano had only been missing for about ten minutes, from his disappearance at the Old Post Office to the reemergence of the phalanx at Seventh Street. You couldn't do major brain surgery in ten minutes.

Ogle kept watching the TV. There was nothing else to do. Eventually the phalanx reached the Capitol and converged on a small entrance on the northern end. No one had been expecting this particular entrance to be used; no camera crew was anywhere near it. But one intrepid minicam operator from CNN managed to get close enough to zoom in on the doorway, just as William A. Cozzano himself entered the building. There was no mistaking him.

Ogle tried the radio link again. Nothing.

The phones in the truck were ringing like mad. He had turned off the ringers a long time ago, but he could tell they were ringing by all the flashing lights. The people at the Network were paranoid: they were into micromanagement, they wanted Cozzano monitored twenty-four hours a day. Which was totally unnecessary. Cozzano was a good politician. He knew how to handle this.

There was nothing more Ogle could do today. In the breast pocket of his suit was a personal invitation, and a pass that would get him a seat on the inaugural platform—the hottest ticket in town. He had been dreading the idea of spending all day sitting in the Eye of Cy. Now he had an excuse to go out there and sit a few chairs away from the Cozzanos and bask in their glory. He grabbed his coat, said goodbye to the guards and to the twenty-four-hour on-site lawyer, and headed into Taft Park, aimed at the West Front of the White House.

*It did not* take a genius to figure out that the entire Inauguration had been set up for the benefit of a tiny minority of rich people. Floyd Wayne Vishniak had arrived well ahead of time and made one complete circuit of the Capitol grounds, strolling down the west bank of the Capitol Reflecting Pool, east on Independence, north on First Street between the Capitol and the Library of Congress, and now westward again on Constitution.

Up to a certain point, an ordinary citizen could walk anywhere he felt like walking, especially if he got all gussied up in nice fancy-looking clothes as Vishniak had. If you wanted to watch the Inauguration from two miles away at the far end of the Mall, that was no problem at all. But if you wanted to actually stand close enough to make out the figure of the new President with the naked eye, you had to enter special zones that were cordoned off and patrolled by cops.

Vishniak had traveled to many parts of the United States, seen many different types of police officers, and even been arrested by a few of them. But he had never seen anything like the variety of cops that were running around this place. It was like a cop zoo or something. Some of the cops had uniforms and some didn't. Some of them looked like souped-up Park Rangers. Some of them looked like glorified mall cops. They had all staked out different parts of different border zones whose sole function was to separate the common people from the rich and powerful scum.

It did not look like there was any way to get within a quarter mile of the inaugural platform without shooting a whole lot of those different cops. This was bound to attract attention, bring in even more cops, and scare away his intended victims. So Vishniak had himself something of a conundrum here. The closest he could get to the platform was on the north side, in a little park north of Constitution. He spent a while reconnoitering this area, looking for gaps in the security, and found none.

Instead he found something even better: a GODS truck. Just like the one he'd glimpsed under the stage at McCormick Place—except this one was practically right across the street from the Capitol. Vishniak began to walk across the park, and even as he did, the door in the back opened and a man climbed out of it.

*Something about the* man with the close-cropped hair and the neatly trimmed beard seemed vaguely familiar to Cy Ogle. He fit the profile for a Secret Service agent. But this man did not behave like Secret Service. He was not scanning the crowd. He was looking straight at Cy Ogle.

Ogle had already reached into his breast pocket and pulled out his engraved invitation. The man in the trench coat was reaching into his breast pocket too. But he hadn't pulled anything out yet.

"Hey," the man said.

"Morning," Ogle said, "excuse me, but I got a party to attend."

"Hold on a sec," the man said, "I recognize you from that article they did about you in *The New York Times Magazine* in 1991. And also from the little article in *Time* magazine last year. They both ran photos of you."

"That's nice," Ogle said. By now he had realized that the man could not possibly be Secret Service.

"Don't you recognize me?" the man asked. "You should. I'm a very important person in your life."

Ogle took a good look at the man's face.

At the face of Floyd Wayne Vishniak.

His lips parted and he felt stunned and weak in the legs, as if he had been struck on the head.

Vishniak grinned and turned sideways to Ogle. He moved his hand inside his trench coat and Ogle could see the barrel of the gun pressing on the fabric from the inside. "I'm covering you with the same gun I used before," he said, "and if you say anything, I'll pull the trigger."

"What do you want?" Ogle said.

"I want to see your truck," Vishniak said, nodding across the park. "You know us farmboys. We're just crazy about big ol' trucks."

Ogle turned his back on the Capitol and started walking back across Taft Park. Every few paces he would look back behind himself hoping that Vishniak would have disappeared. But he was always right there. Almost as bad, he never shut up. "I figured you had to have some kind of secret transmitter to control Cozzano's brain. Because when I busted up your control room at the shopping mall over there, it didn't make any difference at all. Let's go on over there and take a look around."

Ogle crossed Louisiana, climbed up the temporary steps behind the truck, and opened the door to the Eye of Cy. He was thinking of trying to slam it in Vishniak's face, but Vishniak shoved him through and closed the door behind him.

The security men and the lawyer were climbing to their feet.

Ogle saw a white light flashing in the corner of his eye and felt, did not hear, a quick series of explosions pounding him on the side of his head. The three men in front of him jerked, crumpled, cowered, and collapsed to the floor; behind them, blood was showering all over the equipment.

Ogle couldn't hear anything except a pure tone in his ear. He sagged against a wall and closed his eyes, feeling faint.

Vishniak cuffed Ogle's hands behind his back, stepped over the corpses, and proceeded to the Eye of Cy. Ogle could see his lips moving as he commented upon it, but couldn't hear what he was saying.

Vishniak looked around the trailer. His eyes landed on a fire extinguisher mounted to a wall. Vishniak holstered his gun, picked up the fire extinguisher, and then used it as a blunt object to smash all of the screens in the Eye of Cy. At first he worked slowly and methodically, but after a few minutes he really got into it and began to pound away at them in a frenzy. Finally he threw the extinguisher on the floor, battered and scraped.

He turned to Ogle with a triumphant look on his face and said something else. Then he approached. He reached into Ogle's pocket and pulled out the personal invitation. He shoved it into his own pocket. Then Floyd Wayne Vishniak walked out of Cy Ogle's life.

### CHAPTER SIXTY-ONE

William A. Cozzano took the oath of office at twelve noon. Holding the Bible was Mary Catherine. Administering the oath was the Chief Justice of the Supreme Court. After a very intense quarter of an hour running and subwaying across D.C., the Cozzanos had reached the Rotunda in plenty of time and been able to hit the bathrooms and freshen up a little. They looked great and showed little trace of the earlier excitement; television viewers who had heard rumors of wild goings-on up and down the length of Pennsylvania Avenue were comforted to see the Cozzanos looking calm, relaxed, and happy.

Only one detail seemed out of place: as Cozzano had emerged

from the West Front of the Capitol and walked through the passage-way in the center of the stands, he had moved slowly and with a limp. He moved like an old man, not the spry athlete who had become so famous during the campaign. And when he raised his hand and recited the oath of office, his voice sounded different: deeper, slower, not as distinct. He tripped over a few words, something he had never done during the campaign.

But it didn't matter. He looked great. He smiled confidently through the oath, presenting a strong profile for the cameras, towering over the Chief Justice. His daughter was facing directly into the cameras and her face was suffused with joy and pride. She wasn't bothered by her father's gait, or his voice; why should America be?

It was over. President Cozzano shook hands with the Chief Justice and bent down to kiss Mary Catherine on the cheek.

Then he stepped up to the Presidential lectern, still moving slowly and carefully. Before him, the Mall was covered with people, all the way to the Lincoln Memorial, and all of them were applauding. The applause from the invited guests on the platform, and from the lucky few just below, around the Capitol Reflecting Pool, was distinct. Beyond that it merged into a generalized hissing roar, coming from the horizon.

President Cozzano reached into his breast pocket, pulled out a few typewritten sheets folded in half down the middle, and flattened them out on the lectern. He waited for a few moments, smiling to the crowd, as the applause died down.

"Thank you," he said, "thank you." That brought the applause to a close. Then he began to read from the notes on the lectern, calmly, pronouncing the words with conspicuous precision, like a drunken man who is trying not to sound drunk.

"My first act as President is to declare martial law in the District of Columbia and to suspend the following constituted bodies: the Secret Service, the Drug Enforcement Administration, the Bureau of Alcohol, Tobacco, and Firearms, the U.S. Marshals Service, the Park Police, and the Capitol Police. The CIA is reminded that their activities begin at the water's edge. Any violation of martial law may be penalized by summary execution. In their place, to maintain order among executive branch and the government, I federalize the police force of the District of Columbia for a period of one week and place it at the disposal of the Department of Justice."

At this moment, half of the men on and around the platform stood up and stripped off their jackets and dress shirts to reveal black T-shirts emblazoned with white stars on the front and "Dept. of JUSTICE" across the back. As Cozzano continued his address, these men converged on all of the uniformed Capitol police officers in the area, and on anyone who looked like a Secret Service agent.

The men in the black T-shirts—the Justice Posse—looked as though they were ready for a fight, and they were. Some of them actually got into fights. But most of them didn't. The President's words could not have been any clearer.

The Posse men were not very discriminating. They went after anyone in a uniform and anyone who looked like Secret Service: that is, men with earplugs. Unfortunately that included one or two journalists. The journalists put up a scuffle. The scuffles ended pretty quickly.

All of these movements took place against a backdrop of dead silence. Everyone else, within a quarter-mile radius of President Cozzano, was utterly motionless and perfectly silent. Everyone was in shock. Beyond that, out on the Mall, it was possible to hear murmuring from the crowd, and even a few screams. But most of the people in the vicinity of the President were directly, personally, massively affected by the words coming out of his mouth. They didn't want to miss anything. Especially since a misinterpretation could lead to summary execution.

Cozzano continued without pause. "The FBI, one of the few federal agencies to live up to its oath to protect, defend, and uphold the Constitution and laws of the United States, will coordinate all security arrangements at all levels during the period of martial law. I hereby designate Melvin Israel Meyer the acting Attorney General and place the FBI and the D.C. Police under his direct authority. In my capacity as Commander in Chief of the Armed Forces, I hereby suspend the authority of the Joint Chiefs of Staff for a period of one week and place all military forces under my direct command. I order the Air Force and all other military aircraft in the continental U.S. grounded immediately and until further notice. I order the Federal

Aviation Administration to ban all air traffic over the District of Columbia, effective immediately, and to close National Airport until further notice. This air traffic moratorium is to be enforced by the new Attorney General."

Men had already begun to appear on the roof of the Capitol and atop other buildings around the Mall, carrying long, bulky equipment cases. They flipped the cases open and pulled out four-foot-long, tubular objects with flat, slotted antennas that unfolded on their tops: Stinger missile launchers.

"I assure our allies and promise our adversaries around the world that this is a purely domestic affair and that the global balance of military power will not be affected.

"I declare a one-week holiday on all banks and stock exchanges. I call upon our financial leaders to cooperate with me so that calm can be restored to the markets as soon as possible.

"Finally, I ask the indulgence of the American people in this time of crisis. While the steps I have just taken are unprecedented and severe, I can assure you all that the peak of the crisis has passed, and that within hours, or at the most days, the government will be returned to an even keel.

"A complete explanation of what has happened to me, my family, and the electoral process of this country would fill a lengthy book. I cannot give you a full account here. But the people deserve an explanation, and so, at this moment, a summary of these events is being transmitted over all wire services worldwide. The same information is being provided to all governmental offices and major military bases. Videotape cassettes are arriving at all major networks and television stations."

Cozzano finally paused for a moment, to draw a breath and to shuffle his notes around. Finally, the silence broke, and a murmur began to sweep through the crowd.

People began to move. The in-crowd on the inaugural platform included a number of high-ranking military officers; several of them got to their feet and strode to the passageway leading back into the Capitol. As soon as they thought they were out of sight of the TV cameras, they broke into a run. A number of nonuniformed officials did the same thing.

Members of the Justice Posse now entered the front row of chairs and converged on four men: the secretaries-designate of Defense, State, Commerce, and Treasury. Each of the four men was strongly encouraged to rise to his feet and then hustled out. Their family members were not allowed to come along; some of them were too stunned to move, some burst into tears, and some tried to get physical. An initial tremor of panic propagated down the Mall.

*Floyd Wayne Vishniak* was watching Cozzano from the crowd below. Ogle's special invitation had gotten him through several layers of security. But he had not actually climbed up onto the inaugural platform itself. His invite supposedly would have gotten him through the final cordon. But he had watched a few of the bigwigs and seen that the final layer of security was especially stringent. He didn't want to take a chance on that, and it wasn't even necessary. From down below, he had a clear view of the entire platform.

He could have picked off any of the bigwigs sitting up there. Any of the people who were controlling Cozzano's mind. It would have been easy. But it would have been pointless. Vishniak had come to an astonishing realization as he had listened to Cozzano's speech: he was too late. Cozzano was lost.

Vishniak had personally demolished the computer control room where Ogle and the other media manipulators were controlling Cozzano's mind. He had set Cozzano free. But Cozzano had started his term as President by declaring martial law and threatening to execute people in the streets. Cozzano was staging a coup d'état. He was turning America's great democratic system into a dictatorship. Right before Vishniak's eyes.

"My fellow Americans, I come to you at a moment of great peril," Cozzano said, trying to use the authority of his voice to quiet the rising anxiety—the ugly fights going on behind him, the murmuring that had grown into a low roar. "We have narrowly averted a disaster. I am speaking to you, now, as a free man, for the first time in a year. Exactly one year ago, as you may know, I was struck down by a stroke. I have been away for a while. Today, I am here to tell you that I am back!"

It was the first thing Cozzano had said, all day long, that

sounded like what a triumphant new president should say. The crowd was enormously relieved. The shrill chattering and nervous buzzing was overwhelmed by a cheer that started in the throats of the Justice Posse and grew explosively until it rang up and down the length of the Mall.

And it did not die down; it grew into an ovation. Those listening to Cozzano had experienced more anxiety during the last couple of minutes than they had since the Cuban Missile Crisis or the Kennedy assassination. Now, Cozzano was telling them that everything was going to be fine. He told them this, not just with his words, but with the deep resonant tone of his voice and with his posture, his facial expression.

No one really knew what was going on. But hearing his words and watching his face, they came to know one thing beyond question: President Cozzano was doing what he had been elected to do. Finally, a leader was in the White House, and he was leading.

The people on the inaugural platform were the last ones to rise to their feet and join in the ovation.

Cozzano was about to resume his speech, but he realized that there was no way to talk over the voices of half a million people. He paused, smiled at the crowd, waited for a couple of moments. The cheering continued. He stepped back away from the lectern, now just a couple of paces in front of his daughter and Eleanor Richmond and her family, and raised both of his arms in the air as if he had just scored a touchdown.

The first bullet did just what it was supposed to. Its teflon coating took it smoothly through the seven layers of bulletproof fabric making up President Cozzano's bulletproof vest. After that, momentum and plain old-fashioned lead did the rest. It passed into his thorax a couple of inches below the right nipple and exploded against a rib, spraying fragments of lead, bone, and teflon through Cozzano's chest cavity. Most of his right lung was turned into hash. Numerous holes were blown through the heart and a major vessel pierced in his left lung. Nothing emerged from the other side of Cozzano's body; the bullet, which was specifically designed to kill human beings wearing bulletproof vests, had been totally efficient in transferring all of its energy into Cozzano's flesh.

Vishniak saw a jet of steam and blood spurt from the entrance wound and knew that Cozzano was dead. He angled the weapon a couple of degrees to the right and took aim at Eleanor Richmond. But just as he was pulling the trigger, a bulky man in a black T-shirt jumped in front of her.

Darryl Garfield, an offensive lineman for the Skins, took the second bullet in his massive upper arm, which was nearly as big as Eleanor's waist. The bullet ricocheted off his humerus and ended up shattering a window in the Rayburn Building, a thousand feet due south, whence it was later recovered. As the bullet exited Garfield's arm it drove before it a shock wave of blood and pulverized muscle tissue that burst out of his body in a crudely hemispherical pattern, spraying Eleanor Richmond with blood.

Vishniak lowered his weapon a bit, surprised by Garfield's sudden intervention, and did not see the precipitous approach of Rufus Bell. Bell threw all of his momentum behind the heel of his right hand, which impacted on the bridge of Vishniak's nose and collapsed the bone structure of his entire face, driving a number of small bone fragments all the way into Vishniak's brain. Vishniak was a vegetable before he hit the ground. Ten minutes later he was dead.

Most of the people on the platform knew only that Darryl Garfield had been shot, because his wound had been so spectacular. In the ensuing confusion, Mary Catherine was the first person to notice that President Cozzano was sitting down behind the lectern, looking stunned and pale.

At first they thought he was just stunned by the near miss. But a look at his face proved otherwise. Pink foam had collected at the corners of his mouth. Mary Catherine, James Cozzano, and Mel all converged on Cozzano at the same moment and helped him to lie on his back. Within a few moments they were surrounded by the Posse.

A few moments after the shooting, Eleanor Richmond had vanished, completely surrounded by huge Posse members who practically encased her in bulletproof vests. The guests on the inaugural platform drained back into the Capitol as though a plug had been pulled and they were being sucked back into the building. Eleanor and her escort were swept along.

Mary Catherine ripped Cozzano's shirt open down the middle and discovered the entrance wound on his thorax. Her eyes met his.

"I'll be okay," Cozzano said.

"One of the guys has called for a chopper," Mel said. "Hang in there, buddy."

Cozzano didn't pay any attention to Mel. He was looking at James and Mary Catherine, kneeling next to him side by side.

"Listen, peanut," the President said. "James will stay with me. You stay with Eleanor."

"No!" Mary Catherine said.

"They have no choice but to kill Eleanor," Cozzano said. "They'll try to do it now. Natural causes. Go! By order of the President."

Tears burst over the rims of Mary Catherine's eyes and cascaded down her face. "I love you more than anything, peanut," Cozzano said.

"I love you too, Dad," Mary Catherine said.

"Now go and do your job," Cozzano said.

Mary Catherine bent down and kissed her father's cheek. Then she stood up, turned, and ran into the Capitol.

*The Rotunda had* gone nuts. Several dozen Capitol Police had been herded into one corner and were being guarded by a couple of Posse members carrying M-16s with fixed bayonets. More Justice men, and several men wearing FBI windbreakers, were stationing themselves around the entrances, trying to establish some control over who came in and who left. A couple of media crews were here, unable to make up their minds what they should be pointing their cameras at; several radio and television reporters were running around seemingly at random, shouting a stream-of-consciousness narration into their microphones. It didn't matter what they said as long as they said it with authority.

But most of the people in the Rotunda were invited guests who had been seated in the rows of chairs on the inaugural platform. It was easy to tell them apart. The men were all wearing intensely formal garb, and the women were dressed, coiffed, and bejeweled to the nines. These people had gathered into knots scattered around the floor of the Rotunda. Each knot consisted of a few people turned inward, slack-faced with shock, jabbering at one another, and a few people, mostly men, constantly craning their necks in all directions, eyes wide and staring, trying to get some sense of what was going on. One or two men were jabbing at cellular phones with stiff index fingers, screaming into them, getting nothing but static. A man in black tie and morning coat slammed his cellular phone onto the floor in frustration and it slid across the polished stone like a hockey puck.

Mary Catherine couldn't see Eleanor anywhere. A Posse member walked in front of her in his black Justice shirt. Mary Catherine jumped forward and put her hand on his shoulder. "Where's Eleanor?" she said.

As soon as he recognized her, he told her: "She went to the ladies' room to clean up. She's got blood on her."

"Who's with her?"

"I dunno," the man said, "we don't have any female deputies in this outfit."

"Where's that bathroom?" Mary Catherine said, kicking off her shoes.

The man pointed. Mary Catherine headed across the floor of the Rotunda, building up to a full sprint.

It wasn't hard to find the bathroom where Eleanor was holed up: the entrance was almost obscured by a knot of black-shirted Posse members. Mary Catherine just aimed at the door and relied on them to recognize her, and to get out of the way.

They did, but she had to slow down to a brisk walk. She entered the women's lounge. The first thing she saw was Eleanor's dress spread out across a couch near the entrance, spattered with blood.

She rounded a corner and saw a row of sinks. Eleanor was bent over one of the sinks, hot water blasting. She had stripped down to a camisole and panties. Her arms were wet up to the shoulder and she was bent over the sink splashing water on her face; flecks of blood were still visible in her hair.

One other woman was in the bathroom: from her appearance, obviously one of the invited guests. Mary Catherine had spent enough time with people of the advanced upper crust to know one when she saw one.

She even recognized this woman. It was Althea Coover. DeWayne Coover's granddaughter. She and Mary Catherine had gone to Stanford together and attended a lot of the same parties. Because of Coover's support of the Radhakrishnan Institute, his family had gotten several invitations to the Inauguration.

Althea Coover was standing at the sink next to Eleanor's. She had put a few small cosmetics containers out on the shelf beneath the mirror, as though she were here to fix her face. But just as Mary Catherine was rounding the corner, Althea was pulling something else out of her bag: a capped hypodermic needle.

Mary Catherine headed straight for her.

Althea saw Mary Catherine and startled. Her eyes jumped to the hypodermic needle, then Eleanor, then up to Mary Catherine's face. She pulled the cap off, exposing the hair-thin needle, and raised it like a dart, aiming it at Eleanor's exposed shoulder.

Then Mary Catherine shoved her stun gun into the side of Althea Coover's neck and pulled the trigger.

Althea dropped the needle, collapsed, and smacked her head into the marble floor with a shocking thud. Eleanor straightened up, blinked water out of her eyes, and jumped to see Mary Catherine suddenly standing there with lightning in her hand, and Althea Coover gone.

*When Mary Catherine* and Eleanor returned to the Rotunda, now surrounded by very nervous and trigger-happy men in black T-shirts, they discovered that the Chief Justice of the Supreme Court had not been as lucky. He was collapsed on the marble floor, unconscious and unresponsive. Immediately before his collapse he had been seen talking to another invited guest who had made a hasty exit; later, an empty hypodermic syringe was found in an ashtray by the door. The Chief Justice was being attended to by a couple of old and distinguished doctors who had made it onto the guest list. A few Posse members picked him up and carried him into the Capitol infirmary.

Anyone wearing white tie or a formal gown was now being viewed with intense suspicion by the Posse. Mary Catherine and Eleanor found themselves dead center in the Rotunda, surrounded by Posse members facing outward, as the remaining guests were herded toward the outside of the room.

Between the knot in the center and the people crowded to the edges, there was a broad, doughnut-shaped, empty space, now occupied by a grand total of three people: a minicam operator from CNN, his sound man, and a bald, middle-aged man in a long black robe. The robe was a flimsy thing made of synthetic fibers and looked as though it had been wadded up into a ball and then sat on for a few days. It was unzipped to reveal a bulletproof vest underneath; beneath the vest, a black T-shirt could be seen. This guy was a member of the Posse.

In his right hand he was carrying a thick black book with the words HOLY BIBLE printed on the cover in gold letters. A single sheet of typing paper was clasped in the front cover.

"Excuse me," said the man in the black robe, standing up on tiptoes trying to see over the shoulders of the bodyguards, "but I could not help but notice that the Chief Justice has been incapacitated. Can I be of some assistance here?"

"Who are you?" Mary Catherine said, peering at him between a couple of Posse members.

"Stanley Kotlarski, Fifth Circuit Court Judge, Cook County, Illinois," the man said. "Mel asked me to hang around in case something happened to the Chief Justice. Are you ready to do the honors, or are we going to stand around here all day?"

The circle of bodyguards opened up to admit Judge Kotlarski and the camera crew. Judge Kotlarski pulled the sheet of paper out of the Bible and then handed the Bible to Mary Catherine. "You know the drill," he said.

She did know it. She had just done it about fifteen minutes before. Now, tear-streaked, blood-stained, barefoot, and disheveled, she did it again: held the Bible out in front of the President-to-be. Eleanor Richmond didn't hesitate. She put one hand on the Bible and held up the other one.

Judge Kotlarski looked at the cameraman. "You ready?"

"We're live to planet Earth," the cameraman said.

Judge Kotlarski began to read from the sheet of paper. "Repeat after me . . ."

In the middle of the oath of office, Eleanor and the Judge had to raise their voices; they were nearly drowned out by the sound of a medevac chopper setting down out front, then, within a few seconds, lifting off again.

Mary Catherine didn't pay much attention to the oath. She was looking out the windows, watching the chopper carry her father away. The first thing she really heard was the voice of the President issuing her first order: "Evacuate and seal the Rotunda."

Then President Richmond bent down, pulled a thick black envelope out of her bag, and ripped it open.

*William A. Cozzano* arrived at the Lady Wilburdon Gunshot Wound Institute via helicopter, roughly fifteen minutes after the bullet had entered his body. By that point, he had lost roughly half of his blood supply. He was trucked straight into a trauma room, where his chest was split open by Dr. Cornelius Gary. The President was in good hands: between his service in the Gulf War and in the trauma centers of D.C., Dr. Gary had personally treated more gunshot wounds than any other physician in the United States.

Before going under anaesthesia, Cozzano's last words to his son, James, were: "You're free now, son. Go out and be a good man."

Dr. Gary worked to mend Cozzano's shattered organs for thirty minutes. William A. Cozzano died on the operating table at 12:58 P.M., having been President for just under one hour.

## CHAPTER SIXTY-TWO

The first document in the black envelope was a one-sentence executive order that continued in force all of the orders made by Cozzano from the inaugural platform.

President Richmond moved her temporary headquarters to the Senate Press Room, which was easier to secure than the Rotunda, and well equipped with communications gear. She ordered a confirmation from all elements affected by Cozzano's orders that they had received, understood, and would obey. She faxed a message to the ops center on the seventh floor of the State Department and told them to send a copy to every other country in the world. The message stated that today's violence was strictly a domestic affair, things were in order, and full disclosure would be made soon.

She called in the Senate and House leadership. Each was examined by a physician. The Speaker of the House, who had suffered a stroke in November and been rehabilitated at the Radhakrishnan Institute in California, was declared to be medically incapacitated— the document stating so was already drawn up inside the black envelope; the senior whip of the majority party took over as acting House Speaker.

She sent out messages to all four network anchors requesting their presence in the Rotunda. They and their crew members were all carefully frisked and then ushered up to the Senate Press Room, where they interviewed President Richmond, who was flanked by the Senate majority leader and the acting Speaker. The most senior Justice on the Supreme Court had by now been rustled up and brought into the room.

The broadcast went live to all the networks at 2:08 P.M. Eleanor led off by making the first official announcement of President Cozzano's death.

Then she said: "You see before you the three branches of the United States government. Our purpose in being here is to reassure you of the continuity of the basic institutions of this government and to respond to the questions of these journalists, which will hopefully reflect the concerns of the nation."

A network anchorwoman raised her hand. Eleanor nodded to her.

The anchorwoman said, "Madame President. How do you *feel* at this moment?"

*Cyrus Rutherford Ogle*, handcuffed in the back of the GODS truck, had no idea what was going on until about 2:30, at which point the doors were suddenly thrown open and he was blinded by a rectangle of pure white light.

Framed in the white rectangle was a man in a black suit. Behind him were several men wearing dark FBI windbreakers. "Ogle," said the man in the black suit, "I've been looking for you."

"Howdy. Who are you?" Ogle said.

"I'm the new Attorney General of the United States," the man said.

"I've been out of touch the last little while," Ogle said apologetically.

"Oh. I'm sorry. My name is Mel Meyer."

Ogle was deeply mortified. Not to mention confused. "I thought that President Cozzano was going to appoint—"

"Change of plans. When you weren't there to keep things in hand at the crucial moment, we had to do a little improvising. I had to step in and fill the vacuum. You know all about filling vacuums, don't you, Mr. Ogle?"

"Well, I've done my share."

"But I think you'll be happy with the results," Mel Meyer said. He waved his hand at the FBI men. "I've directed the FBI to arrest you. I'm sure you understand."

Ogle didn't understand at all. "On what charge?"

"Turning the Attorney General's best friend into a degraded slave," Mel said. "And a number of other charges which I have written out at great length, and which we can discuss in the fullness of time. President Richmond has ordered you held for a few days until we can sort things out."

"President *Richmond!?*"

The FBI agents grabbed Ogle's arms and hauled him up out of the chair where he'd been sitting for the last two hours. His feet almost slipped out from under him on the blood-slickened floor; they gripped his arms tightly and ushered him out the door and down the steps. An FBI chopper was idling on the ground in Taft Park.

"I hope you're not going to use the power of your office to pursue some kind of personal vendetta," Ogle said, shouting back over his shoulder as the agents took him across Louisiana Avenue.

"Oh, on the contrary," Meyer said. "I've gone to great trouble to arrange a cell for you that I think will be to your liking."

"You're not putting me in with crack dealers, are you?"

"Absolutely not," Meyer said. "You'll be with people much like yourself."

"I thank you for that courtesy," Ogle said.

They loaded him onto the chopper, strapped him into the seat, and lifted off, cutting forward across Constitution at a low angle. Ogle had a spectacular view of the Capitol dome out his window.

He had gotten damn close. And now, in some way that no one had bothered to explain to him yet, he had lost.

It was okay. He was tied into the Network now. The Network needed him. As long as that was the case, he'd never have to worry about anything.

The chopper headed due south, crossing over the Southeast Freeway and then over Fort McNair, on the point of land where the Potomac and the Anacostia rivers came together. They cut down the center of the Potomac until they were south of National Airport, then banked into a gentle right turn and headed south-southeast, passing near the spire of the Masonic Memorial in Alexandria.

"Where are we going?" he asked twice. But the FBI agents either couldn't hear him or pretended they couldn't.

They flew for several miles across the suburban sprawl of north-ern Virginia, roughly parallelling I-395. The broad grassy lawns of Fort Belvoir were visible on the left. Perhaps they were using Fort Belvoir as a temporary camp for political prisoners. That wouldn't be so bad; folks in the Army called Belvoir the Country Club.

Instead, they came down in a yard amid enormous, drab build-ings, surrounded by tall fences topped with swirls of razor ribbon.

Lorton. They were putting him in Lorton Reformatory. The Dis-trict of Columbia was so small and so full of criminals that there wasn't room to build a big enough prison; they had built one out in Virginia instead. And now Ogle was going to be an inmate.

He reckoned they would put him in a minimum-security wing somewhere, maybe out in a nice wooded area. But they took him straight into one of the big prison buildings. Straight to a maximum-security wing, where all of the prisoners were locked in their cells all day long.

The prisoners hung on their bars and watched Ogle hungrily as he was led down the corridor in his nice shirt and his polished shoes. They shouted things to him. Disgusting things.

Ogle was almost paralyzed with fear. Meyer had lied to him.

Finally they reached a cell that was empty. Maybe he'd be put there.

But they passed right on by it and continued to the next cell. This cell had one man in it, curled up on the upper bunk, not moving. Ogle just got a quick glimpse of him before he was shoved in through the door: his new roommate was small, stoop-shouldered, late middle-aged, wearing a dress shirt and slacks just like Ogle.

The massive iron door thudded shut behind him.

Ogle turned to greet his new cellmate. The man had risen up to his hands and knees and was now looking down at Ogle from the upper bunk like a jaguar perched in a tree. He was breathing rapidly and raggedly.

A huge bubble of mucous grew from Jeremiah Freel's left nostril and popped.

Freel launched himself from the bunk headfirst, trying to sink his teeth into Ogle's cheek. Ogle instinctively turned his head away and snapped his head back. The impact slammed him back against the bars. Freel tumbled to the floor.

Freel reached for Ogle's groin. Ogle bent over and shoved his finger into one of Freel's eyes. Freel moved his head at the last moment and sank his teeth into Ogle's finger. Ogle stomped on one of Freel's hands.

And then they started fighting. In cells all around them, the convicts from D.C. flocked to the bars shouting, laughing, and pumping their fists in exultation.

*Several hundred feet* beneath Cacher, Oklahoma, Otis Simpson was sitting in a swivel chair in the Communications Center, staring at a wall of dead screens. He had been staring at them ever since roughly 19:08 Greenwich Mean Time. At that moment, President Richmond had gone live to the world, flanked by the leaders of the legislative and judicial branches. Then all the screens had gone black. The faxes had gone silent. The computer links had been cut off. He had tried sending messages to the Network, but all the encryption keys had been changed.

Finally he stood up, harvested a few remaining faxes that had come out of the machines earlier that day, and fed them into the shredder. He typed a command into the computer system that would cause it to re-format all of its disks seven times in a row, destroying all of the information in the system.

Otho was lying in his bed. He had been lying there since earlier today and was now beginning to go into rigor mortis. Otis bent over him and closed his eyes and smoothed back what was left of his hair.

Then he climbed on the lift and took it up to the surface. It was a bleak midwinter day, a strong steady wind coming out of the north-west prairie, whistling and gusting between the heaps of lead tailings as it picked up a load of toxic metal dust. Otis put on his warm coat and his mittens and his hat with the earflaps. Then he started to walk down the shoulder of the highway, headed southward, where he thought it might be warmer.

*Dr. Radhakrishnan V.R.J.V.V.* Gangadhar was poised above his anaesthetized patient, just about to flick the power switch on his bone saw, when the first tendrils of the noise began to infiltrate the reinforced-concrete walls of the Radhakrishnan Institute. It was a noise that was sensed through the soles of the feet—not so much an actual sound as a change in the way the ground felt. Perhaps there had been another earthquake up in Uttar Pradesh. He flicked the switch and pressed the madly vibrating blade of the bone saw against the freshly peeled skull of Sasha Yakutin, a promising young up-and-coming Russian politician who had just been cut down in the prime of his life by a tragic stroke.

When he finished cutting a hatch through Mr. Yakutin's head and turned off the saw, the room became quiet—but not entirely quiet. A palpable noise was penetrating the walls of the operating room.

A nurse entered the operating theater. "Your brother Arun is on the telephone," she said.

"Can't you see I am in the middle of an operation?"

"He says it's an emergency. He says that you should get out of the country."

A tremendous impact reverberated through the structure of the building, causing the steel instruments to vibrate against their trays. Down the hallway, someone screamed.

"Continue with the operation," Dr. Radhakrishnan said to Toyoda, one of his most promising young protégés.

"Doctor?" Toyoda said.

Dr. Radhakrishnan stripped off his gloves and tossed them into a rubbish can.

When he stepped out into the corridor, the noise became louder, but it was still indistinct. He had heard something like this once in Elton. He had been awakened early in the morning by the most frightening noise, a noise that could peel paint from walls, the noise that madmen must hear in their nightmares, and had shivered under the covers for a few moments, thinking it was the end of the world; finally he had peered out under a windowshade and discovered that the trees in his front yard had been taken over by a vast flock of starlings, millions of them, all screeching at the tops of their lungs.

Dr. Radhakrishnan was approaching a closed door at the end of a hallway. The noise was coming through that door, seeping around its edges.

He opened the door. The sound was crushing, maddening, a noise that could cave your skull in. This room was a third-story office with a picture window that faced out onto a major street. But the window had been smashed out. Slivers of smoked glass had been strewn explosively all over the room. A few rocks and bricks littered the floor, looking crude and dirty in this clean high-tech space. Hot polluted air streamed in through the window and blew over Dr. Radhakrishnan's face. He stepped forward, walking carefully on the broken glass, and looked out the window.

The Radhakrishnan Institute had been surrounded by two million people.

They were all pumping their fists in the air and chanting. Like starlings. They covered the ground for miles in every direction, flowing in a smooth carpet around buildings and vehicles, like the monsoon floods.

The mob seemed to have no particular center. But a few hundred yards away, he could see a kind of vortex, a swirling center of activity, moving slowly through the crowd. Moving toward the institute.

It was an elephant. Unlike the mob, most of whom who were poorly, minimally clad, the elephant was stunningly clothed in gold and brightly colored, embroidered silk. A man was sitting on the back of the elephant. Sitting in a chair on the animal's back. Tied into the chair, actually, so he wouldn't flop out.

Dr. Radhakrishnan recognized the man. He was an ex-patient. And then, at last, he figured out what the crowd was chanting.

WUBBA WUBBA WUBBA WUBBA WUBBA WUBBA WUBBA WUBBA WUBBA.

*Zeldo's telephone rang* again in the late afternoon, probably another one of his friends calling to ask him if he had heard about Presidents Cozzano and Richmond. Zeldo didn't have time for it now. He had been at the California branch of the Radhakrishnan Institute for almost twenty-four hours, going over some data from one of their newest patients—one Aaron Green. Green had been committed here around the time of Election Day, plagued by psychological troubles—posttraumatic stress from the Pentagon Towers bloodbath. Finally, he had volunteered to have several chips implanted in his head.

Zeldo jerked the phone out of its cradle. "What?"

"It's me." Zeldo would have known the voice anywhere: it was Mary Catherine Cozzano. "They're covering their tracks. We've been hearing some weird stuff from the Pentagon and we think you're in trouble. Get on that bike of yours and pedal like your life depends upon it, because it does. See you at dinner."

Something in Mary Catherine's voice got Zeldo up out of his chair. He grabbed his backpack, skittered down the stairs, and yanked his mountain bike from the employee bike rack out front. He rode across the small parking lot of the Radhakrishnan Institute and into the entrance of the bicycle path.

He was about half a mile away from the institute when something caught his eye: an airplane. Usually you didn't notice airplanes, they were part of the scenery. But this one drew his attention because it was flying incredibly low. He thought maybe it was coming in for a landing at the airstrip. But it was going way too fast to make a landing. It was streaking across the landscape, actually kicking up a dust trail from the ground. It was very small, and dark.

Zeldo recognized the shape. He had seen a documentary about

these things once, on 60 *Minutes*, a few years ago. It was a Gale Aerospace Stealth Cruise Missile. It had achieved great notoriety for going way off course during its test flights.

The cruise missile shot over the airstrip, made a minor course correction, and then headed directly toward the Radhakrishnan Institute, making no effort to slow down. Finally, to Zeldo's relief, it popped up in the air. It was going to miss the building and fly harmlessly out to sea.

But it didn't. It shot up several hundred feet, then nosed down into a power dive. It covered the last mile of its trajectory in a few seconds and finally entered the Institute through a skylight, which took it straight down a central atrium.

Vast surges of white flame vomited out of every door and window in the Institute. The image was burned onto Zeldo's retina in an instant and then he was blinded for a moment. The shock wave knocked him off his bicycle and sent him sprawling off the bike path, into the dust.

He didn't feel a thing. His mind was stuck on the last thing she'd said: *See you at dinner.*

*President Richmond traveled* up Pennsylvania Avenue and took possession of the White House at five P.M., bringing the party and congressional leaders with her. The first thing she did was to fire all of the administrative assistants and transition team, who had moved into the place during the change of power. Several of these people were also taken into custody by the formidable FBI contingent that was now following her around, under the direction of the Attorney General, scooping up conspirators and loading them into buses en masse.

There was a lot to do. She ensconced herself in the Oval Office even while the FBI men were scanning it for listening devices. At seven o'clock, all the important people in Washington came into the office: the Congressional leaders, party leaders, several of the Joint Chiefs, all of the acting Cabinet members, heads of various major agencies including the CIA and the NSA. She was not in any mood, or any position, to be ceremonious; these people piled into her office like a tour group from Oskaloosa and stood around the edges of the room, staring at her. She stared back at them over a desk piled with cardboard boxes and loose documents from the black envelope.

"I know what you're thinking," she said. "This can't be happening. This bitch can't possibly be our president. It won't last. Well, it is happening. I am the President. And I will continue to be for the next eight years. You'd better get used to it. Thank you for coming in. Now go out there and do your jobs."

There were boxes all over the place. Cozzano's boxes had been moved in this morning. Eleanor's boxes had been moved in at the Naval Observatory. Now Cozzano's boxes were being taken away and Eleanor's boxes were being hustled down and brought into the White House.

She had one of the movers keep his eye out for one item in particular: a very long, skinny one. An eight-foot cardboard tube. Eventually he showed up carrying the tube over his shoulder like a spear. He got the tape off the end for her and then she pulled out what was inside: a strip of cheap wooden molding with a few nails sticking out of it. Eleanor borrowed a hammer from the White House maintenance people and put it up herself, nailing it right into the wall of the Oval Office, to the shock and chagrin of the house-keeping staff, who came running when they heard those pounding noises. It looked flimsy and cheap, and it was. But anyone who came closer could see horizontal lines drawn across it in ballpoint pen, with dates and the names of her children written next to them. Eleanor liked it.

It wasn't until about nine o'clock that she was able to keep her date with Mary Catherine. They met on the steps of the Jefferson Memorial, accompanied by the motley assortment of football players and graying Vietnam vets who had been following them around all day.

The area was checked out and cleared. Eleanor and Mary Catherine climbed up the steps of the Memorial, turned around, and looked out across the Tidal Basin toward the White House, a mile and a half away, brilliant under the lights.

Eleanor and Mary Catherine sat together on the top step, huddled together against a chilly wind coming off the Potomac. Mary

Catherine put her head on Eleanor's shoulder and cried for a while. Eleanor held her patiently, stroking her hair in the way of mothers, and waited for her to get it all out.

Then she waved her arm toward the Mall. "Look. It's beautiful," she said.

The air-traffic moratorium was still in place over D.C. National Airport, just across the river and it was quiet for the first time in decades. Consequently the Tidal Basin was the way it was supposed to be: placid, undisturbed by the shrieking and thundering of 767s veering in for their slam-dunk landings. The sky was cobalt blue and Venus was out, looking exactly like a diamond over the curved towers of the tall buildings in Rosslyn. The ring of half-staffed American flags around the Washington Monument flickered their silhouettes, lower than usual, against the white limestone.

"It is nice," Mary Catherine said, feeling better all of a sudden. "But I'm freezing."

"Me too," Eleanor confessed. Then she nodded across the Mall toward the White House. "Would you like to come over to my place and help me unpack?"